# Melting Worlds

## A Space Opera

# Melting Worlds

By

Dorian Pratt

Transgressive Publishing
2006

Published by:  Transgressive Publishing

transgressivepublishing@yahoo.com

ISBN:  978-0-6151-4452-8

printed in the united states of america

# Contents

# Chapter 1
# The *Empress*

J ess Ichikawa might have thought that the space station floating outside the porthole she was sitting beside resembled a closed water lily, if she had ever seen a water lily. Since she had not, the thought never occurred to her. Actually, were she ever to see a water lily, she would be more likely to think that its roughly spherical flower resembled the station's globular primary structure and its collection of lily pads looked like the station's numerous platter-like hangars than the other way around. She might even have thought, if she ever saw such a flower, that the dragonflies that surely would have been flitting around it resembled the countless vessels currently moving about in the distance before her.

She was not, however, paying much attention to the space station, as it was more or less similar in design to many others she had seen before. Instead, she was staring at Shokai, the planet beneath this construction, and thinking how it looked very much like a gigantic eyeball.

Most of the world was covered by a yellowish-white desert, the featureless uniformity of which was only broken by a few vein-like mountain ranges and, in the extremes of the southern hemisphere, by a muddy sea about a thousand miles across.* The pupil of the eye was a fifteen-hundred-mile-wide black ocean covering the whole of the arctic region, and its iris was a swath of emerald green land stretching from the shores of this body of water to a ring of mountains about eight-hundred miles away that almost completely enclosed the planet's north. The eye was, however, marred by a gap in the mountain range's circuit, where the desert encroached almost to the water's edge, leaving only a thread of green.

While the *Empress*, the ether-ship Jess was traveling on, approached Shokai, it changed its course so that the girl was no longer able to see the planet. With only the inky void beyond the window, Jess lost interest in looking at the local scenery (or at its absence), yawned widely, raised her hands above her head, and stretched her body, all the while making a noise like a cat's lazy purr.

Jess herself was not yet twenty traders' years old, although she did not look even that. She was very short and rather skinny.

As small and unimposing as she was, it was rare for people to fail to notice her. Not only was her shoulder length hair colored cotton candy pink, but she also made it a point to dress in a way that emphasized her slender but gracefully curved figure. At the moment, she was wearing a thin band of black cloth around her breasts and a pair of hip hugging, very brief black shorts.

Just as she finished stretching, the door to the grubby, gloomy mess hall where she was relaxing opened and a toad walked in.

He was almost identical to an earthly Woodhouse's toad, except that his cranium was larger, he walked on his hind legs, his head faced foreword

---

* Measurements have been converted to those of the system in use in the reader's area.

when he did so, and he was five feet tall.[*] His warted, bumpy skin was a chocolaty brown, save for his milky white throat, and his eyes were large and expressive. Although his huge webbed feet were bare, he wore black spats, tight fitting cream colored breeches upon his spindly legs, and, over his nearly spherical body, both a mulitcolored embroidered waistcoat and a long justaucorps brightly printed with green, gold, and brown floral patterns. In his right hand he carried a cane topped with a silver knob (shaped like the head of a fish) and striped like a barber's pole, though in green and white.

This toad, Uluf, who worked as the ship's cook, was as flamboyant as were almost all the members of his species and invariably dressed himself in some outlandish costume or another. He was also Jess's constant companion.

Neither had much to do with the running of the *Empress* and both were outsiders. Jess was not merely excluded, however; she was often actively resented. Since she had come onboard when she met the captain, Tolliver, in the port city on her home world, after she had begun a relationship with him there, the others saw her as the man's sexual plaything. They were admittedly correct, for Jess was that, but she did have another function on the ship.

Jess was as small and as physically unintimidating as any person could be, but she also happened to be an accomplished killer.

Because the craft she was traveling on, while ostensibly a trading vessel, was actually used by the captain to transport drugs, he had need of someone able to resolve disputes that could not be settled in a local court. Her presence onboard was thus required, even if she was rarely put to work. Some members of the crew were nonetheless annoyed by her general indolence. Fortunately, Uluf felt no animosity towards her, as he himself, being a toad, was also usually avoided by the humans.

When Jess heard the door open and saw her immaculately attired companion standing beneath the flickering yellowish lights that half revealed the room's stained metals walls, the filth clogged grates of its floor, and the other squalid details of the place, she smiled, pushed her rickety chair away from the warped plastic table she was sitting at, went over to the amphibian, and took him by the hand.

"Come and sit with me while we make planetfall," she said.

The creature did not croak at her in response, but answered with a mellifluous baritone. "Are you going into the city with the captain after we land, my dear?"

Jess returned to her seat and replied to Uluf once he had sat down across the table from her.

"No. He has something he's doing on his own."

"Yes. Of course. I did overhear him saying – while he was having his lunch – that he had some personal business to attend to there. Has he told you what it is?"

---

[*] The same height Jess was.

"No. Not a word. To tell you the truth, I'm a little worried. I hope he's not getting into something too dangerous."

With a laugh that was so obviously forced it encouraged rather than dismissed Jess's concerns, Uluf leaned back in his chair and put his hands behind his head. "If you are thinking that he is going to make a deal with some rogue gang leader for a shipment of russa, I am quite sure, my dear, that you are mistaken."

"That's why you're mentioning it, then?"

"Well...I admit that the possibility did occur to me. Nonetheless, Tolliver is hardly stupid. Do you honestly believe that he would make trouble with the Seven Families or the Smuggling Syndicate? I personally do not. Whatever he is up to, it is something else. Of that I am entirely confident."

After a moment's pause, Jess arched her back, reached her hands behind her shoulders (to scratch herself like a bored cat), and sighed loudly. "Yeah. I hope so. Anyway, whatever he's doing, he's doing it on his own. He doesn't need me. And that means I'm free to do what I want to."

Having raised her hands above her head and smiled widely, so that she was transformed from a cat into a little girl, Jess announced, "You know what, Uluf? I'm going to take in the sights. Then I'm going to dance, drink, and do things I will definitely regret the next day. Want to come with me?"

"Without a doubt, my dear. Look. You can see Shokai again."

Jess gazed out the porthole. The planet filled almost her entire field of vision and was getting much closer very rapidly.

The *Empress* was soon racing over the tall mountains surrounding Shokai's arctic regions. The two visitors could see how the southern faces of these were barren and lifeless, how the peaks in the middle were wrapped in snow, and how the mountains on the northern edge of the range were covered with thick green forests and loomed over deep valleys whose floors were hidden by impenetrable fogs.

Heavy clouds pressed against the peaks, pushed by the hot winds entering into Shokai's verdant north through the gap in the encircling range. These searing, dusty airs lifted the waters of the ocean into the skies, ever replenishing the clouds the winds drove into the mountains, where the grey masses gave up their waters and fed countless wide and narrow rivers that hurried back to the ocean where they had ultimately originated.

As barren, lifeless, and terrible as was all the world south of the mountains, the lands to their north were almost completely covered by a single forest. Although Jess and Uluf could see, depending on whether they were over a part of the globe covered by night or a part illumined by the sun's rays, either the lights or the smoky pollution of some small city blinking at or dancing for them amongst the depths of this vast jungle, such habitations were separated by substantial tracts of untenanted woodland.

The edge of the ocean, however, was like a coronet made up of one great city after the next. In the night this sparkled as though bejeweled, and, in the day, it formed an impossibly wide grey circle of little spires. There were even a few cities, like glimmering gems that had fallen from this crown, adorning the edges of the islands scattered here and there in the sea's waters.

Uluf pointed out the porthole. "Do you see that city in the middle of the ocean?"

"Yeah. I see it," Jess replied. She was looking at a city that was just then emerging into the light. It was built on the southern edge of a small island, about a fifth of which it covered.

"That is Quanya, my dear, the city of the Seven Families."

"Really? I'd like to go there. I've heard the casinos are huge."

Jess looked at Uluf and went on. "Will you go with me? I mean if Tolliver isn't up to something that's going to get us killed."

"Of course. I am curious to see Quanya myself."

The two looked out the porthole again. Within a few moments, Shokai was just beneath them. They could see a large city perched on a wide hill by the ocean's side. To the east of it was a valley and, on the other side of that, another smaller city.

"That is Jezic, the capital of Tozana," Uluf noted. "We will be landing there shortly. Look. You can see the spaceport to the south of the city."

As the *Empress* raced towards Jezic over an undulating sea of green trees, the toad and the young woman could make out how about a third of the plateau where the city was built had been cleared away.

On the southernmost edge of this wide, empty space was a fantastically tall tower that gleamed orangish-red with the dawn's rays. From its wide base, which divided into separate parts that spread out as though they were the roots of a tree, it twisted like a corkscrew for half its height and then straightened into a tapering needle that reached almost to the clouds.

This cyclopean edifice was used by ether-ships that had made planetfall to launch back into space. Each of these vessels, rendered weightless with its antigravity engine, was placed on a sort of trolley that was made to hurtle up the tower, at an ever increasing speed, so that it was thrown into the sky and did not need to burn rocket fuel to escape the atmosphere.

The rest of the open field was divided between areas where ether-ships could land and places where they could be docked and unloaded.

Most of the latter were clustered in the northern portion of the plain amid innumerable warehouses and government buildings. These were almost all featureless, uninteresting structures. In fact, the only noteworthy building in the port, other than the launching tower, was the sprawling complex housing the port authority, through which every visitor to the planet had to pass and where every captain had to declare his cargo. It was a bright pink, rectangular stone structure with a façade composed of layers of arcades interrupted by graceful spires set at regular intervals.

The *Empress* flew, more and more slowly, towards the port and gently passed over nearly half the field's breadth before it stopped dead still in the air over a large red square painted on the yellowish-brown material used to pave the ground. As the vessel hovered there, Jess could feel the vibrations caused by the extrusion of its landing gear. Once it was ready to do so, the ship slowly descended and, almost without a jolt, rested upon the earth.

After closing her eyes and sticking out her tongue, Jess squeezed her shoulders together, grinned widely, and said, "I always get excited when I go somewhere new. I can't wait to go exploring."

"I have little doubt, my dear, that you will find much to excite you on Shokai."

Although she knew she had some time to wait yet, and so remained in her seat, Jess could not resist squirming about and fidgeting nervously. Before long, she had her nose pressed against the porthole and had grabbed onto its rusting fittings, as if she thought she could use them to push herself through the window and see everything outside more clearly.

She watched while what appeared to be the pavement within the red square rose up (it was actually a trolley set on tracks) and conveyed the *Empress* along a pathway marked by a blue line towards a long building connected to the port authority structure.

Once the ship had arrived there, an extensible corridor emerged from the building and fastened itself to the vessel's starboard hatch.

The captain then spoke to his crew over the ship's loudspeaker. "All crew members must now disembark. Report to the main hatch immediately."

"Shall we?" asked Jess as she stood up and extended her hand to Uluf.

"Of course, my dear," the warty toad replied and took her hand in his.

The pair left the mess hall and made their way down a narrow corridor, past walls covered with peeling blue paint and patches of rust and beneath a ceiling made of a tangle of exposed wires, ducts, and tubes. As they could not walk abreast, Jess went ahead and, still holding her friend's hand, pulled him along behind her. At the end of the hallway was a heavy iron door opened by a metal wheel. This was already ajar, as several of the other crew members had just gone through it and, knowing that some of their fellows could be coming behind them, had not bothered to close it.

Jess and Uluf went through the doorway and entered a large, drab room, the half rusted walls of which, where not lined with lockers or racks of equipment, were slimy with abundant crops of green mold. To the girl's right was the starboard hatch. While it was only about the same size as was the short, narrow doorway she had just stepped through, it was the ship's main entrance. In front of it were fourteen men and women, all of whom appeared to be more than ready to leave the confines of the *Empress*.

A few of these persons looked at the two who had just entered, but none bothered to acknowledge them. The pair went to the wall opposite the hatch and stood beside the doorway that pierced it.

Several minutes later, through the room's last entrance, that opposite the one Jess had used, the ship's engineer stepped forth to join the others. He was followed by the navigator, two other crewmen, and finally by Captain Tolliver.

The last of these was not an especially noticeable individual. He was dressed in a slightly worn grey tunic and stained, ragged trousers he had tucked into his battered boots. He was of medium height and average build. His hair, though once black, was now peppered with grey, and his imperial had almost entirely lost its color. He did not, however, look to be older than forty since his face was unlined and he moved with the agility of a man half that age.

When he saw Jess, Tolliver smiled and walked over to her. Having patted her backside and taken a firm hold of one of her buttocks, he looked at her breasts and said to them, "Sorry I can't spend the day with you. Will you be able to find something to occupy your time?"

"Do you need to ask? I'll just look around at the sights with Uluf."

"Good. Could you wait until I've arranged for our cargo to be unloaded? I'd like to see you for a few minutes."

"Sure."

A shrill whistle sounded from the intercom box set on the wall by the starboard hatch, and a strident, tinny voice spoke through the device.

"Open your hatch and proceed along the corridor to processing."

The captain signaled for the hatch to be opened and the crew members passed from the ship into the corridor outside.

After the crewmen had spent several hours sitting around while local bureaucrats processed their paperwork, they were returned to the *Empress*, which was then taken to the warehouse where its goods would be unloaded.

Most of the members of the crew, no longer being needed, promptly left the vessel, but Jess, though eager to do so herself, made her way to the mess hall. There, in Uluf's company, she stared out a porthole at the world she was eager to explore and waited, with increasing impatience, for the captain to finish giving instructions to the longshoremen working at the warehouse.

A couple of hours after Jess had sat down, Tolliver walked into the room, apologized for the delay, and took her to his quarters.

She plopped down on the edge of the captain's disheveled bed, and he stood across the room from her between a circular porthole and a dilapidated table piled with filthy dishes and stacks of disorganized papers. He crossed his arms, smiled, and leaned against a wall that was mottled green, red, blue, and grey with its patches of mold, rust, chipping paint, and exposed metal.

Tolliver looked nervous, though he was trying to conceal it, and Jess was sure he was up to something. Whatever it was he was planning, she hoped that it was not going to be more than she could handle. While Jess had no doubts about her abilities as a fighter (and had no reason to doubt them since she had never encountered anyone better than she was), she did realize that even she had her limits.

If the captain tried to smuggle a cargo of russa and the Seven Families or the Smuggling Syndicate found out about it, there would be little she could do to help either herself or him. She might be allowed to die fighting, but even that could be denied her. It was quite possible that she would end up being tortured to death for some gangster's entertainment.

No sooner had such a thought crossed Jess's mind than it swept the inside of her torso into an uncomfortable hollow that, as empty as it was, somehow made what remained of her body itch with anxiety. Having shaken her hands to rid them of their nervousness, Jess grabbed her belly and grimaced.

Tolliver, who was staring at her, noticed her expression and realized that she was worried. He called out to her, "Come over here. Let's have a little fun before you go into the city."

Jess stood up and crossed the room to where Tolliver was standing. She put her hands on his shoulders and tried to kiss him, but he caught her arms and lowered her onto her knees. Knowing well what he wanted, she opened his trousers and took him into her mouth.

There was not much that Jess was particularly good at, as she herself was sadly aware, but when it came to killing and to sex, there were few as skilled as she was.

Tolliver was erect almost as soon as she had touched him, and, in a few moments, as she caressed him with her lips and tongue, his whole body was trembling. He pulled her top down with his shaking hands, cupped her breasts in his palms, and squeezed and kneaded them. Jess began to bob her head faster, and Tolliver, now almost insane with pleasure, grabbed ahold of her hair and pushed her face against his crotch. Within seconds of doing so, the captain, unable to restrain himself any longer, ejaculated in her mouth.

Once he had recovered control over his mind and body, Tolliver pushed Jess away and sat down on the edge of the creaking table. Jess lowered herself onto the floor, resting her buttocks on her heels, and looked up at him. Her limbs were trembling, her nostrils quivering, and her eyes becoming watery. She had wanted Tolliver to be pleased with her and was profoundly disappointed that she had robbed him of the chance to have sex before he went off to attend to whatever business it was that he had in Jezic.

Having swallowed audibly, she said, "I'm sorry. I didn't mean to make you come that fast. We can still make love if you feel like it."

"Forget about it."

Tolliver was clearly annoyed with her, but tried to smile as he fastened his trousers. He mussed Jess's hair, took her by the hand, lifted her onto her feet, and sat himself down in a nearby chair. Jess then perched herself on the table's edge, where the captain had been sitting a moment before, and watched as he wrote a note on a slip of torn paper.

He handed this to the girl and said, "This is the address of the Iron Fish. It's a bar in Jezic where we can meet tonight. Give it to Uluf. He's been here before and knows his way around. Even if he doesn't know the address, he can keep your cab driver honest."

Tolliver looked at his wristwatch, thought for a moment, and continued.

"Be there at around nine standard time. That's about sixth watch and a quarter according to the local measure. I'll be done by then. We'll get a room and take a look at the city together tomorrow."

"When are we leaving the planet?"

"I need to be back at the *Empress* by tomorrow evening to get everything ready. Our departure date isn't for another ten days, though. We'll be launching on Saturday after next at second watch and one quarter. That's around...four thirty standard time."

Waving the piece of paper at Tolliver, Jess said, "I'll be there. We'll fuck all night. I promise I won't disappoint you again."

"You never disappoint me. Now, why don't you go get ready? I need to put some paperwork together anyway."

"Okay. I'll see you in a few hours."

Jess hopped off the table, kissed Tolliver, pulled up and arranged her top, and left the room.

She made her way through the narrow, poorly lit corridor that ran between the crew members' quarters to the oval, iron doorway that led to her own room. When she had twisted the metal wheel at the door's center and opened it, a half dozen small creatures, ranging from the size of her thumb to as big as a man's hand, scurried out from the darkened room beyond, scampered up the walls, and disappeared amongst the wires and ducts running along the ceiling.

These hluvess, for so they were called, infested most cargo ships and looked vaguely like woodlice. Each was covered with a translucent grey exoskeleton, through which its pallid internal organs could be seen pumping and squishing, and, at its fore end, each sprouted numerous whitish antennae and feelers.

While hluvess were harmless, they were nasty, dirty pests, and Jess detested them.

To her satisfaction and disgust, she did manage to stamp on the last couple of the creatures that leapt from her room. Then, having used a grate in the floor to scrape their sticky, foul smelling entrails off her feet, the girl stepped inside and switched on the light.

Going over to her wardrobe, she took off her briefs, put on a pair of skintight, dark blue trousers made of a glossy plastic-like material, slipped her feet into a pair of tall black boots, and draped a loose black vest over her shoulders.

Into a concealed pocket on the inside of this last garment, she slid a small metallic rod cast in the shape of a fierce beast that somewhat resembled a centipede, and, in each of her boots, she concealed other, similar tubes, though these were not as adorned as was the first and had rings set in their sides so that they could be held without being grasped.

Then Jess wound round her waist the cords of a pouch decorated with constantly moving and even changing images of various sorts of flowers, birds, insects, and small beasts so that the pouch itself rested upon her hip. The mouth of this apparently little sack opened onto a separate universe that, though small, was able to hold as many things as Jess could thrust into it. Once she had it on, she proceded to shove an impossible number of garments down the pouch's mouth (without increasing its size at all).

Last of all, she inserted passive translators (shaped like tiny buds) into her ears and pinned an enameled active translator about an inch across and shaped like an animal onto her vest. The former were able to translate millions of languages into Jess's own, and the latter picked up her own words and spoke them in whatever language it had been commanded to use on a given occasion.

Having so dressed herself, Jess looked around the small chamber to make sure she had not forgotten anything and noticed her credit wand lying on a shelf.

This small rectangular piece of plastic was electronically imprinted with information about her account in the Imperial Bank. Anywhere Jess traveled in human space, she could use it to acquire coin, and whatever transactions she made would be deducted from her account. The wand, which contained a record of her DNA, was virtually unforgeable and almost completely secure. Most space travelers carried such devices, although few ground dwellers did. Fortunately, all spaceports had machines for withdrawing money, and every world used the same currency, kopecks.

With the wand in the pocket of her vest, Jess left her quarters, went to the end of the corridor outside, and hopped down the spiraling metal stairs at its end. The mess hall and kitchens were on the level below, and Uluf's quarters were at the back of the latter. As the crew members, with the exception of the captain, shared a common toilet, and they did not want to sit on a commode a toad had been squatting upon or find such a creature bathing in the same shower they would be using, Uluf had been given his own room, with his own toilet, in the part of the ship where he worked. Actually, it was more of a pantry than a proper room and was barely larger than the cook's cot.

Jess rapped vigorously upon his door, and Uluf promptly opened it.

"Are you ready?" she asked.

"Of course. Shall we go?"

The girl took the toad by the arm and together the pair left the ship.

# Interlude 1
# Shokai

Shokai was initially surveyed in 235 S.A.( by the members of an expedition headed by Ismael Jaffrey. The world was then called Jaffreylok in accordance with the ancient custom that a planet should receive the name of the captain of the first vessel to land on it.

It was the third planet discovered by humanity with intelligent inhabitants and the first with more than one such species. Initially, however, only one of these, the Jaffrite, was recognized as being sentient.

Settlers began arriving on Shokai from Earth two years after the first survey. The majority of the colonists came from India and China, with smaller numbers originating from Russia, Western Europe, and North America. The entire planet was placed under the jurisdiction of India and colonists from other nations were settled in the same locations as were citizens of the governing state.

---

* Sidereal Age: The era that began with the first interstellar voyage by a human piloted faster than light vessel. Used to count traders' years.

The name of the largest of these early colonies, New Shanghai, later simply Shanghai, was eventually applied to the whole of the planet. The current name of the world, Shokai, is derived from this designation.

After Shokai was given independence by the Commonwealth in 321, a planetary government was established, but, unable to resist the efforts of individual regional colonies to govern themselves, this collapsed within a few years. The states that subsequently emerged have, for the most part, survived until the present day.

During the two-hundred years of isolation that followed independence, most of these nations developed the forms of government and the kinds of societies that have characterized the states of Shokai since that time.

With few exceptions, the planet's nations are ruled by semi-hereditary monarchs assisted by assemblies of prominent citizens. Rulers may inherit their position, be selected by a preceding ruler, be appointed by the country's assembly of notables, or seize power by means of assassination or a coup.

The majority of the world's societies are divided into several non-hereditary estates based on profession and income. In Tozana, which is typical, the highest estate is made up of the wealthy elites. The second estate is constituted of government officials and military officers. The third estate is composed of the bourgeoisie and the educated. The fourth is made up of craftsmen, shop owners, and semiskilled workers, and the lowest of unskilled laborers and the poor.

Laws dictate the locations where the members of a given estate may live, the clothing they may wear, and their civic rights.

Although the various governments of Shokai unanimously agreed to join the League of Planets in 665 and the Confederacy that succeeded it in 721, no single planetary government was established during that time. The collapse of the Confederacy in the first half of the Twelfth Century thus had little effect on Shokai's societies.

During the period when Shokai belonged to the Confederacy, the use of russa, a highly addictive intoxicant composed of Jaffrite semen, became widespread.

Over time, the criminal organizations controlling the production and sale of this drug grew in size and influence. With the help of smugglers operating off world, the distribution of russa was even extended to other planets.

The social disruptions caused by the manufacture and use of russa led the nations of Shokai to form an alliance in 1388 and jointly attempt to fight a war against the organizations controlling the drug trade.

It was while this conflict was being fought that the Jaffrite nations still existing on Shokai were incorporated into the world's human states and efforts began to confine these beings to preserves.

After over twenty years of unsuccessful armed conflict, the governments of Shokai signed the Treaty of Hudaipwa with the seven surviving criminal organizations. This agreement gave those organizations sovereignty over a small island in the ocean, established preserves for the majority of the world's Jaffrite populations, most of which were leased to one or another of the gangs for the production of russa, strictly prohibited the sale or consumption of russa outside of the organizations' island, and forbade the unauthorized production of the drug.

The seven now semi-legitimate organizations, which became known as the Seven Families, built the city of Quanya on the island that had been ceded to them and have governed it as an independent nation since that time. They have refrained from selling russa anywhere on Shokai outside of Quanya and have maintained good relations with the world's other states.

In 2019 the governments of Shokai surrendered to the Pancloan navy without a fight and swore fealty to the emperor. The city of Nyopwa was subsequently built to house the viceroy's administration.

The population of Shokai, according to the census of 2457, is 244,362,000. The number of Jaffrites is estimated to be approximately one-hundred million. The sizes of the feihi and maruvazi populations are not known.

From Pollidor's *Big Blue Book of Knowledge*

# Chapter 2
# In Jezic

While Jess was looking back at the *Empress* through the window of the taxi she was sharing with Uluf, she might then have thought that the enormous black ship, with its rounded back composed of overlapping plates and its short extendable legs, looked like a headless, tailless armadillo, had she ever seen such an animal. As she had not, however, Jess was thinking, as she usually did when looking at the vessel from a distance, that it resembled a gigantic hluvess.

She quickly lost interest in the ship when the cab left the drab warehouses clustered around the spaceport. The vehicle, hurtling down a road raised above the ground on a single row of a spindly pillars and made of what appeared to be a dull, grey metal (though it was actually a metal heavy ceramic), had come upon rows of tall, narrow, bullet shaped adjoining houses built of some pink stone.

While gazing at her surroundings, Jess noticed that all the vehicles moving up and down the thoroughfare, by means magnetism, were roughly similar in design. Each was shaped like a snail, with a flat base, a projecting head, and a domed shell. At the front of every vehicle, however, where the snail's head would be, was a cowcatcher. From either side of this emerged, on thin, twisting stalks, a pair of headlights, and, on the car's side, just before the spiraling portion of the shell, was a door. The vehicles' windows could not be seen from the outside.

As she watched these peculiar machines racing, at incredible speeds, along the grey highway, Jess pointed out the window and asked Uluf, "Why are their cars shaped like that?"

"I am afraid that I have no idea, my dear," he answered. "Although there are actual snails on Shokai – people raise them as food – I cannot say for certain why the locals would want their vehicles to look like the little gastropods. Nonetheless, cars are like that all over the planet. At least, they are wherever I have been."

"I kind of like them."

"As do I. They have a whimsical charm few human artifacts possess."

Jess leaned back against the shiny, dark purple seat and looked out the window again. Within a short time, the cab left the rows of pink, pointed houses and began moving between increasingly impressive towers, many of which were joined to others by a network of thin bridges like impossible flying buttresses.

The spires, and the bridges between them, were built in a dazzling variety of colors. Some were pink, others blue, and still others were green, mauve, fuchsia, teal, lavender, turquoise, orange, or yet another hue. Whatever their color, all of the towers were narrow, cylindrical, and wider at the top than at the bottom.

Seeing these broad apices, that constituted as much as a third of each building's height and looked like flower buds or the caps of morel or shiitake mushrooms, Jess felt as though she were some tiny insect creeping beneath gigantic plants.

This illusion was complemented by the swarming busyness of the world below the odd, high canopy.

The podium of each tower was made up of a rectangular block, and every one of these seemed to be honeycombed with the warren of some sort of small beast, being either surrounded by one to four floors of colonnaded arcades filled with rows of shops or pierced with shops that opened directly onto the pavement running beneath the ranks of skyscrapers. While Jess could not see the people bustling about these places clearly, as her cab was traveling very rapidly, she could tell that there were substantial numbers of pedestrians rushing around, like ants scurrying in and out of their burrows.

Then Jess thought of how the towers resembled certain other things.

Being as sophisticated as she was, she immediately stated her observation out loud. "They look like pricks. Do you think that's on purpose?"

"I am afraid, once again, that I cannot say," Uluf replied.

Jess giggled at the thought of a city of colossal phalli and returned to looking out the window.

A few moments later, Uluf spoke to her.

"We are coming up on the covered market. That is where we will be getting off. If you would be so kind as to look ahead, my dear, you will be able see it."

Jess peered through the cab's front window and saw an enormous rambling building directly ahead of her. It was composed of a formless mass of domes, spires, turrets, and balconies, no two of which seemed to be of the same color.

The taxi slid down a ramp as it came close to the market and pulled into a metal circle set within the broad square in front of that structure.

Having paid the rubber coated driver, Jess and Uluf stepped out of the vehicle and into the sweltering, humid air of Shokai. The pair wasted little time looking at the glowing sun, the shimmering heated air rising from the flagstones, or the sweating locals. Instead, they hurried into the market. Unfortunately, it was almost as hot inside the building as it was outside.

The ground floor of the market was a labyrinth of wide, vaulted stone corridors lined with countless alcoves that were each occupied by a little shop. As large as its hallways were, the market was so crowded with people that it was difficult to move very quickly and impossible to do so without considerable jostling and pushing. What was more, Jess and Uluf's movements were hardly made easier by the attention they were given by nearly everyone around them.

The people of Shokai had dark to wheaten complexions, straight to slightly wavy black hair, and features somewhere between those of the peoples of the ancient terrestrial nations of India and China.

Jess, anyone could tell, was not from their world.

In spite of her uniqueness, she was, however, arousing far less of the locals' curiosity than was her companion. Uluf was the only non-human wandering through the market and was, obviously, of a species not often seen in Jezic. Every child nearby gawked at him, and a great many of the adults did as well.

While the girl and the toad did their best to ignore such reactions and wandered about the market looking at the various items being sold (and there was a wonderful variety of these), Uluf repaid the locals' interest in him and his companion in kind. He pointed to a group of eight persons (two men and two women who were perhaps in their fifties, three young women in their late teens to early twenties, and a young man of about twenty) who were standing in front of a shop selling trinkets admiring the wares and laughing loudly at one another's jokes.

All the men wore brightly printed cassocks (the skirts of which were cut open in the front to a width of about three inches), colorful cloth slippers, and loose trousers. To the crotch of the last of these items, each man had fixed a foot long prow-like codpiece that emerged from the slit in the front of his outer garment and wobbled back and forth before his belly.

The two older women were as vibrantly dressed as were the men, but in long, loose skirts and loose fitting tunics covered with embroidery.

As bewitchingly gaudy as was the clothing of all these persons, it was the garb of the younger women that caught Jess's attention.

Each of those three wore a formfitting, elaborately printed, sleeveless choli that left her midriff bare, cloth slippers like those of the men, and tight fitting trousers that reached to just above the knee. These last, oddly, were each fixed with a codpiece of the same size and design as those worn by the men.

"See those people over there?" the toad asked (in a voice loud enough to be heard over the buzzing of the crowed). "They are members of the third estate, businessmen, professionals, physicians, academics, and the like, as well as their family members."

"Really? How can you tell?" Jess inquired.

"There are laws in Tozana that regulate what the people of each estate may wear. I am consequently able to determine their status from their clothing. Believe me, my dear, everyone's place in society here is obvious from a glance."

"Why would anyone care about something like that?"

"Tozana is very stratified. A person here needs to know another's estate to decide how he will act towards that individual. As arrogant as someone may be to those below him, he will have to be deferential to his superiors and courteous to his equals. None of that is just a matter of etiquette, either. If a person does not respect his superiors, if a laborer, for example, does not bow to officials and scurry out of the way of members of the third estate, he will be taken by the police and beaten. A person must know his place here. That said, it is possible to move from estate to estate by earning money, holding office, or receiving an education. Of course, in reality, I am certain most persons do belong to the same estate their parents do."

"Gods! That's worse than it is where I grew up. I guess people there probably act the same as they do here, but at least there there aren't any laws about it."

Jess shrugged and then asked, "Anyway, what's with the cocks on the women?"

"Well, I suppose the men are trying to show off their virility, their sexual prowess and their ability to dominate others. Machismo is an important virtue in Tozana. If you cannot strut about and show off your potency, you are nothing. That is true even with the women."

Jess had to admit that, at least when they were interacting with their equals or inferiors, the locals were a vain, slightly belligerent people. Not being too concerned about such attitudes, or about seeing how they were being expressed in the efforts of a number of young men who were milling around her and trying to impress her with their domination of their fellows or with the size and fine make of their codpieces, Jess pushed forward to observe other parts of the crowd in the market.

A moment later, she pointed at a team of men and women carrying crates into one of the shops. Each of them was completely naked except for leathern sandals and a string he had tied around his waist to hold a small purse.

"What class are they?"

"Those are laborers. Unless a person of Tozana is registered as a member of one of the four higher estates, he or she is forbidden to wear clothing. You can always spot a poor person here by his nudity. Of course, not everyone you see who is nude is poor."

"Why's that?"

"Gangsters do not wear clothing either. They are not invariably poor, but because of their means of income, they cannot register as members of a higher estate. They do, however, wear a great deal of expensive jewelry. You will see some at some point, I am sure."

Jess looked around again, but the only clothed people she saw who were dressed in garments different from those worn by the persons of the third estate were the shopkeepers (and a fair number of similarly attired individuals examining the goods for sale at different stalls).

These persons, whether male or female, wore a sort of apron that covered the chest, left the sides and back of the torso bare, and was wrapped around the hips so as to form either a skirt or a loincloth. The only difference between the garment worn by the men and that worn by the women was that the latter was fixed with a string below the breasts so that the upper part of the apron could be tightened and so made to support a woman's chest.

"So everybody with those aprons belongs to the fourth estate, right?"

"Yes. You are correct. That is their estate. They are, I should add, the easiest people to deal with here. They are not as pompous as are their betters or as obsequious as those below them. Mind you, since they are shopkeepers, by and large, I suppose they do need to be somewhat courteous."

"What about the first and second estates?"

"I do not see anyone from the second to show you, but you will have no trouble recognizing such a person if you do see one. They always wear solid white cassocks or orange uniforms, depending on whether they are civil officials or military officers. I doubt if we shall see anybody from the first estate. It is quite unlikely that any person so wealthy and important would come to a place like this."

While Uluf searched for an individual belonging to the second (or even the first) estate to show to Jess, a shop located a short distance down the corridor caught his eye.

"Come here. There is something up ahead you will like."

"Take me there, then," Jess replied, grabbing ahold of the toad's hand and beckoning him to lead her to what he had seen.

Squeezing through the throngs of people, Uluf brought the girl to a food stall, where he gestured at a row of wooden buckets set on the top of the counter running across its front.

Uluf went up to one of these and pulled out of it a stick on which was impaled a repulsive creature resembling a maggot that had grown to the size of a mango. From the fore end of this nasty beast emerged a dozen spidery limbs, like the ribs of a dilapidated umbrella, and its whole body was covered with a glistening, gummy coating.

Uluf handed the stick to Jess, who reluctantly held on to it with the tips of her fingers. The toad then picked up another stick skewering another candied maggot for himself, reached into the pocket of his waistcoat, drew out some coins, looked at the prices posted on the back wall of the shop, and called over the owner.

"Two krimhi, please," the toad said to the man and handed him his coins.

Jess, still holding the little monster at a distance from her body and eyeing it with a mixture of revulsion (for its ugliness) and disbelief (that Uluf had purchased it for her), addressed her friend in a slightly tremulous voice.

"Why did you buy these? They're completely disgusting."

"Try it. Krimhi is one of the best loved foods on this planet."

The toad bit into the krimhi he was holding, making an unpleasant noise that combined a sharp cracking with a wet slurping. Hearing that, Jess was not convinced that she could avoid retching if she bit into the bulbous vermin in her own hand. She just kept on watching Uluf as he chewed his bite and took another.

After he had swallowed, the toad wiped his mouth with a lace handkerchief he took from one of his pockets.

"Try it," he insisted. "I know it looks revolting, but I assure you that it is not."

Jess smiled at him in a weak attempt to appear brave. "Well, I suppose I've put worse things than this in my mouth."

Uluf laughed and gestured for Jess to eat the krimhi. Looking at her friend with a slight hint of annoyance, the young woman hesitantly brought the maggot to her lips and took a very small bite. She did feel a stab of nausea when she heard its thin shell cracking and another when the sticky, soft flesh squirted out of its corpse onto her tongue. A second later, however, before her revulsion had overpowered her, she became aware of the flavor of what she had bitten off. It was sweet, but not excessively so, and the meat, though moist and soft, was smooth and slightly peppery.

Seeing her changed expression, Uluf said to her, "Aha, it is not as repugnant as you thought it would be. Take another bite."

Jess did so, feeling far less disgusted than she had been when she first crunched into the krimhi.

"It's not bad," she said with a genuine smile. "Actually, it's pretty good. It's definitely the ugliest thing I've ever eaten, though."

"Come with me. I will take you to a place where we can sit down and enjoy our meal."

The girl took the toad's hand, and he led her to a bronze and glass elevator that conveyed the pair to a wide veranda on the roof of the market. After they had bought drinks at a bar there, the two walked over to a table beside the ornate balustrade. There, having sat in the shade of a wide umbrella while a machine hanging above their heads blasted them with cool air, the girl and the toad ate their meal and gazed across the city that stretched out around them.

To the north was the broad black ocean, now shaded by a mass of heavy grey clouds looming above the waters on its way towards Jezic. To the west, past the tall towers of the city center and across a wide river spanned by numerous bridges, Jess could make out, on a low hill, the many spired palace of the roshpai, the ruler of Tozana, like an exposed, frightened, and bristling hedgehog, and to the east she could see a collection of smaller towers. These last were shaped like the pink houses she had passed earlier but were all a drab light brown color.

As his eyes moved over the landscape stretching out before him, Uluf, almost with a sigh, said, "Just so, just so."

Jess, realizing this was a common expression among toads, who used it to give voice to their appreciation of the intrinsic beauty of the world around them, said to her friend, "You usually say that when you're looking at mountains and forests. I'm surprised you're saying it about a city."

"My dear, what is made by man can be every bit as lovely as is the natural world. You should never let the joys of the universe pass you by."

Jess smiled and replied, "Okay, Uluf, I'll try not to. So, tell me, what am I looking at here?"

"That is the Old Town," Uluf informed her while pointing at the small brown buildings. "Beyond it is the Oditkalee District, where we will be going to meet Tolliver later."

This last area ran along the eastern edge of the plateau whereupon Jezic was built and, even from a distance, appeared to be run down.

Past it, the scenery was even less pleasant, however. The whole of the valley to the east of Jezic, which was split in two by a broad though filthy river, was filled with a wretched shanty town crisscrossed by tall metal bridges ending in the city rising upon the hill on its far side.

"The area between the two cities, Jezic and Castru," Uluf explained, "is the Odivazi Preserve. Everybody calls it Mudtown, though. It used to be the capital of the Jaffrite kingdom that ruled this part of the planet. When Tozana took that over, the city was made into a preserve. That is the Nando River flowing through it, by the way."

With a bit of krimhi flesh dangling from her lips, and while still chewing a large bite, Jess said, "So, anyway, you've been here before. What's there to do?"

"We probably do not have the time for anything else today, and tomorrow you are going to wander around the city with Tolliver. I am sure he will know of more than a few places to take you."

"Can't you suggest some?"

"Go see the palace. It is very impressive. The Old Town and the city center are both interesting. I think, however, that you will like Oditkalee best. It is filled with bars, strange shops, and outlandish shows. You never really know what you are going to find there."

"Are you coming with us?"

"No. I think not. I will leave the two of you to spend some time together. Besides, I was under the impression that you wanted to see Quanya with me. We will have our own fun when we go there."

"What are you going to do tomorrow, then?"

"I shall stay at the *Empress*," the toad stated before wrapping his long tongue around one of the legs of the krimhi he was eating and breaking it off.

"You should go do something fun."

"Not here, at least not on my own."

"Why not?"

"Do you remember that paper you signed at the port authority, the one making you responsible for me?"

"Yes," Jess replied, breaking off one of the legs of her own dinner.

"Here, I am not a person," Uluf explained while Jess bit into the leg she had disattached. It was, she discovered, rather peppery and quite sweet.

Uluf continued as the girl cracked the krimhi's appendage with her teeth.

"I am considered by the locals to be your pet, your property. I have no right to move about the city on my own. I need you to be with me."

"That's stupid. What about in Quanya?"

"My understanding is that anyone with money is welcome there."

"Okay then, we'll have fun in Quanya instead of here. Is there anywhere else on Shokai we can go to?"

"I doubt if we will have time to see anywhere but Quanya."

"How long does it take to get there?"

"By airship, a day or two. I am not entirely sure. I have not been there before."

"You've been to Shokai a few times, though. Where all have you been?"

"This is the third time I have visited Jezic. I have also been to Nyopwa, the viceregal capital, once and to Hwiccho, the big city by the Southern Sea, one time."

"Which do like the best?"

"It is difficult for me to do much in Jezic unless I am with a human, and Hwiccho is horribly dirty and rough, so I suppose I prefer Nyopwa. It is very impressive, very grand, and toads are treated decently there. We shall not, however, have time to visit it before we leave."

The two continued to chat while looking at the sights below them and enjoying their krimhi and drinks.

Once they had finished their meals, the pair went back down into the market and wandered through its upper levels. These, though filled with a great many more shops, also housed numerous theaters, several temples, a library, and much more. While the two did not have the time to visit any of these places, Jess enjoyed the market's lavish ornamentation and Uluf enjoyed watching his friend having such fun.

Some time later, Uluf commented to Jess, "I believe, my dear, that we should probably be leaving now, if we are going to be at the bar in time to meet Tolliver."

# Chapter 3
# Drinking and Dying

Some time after Jess and Uluf had finished eating their dinner on the veranda set amongst the market's countless domes and spires, the dark clouds that had been racing across the ocean arrived at the city and began inundating it with heavy sheets of rain.

While Uluf, being a toad, hardly minded getting wet, he did not want to ruin his expensive clothing, and Jess had no desire to be doused and to spend the rest of the evening soaked. Upon leaving the market, the two consequently ran across the wide square in front of it and leapt hurriedly into the nearest taxi parked in the metal circle in the plaza's middle.

Uluf gave the mechanical driver the address Tolliver had given Jess, and the vehicle sped onto a metal bridge heading toward the east.

The taxi traveled at an incredible speed along the surface of the road – that looked more like a mass of turbulent water in the downpour than a solid object – and soon conveyed its passengers away from the now barely visible skyscrapers of the city center to streets lined with bullet or mushroom shaped towers burning with multicolored neon signs, tacky holograms of naked, gyrating, and beckoning women, and enormous glowing advertisements. Almost all of these structures were in need of repair, and more than a few were half dilapidated. Even the streets between them deteriorated in quality. All these were narrower than were the spacious avenues cutting through the forest of spires of the city center, and the metal bridge running down them was no longer as wide as it had been, having become only broad enough to allow two vehicles to pass one another at a time.

After the taxi had penetrated deep into this garish district (that Uluf identified as Oditkalee), it suddenly slid down a ramp and parked amongst several other vehicles underneath the bridge.

Uluf paid the driver, and he and Jess got out of the cab. They stood under the bridge, from the sides of which water was pouring, and Uluf looked around.

"There," he yelled, trying to make himself heard over the thunderous booming of the heavy rain on the metal structure above him.

He pointed to a tall bullet-like building that was capped with a copper roof and along one side of which slithered a vertical row of flashing electric signs.

"That should be the one," the toad informed the girl. "Come on."

The two, hand in hand, dashed from under the bridge, through the torrential downpour, past rough men and women wearing huge umbrella-like hats, and came to the building Uluf had indicated. He looked for an entrance with a sign but, at first, did not see one. After moving to the tower's side, he noted a narrow flight of metal stairs leading into a hallway piercing the wall below the level of the street. Above this was a sign in the local language.

"The Iron Fish is over here," he said and guided Jess down the stairs into the corridor at their base.

Both of the two were, by this point, completely dowsed. Jess's hair was plastered onto her scalp; her clothing was saturated, and her shoes squirted out little streams of water whenever she took a step. Uluf was no better off. His lace jabot hung limply from his jowly throat; his waistcoat and justaucorps clung to his round body, and his breeches were so bloated with water that his thighs looked like overstuffed sausages.

Uluf went to the door leading to the bar, the Iron Fish, opened it, and, with an ostentatious gesture, invited Jess to enter before him.

The place inside was not much to see. To the right of the entrance was a counter, and the remainder of the poorly lit, almost unadorned room was filled with a number of rude tables set each with a shabby hookah.

All of the bar's patrons clearly belonged to the third estate, as every one of them was completely naked. They were, however, without exception, dripping with copious amounts of lavish jewelry. The men and women alike wore gold and silver necklaces, arm bands, bracelets, anklets, girdles, torques, finger and toe rings, and various other items besides these. Bejeweled combs were stuck in their hair; silver nails were fastened onto their fingertips, and golden spectacles were set in front of their eyes. Further ornaments dangled from piercings in their ears, nostrils, lips, brows, nipples, navels, and genitals. Each woman's breasts were supported, but left uncovered, by a sort of ornamental brassiere, and each man hung bells from rings encircling his penis.

Apparently unconvinced that such display was gaudy enough, every one of the men (and several of the women) in the bar had covered nearly the whole of his body with bold, colorful tattoos of sinuous fish, swirling clouds, grimacing demons, graceful insects, or delicate flowers.

No sooner had Uluf seen this crowd than his entire body was drained of strength. He wanted to leave and felt as though he could barely make himself proceed further into the establishment. Jess too was a little concerned when she saw these individuals, but she doubted that such persons could give her much trouble. She was far more wary of getting the attention of the Tozani authorities if the locals did try to molest her. Even that thought, however, was not going to deter her from waiting in the bar for Tolliver.

She strutted over to the counter, leaving puddles wherever she stepped, and ordered a bottle of liquor. The barkeeper gave it to her, along with two ceramic cups, and she and Uluf walked over to an empty table near the corner opposite the entrance and sat down.

They still had about an hour before Tolliver was due to arrive, so Jess uncorked the bottle and filled both of the cups.

The two sat, usually silently, in the bar and waited. The other patrons, though obviously curious about these foreigners, did not disturb them. While Jess and Uluf received the occasional stare, no one made any attempt to antagonize them, and, after a few draughts of the pungent liquor Jess had purchased, the two had relaxed considerably.

When Tolliver failed to arrive at a quarter past the sixth watch, Jess thought little of it. As her bottle grew emptier, however, she started to wonder what was keeping him. The seventh watch slipped by; the bar grew busier, and Jess, having emptied the bottle she had earlier bought, purchased another for Uluf and herself.

She was a very small person, and she had consumed, by a quarter past the seventh watch, a fair amount of liquor, so that she was by then feeling quite lightheaded. Nonetheless, she was not nearly as relaxed as she ordinarily would have been when she had drunk so much. In fact, Jess was beginning to get both annoyed with Tolliver and worried about him. She was not particularly good at dealing with irritations and squirmed about in her seat, drummed on the table with her fingers, and fidgeted with her still soaked clothing.

Around the middle of the seventh watch, Jess, feeling frustrated and grumpy, grew tired of her drink and began to wonder what it was that some of the people were smoking in the hookahs set on their tables.

"What is that stuff?" she asked Uluf.

"It is called bhank. It is a mild intoxicant. I would not, however, advise you to smoke it. You have already lost much of your ability to defend yourself and may not be up to handling a problem if one arises."

"Don't be scared. If somebody messes with me and I'm too drunk to fight him, I'll just suck him off. Either way, he won't hurt you. I promise. So, do you get it from the barkeep?"

The toad was less than pleased with Jess, but, realizing that there was little he could do to dissuade her from getting entirely inebriated, he gave up his attempts to do so and told her she could purchase bhank at the counter.

She went there and requested the herb, and the barkeeper handed her a small paper pouch filled with a sticky, thorny brown weed.

Jess paid the man, took the pouch back to her table, and put it in the bowl of the hookah there. She began smoking the bhank, inhaling it deeply and blowing great oily rings of bluish, slightly iridescent vapor into the air above her head.

As she sat watching these circles slowly descending onto the table or the floor, where they flitted about and eventually disintegrated, Jess discovered that she enjoyed the euphoric, dizzying effect the bhank had on her. She was not, however, miserly and offered the pipe to Uluf.

Being unable to stop his companion, he decided to enjoy some of the stuff himself and soon was feeling nearly as giddy as she was.

While the two so continued their wait for Tolliver, Jess, her mind clouded and her body tingling, thought of how she had often before waited for the captain in his cabin on the *Empress*. There, she had quietly dreamt of the things she would do for the man when he had finished his shift and had hoped that he would both enjoy those things and like her for so pleasing him. Such thoughts soon conjured up images of the captain's chest rhythmically pushing against her breasts, of his face looking up at her from between her thighs, and of his bare shoulders sparkling with sweat. She could nearly feel his arms around her back, his teeth biting her ears, and his body inside of hers. Remembering how alive she had been at such times, when her existence was interwoven with that of another person, Jess became deliciously excited.

Exhaling loudly, and blowing her bangs away from her forehead, Jess tried to draw her mind to other thoughts. Tolliver was not, after all, there with her at the moment. Fortunately, the weird universe the bhank had created had more than a few delights of its own. It was, in fact, wonderfully soothing and transformed Jess's arousal into a lazy sense of bemused satisfaction.

Eventually, while sheets of variously colored lights played across the walls of the bar and the tattoos of its patrons wiggled and danced about their flesh, Jess's ringed eyes started to itch and her lids grew heavy. The crowd in the Iron Fish had, by that time, thinned, and, as each person yet remaining there enjoyed the sleepy contentment the bhank had given him, the loud noise of conversation diminished to a dull murmur.

Just as Jess was thinking that she and Uluf should themselves be leaving, since Tolliver was plainly not going to meet them, a naked man with long plaited hair and tattoos of schools of shimmering fish all over his torso walked close to their table and let a slip of paper drop from his hand into the empty cup in front of Jess before continuing on his way to the exit.

When this person had left the bar, Jess looked at the paper in her cup without removing it. On it was written, in Twituboch, "Tomorrow at third watch at the green statue in Chaakvoi Square."

Jess turned her gaze to Uluf, who was leaning against the wall with his eyes half closed, and said, "Come on. Let's get a room and get some sleep."

The toad nodded; Jess grabbed the piece of paper, and the two lifted themselves from their seats and staggered out of the bar. The rain had stopped and so the pair walked a short distance down the street to where Uluf, who knew the local script, had seen the sign of a hotel.

Once the two had entered the room they had rented and had stripped off their moist clothes, Jess handed Uluf the slip of paper the man in the bar had given her. As the room was quite warm, the girl sat down naked on top of her cot and spoke to Uluf, who was sitting unclothed on the edge of his own bed.

"What do you make of that?"

"Well, I am sure that it must concern Tolliver in some way, even though I cannot say how. In fact, given that he has clearly been plotting to do something on this planet and has now failed to meet you when he said he would, I would be shocked if this note had nothing to do with him."

"Do you know where Chaakvoi Square is?"

"Yes. It is where the government executes criminals. They make a huge show of killing such persons here. If they are putting some people to death tomorrow, there will be a substantial crowd. That is probably why your mysterious friend wants to meet you there."

"Will you come with me?"

"Of course, my dear."

"Let's get some sleep, then. My head's spinning from the bhank."

With that, Jess lay down, closed her eyes, and quickly fell asleep.

The toad did the same.

\* \* \*

Jess awoke the next morning dripping with sweat. The room she was staying in was unbearably hot and humid. As she wiped the moisture from her face and body, she became aware of a nasty taste in her mouth and remembered how much she had drunk the previous evening. An uncomfortable feeling came over her while she wondered if she had done anything foolish. She was, fortunately, unable to recall any embarrassing stunts and hoped that she was not forgetting something.

"Ah, you are awake, my dear," called out a mellifluous voice.

Jess looked over to her right and saw Uluf standing at the foot of his cot. He had put on his breeches (but was otherwise naked) and was occupied with attempting to press his justaucorps on a rickety table using a pathetic old iron.

"You should get up if you still want to go to Chaakvoi Square."

The girl recalled the note the man had given her in the Iron Fish the previous evening. She also remembered that Tolliver had never arrived there.

Hoping that the captain was well, fearing that he was not, and thinking that the man from the bar could tell her which of these possibilities was the case, Jess dragged herself out of bed and walked over to the open window set in the peeling, cracked green wall of the room. Leaning against the sill and resting her toes against the rotting, worm-eaten wainscoting, she looked outside at the city.

The sun was already high in the sky and shimmering waves of heated air rose up from the earth like sheets of weightless water, twisting and deforming the multicolored towers looming behind them in the distance. The street below her was quiet. Perhaps, she thought, the residents of Oditkalee preferred the night to the day.

Turning around, resting her elbows against the sill, and leaning upon it, the girl said to Uluf, "What do you think's going on? I think Tolliver has gotten into something he can't handle."

"I am afraid that, at this point, I have no idea. It would probably be best if we met with the man from the bar. Incidentally, I contacted the ship while you were still asleep. The captain did not return there."

Jess walked over to where she had tossed her clothes the evening before. They were lying in a crumpled heap on the floor near the foot of her bed. She stooped down, picked up her trousers, felt them to discover if they were still damp, and, finding that they were not, laid them out on her cot.

Sitting down beside them, she asked Uluf, "Well, do you think our new friend could be dangerous?"

"Again, I cannot say. However, I do not believe that he will attempt anything at Chaakvoi Square. If executions are being held there today, it will be thronging with people."

"I don't suppose it matters, anyway. Even if he is up to something, we still have to meet him."

With that, Jess got up, picked up her clothing, and went to the bathroom.

"I'm going to take a shower. Let's head out when I'm done."

"As you desire. I am almost ready."

\* \* \*

Chaakvoi Square was a wide plaza between the city center and the Old Town. To the south it opened onto a wide avenue. To the north it reached to the colonnaded, many spired, copper roofed Palace of Justice, and to the east and west it was bounded by tall walls covered with inscriptions and bas-reliefs depicting the triumph of law.

In front of these, and partially obscuring them, were stone structures supporting tiers of seats that extended along about a third of the length of the square.

Before each of the stands, at its exact middle, was an ornate building (like a small house) with elaborately cast bronze doors. From either of these, between the wide flagstones used to pave the plaza, ran a pathway made of some gleaming white stone. These paths terminated at a raised, balustraded platform where a variety of unpleasant instruments was arranged.

Between the raised area and each of the stands (to either side of the ornate buildings at the middle of both of the latter) were rows of twenty foot tall stone pillars carved into a variety of monstrous shapes. The top of each of these was fitted with an iron ring, and from this hung a chain fastened to a metal collar clamped onto the neck of some naked man or woman sitting at the base of the column.

A short distance to the south of the stands, beyond a low wrought iron fence, was a row of stone statues and, in front of these, resting upon a marble pedestal, a lone green copper statue of an armed man slitting the throat of an insect-like monster that was wrapping the coils of its body around his legs.

Jess realized that this had to be the statue the man from the Iron Fish had mentioned in his note, and she and Uluf made their way to it.

"I feel kind of weird coming here," Jess commented. "It's like we're pretending to be characters in some tacky movie."

"I will concede that this is an odd situation."

"Do you think we're being stupid?"

"My dear, something peculiar is going on. As strange as coming here may seem, we would be unwise not to do so."

"Yeah. I suppose that's true."

Upon coming to the statue, neither the girl nor the toad saw the man from the bar, but they were not troubled, as there still remained a third of a watch before he was due to arrive.

The square was, however, already crowded with people. The stands were completely filled, and the wide space to the south of the fence was teeming with men, women, and children, who were all jostling for a place wherefrom the platform beyond the barrier could be seen. Several young boys were even perched on the green statue's pedestal when Jess and Uluf arrived there. The girl would have liked to have sat where the children were, but, as there was no room for her to do so, she leaned against the great stone while Uluf stood beside her, resting his weight on his striped cane.

"This really is an interesting square, but there are way too many people here," Jess noted.

"Indeed. The press is somewhat overwhelming."

"Yeah. It's hot enough already without the warmth from all these bodies."

Jess paused to wipe the sweat from her face, and then, while tugging at her top to cool herself, continued. "I'm going to wither up like a dried fruit if that man from the bar doesn't show up soon."

The toad, his mouth hanging wide open, replied, "At least you, my dear, can sweat. All I can do to cool myself is huff and wheeze."

Jess laughed and patted her friend's face in sympathy. "I thought amphibians were supposed to like it warm."

"Yes, but even the most pleasant of things can become unpleasant when experienced in excess."

The pair suddenly heard a loud drumming, which was soon complemented by the blaring of horns. A troupe of musicians, accompanied by elaborately, colorfully garbed soldiers, marched out of the Palace of Justice and made its way to just north of the platform. There these persons stood in a row reaching from one of the stands to the other. The crowd became quiet, men lifted their children onto their shoulders so that these could see over the heads of the countless adults assembled, and everybody looked intently at the events occurring before them.

"Ooh," Jess gasped. "I think they're about to start."

Uluf placed his hand upon the girl's shoulder, wishing she was not going to see what she was about to be shown.

From the ground just behind the musicians emerged a shining metallic pole. It was extremely narrow, except at its top, where it widened like a blossoming flower (so that the whole thing resembled a gigantic golf tee). The top of the spire was a sort of crow's nest, and in it was sitting a magistrate wearing a tall conical hat and red robes.

"Is that the ruler of Tozana, the roshpai?" Jess inquired excitedly.

"No one so grand, my dear. He is simply the presiding judge."

"He made quite an entrance, huh?"

"Just wait, my dear. It gets better than that. Of course, it also gets much, much worse."

When the pole had been raised to a considerable height, the magistrate spoke. His voice amplified and made tinny by a loudspeaker, he announced the purpose of his presence, to preside over the punishments being meted out to criminals, and exhorted the onlookers to learn from the examples these unfortunates were setting for them.

As soon as he had finished this speech, the man called upon the gods to take note of how the people of Tozana loved justice and how, in spite of that love, they were so merciful that they could not themselves harm even the most evil of men. Jess did not yet know what the man meant, but she was soon to learn.

The magistrate next announced that the place of execution should be sanctified, and the band at once began playing a loud, raucous tune.

A moment later, a group of men bearing staffs topped with feathers more colorful than those of a peacock and larger and thicker than those of an ostrich and wearing sky blue robes sewn with images of deities and diverse symbols, lace chasubles, and gilded hats shaped like tulips paraded out from behind the eastern stands. They were followed by a priest garbed in even richer vestments (sewn from golden threads), crowned with a ridiculously tall cylindrical hat, and carrying a sort of wand in either hand. Around this person waddled six fat young boys, his acolytes, who were attired in frilly lace gowns and who bore various items on trays and pillows, while, after him, came more men attired and equipped like those before him.

Jess watched these persons with such fascination that she briefly forgot she had come to the square to get information about Tolliver. The Tozanis undoubtedly knew how to create a grand spectacle.

The priest slowly made his way to stand directly in front of the pillar, below the magistrate, who asked the prelate to bless the legal proceedings. Agreeing to do so, the priest bowed to the official.

"What are they going to do?" Jess asked Uluf.

"They are sanctifying this whole place, handing it over to the gods and making it holy. The religion of the people here is very concerned with rules, and this whole rite involves those who broke their rules. The state is preparing to set the universe back in order. For them, executions are religious rites."

The men with the feathered staffs stood to either side of the pillar while the priest, followed by his acolytes, began to circumambulate the platform. With each step, the man waved his wands, recited incantations, and spoke verses in some language Jess's translator was not programmed to understand. At each of the four corners of the structure, and at the midpoints between these, the priest stopped, babbled more incomprehensible words, and scattered flower petals he took from one of the boys. After doing so, he tossed handfuls of an orange powder upon the ground, followed by a twig wrapped with a ribbon, and then sprinkled all of these with water. Having taken such things from five of his acolytes, the priest, before moving on, picked up a book held by the sixth boy. This he simply kissed and replaced on the pillow whence he had taken it.

After the priest had finished with this rite, he returned to stand below the magistrate and made a low bow to the official. A chair was brought for him and placed beside the pillar. The priest sat down in this and his acolytes stood to either side of him. Seeing these persons were settled, the magistrate commanded that the criminals be brought forward.

"Well, this has already been quite a show," Jess remarked.

"Humans do generally make death into a great spectacle."

"Your people do too. I've seen a toad funeral. Now that was a show – wild costumes, puppets, mimes, singing, dancing, bagpipes, sarangis, and a marionette to officiate over the whole thing."

"Ah, but toads relish life and find joy in all experiences, even those that are sorrowful. We do not wallow in what is hateful or unpleasant. When toads make death into a spectacle, we emphasize the loveliness of sorrow. Humans emphasize the thrill of killing."

"That's not always true, Uluf."

"No. I suppose that it is not, but it often is."

"Okay, well, I'll admit that."

While the girl and the toad talked, a long wagon with enormous spoked wheels rolled out from behind the western stand. Its roof was covered with myriads of statues of ugly, leering goblins and fiends, and the whole of its length was composed of a cage, so that it resembled the kind of vehicle used to hold circus animals. Inside, however, were huddled not lions or tigers but about a dozen naked men and women. At the head of this vehicle, perched upon a narrow metal stem, was a glass bubble, wherefrom the driver slowly steered the cart across the plaza, until it was just to the south and the east of the magistrate's pole.

Several of the soldiers standing there went to the back of the wagon, opened the door to the cage upon it, and pulled out a prisoner using a device similar to a shepherd's crook. This person was then made to kneel in front of the magistrate, who read out his sentence.

The judge said, "Siddot Shoka, you have been convicted of theft. Today you will be given over to justice machines that know your misdeeds and will punish you for your crimes. No man commands these engines. Their actions are determined only by your actions. You alone bear the sin and the responsibility for what happens here now. The people and state of Tozana are blameless. Let the sentence be carried out."

Two of the soldiers marched to each of the structures in front of the stands and, at a signal from the magistrate, opened the heavy doors of these.

"Do ready yourself, my dear, for things to get nasty," Uluf informed Jess.

"How nasty?"

"Very."

Music suddenly blared and out of the house-like building to the east stepped a twelve foot tall brass robot shaped like a grinning, fanged demon. His potbelly was covered with bas-reliefs of men and women writhing in billowing flames and being devoured by worms, centipedes, and other unpleasant beasts. His mouth was filled with projecting silver fangs and tusks. His twisted, clawed hands held a trident and saw-toothed sword, and between his bowed legs hung a knobby, twisting penis resembling that of a pig.

At the same time, from out of the other building raced a whole gang of revolting, constantly squirming robots. They were not dissimilar to the first in design, but were as thin as reeds, made all of shining steel, and stood no taller than the average man.

"You've seen an execution here before, right?" Jess asked.

"Yes. It was impressively staged, but utterly sickening."

The brazen giant lumbered onto the platform, and most of the smaller robots arranged themselves around their superior. Two of them, however, with ungainly leaps, hurried to where the prisoner knelt. They grasped him by his throat and hair and dragged him across the flagstones of the square onto the platform, casting him, upon his knees, in front of an iron block shaped like a tree stump. One of the silvery devils then held the man in place as the second grasped his right hand and put it on top of the metal block.

Jess bit her lower lip and closed her right eye in anticipation of what she was about to see.

"This is going to be disgusting, isn't it?" she asked.

"Yes, my dear."

The larger robot stood over the man, set down his weapons, and picked up a gigantic iron mallet. He swung this dramatically around his head to the great amusement of the assembled crowd, especially the children, who hooted and laughed with delight. Then, with tremendous force, the robot brought the hammer down upon the hand of the man kneeling before him, completely pulverizing it.

Jess grimaced and looked at the toad standing beside her.

"How did you watch this before, Uluf?"

"I did not watch much. I spent much of the ceremony looking at my feet."

"Why didn't you just leave?"

"I was with Tolliver and some of the other crew members, and most of them appeared to enjoy the spectacle. I had to wait until it was finished and we could all leave."

The brass demon stepped back and his two smaller fellows lifted the injured convict up, dragged him from the platform to one of the pillars below the stand to the east, and fastened the iron collar at the end of the chain hanging from it around his neck.

Jess, still repulsed by what she had seen and eager to leave Chaakvoi Square, looked around for the man she had seen at the Iron Fish, even though she was not entirely certain that she would be able to recognize him.[*] She did not, however, spot anyone who returned her glance or gave any sign that he recognized her.

"Do you think he's going to come?" she asked Uluf.

"I think that it is probable he will."

"I wish he'd hurry. This is disgusting."

"Yes. I agree. Nevertheless, you must admit that it does have a certain barbaric splendor and a captivating repulsiveness. As horrified as I am, I cannot seem to take my eyes away from the spectacle. In fact, I seem to be mesmerized because of that horror."

While these two were talking, a second man was led from the cage upon the wagon and brought before the magistrate, who identified him as a murderer and handed him over to the robots.

The same two silver ones that had taken hold of the previous man brought his successor to the brass robot and made him kneel before it. This giant picked up a metal disc that was divided into two parts connected by a hinge. Where the halves of the disc joined there were three holes, and the man's hands and head were placed in these.

As soon as the brazen robot closed the device upon its victim and secured this with a heavy lock, it lifted him up with a handle fixed to the disc behind

---

[*] She had been very drunk the previous night.

the opening for the head. The huge fiend then carried the murderer to the back of the platform, to a huge glass cauldron filled with a clear liquid.

The robot lowered the man into the liquid and set the disc on the lip of the cauldron, to which it was perfectly fitted. At once, the victim began screaming horribly and flailing his legs uncontrollably. For a moment Jess did not understand what was happening, but Uluf offered an explanation.

"The vat," he said, "is filled with acid. It is strong enough to eat away a man's skin, then his flesh, and then his internal organs. But it is not so strong that it will do it quickly. He will remain in the vat for some time slowly dissolving."

"Gods! That's horrible!"

Jess might have been a killer, but she was not without compassion, and she certainly never relished seeing anyone in pain.

"If that man doesn't get here soon, I'm leaving. I can't handle much more this," she said in a slightly tremulous voice. In fact, watching the man in the cauldron howling and thrashing was making her feel distinctly sick.

While a second thief was brought out and treated as the first had been, and the cauldron wherein the murderer was melting gradually filled with blood, a man wearing a wide brimmed hat and a blue cassock printed with bright yellow flowers came around the corner of the pedestal and stood to Jess's right.

"Jess Ichikawa?" he asked without looking at her.

She, however, peered up at him intently. Though this person's face was probably that of the man from the bar, his dress was so different from the other's bejeweled nudity that Jess was not certain the two were actually the same.

"I thought it was against the law to dress in the clothes of an estate you don't belong to," she said. "You shouldn't break the law in this country. Look what they do to criminals."

"You needn't worry. I'm actually a member of the third estate, and there's no law forbidding anyone from dressing like a member of the lowest order."

"So, you're the one from the Iron Fish?"

"Yes."

"Who are you?"

"My name's Noyan Hlu."

"What do you want from me?"

"I'm a friend of Tolliver."

Jess looked at the man again. Even though she had already been nearly certain that he wanted to talk to her about the captain, her heart still began to race when she heard him say as much.

The guards dragged a fourth man from the wagon and Jess asked, "Where is he?"

Before Noyan had replied, Jess heard the magistrate say that the person before him had been convicted of assaulting a member of the second estate.

"I don't know," Noyan said as the convict was set upon a metal table in front of the cauldron where the dying murderer's entrails and skin were floating in a soup of bloody acid.

"Why'd you want me to come here, then?"

"Tolliver got in touch with me yesterday and asked me to meet with him."

The brazen demon began sawing off one of the man's feet, and Jess asked the stranger, "What did he say? What's he doing?"

"He was worried about you."

Having cut off both the criminal's feet, followed by his calves and thighs, the brass robot was now removing his arms, beginning with the hands, proceeding to the forearms, and finishing with the stumps hanging from the shoulders. The mechanical executioner then picked up the still living torso, carried it to the fence to the south of the platform, and impaled it on a twelve foot tall spike just to the north of that barrier. The other robots gathered up the man's limbs, brought these to their leader, and gave them to it so that the contraption could impale these on the spike rising above the torso.

"What's going on?" Jess insisted as she wiped away the sweat rolling into her eyes.

"What do mean?" Noyan asked her.

"Where's Tolliver? Is he alive?"

"I'm sorry. I can't answer either of those questions."

Jess was beginning to get angry.

"Why not?" she demanded.

"I haven't seen him since yesterday."

Her brows furrowed, the girl snapped, "What's he up to, then?"

"He didn't tell me. Look. I want to help you. Just listen for a minute. I hadn't seen Tolliver for several years. He called me yesterday and asked me to meet him. I did. He told me he might be in trouble, but he wouldn't say what sort of trouble he was having."

During the time Noyan was speaking, a fifth convict, a rapist, was brought out of the wagon and hung, spread-eagled, from four posts in the middle of the platform. The brazen robot, his corkscrew penis elevated, approached him from behind.

Jess was so surprised by this sight that she was briefly distracted.

"They're not going to do to him what I think they are, are they?" she suddenly inquired.

"Yes," Noyan replied. "I'm afraid they are."

While Jess watched the enormous robot rape the screaming man, her mouth hanging open as though she were trying to catch flies, Noyan continued.

"Tolliver asked me to wait at the Iron Fish to see if he showed up. He said, if he didn't, I should discretely get you to meet with me."

"Why?"

"He gave me this and wanted me to give it to you if he didn't turn up."

Noyan pulled a black metallic rod out of a pocket in his oversized codpiece and handed it to Jess. It was a picture spindle, a kind of visual recorder.

"What's on this?" Jess inquired.

"I have no idea. It's been locked. Tolliver's encoded it with your DNA. Only you can open it."

Jess slipped the device into a pocket in the interior of her vest.

"Thanks," she said.

Noyan took a pen and a slip of paper from the same pocket the recorder had been in. He wrote something down and yelled over the roar of the crowd, the members of which were hooting in unified delight at the treatment of the man on the platform in front of them. "Here's my number. Tolliver asked me to give you any help I could, and I will."

"Thanks again," said Jess as she took the paper.

Then, while the brazen robot impaled the rapist on the spike next to that decorated with the corpse of the last man so treated, she asked Noyan one more time, "Do you have any idea what's going on? Just a guess?"

"I'm sorry. I don't. I haven't seen Tolliver for years. To be honest, if he hadn't wanted me to come see you now, we might never have met up with each other again."

"Well, I appreciate everything. I'll get in touch with you if I need help."

"Don't hesitate to do so," Noyan said. He then made a gesture of farewell, according to the fashion of Tozana, and left.

The body of the murderer having now completely dissolved, the brazen robot picked up the man's head and hands and stuck all three of these on a spike behind the metal fence.

Another criminal was taken from the wagon, but Jess and Uluf did not wait to see how this person would be treated. They left the square and returned to their hotel.

# Interlude 2
# Species of Shokai

There are three sentient species indigenous to Shokai: Jaffrites, feihi, and maruvazi.

## Jaffrites

Jaffrites, more commonly called mudjumpers, are found throughout the northern region of the planet, but their populations have historically been concentrated near bodies of water, whether rivers or the ocean.

Both genders of the species have black, hairless, rubbery skin, a stocky, almost spherical body, a relatively long, thin neck, two arms, and two powerful legs adapted for hopping and swimming. A Jaffrite's feet are long, pointed, and flipper-like, without differentiated digits, although its hands have four fingers and an opposable thumb. The head is large, rounded at the top, and adorned with a bony purplish or reddish crest. The front of the head tapers to a point and is flexible. On the lower side of this snout is the mouth, a sphincter filled with sharp, rasping teeth. The tongue is prehensile and is approximately two feet long. Each of a Jaffrite's fourteen eyes is hemispherical, glossy, and black. Two of these, the largest, are set in the front of the face roughly halfway along its length. To the outside of each of these are three more eyes. Another pair is set further back on the head so that the Jaffrite can see behind itself, and two more pair are placed on the snout, below the main eyes.

The genitals of the female Jaffrite are externally visible only as a bright red sphincter located on the underside of the base of a long, bulbous, but relatively flat tail-like organ at the rear end of her torso. During mating, the male mounts the female from behind as she presses her tail against her back in such a way that he is able to insert his penis into her genital orifice.

The male Jaffrite's penis, which is as much as twice the length of the rest of his body, emerges from his posterior like a tail and is used not only for reproduction, but also for display and balance. For about half its length, the penis is thin and covered with the same rubbery skin as is the rest of the Jaffrite. Its second half is, however, adorned on top with a hard shell composed of a series of overlapping plates that become wider towards the posterior end. From underneath this shell, on both its right and left sides and all along its length, project a series of leaf-like feathers and, beneath each of these, a thin tendril ending in a colorful tuft. The last of the tendrils, at the very end of the shell, are especially large and brightly colored. Between these final tufts, a second, shorter shell decorated with six bony projections extends from below the first shell. On the underside of this second shell is the opening of a tubular ridge that extends along the underside of the penis. From this emerges, when the Jaffrite is stimulated, a long, bumpy tentacle ending in a bulbous knob, out of a hole at the tip of which the male ejaculates.

Jaffrite semen contains a potent intoxicant that produces vivid auditory and visual hallucinations as well as feelings of intense euphoria. When consumed as a drug, usually orally (most often after having been considerably diluted), Jaffrite semen is commonly known as russa.

The production of russa is strictly regulated in all nations on Shokai by the Treaty of Hudaipwa. According to this agreement, Jaffrite semen can only be collected from Jaffrites confined to certain designated preserves that have been leased to one or another of the Seven Families, and none of the semen so collected can be distributed on Shokai itself, except in Quanya.

Prior to the arrival of humans on Shokai, Jaffrites had developed several distinct regional civilizations. While the species made few technological innovations, and never produced metal tools, they did devise numerous systems of writing and used these to record their substantial literature. The earliest of these works are approximately twenty-thousand years old. In addition to historical and literary texts, Jaffrites wrote sophisticated dissertations on astronomy, mathematics, and agriculture.

In the nine-hundred years subsequent to the initial human colonization of Shokai, Jaffrite nations were recognized by treaties and continued to be self-governing. When the hallucinogenic effects of Jaffrite semen were discovered and the consumption of russa became widespread, human governments canceled their treaties with Jaffrite states and imposed restrictions both on trade with these and on travel between their own nations and those of the aboriginals. Over time, much of the territory controlled by the indigenous states was confiscated by their human neighbors, whose governments increasingly assumed authority over those states.

Later, during the Russa War, the human governments of Shokai incorporated what remained of the Jaffrite nations into their own territories. Attempts were subsequently made to confine Jaffrites to heavily policed preserves or even to exterminate them. In spite of such efforts, significant numbers of the species avoided being captured or killed and continued to survive in the wild.

With the adoption of the Treaty of Hudaipwa, the Seven Families were given authority over most Jaffrite preserves. Several of these, however, such as the Odivazi Preserve near Jezic, continued to be administered by the government of whatever nation they were located in.

**Feihi**

Feihi are arboreal creatures inhabiting Shokai's northern region.

Only the females are sentient.

The parasitic, non-intelligent male feihi is approximately three inches long and has a soft, undifferentiated body, the back of which is protected with a chitinous shell. On the underside of its body are four short legs that exude a sticky substance it uses to adhere to the trunk of a tree and, immediately in front of these, a long proboscis with which it is able to suck out the sap of that tree.

When a female of the species is fertile, she emits a pheromone that stimulates nearby males to detach themselves from the tree they are feeding upon. The female is then able to pick up a male and place him upon her genitals so that he can fertilize her with a tendril approximately the diameter of a human hair that he extrudes up to six inches from its base. After mating, the female generally devours her partner. In fact, male feihi are one of the female's dietary staples.

If impregnated, the female will, within a week, lay a clutch of thousands of minuscule eggs on a sturdy tree branch. Most such clutches, which resemble masses of tiny soap bubbles, will be composed exclusively of eggs with male embryos, and these will hatch within thirty to thirty-five days. One out of every six or seven clutches will, however, include a single egg with a female embryo. When a female egg is present, it will absorb the numerous male eggs around it and send out a set of feeding tendrils. These will penetrate the tree whereupon the egg is resting and extract its sap.

After approximately eighty days, a female feihi will emerge from this egg. At the time of hatching, females are around six inches in height but otherwise resemble adults.

At maturity, female feihi stand approximately five feet tall and are remarkably similar in appearance to human females. Their eyes are, however, substantially larger than are those of human beings, occupying roughly one-fifth to one-quarter of the entire vertical extension of the face, and their shoulders exude sheets of a soft, diaphanous film that enwrap their torsos. They are completely without body hair, although they do have blue or green eyebrows and manes.

Feihi, while only marginally less intelligent than human beings, have not developed more than a rudimentary technology or the simplest of societies. To this day, they live in small bands of genetically related individuals and subsist on fruits and the male of their species.

There are thousands of feihi languages, none of which are written. Some of the creatures living near human settlements have been known to learn to communicate in whatever human language is spoken in that area.

The genitals of the female feihi produce an intoxicant with an extreme aphrodisiac effect. As this substance can be absorbed through the skin, female feihi are often captured and sold for use as sexual partners. Human and feihi anatomy are not, however, compatible, and sexual intercourse of a male human with a female feihi is invariably fatal to the latter.

Because the drug that makes intercourse with a feihi intensely pleasurable is highly addictive, unlicensed trapping of and trafficking in feihi is strictly prohibited by all governments on Shokai, and sexual intercourse with a feihi is permitted only in Quanya.

## Maruvazi

Maruvazi inhabit the deserts covering most of the surface of Shokai and are closely related to Jaffrites.

The shape of a maruvazi's body is similar to that of a Jaffrite, although it is somewhat thinner and its neck is shorter and thicker. The maruvazi is covered with overlapping plate-like folds of thick, rough, yellowish-white skin. These flaps can be raised so that heat can be vented by propelling warm air out of numerous small ventricles located beneath them. The creature's arms are strong and bulky, but the forearms are especially large, being noticeably thicker than the upper arms. The two primary eyes are rounded, glossy, and black, and are set in deep sockets, the skin of which is also black. Within each of these sockets, to the outside of the primary eye, are three smaller eyes, and below the eye sockets are two more eyes, one above the other, that are not set in sockets. The maruvazi lacks the backward facing eyes of the Jaffrite.

The genitals of the male maruvazi, like those of the Jaffrite, extend from the posterior of the torso and resemble a tail that can be longer than the remainder of the body. Unlike that of the Jaffrite, the penis of the maruvazi is not ornamented. It is, instead, covered with a series of overlapping, plate-like rings. Semen is ejaculated through a tendril that emerges from the tip of the tail. Maruvazi semen has no psychotropic properties.

The female maruvazi's reproductive organs consist externally of a brownish sphincter located near the base of a long, relatively flat tail-like organ at the back of her torso. Mating among maruvazi is similar to that seen among Jaffrites.

The tail of both the male and the female maruvazi is capable of retaining water and can become substantially enlarged if the creature has regular access to fluids.

Maruvazi use their shovel-like arms to excavate tunnels and remain underground most of the time. Their communities are clustered around the extensive subterranean rivers and reservoirs that occur beneath the deserts of Shokai. When they do travel across the surface, maruvazi move by hopping.

Little is known of maruvazi cultures, although several of the different systems of writing they have developed have been deciphered and a number of the underground cities they have constructed have been explored.

These settlements, in spite of the harsh environment in which the maruvazi live, are occasionally of considerable size, the most extensive of them being sufficiently large to house over a thousand individuals.

Such populations are fed, in part, by hunting, but the maruvazi are also known to cultivate fungi and to be proficient at pisciculture.

From Pollidor's *Big Blue Book of Knowledge*

# Chapter 4
# Visiting

Back in her hotel room, Jess pressed her thumb against a pad located halfway along the length of the picture spindle Noyan had given her. She then set this device on its end on the table in front of her. It immediately opened up like a collapsible fan and started to spin. Lights emerged from its blurring upper edge and rapidly coalesced into a seemingly solid image of Tolliver.

While Jess and Uluf sat upon the latter's cot, the image spoke.

It said, "Jess, I guess you're probably wondering what's become of me. Obviously, if you're seeing this, I've gotten into trouble.

"You must have realized that I had some sort of secret deal going on. Well, I'll come clean with you about that now. During our last voyage, I was forwarded a message by our contractor. He had been contacted by the Llalloi Family. They're a member of the Smuggling Syndicate. What they wanted was for us to deliver to the Sing gang the devices the Seven Families use to spray containers filled with russa with a film that prevents the drug from being detected.

"Apparently, there's a dispute going on between the Llalloi and the Ngo. They're one of the Seven Families, the one the Llalloi smuggle for. Anyway, the Llalloi are trying to set the Sing up with the facilities they'll need to produce russa. Oh yeah, the Sing are a big gang in Jezic. They run prostitution and protection rackets, smuggle goods, and supply illegal drugs. That sort of thing. As I was saying, the Llalloi are hoping that they can put an end to their dependence on the Ngo. They'll have the Sing to provide russa for them.

"On the day we arrive in Jezic, I'm supposed to meet up with a representative of the Sing at the Drunkard's Pleasure. That's a bar. We're going to arrange the transfer of the goods I have on the *Empress*. But I'm not confident about these people. They're not used to dealing with offworlders and I've been told they're pretty unreliable, not to mention violent. If anything happens to me, I don't want you trying to find out about it. I know how good you are at fighting, but even you can't take on a whole gang.

"The cargo's already paid for, and we're going to unload it into a warehouse. It's up to the Sing to collect it. If they pull anything with me, it's their loss. Don't worry about making arrangements if I'm not there. Let them rot.

"There's one other thing I want to tell you, Jess, and I don't want you mentioning a word of this to anyone. That goes for you too, Uluf, since I'm sure you're there as well.

"When I played the transmission from the Llalloi that our contractor gave me, I noticed there was a glitch in the encoding. I thought there might be something encrypted in it so I checked it out. I was kind of right. The message had been encrypted, but it wasn't meant to be deciphered.

"The sender of the message had tampered with its routing details so that it appeared to be coming from one place when it actually originated somewhere else. Of course, I was curious. I played around with it, and I discovered something interesting.

"Right there in the message were the coordinates of the Llalloi's base of operations. For all the hundreds of years they've been smuggling russa, nobody outside of the highest levels of their organization has known where they're based, and here they're telling me. By accident! They messed up good.

"Jess, don't miss this chance. I've written down the coordinates on page 110 of my copy of *Universal Landing Regulations*. Go get them. I've also left a copy in a locker I rented on Tomasine Station, just in case.

"Contact a Llalloi representative and tell him what you have. Also, let him know that you have a second copy. Don't tell him where it is, but make sure he realizes it'll be found if he harms you. It will be too. As soon as my rental of the locker expires, the coordinates, and a description of what they're coordinates of, will be discovered.

"Don't accept less than a billion kopecks for the coordinates. That's nothing for the Llalloi. They'll try to convince you to take a lot less, but stand your ground. You'll be a rich woman, Jess.

"Sorry I can't be there. I can't get out of this meeting. It may not matter if I piss off the Llalloi, but I still can't make the Sing angry. They know we're here and they'll be visiting me if I don't visit them. I guess, if you're watching this, it didn't matter.

"Best of luck, my love."

The image smiled and then dissolved. The spindle stopped spinning, folded itself up, and stood on its end (like an impossibly well balanced pencil) on the top of the table.

Jess turned to Uluf. She was clearly somewhat confused.

"What are you going to do, then?" the toad asked her.

The girl sat in thought for some time before saying, "I don't care what Tolliver says. I'm going to find out what happened to him."

"You heard what he said. He is right too. You cannot fight an entire gang."

"It's not like they're all going to get together and fight me at once."

"I still do not think it is as simple as engaging with one individual at a time."

"I don't care. I'm going to find out what's happened to him. He may not even be dead. Shouldn't I at least try? I could be saving his life."

"I understand, my dear. Whatever you do, I will remain with you. I am always your friend."

"Thanks, Uluf. What do you think I should do first?"

"Contact Noyan and ask him where the Drunkard's Pleasure is. We can go there and find out if anyone saw who Tolliver was with. We also need to go back to the *Empress* and get the coordinates the captain left for you."

"That all sounds good to me. I'll call Noyan first."

Jess stood up and walked over to the telopticon.

This device consisted of a brass horn shaped like a trumpet projecting from the wall. Rising from this, to a height of about two feet, was a sort of brazen lyre (though it had no strings), and, in front of the lyre, there projected a small stem ending in a ball containing a microphone.

Jess spun the crank located at the bottom of the telopticon, powering it up, and recited Noyan's number.

A moment later, a tinny voice coming from the trumpet said, "Hello."

"It's me, Jess Ichikawa."

"One second."

Suddenly there was a flash of light from one of the horns of the lyre to the other, which quickly expanded into a luminous sheet between these and then resolved into an image of Noyan so clear that he appeared to be sitting just on the other side of a window.

"How can I help you?" the man asked.

"I just watched the recording you gave me. Tolliver said he was meeting somebody at a place called Drunkard's Pleasure. Do you know where that is?"

"Yeah. It's on Kaan Street, in Oditkalee. Who was he meeting?"

Jess thought for a second about whether she should tell Noyan, but decided that it no longer mattered who knew about Tolliver's plans. "He was meeting up with somebody from the Sing gang."

"In the Drunkard's Pleasure? Was it about something of value?"

"Yeah. It was."

"Then Tolliver must have been meeting Hanufam Vomo. He's the head of the Sing gang in that part of Kaan Street. If something involving a lot of money was happening, Vomo would've been there. There's no way he would've let somebody else take care of anything big in his part of town. He's a real hothead, though. I'd be surprised if he didn't have something to do with whatever's happened to Tolliver. But why the gang would send him to a meeting with an offworlder, I have no idea."

"Do you know where I can find Vomo?"

"Yes. He runs his little province from a flat near the Drunkard's Pleasure. I wouldn't advise you to visit him there, though. He's a lecherous old man and brutal. Go to the bar instead. Maybe someone saw something there."

"I can take care of myself. Anyway, whatever I do, I need to know where this guy is. Can you tell me?"

"I don't know the address, but if you tell me where you are, I can give you directions."

Jess told Noyan where she and Uluf were staying, and he described the route they should take to get to the building where Vomo would be.

"If you go there," he continued, "you'll be lucky to leave again. He likes young girls and he'll love having an offworlder to play with."

"Like I said, I can take care of myself."

"It's your call. Just remember that I warned you."

"I will. Thanks for your help. If I can ever repay you, I promise I will."

"I'm sure. Best of luck to you both. Feel free to get in touch with me as long as you're in Jezic. I'll do whatever I can to help. Just don't do anything stupid."

"Thanks a lot," said Jess and pressed a button in the middle of the crank on the telepticon. The image of Noyan dissolved like a fog before a wind, and the girl turned to Uluf.

"Let's get going," she announced.

"We should go to the *Empress* first and collect the coordinates the captain mentioned in his message."

"Oh yeah. Let's do that, then."

* * *

As the sun was setting behind the silhouettes of Jezic's skyscrapers, Jess and Uluf got out of a taxi in front of the tower where Vomo's flat was. Like a rotten tooth in an otherwise healthy smile, the grim brick structure created a dark, ugly patch amongst the other buildings of Kaan Street, that were all burning with innumerable neon signs and obscene holograms.

Having told Uluf to hold the taxi, in case she needed it in a hurry, Jess kissed the toad's cheek and made her way to the moldering structure in front of her.

She entered the foyer through a rickety screen door and, in the dim yellow light cast by a single fixture on the ceiling, looked at a directory posted on the wall. It indicated Vomo's flat was located on the top floor. Taking the glass walled elevator that ran up the center of the building's spiraling stairwell, the young woman arrived at a landing leading to a single door covered with metal plating that was cast with various sexual images.

In the center of these was a relief of a woman with her legs spread and her vulva open. Jess looked at it (with a vague feeling of annoyance) and inserted her finger into the image's vagina. She could hear a bell sounding within and leaned against the railing at the top of the stairwell, making certain the crumbling green and black parquet floor did not disintegrate under her feet and send her falling to her death.

An enormous man whose naked tattooed body gleamed with jewelry opened the door. He looked at Jess and smiled. Above her waist, the girl was dressed as she had been earlier in the day, in a thin vest and a tube top, but she had exchanged her trousers for a loose red skirt that reached to just below her crotch and left her thighs bare. Her calves, however, were hidden by her tall, shining black boots. Jess knew she looked sexy and so, as soon as she was no longer alone, struck a sultry pose that she was sure would tempt any man who saw her.

Since the individual standing in the doorway was entirely unclothed, Jess knew within seconds that her attitude had had the effect she desired.

While his interest in her grew, the man asked in a rough voice, "Who are you?"

"My name's Jess. I want to talk to Hanufam Vomo."

"What business do you have with Mr. Vomo?"

"Does it matter? Don't you think he'll want to see me?"

The man smiled widely, baring his gold plated teeth, all of which had been filed into triangular fangs. With a painfully obvious meaning, he said, "Oh, he'll want to see you. Come in."

The gangster opened the door and Jess walked past him, swinging her hips as dramatically as she could.

Inside was a drab room completely covered with formerly white tiles. Many of these had, however, been broken off and those that remained were so filthy they were usually more yellow or even brown than they were white. To the left of the door was a table, where two more nude, tattooed men were sitting playing some game that involved casting small bean-like objects onto a diagram, and, directly opposite the entrance, was a second door, this one made of featureless metal.

Jess waited in the middle of the room while the man who had let her in closed the outer door. He told her to sit down on a stool propped against the wall to her right, across from the table, and then left the room through the interior door.

The men playing the game with the beans stared at Jess as she sat on her stool, her knees together, her feet apart, and her lips pouting. She twisted her pink hair around her finger, looked at the men with her face slightly cast down, and generally had fun teasing them.

She did not enjoy this diversion for long, as the inner door soon reopened and the same man who had let her into the flat beckoned for her to come with him.

Shutting the heavy, iron door behind him, the thug told Jess to continue down the hallway to the last door on the left.

Her feet sinking into the two inch deep carpet, Jess walked past three-dimensional images of women performing various sexual acts that were hung in grotesquely gaudy frames on the painfully magenta walls. When she came to the room she was supposed to enter, her gold toothed companion, who had been following immediately behind her, opened the door and told her to go inside.

Except for where Jess was standing, a divan ran around the whole of the circumference of the oval room before her. Above this, directly opposite the entrance, was a tall window that reached to the domed ceiling and presented an impressive view of all the city to the north. To the right and left, the walls above the divan were recessed and the shelves so created were occupied by remarkably realistic mechanical statues of beautiful young women dancing lasciviously, contorting themselves into obscene postures, or performing some seemingly unpleasant sexual act or another. On the walls to either side of the door were larger versions of the pornographic holograms found in the hallway.

To Jess's left was an ornate table dripping with fake gilding and littered with bottles, hookahs, and vials containing different drugs. Behind this, on the divan, sat two young, nude women. Neither was wearing any jewelry, although both were elaborately tattooed. Between them reclined a naked, obese man of about sixty around whose torso was twined a colorful tattoo of a ferocious dragon. Further along the divan, to this man's right and left, were more burly thugs, five altogether, all of whom were unclothed, tattooed, and tangled in vast amounts of jewelry.

Jess walked to the middle of the room, twitched her nose, and then pinched it as she felt the stench of stale alcohol, noxious chemicals, burnt weeds, sweat, and semen stabbing into her skull.

The fat old man looked at her intently for an uncomfortably long time. Finally, he said, "What brings you here?"

Rubbing her nose energetically, Jess answered him with a question of her own. "Are you Hanufam Vomo?"

"Yes," he replied. "And who are you?"

"My name's Jess. I want to talk to you about your meeting with Tolliver yesterday."

"Who's that, then?"

"He's the captain of the *Empress*. You had a meeting with him at the Drunkard's Pleasure yesterday afternoon."

"I'm sorry. I can't seem to recall any such thing. Perhaps if I thought about it a while I might remember. Why don't you stay for a spell and help to jar my memory? It's getting so bad as I grow older. Come over here now. Sit with your daddy."

"Why don't you just tell me what you did with Tolliver? I'm not going to suck your cock or whatever you think you can get me to do."

"That's no way to make friends, my girl, and I think you need to be friendly with me right now."

"Fine, let's be friends. Now, let's gossip about a mutual acquaintance. So, how's Tolliver? Seen him lately?"

"You can grow tiresome, my girl. I'm not interested in talking right now. Take care of daddy and he'll take care of you."

Jess was beginning to lose patience with this discourse.

Her voice tremulous with anger and disgust, she snapped, "Look, you nasty old fuck, there is no part of your disgusting body that I'm going to let you put inside of me."

Vomo was clearly annoyed by her insult and, gesturing to the men around him, bid them get up.

"Strip her," he barked. "Strip her and bring her over here."


# Chapter 5
# Growing Up

Jess could not remember her father. She was not even sure that she had ever met him. Since her mother had no idea who the man was, there was really no way for Jess to know either. It was, of course, possible that she had seen or even spoken with him, maybe many times, but, if she had, she had not guessed who he really was.

Jess did, however, remember her mother and her habits, although she often wished that she did not. She might, admittedly, have been unable to answer anyone who asked her what the woman's name was, but she could not rid herself of phantoms that, taking the shape of her mother or of occurrences relating to her, often snuck uninvited into her mind. Recalling, against her will, how she had been forced to mix doses of telheq, the drug her mother had used, Jess would see images of oily streams of that substance pouring from vials and forming translucent spirals in cups of water. She would often, in spite of all her efforts, find herself presented with visions of her fragile, tired mother lying on her bed, in a chair, or on the floor in a babbling, drooling stupor. At yet other times, she would, without any desire to do so, picture some man or another having sex with the inebriated woman, whether she was awake and needed money or was unconscious and helpless.

Jess had especially hated those times when men had come to the concrete flat she had shared with her mother in a tall tower facing countless other identical towers in Hosak, the city where they had lived. Some of the men ignored her and did what they came to do while Jess sat in a corner and pretended she was not aware of anything. Others, however, did not like having her in the room while they were having sex. When those men came, Jess's mother threw her out. Sometimes she would wander about and try to find something to occupy her time, but usually she just sat in the corridor outside and waited until she heard the grunts that always preceded a male visitor's departure.

What money Jess and her mother had the latter got from those men who came to visit her, but most of it went to pay for each day's supply of telheq.

Even in the slum where the two lived, where nearly all the children were dirty and scrawny, Jess was unusually filthy and exceptionally skinny.

Consequently, when Sechun started sleeping at their flat and bringing food home with him, the young girl was pleased with her changed circumstances. She soon grew stronger, and Sechun eventually insisted that she bathe and attend school. While she did not like being too close to him, since he had an odd smell, she certainly preferred the way things were since he had moved in to what they had been before.

Besides, he was always kind to her. He often sat with her when he and Jess's mother were not injecting telheq. He frequently asked her about her life, about what she had done at school, and about the things she had learned there. He even played games with her.

After a few months, in fact, he was spending more time with Jess than he was with her mother, and that was when things became much worse.

Jess made every effort not to remember any of the events that followed. Although she had clean clothes, food to eat, and toys to play with, her life went from being noticeably better to being infinitely more horrible than it had ever been previously. Even her mother made her existence more difficult. Before, the woman had been indifferent. Now, she was always angry at Jess and constantly demeaned and struck her.

Finally, when she was twelve traders' years old, Jess had had enough and left her mother and Sechun to find ways to amuse one another without her.

For some time, she made do by sleeping in alleys, under bridges, behind piles of rubbish, or in any other place where she could and by stealing whatever she was able to get her hands on. Then, one day, she met a boy a few years older than herself who was squatting in a dilapidated factory and earning a few kopecks by selling telheq. She remained with him for half a year.

Though Jess made enough money dealing drugs and stealing to buy her clothes and food, it was during this time that she realized that there were innumerable men who would pay her well for her favors. Her companion, though he was happy enough to spend her greatly increased income for her, was often angered by the way she made it and almost as often treated her roughly. On those occasions when he was especially rough with her, she was, of course, left unable to earn any money for some time, but that irritated him more than the way she got her money.

Jess eventually decided not to put up with such treatment any longer and left the encampment she shared in the ruined factory with her young companion. She then resolved to earn a living at what she had learned she was best at and so made her way to one of the many brothels situated in the outskirts of Hosak.

The city was located on the northern coast of a large but sparsely inhabited continent on the planet Koismai. There were numerous mining colonies and small settlements scattered throughout this landmass, but the only city there was Hosak. Consequently, not only did all the continent's trade with the world's population centers pass through that metropolis, but the rough men who made their living in the wilderness also came there from time to time to entertain themselves.

Having been isolated from the company of women, and even from other men, these persons, most of whom were themselves wild and barely civilized, desired raucous fun, plentiful drink, and available whores when they entered the city. Fortunately for them, Hosak had more than a sufficient number of establishments that catered to their desires.

Jess was young and attractive and had little trouble selling herself to a procurer, who purchased her services for a period of ten years. While she could hardly say that she enjoyed being smothered by the filthy, brutal men who visited the establishment where she lived and toiled, she earned a reasonable income and had far better accommodations than she had ever had before.

For two years she remained at the whorehouse, servicing how many thousands of men she could not guess, until, one day, an odd old codger consumed too much wine in the bar on the brothel's ground floor.

He had been drinking continuously there the whole day, and, by the coming of evening and the arrival of substantial crowds, he was so inebriated he fell asleep on the floor. At some point, it occurred to somebody in the bar that it might be entertaining to urinate on the unconscious drunkard. When, after being so treated, the old man failed to regain consciousness, the patrons of the bar began having more fun with him. They threw food, rubbish, stones, and filth at him, painted his face, stripped off his clothes, dressed him like a whore, and did whatever they could think of to try to wake him up.

Nobody made any attempt to defend this person for some while, until Jess came down the stairs to see if she could wheedle some money out of a drunken patron or two. Even though she had hardly been treated with compassion by any person she had ever met, when she saw the old man being degraded and laughed at, she felt sorry for him.

She was a feisty girl and raised so much noise that the crowd released the drunk into her custody and even helped her drag him into an empty room where he could sleep off his liquor.

The following day, the man awoke, found himself reeking of other men's urine, covered with filth, and pathetically disheveled. He demanded the employees at the brothel tell him what had happened to him, and they gladly, and with laughter, related every detail. When he heard how Jess had come to his aid, the aged drunkard, whose name was Seizho Takenac, insisted upon buying out her contract and taking her with him when he departed.

While the girl was less than ecstatic to hear that this red nosed old man now had the rights to her favors for eight years, she had little choice but to leave the brothel with him.

Takenac took her across the sea to Hasakyur, the capital of the kingdom of Fukwohak, and to his large, sprawling, if slightly dilapidated house set in an extensive walled garden nestled in a valley between two mountains outside of that city.

There, Jess was surprised to learn that the bleary eyed codger who now owned her taught combat techniques to a number of aristocratic young men who lived in a dormitory on the grounds of his house.

Although Jess was not made to work, as Takenac had more than a sufficient number of servants, she was discontented with her lot. Each day, her owner left her alone while he taught his students how to fight with their hands or with various weapons, but each night he remained with her. He often drank so much in the evening that he fell asleep beside her, but he was so entirely infatuated with Jess that he never failed to spend whatever time he was not with his pupils with her. On those nights when Takenac did not collapse in a drunken stupor, he insisted upon having sex with Jess, and even when he was left impotent by his consumption of alcohol, he still demanded that she entertain him by taking his flaccid, withered member into her mouth. Jess was certainly more than accustomed to having such relations with nastier individuals than her latest partner, but she did find that having to perform on one such person over and over again got increasingly bothersome.

She was, however, curious about who Takenac really was and took to questioning him when his bouts of drinking had made him garrulous. In time, she discovered that the man had once been an assassin. He even claimed to have been the most skilled killer on the planet and said that his services had been sought by the rulers of many, even most of the numerous quarrelsome little states between which the world was divided. Only after he had grown older, and his lifelong love of wine had somewhat dulled his abilities, had he given up his occupation and used the substantial money he had earned from murdering one wealthy man for the benefit of another to purchase the estate where he now lived.

Since his retirement, he had busied himself by taking on a number of students from various aristocratic or royal families. Though he said he never taught any of them all he knew, what he did teach them, he claimed, made them some of the most lethal fighters on the planet. He was thus able to earn a substantial income without endangering himself.

Jess was intrigued by Takenac's tale, and, with little to do to occupy her time, she eventually took to watching him train his students. After a while, she even began to desire to learn some of the skills they were mastering.

When she had been at the old man's house for around six months, she approached him about teaching her, but he refused, spoke condescendingly to her, drank some wine, removed her clothing, and had sex with her.

In spite of such a reply, Jess was so intrigued by the idea of learning to fight that she resolved that she would find some way to do so. Soon thereafter, she went up to one of Takenac's students, though her owner had forbidden her ever to speak with any of these young men, and asked him to train her secretly. Seeing he was reluctant to comply with her desire, and having no money with which to pay him, Jess offered him the only thing she had that he was interested in. Fortunately, since she was already an attractive young woman, she had little trouble tempting her potential instructor. She allowed him a sufficient number of glances at and gropes of what he could later have if he taught her some of the skills Takenac had imparted to him to ensure that he would show them to her. Of course, the young man, being more than a little dizzy with lust, agreed to introduce Jess to the martial arts.

Within a few days, Jess had come to agreements with all of Takenac's students. Whenever Takenac was occupied elsewhere and one of these young men was free, he and Jess would meet. The youth would teach the girl what he could, after which she would pay him as much as she thought his lesson was worth. She so purchased simple exercises with her hand, help with skills she had already learned with her mouth, new skills with more intimate embraces, and special techniques with whatever the student desired of her.

Jess's training continued so for over three months, until, one afternoon, Takenac, hearing a noise behind a hedge in his garden, happened to find her lying on her back with her legs wrapped around one of his pupils. He was so overcome with rage that he began pounding upon the youth with the staff he was carrying, bloodying and bruising the boy while ignoring his pleas for forgiveness. Before he had killed his student, however, Takenac regained his composure, had his servants cast the nearly unconscious individual out the front gate, and bid the wrongdoer never return.

While the old man battered her teacher, Jess was nearly overcome with terror at the thought of what Takenac would do to her, but, when the gate was closed and he turned towards the terrified girl, he did not strike her. The furious, trembling old killer did, at first, raise his staff as though he planned to do so, but before he had brought it down upon her skull, he stayed his hand. Pointing at her with a trembling finger, Takenac told Jess not to return to her chambers that night, that she was, instead, to sleep with the servants.

The following day, Jess was informed that she would thereafter have to work to earn her keep and was hardly surprised to hear what her new duties would be. She was assigned the most unpleasant and the most arduous chores on the estate. The more difficult or disgusting a job was, the more likely it was that she would have to do it. For the next week, she cleaned up after the livestock and birds Takenac kept, scrubbed toilets, pruned roses, and carried heavy burdens.

Jess, who hated her new condition even more than she had disliked some of her previous chores, quickly resolved to win back her owner's favor. Unfortunately, Takenac never came near her and prohibited her from coming to any place where he would be.

Eight days after Takenac had discovered her infidelity, Jess, while raking leaves, saw him sitting in a pavilion near a pond in his gardens. She immediately ran to him, cast herself at his feet, grasped his legs with her arms, and pleaded with him to forgive her. With salty tears rolling down her cheeks, her face darkened with sadness, and her mouth contorted with the extremes of her emotions, she told him she had so wanted to learn the skills he was teaching his students that she had used her only asset to gain access to them.

At first, Takenac had wanted to push the girl away, but, as he watched her body heave with sobs and listened to her tremulous voice, his heart softened while, simultaneously, something else hardened. He stroked her long black hair, lifted up her chin, and agreed both to forgive her and to train her as he did his other students.

Jess was overjoyed to hear this and threw her arms around his waist. The old cuckold, thinking that he had rid himself of the one student with whom Jess had secretly had relations, felt the tide of his previous jealousy recede and his old lust for the girl surging up again through his body. When she began to tell him how grateful she was, he silenced her, informing her that she need say nothing, and gave her something else to do with her lips.

Takenac subsequently taught Jess the basics of both unarmed and armed combat. He showed her how to perform acrobatic leaps, how to move unseen, how to predict an opponent's moves, and how to harden her body so that she could successfully engage in any strenuous activity.

During this time, the man came to realize that Jess was remarkably talented and learned far faster than did any of his other pupils. He also became even more infatuated with her than he had been before. Now that she was doing something that excited her, she was far more vivacious than she had previously been, and far more willing to please Takenac. The lust she was able to stir up in him soon so consumed the man that there was little he would not have done for the girl.

Eight months after her training had begun, Takenac took her into the chapel of Haya, the war goddess, a place he had never before entered in the company of another person. There, he offered oblations to his fierce deity, bid Jess do the same, and asked the girl if she would be willing to accept his highest training, which he had never offered to any other person.

Jess immediately accepted this honor, but as soon as she had, Takenac told her that if he were to train her, she must first swear to keep secret all he would reveal. With an offering of her own blood, Jess vowed before the goddess to remain quiet and was made one of her most intimate disciples.

Having drunk wine suffused with Haya's essence and having had her own life's breath replaced by that of the deity, so that, from the tips of her fingers to the marrow of her bones, she had been ritually possessed by the goddess, Jess was readied for the darkest teachings of the arts of war.

The very next day, Takenac again took the girl, whose naked body was adorned with myriads of magical diagrams, to the chapel, and there, while the two knelt face to face before the goddess's image, the old man drew an ornately carved box out from under his robe and placed it on the floor between himself and his student.

Saying a few words in some language Jess did not know, Takenac opened the box and lifted from it a thin black thread that had apparently been knotted at numerous points along its length.

He told his disciple that what he held was an artifact left by the ancients that had been discovered by men.

He said, "This thread is able to arouse an awareness of the true nature of reality, that the mind does not exist in the universe but the universe in the mind. Like a serpent that, biting its own tail, devours itself, this thread consumes the external world that is actually already within it. When raised, it reveals how what appears to be the container is actually the contained and how what appears to be the contained is actually the container. It pulls the universe inside out just as a fishmonger tears the skin from a fish.

"Now, turn your back to me and rest your brow upon the floor."

Jess did as the man told her and felt him place his hands upon her body just below the base of her spine. Suddenly she experienced a cold piercing sensation and intuitively realized that she was feeling the thread entering into her body. A rush of terror came over her, but she did not budge. A moment later, Takenac instructed her to face him again, and she resumed her previous posture.

He continued his instructions, saying, "The thread within you is now dormant, resting coiled above your perineum. With the training I will give you, you will learn to rouse it from its sleep and to force it to race up through your spine, like a flash of lightening that burns away your false perceptions and reveals things as they really are.

"The thread, having produced a powerful true cognition, that causes the potency resident in it to become your own, will enable you to see that the objects apparently outside of yourself are actually within you and that you can form and change them according to your will, just as you already do with those you now recognize as being produced by your own imagination.

"Instead of moving your body, you will move the universe. Instead of being enslaved to the passage of time, time will move according to your desire. There will be no physical feat you cannot perform. There will be no enemy who does not crawl while you rush like raging water.

"This thread is the secret behind my unsurpassed skills. While I am as talented as is any other fighter, I am but an ordinary man without the thread. With it, my skills make me invincible. It will be the same with you if you learn to use it.

"Do you have any questions you would now like to ask me?"

"Yes," Jess replied. "Are you giving me the thread?"

"I am."

"What about you? Don't you need it?"

"No. My days as an assassin are long past. I am now enjoying the peace that comes with the end of life. What else do you want to know?"

"How did you get the thread?"

"It has been passed on through a line of teachers and students from the time it was discovered less than four-hundred years after the colonization of this planet."

"Doesn't anyone know anything about it?"

"Its existence has been revealed to no one outside of our lineage. Although I am sure other threads exist elsewhere, what others know of these I myself cannot say. I merely know that none know of this thread besides a single person and his or her teacher."

After Takenac had spoken these words, Jess thanked him for favoring her. He then explained more about the thread. The old man told her how to concentrate on it as it lay coiled at the base of her torso, how she was to focus her will upon it to stir it from its slumber, and how she was to draw it up through the length of her spine so that it transformed both herself and the universe that existed within her.

Although, on her first several attempts to awaken the thread, Jess could not move it at all, within a few days, she was able to pull it up as far as her navel, and, over time, she was able to make it to shoot up into her skull so that it pervaded the whole of her body, flooding her every cell with some ambrosial liquor that left her intoxicated with a sense of endless power and bliss.

When the thread, piercing her body from her perineum to her brow, vibrated inside of her, Jess felt as though she were possessed by it, as though it swallowed her up. The strange, wriggling worm penetrated the whole of her being and merged itself and her into a single ravenous beast that, turning upon and devouring the external world, obliterated everything beyond itself, melting the universe into Jess's own flesh.

Sensing that each entity before her was her own creation, Jess was able both to cause the ground to rise up beneath her and to hurl the earth away from her. She then no longer needed to leap across any obstacle and could easily descend from incredible heights. Time too was hers to rule. She could slow it down to half its ordinary speed or more, preventing any opponent from being able to match the rapidity of her motions. She could even, though the effort exhausted her, nearly freeze time, thereby allowing her to move unseen though surrounded by countless eyes.

Takenac was pleased to see the progress Jess made in her training, and, some four months after he had given her the thread, he took her once more to the chapel of Haya.

There, sitting face to face with his student before the goddess's altar, the red nosed old man said to the young girl, "Jess, you are the most talented pupil I have ever had. But remember, though you have chosen the bloody path, do not kill for the love of killing, kill for the love of Haya. Offer up to the goddess the blood and soul of every being whose life you take, and she will reward you. Now, I have another gift to give to you."

He handed Jess a slender metallic rod ornately cast with the image of a centipede-like creature.

"This," Takenac explained, "is Dawn's Spine. It is my sword as it was my master's before me and his before him. Press the nodule here."

Jess did as he commanded her, and from the rod shot out a grey, slightly curved blade composed of a series of segments each of which emerged from that below it, like the sections of a collapsible telescope. When the blade had so extended itself, its parts were still distinguishable so that it vaguely resembled a metal tapeworm.

Takenac spoke again.

"When the blade has been drawn out of the hilt, it is encased in a force field. It is, consequently, unbreakable, impossibly sharp, and incapable of being dulled. I give Dawn's Spine to you today, Jess. From now until you yourself die or pass it on to another, it is yours."

After the girl had received the blade from Takenac, he trained her how to use it, and, within a short while, she had become a proficient swordswoman. Even her teacher, as skilled as he was, was surprised by her abilities.

Four months later, however, Takenac, while enjoying a bottle of wine as he reclined in a boat floating upon the pond in his garden, happened to need to urinate. He stood upon the rocking vessel to relieve himself in the waters, but, when he did so, he lost his balance, fell in, and drowned.

As much as she had hated living with Takenac when she first arrived at the old man's home, Jess had learned much from him and had come to feel affection for the libidinous drunkard. She was, consequently, deeply saddened by his death.

Once Takenac's funeral had been performed, Jess resolved to earn her living not as a prostitute but as an assassin, now that she had the skills and tools to do so.

She left her teacher's estate and made her way to Hwakash, Koismai's largest city and the location of its sole spaceport.

There she discovered that she had absolutely no idea how to offer her services as an assassin and was forced to rely on her other talents to earn enough money to pay for a room to live in and food to eat.

Fortunately, while visiting one of the rough bars patronized by the city's gangs, she met a petty drug dealer and quickly became involved with him. Soon thereafter, her new lover introduced her to his employer, Masawa Tauk, the boss of the local Raisu gang, and Jess, taking advantage of her charms, easily aroused that man's interest in her. Within half an hour of their meeting, the gang lord had sampled Jess's amorous skills and had taken her as his lover.

Realizing that he was entirely infatuated with her, Jess asked Masawa to let her fight for him. As drunk with lust as he was for his new plaything, the boss, seeing how small and slight this girl was, merely laughed at the idea. She insisted, nonetheless, begging him in a pouty, enticing way to let her fight with one of his own men to prove her skills.

Masawa, unsure of what exactly to do, agreed to her request and, bringing Jess to a bar where many of the Raisu gang spent their time, bid one of his smaller and less intimidating underlings fight with her. Jess dispatched the man with such speed and ease that Masawa and his followers were all astonished. When Jess requested that she be allowed to take on someone more dangerous, Masawa sent one of his most brutish goons against her. She sent this musclebound oaf crashing, unconscious, bloodied, and bruised, to the floor as handily as she had the first man and so convinced her lover that she could be a valuable soldier for him.

Over the next several months, Jess was sent to bring Masawa's more difficult business associates into line with his way of thinking, to convince local merchants that they ought to be fearful of the Raisu gang, and to remove individuals who opposed or annoyed that group. All the while, she both won considerable notoriety throughout the city's underworld and became indispensable to Masawa, who invariably relied upon her whenever he required force.

Thus, when he and another gang lord were to meet with the captain of a smuggling vessel, who was selling drugs imported from another world to both of them, Masawa naturally brought Jess with him. He neither trusted this captain, a man named Tolliver, or the other boss, who was often his rival, and suspected one or both of them could attempt violence.

Masawa's rival did, in fact, prove to be unreliable, and, at the meeting, he tried to murder both Tolliver and his local enemy. Unfortunately for him, Jess's patron and lover underestimated the abilities of his foes and failed to react quickly when these thugs attacked. Masawa was so killed, as was Tolliver's bodyguard. In spite of such successes, however, those individuals' murderers were no match for Jess and she managed to butcher them and their boss. Tolliver and Masawa's successor then concluded their own deal.

The following day, the captain of the ether-ship contacted Jess and asked her to have a drink with him. She, having had little contact with anyone from another world, agreed, and the two met that evening. Being convinced that the best way to interest a man was by not being reluctant about sharing her body with him, Jess did just that and spent the whole of the night with her new acquaintance.

For the next several days, she spent nearly all of her time with Tolliver, who was increasingly mesmerized by this deadly and charming young woman he had encountered. Before his ship left, he asked her to come with him, to replace the bodyguard who had been killed at the meeting where Masawa had died.

Jess was captivated by the possibility of traveling to other worlds, thrilled that she would have the opportunity to make a living with the skills Takenac had taught her, and overjoyed that she had met a man who appeared to like her. She readily agreed to Tolliver's offer and left with him aboard his ship, the *Empress*.

# Interlude 3
# Ancient Species

Approximately seven million years ago, a species known to humans as shiyu developed space travel and began to colonize the rim of the Milky Way. Since that time, their empire has expanded to include a substantial portion of the edge of the galaxy, although the exact extent of their dominion remains unknown.

The shiyu currently generally avoid contact with species living outside of the area they inhabit. The sole exception to this avoidance is their relationship with the huviho. This species, which controls the region to the east of the Earth, was contacted by the shiyu roughly two-hundred-thousand

---

* Sidereal directions have been set as follows: The direction of the galactic core from the Earth is north. The opposite direction is south. The direction towards

years ago. The huviho had not, at that time, developed space travel, but the shiyu provided them with a considerable amount of advanced technology and transformed them into a spacefaring race. Under shiyu guidance, the huviho subsequently expanded along the northern border of their benefactors' domains. Their own empire thus formed a barrier between that of the shiyu and those of other species.

Almost the whole of human knowledge of shiyu history and culture has been provided by the huviho. Even that species' knowledge of the shiyu is, however, limited by the shiyu's unwillingness to share much information about themselves with others.

Mankind has, nonetheless, learned from the huviho that about three and a half million years in the past, another species, the veiac, who are often referred to simply as the ancients, developed space travel and colonized an area of the galaxy bordering shiyu space to the west of the Earth. For over a million years, the veiac co-existed peacefully with the shiyu, but, for reasons that remain unknown, they eventually became involved in a war with their older neighbors.

This conflict cost the shiyu dearly, as the veiac, through trade and their own efforts, had developed a technology nearly as advanced as that of their opponents. The shiyu, consequently, took extreme measures. They waged a war of extermination and entirely wiped out the veiac species.

With their enemy eradicated, the shiyu, intending to prevent any other species from gaining access to veiac technology, forbade all entry into the region formerly colonized by that race. This area of space, often called the Wilderness, remains entirely uninhabited to this day.

The shiyu, usually employing the huviho as intermediaries, regularly inform any species traveling through space in that part of the galaxy near their own territories that the entrance of any vessel into the Wilderness will result in the extermination by the shiyu military of the entire species that sent that vessel.

Entrance into a significant region of space surrounding the Wilderness was also forbidden by the shiyu. They did not, however, prohibit any species that evolved on a planet within this border region from developing space travel and colonizing neighboring worlds.

As the Earth is located within this restricted area of space, no other species either made contact with mankind prior to his expansion beyond his home world or interfered with his colonization of other planets within that region. Humanity was thus able to establish settlements over an extensive area of space prior to interacting with any species that had long been capable of space travel.

Many of the worlds so colonized by mankind had previously been visited by veiac ships, although none had been settled by that race. Inevitably, artifacts left behind by the veiac were discovered. Most of these were of

---

which the galaxy is spinning is west. The opposite direction is east. The two directions from the Earth that are ninety degrees from the plane formed by the four previous directions are up and down.

historical value only, but some were of more pragmatic use. Even though human scientists were rarely able to understand the workings of veiac technology, human beings were able to discover how to use some of the devices they had discovered. What is more, a number of records were found over time and, following the partial decipherment of several veiac scripts and languages, these did add to mankind's knowledge of the Milky Way's ancient history.

From Pollidor's *Big Blue Book of Knowledge*

# Chapter 6
# Down to Mudtown

"Strip her," Vomo barked. "Strip her and bring her over here."

Before the gangster's lackeys had even reacted to their master's command, Jess spun around and landed a kick on the genitals of the man standing behind her.

As she did so, Jess focused on the thread coiled above her perineum and roused it from its sleep so that it shot up through her spine like a bolt of lightening that burnt away everything but its own radiance.

The efficacy of her will so expanded, Jess slowed time as she might restrict her breath and bent the world around her rather than contorting her own body. From her point of view, she placed the doubled over man beside her upon her hands and thrust him and the rest of the universe beneath her body. From the perspective of those watching her, however, she lifted herself upon him, tumbled over his back, her feet in the air, and smashed her heels into the chin of one of Vomo's goons, who had half risen from where he was sitting.

Flipping over this person, Jess landed on the shelf above the couch, between two wiggling pornographic sculptures, pulled a dagger from one of her boots, and extended the blade. Like a spider lunging at its prey, she jumped onto the floor before the couch, simultaneously opening up her bloodied victim's belly and causing his intestines to slide out onto his feet.

Jess allowed time to speed up nearly to its normal rate for an instant, giving the four remaining thugs a chance to stand. When they had, however, she again reduced their perceptions to a useless crawl and made them as helpless as they would have been had they been asleep.

She drew Dawn's Spine from her vest and activated it. The telescoping blade extended out from the hilt, and Jess swung it about her head and brought it down upon the crown of the man nearest her. With a single motion, she split his body in half so that, in the inert reality she had created, her victim's right side stood next to his left though the two were no longer connected at any point.

Again Jess let time rush forward. She planned to make an impression on Vomo as she slaughtered his henchmen and thought that permittting several of them to realize that they were dying, and so filling them with terror, would have the appropriate effect.

As the split gangster's cadaver fell in two parts, his fellows did look on in horror. They were, in fact, so shocked that Jess did not even need to slow time to keep them from moving.

Taking advantage of her opportunity, she jumped over the pile of entrails sliding about on the floor in front of her, grabbed the man who had been standing behind the deceased by the hair (using the hand she was holding her dagger in), and, with a flourish, severed his head from his torso.

There was now no one between Jess and Vomo except one of the women with whom he had been amusing himself.

While Jess wiped from her lips and teeth the salty blood that had splattered on her when she had decapitated her last victim, the gang lord, who was squirting a stream of urine onto the floor, where it splashed into the sheets of blood accumulating there, pushed the woman beside him into Jess's arms.

The wretched tattooed girl was so frightened that she did not scream or attempt to escape. She merely made a soft, whining sort of noise in her throat and grabbed ahold of Jess, clutching her attacker's arms as though she expected this person would save her.

Jess was somewhat surprised by the woman's actions, as well as by the sight of her face as she looked into Jess's own, and, for a moment, forgot to slow time again. Seeing Jess's momentary confusion, Vomo, his masses of flesh wobbling madly, leapt over the table in front of him and rushed towards the still open door.

When she saw her prey so escaping, Jess recovered her wits, struck the woman grasping her with the severed head she was still holding, knocking this terrified individual onto the couch behind her, and tossed the head into her lap. That did make her scream.

Jess paid the woman little heed, poured temporal treacle upon her foes, and jumped at the man standing behind the second woman. Paralyzed, he waited unknowingly for Jess to separate his torso into halves at the waist and courteously remained stock still while his killer spun around him, raised her sword up beside her ear, and drove it into the heart of the man behind him.

Drawing her blade out from the corpse, though it had not yet realized it was dead, Jess wheeled around and looked at the two women who were still alive. She realized that she could not allow them to remain so, even if she had no desire to kill them, and so mentally offered their blood to Haya, that she might alleviate the goddess's thirst.

One woman, who was standing, Jess beheaded with a casual gesture, and the second, who was sprawled on the couch with a head in her lap, she dispatched by cleaving her skull in half all the way to its chin.

With time still barely flowing, Jess calmly walked over to the bent over man standing in the doorway, whose now upraised face was limp with fear. As he watched her approach with what appeared to him to be impossible speed, he, like his boss, urinated upon his feet. In an instant, Jess was standing over him, looking him in his eyes and grabbing one of his ears. She pulled him up abruptly and, at the same time, swung her sword upwards between his legs splitting his body from his crotch to his jaw.

Jess pushed the man to the side, leapt over the pile of viscera that had spilled out of his body onto the floor, and hurled herself through the doorway, or rather hurled it around herself. She landed upon the wall opposite the entrance to the room she had made into an abattoir and ran along the hallway's length, having given up the delusional belief that there is such a thing as gravity. Nearing the corridor's end, she fell forward onto her hands, flipped backwards, and struck the closed doorway before her with her feet. It burst open and Jess, spinning in the air, landed upon the floor in the middle of the tiled foyer.

The two men who had been gaming there when she had entered the flat were both now standing and waiting for her.

Each of them bore a needle gun, a weapon consisting of a thin metal barrel – set in a wooden stock shaped like that of a flintlock pistol – that used a magnetic pulse to shoot a small metal needle at an extremely high velocity.

Before either could fire, Jess whipped around on the ball of one foot, swung her other leg in a wide arc, and kicked the gun out of the hand of the closer of the men. As the weapon wafted through the air, like a leaf blown by a gentle breeze, the other guard squeezed the trigger of his own gun.

While Jess had some control over time, there were limits to how much she could impede its passage. The needle was simply moving too fast for her to dodge it. Fortunately, however, the gunman had not had particularly good aim and missed her. The projectile zipped past Jess's head, ricocheted off the tile wall behind her, and returned to strike the disarmed man in the leg.

As the blood squirting from his veins speckled the white floor with red polka dots, Jess sliced through the injured hoodlum's eyes with her dagger, causing them to empty the jelly with which they were filled onto his cheeks and nose, and used his body as a lever to twist the world and send herself hurtling over him and onto the floor.

She raised her sword while she slid across the bloody tiles, and, as she passed beneath the other man, she cleft his body from his groin to his breastbone. Barely avoiding the cascade of intestines that poured out of the corpse she had made, Jess slid on past him and rebounded from the nearest wall to land on her feet.

She hurried to the blinded man, who had fallen screaming onto his hands and knees, jumped over his body, cutting it in half just below his rib cage as she did so, and landed next to the front doorway.

Realizing that Vomo must surely be attempting to flee, Jess hurried outside his flat and dashed to the railing of the landing that overlooked the lobby below. She immediately saw her victim in the elevator, which was still making its way down the metal column around which the stairs wound their way from the top to the bottom of the building. Not wanting to waste time, Jess, sheathing her dagger, leapt over the railing and gently fell the distance of the height of the multistoried stairwell.

She came to rest in a squat on the green and black tile floor of the lobby just as the elevator arrived there. Vomo saw her looking at him through the glass walls of this device and felt his jaw drop in terrified surprise. Before he could react in a more effective way, Jess rushed to the elevator, flung open the door, and pulled him out.

The girl let time return to its ordinary pace as she hurled the man onto the ground and jumped upon him. She sat on his chest, on his massive, pendulous, hirsute breasts, her sword just above his brow, and smiled at him.

Vomo clearly expected to die within seconds and was shivering with fear. Jess could hear the splashing of urine on the tiles of the floor as the man lost control of himself. She hoped none of the liquid would get on her boots, but, having other concerns than the possibility of having to clean these, she turned her mind back to her hostage.

Brushing her now disheveled pink hair out of her eyes, she asked, "So, you want to talk about your meeting with Tolliver yesterday?"

The man merely sniveled, grunted, and trembled in response.

"Come on now. Let's not make this difficult."

"Please," the hood blurted out, "don't kill me. I'll give you whatever you want. I've got money."

"Oh, come on. I'm not interested in your money, obviously. Tell me about your meeting with Tolliver yesterday."

"Whatever you're being paid to do this, I'll pay you more. I've got a vault upstairs. We can go open it now. Take it all, cash, jewels, everything."

"Would you shut up about that," Jess snapped in exasperation. "I don't give a damn about your money and I'm not being paid by anyone. I want to know about your meeting with the captain of the *Empress* yesterday. So, you can either start telling me about it or I can start cutting things off of you. We can start with your fingers, then..hmm..maybe the toes, then your little wiggly worm. I'll let him go swimming in the pond he made."

"Please don't," the man squawked in a tone of near panic. "I met with Tolliver at the Drunkard's Pleasure. He was delivering some goods to my boss and I was supposed to make arrangements for us to retrieve them from the warehouse at the spaceport. That's all I did. I swear."

"Are you sure?"

"Yes. I swear. Truly, I swear."

"Where is he now, then?"

"I don't know."

"Don't you think it's a little odd that he disappeared right after meeting you? Don't you think that's a little suspicious? Maybe you had something to do with that, huh?"

"No! No. I swear. Why would I do anything to him? He was delivering goods we wanted."

"So, what happened to him?"

"I don't really know, but I heard the crier on the picture vat saying that some man was seen being grabbed yesterday by a couple of mudjumpers outside of the Drunkard's Pleasure. It could have been Tolliver. We didn't leave together and I didn't see where he went."

Though she had little faith in her new acquaintance's honesty, Jess did think that it was likely that he was telling the truth. He was entirely too terrified at the moment to make much of anything up.

"Why are some aliens going to attack Tolliver?" she asked.

"All I can tell you is what I saw on the news broadcast. The crier said some man, an offworlder, was seen being abducted by a pair of mudjumpers. Go back to your ship and watch it. You'll see I'm not lying."

"What's that going to prove? Do you think if I watch it it'll get you off the hook? As far as I know, the mudjumpers are working for you."

"No. The Sing gang doesn't use those dirty animals, except as cattle. Look, if you want to find out about them, I'll tell you who you need to ask."

"Go on," she said.

"The biggest boss in Mudtown is a creature everybody calls Kon Kutta. He's the one you should talk to, not me. If somebody used some mudjumpers to kidnap or kill anyone, he'd have heard about it. He probably set it up. I don't have anything to do with any of this."

"Alright then, where can I find Kon Kutta?"

"He lives in Mudtown. He has a big complex near the palace. I'll draw you a map."

"No. That's not going to do. You can take me there."

As probable as she believed it was that Vomo was speaking the truth, Jess saw no point in taking an unnecessary risk by leaving him to his own devices. Though she had already resolved to see this Kon Kutta, she was going to take Vomo with her.

"Come on," she said. "Let's go pay Kon Kutta a visit."

With that, Jess began to stand up, but, as she did so, she slipped in the puddle of Vomo's urine. It had flowed, while she and the man were talking, under one of his legs and under one of hers. She nearly fell over as she lost her footing, but managed to regain her balance and secure her upright position by planting her other knee in Vomo's chest. Though the man first let out a mousy squeak and then a louder squeal when the girl struck him, seeing Jess's sword still hovering over his face, he did nothing more.

For her part, Jess looked at the man with irritation and stood up again. She backed a few feet away from him and bid him stand himself. The pathetic creature's flabby belly wobbled and shook as he heaved himself to his feet and looked sheepishly at his diminutive conqueror.

"Let's go to your car," she told him and gestured for the man to lead the way.

Pushing her hostage in front of her, Jess exited the building to find herself beneath a grey twilight sky that was bathing the city with a soft, cooling drizzle.

She walked over to where Uluf was standing beside the cab he was holding and said to him, "We don't need that anymore. My new friend here has agreed to give us a ride."

Jess then looked at Vomo and, gesturing towards the taxi with her head, told him, "Why don't you pay the driver, dear?"

Without a word of argument, but with a look of definite hatred directed towards Jess, the man pulled some coins from a purse hanging at his waist and handed these to the driver.

"Let's go," Jess said to her companions.

Vomo led the girl and the toad to his own car, which was parked beneath the metallic road. It was a gaudy thing adorned with gold trim and paintings of nude women in various impossible but very revealing positions. Jess beckoned for Uluf to get in first and then motioned for Vomo to follow him. When both were inside, she slipped into the vehicle, wiped the rainwater from her face, and had her captive give the mechanical driver instructions on where he was to go.

The car leapt onto the nearest ramp, sped across the motorway running along Kaan Street, and then hurried towards Mudtown. Soon after leaving Oditkalee, the driver, rather than passing over the wide valley to the east of Jezic, took one of the final ramps before the long bridges spanning the mudjumper preserve and moved along a narrow road built only inches above the ground.

The car rushed across an open space filled with ragged vegetation and scattered rubbish and, at the base of the hill, through an open gate set in the dilapidated fence encircling Mudtown, beside which stood an untenanted sentry box. Having entered the preserve, the vehicle began moving more slowly, as the buildings of the place were built immediately next to the road and, in some cases, actually leaned over it.

Jess and her companions soon arrived at a small square, where the road ended in a cul-de-sac.

"If you want to go see Kon Kutta, you'll have to walk through Mudtown," Vomo told Jess.

"That's fine. I'll have you to protect me. Let's go."

The pink haired girl got out of the car, followed by Vomo and Uluf. It was raining harder than it had been before and the remnants of the day were fading quickly. Vomo looked chagrined at the prospect of entering Mudtown in such conditions, but Jess was unconcerned and motioned for him to lead the way.

To the north of the plaza was a large edifice, the palace of the kings of the Jaffrite nation that had once ruled over the region of Shokai now controlled by Tozana. It was a hideous pastiche built in an attempt to emulate the style of human habitations. Though the roof was composed of innumerable domes, it was pierced by several towers, and the colonnaded façade of the structure was interrupted by a row of even taller and very brightly colored pinnacles composed of a series of sculptures of distorted Jaffrite faces and diverse outlandish monstrosities.

It was significantly different from any of the other structures of the mudjumpers' preserve. Some of these were constructed with stone or reeds, but others were wretched shanties built with whatever material happened to be available to their denizens. Some were traditional igloo-like Jaffrite domes, but others were pathetic boxes or lean-tos. Whatever these buildings' form and whatever they were made of, there were set up, in front of many of them, tall poles topped each with a sculpture of some peculiar creature or another.

The sky was not yet completely dark, and both of Shokai's moons were already visible, the clouds having partially parted to allow their light to filter into the city. Nonetheless, Jess had some difficulty navigating through the unlit, unpaved, mud choked, and garbage strewn streets of the preserve. She kept Vomo in front of her so that if there were any obstacle in their path he rather than she would be presented with it.

There were a fair number of Jaffrites hopping through the narrow, muddy lanes, and while many of them looked at Jess and her companions as they went by, none of the beasts paused when doing so. They merely crept or jumped away.

Jess was intrigued by these odd creatures, as she had never seen any member of their species before, but she had other concerns at that time that trumped her curiosity. She was especially intent upon keeping an eye on Vomo and never allowed her gaze to stray long from him as she repeatedly pushed him in the small of the back to encourage him to maintain a brisk pace. As focused as she was, however, Jess did note that none of the Jaffrites wore any clothing and that a few of them were adorned with conspicuous amounts of jewelry that was very similar to that worn by Jezic's human gangsters.

After the girl and her companions had wandered through the labyrinth of Mudtown's filthy alleys for about fifteen minutes, they came to a complex of domes that were either built against each other or connected with short passages. One especially large dome on the edge of the street did not have the narrow entranceway most similar Jaffrite buildings had. Instead, from the front of it projected a substantial, gabled wooden structure. At either corner of this was a pole topped with a sculpture of an odd monster. The façade itself was colorfully painted with a stylized representation of a Jaffrite's face, and, at its center, there was a narrow tower composed of a series of sculptures set one on top of another. At the base of this pinnacle, between the legs of some fanciful beast, was a round doorway.

"You first," Jess told Vomo, and the man passed into the dark entrance, followed by Jess and then by Uluf.

The room within was fairly large, though it was so gloomy it seemed oppressively small. The rectangular structure opened up onto a larger domed area, the ceiling of which was supported by a number of wooden columns.

Near where the vestibule joined the main part of the room, a decrepit looking Jaffrite (whose legs had, at some time, been so severely injured that little now remained of them other than shapeless hunks of meat) was squatting on a wooden plank fixed with little wheels beside a bhank filled hookah and blowing out clouds of greasy smoke. In the larger room, that was lit with a single kerosene lantern hung from a hook in the ceiling, several healthier Jaffrites sitting around a cauldron filled with water, weeds, and some kind of feathery crinoid-like animal stopped spearing these last with long metal needles and looked up at the newcomers.

The old Jaffrite picked up a roughly hewn wooden staff, to the top of which was affixed a translator shaped like a microphone, and used this (as one would a punt pole) to drag himself nearer to the three persons standing in front of him.

When he was nearly under their feet, he brought the translator close to his mouth and spoke into it in his own language. This series of variously pitched whistles, pops, and clicks was rapidly converted into Tozani, and Jess's translator rendered this into her own language.

The mudjumper said, "Good evening. Will my lord and my lady please do me the honor of informing me of the purpose of their business here?"

Jess answered him. "We've come to see Kon Kutta. Would you take us to him?"

The Jaffrite's translator sputtered and burped for a few seconds before it began whistling to him in his language. When it had finished, the Jaffrite spoke again.

"Would your lordship and your ladyship please wait here for one moment?"

"Okay," Jess replied, "but don't take too long."

The Jaffrite used his staff to wheel the plank he was squatting on around and then dragged himself over to where the others of his kind were sitting. They spoke to each other in low whistles for a moment. Then one of them crept away through a door at the far side of the dome while a second, who took in his hand the old cripple's staff, made his way, half hopping and half creeping, to where Jess and the others were standing.

Using the translator, he addressed them, saying, "My noble sirs and madam, if you would please do me the honor of accompanying me, I am eager to provide for your comfort while Kon Kutta is being fetched to serve you."

Although she noticed that Vomo was looking even more nervous than he had been earlier, Jess bid the Jaffrite lead her where he would. The creature bowed to her, turned around, and guided them to the door at the other side of the dome through which the other Jaffrite had passed a few moments earlier.

This opened into a short low passage that itself opened onto a second dome. This was much like the first, except that there was a sort of divan (whereupon about two dozen human men were reclining) that ran around the room's circuit. A solitary Jaffrite was wandering through the flickering rays of a single lantern from one of these persons to the next pushing a trolley on which was a glass pot filled with a greyish, viscous liquid, russa diluted in liquor. When he came to one of the men, the Jaffrite would speak to him in an airy singsong, asking him if he would like more of the drug. If the man did, he would hand the waiter a few coins, and the Jaffrite, dropping these in a box hanging from the side of his trolley, would pick up a long handled wooden spoon, dip it into the pot, and hold it in front of the man so that he could take it in his mouth and consume the russa.

The Jaffrite guiding Jess and the others took them past his fellow to another narrow passage on the other side of the second dome, where he was met by another of his race. After the two had spoken briefly, the first Jaffrite turned to his guests and addressed them.

His translator, though sputtering and whining, rendered his whistles into a tinny voice that said, "May I be so bold as to ask who it is among your esteemed party, my lords, my lady, that is honoring Kon Kutta with an audience this evening?"

Jess replied, "I am."

"If my lady will then go through here," the translator said as the mudjumper indicated that she should enter the narrow passage in front of her.

Looking briefly at Vomo, and then at Uluf, to let the latter know he should watch the former carefully as she went on ahead, Jess entered into the connecting hallway.

No sooner was she within it than the Jaffrite standing before her, at the entrance to the next chamber, leapt upon her.

Caught in this strange, gloomy warren by a host of multi-eyed aliens, Jess was briefly overcome by fear in a way she had not been since she had been trained by Takenac. She reached for her sword and took it out from her vest, but she was entirely unable to focus upon the thread within her and so rouse it from its slumber.

Almost immediately, she had, however, activated Dawn's Spine, even though she could not use it properly within the confined space of the passage.

Her attacker was already grasping her other arm when the blade shot out from its ornate hilt, and just as she began to swing it, he took hold of her right arm as well.

Jess, seeing her predicament, let the Jaffrite himself support her weight and kicked him in the chin first with one foot and then with the other. The creature involuntarily loosened his grip on the girl, and she was able to shove her blade into his throat, twist it, and lop off his head.

Though the Jaffrite was dead, he was not finished giving Jess trouble, for his bulky body fell on top of her, knocking her backwards into the arms of the Jaffrite who had led her to the passage. This creature immediately wrapped one of his arms around the girl's waist while, with the other, he thrust a dagger at her chest. Again, Jess reacted quickly, severing her assailant's hand before his knife could reach her. The beast produced a piercing whistle, his cry of pain, but his misery did not last long, for Jess swung her sword over her shoulder and stabbed the Jaffrite in his head.

The creature began to convulse and his legs contracted and straightened spasmodically, causing his body to lunge against Jess and push her onto the ground. The impact of the fall briefly left her winded and confused.

When Jess regained her senses and tried to jump up she found she could not. The body of her opponent was lying on top of her while her own head and shoulders were resting on the corpse of the first Jaffrite she had killed. She could not even cut herself loose. Her sword hand was pinned beneath the body on top of her and immobilized, and the blades hidden in her boots were inaccessible, since her legs were buried under masses of rubbery Jaffrite flesh.

Before she had the chance to think of some way to escape from her present troubles, Jess stopped her wriggling and lay dead still. Two Jaffrites were standing at the entrance to the passage leading out and three more stood at its other end. All of them were holding spears made from some bamboo-like cane, and the sharp blades of these were all resting upon or inches from Jess's head or breast.

# Chapter 7
# Up from Mudtown

As Jess lay on top of one Jaffrite corpse while another lay on top of her and the blades of five spears pointed at her face and heart, she felt all her strength leak out of her body. Her limbs became as heavy as lead and she let her head fall back onto the bloody flesh underneath it. Devastated by regret, she closed her eyes to restrain her tears, but they slipped out from beneath her lids in spite of such efforts.

She hoped that her death would come soon, to put an end to the sadness she felt, but though she expected to feel the hovering blades above her piercing into her skin at any moment, she instead heard the sounds of movement coming from the corridor leading deeper into the complex. Opening her eyes and arching her neck, in order to discover what was happening behind her, Jess saw that the three armed Jaffrites standing above her in that direction had moved aside to permit a fourth to look at the girl.

This individual was covered with a gaudy mass of jewelry and crowned with a tall feather bound to the crest on his head with a bright blue ribbon tied in a bow fastened with a diamond encrusted pin. He held a translator on a short, bejeweled wand and whistled into it.

He said, "Please tell your toad to calm himself."

Jess raised her head to look back into the room whence she had come and there saw, behind the two Jaffrites pointing spears at her, another holding both of Vomo's hands together behind the man's back and still another trying to get a grip on Uluf. He only held one of the toad's hands, however, and could not grab the other. Uluf was wriggling and jumping about frenetically and repeatedly striking his assailant over the head with his cane.

Even though she could not help but smile a little at the sight, Jess was still disheartened and so called out to her friend, asking him to cease his struggle.

Uluf looked at her with surprise. He had never known Jess to surrender and was saddened to see her give up now. Losing his own desire to fight on, he lowered his weapon and submitted to his captor.

"Thank you," said the ornamented Jaffrite. "You are an offworlder, are you not?"

"Yes," replied Jess.

"Why have you come to see me, and why are you with a member of the Sing gang?"

"He's not my friend, if that's what you're thinking."

"Go on."

"I'm a member of the crew of a freighter that made planetfall yesterday. My captain disappeared after he had a meeting with this man. I went to see him, and he told me that an offworlder had been seen being taken away by some mudjumpers. He said Kon Kutta would know about it so I made him take me here. Are you Kon Kutta?"

"That's what the humans call me, yes.

"Did you kidnap Tolliver, my captain?"

"I had nothing to do with your captain's abduction, though I have heard about a man who was snatched by a couple of my people outside of a bar in Jezic. Is he the one you're looking for?"

"Yeah."

"I had nothing to do with that, nor do I know with certainty who did. Nonetheless, I can say that it is unlikely that any other leader among my people was behind the abduction. The Jaffrites who took him must have been desperate, unattached individuals, and I'm sure that they were employed by humans who wanted to do injury to my people."

Pointing at Vomo, Kon continued. "If you want to find a likely suspect, look at this man's gang. We haven't had any outright quarrels with them, but we're still competitors. They wouldn't mind if we were gone, and stirring up a little hatred for my people among their kind could get their government to attack us. I assure you, no Jaffrite organization had anything to do with taking your captain."

"How do I know you're telling the truth?"

"You know because I'm not going to kill you. I'm letting you go."

"Really?"

"I know what the consequences are for harming a human – and I have no quarrel with you – so I don't desire to do you harm. I do, however, want to apologize for my underlings' behavior. They recognized your companion and assumed you were sent by the Sing gang to do me harm."

Kon Kutta whistled to his followers, and the two standing at Jess's feet put down their spears and pulled the corpse of their fellow off of her. Jess exhaled loudly, sat up, retracted the blade of her sword, and put the hilt back in the pocket in her vest. Having done so, she stood up, bowed to Kon Kutta, thanked him for his courtesy, and walked over to Uluf, who had been released by the Jaffrite holding him.

Jess turned around to face the Jaffrite boss, who had entered the room where the waiter with the bowl of russa stood (though all of his conscious customers had fled), and addressed him.

"So, how do you think I can find out who kidnapped Tolliver?"

Gesturing at Vomo, he replied, "Ask this one. We will help you."

"Thanks. But why?"

"I told you. If the Sing are trying to stir up animosity for my kind among your kind, we need to know. By bringing this man to me, you have saved my dependents from needing to make a great number of inquiries."

Kon ordered his underlings to take Vomo through the passage where Jess had been ambushed and then motioned for Jess and Uluf to follow these individuals. He himself came behind them with the Jaffrite who had restrained the toad.

They took Vomo through a maze of chambers, until they came to one in the center of which stood a potbellied stove. The Jaffrites tied the gangster to one of the pillars supporting the domed roof and thrust a number of iron tongs and pokers into the fire burning in the oven.

Kon said to Vomo, "Tell this girl what she wants to know or we will torture you until you do or until you die. What happened to her captain? Who hired the Jaffrites who kidnapped him?"

Vomo, tears welling up in his eyes, blurted out, "I already said that I don't know. I really don't. Please don't hurt me. I have nothing against your sort."

A few minutes later, after the tongs and pokers were glowing red, one of Kon's subordinates, holding them with a pair of thick mittens (for Jaffrites are averse to fire), began to torment the prisoner. While this creature tore off bits of the man's flesh, branded him in various places, peeled away his skin, and inflicted diverse other injuries upon him, Kon continued to ask the gangster the same questions he had before. Vomo, though he howled and pled for his life, refused to give his interrogator any answer.

Jess was soon feeling distinctly sick from watching the happenings occurring before her, but they did not last as long as she feared they would. While Vomo's torturer was using his tongs to twist off one of his victim's fingers, the man began to convulse and expectorate foamy spittle. A few seconds later he was dead.

Kon turned to the girl and said, "You will have to get your information elsewhere. This one was very stubborn and very fragile."

Jess, being queasy from the show she had been watching, merely nodded her head in acknowledgment of the Jaffrite's words.

Uluf said, "We offer you our thanks for your efforts and for your courtesy. You could have taken our lives, but you did not, demonstrating your grace and decency."

The toad bowed dramatically to Kon Kutta, and Jess bowed to him in a more restrained manner. The two were then escorted from the gangster's complex back into the street outside.

There were no Jaffrites about any longer, and Mudtown was silent and dark. Shokai's two moons provided enough light for Jess and Uluf to see, but populated the squalid shanty town with armies of somewhat menacing shadows.

"Well, Uluf," Jess said, "we don't have Vomo to activate the car for us. I guess we'll have to walk back."

"I am afraid that you are right. Shall we?"

The toad offered his companion his arm; she took it with her own, and the pair set out down the street in the direction of Jezic. It took them over an hour to reach the outskirts of the human city, but, once they had, they were able to hail a taxi and continue on more quickly to their hotel.

There, Uluf undressed and went directly to bed while Jess, dowsed with sweat from her long walk through the warm and humid night, kicked her boots off onto the floor, dropped her skirt and vest beside them, and went to the bathroom to take a shower.

As the streams of water poured over her body, relaxing her aching muscles, drumming upon her nerves, and gliding down her skin, Jess let whatever images came to her play out before her mind's eye. Feeling a little drunk with exhaustion and vaguely physically stimulated, she thought of the times she and Tolliver had spent lying together in his bed, their naked bodies, at once slick and sticky with their sweat and sexual fluids, pressed against each other so closely that the vibrations of one person's breath or heartbeat penetrated the other. A wave of excitement prompted by such images surged through her body, but as quickly as it aroused her, the thought that she might have permanently lost her lover sent a wave of icy desolation after it, and that left her even more tired and ready for sleep than she had been when she had arrived back at the room.

* * *

Jess was awakened at some time the following morning by an urgent need to urinate. She was more than a little annoyed about having to drag herself from her bed, but realized she would not be able to return to sleep until she had done so.

It was light when she got up, though Jess had no idea what time of day it was and could not have cared less. Wiping away some of the sweat that was pooled upon her naked body as she staggered across the already sweltering room, the girl made her way to the bathroom, closed the door behind her, and sat upon the toilet. She was so tired from the exertions of the previous day and night that even while she relieved herself, she let her head rest upon the wall beside her and dozed off.

Sometime later, Jess stirred herself, wiped her eyes, and remembered where she was. She decided to urinate a little more before returning to bed since she did not want to have to get up again before she was ready to face the day.

While she was doing so, Jess heard the bathroom door creak. Sleepy though she was, she looked up and noticed the shadow of a foot against the jamb. Her mind was suddenly alert, and she immediately directed her attention to the thread resting inside of her body.

A moment later, a nude man covered with tattoos of dragonflies flung open the door, but, as he did, Jess grabbed ahold of time as it attempted to escape and kept it from racing forward. Leaping up from the toilet, and wetting herself a little in the process, Jess hurtled across the room, landed upon the floor, and slid between the legs of the man in front of her. As she passed beneath him, she seized his testicles in her hand and squeezed them with all her strength, cracking them like peanuts.

In the room beyond there were four more men, all of whom, like their neutered fellow, were nude, tattooed, and covered with jewelry. One of these persons was poking at Uluf's bed with a long poniard, though the toad himself was nowhere in sight. A second was on his knees, looking under Jess's bed, and the remaining two were standing near the door leading into the hallway outside.

The man occupied with Uluf's bed was nearest her, but Jess turned her attention to the pair beside the door as both of these, unlike the others, had needle guns in their hands.

Though she briefly wondered what had happened to the toad – and felt as if she had been gutted when she thought that he might have come to some harm – Jess had no time to answer such a question. Most likely, she reassured herself, he had left the room before the gangsters had arrived. There was, after all, no sign of his having struggled with them.

She pushed the floor away from her, so that, from the perspective of the others, she jumped into the air. Both her feet struck one of the men in the stomach. Then, recoiling from him, Jess kicked the needle gun from his hand, arched her back, pointed her head downwards, planted her hands upon the floor, and, from a handstand, flipped herself upright.

As slowly as time was moving, the second man had still managed to turn his gun upon Jess while she was regaining her feet, though he had not yet pulled the trigger. She kicked the gun from his grasp and, swinging her entire body in a circle, kicked him in the groin. With both of the men doubled over, one from being winded and the other from nearly being emasculated, Jess grabbed their heads and slammed them together with all her strength.

By this time, the individual who had been searching under her bed had looked up. While he was rising from all fours, Jess noticed that he too had a needle gun. She rushed at him, leapt, and kicked him in the nose. Droplets of blood floated apparently weightlessly through the air.

Landing upon the floor in front of the man, Jess kicked him in the face again and again. Then, as his mouth hung open, dripping slobbery gore onto his assailant's skirt, which was lying on the floor in front of him, Jess spun round and kicked him in the side of the head, snapping his neck with the blow.

Finished with another enemy, Jess turned to face her final opponent, but, as she did so, she saw that the door to the room was opening and that a large number of men (she could not tell how many) were standing in the hallway. They all seemed to be holding needle guns and Jess, realizing that even she could not take on so many persons with such weapons, decided to make her escape as quickly as possible. She even decided to flee without her weapons, as she knew that, in the time it would take her to retrieve them, her attackers would be able to put her in their sights.

Naked as she still was, she jumped onto the window sill and then, even as she heard the sound of needles striking the wall beside her, out the window itself. Her room was several floors up, but she did not let the ground rush to her with undue rapidity. Nonetheless, her first sensation upon landing was one of pain. The sun had so heated the pavement that standing upon it with bare feet, as Jess was now doing, was agonizing. The girl leapt up at once, jumped about a bit, and looked up at the window of her room. There she saw several armed men looking back at her.

Though their faces revealed their astonishment that their prey had not splattered when she hit the ground, one of them still had the presence of mind to aim at her. As he shot, Jess took off running. She moved her legs as fast as she could, not simply to distance herself from the man who was about to shoot at her, but also to minimize the time her toes were in contact with the burning pavement. Unfortunately, her ability to run was considerably impeded by the many obstacles in her way. The ground was strewn with rubbish, and Jess had to be careful not to step upon shards of broken glass, bags filled with she had no idea what, and other things she preferred not to speculate about.

While running, Jess heard a needle ricocheting behind her and decided to get off of the main street as soon as possible. Almost at once, she saw a narrow side street to her left and turned into it. This winding alley was lined with little shops and stalls, over and in front of which were gaudily painted placards and blinking neon signs. She rushed past the few people making their way down this street and passed from it to another exactly like it.

Within a few minutes, and after a few more turns onto even more identical paths, Jess realized that she was completely lost. Perhaps, she thought, that was for the best, as she might have taken so complicated a route that her pursuers would be unable to track her. Perhaps, however, they knew their way around this neighborhood so much better than she did that her being lost would only be a problem for her.

Whatever her odds of evading the gangsters were, Jess continued her dash through Oditkalee's side streets.

All the while, she felt her heart racing and her stomach heaving not only from her exertions but also from her increasing fear. She was running unarmed and naked through a city where she could not even understand the language. What was even worse than that, however, was that she had no idea what had happened to Uluf. He could well be fine (and probably was), but she could not shake from her mind the thought that he might have been hurt or even killed. Such ideas were soon tormenting her even more than her physical stresses and worries for herself were.

Then she heard raucous music and the sounds of a crowd coming from her right. She turned upon the next alley she came across leading in that direction and saw that this opened onto a wide pedestrian street (one without a raised metallic road running down its center) whereupon a large number of people were gathered.

Jess hurried to the end of the garbage choked alley and looked at what was going on, though she tried not to reveal herself as she did so.

A large procession made of an assortment of often costumed individuals performing a variety of ritual functions was making its way down the street in front of her, and all around such marchers wandered both countless spectators of all ages and sexes as well as numerous musicians loudly playing upon shawms, crumhorns, serpents, and drums.

Though Jess did not know it, she had stumbled upon the March of the Dead, Tozana's most important religious festival, during which the corpses of all those who had died in the preceding year were taken from the charnel house where they had been kept and conveyed to a local temple to be cremated.

While she might not have been concerned about the practices of the local people at that moment, Jess was pleased to note that many of the onlookers at the celebration of this feast, those who were mourning for someone who had died in the previous year, were dressed in long, flowing white robes and tall, pointed white hoods that completely concealed their faces.

She at once had an idea. Looking around, Jess discovered a person, clearly a woman, dressed in such an outfit who was roughly the same height she was and who was walking in her direction on the same side of the street that she was standing on.

Moving to hide herself behind a pile of rubbish beside the wall near this approaching individual (and so concealing herself from the woman's eyes), Jess picked up a stone and waited. When the woman walked into view, Jess slowed time nearly to a standstill, leapt out from where she was hiding, grabbed her victim, struck her head with the stone she had picked up, and pulled her into the alley. By acting quickly, Jess hoped that her movements would be virtually imperceptible and that no one would have any idea of what she had done. The woman, as though spirited away, would simply disappear in the twinkling of an eye.

Jess dragged her victim into a second alley branching off the first, dropped her behind a heap of refuse, and removed her robe and hood. Both of these the naked fugitive donned herself and then took the woman's shoes from her feet. As these were much too big for her, Jess stuffed them with some discarded paper she picked up off of the ground.

So disguised, Jess searched for something she could use to bind her unconscious victim. She quickly found some scraps of cloth, which she tore into strips. With some of these she then tied the woman's wrists and ankles and with another she gagged her.

Looking down at the helpless individual lying at her feet (who was about the same age she was herself), Jess felt both sad and guilty. She had compassion for the girl, but, at the same time, she did not want to be murdered by the men who were hunting her.

Jess's worry and fear were, in fact, causing her heart to pound and her innards to tear themselves apart. She took a deep, calming breath, left the alley, and returned to the street along which the March of the Dead was making its way. There she saw that the end of the procession was about fifty yards distant from the side street where she was standing and that it was slowly moving away from her. Thinking that she would probably be safe in this crowd, and growing weary from concentrating on the thread for so long,

Jess let go of time, permitting it to race away, and plunged into the river of men and women flowing past her.

Fortunately, these individuals were so caught up in the emotional excesses of the celebration that they paid her little heed. Some of them were shouting joyously, adding to the din of the blaring horns and thundering drums; some of them were weeping gratuitously, beating their breasts and tearing their hair, and still others were making loud ululations.

Being small and agile, Jess was able to squirm between the innumerable people pressed together in the wide street and so came to the end of the procession, which was made up of a troupe of clowns who were cutting capers, striking comical poses, and generally making merry, lightening the dark atmosphere around them.

They were all men whose nearly naked bodies and limbs were completely painted green. On his head each wore a loose green cap topped with a pair of long, thick, pointed stuffed socks, and each covered his face with a ridiculous mask shaped like a contorted human countenance, the goggle eyes of which were crossed, the nose of which was askew, and the tongue of which hung out of its open mouth. The only other thing the men wore was a kind of thong that made them appear to have no genitals.

As these performers wound down the street, they repeatedly grabbed some person or another, usually a young and attractive woman (but often an older woman, a man, or even a hooded mourner), and either acted out some comical part with this individual or attempted to dance with her, generally in an outrageously lewd manner.

Jess could not clearly see what the clowns were doing through the bodies of the people surrounding her and so was somewhat surprised when, as she was trying to pass beside them, one of these fellows seized her head in his hands, thrust his grotesque, misshapen mask into her face, and stared intently at her. At first she was startled, but then she remembered that the man could not even see her eyes, as the hood she had on her head was provided with mesh patches only the wearer could see through.

The clown hooted wildly, took one of his hands from Jess's head, and wrapped it around her waist. Pulling her body against his, the man began rubbing his crotch against Jess's belly while turning his face to the sky and howling like a lunatic. Jess, focused on the inner pains brought about by her anxieties, tried to pull away from him, but the man only waggled his finger at her as though she had been a naughty girl. Then he suddenly pinched her breasts.

As the clown did so, Jess gathered her wits and noticed how other women were reacting to these persons' advances. Some leaned forward and jiggled their breasts. Others turned their backs to the men, bent over, and wiggled or spread their buttocks. Still others pressed their bodies against those of the clowns and writhed about lasciviously. While so tempting and teasing the clowns, the women of the higher estates and those dressed in robes like those Jess had donned lifted up or pulled down their garments to let the clowns enjoy their charms.

Though she was concerned about the gangsters chasing her and her heart was still drumming loudly within her empty torso, Jess could not help but feel herself being carried away by the throbbing music that filled the air of the street and by the ribald fun the celebrants were indulging in. Moreover, she thought that it would be wise to do as everyone else was doing so as not to draw attention to herself. She dared not, however, lift up her robes, for, if she did so, she would reveal to anyone who saw her bare skin that she was not from Tozana.

She grabbed ahold of the clown in front of her, pulled him against her, placed his hand upon her crotch, and rubbed his body with hers with considerable fervor. As the shawms, crumhorns, and serpents wailed and the drums sounded their complex rhythms, Jess wriggled against the clown and drew his hands across her every curve.

Like all his fellows did, the clown, when he had become thoroughly aroused, drew away from Jess, beat his hands against the sky, and generally behaved as though he were utterly distraught. He drew attention to his supposed lack of genitals, pretending to weep piteously for their absence and for his consequent inability to complete the pleasures he had begun with Jess.

Doing as the other women did, Jess acted as though she had sympathy for the man and, to show her feelings, kissed the cheek of his mask. To complete his part, the man next turned around, bent over, and offered Jess his rump. She kissed him upon each of those cheeks as well and gave him a hard smack with the palm of her hand, which sent the clown running back to join his fellows.

The thrill of the crowd continuing to flood over her worries and fears, Jess remained excited. She was, at least briefly, actually able to enjoy herself. Half skipping and half merely jumping up and down, she pressed on through the multitude towards the front of the procession.

Ahead of the clowns, staggered, walked, or even strutted a great many men and women who, fearful of the consequences they would have to endure after death for their actions in this life, were performing agonizing penances. Some of these persons cut their skin with knives; others flagellated themselves or skewered their cheeks with huge needles, and still others drew thorned cords through holes they had drilled into their tongues.

Jess spent little time watching this much less entertaining group and kept on making her way along the street. Her fears returned to her immediate awareness and her mood darkened again. Concern for Uluf surged through her body, nearly taking her breath away, and an awareness of the dangerousness of her present situation made her heart race frantically.

Pushing past the persons walking around the penitents, who were either berating them as evil-doers or encouraging them to atone for their misdeeds, Jess continued to jump up from time to time. Now, however, she was not doing so from excitement, but out of a desire to see if she could spot anyone who might have chased after her. She did, in fact, see a number of tattooed men wearing jewelry, but these were further ahead of her and appeared to have come to the street to watch the procession rather than to hunt her.

Though she felt reasonably safe for the moment, so that her worries about Uluf dominated her thoughts instead of her concerns about her own immediate survival, Jess moved further forward, leaving the penitents behind her and coming to the next group. These were even more grisly than were those following them.

Each pair of these numerous men was bearing a dried, half-mummified corpse upon a bier, often while making wild ululations or howling horribly.

The bodies so being carried belonged to all those individuals who had died in this part of Jezic in the year since the last March of the Dead. Now, having been stored in charnel houses, where they had been smoked and preserved, they were being conveyed by their closest male relatives to the temple where they would be burned.

As repulsive as Jess found this sight, she had an especially difficult time getting past this part of the procession. Not only were there a substantial number of sweaty, often exhausted, and sometimes stumbling persons carrying jerked cadavers, but the crowd around them, which was composed almost entirely of persons wearing hooded robes, was also thicker than it was elsewhere.

All those who had lost a loved one in the last year were staying close to that individual's body, watching as it was borne through the streets and crying piteously all the while. Every now and then some woman in this throng, overcome with despair, would fall upon the earth or attempt to cast herself in front of the feet of others so that she might be trampled to death and sent after whoever she had lost. Most such persons were lifted up by their relatives, although often with difficulty, but a few were left alone and crushed by the feet of those marching behind them. Because of such activities, Jess had a very hard time making it further down the street.

She squirmed under men's arms, hopped over fallen widows, and pushed past curious children, but, from time to time, she found her way entirely blocked by some congregation through which she simply could find no route. While she waited for these knots of people to undo themselves, Jess would jump up or do whatever she could to peer around for her pursuers. Happily, she did not see anyone who looked dangerous.

Then, when she was only about fifteen feet from the front of the army of men bearing their deceased relatives, she found herself hopelessly stuck behind a large family that was trying to lift up a grossly fat woman from the ground, where she was wallowing about and interspersing her wails with loud gurgling noises.

Hopping into the air and twisting her head around while waiting for these persons to raise the overwrought woman up, Jess saw four tattooed men with serious expressions shoving their way through the crowd on the other side of the street.

Her heart sank as she realized that these men were searching for her.

Worried that there might be others, Jess jumped up several more times and spied three men close to but behind the first group. After seeing them, she hopped once more and spotted another five making their way down the same side of the street she was on. These last, as they were now only a few yards behind her, especially concerned and surprised Jess, who had no idea how they had come so close to her.

# Chapter 8
# The March of the Dead

Still unable to move forward because of the press in front of her, Jess resolved not to wait to deal with the nearest group of her pursuers. She crouched as low as she could, wriggled backwards through the crowd, and made her way around the gangsters so that they were in front of her. Hiding behind a man standing just in back of the last member of this lot, Jess watched them for a moment and thought about what she needed to do. The men probably knew their prey was nearby, but they had not seen her approach. It was, therefore, possible that she could dispatch them all before they realized she was upon them.

With all her will, Jess focused upon the thread, seeking to stagnate time, and brought it as close to a standstill as she ever had. She would now be able to move so rapidly that to others she would appear as little more than a smudge, a mirage or a trick of the eyes, and could, perhaps, kill all five of her enemies without their or anyone else's knowing what had happened. She certainly acted so fast that the telling of what she did takes far longer than did the actions themselves. These were started and finished before a man could even open his mouth to begin relating them.

Moving as quickly as she could, Jess slid around the man behind whom she had concealed herself, reached up, grabbed the head of the last of the individuals hunting her, and twisted it with all her might. She felt his spine snap and pushed him forward so that, though he descended like a sheet cast into the wind, he began to fall towards the ground. He would so, Jess hoped, merely appear to be mourning for some cadaver being carried by the sweaty bearers marching in the procession.

Three celebrants were standing so close to the second gangster, between him and the next year's participant in the March of the Dead, that Jess was not able to attack him from behind. She therefore ducked between the feet of yet another mourner standing ahead of her and to her left and emerged in front both of the man she planned to kill next and two of his fellows, who, though walking before him, had turned around to speak to their comrade.

Jess grasped the head of the individual she had initially been trying to reach, broke his neck with a swift motion, and pulled on his nose to make him fall forward as though in despair.

The eyes of the other two speaking to this man were slowly moving towards Jess. Though she seemed to them to be some lightening fast specter, they were able to see her. She was, however, racing through time so much quicker than they were that there was simply no way for their muscles to move rapidly enough for them to stop her or even for their minds to work out what they were seeing.

The girl spun around while the two gazed at her and saw how one of the men was beginning to contort his face into an expression of terrified surprise. He did little else, for, before he could, Jess had broken both his neck and that of his companion.

Instead of pushing these two down, as she had the others, Jess decided to allow them to stand a few seconds longer, as she had something else she needed to do.

While she wanted onlookers to think, at first, that these persons had merely thrown themselves upon the ground, she knew it might not take long for someone to notice that they were dead, and she wanted to make their ends seem as unmysterious as she could.

Jess reached into the pouch hanging from the tacky gold belt around the waist of one of the corpses and found his needle gun. She took the weapon out and used it to shoot two of the dead men, each in one eye, and then wrapped the third man's fingers around its handle and left it to him.

Only one of her enemies remained from the lot that had been approaching her, but, as Jess left those she had already dealt with in order to treat him in the same way, she noticed that a man and woman standing beside the corpses she had just made were looking directly at her. She might have slowed time, but she had not stopped it and so could be seen by others, especially if she did not constantly move. When Jess realized that these two were themselves realizing that they were watching a person in a robe killing four men, she knew they could not be allowed to continue living.

Once she had kicked the male onlooker in the groin and knocked the female's feet out from under her, so that both started to fall towards the ground, she turned away from the pair.

So leaving them for the moment, Jess slid between two persons standing between her and her last pursuer, took ahold of that man's wrist and waist, and spun him around to make him face his companions. While his body twisted, he looked down at Jess and, as slowly as a sluggish, half-conscious drunkard, began to reach for his gun. She helped him to do so. Pulling on his hand, she enabled him to move it through her own time and reach into his pouch. She wrapped his fingers around the weapon and helped him draw it out. His jaw was dropping and his eyes widening as he felt his body moving at an incredible speed and watched the hooded figure before him controlling it.

In spite of his knowledge of what was happening to him, the man was unable to act in time to save his life. Jess turned his gun towards his face, pressed his finger, and made him shoot himself in one of his eyes. She then pointed the pistol at the nearby gangster she had not shot and sent a needle into his heart.

People finding these individuals would, the girl hoped, simply think that they had fallen out with one another and resorted to their guns to resolve their disagreement.⁽

---

* She could, of course, have simply left her victims upon the ground with broken necks since people, upon discovering they were dead, would have thought that they had suffered such injuries from being trampled by the crowd. But Jess never thought of that.

All of her enemies dead, Jess (with a sincerely regretful sigh) fired two more projectiles into the faces of the man and woman who had seen her. Then she yanked on the nose of the corpse whose gun she was holding to send him falling forward.

She prayed that it would take a few seconds before anyone realized these people were dead, so giving her enough time to get away, but she knew she might not even get that. As fast as she could, Jess writhed through the crowd, eventually coming to and jumping over the woman lying upon the earth who had earlier been blocking her way and who had not yet been lifted up by her family members.

Still holding back time, though the effort required to do so was beginning to exhaust her, Jess, now so doused with sweat that her robe clung to every part of her body, left the men carrying their dead relatives behind and found the procession made up of a new group.

Ahead of the mourners there marched a host of men adorned with ten foot tall masks from which were draped heavy brocaded robes that made their wearers appear to be giants. These individuals, who impersonated the attendants of Hyum, the psychopomp of the Tozanis, surrounded a palanquin whereupon was being borne a bull headed image of that deity crowned with a jewel encrusted tiara, garbed in richly embroidered multicolored robes, and holding a noose in one hand and a shepherd's crook in the other.

Jess, seeing the ornate image and its outlandish court, wished she could have watched the procession under more pleasant circumstances. She had a fondness for colorful, vibrant events and had little trouble letting herself get carried away. Unfortunately, at the moment, she could not give in to the excitement of the revelers. She was simply too concerned about her own survival and about what had happened to Uluf. She had no idea what had become of her friend, and her recent violent activities were inclining her towards unpleasant speculations she was unable to ignore.

Leaving behind the god and his attendants, Jess came upon a priest attired like the one she had earlier seen officiating at the executions in Chaakvoi Square, except that this individual carried a staff topped with a rattle composed of countless images of tiny fiends and vicious beasts suspended from a metal framework.

Unlike everyone else around him, all of whom were walking under the burning sun, the priest made his way down the street shaded by a baldachin supported on poles held by four of the numerous young acolytes who were circling him.

As she was passing by the priest, Jess, growing ever more tired and anxious, decided to permit time to move along at its normal pace. When she released it from her power, she jumped up and turned her head in order to look behind her. She saw the five gangsters and two bystanders she had killed crumble onto the ground. Again she jumped, and this time she noticed that no one was paying much heed to those fallen individuals. Most stepped over them and many simply trod upon their bodies. No one seemed in the least concerned, and no one seemed to realize that anything unusual had happened.

Feeling a little relieved, Jess continued to press forward through the crowd. She was now nearing the front of the procession, but the throng of people was just as close as it was everywhere else, except near the mourners carrying the bodies.

The priest Jess had left behind was preceded by a troupe of men who had dressed themselves as warriors and had painted their faces red. Each of them carried a weapon, whether this was a trident, a spear, a staff, or a whip, and with it harried the villains in front of him.

These revelers were all disguised as demons, and each of them held onto a leash fastened to a collar secured around the neck of one of the persons at the very front of the procession, who were all imitating various sorts of sinners. Some of them acted as though they were gluttons, others behaved as thieves, and still others pretended to be murderers, sluggards, or drunks.

The onlookers seemed to be particularly involved with this group, many of them casting rotten fruit, moldy vegetables, dirty water, or even pebbles at these persons while shouting imprecations that Jess, being without her translator, was unable to understand.

As she was watching these individuals attack the persons in the procession, Jess saw, but a short distance away, a man wearing a wide conical hat topped by a spike adorned with a red horse hair plume. He had shoes with upturned toes, enormous, billowing red trousers (to the crotch of which was fixed an oversized armored codpiece), and a dark blue fitted tunic with swallow tails, loose sleeves that were tied with a cord at the wrist, and a wide red collar. Hanging from his belt were a needle gun and a truncheon, and in his hand was a halberd decorated with another red horse hair plume and a banner sewn with words in the local script.

Jess had seen many others similarly dressed at the spaceport and knew this individual was a policeman. He had surely been placed at this point in the procession to prevent the bystanders from doing injury to those they were attacking with refuse.

Whatever his purpose there, Jess felt somewhat disgusted with herself when she spied him. Had she known he was there, she would certainly not have taken so risky an action as killing her opponents in the midst of a large crowd. She could simply have gone to the policeman and remained near him. It was unlikely that anybody would then have troubled her. The gangsters might scrutinize many of the persons participating in the festival, but those nearest the policeman would, very likely, receive far less of their attention.

Even though she might not have found him in time to avoid her earlier act of butchery, Jess still thought she could use the constable to avoid any further such incidents and so made her way over to him. As the policeman marched along with the crowd, Jess followed near to him, trying all the while to act as everyone around her was acting. She, nonetheless, leapt up from time to time, when her unwitting protector was not looking in her direction, and tried to see the other groups of her pursuers. Both were still on the other side of the street, but both had come far closer to the front of the procession.

None of the gangsters had noticed that five of their fellows were no longer with them, which made Jess feel a little better, even if their failure to discover these disappearances occured only because they were so focused on their search. They peered at the face of nearly every person they passed, and, when they came upon a hooded mourner who was slightly built and female, they would lift up that individual's garments and look at her face or hands.

Within a few minutes, as the gangsters continued their hunt, the procession reached its destination, a wide square before a substantial temple that extended from a broad, ornate façade to a tall, beehive shaped tower at its rear.

In front of the temple was a mountain of wood. To the right of this were two balustraded stone platforms, and, to its other side, was a series of tall poles topped with effigies of robed demons.

The crowd soon filled the square and much of the procession dissolved into this multitude. The priest and his acolytes, however, made their way onto one of the platforms, where, beside a brazier wherein burnt a fire, they stood overlooking the arrival of those following after them. The palanquin bearing the icon of Hyum was taken to the other platform, and there it was set upon a dais and surrounded by its giant attendants.

As these persons found their ways to their designated places, Jess's worries about Uluf were becoming so great and were so overwhelming her thoughts that every nerve in her body crawled with such anxiety it seemed her skin and muscles were about to leap away from her bones. Realizing the intensity of her emotional state, Jess grabbed ahold of her breath and strove to calm herself, so as not to panic.

Feeling a little better, Jess followed the policeman to a slightly elevated area in the middle of the square. There she was able to look around and saw that some of her pursuers were milling about near the priest's platform and that others, though now fairly close to her, were not showing any sign that they would be coming any nearer. Some of her hunters, however, had disappeared amongst the throng of people and Jess could not find them.

Meanwhile, the now fatigued men bearing the bodies of their dead relatives staggered across the square, under the blazing yellow sun and through the shimmering waves of heat rising from the scorching cobblestones, and crossed over to the pyre itself, whereupon they placed the corpses they were carrying.

When the last of these had been laid upon the great heap of wood, and the last of the mourners had exited the fenced area encircling this, the priest upon the platform gave a sign and all the shawm, serpent, and crumhorn players sounded a drawn out note upon their instruments and all the drummers beat heartily upon theirs.

The crowd became silent and the musicians, at another sign from the priest, did as well. Then that man began to speak, though Jess had no idea what he was saying, and performed, with the help of his acolytes, an elaborate ritual. At the end of this, he was handed a brand by one of his acolytes, lit it from the fire in the brazier beside him, and handed it to another acolyte, who ran with it from the platform to the pyre. He set the pile of wood alight in numerous places, and it was soon engulfed in a terrible conflagration.

While the cadavers burned in the bonfire, the festivities continued. The blaring music started up again, people danced and shouted, and young men endeavored to shimmy up the poles with the images of the fiends atop them. When one such person succeeded at reaching the top of one of these, he would take hold of the effigy and toss it into the fire to the great delight of the crowd.

Seeing that the gangsters trying to find her seemed now to have entirely given up, and were simply watching the tall flames rising up from the great pyre in front of them, Jess decided that the time had come for her to make her way elsewhere (and hopefully find the friend she had left behind alive and unharmed). Most of her enemies, perhaps all of them, were to her right, so she decided to head to her left, past the poles topped with demonic images and down a street she saw connecting to that side of the plaza.

There were so many people pressing forward to watch the pyre that Jess had a difficult time wriggling through them, and the heat from their bodies, the sun, and the gigantic fire before her was nearly overwhelming. Jess's robes were soaked with her sweat, and she was beginning to feel as though she could endure little more of this place. A definite sense of panic was taking hold of her mind, which prompted her to push and shove with all her strength and to squeeze through whatever claustrophobic path she could force her way into.

Unfortunately, her discomfort and growing anxiety so overwhelmed her reason that she failed to pay enough attention to where she was going. When she emerged from between two laborers, who seemed to be trying to press their bodies against hers for their own satisfaction, Jess fell forward onto the chest of a tattooed gangster.

He looked down at her, but did nothing else. For a brief moment Jess was still, resting her head and hands upon the man's bosom. She knew she was going to have to fight. The man said something to her, though she could not understand what, and she recovered her wits enough to back away from him and ready herself to attack.

She started to focus on the thread within her, but before she had roused it, the man turned away from her and looked at the pyre. For whatever reason, he did not realize he had encountered the very person he was searching for.

Not wanting to waste the opportunity luck had given her, Jess hurried on past him and continued pushing through the crowd.

After she had gone some way, she looked back, as she was still worried about the man she had run into. He was now watching her with a slightly perplexed expression. Perhaps, Jess thought, it had occurred to him that the hooded figure now moving away from him could be his quarry.

Jess was a good distance ahead of the man when he began to follow her, but she would have liked to increase that distance further. Unfortunately, she had so wearied her mind by her earlier excessive slowing of time that she was having difficulty awakening the thread. After a couple of failed attempts, and a couple of brief successes, she decided to save her strength and let time continue to move as it would. If she had to fight, she would lift up the thread then.

Once she had pushed and squirmed for a while, Jess made it to the street that had been her goal. Although there were still a fair number of people milling about there, the crowd was far thinner, and Jess, having removed her hood, was able to take off running.

She had not gone far when, craning her head over her shoulder, she saw the gangster chasing after her. He was bigger than Jess was and so, having longer legs, was rapidly gaining on her. If she used the thread to try to flee from him, she would certainly succeed in escaping, but her pursuer would probably return to his fellows and, with them, continue hunting her. If she did not, however, she would certainly have to fight him. At least, in the latter case, she would have but a single opponent to deal with. With that fact in her mind, Jess turned into the first alleyway she came upon.

There, dropping the hood in her hand upon the ground and resting her elbows upon her knees in order to catch her breath, she waited behind a heap of rubbish taller than she was.

Within a few moments, she heard her pursuer enter into the alley. She did not wait until he found her, but instead, with all her remaining mental strength, drew the thread up into her spine so that it pierced through the very core of her being and turned the world inside out. She grabbed ahold of time, restrained it as best she could (though her concentration was flickering and unsteady), and leapt out from behind the pile of rotting vegetables, dead animals, and waste paper.

The man in front of her moved as though his every muscle was burdened with great weights, but he already had his needle gun drawn and pointed in Jess's general direction. She saw the weapon and moved to one side, keeping the man from being able to aim it at her before she reached him.

Jess jumped into the air, directed her left foot at the man's hand, and knocked the pistol from his grip. No sooner were the toes of her foot on the ground than, with the other, she kicked the man a second time, now in his groin.

The gangster began to double over, and Jess kneed him in the nose twice, splattering his blood across her robe. The man looked up at her, his face covered with streaming gore, but Jess did not dare be merciful to him. Instead, she seized him by one of his ears, lifted up his head, and jabbed a finger into his left eye.

Now that he was nearly incapacitated (and screaming loudly), Jess spun around to stand at his back and kicked his feet out from under him. The hoodlum collapsed upon his face in a murky puddle in the middle of the alley, and Jess, having picked up his needle gun, fell upon his back, pointed the weapon at his head, and permitted time to return to its ordinary pace.

"Okay," she snarled, "you speak Twituboch or Uopa? I hope you do, for your sake."

The man merely howled in agony and despair.

"I don't really have time to waste right now. You'd better tell me."

The man still refused to answer.

"Let's have some fun, then," Jess informed her victim as she struck his temple with the butt of his own gun several times.

While blood drained out of his flesh, Jess inquired again, "So, do you speak Twituboch or Uopa?"

The man only insulted her in Tozani.

"I hope you know this could get really unpleasant for you if you don't answer me."

Jess lifted the gangster's head and struck him in the mouth with the butt of the pistol, knocking out several of his triangular, gold capped teeth.

"The nose is next. If I were you and I knew Uopa or Twituboch, I'd start talking."

The man failed to reply so Jess raised his head again and smashed the bridge of his nose with the pistol. He tried to scream in pain, but his tormentor thrust his face into the puddle to keep him quiet.

Lifting the gangster's face up before he drowned and looking at his remaining eye, Jess smiled.

"I see you're sitting on a couple of eggs. Maybe it's time to crack them open now. I really hope you can speak Uopa or Twituboch so you can ask me to stop."

"Stop! Don't do it," the man pled in Twituboch.

"Well, that's my good little boy."

"Fuck you, you clot!" he shouted at her in that same tongue.

"Not just at the moment. Thanks for the offer, though. Right now, you need to tell me who sent you."

The man began to scream, but his captor bashed his forehead against the paving a sufficient number of times to convince him to stop.

"I'm waiting for an answer," she informed him.

He started insulting her in Tozani again.

"Fine," Jess said and, shoving the man's face into the pool of grey, syrupy water, broke one of his fingers.

She held his head in the puddle for a few moments, so that his shouts would not draw attention. When she thought it was safe, she let him breathe again and again asked him, "You want to tell me who sent you to kill me?"

Since he still would not answer her, Jess pushed the gangster's face back into the water, twisted her torso around, set the needle gun on her thigh, pulled the man's testicles out from between his legs, picked up the gun, and shot one of them off.

The hood kicked, shook his body, and blew bubbles in the water. He even managed to throw Jess off of his back.

She kept the gun pointed at him, and, when he rolled over onto his side, he saw it and did not get up.

Crouching in front of the man, ready to react to anything he might try, Jess repeated her question. Instead of answering it, the gangster lunged at her. She shot him in the knee and he fell back down.

Jess stood up, walked behind the man, kicked him onto his belly again, placed her feet on either side of his head, squatted down over him, and repeated her question one more time.

"Please," he said, "stop it. Gople Sing sent me."

"Who?"

"The boss of the Sing gang. He said you killed Vomo."

"How'd he find out about that?"

"I have no idea. I swear."

"Fine. So, where can I find Gople?"

"He lives in the penthouse in Sunshine Towers on Sotru Square."

"You think he'll be in today? I'd like to drop by for a chat."

"Yes, yes, of course."

"Thanks, you're a big help," Jess told the man. Then she grabbed ahold of his temple and his chin and snapped his neck.

As soon as his face had fallen upon the ground, Jess dragged her victim further into the alley, hiding him behind the same pile of pungent rubbish where she herself had been hiding moments before.

She picked up the hood she had dropped, put it over her head, tucked her new gun under her arm (hiding it beneath her robe), and continued on to the end of the alley, which opened up onto a narrow side street crammed with shops, though, like before, there were few people wandering about it.

Jess was uncertain what she should do next, but she was worried about Uluf and did regret leaving Dawn's Spine behind. Whatever the consequences, she decided to head back to her hotel.

Being unable to ask anyone for directions, the girl wandered about Oditkalee for some time. Eventually, however, she chanced upon Kaan Street, and, once there, she easily found the hotel where she had been staying. She cautiously entered the lobby, still wearing her hood, and looked around. There was no one in sight who looked dangerous to her, so she made her way towards the stairs at their back. Halfway there, she turned to her left to peer into the hotel bar, and there she saw Uluf sitting and drinking a cup of wine.

She at once removed her hood, hurried into the room, and sat down next to her friend. He looked at her with surprise and joy.

"Ah, you are back, my dear," he exclaimed. "What happened to you?"

"What do you mean?" Jess asked him.

"Where did you go this morning? I thought something might have happened to you. I was terribly worried."

"You don't know what happened?"

"I am sorry, my dear. I do not."

Jess could not help but laugh.

Wiping the sweat from her eyes and her saturated hair from her face, she said with a chuckle, "Would you get me a drink? I don't have a groat on me and I'm dying of thirst."

"Of course," Uluf said and called over a waiter. When this man came, the toad ordered a glass of fruit juice for Jess.

The waiter left and Uluf asked his friend, "Now, what happened to you today, my dear?"

"First," Jess said, "you have to tell me what happened to you. Where did you go this morning?"

"I woke up just before midday and needed to use the toilet. You were sitting on it sound asleep, so I got dressed and came downstairs to the bar to use the one here. Since, after I had readied and relieved myself, I was wide awake, I decided to order my breakfast. When I got back upstairs, I found the room a mess and you gone."

Jess laughed again. "So that's what happened to you."

The waiter arrived with Jess's drink and Uluf tossed him a few coins. The girl gulped down half of her juice in a single swallow and leaned back in her chair as though relieved, which she was.

"Now, my dear, you must tell me your story," Uluf said to her.

"Okay," replied Jess as she grabbed the collar of her saturated robe and rhythmically tugged on it, trying so to fan herself.

"While I was pissing this morning, a bunch of men broke into our room and tried to kill me."

"Oh dear," exclaimed Uluf. "I am glad to see that you are all right."

"Yeah, I'm fine. But when I saw you weren't in the room – after I got out of the toilet – I thought they'd taken you somewhere. I'm happy I didn't lose another friend. You and Tolliver are the only people I have."

Getting a little choked up and teary, she continued. "Now that he's gone, you're my only friend, Uluf. I'd be totally lost without you"

"You are too kind, Jess."

"No. It's true. I couldn't make it without you. I'm sorry. I'm getting too emotional here. It just scares me when I think I might lose you."

Jess wiped her moist eyes and smiled. "Anyway, if you were down here, that explains why I didn't see you earlier."

Uluf patted his friend's hand and she exhaled loudly.

"So, as I was saying, I fought off a few of the guys who attacked me, but there were a lot more of them in the hall, and they all had needle guns. There was no way I could get them all. I couldn't even reach my sword. All I could do was try to get away. I jumped out the window and tried to lose them in the streets. I wound up having to kill a few more of them, but I did eventually throw them off my tracks. When I had, I decided to come back here to see if I could find out what had happened to you and Dawn's Spine. Where is my sword, anyway? Is it in the room or did those hoods take it?"

"Neither," answered Uluf. "I have it here, and your other belongings as well. I assumed something serious had happened when I returned to the room and found things like I did."

"Why didn't you go back to the ship? You'd have been safer there."

"I am not going to abandon you, Jess. You are precious to me as well."

She leaned over the table, grabbed Uluf's hands in her own, and said, "Thanks, Uluf. That means a lot to me. You took a risk staying here."

"And you took a risk coming back."

"It's nothing. So, anyway, what I want to know is: What'd they do with the body I left in the room? Did you see?"

"No. I am afraid that I did not. I suppose the persons who attacked you entered and left the building through a back entrance. That makes me think that someone working or staying here must have told them you had a room, and that makes me think that we ought to leave as soon as possible."

"You're right. Let's get going. First, though, do you have my clothes?"

"I have your bottomless pouch in my bag down here," Uluf told her while pointing to the floor beside his chair.

"Thanks," Jess said while standing up. "Do you know anywhere we can eat? I'm starving."

# Interlude 4
# The Religion of Tozana

The religious practices of the people of Tozana are broadly similar to those of many of the other nations of Shokai, having, like those, been gradually developed from the customs of the original colonists.

The Tozanis believe that after death the virtuous will be reborn in a heaven where they will enjoy the fruits of their good deeds and the sinful in a hell where they will be punished for their crimes. When such persons have exhausted their store of merit or demerit, they are reborn as human beings. Those individuals who have been especially virtuous are not, however, reincarnated. It is held that they are instead given positions in the celestial bureaucracy and charged with running the universe for mankind's benefit. Such individuals are, in fact, worshiped as deities in temples across Tozana.

These gods and the other supernatural powers that are understood to govern the universe are organized into hierarchies under the authority of the Flowery King, and each has authority over some sphere of life or some aspect of nature. In certain cases, this connection reflects an historical reality, as most if not all of the nation's deities are believed to have formerly been human beings, including the Flowery King himself. A person who achieved repute in a particular field will thus sometimes be worshipped after his death as the ruler of that field. Kavipai, the god of poetry, for example, is the apotheosized Hravi Padu, Tozana's most renowned early poet. Others, such as the Flowery King and Zhuneihi, the god of war, are identified with purely legendary figures who have no historical foundation. A number of deities, although connected with real or legendary human beings, are actually derived from gods that had been worshipped on Earth. Povai, the goddess of compassion, for example, originated from the Indian deity Parvati, and Sakshi, the god who watches over man's misdeeds and reports these to the Flowery King, evolved from the Chinese Kitchen God.

The rites by which these deities are venerated or propitiated are performed both privately and in temples, depending on the nature, purpose, and grandeur of the ritual. Professional priests do exist and are employed on important occasions. Most such persons are associated with a given temple.

Generally, temples exist as independent institutions supported either by property they own, by donations, or by fees paid for rites performed by affiliated priests.

There is no overarching organization governing Tozana's religious institutions as there are in several of the other nations of Shokai. Some sectarian movements are, however, ruled by a hierarchy of priests, and several of these do control substantial numbers of temples.

Just as there is no single body governing the religious institutions of Tozana, there is no universally acknowledged canon of scripture in that country. Certain texts are accepted as being sacred only by small numbers of persons while others are accepted even beyond Tozana's borders.

Several widely regarded texts are, in fact, revered in nearly all of Shokai's nations. Some, though current only in Tozana, are venerated throughout that country, and others are accepted only in specific regions of Tozana. Still other texts are restricted in use to particular sects or temples.

Like the scriptures of the planet generally, those accepted in Tozana are, for the most part, concerned with relating myths and legends, providing detailed moral codes, and giving instructions for the performance of rituals. There is scant attention paid in them to the establishment of doctrines or to metaphysical speculations, which play little or no part in Tozani religious life.

As a rule, religion in Tozana consists of the propitiation of deities in the hope of gaining benefits or avoiding misfortunes, the performance of calendrical rituals and rites of passage, the adherence to moral injunctions, and the performance of penances when these are violated.

Numerous religious festivals are celebrated in Tozana. The most important of these is, undoubtedly, the March of the Dead. When a person dies in that country, his body is taken to a charnel house, where it is smoked, partially mummified, and stored until the next March of the Dead. Upon the day of this feast, all the corpses being kept in charnel houses, that is to say, those of all the persons who died in the preceding year, are conveyed to the nearest funerary temple, where they are cremated in a mass pyre.

Other important public or private rituals include Shojwa, a spring festival, Nafaraatru, when the Flowery King's consort, Taro, is venerated, and Gnwel, during which Sakshi is propitiated and gifts are exchanged.

From Pollidor's *Big Blue Book of Knowledge*

# Chapter 9
# Gople Sing

After they had left Kaan Street behind and were a good distance from the hotel, Jess asked Uluf for her clothes. He took the girl's bottomless pouch from the bag he was carrying, and, once he had handed it to her, she rifled through it.

While a drunken vagrant watched her intently from where he lay half buried under a heap of refuse, Jess stripped off the sticky robe she was wearing and put on a skintight black halter-top made of a substance that looked like rubber, a pair of bright pink shorts that covered most of her buttocks, and the same pair of tall boots she had worn the day before. On her breast she then pinned her translator, and from her waist she hung her ornate (and very useful) pouch. In this she placed her usual weapons and the needle gun she had acquired earlier that morning.

Even though she had not bathed after all her previous exertions, she felt better once she was wearing new clothes and resumed her walk down the street to the restaurant Uluf had recommended to her.

This place, a ramshackle dive that, were it not for the thin curtain hanging across its front, would have opened directly onto the street, was filled with rickety wooden tables set in front of a worm-eaten wooden bar and served only bowls of noodles mixed with various strange looking creatures that had formerly inhabited Shokai's ocean. As suspicious as she was both of the restaurant's ruinous state and of the odd animals swimming in its food, Jess was happy to discover that she enjoyed the soup as much as she had enjoyed the krimhi she had earlier had at the market.

While slurping up her noodles, Jess spoke quietly to Uluf, telling him who had sent the men to their hotel room.

"I know he's probably expecting me," she continued, "but I'm going to go pay him a visit, anyway. This can't go on. I need to find out what happened to Tolliver, and I need to do it before Sing or whoever it was that got him gets me."

"I realize that I shall not be able to dissuade you, my dear, but I do not think that what you are doing is wise. At the least, please do be careful."

"I will, Uluf. Now, can you tell me where Sotru Square is?"

"Yes. Just a moment."

Uluf fished about in his pockets and eventually took out a pen and a piece of paper. He drew a rough map for Jess and told her where she was, where Sotru Square was, and how to get from the one to the other.

"I am sorry that I am of no use to you in situations like this," the toad said.

"Don't worry about it. Just tell me where we can meet up when I get back."

"I will go the Kol Theater. They serve food and drink and provide musical and dance performances. It is a pleasant place to spend a few hours. I went there on my last visit here and have since wanted to return. I will remain at the theater until you arrive or it closes for the evening. If the latter is the case, I will return to the *Empress* and wait for you there."

"Will it be okay for you to wander around the city by yourself? I thought you said you weren't allowed to?" Jess asked him.

"I will hire a prostitute off Kaan Street to accompany me. As long as I am not alone while I am in public, I do not believe I shall be bothered."

"You promise?"

"I cannot do that, but you should not worry."

"I'll try not to, but I can't promise that either," said Jess as she stood up.

She walked around the table, put her arms around Uluf's neck while he was still sitting, kissed him upon his cheek, and placed her own cheek upon his brow. He reached up, grasped her arm, and said, "Please do take care, Jess."

"I will. I never get killed, anyway. I'm too adorable to die. I'll see you later, Uluf."

With that, Jess left the restaurant, walked to the edge of the pavement beside the parking area beneath the elevated metallic road, and stood beside what looked like a lamppost. She pulled a lever on the side of this and the light on top came on, burning with a bright green glow.

This device, as Jess had noticed many times since her arrival on Shokai, was used to hail taxis. Whenever a passing driver saw a green light on, he would pull off of the bridge and pick up the person standing next to it. If there was no such light, the traveler could wave at passing taxis, and one of their drivers (all of whom, whether human or mechanical, were very keen eyed when it came to spying fares) would stop if he did not already have a passenger. The lights, however, were much more convenient.

Within moments, a cab slid down the nearest ramp from the bridge and came to a stop beside the pavement where Jess was standing. She bid the driver take her to just outside Sotru Square, and the vehicle returned to the road and sped off towards her destination.

\* \* \*

Jess located Sunshine Towers easily enough and did not have any difficulty finding a way in through the back of the building. There were several entrances for the servants of the residents and these were neither watched nor locked. Inside, having taken the hilt of her sword in her hand, though without extending its blade, she slunk past whatever persons she chanced upon and eventually spotted an elevator. She took this to the level of the penthouse and discovered that it opened onto a room filled with skips overflowing with rubbish.

Now she readied her sword, letting its telescoping segments slide out from their container so that, should she suddenly encounter any of her foes, she would be prepared to deal with them.

At the far side of the stinking chamber was a door, and Jess checked it to find out if it was unlocked. It was.

She slowed time and entered the room beyond. It was a large kitchen. Fortunately, there was no one there, and she continued to the next door. This led to a dining room that was as empty as was the kitchen.

The girl crossed the room cautiously and checked the nearest door. It was locked, and so she moved to the second, that directly across from the entrance to the kitchen. Slowly opening this, a swinging wooden door, she peered through the crack between it and the jamb.

Beyond was a large lounge with a tall ceiling adorned with an image screen that made it appear to be a blue sky across which clouds sailed and fantastic winged monsters flew. The blue, wood paneled walls were decorated with more such screens set in ornately carved and richly gilded picture frames, and these presented images of diverse beautiful or fanciful landscapes that were so real the screens seemed to be windows opening onto such places.

The lounge itself was filled with luxurious sofas and plush chairs that were made of the hides of different animals, rested upon those beasts' feet, incorporated their legs as armrests, and were adorned, in some way or another, with the dead creatures' heads or horns.

Such furnishings were arranged, more or less, in a circle around a tall glass cylinder, a picture vat, that, were it not for its elaborately carved wooden cap, would have been entirely invisible, as it had transformed itself, with remarkable verisimilitude, into three-dimensional moving images of some kind of sporting event. This involved a man dressed in richly embroidered garments, seated atop a tall porcine mount, and armed with a long spear engaging in ritualized combat with a huge animal vaguely like a featherless four-legged chicken with the head of an aardvark, from whose body dripped copious amounts of blood from innumerable wounds.

Watching this spectacle while reclining upon the various sofas and chairs in the room, and frequently hooting with delight whenever one of the combatants injured his enemy, were about a dozen tattooed gangsters. Jess could not clearly see those sitting with their backs to her, but the others, she noticed, were armed both with needle guns and daggers.

There was no other way for her to leave the dinning room and so she resolved to be done with these persons as quickly as she could and, perhaps, to use one of them to locate Sing.

Jess took a deep breath and exhaled slowly, readying herself for the violence about to come. Her heart hardened, her compassion cast away, and her will fixed, she offered up the lives of her victims to the goddess Haya, asking her to accept the blood of her own children and to bring them back into her own being.

Without delaying any longer, Jess slowed time as much as she could, though her exertions earlier in the day prevented her from being able to control the thread effectively and impeding time as much as she would ordinarily have done in such a situation.

She pushed the door open and leapt from where she stood over the sofa directly in front of her, slicing off the head of the man sitting there. She landed in the middle of the room, next to the cylindrical picture vat, putting her back to it so that she could not be shot from behind while she dealt with the other two men reclining between where she stood and the dining room.

Both of these were in the process of standing, but the first would not complete his movements. Jess lunged at him and split his body in half at his waist. The second fared no better. Though he was upon his feet while his fellow died, he had not yet drawn his gun (as he was trying to do) when Jess opened his throat with a swing of her blade, splattering his blood across the sofas and picture vat in front of him.

A sudden sensation of chagrined horror then raced through Jess's body as she felt a hand grab ahold of the back of her shorts, yanking on them and, in the process, pulling them halfway down her buttocks. She whipped around and saw a man lying on one of the sofas behind her. He had not been visible earlier, but now was simultaneously trying to lift himself up by pulling Jess towards him and to draw his gun from its holster.

The barrel was nearly pointed at her when Jess severed the hoodlum's hand. Shocked by this amputation and immersed in a mess of sticky time, the man kept on tugging on Jess's shorts, so she, with another motion, removed his cranium above the bridge of his nose.

While Jess's attack on the persons on the other side of the room was delayed by the previously unseen thug, two of these, who were standing to her right (after she had spun around), armed themselves with needle guns and aimed their weapons at the girl. To avoid their fire, Jess thrust the world downwards, leapt onto the ceiling, rolled, and, upside down, dashed across it. She sprang down at the feet of her two adversaries, brandished her sword, and cut their outstretched hands from their wrists.

As these two screamed horrifically, another gangster, having risen from a chair just to the left of his maimed comrades (to their right), shouted and threw his dagger at her. She was able to duck in time and it harmlessly pierced the couch behind her. The same man, while pulling out his needle gun, dove to his right in order to hide at the back of a chair close to another three men.

Jess followed him, even as she noticed two more gangsters (who had been sitting on the side of the room opposite the dining hall) moving near the picture vat in an effort to get behind her.

While she jumped upon her quarry, as a lioness upon its prey, opening up his jugular with her blade as the big cat would tear open the neck of its victim with its fangs, Jess felt a sudden motion in the air beside her. She looked down and saw a hole in her now dead enemy's stomach. One of the men behind her had fired his needle gun and the projectile had narrowly missed her.

Leaping up and using all her will to slow time as much as she could, Jess hurtled through the air and fell upon one of the men in front of the vat. In a moment of carelessness, she allowed her blade to chop not only through her enemy's neck, but through the glass picture vat behind him as well. The device sputtered, shot out sparks, and went grey over a large part of its circumference. As the whole thing did not, however, go out, the pictures it subsequently projected appeared to be partially covered by some strange opaque fog.

Two of the men standing above the person from whose body Jess had just jumped promptly fired their needle guns. Fortunately for her, both missed. One shot the individual standing beside his target between two of his ribs and the second hit the picture vat, opening up a jagged, sparking hole in its side.

Knowing that she would be unable to reach them before they had a chance to fire again, Jess fell to the floor and rolled between two sofas on the side of the room opposite the dining hall. She had not, however, noticed that three of the remaining gangsters had made their way from where they had been sitting (across from the men shooting at her) to where she now was.

One of these persons wrapped his arm around Jess's throat while she crouched on the floor and lifted her up. He immediately cried out to the others who had just shot at the girl to fire again, but, before they did, she spun the man around and he himself was struck by two of the needles. Jess felt his leg flinch and his shoulder heave and knew he had been hit in both those places. He was not dead, however, and with his free hand he tried to jab his fingers into Jess's eyes. With a quick motion, she severed the man's digits and prepared to stab him in his face.

Before she did so, a loud, deep voice called out, "Stop!"

The thug holding onto Jess immediately let go of her throat and the other two near her fell back.

Jess looked in the direction whence the command had come. In a doorway behind the persons who had been shooting at her stood a pair of nude men. The one who had spoken, who was positioned in front of the other, was in his mid-thirties, muscled, and handsome, though his body was so weighed down with bejeweled gold ornaments Jess could hardly believe he was able to stand.

The whole of the top of his bald head was covered with a tattoo of a lotus. Around his lips were tattooed the petals of another lotus, and around this were both smaller lotuses set on intertwined stalks and myriads of swarming bees and dragonflies. His body was as ornately decorated as was his head, being adorned with pictures of various flying insects with iridescent wings flitting through a forest of gracefully bending reeds and flowers that emerged from a pool teeming with fish, larvae, and prawns.

"There is no need for this," he continued in a booming, impressive bass once the fighting had ceased (though the moans and cries of the mutilated had not). "You came here because you think I killed or abducted Tolliver. Isn't that right?"

"Who are you?" Jess shouted back to him in a confrontational manner while wiping away the blood that had splattered across her face.

"I am Gople Sing. Am I right? You think I did something to Tolliver?"

"Are you saying you didn't?"

"I did not. What is more, the people who have harmed him are my enemies as much as they are yours."

"What are you talking about?"

"You are being duped."

"Like I said, what are you talking about?"

"Someone who wants to ruin me has arranged for all of this. You're just the tool he's using."

"That doesn't sound very likely."

"Be that as it may, it is true. I'll prove it to you too."

Now Jess was curious.

"How?" she asked.

"I've got a video of Tolliver's kidnapping. I know who grabbed him."

"Show me, then."

"Fine. Put down your weapon and come with me."

"I'll go with you, but I'm not putting down my sword until I know you're telling the truth."

"As you wish, but my men will have their weapons ready as well."

Gople, accompanied by the man who had followed him into the lounge, and by the three who had shot at Jess, made his way over to a door near where the girl was standing.

When he had opened it, Gople looked back and around and commented, "You certainly made a mess of my sitting room. It's going to cost a fortune to replace or clean all of this."

He then gestured for Jess to follow him and, with his fellow, walked through the door. She went after them, as did the two remaining uninjured thugs she had been fighting. The man who had been shot and the groaning, weeping amputees stayed behind.

On the other side of the door was a hallway running to the right and left. Gople went to the left and passed through another door on his left hand side. This led to a room filled with desks where a number of women of the fourth estate were performing various clerical duties. Gople turned to his right and led the others through another door, which opened onto a large office.

The wall to the left was pierced by a series of tall bay windows and that to the right was composed entirely of a fish<sup></sup> tank filled with myriads of colorful and outlandish sea beasts. Along the wall opposite the door was a highly polished wooden desk that was so long it was more like a counter.

As they walked through this large office, Gople said to Jess, "I think you will see that what we have in common more than outweighs our differences, even if you have killed a great many of my men."

"We'll see," Jess answered him warily.

When Gople reached the room's far end, he whistled for his computer and it came walking over to him across the countertop.

The central part of this device was shaped like and about the same size as a toaster. On its bronze front were four round brass knobs, each of which was set in a vertical slit extending from the machine's top to about halfway down its height. From behind the body of the computer projected, in the spaces between the four slits, three glass cylinders topped with copper lids. Below the slits, and set off from them by a raised seam running around three sides of a slightly recessed rectangular niche, was a series of chrome plated metal tubes. Each of these was attached at its base to a copper valve that was itself attached to a bronze tab-like key. In the middle of these tubes was a small round plate, like the chestpiece of a stethoscope.

---

* Terms for types of terrestrial animals have, throughout human space, been applied to animals occupying similar environments or having vaguely similar characteristics. The term "fish" thus refers to any animal that lives in the water and does not breathe air. "Bird" refers to any animal that flies. "Insect" refers to any animal with an exoskeleton, and so on.

At the computer's right hand side was a nacre handled lever like that of a slot machine, and at its left hand side a long, brazen, S-shaped neck that grew ever wider and ended in a large bell, like that of a French horn.

In the mouth of this bell was set a convex, lavender glass screen etched around its edge with images of swirling leaves, flowers, and ribbons.

The whole contraption was set on four short but movable legs ending in feet cast to resemble those of a lion.

Sing drew out the disc between the tubes out of the computer, to which it remained attached with an extendible rubber hose like that of a voicepipe. He then pulled on the lever at the computer's side and spoke into the disc (which was actually a microphone) while holding it close to his mouth.

He said, "Show the video from the Drunkard's Pleasure," and pulled the lever a second time.

The neck of the computer turned the screen at its end towards the people standing in front of it, and the lavender glass seemed to disappear, dissolving into a vision of a narrow street in front of a bar.

Jess looked intently at the images and saw how a man emerged from the entrance to the bar. While the picture was not perfect, it was clear that the man was Tolliver.

The captain had walked only a few paces when a Jaffrite hopped from off screen to grab him by the neck and strike his head with some dark object. Tolliver immediately fell onto the ground unconscious; a second Jaffrite joined the first, and the two stood over the man's body. They appeared to be discussing something for a few seconds, but then each grabbed one of Tolliver's arms and dragged him out of sight.

Gople pulled the computer's lever and spoke into the microphone in his hand.

"Pan to the top and continue the video," he said and yanked on the lever again.

The screen showed the Jaffrites pulling Tolliver down the alley. When they had reached its end, a freight vehicle pulled up; its door opened; a man wearing a cassock and a wide brimmed hat that covered his face leaned out and spoke to the Jaffrites, and they put Tolliver inside. The creatures jumped in after him and the man looked out again before closing the door and driving off.

Jess's whole body seemed to be emptied in a second. She recognized the man in the vehicle. It was Noyan. She did not, however, say a word about knowing him.

Gople pulled the lever of his computer again, spoke into the microphone, telling it to stop playing the video, and tugged the lever one last time.

With a gesture, he invited Jess to have a seat in one of the plush chairs in the room. She did, though with her still drawn sword lying across her lap, and Gople sat down near her.

He looked at his guest and explained. "The man you saw there is known to work for the Ngo Family, one of the Seven Families. He's the one who kidnapped Tolliver, not me. You can take the video and have it authenticated if you don't trust me."

"Where'd you get this?" Jess asked him.

"The owner of the Drunkard's Pleasure gave it to me. He had a camera hidden outside his bar. The kidnappers must not have known about it."

"Okay, so, if you knew about the video, why'd you send your men to kill me?"

"I didn't know about it when I sent them. I didn't even know who you were yet. I only received the video and information about you this afternoon. Before that, all I knew was that you'd slaughtered Vomo and his whole crew."

"So, why're you being friendly now?"

"You, love, are unbelievably deadly. Like I just said, you slaughtered Vomo and his crew. Just now you wiped out half of my own bodyguards, and they're some of the best men I have. When I saw the video, I knew who I was up against and I knew I'd need the best people I could get to deal with him."

"And you want me to help you."

"Yes."

"Why would I do that?"

"The same reason you took me on, to find Tolliver. Before, you were wasting your time hunting around for some mysterious phantom. Now you know who's got him."

"Okay, that's true enough, but I still don't know why the Ngo are going to all this trouble."

"Oh, you know, at least you can figure it out. I made a deal with the Llalloi to supply them with russa. There's going to be a war with us and the Llalloi on one side and the Ngo on the other. The Ngo are just hoping to put an end to me without having to get their own hands bloody. They have Tolliver abducted, make sure some people see that he was taken by mudjumpers, and then stir up some fear of the dumb creatures in Jezic. There've already been several protests, one in front of the roshpai's palace earlier today. I heard a couple of people were even killed when the police tried to break it up. Pretty soon, if the Ngo play it right, the government'll have to give in to public pressure just to keep the peace. Then they'll crack down on us and the mudjumpers. If they make things too tough for us, they might even put us out of business."

"All that's supposed to happen from one kidnapping?"

"Tolliver was hardly the first person attacked by a mudjumper recently, and I doubt if he'll be the last. The Ngo will keep on until they get the reaction they want. I'm sure they have other agents stirring things up in other ways too."

Jess was beginning to think teaming with Sing was what she should do, and so she said to him, "Let's say we join up. What's your plan? Are you going to find the man in the video?"

"No," Gople replied. "I've already tried to locate him. He's nowhere to be found. I suspect he's left Jezic. Even if he didn't know about the camera, he's not so stupid that he's going to think we wouldn't find out about what he did."

"So," Jess asked with a little disappointment, "what are you planning to do, then?"

"I'm going to send a couple of my assistants to Quanya to kill Tsoi Ngo, the head of the family. I'd like for you to go with them. Maybe you can find out if Tolliver's been taken there, or, at least, what they've done with him."

"Who are you planning to send with me?"

With a gesture, Sing indicated the man who had been behind him when he had entered the sitting room.

"Ofu Not, for one. He's one of the best fighters I have."

Jess looked closely at this person now for the first time. His enormous, muscled body was covered with tattoos of bear and spider-like creatures from whose bodies sprouted the man's own abundant hair. His teeth were all filed to triangular points, and his remarkably ugly face was made weirdly ferocious by a wide grin.

"My sister, Eshwurhiyo, and her lover, Syo, will also be traveling with you. I believe you will find both of them more than adequate in a difficult situation. Are you interested?"

"I'll go."

"That's good."

Gople got up, pulled the lever on the computer on his desk, and spoke into its microphone, telling it to assume its interactive mode. Then he pulled the lever again and resumed his seat.

A pair of great lids slid over the computer's screen from above and below, completely covering it. These promptly changed shape, as though they were made of clay that was being molded by invisible hands, and took on the appearance of the face of a young woman. This looked at Gople with its brass eyes and, with its brazen lips, teeth, and tongue, asked him what he would like.

Gople said, "Book four standard tickets on a skyliner leaving tomorrow from Jezic to Quanya."

"Five," Jess interrupted.

"Why five?" Sing asked.

"I've got a friend who's going to want to come with me."

"The toad?"

"Yes."

"That's fine. Computer, book five tickets."

The machine replied in a sensuous feminine voice. "Five standard tickets have been booked for passage on the *Cloud Cutter*. Your departure time is a quarter past fourth watch tomorrow. Would you like me to print the tickets?"

Sing told the computer to do so, and, with a whirring, clicking noise, it produced the tickets from a slot beneath its nacre handled lever. When she saw this, Jess, being the sophisticated young woman that she was, could not help but think that the machine looked like some strange animal defecting. She snickered a little, but tried not to call attention to herself.

"Bring those here," Gople instructed one of his underlings, who did as he was told. The gangster looked at them, handed two to Jess, took two himself, and bid the man who had fetched them give the last one to Ofu.

Jess finally closed her sword, stood up, and looked at Sing.

"I better go," she said. "I have to meet up with my friend tonight."

"Just make sure you're at the airport before the skyliner departs."

"I'll be there."

Jess started to leave the room, but, at the door, she turned around.

"One little thing I'd like to know," she said.

"What's that?" Gople replied.

"How'd you find out who I am?"

"The clerk at the hotel where you were staying. He told us who you are, Jess Ichikawa."

"And how'd you find out what hotel I was at?"

"There aren't that many offworlder women with bright pink hair staying in Oditkalee."

Jess nodded her head and left the room.

Once outside Sunshine Towers, she hailed a taxi and went to the Kol Theater.

Inside that place, Jess passed through a thin sliding door and entered into a large chamber with a stage at one end. Before this was a sort of checkerboard formed by a gridiron of narrow wooden planks separating slightly sunken pits. The members of the audience were reclining on pillows arranged on low couches placed in these pits while eating and drinking from squat, lacquered tables set in front of them.

On the stage itself, in front of a screen covered with gold leaf that accentuated the billowing tree painted at one side of it, as well as the branches of the tree that were streaming across the whole of the screen's width, sat a small orchestra, and this provided the music for a single female vocalist and a solitary female dancer. As the former of these recited some narrative, the second, an attractive young woman, enacted the events so described with graceful, stylized motions.

For a moment, Jess was enthralled by the half visible movements of the dancer's legs under her transparent bell-shaped skirt (that was supported on a frame of metal wires from which were suspended little bells that tinkled as she moved). She was delighted by the woman's long, dagger-like, colorfully enameled nails as these twirled about in the air like the feathers of a bird's wing. She was mesmerized by the complex images sewn onto the length of cloth wrapped around the woman's torso and fastened at her back in an oversized bow. She was even thrilled by how, as the woman frenziedly flung her head in different directions, her long, plaited hair lashed about wildly beneath the colorful, plumed comb upon her brow.

It took a while before Jess was able to disengage from this spectacle and bring herself to remember why she had come to the theater. She looked around and spotted Uluf easily enough. There was no one else like him watching the performance.

Jess walked along the planks of wood in front of the stage and stepped down into the pit where Uluf was sitting by himself (he had apparently already dismissed the prostitute he had said he was going to hire to accompany him through Jezic's streets).

The toad was clearly pleased to see that his friend was still alive and embraced her fondly. Then, when he felt so assured that she was really in front of him, he asked her what had happened, and she quietly related the events of the afternoon.

Uluf, hearing her tale, told her he was glad that she had insisted he come with her to Quanya and promised to help her in whatever limited way he could.

"Most of all," the toad added, "I am just relieved that you are alive and well."

With a chuckle, he continued. "Not only that, but it also looks like we will be able to visit Quanya after all."

"Yeah," Jess answered while laughing a little herself. "Who knows, maybe this'll all work out in the end. I have to admit, our visit to Shokai has been pretty rotten so far."

"You have faced some tough people before, though. Were they that much worse here?"

Turning her eyes away from Uluf, to look at the woman on the stage alternate from slow, graceful gestures to wild, ecstatic convulsions, Jess went on.

"That's not what I meant. It scares me to think I might have lost Tolliver. Like I said before, you and him are the only two people I have. The rest of the universe couldn't care less if I died today."

"You should not assume he is dead yet. Since I first met you, I have been impressed by your abilities to solve difficulties and to persuade others to do as you wish them to. I would not be surprised if you located Tolliver and brought him back."

"I hope I can, but everything that's happened here is really bothering me. From the time I was a little girl until just a couple of years ago, people did to me whatever they wanted to, and there wasn't anything I could do about it. After I trained under Takenac, I was able to fight back. People couldn't just treat me like I was nothing. If they tried to, believe me, I made sure they knew I was worth more than that. Now, here I am feeling that I might be as helpless as I was when I was a little girl. Maybe I can't help Tolliver. Maybe I'm just useless and he's dead or going to die."

"Jess, my dear, if the captain is alive, I am certain you will save him. There is no one who is more able to do so than you."

"Thanks, Uluf," said Jess, moving her gaze from the stage to her friend. "I really don't know what I'd do without you."

The two then turned their attention back to the stage, and while they dined on food brought to them during the intermissions separating the acts of the performance, they found themselves enthralled by the music, the dancing, and the ancient tale being related about the tragic love of an honest prince and a beautiful goddess.

They heard of how, in the ancient past, when Tozana was still young and the roshpai resided in the city of Mozei, one such ruler had three sons. The first was brave and skilled at arms. The second was wise and learned. The third, Sajjit, though handsome and kind, was also lazy, ignorant, and weak.

One day, while these youths were out hunting in the forests beyond Mozei, they chased after their quarry so vigorously that they lost their way and found themselves wandering without direction amongst the dark passageways beneath the interwoven limbs of the trees.

Having grown weary and thirsty, the three heard a stream flowing a short distance away and made their way towards it. There, hidden by the dense foliage flourishing at the water's edge, the men spied a young woman bathing in the river before them accompanied by a band of female attendants.

Each and every one of them was more beautiful than a human being could ever be, with eyes that shone brighter than any star, hair blacker than space but as glossy as the finest mirror, a body slimmer and more flexible than a weasel's, and nutmeg hued features more delicate than any eggshell. There was nothing about these heavenly women that was not captivating. Their breasts were like pomegranates, their nipples like brazen crowns, their graceful limbs like hanging vines, and their mouths like rose petals dipped in honey.

As fair as all of these beings were, the first of them surpassed her attendants to the same degree that they surpassed every mortal woman who had ever lived. All three of the princes immediately loved her and all desired to possess her.

They did not, however, know how to win her and so remained concealed, contenting themselves with the sight of her impossible beauty.

After some time, the celestial nymph said to one of her attendants, "I have forgotten my comb. Go and fetch it for me."

The serving girl rose up from the waters, stepped onto the shore, and picked up a cloak of feathers hanging over the branch of a tree. She draped this around her shoulders and suddenly transformed into a bird, which flew away into the sky to do her mistress's bidding.

The youths knew at once what they should do and stealthily removed all the other feathery cloaks hung near where the one the serving girl had just taken had been. Keeping these with them, the three waited concealed until the other maidens decided to come out of the waters and lie upon the stones along the shore.

When they saw the naked shapes of the heavenly women glistening under the sun, the men were no longer able to restrain themselves and rushed forth to profess their love. The women, panicking, fled from them, but finding that their garments had been taken, did not know what to do.

The men showed them the cloaks and swore that they would return them if the single woman they all three loved would agree to remain behind and marry one of them. Though, at first, she would not consent, when she saw that her suitors would not otherwise release either her or her handmaidens, she gave in to their demands.

She said, "My name is Jezic, and although I am a resident of the kingdom of the gods, I admit that you now have power over me. I will marry one of you and, leaving my home in the heavens, reside here in the universe of men. However, you must agree to three conditions. First, I will choose which of you I will marry. Second, you will return to me my cloak, and, third, whoever I select must swear never to look at me while I am naked after the sun has set."

The three agreed to these terms and each began trying to demonstrate his worth. The eldest youth showed off his strength and skill with weapons, killing several animals and presenting the nymph with their vivisected corpses. The second displayed his knowledge, regaling his beloved with longwinded lectures on a variety of topics. The third, being meek and ignorant, made no attempt to awe the heavenly woman. He simply told her that he was so intoxicated by her unearthly beauty, her gentle smile, and her vivacious manner that he would spend every moment he had remaining to him loving her.

Though the elder brothers were stunned by Jezic's choice, she was charmed by Sajjit's simple love and honest words and selected him to be her husband.

On their way back to their father's palace, Sajjit's brothers resolved to be rid of him and once tried to drown him, once tried to lure him into the den of a deadly beast, and once tried to cast him into a deep pit, but each time he survived.

Unwise as the youth was, he did realize that the troubles he had experienced after winning Jezic had been attempts to take his life. Consequently, once he had married her, he begged his father for estates of his own and took up residence with his wife upon these.

In her new home, Jezic eventually bore her husband a son and a daughter, and together the four lived contentedly for many years.

Then, one moonless night, the married couple went to a cottage they owned in the jungle and, in the darkness, bathed in a nearby spring. Thunderheads rolled overhead and obscured the stars above, interrupting their amorous play. Seeing these, Jezic begged her husband to take her home, but he refused and embraced her closely as they lay together upon a mossy stone.

Suddenly, a flash of lightning cut through the sky, illumining all the pond and revealing Jezic's naked form. Sajjit clearly saw that his wife's feet were like those of a chicken, that a writhing tail emerged from the base of her spine, and that down grew where pubic hair should have.

He recoiled in horror and fled from Jezic back to his cottage. There he repented of his cowardice and hurried back to her. She, however, had gone. Sajjit sought her throughout the night, but as he did not find her, he continued searching through the jungle for the next seven days.

Still failing to discover his love, he returned to his home, left his children in the care of his castellan, and began wandering across Shokai looking for Jezic. Though he circled the ocean three times and made journeys to a dozen different planets, Sajjit never found Jezic, nor even met a person who had seen her.

After thirty years, Sajjit, grown grey and haggard, finally despaired and returned to his estates. He took up residence on a plateau above a Jaffrite city and earned his food by trading with the aliens. When his children learned of their father's new home, they came to live with him, and after them came their followers. Others yet came after these. In time, a town grew up around the man's humble house, and this he called Jezicpwa, Jezic's City, after the woman he had loved and lost.

Long after the city had grown rich and had come to be known simply as Jezic, its lords, Sajjit's heirs, succeeded to the throne, the elder line of their family having died out, and made their home the capital of Tozana.

Jess, saddened by this tale, left the theater grasping Uluf tightly. She thought of how she herself had lost her love and was now searching for him. She also wondered if she, like Sajjit, might not end her days alone, having discovered neither the one person who had cared for her nor any other person who would embrace her as he had.

# Chapter 10
## Scheming

Tsoi Ngo might have thought that the face of the feihi gazing up at him resembled that of an anime character drawn in the first years of the Twenty-First Century (of the ancient calendar), if he had ever seen such a work. Since he had not, the thought never occurred to him. What Tsoi was thinking as he gazed upon the huge eyes and tiny mouth of this being's face was that it was a shame that he would not be able to have sex with her again before she died.

He stroked her abundant, soft, blue tresses and gazed regretfully at the graceful curves of her body, that were clearly visible beneath the sheets of translucent film hanging from her shoulders. Every detail of her form enthralled him.

The entirety of his own body still tingled with the excitement only sex with a feihi could produce. The world beyond his bed seemed to spin around in a confused vortex of colors. Only what was within a few feet of him had any tangible reality, but what reality such things had was so heightened in intensity that the pleasure each touch, each glance, and each smell gave him left him utterly intoxicated and nearly deranged with lust.

Tsoi had no idea how many times he had achieved an orgasm in the last few hours, but thanks to the aphrodisiac effect of the drug produced by the feihi's genitals, he had been so stimulated that he had never had any desire or need to rest. Unfortunately, though sex with his pretty toy transported him to a timeless universe that did not extend beyond his body and hers, since the feihi's internal structure was not entirely compatible with a human male's genitals, that apparent eternity was bound to end. Her reproductive organs had been wrecked by their intercourse, and such damage had been exacerbated, as it always was, by the consequences of the maddened excitement the drug produced in the man who was using such a being, as that ecstasy had led him to overly energetic and unceasing exertions. The feihi did not, therefore, have long to live now – she would surely be dead within a quarter to a half of a watch.

As much as he hated to waste his last moments with his pet, Tsoi had just been informed that Soniyo Dogrue had arrived and was insisting upon speaking with him. Now, not only would he have to see that woman, though he had no desire to so – he despised dealing with her – but he would also be unable to spend any more time in the company of his feihi. Unfortunately, he could hardly afford to ignore Soniyo at this point.

With a sigh, Tsoi lifted himself from his bed and sat upon its edge. The touch of the cool atmosphere of his air conditioned palace on his naked body made him shiver. Rubbing his arms for a little warmth, he looked back one last time at the feihi. She had lain back down, resting her head on her hands and her hands on her pillow while staring blankly ahead.

It was a shame, Tsoi thought, that the creatures died so easily. He did not mind paying for them, as expensive as they were, since he had more money than did any other human being except a member of the imperial family. They were just so adorable and sexy that it bothered him a little to see one dying.

Although such concern was, he reflected, only natural in a tender hearted person, he resolved not to let that sort of sentiment trouble him unduly. A dying feihi was, after all, merely like some cute toy that had been ruined and needed to be thrown in the rubbish. Besides, he had sex with at least one or two of them every day.

The man was pleased with his sensitivity and thought the melancholy that tinged his perceptions as he watched such lovely beings giving up their lives enriched his, both adding to his refinement and allowing him a deeper experience of his emotions.

It was certainly for the best, Tsoi thought, that feihi were not too readily available. The pleasures they were capable of providing would simply be squandered by most people. Although the lovely creatures could suffuse a man's existence with joys that were not only incomprehensibly intense but which were also able to transform the core of one's being, there were few persons who were not wholly closed to the relishing of such refined bliss.

As Tsoi himself could relish that bliss, it was no wonder that he no longer had any interest in human women. Compared to feihi, there was an utter crudeness about them. Of course, being completely addicted to the drug the feihi produced did help him to maintain that aversion.

Tsoi stood up, walked over to a tasseled ribbon hanging from the ceiling, and pulled on it. A moment later, two of his valets entered the room and, following their master to his bureau, combed his long hair and plaited it at his brows. Having washed his face and hands, one of them plastered the man's handsome countenance (that looked far younger than that of a person of nearly thirty years) with thick white powder, painted his eyes with kohl (as though he were an ancient Egyptian Pharaoh), and darkened his lips with a purple dye. The other man, meanwhile, traced complex floral patterns in henna upon his lord's hands and slipped onto his fingers six inch long artificial nails made of gold and decorated with cloisonné roses.

Having finished with their master's toilet, the valets fetched his clothes from an adjoining room and began to dress him.

They attired Tsoi in baggy white silk trousers colorfully printed with images of flowers. Over his shoulders they draped a long frock coat made from the hide of some creature whose spotted fur had an iridescent sheen. They fastened the gold, nacre inlaid buckles of this across his chest, closed its embroidered mandarin collar, and tidied and arranged the coat's lace trim and the long lace cuffs that completely concealed Tsoi's hands. One of the valets then fetched from a closet a wide conical hat surmounted by a bejeweled bulb shaped like an onion and placed it on Tsoi's brow while his fellow wrapped around that man's neck a stole made of some thick luxurious fur.

When he was dressed, Tsoi said to the more senior of the valets, "Dispose of the feihi. It will be dead soon."

The two men picked the creature up by her arms and dragged her over to a sliding door like that of a dumbwaiter. While the feihi looked at Tsoi with her wide, expressive eyes, the valets opened the door and hoisted her into the black vertical shaft on its other side. Too tired and weak to move her limp arms or legs, she fell quickly down the shaft, though now and then banging against its sides, until she came to the furnace at its base, where she died and was incinerated.

The valets closed the door to the shaft, hurried past Tsoi, and opened the door to the bedroom so that he could leave.

Outside, around a litter strewn with cushions, were standing eight homunculi, who were like men with the hides and heads of Indian rhinoceroses.

Tsoi sat himself upon the palanquin, and four of the beasts lifted him up. Three of the others walked in front of him, one carrying a censer from which wafted swirling scented smoke and two bearing halberds adorned with bright plumes. The last two followed behind armed as were the pair ahead of their master.

Through the wide, garishly decorated halls of his palace, Tsoi was carried by this group, until they reached a pair of tall doors set in a marble portal. There they set the litter down, helped Tsoi to stand, and opened the doors for him.

Beyond was a long room beneath a high glass barrel vault supported by thin columns. The whole of the length of this great chamber, that was as cool and pleasant as was the rest of Tsoi's palace, was filled with a variety of earthly plants, including beds of flowers, rose bushes, and fantastic topiary. Between these ran a path lined with rows of birches that led to a domed pavilion at the very middle of the room. This was furnished with a number of couches that apparently consisted of cushions placed directly on the backs of naked young women who were crouching on their hands and knees. In fact, the seats of the sofas, while bound to the women's backs with collars fastened round their necks and waists, were supported on thin corkscrew-like legs that wrapped around the women's limbs and appeared merely to be jewelry.

Tsoi walked down the path with the slow, mincing steps affected by the elites of Quanya (but which were currently also necessitated by the dizziness lingering from his intercourse with the now dead feihi).

When he neared the pavilion, he saw a woman in her early thirties sitting therein upon a couch. It was Soniyo Dogrue.

She was gorgeously attired in a long sleeved, formfitting, printed hot pink choli that left her midriff bare and a tight, printed pink skirt that was laced up the back (from the hem to the waist) with a blue ribbon tied in a bow at the small of her back. Her pink embroidered shoes had very thick soles (that made her seem much taller than she actually was) and were curled up at the tip.

As lovely as were her garments, she was still somewhat odd to look at as a result of the custom prevalent amongst the members of Tozana's first estate to shape the heads of their children. The woman's forehead was, consequently, flat and sloping, and her cranium rose to a high, conical peak. Atop her pointed head, her hair was arranged into a huge whorl wrapped around a circular frame.

In her arms she held a genetically modified dog, an hadishyen (as such creatures were known in Tozana). Its body was entirely hairless, though its cranium was adorned with a thick mane. Beneath this fur was a slot into which a small computer could be inserted and the end of it concealed. The animal's brain had been altered in such a way that it was able to connect directly with the computer. This so enhanced the hadishyen's intelligence that, with its modified lips, it was able to speak. Naturally, such creatures were given subservient personalities and a fondness for complimenting their masters. Tsoi found them horribly annoying.

Soniyo was tapping impatiently upon the hadishyen's head, causing it to blink with each blow, when Tsoi stepped into the pavilion and reclined lazily, like a languid cat, on a couch across from her.

"I am glad to see you again, Lady Soniyo," he said as a young, naked, but bejeweled serving girl brought him a lit pipe with a three foot long stem and then retreated to squat in an alcove where several other young women were waiting for orders. Meanwhile, another woman sitting unclothed (except for her brightly colored ribbons and shining jewelry) in a second alcove began to play upon a zither.

"What, may I ask, brings you here?"

"I am concerned about recent rumors I have heard."

Tsoi tried to conceal his irritation. He detested Soniyo. Not only did he find her rather stupid, but he was certain that she despised him, looking at him as if he were merely some rich gangster.[*]

---

[*] This suspicion was especially irritating to Tsoi because, of course, that was exactly what he was.

"What then are these?" he asked her.

"It has been brought to my attention that Sing has begun collecting arms and that the Llalloi have bought new friends in the military."

Tsoi's exasperation increased as Soniyo spoke. She was one of Tozana's wealthiest citizens and descended from one of its oldest families, but she was both painfully slow and entirely convinced of her own insightfulness.

As he exhaled a cloud of smoke drawn from his pipe and felt its euphoric effect spread throughout his body, pervading every cell of his being with a joyous lightness, Tsoi responded to her.

"Lady Soniyo, you needn't worry. I am well aware of the situation. The Sing are gathering arms and the Llalloi are buying allies. Our enemies, you see, are planning a coup of their own."

"You know?" she exclaimed with such energy that her hadishyen looked up at her.

With a high-pitched voice it said, "You are beautiful, my lady. You are so lovely in this light."

While Soniyo, to quiet the poor beast, slapped her pet upon his brow and hissed at him, Tsoi explained.

"Yes, I do know what they're doing. You didn't imagine that they would allow the present regime to survive and threaten their own plans, did you? They're plotting to make a roshpai of their own, just as we are."

"What are you going to do about it?" Soniyo insisted.

"Nothing. There's no need. If we act first, we'll simply kill everyone who stands against us. If they act before we're ready, I've made arrangements to step up the disturbances in Jezic. Whatever the Llalloi do, we'll make things so bad our own coup will be easy to orchestrate. Either way, we'll win."

Besides, Tsoi thought to himself, I have other allies who will ensure that everything proceeds as I desire it to. You, however, need not be concerned with that.

"What about me, then?" Soniyo insisted. "If the Sing take over, they'll have me executed."

"My lady is exquisite today. Her smile fills the room with more light than does the sun," the hadishyen interjected.

Soniyo smacked him on his head again and snapped, "Hush!"

"Again, Lady Soniyo, you need not worry," Tsoi assured her. "If you don't feel comfortable remaining in Jezic, say that you aren't well and return to your estates to recuperate. No one will touch your allies, whether there is a coup or not, and no one will be able to harm you while you are on your own lands. I'm sure you have as many soldiers at your disposal as does the roshpai himself. Besides, you are a clever woman. I doubt if anyone in Tozana is going to be able to outwit you. Think about how carefully we've planned everything. Is someone going to outmaneuver us?"

Feeling somewhat reassured, but being somewhat annoyed that she did feel better, Soniyo objected. "We've made plans and put a great deal of effort into this. I don't want to see everything unravel now."

Tsoi blew out another cloud of smoke. "Lady Soniyo, if anything, our position is stronger than it has ever been before."

The gangster's head now seemed to be filled with helium and every object before his eyes amused him. What was more, the smoke swirling about in his lungs was reinvigorating the small amounts of the drug from the feihi's vagina that were lingering in his system. He was, consequently, beginning to be aroused by the woman in front of him. In spite of her pointed head, she was shapely and did have attractive features.

As he rested his hand in his lap so that he could stimulate himself though his clothes, which activity Soniyo noticed with chagrin, Tsoi thoughtlessly explained to his guest, "I have recently acquired a bit of especially valuable information. No matter what happens, we cannot lose now."

Repulsed though she was by her increasingly inebriated host's behavior, Soniyo was intrigued by this comment. "What information?"

"I know where the Llalloi's base is."

Soniyo's eyes widened. "You do? How?"

"Well, that doesn't matter. What's important is that I've already arranged for some new helpers who can deal with them."

"Who?"

"I can't tell you that. I don't want to spoil your fun. Won't it be more exciting if you get to hear the details about our victory all at once and after it's been accomplished?"

"As you wish," she said, slightly disappointed.

"Now don't be sad, Lady Soniyo. I'm only thinking of your pleasure."

"Don't patronize me. Besides, except insofar as your plots affect what's going on here, I really couldn't care less about them."

Stupid woman, Tsoi thought. For all her conceit, her universe doesn't go beyond the parties and dinners of her little circle of aristocratic friends.

He said to her, "I assure you, what happens with the Llalloi will decide everything in Tozana. Without the Llalloi, the Sing are impotent. If we break the smugglers, we can't lose."

"Still," the woman insisted, "even if you beat those people today, there's no telling how long news of that will take to get to Tozana. You can't say what'll happen in the interim."

"As I told you, take what precautions you feel you should take."

"Oh, I will, but that's not what I'm getting at."

"Would you mind explaining, then?"

"Of course not. You go out and kill your smugglers. I really don't care about a bunch of gangsters, so that's your business. Mine is with the so-called roshpai. If you don't help me with him, then you're useless to me."

Soniyo's family had for several generations been feuding with the Kuma, another aristocratic clan. Since a member of that family had seized power and made himself roshpai about forty years earlier, the Dogrues had been seething with jealousy and hoping for a chance to undo their enemy's success. Tsoi was less than concerned about Soniyo's plans to be rid of a Kuma roshpai, but he needed a friendly ruler in Tozana to break the power of his own enemies there. He was, consequently, more than willing to help

Soniyo make herself ruler of that country, so long as she then ensured that those he wanted destroyed were broken.

"Our interests are in complete accord on this matter," Tsoi assured her. "You'll be roshpatni and I'll bring a new era to the universe. We will be like Antony and Cleopatra were in ancient times, a visionary leader and a beautiful queen, and like them we will be undefeatable. Just as they crushed their enemies and presided over brilliant courts, so we will divide Shokai between us and become like twin suns that will outshine even that burning in the sky. Just don't forget who helped put you on the throne."

Seeing Tsoi's conciliatory manner (and noticing that she had been able to worry him enough to distract him from touching himself as he had been before), Soniyo said with a smile, "I won't, but, before I'm there, you should remember that even with these Llalloi of yours dead, our enemies in Jezic can still act with the money they got from them. They can still use it to ruin everything for us."

Growing increasingly weary of his guest, and no longer feeling excited, Tsoi filled his lungs with smoke from his pipe and then exhaled this in a great cloud he directed towards Soniyo.

She tried vainly to fan the inky mist away from her eyes, and her hadishyen coughed.

Tsoi smirked. "I promise you, every precaution is being taken to guarantee the outcome we both desire. Besides, my understanding is that things are going well in Jezic. I've been informed that there have been several protests, some coming close to becoming riots. People there are getting tired of bands of thugs doing what they want and making life unsafe for ordinary folk. They're sick of mudjumpers enriching themselves by selling their semen and arrogantly murdering human beings. Somebody's going to have to restore order soon."

"All that's true. Things are pretty bad in Jezic right now. I heard that a new gang war is starting up too. Is that your doing?"

"No, but I'm not surprised to hear it. As things deteriorate, people will get more desperate and start doing foolish things. That, of course, is fine by me. I hope they behave as stupidly and recklessly as they can. It only helps us."

Stroking her hadishyen's head, prompting it to praise her beauty one more time, Soniyo added, "I'm glad everything's under control. Make sure it stays that way. I was very worried when I received news that the Sing have friends in the government. It wouldn't bother me if they killed that moron roshpai, but I don't want to see some crass, uneducated gangster ruling Tozana."

Tsoi kept quiet, though annoyed by her insult. He drew another breath of smoke from his pipe and asked Soniyo, "Are you staying in Quanya for a while?"

"No. I'm on my way to Min to visit my sister there. When I heard that there could be a coup to forestall ours, I thought it would be wise to travel for a short time."

"I'm sorry to hear I won't be able to enjoy your company for longer. I do hope you have a pleasant journey."

"I'm sure I will, and thank you for your courtesy. I wish I could enjoy your hospitality for a few days more, but as much as I like your home, I detest Quanya. It is the most revolting, noisy city I have ever had the displeasure of visiting. I simply could not remain there."

"Well then, I suppose you will be leaving."

"Yes," Soniyo said, and both she and Tsoi stood up.

The pair bowed to one another, and Soniyo left the pavilion, making her way down the path between the rows of birches while her hairless pet continuously lauded her charms.

Once she was gone, Tsoi sat down again and resumed smoking his pipe.

He was a little irritated with himself for telling Soniyo about his plan to destroy the Llalloi. Fortunately, she did not seem to realize how greatly this new development reduced her usefulness. She could be painfully shortsighted. That trait was generally a nuisance, but, at least on this occasion, it was not.

If he could wipe out the Llalloi, Tsoi thought, he would have little need of Soniyo. He was not, however, ready to dispense with her yet. As much as he hoped that he would not have to endure her for much longer, he knew it would be foolish of him to act precipitously.

Turning to the servant girls squatting in the alcove near him, Tsoi beckoned to one of them, who rushed out of her hole and knelt in front of her master. On her brow was a circlet on which was mounted a small brass telopticon. Tsoi cranked the handle of this and spoke a number into the antenna-like microphone.

A moment later, he was looking at the image of a man forming between the two horns projecting from the device upon the woman's head. "Has my agent from Jezic sent any word yet?"

The man replied, his voice made tinny by the trumpet reproducing it. "He reported in less than half a watch ago, my lord."

"Patch me through to him."

"Yes, my lord."

Within seconds, Noyan's face hung weightlessly in the image harp.

"How's the situation in Jezic?"

"That girl has been a wonder. She's caused more devastation in two days than we could have brought about in a month. She killed a whole crew of Sing's men, attacked one of the big mudjumper bosses, and then butchered a half dozen of the thugs Sing sent to kill her. Not only that, she also managed to kill a couple of bystanders while doing so. People think the city's turned into a battlefield."

Tsoi smiled broadly. "That is wonderful news to hear. My congratulations on your success."

"Thank you, my lord, but I'm afraid that I just received a worrying report from one of my contacts."

Drawing a great draught from his pipe and exhaling it slowly, Tsoi asked, "What?"

"I heard that she went to Sing's penthouse earlier and left without killing him. I'm afraid that one of them might have found something out and that they came to an agreement."

"Don't ruin this, Noyan."

"You needn't worry, my lord. I've had one of my people keeping an eye on the girl since I met with her. He's sticking close to her, and he'll report the details of whatever she's up to later."

"If things have gone wrong, make sure you deal with it. That girl's been a tremendous help so far, and could still be very useful in the future, but she could also be a pest. If she starts making trouble, dispose of her."

"As you wish, my lord. If she makes any threatening move, she'll be killed."

Tsoi switched off the telopticon, motioned for the girl carrying it to return to her place, and pulled on the cord hanging near him from the ceiling. A few minutes later, a servant entered the pavilion to stand in front of him.

After the man had bowed, Tsoi instructed him, "Bring a feihi here, one with green hair."

# Chapter 11
## The *Cloud Cutter*

Jess and Uluf took a taxi from their hotel to the airport to the west of the roshpai's palace. Once they had presented their papers to the authorities there, they were directed to the wide paved field behind the main building.

While flocks of ornithopters flew overhead, some of which were landing at other parts of the airport and some of which were leaving on journeys to various distant places, the pair crossed this broad open space in a vehicle shaped like a stagecoach that moved on six long, arched, articulated legs resembling those of a spider.

Within a few minutes, it had taken them to the wooden pavilion where they were to wait until the *Cloud Cutter* was ready to board passengers. The ship itself was resting upon the field just a short distance away and was surrounded by a host of naked, toiling men, who were tugging on and checking great lines fastening it to the earth, bearing heavy burdens into its hold, unloading others onto waiting transports, or engaging in yet other activities.

The vessel itself was about three-hundred feet in length and was similar to an ancient carrack, although its flat base rested on the ground and its hull was adorned with elaborate pilasters, bas-reliefs, and murals, all of which were shining with vividly colored paint, gold leaf, chrome, brass, and the like. The top of the vessel rose up into a tall, fantastically ornate forecastle and an equally impressive sterncastle. Between these was a balustraded deck crowned with a pair of iron smoke stacks decorated at their tops with cast iron filigree flowers. At the front of the vessel was a colorful figurehead shaped like a naked, winged woman, and from both sides and the back of the craft emerged sinuous metal poles ending in large propellers.

As she leaned on the railing at the edge of the pavilion, looking at the skyliner in front of her (and the several others scattered here and there across the field like great metallic castles), Jess, who was back in the tube top and shorts she had been wearing when she arrived on Shokai, noticed three persons walking towards her and Uluf, who was standing close behind her. Jess stared at them and immediately recognized one as Ofu Not, though the two women with him were new to her.

Both of the women were naked, draped with copious amounts of jewelry, and covered with elaborate tattoos. One of them, who was, perhaps, in her late twenties or early thirties and whose body was decorated with images of many legged dragon-like insects intertwining with one another and with diverse sorts of blossoming flowers, strutted through the pavilion with an air of importance. She was attractive (if somewhat heavily muscled), but seemed arrogant and tough.

The other woman, who was holding the arm of the first in an affectionate though deferential manner, was about ten years younger than her companion. She was also slimmer and bustier, besides being, Jess thought, stunningly beautiful, even if her body did glow with the bright colors of her tattoos of young armed women fighting and posturing upon clouds gliding before a mountain range.

When Ofu and his two companions had reached Jess, the man turned to the older woman and said, "This is Jess Ichikawa."

The woman let her gaze stray across Jess's body, from her toes to her face, and then brusquely informed her, "I'm Eshwurhiyo Sing, Gople's sister, and this is my partner, Syo."

Jess crossed her arms and, indicating her companion with a nod of her head, replied, "This is Uluf, my friend. He's coming with me."

"I've never seen a toad this close before," Eshwurhiyo said and went to stand close to Uluf, looking at him from warted brow to webbed toe.

"There are sometimes toads in Quanya," she continued, "but we don't see much of them in Jezic."

"Maybe," added Jess, "that's because everything is so restricted here."

"That's true enough," said Ofu with a gruff laugh.

Eshwurhiyo glared at him. "Some restrictions are still important."

"And those that aren't could change," Syo commented.

Gople's sister looked at her partner, and Syo turned her eyes towards the ground.

For a brief moment, there was an uncomfortable silence. Then Jess announced with a cheery voice, "They're letting passengers onto the ship."

Everyone looked towards the *Cloud Cutter* and saw that indeed a number of people were walking up the low ramp and through the ornate portal near the ship's bottom. A second later, a voice on an intercom bid those waiting in the pavilion make their way to the vessel.

"Shall we board?" Uluf asked.

Eshwurhiyo looked at the toad and, with a gesture of her hand, motioned for the group to cross the field and get on the ship.

Jess and Uluf were quartered together and went first to their cabin to store their belongings. When they had done so, the pair, before the vessel had launched, made their way to the *Cloud Cutter*'s poop deck.

Leaning side by side over the balustrade, they watched as the enormous metal ship, made weightless by its antigravity engines, was lifted from the earth with its propellers. The ground receded below them and the vessel sailed first above the outskirts of Jezic and then away from that city out over the ocean to its north. Gradually, the tall, multicolored towers of Tozana's capital shrank away, until they disappeared beneath the horizon.

Several hours later, Jess and Uluf were still relaxing on the poop deck, though they were now sitting in deck chairs and sipping drinks. The *Cloud Cutter* was traveling slowly through the sky over the waves of Shokai's great dark ocean. The ship had not yet moved far from land, and the coast was still clearly visible. Along the water's edge were innumerable small towns and cities, and, beyond these, was a dense mass of green forests.

Most of the cities were similar to Jezic in appearance (being centered around tall, vibrantly hued towers that were larger at their upper end than at their lower), although none of these places were as impressive as was the capital.

The larger towns sometimes had a spire or two as well, but they were mostly composed of brightly painted wooden houses with wide, upturned eaves hung with lanterns. Many of the towns, Jess noted, were built more over the water than upon the land, their colorful houses being gracefully perched upon spindly stilts.

Enraptured by these visions, Uluf softly said to himself, "Just so, just so."

Jess heard the toad speak, looked at him, and smiled.

"Do you see," Uluf asked his friend when he noticed her glance, "those square, purplish blotches in the ocean, the ones near the shore?"

Jess looked and saw rectangular areas surrounded by partially submerged fences where the water was almost magenta.

"Yeah. I see them."

"Those are hunna fields."

"What's that?" the toad's young friend asked as she sauntered over to the balustrade and leaned dangerously far over it for a better view.

While getting up and joining Jess so that he could put his arms around her and pull her back a little from her precarious position, Uluf explained. "Hunna is the staple here. It is an aquatic plant and is both easy to process and very nutritious. Since its potential flavors are extremely variable and a diet of hunna needs to be supplemented with little else, it provides the bulk of the people's diet here."

"We had krimhi in Jezic."

"Well, people do eat other things."

"Ah," said Jess. "They grow it in the water, huh?"

"Yes. It is an aquatic plant."

"I guess that's why there are so many forests here. They don't clear them to grow crops. That's good."

"I suppose that is the reason."

Jess looked down at the underwater fields and watched as men in skiffs wandered across them, tending their crops. She noted how, here and there, farmers rested upon small platforms that rose from the wine colored water (some of these were topped with little buildings), chatting there with their fellows or relaxing with only a pipe or a drink to keep them company.

"It's actually very pretty," she said, more to herself than to Uluf.

Just then Ofu and Syo appeared on the poop deck and crossed over to Jess and Uluf.

The two were no longer nude, having dressed like members of Tozana's third estate.

Ofu wore a long purple cassock and loose trousers decorated with a gigantic codpiece covered with metal studs and hung with little silver bells.

Syo was dressed in a colorful, formfitting, long sleeved blouse and equally bright skintight shorts that reached to just above her knees and were fitted with a foot long, bejeweled codpiece.

Both, Jess noticed, had completely covered their numerous tattoos.

The gangsters sat down in chairs near their traveling companions, and Syo asked Jess, who was leaning against the balustrade with her arm around Uluf, "Have you ever been on an airship before?"

"A few times, but never a nice one like this."

"I suppose," Syo went on, "you've been around a lot more than I have."

"Maybe, I guess. I never get to stay anywhere for long, though."

"I love sailing like this," said Syo. "It's so peaceful and beautiful up here. You feel like you've escaped from all the dirt and suffering of life, like you've left it all on the ground and you're soaring up to the heavens."

Jess liked the way Syo described her feelings and did not have the heart to tell her that above the clouds life was just as nasty as it was below.

This thought made Jess a little sad, but she herself still felt something similar to what Syo did, even if having such emotions went against her better judgment.

Looking out across the waves at the endless forest, like a range of miniature green mountaintops, Jess was a little overcome by the beauty of these things.

She said, "It really is nice up here."

For a moment there was silence; then Jess asked Syo, "Why'd you change into those clothes?"

"There's no reason we should announce who we are."

"That makes sense," Jess replied. "They cover your tattoos, though."

Ofu answered her this time. "If anyone sees the tattoos, they'll know we're members of a gang."

"Oh, I see."

Syo added, "When we get to Quanya, we'll change again. We'll put on something in the local style. Nobody'll even know we're from Jezic."

"What about your language? Will people not recognize that you are speaking Tozani?" Uluf inquired.

Syo responded. "We all know Juheyu.ᶜ We'll speak that while we're there."

"Even so, won't you get into trouble now?" Jess asked her. "I thought there were laws about what everybody in Tozana can wear."

"There are," Syo told her, "but we're not in Tozana now."

Again the group fell quiet, until Syo said to Uluf, "You're the first toad I've met. I've seen other toads in Quanya before, and some in Nyopwa, but I never talked to any of them."

"Well, you have met one of us now." Uluf doffed his plumed chapeau bras and bowed to the young woman. "I only hope that you will forgive my inelegance and not form any bias against my kind because of me."

"I heard that toads are supposed to be really good singers. Is that true?"

"Some are better than others, but there is no toad who will not endeavor to bring as much beauty into the world as he can."

"Could you sing me a song?"

Never willing to let an opportunity to perform pass him by, Uluf replied that he would be happy to do so.

He sat upon a mooring bollard near the edge of the deck and took from the pocket of his green, embroidered justaucorps a rectangular object about the size of a book that was wrapped with a thin band and that apparently contained, instead of pages, a great numbers of wooden pins which projected out its top and bottom ends.

Uluf undid a clasp fastening the band, and this quickly straightened itself into a bow. As it did so, the rectangular object expanded like a concertina, transforming itself into a solid block about two feet long. Near the top of this was a sort of rod, and Uluf drew this, along with the forty strings attached to it, from where it was fixed to the topmost of the pins and fastened it to the base of his box-like object.

The toad then positioned the collapsible sarangi (for that was what he was holding) in front of him and said, "The sound is not, by any means, the same as that of a proper sarangi, but this is all I am able to carry with me. I hope you will, therefore, forgive the limitations of the instrument. I will not, of course, ask that you make allowances for the performer's lack of skill."

That request made, Uluf brought his bow to the sarangi's strings and began to play upon it. Each string made the others resonate, and a poignant music filled the air of the *Cloud Cutter*'s deck, its plaintive beauty at once captivating both Jess and Syo. Each listened intently as Uluf gave life to sorrow and suffused the undulating waves of the ocean, the turbulently moving leaves of the forests, and the ornate airship upon which the travelers were sitting with a bewitching sense of melancholy

Within a few moments the toad supplemented the sounds of his instrument with his own mellifluous voice, which had a range and timbre that could not be matched by that of any human being.

---

* The language of Juhei, the country bordering Tozana to the east.

As Jess gazed at the wonders about her, and was mesmerized by their loveliness (that seemed only to be enhanced by the sadness of the sounds now possessing her), the toad sang a madrigal-like song.

*The fish may dream of the stars above*
    *And gaze at the passing clouds,*
*But they will dance when a man despairs*
    *Of winning his heart's desire.*

*Although they want the marvelous lights*
    *That burn in their shaking roof,*
*The scaly fish do not mourn their fate –*
    *They savor the thrills of life.*

*And so it was that when schools of fish*
    *Discovered a wondrous treat,*
*They turned their thoughts to their present joys*
    *And gathered around to dine.*

*For underwater a bluish face*
    *Was shedding a salty tear,*
*And fish could nibble its juicy meat*
    *While tasting its pungent breath.*

*Their wretched food never felt a bite*
    *But suffered from madding pain.*
*Forsaking life for an empty hope,*
    *He stared at the speckled sky.*

*Past leaves, like navies of little ships*
    *That floated from here to there,*
*He caught a glimpse of the stars above*
    *And thought he had glimpsed her eyes.*

*He saw the girl he had loved before*
    *And wished she had loved him too.*
*Like twinkling candles her eyes had shone,*
    *Though they'd never burned for him.*

*While flower petals were rained by gods,*
    *Who merrily laughed the while,*
*From starry heavens and empty voids*
    *Gelatinous ladders fell.*

*The bubbles scented with wine and beer*
    *Had ended their steady flow.*
*In quiet, painless repose he slept,*

*His agony washed away.*

*And so he died as the carp rejoiced,*
*Not knowing this simple truth:*
*It's best to love what is here and now*
*Not vacant or foolish dreams.*

When the toad had finished, Jess, who found herself surprisingly moved, sat silently looking at Uluf with admiration for his musical talents. Syo too seemed to be touched. Ofu, on the other hand, was pretty obviously bored by the performance.

"That was very nice," Syo said. "Would you play for me again some time?"

"Of course. It is always my pleasure to sing and play. I am afraid that I have far fewer opportunities to do so than I would like to have."

As he was saying this, Eshwurhiyo arrived on the deck still naked and covered with jewelry as she had been before.

"I heard the end of your song," she told Uluf. "It was pretty. I'd like to hear you sing some time myself."

"I would be more than happy to do so," Uluf told her graciously as he collapsed his sarangi back into a little package so that he could replace it in his pocket.

Turning to Syo, Eshwurhiyo said, "It's about time to eat. Do you want to go to the dining hall with me?"

Syo smiled, stood up, walked over to Eshwurhiyo, and wrapped her arm around that woman's elbow.

"Let's go eat," she said.

The pair left, and Ofu sat looking taciturnly across the ocean as Jess and Uluf went back to their deck chairs and finished their drinks. When she was nearly done with hers, Jess said to Uluf, "I'm hungry too. Do you want to get something to eat?"

"Yes. Let us go."

As he and Jess stood, the latter looked back at Ofu and then at Uluf. The toad turned and addressed the man. "Would you care to join us for dinner?"

The gangster, though obviously not ecstatic about eating with these two, nonetheless nodded, got up, and followed after them as they crossed the poop deck to a small structure near its forward end. Uluf pulled the cord hanging from the upturned eave of this and watched as the hand on the dial above the door moved clockwise. When the hand had arrived at the dial's far right side, Uluf swung the door open and gestured for Jess to enter. She slid the metal screen to the side and stepped into the elevator, followed by Ofu and Uluf.

Inside, the toad turned a knob on the wall to a small sign indicating the floor with the dining room, which was near the bottom of the vessel, and pulled a lever to show he had so made his selection. With a groan, the elevator conveyed its passengers to their destination.

The dining hall of the *Cloud Cutter* occupied a substantial part of one deck and was strikingly sumptuous. A forest of pillars of shining red marble crowned with gilt capitals supported a groined roof alive with countless paintings, and the walls were decorated with tinted bas-reliefs set below rows of outlandish grotesques and between copper pilasters ornamented with medallions bearing beautifully cast figures. Throughout this elegant chamber were scattered low tables of lacquered wood around which were arranged couches piled with pillows. All of these things were illumined by lanterns hung from numerous lampposts shaped like sinuous, naked young women that were so situated amongst the pillars that they seemed to be playing or dancing with one another.

Jess and her companions were escorted by a liveried waiter to one of the tables, where Ofu ordered his meal and Uluf ordered his and Jess's.* While they waited for their food to arrive, Jess began to grow uncomfortable.

She turned to Uluf and said, "I need to poop. Have you seen the toilet?"

After Uluf pointed her in the right direction, she stood up and, with arms akimbo, announced, "I guess I've got to get rid of the old to make room for the new."

Then she headed for the toilet.

The lavatory was as gorgeous (or as tacky) as was every other part of the ship and stunned Jess when she saw it. Three of its walls were composed of a series of mirrors set between black marble pilasters, and the fourth, that opposite the entrance, of a row of shining brass doors that were also set in black marble.

Walking around the counter with the sinks in the middle of the room, Jess went to one of these doors and opened it.

Within was a sort of garderobe. At its back was a niche that projected from the side of the ship. The bottom of this was an ornamented bench with wide armrests and, in the middle of its seat, a round hole. Curious, Jess looked through the hole and saw the ocean far below her. As she was examining the facilities, she noticed in the side of the niche a little arch that opened into a sort of cupboard wherein were standing a pair of small creatures like potbellied pigs, though they walked upon their hind legs, had hands like a man's, and were only about a foot tall.

Jess was a little surprised by these beasts, as she had never seen their kind previously (though she knew at once that they must be homunculi of some sort). Whatever they were, she had no idea why they had been placed where they were. Before she could guess their purpose, however, one of them turned a crank on a wooden box beside the arch, and this produced a voice.

The voice said: "Please sit down and relieve yourself. When you are finished, give our house a tap and we will attend to your cleanliness."

Accepting this promise and pulling her shorts down to her ankles, Jess hopped onto the bottomless seat and let her buttocks hung out the skyliner over the sea.

---

* Even if Jess had been able to read the local script in which the menu was written, she would still have had no idea what the dishes offered were. There was no telling what she could have wound up with to eat had she ordered herself.

When she had done what she had come to do, Jess rapped upon the wall beside the little house and the two pigs came out. One gestured for Jess to raise her backside, and, when she had, he held her buttocks and moved them about to allow his fellow to clean them with a damp cloth.

The pigs were busy with such work when Jess heard someone enter the lavatory. A few seconds later, a woman in her fifties opened the door to the stall where Jess was sitting and looked in.

With an expression of surprise, this person quickly said, "Oh, I'm terribly sorry. I thought this one was vacant."

Jess smiled, turned red, and answered, "Don't worry about it."

For a second Jess looked down, feeling a little embarrassed, but the woman, instead of leaving the room, leapt upon her and blew some powder she held in her hand into Jess's face.


# Interlude 5
# Technology

In order to prevent the worlds over which it rules from rebelling, as well as to minimize the destruction that the nations of a given world may cause to one another, the Pancloan government has placed restrictions on the production of a variety of technological items.

The manufacture of vessels capable of space travel is strictly regulated. Any such vessel produced must be registered with the Pancloan government and cannot be provided with any armaments, unless it is being built for the navy. Severe penalties are rigorously applied to those engaged in or supervising the unlicensed production of unarmed or armed ether-ships.

The ruler of a state in which such manufacture has occurred is held personally responsible for that violation of the law by the Pancloan government. When armed ether-craft are found to have been built in a given state, its ruler is subjected to public execution by torture.

The manufacture of any propulsion system that could be used for space travel is similarly forbidden, although violations of such regulations do not carry the same penalties for the ruler of a state where such manufacture is discovered as are applied when the manufacture of prohibited ether-craft is uncovered.

The production of jet engines, even for the use of aircraft, is prohibited under this rule. Vessels lifted with antigravity engines, whether ornithopters or airships moved by propellers, are thus the primary means of air travel on worlds within the empire. The former are generally smaller and faster, while the latter may either be small but slow craft or large cargo or passenger transports. Although antigravity engines can be employed to allow vessels to be propelled by means that otherwise would not have been effective, as these devices are not themselves capable of moving vessels, their manufacture is not prohibited.

The most important restrictions on technology, other than those on means of propulsion, are those on weapons. The creation and use of all biological and chemical weapons, as well as of all powerful explosives, including nuclear arms, are forbidden. Such regulations are justified by the government on the grounds that they prevent its subject states from waging unnecessarily destructive wars against one another.

Several other technologies are regulated in addition to those given above. Surveillance satellites are proscribed, as these could be utilized to detect Pancloan vessels and troops and could, therefore, be useful in a rebellion. Certain devices and techniques that can be employed to conceal objects or encode information are forbidden, and, in accordance with long established taboos existing on virtually every human world, the genetic engineering of human beings is outlawed.

From Pollidor's *Big Blue Book of Knowledge*

# Chapter 12
## Adventures in the Sky

B efore she could react in any way to the strange woman's having blown a cloud of stinging powder in her face, Jess felt a fog fall upon her mind, leaving her confused and dizzy. She still had enough of her wits to try to move, but her limbs felt like strings of sausages waggling about limply from her shoulders.

The woman slapped her face, pulled the lids of one of her eyes apart, and gazed intently at her pupil. Then she turned around and said something that to Jess sounded like the groans of a dying machine.

Two men dressed in aprons similar to but much richer than those worn in Jezic by persons of the fourth estate entered the stall. Both stared at Jess, glanced at one another, and grinned.

The woman spoke to them in a loud voice, and though Jess could not understand all that her attacker said, she could make out the words, "We're here to kill her," and "Don't waste your time. The effect of the poison won't last long."

"Long enough," said one of the men and pushed past the woman to stand in front of Jess. He grabbed her legs, lifted them into the air, and, spreading her thighs, thrust himself between them. Jess could see him moving his apron away from his crotch and soon felt him inside of her body.

As angry as she was, Jess could barely move. Even if she had been able to resist her grunting, wheezing assailant, however, the second man was now standing over her, kneading her breasts and holding a kriss to her throat. There was nothing she could do to disable him in less time than it would take for him to slit her jugular.

Suddenly, a cry of pain came from outside the stall, followed by a thud, like that made by a falling body. The man inside of Jess immediately withdrew from her and spun around, while his fellow, in order to look at the door himself, leaned back and craned his neck.

Woozy and weak as she was, Jess used all her will to lift her limp hands from where they lay and to seize her second attacker by the wrist, hoping to keep his knife away from her. He reacted without thought when he felt her touch, striking her with his other hand across her face and knocking her to the back of the niche.

He immediately realized his mistake and bent over the toilet to grab Jess by her hair. Just as he had a bunch of her tresses in his hands and was tugging on them, however, the door to the stall opened.

Announced only by the click of a trigger, a needle shot out of the gun Uluf was holding and penetrated the chest of the man holding on to Jess. He collapsed onto the toilet and slid down to the floor.

The other man, shoving the woman with him against the wall, leapt upon his new enemy, hitting the toad in the stomach with his fist. Uluf doubled over and fell onto his knees. The man ran past him and was jumping over the counter in the middle of the room when the door to the dining hall opened and Eshwurhiyo and Syo entered.

The escaping man tried to thrust the former of these two to the side, but she, instead, seized him by the wrist and ended his flight.

Almost as soon as Eshwurhiyo had grasped her foe, the tattoo of the centipede-like monster that was wrapped around her arm began to wiggle its legs and twist its coils. It raced down her forearm, over her hand, and crossed onto the arm of the man she held.

At once, he opened his mouth to shout, but Syo thrust a wand, a stinger (a pain inducing device), she had produced from her pocket down his throat and closed his jaw upon it with a blow of her hand.

The tattoo centipede writhed about on the man's arm, seeming to jab him with its venomous legs and to bite him with its sharp mandibles. As it did so, the flesh of its victim's arm dissolved and dropped onto the ground in smoky chunks. His panicky flailing enabled him to get away from Eshwurhiyo, who released him from her grip without much of a struggle when she saw how he was nearly mad with pain, but he could not shake the centipede from his arm. Nor could he dislodge Syo, who had now wrapped her arms around his head so that she could keep the rod thrust into his mouth, thereby both gagging him and searing every nerve running through his face and jaw.

He hurled himself about as the tattoo monster crawled over his shoulder, sending pieces of meat tumbling across his chest, and made its way up his throat and onto his face. While holes opened up in his cheeks and the tip of his nose burned off, the man began to convulse in agony and lose control of his body. In a few moments, he lay unconscious on the floor.

Eshwurhiyo pressed her hand upon the man's face and the centipede crawled back onto her arm, where it ceased its motions and returned to its lifeless slumber.

While this gruesome scene was playing itself out, Uluf managed to raise his gun again and pointed it at the woman who was still standing in the stall with Jess. He motioned for her to enter another stall and closed the door behind her. Then he called to Jess and asked her if she could stand.

With a slurred voice, she replied she could and lifted herself from the toilet.

Once she was back on her feet, even though she was more than a little unsteady, Jess picked up the kriss that had shortly before been at her throat and staggered over to where her mutilated assailant lay on the ground.

"Is he alive?" she asked Eshwurhiyo.

"You'll have to check."

Jess touched the man's chest to feel his breathing. He was not dead yet. The girl leaned against the counter and tried to regain control of her body. When she felt that she had her balance back, she kicked the man lying in front of her until he began to stir.

As soon as his eyes had opened and widened with dread, Jess kicked him again, this time much harder than she had before.

With a snarl, she jumped upon her attacker, as a lioness upon her prey, and, grabbing and twisting his penis with one hand, brandished the kriss in front of his eyes with the other.

Her voice slurred and trembling, Jess snapped, "You really shouldn't have done that to me. There's no way you're getting away without paying for it."

Taking the stinger from Syo and shoving it into the mouth of the man beneath her, Jess dug her blade into the hole where his nose had once been and relished the sight of him twitching.

As soon as she had withdrawn the kriss from his sinuses and handed the stinger to Syo (who held it where it was), Jess poked the man's brow with the dagger and warned him, "Oh, that was nothing. There's much worse to come."

She snatched up his penis again, pulled on it as hard as she could, and sawed it off with the knife. The man's body lashed so fiercely that, were it not for the help Eshwurhiyo and Syo gave Jess, the girl would have been knocked off of him.

Once her victim had calmed a little, Jess shook his severed organ in front of his eyes and laughed. She slapped him with the piece of meat, grabbed Syo's stinger, and pulled it from his mouth. He started to scream, but she dropped his penis onto his tongue and pushed it down his throat with the wand before he could make a noise.

She was about to stab the man and be done with him when Eshwurhiyo stayed her hand.

"Wait," that woman said. "We have to get him, his friend, and the two bodies out of here."

Jess had not thought about what would happen were the remains of her assailants discovered, but she had no idea what she and her allies could do to clean up the mess they had made.

"How are we going to do that?" Jess asked.

"Syo, take care of the corpses," Eshwurhiyo ordered.

The other woman took from her pocket a pair of six inch long metal spikes, walked over to the body of the man Uluf had shot when he had first entered the bathroom, rolled it onto its back, and drove the spike into its brain from the base of its skull. Almost immediately, the body trembled.

"Get up," Eshwurhiyo commanded it, and the cadaver rose to its feet.

While Syo went to insert a similar spike into the corpse in the stall, Eshwurhiyo explained to Jess, "When you jab one of those in someone, whether a person's alive or dead, it'll take control of his central nervous system. Most of his higher mental functions will be limited, but he can still move and obey commands. Control spikes are a great way of getting rid of bodies and making hostages do what you want them to."

Once Uluf had joined Jess (along with the surviving woman – at whose back he held his gun) and Syo had returned with the second corpse, Eshwurhiyo poked her head out of the door leading to the dining room and summoned Ofu, who had positioned himself nearby to make sure no one disturbed his comrades.

When he had entered the toilets, Eshwurhiyo bid him take off his coat and put it on the eunuch lying on the floor. Ofu did as she told him and then tried to cover the man's face by arranging Uluf's jabot (which the toad had handed to him) around it.

Eshwurhiyo meanwhile turned her attention to the woman standing in front of the toad and asked her, "Who sent you?"

The woman did not reply.

"Well, you keep your mouth shut, then," Eshwurhiyo continued. "I'm afraid I don't have the time to torture you right now. But, since I'm sure that you're working for Ngo, whether directly or indirectly, I guess getting you to admit that doesn't really matter anyway."

The woman remained silent and Eshwurhiyo went over to Syo and put her hand upon her partner's shoulder.

"Syo, take care of these two."

The younger woman nodded and thrust a control spike into the back of the head of each of the prisoners.

"Okay," said Jess, "let's get rid of this lot."

"My dear," interjected Uluf, "do not forget your shorts."

Jess looked down. She had forgotten to put them back on. Though still a little unsteady, she skipped over to the stall, retrieved her garment, dressed herself, and rejoined the others.

"Stay behind and clean this up," Eshwurhiyo told Syo.

"Alright."

Uluf looked at the puddles of blood on the floor, smelled their salty smell, and asked, "How are you going to be able to clean all of this up? Someone could easily come in on you. There are, after all, a few people in the dining room already."

Syo smiled. "Don't worry about it. I've got this."

She pulled from a bag hanging at her hip a foot long but emaciated plecostomus-like creature (a slurp cat) and waggled it about in the air by its urodelous tail.

"No killer should be without one," she said while dropping the animal onto the floor.

"What will it do?"

"Look."

The slimy beast was writhing about and sucking up the blood remarkably quickly.

"Come on," interjected Eshwurhiyo. "We don't have time to watch this."

The group left the toilets and walked calmly to the elevator connected to the middle deck. Fortunately, this was located nearby and they did not have to cross the dining hall. Syo, meanwhile, remained behind to finish cleaning up the flesh and blood left by their recent activities.

The group made its way onto the middle deck, which, luckily, was deserted, as the sun had set, the twilight was fading, and the ship's lanterns had not yet been lit.

After the zombies had been herded over to the balustrade, Eshwurhiyo ordered them to stand in front of it. Ofu removed the spike from the back of each person's neck and pushed him over the railing into the sea. When he came to the somnambulist without a nose, however, he first removed his jacket from the man's shoulders and only then pulled the spike out of his brain. When he had, he did not push the man himself, but rather allowed Jess (whose eyes were downcast, whose brow was furrowed, and who looked as though she were going to cry) the pleasure of giving him the shove that sent him plummeting and screaming to his end.

"I hope no one saw us," said Uluf.

"We'll find out soon enough," Eshwurhiyo assured him.

Jess, her eyes moist and red, looked at her and then at Uluf. "Thanks, all of you. I owe you."

"Please, my dear," Uluf responded. "Do not trouble yourself about it."

Smiling at the toad, Jess took his hand and squeezed it.

"I just about got killed in there," she told him, adding with a shaky laugh, "People on this planet keep attacking me while I'm on the toilet. I guess I can't shit or piss until I leave."

Jess, having swallowed with a slight whimpering sound, turned her gaze to Eshwurhiyo and, changing the subject, asked her, "By the way, what is that thing on your arm, the tattoo?"

"It's made up of micromachines. They're powered by my body and use my tissue to produce an acid that burns the skin and a stimulant that induces severe pain. Tattoos like this are pretty expensive, but I've got the money."

Expensive though Eshwurhiyo's tattoo might have been, and as inefficient as it certainly was as a weapon, Jess still liked it and thought she may find out about getting one herself if she ever had the chance to do so.

Syo interrupted Jess's musings when she arrived on the deck, walked up to the others, and wrapped her arm around Eshwurhiyo's waist. The older woman turned to her lover, kissed her, and said, "Shall we return to our meal?"

Syo nodded and the pair left.

Uluf looked at Jess (who still appeared to be more than a little unsteady and distraught). "And you, my dear, would you like to go back for our dinner? It may be ready by now."

"No. I'm not really hungry. Besides, I don't really feel well right now. Maybe I'm sick from the poison that woman used on me. Could you go down and ask them to package mine for me? I'll eat it later."

"Of course."

"I'm going to go eat," interjected Ofu as he finished buckling his jacket.

"I will be there in a moment to collect our food," Uluf informed him.

Ofu nodded and left the girl and the toad alone on the deck.

"You can go eat if you'd like," Jess told her friend.

"I will collect both our meals in a few minutes. I would rather eat with you later than with our convivial friend now."

"Thanks, Uluf," Jess said quietly as she rested her elbows on the balustrade and gazed down at the glints of light reflecting on the waves of the dark waters of the ocean.

"This whole thing is going from bad to worse," she sighed. "I can't believe what just happened to me. It's not like I haven't been in situations like that before, but it's been a long time since I have. I thought I was past all that. I guess I'm still helpless after all."

"Jess," asserted Uluf with a tone that was at once soft and firm, "you are far from helpless. You are the strongest person I have ever encountered. Not only can you fight, but you can also endure just about anything. You really are quite an amazing individual."

With a smile, Jess took her friend's hand in her own. "Thanks for stroking my ego. I need it sometimes. Let's go back to our cabin. I need to take a shower and relax. Once I'm clean and lying down, I'll probably feel a lot better. Hopefully, nobody else'll try to kill me tonight."

"We will be as careful as we can be to avoid any surprises."

"I'd like to know who sent them."

"Ngo perhaps?"

"It could be. Somebody could've betrayed Sing and told him we were coming. It could be someone else, though. What if somebody was tailing us in Jezic? Anyway, whoever sent that last group could've sent some more. There could be more of those people onboard."

"Like I said, Jess, we will take every precaution. Would you like to go back to the cabin now? I will walk there with you and then return to the dining room for our food."

"That sounds great, Uluf."

With that, Jess put her arm around the toad and the two set out for their cabin.

* * *

While Jess and Uluf spent the evening by themselves, Eshwurhiyo and Syo sat together in the dining room enjoying their meal. Fortunately, the waiters did not bring it until shortly after the two had returned.

As she ate, Eshwurhiyo said to her companion, "I hope that girl isn't going to be a problem. She's not as tough as I thought she was going to be."

Syo answered, "Yeah. She seems really fragile, physically and emotionally."

"Don't let her put you in danger. If she can't handle herself, forget about her. I'd much rather she die than you."

"Okay."

"In fact, if you have to, you should be ready to kill her yourself. She worries me. I think she's got some sort of mental problem."

"I thought she was supposed to be able to fight, though."

"Yeah," replied Eshwurhiyo, "she can. I saw the mess in Gople's penthouse. She massacred his men. I've never seen anything like it before. It's hard to square that with the girl we met. I can't make sense of her."

"You think she could be trouble, though?"

"Didn't you see how she was acting on the deck?"

"Yeah. She seemed upset."

"More than that. I thought she was going to cry or have a breakdown."

"I'm pretty sure that man we fought did something to her in the toilet."

"I'm sure he did," snapped Eshwurhiyo. "He raped her."

"Well, it'll take her a while to pull herself together after that."

"She doesn't have a while. We'll be in Quanya tomorrow night. Besides, I don't think her problem is just what happened in the toilet. Like you said, she seems fragile. Suppose she snaps at the wrong moment. She could get us killed."

"Your brother thought she could help."

Eshwurhiyo frowned at her companion. "He was impressed that such a tiny girl could take on so many men. He doesn't have any insight into people."

"Well," said Syo, "I'll be careful. You too, though."

\* \* \*

The next day, after a night's sleep and a good breakfast, Jess did feel better, and she and Uluf spent most of the morning and afternoon relaxing on the poop deck.

The sun glared down at them and charged the atmosphere with a heat so intense it almost seemed to cook the flesh of any person who dared challenge its maker's possession of the world. Both the girl and the toad stripped off their clothing and lay naked upon the deck chairs, enjoying the cool wind blowing on their bodies (and horripilating their skins) from an air conditioning unit hanging underneath the umbrella shading them.

Though she knew it was far from wise, given the danger of her present situation, Jess wiled away her time consuming one drink after another. Eventually, her mind grew a little sluggish and a hazy peacefulness descended upon her. She forgot the unpleasantness of the preceding day and merely enjoyed her body's inebriated rocking and the diverse sights and sounds around her. She watched ships traveling upon the waves of the ocean and sky barges floating past the clouds. The latter, she noted, having been freed from the planet's pull by antigravity engines, were moved with propellers as was the *Cloud Cutter*. Such vessels were, however, flat and unadorned, and their wide decks were heaped with crates.

As the barges made their way to whatever destinations lay ahead of them, Jess either listened to the wind as it swirled about the deck or, when Uluf was moved to take out his sarangi and sing, to her companion's beautiful voice and the haunting tones he produced on his instrument.

Towards the end of the afternoon, the ship passed under a roof of gloomy clouds that vomited out great quantities of rain and drove Jess and Uluf from the poop deck.

Having made their way to the veranda on the middle deck that ran along the lowest floor of the aftcastle, the two dressed themselves, she in a skintight pink catsuit and he in a lavender, swallow tailed tuxedo and white breeches. They then went below deck and found refuge in a lounge decorated with green velvet wallpaper and filled with green sofas arranged between a polished wooden bar and a series of wide portholes. There the pair bought drinks and continued to relax while sitting and watching the rains fall outside the vessel's windows.

Eventually, Syo spied the girl and the toad and joined them.

"Jess," she said, "if you don't mind my asking, why are you going to all this trouble?"

"I've got to find out what happened to Tolliver, the man who was kidnapped by the mudjumpers. You know about him, right?"

"Yeah," Syo responded with a nod. "I heard about what happened. Was he your lover?"

"He was."

"You're really loyal."

"No, not really, but I'm not just going to let him die and do nothing about it. There aren't a lot of people who care about me so I don't want to lose any of them. Life's hard enough as it is without having to face it by yourself."

"Well," laughed Syo, "that's true enough, but I still think you're pretty loyal. After all, you're going to try to kill the head of one of the Seven Families to help this guy, and you don't even know if there's anything you can do for him, or even if he's still alive."

Jess leaned back in the sofa, reached her arms above her head, and stretched her body like a cat. She then blinked her eyes, trying to dry up the alcohol with which every cell of her body was soaked, and said, "What about you? Why are you here?"

"I guess it's the same as with you. I'm going to stick with Eshwurhiyo no matter what. There's no way I'd ever abandon her. Like you said, you can't afford to lose anyone who cares about you."

"How long have you two been lovers?" Jess asked Syo.

"Five traders' years. She's been my whole universe since we met."

"May I inquire," Uluf asked her, "about how the two of you met? I am sorry, but you do seem to care a great deal for her, and I do love a romantic story."

"I don't mind telling you. When I was still a little girl, I joined a street gang. We were all about the same age and did the usual stuff, stole, made trouble, loitered, that sort of thing. When we got older, we started trying to make more money with a little whoring and a little more serious stealing. Sometimes we'd beat up some poor sod and take his money; sometimes we'd just pick on someone because we thought we were tough. We were just kids, though. It was nothing too serious. But we did get the attention of the boss of the local Sing crew, and he started using us to run errands, deliver goods, and even, sometimes, rough up some shop owner or junkie who crossed him.

"Anyway, that's how I wound up meeting Eshwurhiyo. One day, when I was fifteen, she came down to talk to the guy who hired us sometimes and saw me. We were together almost right away and we have been since.

"She's given me everything I have. She even taught me to fight. Before I could throw some punches and take on some other kid, but she's shown me so much more. Eshwurhiyo's really incredible, though. She's tougher than Gople, and smarter too. He always relies on her when things get violent. She's the one who can handle all that, not him."

"You certainly are devoted to her," said Uluf.

"Yeah, of course. Like I said, she's everything I have."

Jess looked at Syo with real affection and felt a definite connection with the woman.

Although there was a toughness to Syo's mannerisms (and her muscular body and vaguely predatory movements gave her an aura of dangerousness), she was still genuinely likeable. She was, in fact, both friendly and interested in others in a way that readily drew Jess and Uluf to her. Syo was surely the center of attention wherever she went.

"That's a great story," Jess said with a smile.

Syo smiled back at her, but felt a sense of unease. She did not want to get close to Jess in case she had to act against her.

At that moment, Eshwurhiyo entered the lounge, walked up behind Syo, leaned over, and rested her elbows on the younger woman's shoulders.

"What are you talking about?" Eshwurhiyo asked.

"I was telling them about how we met."

"Oh. Well, I need to talk to you two as well."

Eshwurhiyo walked around the sofa, sat down next to Syo, and addressed Jess and Uluf.

In a low voice, she said, "When we get to Quanya tonight, we're going to meet with a contact Gople and I have there. He can give us the information we'll need about where Ngo is and what he's doing. It's possible he'll even know how we can get access to him. At least, he'll be able to make suggestions about what'll work and what won't. He's also going to find places for us to stay while we're waiting for our chance. I don't want to get rooms in one of the big hotels. It's just too likely that somebody will see one of us if we do."

"That sounds fine with me," Jess said.

"Well, that's good, since it's what we're doing," Eshwurhiyo replied.

Jess looked at her with an expression of annoyance, but Eshwurhiyo leaned forward and spoke to the girl in a low tone.

"I don't know if you've noticed it or not, but there's a man sitting at the bar keeping an eye on you."

Without reflection, Jess gazed up at the bar and her eyes briefly met those of a man sitting there wearing the garments of a person of Tozana's third estate. Both quickly averted their eyes from one another, though it was pointless for them to do so.

"He knows we're on to him now, doesn't he?" asked Eshwurhiyo as she started to rise.

Jess motioned for her to remain seated. "I'll take care of this."

Before she was standing, however, the man had put down his drink and walked around a corner at the far side of the bar. Jess followed him, and, though she discovered her quarry had gone, she did see a spiral staircase at the end of the further section of the lounge. She hurried to this exit and craned her head back to see if the man had gone up. There was no sign of him so she looked down and chanced to see the slightest motion on the deck below.

Virtually leaping down the stairs, Jess chased after her prey, rushing through the door she had seen something passing through.

The dining room was beyond this, but, as it was the middle of the afternoon, it was closed and all the lamps were off. Enough light was, nonetheless, entering through a couple of open doors so that the wide hall, though alive with deep shadows, was not completely dark.

Jess reached her hand into the bottomless bag strapped to her hip and took out Dawn's Spine, although she did not yet extend its blade. Focusing on the thread within her, she slowed time enough to make sure that, were she attacked, she would easily be able to defend herself.

So readied, Jess slowly stalked through the forest of pillars and the hosts of dancing statues playing hide and seek with one another in the gloomy room. She did not see the man anywhere, but she knew he could be concealed behind any pillar or couch.

Her heart was racing and droplets of sweat crept down her brow and along her nose. Though she would not ordinarily have been so nervous, Jess's recent difficulties had somewhat sapped her confidence.

The room was entirely empty and completely quiet, except for the low, rhythmic rumbling of the ship's machinery, but that, like the heartbeat of some great and terrible beast, caused the air of the room to reverberate as though it were trembling with anxiety.

As sweaty anticipation gripped her body, vague figures repeatedly caught Jess's attention, although these, when examined, would reveal themselves merely to be some statue or patch of darkness.

The girl peered behind each pillar and couch she passed, though without luck. She feared that perhaps her quarry had left the room through some passage she was unaware of and had so escaped her, at least for the moment. Then she heard a loud creak ahead of her, like the sound a piece of wooden furniture makes when a person leans upon it.

Suddenly, the man leapt out from behind a couch and ran away from his pursuer to another stairwell at the dining hall's far end.

Jess hurried after him, but did not slow time further in case she happened to pass someone on the stairs. Instead, she vaulted up these after her quarry with all her might and followed him onto the middle deck.

The rain was so thick Jess could barely see through it and so hard the droplets pummeled her body. Within seconds, her clothing was saturated and her hair was plastered to her head.

The deck appeared to be empty, so Jess pressed the activation switch on Dawn's Spine and its telescopic blade rushed out of the hilt. She peered through the downpour, searching for the man who had fled from her, but, as he was nowhere to be seen, she began to move cautiously across the slippery surface of the flooring, over which a river of water was gushing. She checked the veranda where she and Uluf had earlier taken shelter to dress themselves, but the man was not there, nor was he in the room that opened onto this.

Looking around, Jess noticed a pair of statues bearing lanterns on either side of the ship and realized that these were large enough to conceal a man. She cautiously made her way to the nearest of these, readied her sword, and peeked behind it.

The man was not there, but, to her surprise, Jess felt a terrible pain in her side from a blow to her kidneys. She lost her balance on the wet wood of the deck and crashed to her knees.

As she fell, she was still able to spin around and saw her enemy standing over her. There was a recess in the wall of the aftcastle between the edge of the veranda and the balustrade that Jess had not noticed, and the man had managed to secret himself there.

While she was still clutching her side, the man kicked Jess in the stomach, knocking her onto her back. She did not, however, forget herself, but instead slowed time and bent space to her will.

From where she lay, Jess thrust the universe downwards and spun it over her head so that, to the man before her, she seemed to leap up, flip backwards, and land on her feet in front of him.

He was so astonished by this action he did not react to it. Jess did not give him a second chance. With a single swing of her sword, she lopped off the hand he had extended in front of him.

The man looked down at his new stump and started to howl. Jess again took advantage of his inaction and jumped upon him. She seized her opponent by his throat, slid her blade between his legs, and pushed him against the balustrade.

"This is the end of the journey for you," she shouted over the noise of the rain.

Then she shoved the man over the railing and, as he fell, split him with her sword from his perineum to his navel.

After she had watched the man disappear into the grey sky below the *Cloud Cutter*, and had kicked his severed hand after him, Jess returned dripping wet to the lounge. All four of her companions were now sitting there. The three from Jezic were laughing and chatting, but Uluf looked very nervous.

She walked over to them and said, "He won't be trying anything now. I'm going to go put on some dry clothes."

* * *

Once night had fallen, the day's earlier downpours diminished into a gentle drizzle and the girl and the toad went to the foredeck. In the distance they saw the lights of Quanya shining dimly through the mist and rain.

Jess, feeling tired and dreamy and being enchanted by the shimmering glow of the metropolis ahead of her, let a pleasant melancholy chill her nerves and moisten the edges of her eyes.

With her lids wide open, and the marvels and sorrows of the present world entirely clear to her, the girl, at the same time, discovered that images of her past were drifting by just as clearly. Quanya sparkled before her, the stars above her, and the ocean below her, but Jess, nonetheless, found herself lying on Tolliver's bed, watching him working at his table and waiting for him to finish. She was bored, not having much to do, but she was still content, knowing that she was not alone, that another person would soon be holding her in his arms and pressing his body against hers. She could almost feel him penetrating her and could nearly taste his fluids as they filled her mouth.

She felt the joy of such moments so poignantly that, even with Tolliver gone, maybe forever, she was happy knowing that she had not spent her whole life by herself.

Perhaps, she thought, Tolliver could still be rescued and the wonderful hours she had spent with him would have sequels. Unfortunately, as soon as such a hope presented itself to her, she reflected that it was possible she truly had lost her love and that those times were already irrecoverable.

Her nostalgic happiness was so replaced with sadness, although also with a resolve to fight for her love, whether she was going to be saving him or merely avenging him.

Jess grasped Uluf's arm and squeezed it while trying to focus on the world before her and what she had to do. He touched her hand with his soft, nailless fingers in return. At least she was not completely alone.

As time passed, the vast city ahead of the airliner became clearer. Along its center, in a straight line that ran from the southern tip of the island where Quanya was located almost to the northern edge of the built up area, there were innumerable skyscrapers, each of which was bathed in an array of multicolored lights and bejeweled with glowing holograms. Near these were other structures that, though smaller, were nearly equally brightly lit. The greater part of the city was, however, surprisingly dark.

A short distance to the south and east of the urbanized island was a second, smaller isle, where both the spaceport and the airport were situated, and it was towards this that the *Cloud Cutter* was heading.

# Chapter 13
# Quanya

After Jess and her companions had disembarked the *Cloud Cutter*, they presented evidence that they had money to spend and were provided with passes that gave them access to the center of Quanya.

The group was conveyed from the airport to the city on a cigar-shaped carriage that was perched on the top of a single wire (itself suspended in the air from a row of spindly poles) and was moved by a pair of propellers attached to its back end.

During the journey across the strait between the isle where the airport was and that where Quanya was built, Jess peered out of one of the round portholes along the side of the carriage and saw behind her the needle of the launching spire in the spaceport reaching to the sky. Then, redirecting her gaze ahead of her, she noticed, rising from the waters a short distance from the shore of the larger island, a series of much smaller but still tall towers that appeared to ring that landmass and that were each capped by an enormous gun turret.

The carriage raced past these and approached a passageway that pierced a vast illuminated ziggurat located at the southernmost end of the city. Out of this structure there also emerged, from a point near to the tunnel towards which the carriage was heading, a bridge set atop tall, thin pillars that formed elegant arches, and this stretched across the ocean and over the horizon. Though Jess did not know it, the bridge reached all the way to the mainland.

Once Jess and the others had arrived at this impressive station, they disembarked and walked through its crowded, cyclopean halls to stand in the gentle drizzle on a balcony overlooking the city.

Stretching out before them, on either side of a wide boulevard that extended from one end of Quanya to the other, were rows of skyscrapers as weirdly shaped as half melted candles or as top heavy as wine glasses. Every one of these was adorned with blazing neon signs, lurid holograms, and flashing lights, and upon each shone myriads of still or moving spotlights, no two of which seemed to be of the same color.

Not far from the station, in the southern part of the city, the boulevard split in two and its halves, before rejoining, circled around a fabulous building that dominated the newcomer's view from the ziggurat. This structure was of almost impossible size and consisted of an assemblage of great disks and spheres perched on numerous slim or thick towers. The whole thing looked like a sort of gargantuan banyan tree.

"That," said Eshwurhiyo to Jess and Uluf, "is the Reef in the Sky, the Ngo family's biggest resort. There are hotels, casinos, brothels, amusement parks, russa dens, and who knows what else in there. That's also where we might be able to catch Tsoi."

"Are we going there now?" Jess asked her while adjusting her tube top and tugging at the edge of her pink hot pants.

"No. I don't want to risk being recognized. We're going to see my brother's agent here, the one I mentioned to you on the *Cloud Cutter*. He owns a russa den outside of the Serpent, the area around the main road, so it's not likely anybody will notice us. No one pays attention to what goes on in those parts of the city. He's over there."

Eshwurhiyo pointed towards the outskirts of the city to her right, and Jess, following her finger, now noticed the structures beyond those of the Serpent.

The buildings of that gaudy street were entirely enclosed by a low wall, and those beyond it were more modest, though even these were brightly lit and apparently tenanted, at least in part, by affluent individuals.

Beyond these, however, was another wall, and the structures on the other side of that seemed to be almost entirely shrouded in gloom. Here or there a light shone in this area, or even a street full of lights, but, as a whole, the region seemed forlorn and impoverished.

The group left the station and hired a taxi that rushed them along the metallic boulevard running along the Serpent's back. Eventually, it turned onto a side street, though still a wide one, and passed through the first wall. No one stopped them as they went through the gate piercing this, but Jess noticed that there was a guardhouse there and retractable bollards that would prevent any vehicle from entering the Serpent without first stopping and receiving permission to do so.

The taxi continued on through this area for some time, until it came to another wall, that dividing the second part of the city from its outermost areas. Here they did stop, as the metal road came to an end in front of the gate into the last region.

The group got out and passed through a barred portal under the watchful eyes of guards sitting in sentry boxes nearby. On the other side of the wall was a grim, unlighted slum where the best buildings were made of crumbling brick or wood and the worst were shanties constructed out of sheets of corrugated metal, pieces of discarded boxes, or scraps of lumber.

The gentle rain was still falling and cooling the air so that Jess was not uncomfortable as she made her way through the gloomy alleys, though she was wary of any potential dangers the dark could be hiding from her.

She did not, however, have to remain in the shadows for long. Having passed a cluster of several of the district's larger buildings, she came upon a fairly wide street illuminated by numerous neon signs and holograms.

While music blared from open doors leading to clubs in the moldering structures there, hordes of male, female, and transgendered prostitutes of every age from very young to decrepitly old loitered in the street. Some of these wiggled seductively, others strutted about arrogantly, and still others accosted any man or woman who chanced to pass them by.

Following Eshwurhiyo, Jess and the others pushed their way through the inebriated crowd of impoverished addicts, petty criminals, and other pariahs until they came to a tall building near the end of the street. Most of the front of the ground floor of this structure was open, revealing a wide room filled with men and women lying in heaps upon one another, their eyes focused on worlds only they could see, and others reclining in front of hookahs and bantering loudly. Next to this establishment there was a narrow entrance leading to a stairway.

Eshwurhiyo took the others up these stairs, which were lit by a dim greenish light, to a landing in front of a single metal door. On the wall beside this was a gold sculpture of a man's face. Eshwurhiyo went to this and flipped a switch below its chin. The sculpture's eyes immediately opened and its features moved as though it were alive.

After a croaking, a whirring, and an extended groan, the face said, "What is your business?"

Eshwurhiyo replied, "We come from the far side of the sun."

Obviously recognizing this as a pass phrase, the face replied, "Who are you?"

"I'm Gople's sister, Eshwurhiyo."

"Please come in," the sculpture told her.

The iron door unlocked with a loud clank and swung open.

While the face watched them with its golden eyes, the members of the group passed through the doorway. Inside was a filthy room with chipped, molding walls, a ceiling blackened with fungal growths, and various items of rubbish, many of which were unidentifiable, strewn about the floor.

From a second doorway across from the first emerged a middle aged man dressed in the style favored in Quanya, though his garments were more than a little threadbare.

He saw Eshwurhiyo, spread his arms wide, as though in joy, and exclaimed, "My dear Eshwurhiyo, it is a pleasure to see you after all this time. What can I do for you?"

"Didn't Gople get in touch with you?"

"He did. He said he was sending some people here to do something very important, but that's all. He didn't say that it was going to be you."

"Well, it's me he sent, and what he wants me to do is pretty important."

"What is it?"

"Before I tell you, Vijeihi, I have to warn you. Once we do what we came here to do, you'll have to get out of Quanya. If you stay, there's a good chance you'll be killed. My brother's set up an account for you in Jotpwa. Go there; you'll have plenty of money. Don't waste time here. If you do, you could well be dead. Do you understand?"

Vijeihi no longer looked happy, but he nodded and said, "I understand. What do you want me to do?"

"You've lived here a long time," Eshwurhiyo said. "You know the ins and outs of Quanya. We need your expertise."

"You'll still have to tell me what you're planning to do."

"We came here to kill Tsoi Ngo."

"Oh shit."

Eshwurhiyo smiled and continued. "We need for you to tell us the best way to get to him."

"That's not going to be easy. Most of the time, he stays on the island south of Quanya where his palace is. There's no way you'll be able to get him there. The place is enormous. It's as big as a city, and I doubt if there's anyone who knows the whole layout. Those who do know anything worthwhile would never tell me. Besides, the palace is well guarded. You'd just be committing suicide if you attacked him there."

"Okay." Eshwurhiyo inquired, "Where can we get to him?"

"Hmm. He often takes excursions on his pleasure barge. He'll just float around the skies over the sea. There are always armed barges and ornithopters nearby, though. Even if you could get on his barge, I can't imagine how you'd escape. I suppose the best way would be to get him while he's at the Reef.

"Come here," he said while gesturing for the others to follow him to a window. From there he pointed to the Reef, which was visible in the distance.

"Do you see that crown-like structure on the top of the large disc in the middle of the complex?" he asked. "The one with the little towers and balconies."

"Yes," Eshwurhiyo replied.

"That's Ngo's penthouse. He stays there when he comes to Quanya. You might be able to get in there. It'll be difficult, though. No. I've got a better idea."

"Which is?" Eshwurhiyo asked.

"Just about every Tuesday and Thursday, Ngo goes to the big casino in the Reef and gambles with his richest guests. He has a special room in the very center of the casino where he can entertain them. The day after tomorrow's Tuesday, so he should be there the night after tomorrow night. It's possible you could get into his private room and kill him."

Vijeihi turned to Jess and began examining her body, first looking at her front and then turning her around to look at her back.

"You'll be perfect. You've got a nice body. You're from another world, and you don't have any tattoos that'll give you away."

"What is it I'm perfect for?"

Vijeihi answered. "I know the man who supplies Ngo with the toilet attendants for his casino. He'll sell you to Ngo if I bring you to him. He won't know what you're going to do, but that'll probably be best for him. The manager at the casino will put you in the public toilets, but once you're in with the other attendants, you should be able to change places with one of the girls working in Ngo's private toilets. If you can get that far, you might be able to let your companions in and attack him."

"Do you think that'll work?" Eshwurhiyo asked.

"I have no idea. It all depends on your skill and how much the gods favor you. You could be discovered and killed or you could kill Ngo. I can't say. One thing I will say is that I can't imagine how you're going to escape. Ngo is always surrounded by guards and the Reef has more security than the viceroy's palace does."

"We'll manage," Eshwurhiyo told him. "Make the arrangements to sell Jess to your acquaintance."

"First of all," Vijeihi said while turning to address Jess. "Is this toad yours?"

"He's my friend, if that's what you mean."

"Okay. Do you trust it?"

Jess was starting to get annoyed with Vijeihi. He clearly thought that Uluf was some kind of pet. Her brows furrowed and she snapped, "I'd trust him with my life."

"Good. Transfer all your money to him either tomorrow or Tuesday morning. I'll take you to a machine. There are plenty of them around this town. Everyone needs money to pay their gambling bills, after all."

"Why do I need to do that?"

"Lots of people come here and spend too much or lose their money. When they do, they have to earn some more quickly. For an attractive woman like yourself, there are plenty of opportunities in this city. Some women become whores, others dance. Some get jobs as waitresses or attendants. Nobody'll be surprised if you sell yourself to the Reef to be an attendant there. I'll just tell my contact that you got a little carried away in a russa den, made a bet with a toad, and lost everything. He'll give me a little commission for finding you and won't think more of it. We just have to make sure you're penniless in case anybody checks up on you."

"I'll do it," Jess said. "But first I want to know how all this is going to help me find Tolliver, or find out what happened to him."

"If we kill Tsoi," Eshwurhiyo explained, "we'll cut off his head and take it back to Jezic. We can revive it there and put it in a juicer."

Such a device, Jess knew, was able to revivify a brain to a certain degree so that it could be interrogated through a processor that either controlled its vocal apparatus or rerouted the impulses created by the brain into a vocal imitator or a readout screen. Because the machine was able to manipulate and even control many of the brain's functions, it almost completely eliminated the possibility that any of the information extracted would be deceitful. Unfortunately, while a brain put in a juicer would not lie, and would provide answers to any questions it was asked, the more it had decayed, the less it would be able to answer. Jess would have to interrogate Tsoi's head quickly or would, at least, have to preserve it until she could put it in the machine. Otherwise, it would be useless. She still thought it would be worth trying.

"Okay, I'm fine with that, but I'm not leaving without his head. You'll need to get something to pickle it in."

"We'll pick up some sleeping jelly and inject the head with that," said Eshwurhiyo.

"I'm in, then."

"Great," Eshwurhiyo replied and then turned to Vijeihi. "Now that all that's settled, do you have a place for us to sleep tonight?"

"Yes," he informed her. "You and Syo can stay here in my flat."

"That's fine with me," Eshwurhiyo told him. "I need to discuss our plans for Tuesday with you, anyway."

Vijeihi nodded.

"Your friend," he said pointing to Ofu, "can stay with one of my men. The offworlder girl and the toad can sleep behind my russa den. There's a room there."

Vijeihi turned towards the door through which he had entered the room earlier and shouted, "Priyoko, come here."

A moment later a lithe young kathoey appeared and leaned her graceful naked body against the jamb.

"What do you want, darling?" she asked.

Vijeihi answered, "Show this young woman...What is your name?"

"I'm Jess and this is Uluf."

"Show Jess and Uluf to the room behind the russa den. They'll be staying there tonight."

"Anything you want, darling," Priyoko replied. She then picked up a brocaded sarong from the back of a sofa, wrapped it around her waist, and fastened over her torso a halterneck that supported her ample breasts while leaving them uncovered.

She looked at Jess and Uluf as she walked across the room, swinging her hips in an exaggerated way, and said to them, "Come with me, sweeties. I'll take you to your room."

Priyoko led the two from Vijeihi's flat, into the street, and to a building some distance further down its opposite side. There she brought them up a wrought iron stairway at the structure's side to a wide balcony opening into a large but bare room filled with a great many men (and a few women) who were mostly sprawling across the floor or leaning against the graffiti covered walls or pillars.

The group picked its way through the thicket of inebriated flesh and came to a small door on the other side of the room.

Nearby, a drooping and desiccated Jaffrite squatted on the floor, his tail coiled around his legs and a feedbag-like pouch hanging in front of his nostrils so that he could inhale the female aromas with which it was filled. Since Jaffrites were more aroused by their sense of smell than by their sense of sight, the wretched creature in the den was so being kept in a constant state of excitation. To relieve himself, he held his serpentine penis in his hands and masturbated into a bowl over the rim of which the tip of his organ dangled like a withered flower.

Between this beast and the door to the back room there sat an old woman smoking a hookah and ladling russa into small clay cups from a battered cauldron.

Priyoko said to her, "Vijeihi is letting these two stay here tonight."

The old woman puckered her hairy lips and nodded to the kathoey in acknowledgement.

Resting her wrist on her hip, Priyoko told Jess, "There are a couple of beds in there, so you two don't have to sleep together if you don't want to. Sometimes, Vijeihi brings his sluts over here, so there should be some food in there too. Help yourself to whatever you want. Oh, and there's a telopticon if you need to call anyone."

"Thanks," Jess said. "Is there a lock on the door?"

"Yeah." Priyoko turned to the old woman. "Hey, Leilo, give me the key for the door."

The crone pulled a huge ring of keys from the folds of her baggy robe, took one off, and gave it to Priyoko, who gave it to Jess.

"Well, I guess that's all I can do for you," Priyoko said. "If there's anything else you need, just ask Leilo, the old escapee from the land of the dead here. She'll get you whatever you want. Okay then, I'm off."

With that, Priyoko left them and Jess and Uluf entered the room. It was small and dirty, but no worse than many of the other places the two had stayed in before.

Jess sat down on the bed, looked up at Uluf, and asked, "Are those people out there on russa?"

"Yes."

"They really look out of it."

"I am sure they have all escaped to their own imaginary worlds and are enjoying feverish, liquid dreams."

Jess knew it would not be very wise to try russa on this particular night, but she was so curious about its effects she could not stop herself from thinking about it.

Eventually, she was no longer able to endure the temptation, got up, and informed Uluf, "I'm going to try some russa. Do you want any?"

"No thank you. Jess, is it..." Uluf began to ask, but his friend interrupted him.

"Honestly," she said, "it's stupid, but I'm going to take some anyway. You know I have no willpower."

Uluf nodded to her. Though the toad was concerned that, should Jess take the drug, she would be completely helpless, he was not willing to keep any person from enjoying life's pleasures. Nor could he have stopped her, anyway.

Jess went into the den outside, purchased a cup no bigger than a thimble full of russa from the crone behind the cauldron, and returned to the room, locking the door behind her.

She reclined on one of the beds and drank the thick, sticky liquid in a single gulp. It was overpoweringly salty and nauseatingly bitter. She almost gagged as the foul substance slid like a salted slug down her throat.

"Ah. I hope it gets better than that. That was really disguising!" she exclaimed.

Within seconds, Jess did start enjoying herself. She began to feel a pleasant tingling in her mouth that gradually ran all the way down to her stomach. This sensation slowly spread throughout her body and grew in intensity.

Before too much time had passed, Jess was overcome with dizziness and had to rest her head against the headboard behind her. She looked around as she lay back and noticed that the walls of the room were pulsating as though she were inside of an enormous heart and that the bed she was lying on refused to stay beneath her.

The tingling permeating her body burned away the matter from which it was made, so that Jess became weightless and started floating towards the undulating ceiling. The walls bulged and rushed towards her. Like sumo wrestlers, they pushed her away from the ceiling and sent her spinning to bounce from one of them to another as though she were a rubber ball being tossed by a child.

Far below her, Jess saw Uluf sitting on his bed eating some kind of spiky insect. In her dizzy confusion, she forgot who she was, dove into that insect, and found herself being tossed into the toad's huge, gaping mouth. Panic raced through her whole being like an electric shock as she plunged down her friend's throat. The tingling sensation produced by the wind rushing past her, however, was so agreeable that, in spite of hurtling through a wet pinkish tunnel ending in a vat of acid, all she could notice was that feeling.

As before, the sensation spread through her body and became more and more intense, until Jess was swallowed up in an ecstatic blissfulness unlike anything she had ever known before. Her body trembled and occasionally convulsed with orgasmic delight.

Suddenly, she reached the bottom of Uluf's esophagus and fell into her own body lying on the bed in front of him. She was back in the room she had been in before, but the room was no longer in the same universe.

What had been distinct, unified entities in the old universe were not so in the new. Jess's world had been transformed into a mass of spongy balls upon which images of everything in her field of vision had been painted. What was even more (deliciously) disconcerting, however, was that every one of the entities of her former reality had been divided up amongst several balls, some part of each having been applied to one ball and another part to a second. Uluf was no longer Uluf and a wall was no longer a wall. Instead, some piece of Uluf and some part of the wall were present on one ball while other parts of these were present on different balls. It was the balls that were now the distinct parts of the world.

Even movement had become dependent upon such new realities, being produced when balls, rolling about on top of one another, covered and uncovered portions of the images upon them and altered the images' relationships to one another.

For a while, Jess was captivated by her new universe and by the joy it spontaneously infused into her body, but, eventually, she realized that her pleasure had become so extreme that she was bathed in sweat.

Thousands upon thousands of tiny eyes had opened in her skin and each poured forth a stream of salty tears. The quantity of water they shed soon emptied her flesh of its substance and left her as a thin, electrified mist composed only of an intoxicating delight.

Even with her body gone, tears continued to issue from its ghostly afterglow, and these flowed in deadly currents along the deep valleys of her immaterial form and across its wide plains, where tiny men and women with the heads of chickens sang songs about pork pies and farted out spectacular fireworks displays. Then, leaving this fabulous land, the rivers of sweat spilled upon the floor of the room where Jess was lying and formed great puddles. These grew and grew and soon coalesced into a vast ocean that reached to the very edge of the universe, where it was held in place by the coils of an encircling pink dragon who was eating cheese he found stuck in his walrus-like mustache.

From the deep, salty ocean plastic flowers rose, forming a bed around and under Jess, enabling her to float across the waters as these lapped against her body and made her shake with pleasure.

In the throws of her unending orgasm, Jess grabbed a bunch of the flowers with her right hand, squeezing the blossoms into a jelly that turned into a fiery bird that soared away into the sky. With her left hand, she reached to grab more of the flowers, but her fingers came to rest instead upon a scaly fish with a face like Uluf's that was sitting beside her. This creature was immediately joined by countless others just like it, and they all began to lick Jess's body with their long, prehensile green tongues.

As overcome with pleasure as she had been before, what she felt now so surpassed that that she swooned in her ecstasy. All images, sounds, smells, tastes, and feelings merged into a single passion so incredible she lost herself in it as though she had died.

Tears rolled out of her eyes. Her back arched, and her hands, feet, shoulders, and buttocks pressed against the flowery bed she was lying on with such force that it was thrust beneath the waters of the ocean. Jess herself sank into the warm liquid that was composed, she now saw, of swarms of glass mermaids writhing around one another. These slid into every orifice of her body and caressed each nerve cell they found therein, so increasing her pleasure even further.

When she exhaled, the waters that flowed through her mouth emerged as one iridescent soap bubble after another and these danced about in the air in front of her. Captivated by this new sight, Jess saw how, in each, a whole new universe entirely different from anything that ever had or ever would exist anywhere else came into being. Then, within these, an infinite number of entities were born, lived, and died as Jess watched them and immersed herself in their troubles and adventures.

Countless billions of years later, she realized such worlds were produced from her own imagination and so blew more shining, variegated bubbles from her mouth, taking delight in her own marvelous ingenuity. She thought up and became each and every living thing upon each planet of each universe and relished and experienced those creatures' diverse joys and sorrows. Like a girl playing with her dolls, she played with creation.

Eventually, however, she noticed, at the far edge of the sea, a host of gods born from the tiny parasites that had been living on her skin. The body of each of these was carved of a single great jewel, but was as soft and pliable as any made of flesh.

From the waters between these ruby, emerald, sapphire, diamond, and amethyst beings, a huge fish with goggle eyes rose. It opened its mouth and a beautiful young woman emerged from its throat and passed through its lips. Her belly swelled and she gave birth to a child which she held to her breast that it might suckle there. Then, as it fed, the woman transformed herself into a withered crone from whose brow horns rose and whose fingers ended in talons. She raised the baby to her tusked mouth and with great bites devoured it. When she had crushed the last of the infant's bones between her fangs and swallowed the last of its marrow, she wiped away the blood that bespattered and concealed her face, so revealing her earlier beautiful form.

She smiled, lifted up a sword given her by an emerald deity, and struck off her own head. Then, as the woman held it in her hand, the head lapped up the streams of blood that spurted from her neck.

Jess shuddered in thrilled, strangely jubilant terror, but, before she could react, the woman had leapt across the ocean and was resting on all fours on top of her. Though she knew that she was about to die, Jess was not afraid. She longed to be eaten. She wanted to surrender and be devoured. In fact, her body trembled ecstatically at the prospect. She looked up at the woman on top of her, whose head was now back upon her shoulders, and that woman smiled down at her as an areole of raging flames encircled her face.

While a joyous fear pervaded her body, Jess, her eyes closed in anticipation, felt the woman grab ahold of her and lift her up. She felt the woman thrusting her into her mouth, and she felt the woman devouring her flesh.

Once she had died, Jess opened her eyes again to discover herself standing in the woman's mouth, that was like a cavern vaster than any world. There she saw within the woman's mountainous teeth great cities and beautiful wildernesses. She saw armies marching upon the woman's tongue, past grazing animals and waving trees, and she saw all these things annihilated and swept away as the woman gnashed her teeth and swallowed.

Drawn in by the gulp that destroyed this peculiar world, Jess fell down the woman's gullet, where she hurtled past stars and moons and planets. At last, she emerged in the woman's belly, wherein was confined the whole of the beginningless, endless, and infinite universe. Jess looked around in awe as galaxies fluttered past her brows like butterflies and subatomic particles hurtled overhead like flying mountains.

Then, without warning, the balls that formed this universe flew apart, revealing behind them a chamber exactly like that Jess had been in before, except that this one was entirely composed of tiny insects whose bodies were made of gems, and these were constantly crawling about so that the room was always in motion.

Their dancing about began to hypnotize Jess, who felt the intense bliss she had been experiencing fade into a pleasant contentment. Obese crocodiles crept out from under her bed, pressed their soft blue and green coils against her sides, nuzzled her cheeks with kisses, and sang incomprehensible lullabies into her ears. Before long, Jess's eyes grew heavy as the swirling colors around her made her dizzy and confused and the quiet reptilian songs calmed her. She closed her eyes and drifted off into a sleep alive with wild, impossible dreams.

# Interlude 6
# Toads and Scorpions

During the last major conflict fought on the Earth prior to the end of the Terrestrial Age, that between North Australia and Java, the former government, short of ground troops, decided to genetically engineer its soldiers. Since making genetic alterations to humans had long been forbidden by international treaty and had already become a taboo as strong as more ancient prohibitions on incest and cannibalism, North Australian scientists primarily made use of scorpion and horse DNA. Although some structures present in the human genetic code were incorporated into the soldiers these scientists created to give them a modicum of intelligence and the ability to understand language, the creatures were essentially scorpions as large as horses whose bodies were supported by internal skeletons.

The new soldiers were effectively used in the conflict and prevented North Australia from being defeated.

Within ten years, both nations had joined the International Commonwealth, as had every other terrestrial state in the quarter century following the end of the war, but several nations nonetheless preserved the genetic blueprint of the soldier scorpions developed by North Australia. As conventional armies were severely restricted in size, and most nations desired a readily available force of ground troops, the refinement of scorpions continued throughout the period of the International Commonwealth.

When faster than light interstellar travel was developed and large scale human colonization of other worlds began, the technologies developed for the creation of the scorpions were employed to create labor forces able to rapidly build infrastructures on newly settled planets. Later, when immigration to other worlds had so increased that it diminished the population of the Earth and led to a labor shortage on that planet, such workers were also used to fill vacant jobs there.

Like the soldiers of the Austro-Javanese War, these workers were created by altering the DNA of non-human species, often by modifying the DNA of one species with structures found either in the DNA of other non-human species or in that of humans.

Several different species were employed to provide the basic models for the various types of workers. All species, however, were significantly altered so that they were reasonably intelligent and capable of understanding speech. Most were also made bipedal and given human-like hands. Collectively these new beings came to be referred to as homunculi.

By the end of the Interplanetary Commonwealth, many of these invented species had been confined to performing only specialized functions. Human populations on colonized worlds had grown sufficiently large and the societies existing on those planets had become sufficiently stable for the use of such workers to be limited. Several species did, nonetheless, continue to be employed in substantial numbers on the Earth, where the population was continuously declining, as well as on the most recent colonies. Even on those planets, the majority of the species of homunculi had become severely restricted in use by the time the Confederacy was founded.

Two species have, however, remained important up to the present day: scorpions and toads.

## Scorpions

The use of scorpions by any private person or tributary government is forbidden by edict, but the creatures do form an important part of the Pancloan military. Every viceroy, in fact, maintains an army of scorpions in stasis in case of civil unrest or rebellion.

The scorpions currently employed are externally different from the original terrestrial animal only in that they have the enormous chelicerae of solifugids and in that one of their pincers has been made larger than the other. The smaller pincer is of a size able to hold a firearm and the larger pincer is capable of inflicting severe damage on an opponent in close combat.

Internally, the body of such a creature is much like that of one of North Australia's ancient scorpion soldiers. There is an internal skeleton, including a backbone, altered organs able to support a large animal, and a substantial brain capable of understanding orders and operating simple machinery.

Although unable to speak, scorpions are often fitted with cameras that allow commanders to see the activities of their soldiers.

All scorpions are male. The production of female scorpions is strictly prohibited.

## Toads

Woodhouse's toads were one of the species originally used by scientists in the experiments conducted to develop the techniques used to create genetically engineered workers, although no race of workers was ever derived from these creatures. Beginning in 36 S.A., however, toads were offered for sale as entertainers.

These beings resemble Woodhouse's toads, except that they are bipedal, have a forward facing head, and an enlarged cranium. They have also been internally altered so that their vocal apparatus is capable of producing a range of notes and sounds considerably beyond that of human beings.

The corporation responsible for producing this species initially marketed them as singers and was very successful at doing so. Toads quickly displaced human singers and, before long, other human musicians. Moreover, they proved to be as popular on many colonies as they were on the Earth.

Within twenty years of the creation of the first toad, demand for the creatures as musicians had so increased that the Commonwealth government required the company controlling their production to create female toads. Previously, only males had been produced.

The legal status of toads differs from world to world and even from nation to nation. In some states they are considered to be animals and can be owned by human beings. Other countries forbid their being imported, their immigrating, or both. Still other governments accord toads certain rights, and a few states grant them citizenship. The Pancloan government does not accept toads into the military or the civil service, although they are granted most of the rights humans have. On worlds where toads have citizenship or own property, they are taxed by the empire.

Unlike many other engineered species, toads are as intelligent as are humans and have evolved several distinctive cultures.

Nearly all toads display an interest in the arts, and most are especially proficient at music. Their musical traditions are, consequently, extremely rich. Forms of elaborate musical drama are common to most toad cultures.

Toads are also fond of display. Their cities or neighborhoods are distinguished by florid and very colorful architecture, and their clothing tends to be flamboyant, exaggerated, and rich.

Their love of sounds is often expressed in their linguistic playfulness. Toads have developed numerous artificial languages, and a given toad will frequently speak several of these. The majority of such languages disappear within a generation or two of their creation, but several of them have endured for hundreds of years.

While toads gravitate to careers in the arts, many, even most, are employed in other occupations. Most of the members of the species do not, however, abandon their interest in singing, instrumental performance, musical composition, painting, or some other art and continue to labor in such fields even if employed at a different job. Artistic endeavors consequently permeate all toad societies, and skill at one's art remains a toad's highest achievement.

The total population of toads throughout the Pancloan Empire is estimated at eight hundred million. Hyupo, with approximately thirty million resident toads, has the largest toad population of any single world. Toads have been granted citizenship on Hyupo and there enjoy rights equal to those of humans.

From Pollidor's *Big Blue Book of Knowledge*

# Chapter 14
## Relaxing and Preparing

"Well, my dear, what did you think of your first experience with russa?" Uluf asked Jess when she woke up the next morning.

Jess rubbed her eyes, started stripping off her dirty clothes, and said, "It was like nothing else I've ever tried before. It was amazing. When I was a kid, I injected telheq a couple of times. That makes you feel good, but it was nothing compared to russa. Each second was like having a thousand orgasms at the same time, except that they didn't stop. It seemed like it lasted a million years. I didn't think anything could feel that good. And you wouldn't believe the things I saw."

"I have tried it before and had an amazing experience," Uluf told her as she began dressing herself in her red skirt and halter-top. "I suppose everyone does. That is, undoubtedly, the reason why it is so popular and so expensive."

"I can definitely understand why people would want to take it, but I don't think I'll ever do it again. My mom was a complete junkie. She wasted her life and made mine hell. No matter what, I don't want to be like her, and I'm afraid if I ever took russa again I wouldn't be able to keep myself from doing it again and again. Once is enough."

"I am glad to hear it, Jess. Russa is horribly addictive, physically and psychologically. If you keep taking it, you will inevitably wind up as human garbage like those people in the den. The only thing they care about is russa. If they do not have it, they will do whatever they have to in order to earn the money to buy some. Their whole existence is a stupor."

"I know, Uluf. Don't worry about me. I'm not stupid. Okay?"

"I am sorry, Jess. I am just concerned about you."

"I appreciate that. So, you want to go look around Quanya today?"

Realizing that this could be the last day of his life, Uluf had no desire to miss out on whatever pleasure he could experience.

"Without a doubt, my dear," he replied

"Okay. It's settled. We've got a plan, but, right now, I'm dying of starvation. What's Vijeihi got to eat in here?"

\* \* \*

Beautiful young women and high ranking gangsters wandered about the balcony projecting from and encircling the arcaded side of the ornately sculpted, brightly painted hull of the pleasure barge floating through the skies over the ocean. Above these persons, past a row of windows, even more important individuals chatted amongst themselves while standing upon the vessel's wide, oval deck, which was surrounded by a brass railing and surmounted by a pair of colonnaded, red roofed buildings, one to the fore and one to the aft. Between these, below a canopy that itself was situated beneath rows of banners blowing in the wind from the tops of tall poles, Tsoi reclined upon a couch smoking his long stemmed pipe and listening to a pair of young woman singing to the accompaniment of a zither, a drum, and a tambura.

He was looking out across the waters watching an antigravity sled moved by a propeller at its back approach beneath the armed barges and circling ornithopters that surrounded his own craft.

After this little vessel had landed, Tsoi's aged, crooked, and wrinkled major-domo came to him and announced, "Your uncle and cousins have arrived, my lord."

"Bring them to me," Tsoi answered.

A few minutes later, the major-domo returned followed by a portly but heavily muscled man in his mid fifties, a handsome, athletic man in his mid twenties, and a stunningly beautiful woman in her early twenties. All were dressed according to the style favored in Quanya and in the most luxurious of garments. The men wore long frock coats fastened with buckles, baggy trousers, and conical hats, and the woman was attired in a tight, open chested blouse and a long bell-shaped skirt.

The older man, Lo, was Tsoi's uncle, and the other two that man's son, Huazheen, and his daughter, Hyan.

Tsoi despised Lo and would have been glad to kill him. The man was a brutal oaf who lacked any imagination. He had learned to do things a certain way and had no ability to see that they might be done differently. Worse than that, he was so stupid and crude that, even if he were amenable to Tsoi's radical plans, any efforts he made to carry them out were sure to be done with such an absence of subtlety that he would still be more likely to be a hindrance than a help. At least his crudeness and simplemindedness kept him from being much of a threat to Tsoi, even though he detested his nephew as much as Tsoi detested him. Unfortunately, any attempt to dispose of Lo could have severe consequences. The man was both jovial and rough, and those traits ensured that he was well liked and admired by many members of the Ngo gang.

Lo's children were also fiercely loyal to their father, but both hated him nonetheless. Hyan looked at the man in the same way Tsoi did, and Huazheen, though as dimwitted as his father, was so devoted to his sister that he adopted all of her opinions and prejudices without reflection.

Tsoi might not have been fond of Lo, but he did like both Huazheen and Hyan. In fact, he relied upon the latter of his two cousins more than he did on any other person. She was as farsighted as Lo was blind and as clever as he was thick. Admittedly, her own ambition and her usefulness to her father's did concern Tsoi, who realized that both those two wanted him to marry Hyan. Lo hoped thereby to ensure his grandchild would become head of the Ngo family, and Hyan hoped to gain control over Tsoi and rule the family through him. As dangerous as she was, Tsoi could not, however, dispense with her. She was his staunchest supporter in his family and the most intelligent of his subordinates.

What was more, she and Huazheen were Tsoi's best fighters. The young man, in particular, was horribly dangerous, having been given the thread that had been passed down in the family for five-hundred years. He was virtually unbeatable in battle.

The only person who could possibly have defeated him was, in Tsoi's opinion, Hyan. She did not have a thread, but she had been trained to use a resonator to accomplish many of the feats that were normally possible only for a person with the ancients' strange tool.

This resonator was a sort of U-shaped metallic collar that was imbedded in her skin. Its two prongs, which were draped over her shoulders, met in a knob that emerged from the back of her neck and led to a series of nodes that pierced her spine. With it, Hyan could cause specific pervasive forces that determined the nature of the experienced universe (including such forces as those determining temporal and spatial relations) to instantiate themselves as particular sounds. Having done so, she could magnify, subjugate, and internalize those manifested powers. She was so able to bend time and space to her will, even if she could not do so with the ease of a person with a thread.

Tsoi gestured for the three to sit in a sofa that was being placed in front of his own by a gang of scurrying servants.

His uncle looked at him and asked, "Are you sure it's wise to be floating around over the ocean like this? Do you have enough protection? Somebody could easily attack you here."

"Don't worry, my dear uncle," Tsoi said. "If a man doesn't expose himself to a little danger and take a few risks, he's as good as dead. Besides, the sea breeze is wonderfully invigorating. You may not have realized it, but all the great men of history spent much of their lives on the sea. Genghis Khan, Stalin, Samudragupta, they were all lovers of the salty waters. The oceanic vapors, you see, produce a hard sheath, an armored plating, inside the body, around each cell, that makes a man's physical constitution much firmer. Of course, the body affects the mind, so by hardening his body, a man hardens his mind as well. Not only that, but the qualities of the sea are transferred to him by such vapors. He acquires all the ocean's profundity, mystery, and dangerousness."

Lo looked unconvinced, but before Tsoi could be too annoyed, Hyan smiled at him and spoke.

"My lord, we were told that you had something you wanted us to do."

Tsoi watched Hyan as she positioned herself so that various parts of her body pressed against or emerged from underneath her clothing in distinctly alluring ways.

Placing his hand in his lap, to help maintain the excitement Hyan had aroused in him, Tsoi replied. "Yes. Yes, I do have something for you to do."

"What is it, then?" Lo asked.

"Our new allies are now on their way to deal with the Llalloi. I am not, however, confident about them. They are so mercurial, and so oblivious to everything but their own pleasure, I do not think it would be wise to rely exclusively upon them to carry out our desires."

"You're right about that," Lo interjected. "They could be the end of us. You should reconsider this whole adventure before they are."

Tsoi could have leapt from his seat and killed Lo at that moment, though he was not so stupid as actually to do so.

He took a draught from his pipe, calmed himself, and exhaled. "No. We will continue. I am not some child who longs to cross a stream but refuses to do so because the current scares him. I will judge the strength of the current, make sure my footing is firm, and cross. Only a fool does not try to acquire what he desires because he is afraid his efforts may not be fruitful."

Lo looked at Tsoi angrily while Hyan unsuccessfully attempted to suppress a smile.

With hints of laughter in her voice, she asked, "How can we help make sure our footing is firm in this case, my lord?"

"I have acquired an armed ether-ship," Tsoi announced and inhaled a mouthful of smoke as he watched the others' reactions.

"Are you insane?" Lo nearly shouted. "If the Pancloans find out, they'll wipe out our entire family. This could be the end of all of us."

"That, dear uncle, is why I am putting you in command of it. You will exercise your usual prudence and ensure that we are not discovered."

"Ah! I don't like this."

"And that's why you'll succeed. I have complete faith in you, uncle. You will keep the ship hidden. I assure you, I have no desire to be tortured to death in front of the viceroy's palace in Nyopwa for the amusement of a crowd of noblemen and bureaucrats. If I didn't think you could do this, I wouldn't give you the assignment."

Lo scowled at his nephew, his face red with anger.

Tsoi asked him, "Will you do it?"

Though Lo had no desire to accept the job, he did not want to rely on anyone else to do it and so nodded his head.

"Good," Tsoi said and turned his gaze to his cousins. "Hyan, you will accompany your father. I'm placing you in charge of the attack itself. Our allies are to report to you, and you will be responsible for making certain that they accomplish our objectives. I want as many of the top ranking Llalloi captured as you can get your hands on, and all of the rest of the lot butchered. Make sure you destroy whatever stores of russa they have at their base as well."

Hyan smiled and coyly brushed her long hair from her dark eyes. It was plaited in cornrows and flitted wildly about her face in the strong wind blowing across the deck of the barge.

She saw how Tsoi looked at her and thought that, perhaps, she might be able to cure him of his addiction to feihi.

For a few seconds, Tsoi stared at her while stroking his crotch. When he finally recovered his wits, he said, with a slight croak, "Yes, you will be in command of the soldiers I am sending and of the ship during battle, if it comes to that, of course. I must insist that you do attack the Llalloi's base and destroy both it and them, but, in every other situation, you have the authority to decide when fighting is necessary. Nonetheless, although you may engage any craft if battle is the only way to avoid detection, you should still exercise caution. I cannot begin to stress sufficiently how important it is for us not to be discovered."

Hyan arched her spine, put her elbows on the back of the couch, and let her braids play across her face, before her dark, kohl-lined eyes. "I'll take care of everything. You can rely on me."

"Yes, I know I can," Tsoi told her.

He continued to stare at her for some time before he spoke to Huazheen.

"Cousin," he eventually said to the young man, "I want you to protect your father and sister. You're the best fighter I have, and you're the only person I can trust to make sure they stay safe. Can you do that for me?"

"Of course, my lord," Huazheen replied.

Addressing the three of them, Tsoi said, "You will leave immediately. I have a ship waiting to take you to the orbital station. From there, you'll be conveyed to the armed ship I acquired. It's in another system now, so you'll have to board it there. You should get whatever you need before you depart. Your transport from Quanya is leaving in two watches."

The three stood up, bowed to Tsoi, and left.

* * *

Eshwurhiyo was not pleased with Jess's plan to take in the sights of Quanya, but she quickly realized that there was little she could say to dissuade the girl.

With a tone of exasperation, she told Jess, "At least take Ofu with you and stay out of Ngo's part of the city."

"What do you mean?" Jess asked.

"Each of the Seven Families controls one section of the city, either on the right or the left of the Serpentine Path, the boulevard in the middle of the Serpent. The Ngo are the exception. They control the whole southern end of the city, to the right and the left of the street. Just stay out of the south, okay?"

"Don't worry," Jess reassured her. "I'm not going to do anything to get caught. I came here for a reason, you know."

Eshwurhiyo nodded her assent and gestured for Ofu to get up from the soiled couch where he was sitting in his new garments, which were cut in the local fashion. He now wore a long green frock coat that was fastened with a row of buckles extending from his waist to the stand-up collar around his throat, a pair of baggy green trousers, shoes with upturned toes, and a conical hat topped with an onion-shaped bulb.

The man stood, and he, Jess, and Uluf left Vijeihi's flat.

They went to the entryway set in the wall around the slums where they were staying. The guards posted there stopped them and demanded to see their passes. The three presented these and the sentries opened the gates and let them through.

As they walked to the nearby road, Jess asked Ofu, "What if we didn't have passes?"

"They wouldn't have let us through."

"Are they just going to trap us there until we die?"

"The Ngo have offices there. If you got mugged or something like that and your pass was stolen, they could get you out, as long as you could prove who you are somehow. Or, if you earned enough money there, you could buy a pass. Otherwise, yeah, you'd be stuck there."

"Why do they do that?"

"There are a lot of junkies in Quanya. They don't want those people coming to the Serpent. Half of them would try to steal from the tourists and most of the rest would beg. That's not good for business. If you want to be an impoverished russa addict, you'll have to stay where you don't cost the Ngo any money. Mind you, they're more than happy to supply the junkies with russa and to sell them alcohol, whores, or whatever. They even own half the buildings in the slums. It's a great set up for the Ngo."

"Sounds pretty sleazy to me."

"Anyway, where do you want to go?" Ofu asked the girl as they came to the nearest taxi.

"First of all, I want to see the sights."

"We'll go to the station at the southern tip of the city and take the train that runs down the center of the Serpent."

"I thought Eshwurhiyo doesn't want us going to the south."

"The station is fine. It's no-man's-land. The Seven Families run it, the trains, the air and space ports, and the Serpentine Path itself jointly."

"Okay then. Let's go," Jess replied with a grin and hopped into a cab.

The mechanical driver took them to the vast ziggurat at Quanya's southernmost point and there the group bought tickets to ride the train that ran through the city's center.

This vehicle was not actually a train Jess discovered, but a rectangular box made entirely out of glass. At each of its four corners was a black, elaborately cast pole that was connected to one of two parallel rails that ran directly above the transparent cabin and from which it was suspended.

The three boarded one of these glass hexahedra and sat upon the glass-like but surprisingly soft seats inside it.

Then, with Uluf's hand in her own, Jess excitedly watched as the train emerged from a tunnel high in the ziggurat and glided down the spine of the city upon its twin rails.

These were hung from beams extending from the tops of impossibly thin spires that supported, on their opposite side, other rails along which other trains were moving to the south. All of these vehicles passed, at regular intervals, through towers where they would stop to let their passengers on and off.

Below her, to the right of the spires supporting the train, Jess saw a metal bridge bustling with snail shaped cars moving to the south, and, to the left of the spires, she saw another such bridge covered with cars heading towards the north.

Just past these were wide, tree lined sidewalks that ran beneath various outlandish and ridiculously gaudy structures.

Ahead was the enormous Reef in the Sky, which, Jess noted, they were rapidly approaching. She felt a little worried as they did so, but she was still enthralled as the train slid under the resort's huge spheres and discs perched atop a forest of towers and piers. Not only did all of these structures combine to form an ornate, astonishing whole, but, moreover, they were adorned with such a variety of balconies, neon signs, holograms, and monumental sculptures and were topped with so many minaret-like spires, wide gardens, and glass roofed conservatories that they were just as bewitching in their details. The place was like some impossible fairy palace.

While the train entered into tunnels piercing several of the towers of the Reef and slithered by the sides of others or under or above innumerable bridges connecting these, Jess's face remained plastered against the glass wall in front of her, her buttocks barely remaining on her seat, her nose bent sidewise onto her cheek, and her eyes as wide as a fish's.

Leaving this weird elfin castle behind, the glass train continued on its way down the middle of the Serpentine Path far below its passengers' feet.

Ofu, who was sitting with his arms crossed upon his chest next to Uluf, said, "We should be leaving Ngo's quarter. Wait until we pass a couple more stops before you get off, though."

"I want to go all the way to the end of the line," Jess responded. "It loops back around doesn't it?"

Ofu nodded.

"Good, let's look around," Jess exclaimed with a smile. "What do you want to do, Uluf?"

"I understand that there are numerous venues for musical and dramatic performances in styles from various cultures from many different worlds in Quanya. I would like to take in something of a kind I have never before encountered. After all, without the sweet waters of diversity flooding through one's experiences from time to time – and without a willingness to drink of these – even a toad may find his heart and mind so desiccated that he is transformed into a lazy lizard who glares stupidly at the waste around him."

"Okay then, we'll go listen to some music."

"What would you like to do, my dear?"

"I want to see the sights, have something to drink, and then, when I'm a little tipsy, I want to lose some of my hard earned money gambling."

Uluf looked at the girl, his affection for her clearly visible in his moist, goggle eyes.

Jess smiled at him in return and then pressed her nose against the glass wall again, though without releasing the toad's hand.

In front of and around the top-heavy towers lining the Serpentine Path, Jess saw one gigantic animatronic sculpture after another. Some were shaped like odd animals, aliens, or monsters, others like fictional or historic characters, and still others like religious figures venerated on one world or another. Some beckoned to the crowds milling around their feet to enter whatever establishment they were erected in front of. Others acted out some routine or gave some speech, and still others engaged in mock battles with one another.

Jess was absolutely delighted by these moving sculptures, a few of which were as tall as skyscrapers, and could not keep herself from pointing one after another of them out to Uluf, even though she realized he would certainly see them even without her help.

As entertained as she was by these mechanical giants, Jess still noticed the myriads of casinos the train passed and tried to remember which of these looked the most appealing to her.

Unfortunately, since most of them were relatively similar to one another, she soon found that she was having a hard time keeping them straight in her mind. It did not really matter, however, as she was far more intrigued by some of the Serpent's other buildings. About a third of the structures in

Quanya's center were so outlandish that they consistently distracted Jess from those around them.

Some, whether as small as a house or as big as a skyscraper, were shaped like elephants, owls, dogs, walruses, or some different sort of animal from the Earth or Shokai. Others were covered with armies of brightly colored animatronic sculptures, and still others were adorned with holograms that made them appear to be, rather than solid structures, gateways into other worlds filled with magical spectacles, sporting events, or stages for dancing women a hundred feet tall.

About halfway through the city, Jess spied to her right a building shaped like an incredibly realistic naked woman resting on her haunches and using her arms (that were stretched behind her) to support her arched torso with its jiggling, dome-like breasts. From her head long black tresses fluttered in the breeze, and crowds of people entered and exited her through her gaping genitals, that opened onto a plaza between her wide spread legs.

"Oh dear," Jess exclaimed while pointing at this structure. "What's that?"

"I am afraid that I do not know," Uluf replied.

Ofu, without taking his eyes from the building, explained. "It's a brothel."

"Ah," Jess responded. "That makes sense."

She felt strangely uncomfortable looking at the structure after Ofu's statement. An acute sadness passed over her body like a cold wind, but it quickly gave way to the warmth of embarrassment.

"Okay, that's enough of that," she murmured to herself and looked around.

On the other side of the boulevard was a forest of two-hundred-foot-tall artificial trees topped with great masses of pink, yellow, and blue leaves. The trunks of these formed a colonnade and multitudes of people, most of whom were accompanied by children, wandered into and out of the imitation wood.

Beyond the trees Jess saw a jumble of brightly lit, constantly moving amusement rides. There were roller coasters, carousels, tumble bugs, funhouses, Ferris wheels, witch's wheels, gyro towers, observation towers, and more.

"Ooh," she exclaimed. "That looks fun. I want to go there."

Ofu glared at her with a combination of surprise, disdain, and dread.

"That's for children, you know," he told the girl.

"I don't care. I'm still a kid in my way."

"I'm not."

Jess frowned.

"If you want to follow us around, you're going to have to go there."

Ofu was not happy. Actually, he looked a little angry.

Jess furrowed her brows at him for a few moments more, until something else caught her attention.

A short distance ahead of her, to her right, was a building like a castle, with tall walls and countless turrets, and, in front of it, marched armies of animals dressed in armor.

"What's that?" she asked Ofu.

"That's a fantasy place. You tell them whatever fantasy you have, and they'll take you to a room and let you live it out."

Uluf's curiosity was piqued by this explanation, and he asked, "How then do the proprietors of that place go about fulfilling their customers' dreams?"

"They use holograms and golems."

Golems were artificial beings made out of plastic. A small computer capable of whatever amount of thought was desired for a particular golem was placed in a mold and attached to a framework of wires appropriate to the size of that mold. A special kind of plastic that could be made more or less rigid by the application of electrical currents was then poured into the mold. Once the plastic had solidified, the computer was able to direct a current to different parts of its body and soften these, either to make them move or simply to give them the feel of human tissue. The resulting machine, a golem, could later be melted down if it was damaged or had fulfilled its purpose, and the computer inside of it could be used to create another golem.

"What kinds of fantasies can they fulfill?" Jess asked.

"Just about anything, I guess."

"Like what?"

"If you want to have sex with some actress or singer, they can make a golem look like her."

"Is that all?" Jess asked, somewhat disappointed.

"You could climb a mountain, be a celebrity, swim to the bottom of the sea, visit alien planets, whatever."

"What else?"

"I don't know. I suppose if you want to pretend to be a hero from an epic, they could create a dream world of castles and princesses and let you fight monsters and armies. It depends on what you want. They can make you see whatever you need to see for your fantasy with holograms, and, if you're going to touch someone in it, they can make that person with a golem. It can be as wild as you want it to be."

Jess was very excited about this new place.

"Forget the amusement park. Let's go there. How much does it cost?"

"It depends mostly on how many golems they have to make for you. It's usually pretty pricey, though."

"That sucks. Oh well, we can still go to the amusement park."

The train continued on its journey north, passing more casinos, more brothels, and more parks, as well as innumerable theaters, russa dens, and stadiums.

In front of some of the last of these were animatronic giants enacting the events occurring inside or great holograms showing passersby what they could see with their own eyes if they were willing to pay for tickets.

About half of the displays in front of the domed arenas were of men armed with spears wearing elaborately embroidered costumes and riding upon pig-like creatures festooned with ribbons and tassels. Each of these persons, while so garbed and mounted, was fighting with a gigantic, naked, quadrupedal chicken whose head ended in a long trumpet-like snout.

Ofu stared at such scenes as the train passed them by, and Jess, noticing his interest, asked him, "What is that they're doing? I saw the men in Sing's place watching the same thing."

"The men you killed?"

"Yeah. So what's that they're watching over there?"

"It's mwag fighting."

"What's the point?"

"A man fights a mwag. It's popular over most of Shokai."

"That's where you want to be?"

"I'd rather go there than play on children's rides."

"I'd rather play on the children's rides. Good thing I'm deciding, huh?"

The rails from which the train was hung made a U-turn at the city's northernmost end. At that point, Jess could see that the rest of the island was heavily wooded and almost entirely uninhabited, being divided into the personal estates of the heads of the Seven Families, with the exception of the boss of the Ngo, whose palace was on a separate island to the south.

# Chapter 15
## Out on the Town

When the train arrived at the tower nearest the amusement park, Jess, Uluf, and Ofu got off and took the elevator within this spire to the ground.

It was hot outside, but it was not sweltering like it had been in Jezic, and the warmth filled Jess with a buoyant energy. She ran across the sidewalk, dragging Uluf by the hand behind her, to the amusement park. There she bought tickets for various rides from a twelve foot tall robotic vender shaped like a grotesquely fat man with an oversized head and a gaping, toothy grin that literally reached from one ear to the other. Then she rode as many of the rides as she could.

Jess invariably pled with Uluf to accompany her on each of these, and, though he was not always pleased to do so, the toad was rarely able to convince his friend to allow him merely to watch her having fun.

She asked Ofu to come with her a few times as well, but he firmly rejected her offers and remained on the ground. He spent most of the day scowling and scratching the back of his thick, hirsute neck impatiently. Occasionally, however, he was able to watch a telecast of a mwag fight, if there happened to be an image screen nearby. Fortunately for the irritable gangster, there were many of these throughout the park, tempting bored fathers to spend the odd moment away from their families.

While Ofu grumbled, Jess, pulling Uluf along behind her through a tumult of people from all over Shokai, and from many other worlds as well, purchased a great mass of cotton candy on a stick, jumped with excitement at the sight of several rides, and had more fun riding these than did most of the children around her.

From time to time, razorblade images of the man who had attacked her on the *Cloud Cutter* would slash through Jess's mind, but, when they did, she drove them away by focusing as intently as she could upon the enjoyable things around her. Consequently, though the repeated intrusion of such visions, and of worries about the dangers that she would have to face the following night, tinged her experiences with a poignant melancholy, these thoughts did not ruin Jess's fun, and she remained ebullient throughout that day.

Uluf, though hardly a great admirer of amusement parks, was nearly as happy as Jess was. He was always delighted to see her smile, and was especially pleased to see her joy on this particular day. She had experienced entirely too much pain over the last few days and could well be facing death on the morrow.

By about the middle of the afternoon, Jess had ridden about as many of the rides as she cared to and was beginning to get tired. The air was hot and her constantly running around and struggling through the thick crowds of rowdy children and exasperated parents had left her doused with sweat.

After she got off one last roller coaster, onto which Uluf had refused to accompany her, Jess went to her friend, wiped her dripping pink hair from her face, and asked him if he would like to do some gambling before they went to the theater that evening. He said he would and so the pair, followed by Ofu, left the amusement park to find a casino, stopping off at a street vendor's stall to purchase krimhi for their lunch.

The gigantic domed foyer of the casino they went to opened onto three other rooms. To the left were a dining hall and a bar. To the right was a russa den, and straight ahead was the casino itself.

Dazzled by the multitudes of people there from various different worlds wearing an endless assortment of garments, Jess stood in the foyer and looked around. She was shocked both by the diversity of these individuals (amongst whom she even saw a few aliens and homunculi) and by the opulence of the place they had come to.

When she spied the russa den, Jess pulled on Uluf's sleeve and dragged him into it so that she could examine it more carefully.

It was a circular room filled with plush couches upon which inebriated men and women lay enjoying their mad dreams. Near the front of the room, behind a polished wooden counter, a team of liveried young women ladled russa from great polished metal cauldrons into thimbles for their customers. Looking down upon this scene were fifty or more Jaffrites confined behind glass doors in niches set above a divan that ran around the room's circumference. Each of these creatures was provided with a pheromone drenched nose bag and each was continuously masturbating into a bowl set in front of him.

Jess was surprised by the luxury of this chamber, but had no desire to imbibe russa again. She led Uluf from the room and went with him to the casino.

Like the russa den, the gambling hall was round and domed, but, except for a walkway around its perimeter, it was entirely flooded. Floating in this pool was a multistoried ship covered with painted or gilt sculptures.

The casino's guests made their way to one or another of the piers projecting into this lagoon, and from these they embarked upon shell shaped craft drawn by homunculi created from fish, otters, or seals. Such vessels took them to the fanciful ship in the middle of the room.

Jess and her companions followed these others and, joining a group of grossly obese reptilian fugazzi with ornate feathery crests upon their pink and green beaded brows, traveled over the waters, above miniature submarine castles built from semiprecious stones, to the ship, the whole of which was filled with tables for playing various games of chance or skill.

Before she sat down to play any of these, Jess found a bar and purchased the most outrageously bizarre drink she could see being served. It was a bluish liquid topped by a fizzing foam served in the shell of a potbellied prawn the size of a grapefruit. Still being sweaty and overheated, she drank this quickly and ordered another. As the barkeep made Jess's second order, Uluf tried to wipe her lips with his handkerchief. They had been stained bright blue by the first drink. The stain did not come off, but Jess did not care. She was having entirely too much fun.

After her new drink was ready, Jess took it with her to one of the gaming tables, where she discovered that the waitresses wandering about the ship would take her order without her needing to return to the bar. While making use of their services and downing one drink after another, until she was more than a little dizzy and was having trouble focusing her eyes, Jess played several games she had seen before and had Ofu or Uluf show her how to play several others that were new to her. She was, however, terrible at such things and, whether she was familiar with a game or not, consistently lost. Fortunately, she did not really care and had a tremendous amount of fun that day.

As evening approached, Jess and her companions grew hungry and decided to leave the casino to get something to eat. They went to the large dining hall in the same building, that across from the russa den.

Like the other major rooms of the establishment, the dining hall was circular and domed. To the right of the entrance was a long bar where drinks were being served, but most of the place's patrons, whether they were eating or merely drinking, were sitting at tables placed on the annular tiers of an arena. At the very center of this inverted cone was a wide, round screen on which were projected images of such clarity that had Uluf not mentioned what it was, Jess would have believed that the things she saw there were physically present in the restaurant.

The group found a table about midway down the arena and ordered food from a waitress who attended to them.

They then turned to the images being displayed on the screen below.

"Ah!" exclaimed Ofu with joy. "You're going to get to see a mwag fight after all. Look. It's beginning."

While Jess squinted her eyes at the scene before her, trying to see if she could tell that it was an image screen, a gate opened in the side of the circular area being shown.

Two men carrying banners followed by a pair of boys swinging censers emerged from this amid the blaring of horns and the thunder of drums. Behind these individuals, a priest dressed in a fashion similar to that of the clerics of Tozana slowly walked and, after him, two more acolytes leading an animal vaguely like a four legged guinea fowl with the neck of a giraffe and a salamandrine head. Another two boys followed carrying trays, on one of which was a curved sword and on the other of which a heavy book. A third man with a banner brought up the end of the procession.

"What's going on? What are they doing?" Jess asked Ofu.

He shushed her and said, "This is sacred. You need to be quiet."

Jess crossed her arms and glared at the man.

After the persons who had entered the arena had circled it, the priest went to stand at its very center, in front of the men with the banners and flanked by the acolytes with the trays, who were themselves flanked by those holding the censers. The two leading the animal stood in front of the priest making sure their charge remained calm.

Once the members of this group had arranged themselves, a second set of wide doors, this situated behind a sort of wooden lych gate, opened and two men with banners walked out followed by four young men who were naked except for circlets of leafy twigs.

Ofu, seeing these individuals, and clearly excited by the prospect of being able to watch a mwag fight, explained to Jess and Uluf that they were apprentice mwag-naritka.[*]

Jess, looking at him out of the corners of her eyes, grunted in response.

Behind the youths two more men wearing bulky, bulbous suits of armor covered with spikes and painted bright red entered the arena. One of them was carrying a long spear.

They were followed by a naked man whose skin was dyed green, on whose head was a loose green cap adorned with a pair of long stuffed socks, and whose face was concealed by a grotesque mask. While all the others moved with the utmost gravity, this person danced about and gesticulated like a deranged fool.

Jess recognized him at once as a clown and, tugging on Uluf's sleeve, announced, "Ooh, look. It's a clown."

The next person to emerge from the gate was riding atop of a great porcine creature that was protected with brightly painted armor covered, like that of the men ahead, with innumerable spikes.

The rider himself wore upon his brow a round hat, the wide brim of which was piled high with red flowers, and, over his torso, a tunic embroidered with images of deities and various words in a script Jess could

---

[*] Mwag fighters.

not read. Around this, just below his armpits, a blue sash was tied, into which a curved dagger was stuck. Upon his legs were brightly printed hose and, upon his feet, colorful, fringed gaiters adorned with bells. In one of his hands was a wand shaped like a shepherd's crook and, in the other, above a shield no bigger than a dinner plate that was strapped to his arm, a long knobkerrie. To his back was fixed a pair of quivers and, in each of these, were three lances topped with banners that fluttered in the wind.

"That's the mwag-naritka," Ofu told his companions. "He's called the prince right now. The mwag is called the king. If the prince kills the king, he gets the crown. Watch him ride. He has reins, but if he's skilled he won't use them. He'll get his mount to go where he wants it to by using his feet and legs only."

The group that had entered the arena circled it as had those who had come before and went to stand across from and facing the others.

Once they had bowed to the priest, that man, holding the book one of his acolytes had brought with him, intoned some mystical chant and made various signs with his hands over the tethered animal in front of him.

"He's sanctifying the arena," Ofu said. "Everything that happens there will now be an offering to the gods."

The priest, having returned the book he held to the acolyte who had brought it, took the sword from the other and blessed it. Then, with a single blow, he decapitated the animal standing in front of him.

"Ugh!" Jess exclaimed.

Uluf patted her arm, and Ofu looked at her with a frown. "That disgusts you?"

"Yeah."

"You did a lot worse to Sing's men."

"Maybe, but that," she said pointing to the screen, "was totally unnecessary."

Ofu grimaced and retuned his gaze to the arena.

The priest had resumed his incantations, which went on for a few minutes, then dipped the tasseled end of the sash he was wearing in the puddle of blood that had accumulated on the ground. Walking up to the man on the armored mount, who leaned down over its side, the priest wiped the blood onto that person's brow and cheeks.

The ritual completed, the priest undid his sash and gave it to the acolytes who had led the animal out. They opened it up, wrapped the beast's corpse in it and, so carrying the dead creature, followed the others in their group back through the gate whence they had originally come.

When they were gone, more horns were sounded and a third gate was flung open. From this emerged two men wearing bulbous, spiked suits of armor (like those of the men who had come out in the procession before them) and leading on ropes a featherless four legged chicken that stood six feet tall at the shoulder.

Its body was draped with bright sheets of cloth festooned from medallions (from which numerous tassels and ribbons also hung), and its skin was colorfully painted with diverse abstract floral and magical designs.

Over its long, funnel-like mouth a muzzle was fitted, and on top of its brow was a wreath of red flowers.

"That's the mwag," Ofu told the others. "They'll bring him up to the fighter so he can show his respect to the beast. Once he's bowed to it, the fighter will retire and let the apprentices dance with the creature. They'll get a chance to develop their agility, and he'll get a chance to size up his opponent."

After this greeting was done, each of the four apprentices was given a hook fitted onto a bracelet (by the man in red armor who was not carrying the spear) and dipped his hands into a box that same person was holding, covering his palms with a red paste kept inside that container. Each then placed the bracelet on one of his wrists and went to stand beneath the arena's wall at a regular interval from the others.

The men leading the mwag unfastened the ropes holding it and retreated to where the other persons were clustered near the fighter.

"Watch now," Ofu said with a grin on his face. "The apprentices will take turns running at the mwag. They'll try to somersault over the creature and put a red palm print on its back. If they can, they'll only use their hands, but they can use their hooks if they have to. It's just much less praiseworthy if they do. After he's jumped the mwag three times, an apprentice can try to grab the wreath of flowers on its head. Once one of them has the wreath, the other three have to try to leap on top of its back and undo the muzzle it's wearing."

"What do they get if they can do all that?" Jess asked.

"The one who undoes the muzzle gets a purse of kopecks. The one who gets the wreath becomes the mwag-naritka's wife. If the fighter wins, the apprentice becomes his queen."

"Hmm?" Jess asked.

"Mwag fighters don't marry women. They can once they retire, but not while they're fighting. Women only weaken a man, they say. Anyway, what the fighters do is marry apprentices instead. Until the fighter's next competition, the apprentice who gets the wreath here will be that man's queen, his wife. During that time, the fighter'll teach his bride how to become a fighter himself, and the apprentice'll attend to the fighter's needs."

"What about the others?" Uluf inquired.

"They live in schools together if they don't have a king. They still train, but it's not the same. Ah, look. They're starting."

One of the apprentices ran from where he stood, towards the mwag's face, and jumped when he had come close to the animal. Placing his hands upon the creature's shoulders, he somersaulted over its back and landed on his feet behind it.

The second apprentice did the same, but the third, unable to place his hands high enough upon the mwag's back, was forced to dig his hook into its flesh. The beast, already growing angry, began to thrash about and look with hostility upon the men who were antagonizing it.

The fourth apprentice was, despite the mwag's jittery motions, able to clear it. The first, however, was struck during his jump by the creature's snout and knocked onto the ground. At once, the mwag turned upon him and clawed at him with the long talons upon its chicken-like feet. The man rolled to one side and was merely scratched upon his shoulder.

The mwag chased after the apprentice, but the green clown ran from where he stood and kicked and punched the beast upon its flank until it turned and pursued him instead. The clown, with comically exaggerated strides, hurried to hide behind a screen erected close to the wall.

While the mwag sought to reach the clown with its clawed feet, the second apprentice jumped its back. The creature turned as the third man did the same. It ran towards the first person it saw, the second apprentice, and, as it did so, the fourth apprentice placed his palms upon its shoulders and spun showily over its spine.

"Actually," Jess exclaimed. "This is pretty interesting."

"Oh, yes," Ofu assured her. "It is."

The first apprentice jumped the mwag a second time, though he had to use his hook to do so, causing the animal to buck and writhe with terrible anger.

Ofu pointed to the second apprentice and said, "If he can make it over, he can try for the wreath on his next turn."

The man did succeed, though, like his fellow, he had to stab the mwag with his hook.

The third apprentice ran towards the infuriated creature, but his hand slipped while he jumped and he fell onto the ground. The mwag turned upon him and struck him such a blow upon his belly and chest that the man's viscera squirted out the side of his torso.

Ofu howled with delight.

"Ha! He won't be dancing again."

The next two men cleared the mwag with ease, but the second apprentice lost his footing when, having unsuccessfully attempted to snatch the wreath, he landed on top of his fellow's intestines. He would have died at that same spot had the clown not jumped onto the mwag's back and slapped its sides so heartily that the creature was distracted long enough for the young man to stand up and run away. The mwag bucked frantically, knocking the clown to the ground. Fortunately for him, he was able to scurry to cover before the mwag could catch him.

After the fourth apprentice tried and failed to seize the wreath upon the mwag's brow, the first apprentice jumped again, attempting to do the same, and nearly had it. The second followed him, but missed entirely, as did the fourth. Upon his next jump, his chest now streaming with the blood flowing from the wounds he had acquired earlier, the first man did grab the wreath and ran with it to where the fighter was standing. That man touched the youth with his crook in acknowledgment of his accomplishment, and both turned to watch as the other two apprentices endeavored to unmuzzle the mwag.

Taking turns risking their lives, each of these two sought to mount upon the mwag's back. Each failed upon his first try, but the second man succeeded on his next attempt and unfastened the muzzle. While the creature shook this from his face, both the apprentices hurried away from it to stand behind the fighter.

He did not remain at the edge of the arena for long, however, but hurried to face his opponent.

"Now it gets good," said Ofu while almost salivating.

Unluckily for him, a waitress brought their food at that moment and Ofu was not able to watch the spectacle for a few minutes.

Jess, looking around the waitress's side, saw how the fighter circled the mwag upon his mount, tapping the creature with his knobkerrie in an attempt to make it even angrier than it already was.

As intrigued as she was by the battle being displayed on the screen before her, Jess was distracted from it when she caught a glimpse of Ofu's meal.

On his plate lay a small sausage shaped animal whose hairless skin had been decorated with swirls of colored condiments, whose legs had been broken, and whose pink, hand-like feet had been impaled on little spikes.

The poor creature was still alive and began rolling its huge spherical eyes and opening and shutting the thick lipped mouth at the end of its long snout when Ofu cut into its belly with his knife.

Jess, seeing this, felt her skin transformed into a thin, fragile shell encasing a quivering hollow. Her nose wrinkled involuntarily; her nostrils flared, and her throat knotted. She wanted to say something, but found herself, at least briefly, without her voice.

Instead, she picked up her napkin and set it over the gasping face of Ofu's agonized dinner so that she need not watch its pathetic expressions as the man sliced open its belly and tore out pieces of its innards to shove them between his hairy lips.

He scowled at the girl, but she scowled back. The man decided to leave the napkin where it was and continued vivisecting his food.

Turning her gaze back to the screen at the center of the room and trying to forget what her companion was devouring, Jess saw how the mwag had reared up upon its hind legs.

It promptly, though briefly, placed one of its forefeet upon the side of the fighter's mount in order to grab the man with the other. When it did so, however, the spikes upon the prince's steed poked the mwag's flesh, causing it to jump away. It hurled itself to the far side of the arena and then came running back.

Once it had covered about half the distance between the wall and its attacker, the mwag raised its snout and shot out its enormous chameleon-like tongue. This was as long as the whole of the mwag's body and would have struck the fighter had he not adroitly avoided it.

"Ah!" shouted Ofu. "That was good. It's not often you see somebody actually duck a mwag's tongue."

"What's going on now?" Jess asked while sucking up a mouthful of noodles from the bowl in front of her.

"This is called 'The Silencing of the Mwag.' The prince is trying to cut off its tongue so he can proceed with his killing of the beast. If the mwag hits him, it could drag him into its mouth and tear him apart with its fangs. It does happen sometimes. The tongue is very sticky and, if the mwag can unseat a rider, it can draw him in."

Looking at the screen below her to avoid seeing the man's convulsing, mutilated meal, Jess nodded to acknowledge Ofu's words. She was, however, barely paying attention to the fight, being more concerned with a lump of some sea creature that had been included with her noodles but was now stuck between her teeth. With her finger thrust into her mouth (she was, after all, a sophisticated young woman), she dug fiercely at the piece of meat (while drooling a little on her chin), until the flesh was dislodged and she could concentrate on other things.

The mwag circled round the man and shot out its tongue once again. This time the fighter held out his shield and the tongue struck its surface and adhered thereto. The beast reared back and tried to pull the man towards it, but he leaned back himself and gripped his steed with his legs. While doing so, the prince threw down his knobkerrie and drew his dagger from his sash.

He pulled his shield arm close to his torso, seized the tongue with the crook he held in his other hand, and wrapped it around his chest several times.

Ofu explained. "The more of the tongue he can loop around his body the more honor he'll win, and the bigger his purse will be. Of course, the more of it that's around him the closer he is to the mwag's mouth. Plus, if something goes wrong, it'll be hard for him to get loose."

Whatever the danger the man was placing himself in, he continued to drape himself in the coils of the mwag's long purplish tongue.

When the animal saw that it was not going to be able to pull its prey into its mouth, it lunged at the man, but he kicked the beast under its chin and, so raising its snout, jabbed his dagger into its mouth. The mwag immediately jumped back, and the fighter, holding the tongue with his crook, severed it with his dagger.

"Ha! This fellow's good," Ofu exclaimed.

Jess and Uluf felt disgusted. Jess even had to look away before she could continue with her meal.

"This is just cruel," she said, though Ofu did not pay any attention to her words.

With the mwag's tongue looped around him, the fighter rode away from the creature to meet with the armored man who had earlier provided the hooks to the apprentices, giving that person his dagger and his crook.

While he rode back towards the monster, the prince reached over his shoulder and took hold of one of the banner adorned lances that was in a quiver on his back. Its lower end was tipped with a sharp blade.

"Now," Ofu said, "he has to jab all six of those into the mwag. If he can, he'll only stab it in places that are marked by the handprints of the apprentices. This fellow's good. He should be able to do it."

Ofu was right. The man circled the mwag, rode close to its side, lifted himself from his saddle, and thrust the short spear into one of the handprints on the animal's back. Two more times he did this, each time avoiding the mwag's efforts to lunge at him and defend itself. On his fourth attempt, however, the beast was able to place its foot upon the side of the fighter's mount and from there sought to grab him again. It was now so maddened by the pain of its wounds that it did not seem to notice the spikes that were piercing its toes.

Jess, trying to avoid looking at the fight, or at Ofu gouging out one of his now barely living meal's eyeballs and popping it into his mouth, concentrated on picking a vegetable dumpling from Uluf's plate. Her gaze firmly directed at her dinner, she dunked the dumpling in her own broth and nibbled its edges with awkward intentness.

The prince, meanwhile, drove the spear he was holding into the bottom of the mwag's foot, twisted it round, and forced the wounded beast to retreat before it was able to harm him. He then proceeded to stab the creature with the same spear as it ran away. The mwag turned and reared up again, and again the fighter stabbed it with a spear, this time in its snout. The blow caused the animal to shudder wildly, but it was still able to strike its attacker with its claws, opening huge, bloody gashes upon his chest.

The man retreated now, but he quickly recovered and drove his remaining spears into the mwag's back.

As the injured beast leapt wildly about, shaking the fluttering banners rising from its bloody wounds, the fighter rode to where the armored man holding the lance was standing and took that weapon from him.

So armed, he returned to fight his foe.

"It's getting to the end now," Ofu explained. "He'll try to stab the mwag in its heart. I like this one. He's pretty good. I haven't seen him before, though. He must not fight in Jezic. That's a shame."

Jess snorted at him and sucked up some more noodles, although they no longer tasted especially good to her.

The prince once more circled the mwag, avoiding its leaps and stabbing it again and again whenever it approached him. As the animal grew increasingly tired and weak from loss of blood, it grew more desperate as well. Eventually, it jumped upon the side of the man's mount as it had done before and this time it seized him in its claws. The fighter jabbed it in its chest and extended limb, but it did not let him go. It thrust its snout at him and tried to take him into its mouth. Fortunately for the man, he was able to plunge his lance into its throat and hold it back. The mwag took a swipe at him with its other leg, though this had been mutilated by the spikes on the porcine beast's armor. As wounded as it was, the mwag was still able to shred its opponent's shoulders with its claws.

Jess, now feeling thoroughly repulsed, was no longer enjoying her meal. She was spending more time playing with her noodles than putting them in her mouth.

The clown ran to the mwag and started kicking and hitting it from behind. He even bit it a couple of times. The mwag turned around and started to chase the clown, giving the fighter another chance to attack. He hurried after the mwag, caused his mount to jump in front of it, and drove his lance into its chest. The creature raised itself up upon its hind legs, but was unable to do much else. It fell over onto its back convulsing horribly. The man drew out his spear and stabbed it into the mwag's throat, allowing a river of blood to spurt out onto the ground.

"Now that was a good fight," Ofu informed the others before cracking open the skull of his deceased dinner to get at its brain.

Jess and Uluf had both stopped eating. Neither had much of an appetite after the spectacle they had witnessed. Noting their displeasure, Ofu grimaced, exhaled with disgust, and sucked the brains from the skull of the animal he had been consuming.

"I'm going to get something to drink," Jess declared. "I need something alcoholic after that. Uluf, do you want anything?"

"Yes. Something strong."

"I'll be right back."

After Jess and Uluf had finished the drinks the former had bought at the bar, they felt a little better. Happily, the screen below them had started showing creatures like green harvestmen racing. The girl and the toad recovered their appetites and finished their meals while cheering for one or another of the ungainly animals hurtling round the track below them.

Once they had dined, Jess and the others left the casino and wandered along the Serpentine Path looking for a performance that interested Uluf.

They strolled past rows of booths covered with pornographic paintings and topped by blazing neon signs in front of which wiggling, posing human or golem prostitutes stood calling out to passersby, trying to convince one or another of these persons to join them in the little structures for a brief tryst. As they did so, the human whores, all of whom were naked and many of whom were offworlders, repeatedly blew upon little amulets they wore in the belief (or, at least, in the desperate hope) that these would magically make them irresistible, while the golems, who were cast with the faces and bodies of celebrities from mankind's present and past, mimicked the behavior of those they were modeled on, seeking to tempt pedestrians to fulfill their fantasies.

Many such persons were stumbling out of countless bars so inebriated that they readily succumbed to the glances of these real and artificial men, women, kathoeys, and others. Some of the drunkards, dressed in the bright frock coats favored amongst the gangsters of Quanya, were, however, more interested in strutting about and displaying their own importance. Fortunately, they did not trouble the tourists, since they would have won the displeasure of their superiors had they done so, and contented themselves by striking poses for each other. Nonetheless, one or another of them would occasionally refuse to defer to one of his more pompous compatriots and the pair would then either act out a ridiculous display of machismo or actually begin fighting.

Jess, Uluf, and Ofu ignored those individuals and continued on their way, enjoying the colorful scenery around them. There was hardly a place where they cast their eyes where they were not presented with some outlandish sight.

At numerous locations along the teeming boulevard, Jess and her companions were regaled by the shouts, grunts, lows, crows, and other calls of various homunculi vendors. There were porcine and bovine hawkers selling sausages, gallinaceous and caprine hawkers selling kebabs, and chelonian and hippopotamus-like hawkers selling other foods, including soups, sweets, and pastries. Seeing what each of these was promoting, Jess wondered what the sources of their wares were, whether they came from the original terrestrial animals or from unsuccessful or retired vendors. She would have been right had she guessed the latter.

While so reflecting, the girl sauntered under a pair of fifty foot tall animatronic figures having sex (that advertised a brothel) and below numerous holograms of young women dancing, either naked or dressed in fantastically elaborate but invariably skimpy costumes, until Uluf eventually discovered a theater offering a performance that caught his fancy.

Jess was surprised by her friend's choice, which looked tacky even to her.

Noticing her expression, Uluf, as he entered the establishment, said, "A stupid person looks at something clever and says that it is stupid. A person of mediocre intelligence will proclaim both clever works and those that are silly or childish to be stupid. He will only admire what is itself mediocre. An intelligent person, however, can take pleasure in what is clever, ordinary, or silly. He is not so immature or blind as to think that simple pleasures are beneath him. He merely enjoys them. I will give you an example. On my own world, as on many others, sophisticated movies are always animated, and live actors are used only in children's movies. Most adults consequently feel embarrassed to watch a movie featuring actors. They think that it is childish to do so. They are, however, mistaken. Maturity and sophistication entail an ability to appreciate beauty in whatever form it takes and not to be deluded by prejudices. Those people who disdain such movies only reveal their own childishness."

Jess smiled at her friend's words and nodded in agreement. She was always impressed with Uluf's wisdom.

Taking his hand in her own to show her affection, she walked with him into the auditorium.

Having seated themselves before the wide stage, in a booth furnished with a table in the middle of which was a hole containing a glass hookah, all three ordered drinks (and Jess ordered a quantity of bhank) from a waitress making her rounds through the theater.

They then watched as a host of naked kathoeys adorned with feather headdresses nearly as tall as they were themselves and draped in sparkling jewelry marched onto the stage and gyrated wildly while a young woman borne on a palanquin carried by homunculi like hedgehogs and vocally accompanied by a troupe of toads who were goose stepping behind her sang a lascivious song.

This was followed by a number performed entirely by homunculi created from different kinds of birds and cats. The former whistled and sang beautifully and danced with considerable energy as the latter sought to devour them (and frequently succeeded in their efforts).

Jess did not care for that particular performance, but she enjoyed most of those that followed. Of course, as she was smoking copious amounts of bhank, she was amendable to appreciating most anything with which she was presented.

The acrobats, the endless groups of dancers, and even the diverse sorts of weird homunculi were all wonderfully entertaining to her, but the procession with which the show concluded was the best part of the whole thing so far as Jess was concerned.

She was thrilled by the outlandish floats shaped like snails, fish, reptiles, crustaceans, and innumerable fanciful animals, and by the brightly costumed women and kathoeys dancing upon and around these to the pulsating music that filled the whole of the auditorium. Jess was actually so carried away that she got up and danced a little herself. She was glad to notice, when the music was done, that many of the other members of the audience had done the same.

When the performance had come to an end, Jess and her companions, tired from their day out, hailed a taxi and returned to the gate near Vijeihi's flat.

Jess and Uluf then went back to the room behind the russa den, where each collapsed and fell into a peaceful slumber.

# Interlude 7
# The Seven Families

The production of russa is monopolized by a cartel of semi-criminal organizations, the Seven Families. In spite of its name, this group is actually composed of eight gangs, one of the original seven, the Hri, having split into rival groups, the Blue Hri and the White Hri.

### Names
Each of these organizations, called a family, was originally referred to by the surname of its boss. There were thus such gangs as the Ngo Family, the Syong Family, and the Fuypang Family. In spite of this, it was rare for a boss to be able to pass control of his organization to his children. Even in instances where a "family" retained the name of a boss after his death, persons other than his descendents usually controlled it. The only gang that is currently ruled by the heirs of the boss who ran it when the Treaty of Hudaipwa was signed is the Ngo Family.

The term "Ngo Family" can thus refer either to the descendents of Lei Ngo or to the organization these individuals control, including the unrelated members of that organization. The other seven gangs are also referred to as families, and each has a traditional name (one is the Liyu Family, for example, and another is the O Family), but none of the bosses controlling these organizations are descended from the founding bosses.

### Origins of the Seven Families

Eleven-hundred years ago, numerous gangs were involved in the production of russa, although eleven of these were substantially larger and more powerful than the others.

Across the nations of Shokai, addiction to russa had become such a severe problem that all but two of the governments of that world formed an alliance, formalized in the Treaty of Lihaung, in order to wipe out the gangs supplying the drug.

In 1388 military assaults were simultaneously launched in all the signatory states on gang strongholds, most of which were located in the jungles or mountains and were distant from the population centers around the sea.

At the same time, property belonging to gang bosses and their followers was confiscated, including bank accounts, warehouses, distribution facilities, vehicles, and weapons.

Such attacks seriously weakened the gangs, but these were able to retreat further into the wilderness and continue the production of russa. Even with the greatly increased military patrols of that time, the drug proved to be easily smuggled through Shokai's dense and sparsely populated jungles.

Three years after the commencement of this conflict, which had, by then, come to be known as the Russa War, the states comprising the Lihaung Alliance agreed that they needed to take steps to curtail the gangs' access to Jaffrites.

Independent aboriginal states were annexed by human states and the populations of the former were relocated to preserves where they could be guarded.

The number of wild Jaffrites remained substantial, and in 1399 the government of Min began the systematic extermination of Jaffrites within its borders. This policy was promptly adopted by the other members of the alliance. Its successfulness was, however, limited. The majority of Jaffrites culled came from preserves, to which the gangs had limited access. Wild Jaffrites were far more difficult to liquidate. Military hunting parties were expensive and inefficient, and civilian parties were frequently implicated in russa smuggling.

While operations by the governments of the alliance did not immediately destroy the gangs they were directed against, they did further weaken those gangs.

The difficulties the criminal organizations experienced were compounded by their initial inability to cooperate with one another. One gang would rarely help any of the others in their struggles against Shokai's governments. Most, on occasion, even assisted those governments when these were engaged in hostilities with a competing gang.

Several of the gangs were eventually destroyed, including the Sidrong Family, which had, prior to the war, been by far the largest of these, having been responsible for the production of approximately one-third of all russa then consumed. While the Sidrong were specifically targeted by the militaries of Min and Sugudish, their demise, at least in part, resulted from their often violent rivalries with other gangs.

In 1402, fourteen years after the beginning of the Russa War, Lei Ngo succeeded his father Tyoma as the head of the Ngo Family. Almost immediately thereafter, he adopted a strategy different from that pursued by any of his fellow bosses.

In Panjua, the nation where the Ngo operated, Lei made use of mercenaries to fight the soldiers sent against him. These troops were soon supplemented by others hired from among the impoverished tribes inhabiting the jungles.

The resulting guerrilla war cost the Panjuan government dearly, but did not motivate it to end the conflict. Lei Ngo again changed his strategy. From 1405 he waged a protracted campaign of terror. The inhabitants of villages that aided the military were massacred. Guerrillas attacking towns would engage in mass rapes and systematic killings of government officials and supporters of the government. Captured soldiers were tortured and their bodies left where they could be seen by the nation's citizens, and bombings of public places became routine. In one particularly gruesome incident, guerillas employed by the Ngo hung the bodies of murdered infants from the lampposts of Panjua's capital to announce a new offensive.

The Russa War became increasingly unpopular in Panjua, but neither Lei Ngo's tactics nor the government's response to them appeared to bring the conflict closer to an end.

The turning point came when Ngo began efforts to bring the seven remaining major gangs into an alliance. In 1407 he succeeded in doing so, and the various gangs, having already adopted Ngo's tactics, began to coordinate their efforts.

When public dissatisfaction with the war in several of Shokai's nations had increased to such a level that a number of governments were threatened with revolution and one, that of Min, was overthrown in a military coup, Ngo sought a negotiated peace.

This was achieved by the Treaty of Hudaipwa signed in 1409.

By this agreement, the seven surviving gangs, which would eventually come to be called the Seven Families, would be ceded Jongjo, an island in the middle of the ocean, that would thereafter be an independent nation. A council composed of the heads of the families would make decisions on matters relating to the island as a whole, though each of the seven would be given direct and exclusive authority over two of the fourteen sections into which the island was to be divided. One of these would be a part of a city, the future Quanya, that was to be built on the island's southern tip. The other part would be the personal estate of the boss of the gang.

Additionally, the Seven Families would be permitted to continue producing russa in all the nations of Shokai. They were even to be given the right to manage and exploit nearly all the Jaffrite preserves that had been created during the war.

In return for these concessions, the Seven Families agreed not to sell russa in any state on Shokai, except Quanya, and to cease all violent activities within the borders of those other nations.

Since that time, smaller gangs have arisen in the different countries of Shokai to supply russa to those desiring it, but these, faced not only with the hostility of their own governments, but also with that of the Seven Families, have never grown especially large or powerful. Because of such opposition, none of these gangs has been able to export russa from Shokai successfully. The Seven Families have maintained their monopoly.

From Pollidor's *Big Blue Book of Knowledge*

# Chapter 16
# Working Girl

The morning following their foray into the Serpent, Jess and Uluf went over to Vijeihi's flat, after having eaten breakfast and dressed themselves (in a pink catsuit and a green redingote and tan breeches, respectively).

Ofu was attired as he had been the preceding day, and Eshwurhiyo and Syo had both put on formfitting blouses and ankle length, bell shaped skirts. Each of the women had also now gathered her long, plaited hair, every braid of which was tipped with a tinkling bell, into two bundles (that rested upon her shoulders) using colorful, six inch wide bands.

Eshwurhiyo, gesturing to the new arrivals, bid them sit down.

"We've been discussing exactly what we're going to do," she said, "and this is what we came up with. Jess, you'll go with Vijeihi this morning. First, you'll transfer your money to Uluf. Then Vijeihi will sell you to his contact. Once you're working in the Reef, just do the job they give you, until tonight. When you know that Ngo is in his private room in the casino gambling, find some way to exchange places with one of the women working the toilets there. It doesn't matter what you do, just don't get caught. Once you're in, find a way to unlock the doors leading to the main room of the casino. When you do that, give us some kind of signal. There's a huksh table near the entrance. We'll be there. After we're in, we should be able to get to Ngo. Vijeihi says there'll be a few guards, but it shouldn't be more than we can handle, and he won't have any heavy weaponry around him.

"It's after we've killed him that things get tricky. If we can, we'll make him into a zombie and have him take us to the ornithopter nest in his penthouse. Of course, we'll still have to make sure nobody knows he's dead for at least as long as it takes us to get out of the range of the guns around the city. It won't be easy. If we can't hide what we've done, the best we can hope for is either to zombify Ngo or cut off his head, then make a run for our lives straight through the casino. Should we have to do that, we'll give a sign to a man Vijeihi's going to have waiting in the casino, and he'll call a driver who'll be cruising around nearby. The driver'll come to the casino and take us into another part of the city where we can get into another car. We'll have a few more cars waiting after that, and we'll keep changing them to throw any pursuers off our trail. There's a safe house arranged for us where we can stay until we can figure out how to get out of Quanya. And don't worry, Jess, Vijeihi's already supplied me with enough sleeping jelly to keep Ngo's head from rotting. Is everyone clear on what we'll be doing?"

The others all nodded.

"Good," Eshwurhiyo continued. "Jess, give Ofu your sword. He'll find you in the casino and give it back to you there."

Jess was not happy about handing Dawn's Spine to Ofu.

"I'll give it to Uluf. He can return it to me. If he can't, then he'll give it to Ofu and he can."

"Fine," Eshwurhiyo told her.

Jess handed her weapons to Uluf, who concealed them in the pockets of his redingote.

Eshwurhiyo, looking at Vijeihi, asked him, "Do you have anything less foreign you can give the girl to wear?"

"Priyoko!" he called out imperiously.

When the man's lover had appeared, Vijeihi told her, "Bring me something for this girl to put on."

"Sure thing, darling."

The kathoey left the room, returning after a couple of minutes with some clothes for Jess.

"These," Priyoko said, "should be less conspicuous. Why don't you try them on, sweetie?"

Having given Uluf her bottomless pouch, and having stripped off her own garments and given these to Uluf, Jess, with Priyoko's help, dressed herself in a bell-shaped skirt and a tight blouse with a very low neckline.

"Now, the first thing we need to do is to sell Jess to Vijeihi's friend," said Eshwurhiyo as soon as she saw the girl was almost finished changing her attire.

Then, looking at both Jess and Vijeihi, she asked, "Are you two ready?"

Both indicated they were, and so, along with Uluf, they got up and left the room.

Vijeihi took the girl and the toad to a machine where the former could transfer her money to her friend, which she did.

Before returning to Vijeihi's flat, Uluf wished Jess luck. She kissed his wide, warty cheek, watched him walk away, and accompanied Vijeihi through a maze of filthy streets, past dozing junkies and sleepy whores, until the pair came to a structure with a gigantic neon sign that covered nearly the whole of its façade. Although Jess could not read the script in which the sign was written, she assumed that it must indicate that the business behind it bought and sold women who were in desperate need of money. She was, of course, correct.

Inside, Vijeihi presented Jess to an aging man who examined her thoroughly and then informed her that he would be willing to buy her. She thanked him, and he explained that he would sell her to the Reef to work as a toilet attendant. Once she had worked off the price the Reef paid for her contract, as well as the cost of purchasing passage back to her own world, she would be released. Until that time, she would be the property of the resort. He asked her if she agreed to those terms. She said she did and he had her sign a document.

Vijeihi left, and the man who had bought Jess locked her in a room behind his store. A quarter of a watch later, at around noon, a second man arrived, took Jess out, led her to a truck, and drove her to the Reef.

There she was taken into an office and her face and body examined by a hotel worker. He purchased Jess's contract, gave her a copy of a document detailing her new status, and handed her over to another man. This person led her deep into the building, through the dormitory where Jess would have slept (had she actually retained her new job), to a large room next to this, where the toilet attendants were prepared for their duties by a team of gaudily painted, continuously squawking crones.

Jess, having been placed in the custody of these women, was stripped naked, her body carefully and entirely depilated, and every inch of her skin covered with white powder. Kohl was applied to nearly the whole of each of her eye sockets, all the way to her eyebrows, at the corners of which this make-up was shaped into a point. A thin black line was drawn from one eyebrow, along the edge of the bridge of her nose, round its tip, and back up the other side of the bridge to the end of the other eyebrow. A square of dark purple lipstick the width of a finger was painted upon the center of her lips, which were otherwise covered with the white powder that coated most of her form, and both of her nipples and aureoles were gilt. A tiny translator was next stuck to her shoulder blade; a bejeweled ornament was fixed to her navel, dangling earrings were placed in her ears, and an auspicious mark was drawn upon her forehead. Once the women in charge of readying Jess had finished with her body, one of them placed on the new attendant's head a black wig piled up into a tall beehive.

The other female attendants, Jess noted, were all adorned much as she was, though not all were covered with white powder. The bodies of some were pale blue. Others were pink. Still others were green, yellow, lavender, or some other color. Their wigs, likewise, were shaped as was Jess's, but were of various different colors.

She was, however, far more interested in watching the male attendants than in looking at the other women. She gazed at them as each man's body was covered in brightly colored powder, his face entirely painted with an oval of another color, and a wig of tight black curls set upon his scalp. As much as such things intrigued her, what Jess especially enjoyed was seeing how each man's genitals and nipples were gilt. In spite of herself, she was soon moist with excitement.

Unfortunately, once she had been readied, Jess had to leave off her appreciation of her colleagues' forms as she was then addressed by the woman who had prepared her.

This person said, "You will be posted in one of the toilets in the central casino. When you get there, you'll see a row of attendants standing along one wall. Stand at the end of that line. Every time a man enters the toilet, the first attendant in the line will help him. After she's done, she'll go the end of the queue and the next girl will move up. If a man chooses a different girl, instead of the one at the front, she goes with him, even if it's not her turn. Got it?"

Jess nodded and the woman continued. "When you're up, follow the man to the stall, open the door for him, and ask him what he needs to do. If he needs to shit, take out his backside and clean him when he's finished. If he just has to piss, take out his penis, hold it for him, and shake it when he's done. Make sure you squeeze out every drop. If he likes the way that feels, take care of his needs. Just remember, always wash your hands when you're done. Do you understand?"

Jess nodded again and the woman directed her to follow another girl, whose body was colored green and who was just leaving for the toilets.

"You'll be working in the same place she is," the woman explained. "Just stay there and do your job. You get a break for dinner later this evening. There's a lamp hanging in the toilet that changes color. You'll see it. When it turns the color you're painted, you can go and eat in the refectory. There are signs in the hallways that'll direct you there. Now go."

Jess bowed and darted off down a passage under the resort, hurrying after the emerald skinned woman ahead of her, until she came to a stairway that led to a door opening into the toilet.

This huge, marble walled room was, at once, wildly luxurious and astonishingly tacky. In its center was a fountain filled with hideous sculptures. To the right of this were the heavy wooden doors leading to the casino. In the space between the doors and the fountain, arranged around a lamppost whose light changed color about once every eighth of a watch, were a number of grotesquely ornamented sofas and chairs where the resort's visitors could rest. Against the far wall, behind these pieces of furniture, stood a row of male attendants, opposite whom, against the wall pierced by the door wherein Jess was standing, was a row of female attendants. To the left of the fountain were a number of solid gold counters set with rows of sinks, and around the walls of this end of the room were the polished, green stone doors of the toilet stalls, each of which was embellished with golden images. Looking down on all this gaudiness were a plethora of equally atrocious figures resting on billowing clouds painted across the ceiling.

Jess continued to follow the woman in front of her and took her place in the line of female attendants.

The casino was very busy, and Jess did not have to wait long until she had to take care of one of its guests. As repulsive as she found her new job, Jess persevered throughout the afternoon, though, being shut up in the toilet, she had only a vague sense of how much time had passed since her arrival there.

She was beginning to get weary and irritable when the huge wooden doors were thrown open by Uluf. Jess at once felt a sense of relief like a cool breeze that penetrated every part of her body when she saw him.

The toad walked over to the row of women and inspected each of them in turn. When he came to Jess, he said, "Ah, now this one is graceful. Her lines are elegant, her curves refined, and her skin smooth and soft. Just look at her lovely eyes, brighter than the sky yet darker than any cave, her enchanting features, so delicate and yet radiating such vivacity, and her perfect body, thinner and more supple than a ferret's. Now she is indeed a pleasure to see. You, my dear, may come with me."

With a gesture, he indicated for Jess to follow him, and she scampered behind the toad to one of the stalls. Once they were inside, Jess put her arms around her friend's neck and gave him a kiss on his cheek.

In a quiet voice, Jess said, "I'm so glad you're here, Uluf. I feel like I've been in this disgusting room forever."

"It is horribly tacky," the toad replied, entirely missing Jess's point. "Hopefully, you will not have to stay here much longer."

"Has Ngo arrived yet?"

"No, I am afraid that he has not. I have brought you your sword, however."

Uluf reached into his pocket and took out Dawn's Spine, handing it to Jess. She lifted up her beehive wig and hid the blade underneath it.

"When Ngo shows up, one of us will come to the toilet and inform you," the toad said.

"Well, I'll be here."

"I will see you shortly, then."

Uluf embraced Jess and the two left the stall, the former to return to the casino and the latter to rejoin the line of attendants.

It was several hours later when Ofu finally came into the toilet. Like Uluf, he inspected each of the women in the row of attendants, but he did not select Jess; he chose the girl beside her. As the two walked away together towards a stall, Ofu commented to the girl, "Everything here is certainly showy. I thought the way your master turned up was spectacular, but this place is even better."

For the second time that evening, Jess felt relieved. All she needed to do now was to wait for the lantern in front of her to turn white.

Annoyingly, however, for most of the time that followed Ofu's visit, the lamp remained a color different from that of any of the attendants, and when it did change, it turned blue, yellow, and then green. Jess was beginning to grow impatient again when it finally shone white and she was able to leave her place in line and make her way down the stairway behind her into the corridors that ran under the casino.

There were signs in several scripts posted on the walls indicating where different rooms were located, and she saw the one pointing towards the refectory almost immediately. She briefly thought of going there to eat something, since she had not had a bite since breakfast, but she realized that she could not afford to waste any time. It was possible that, sooner or later, somebody would miss her and wonder why she had not returned to her duties. When that happened, someone might be sent to look for her, and that could prove to be a problem.

Jess continued to inspect the signs and soon found one indicating the route to Ngo's private toilet. She hurried along the appropriate corridor, though she did so as stealthily as she could in case she should chance upon a guard. To her surprise, there was no one blocking her way, and, after a short time, she arrived at a stairway ending in a door.

Jess cracked this open and peeked into Ngo's toilet. It was even tackier than that available to the resort's guests, but was completely empty except for a single pink skinned woman standing underneath a golden arch.

Seeing that this person was alone, Jess opened the door wide and walked over to her.

"Who are you?" the woman asked. "Is it time for me to be relieved already?"

"Yes," Jess replied. "They want you for something else tonight."

"What's that?"

"I don't know. Ask them."

The woman seemed confused and unsure whether she should leave or not. She did not want to be accused of deserting her station, but neither did she want to stay and be reprimanded for not showing up where she was needed.

She walked past Jess and started for the door.

Before she made it there, Jess turned her mind to the thread within her and lifted it up just enough to slow time. She did not expect a fight, but she did not want to take any chances either. With a sudden leap, Jess was upon the pink powdered attendant, and, seizing her head with both her hands, she snapped her neck with a single quick motion.

"I really am sorry about that," Jess said (and she was).

Sighing with regret for what she had needed to do, Jess grabbed the woman's feet and dragged her body into a janitor's closet, concealing it behind a heap of buckets, mops, brooms, rags, and cleansers. She then made a cut in the woman's throat and offered her life and her blood to Haya for the goddess to consume.

Her chore finished, Jess slowed time even further, intending to make her next move nearly invisible, and peeked out the door leading from the toilet.

Outside was a large room with dark, wooden walls set between red pilasters, and in the middle of each of the three walls facing her was a door covered with metal panels cast in bas-reliefs. There were two guards standing in front of the door to her left and two more men dressed in the fashion of Quanya in the center of the room.

One of the latter pair was addressing the other when Jess noticed them. She allowed time to return to its normal pace so that she could understand the speaker's words.

He said, "...as planned. Hyan has left to take charge of the destruction of the Llalloi, however, so you will be in charge of dealing with Soniyo. If the popular mood in Jezic is ugly enough and the circumstances favorable, allow her to act, but try to keep her from doing anything precipitous. I want to make sure the Llalloi won't have anything to fall back onto. They'll still have all their ships and contacts even if their leaders are killed. After we cut off their head, we must burn their neck so they don't grow a new one. You may leave."

The man who had been speaking (Ngo perhaps? thought Jess) went through the guarded door and the other left through the door opposite that.

Jess slowed time again and closed the door to the toilet. She did not want to begin a fight until she was ready to let the others in, and, before she did that, she wanted to see what she was getting into. Thinking about her next move, Jess leaned against the counter where the golden sink was set, rested her hands upon a spigot shaped like some kind of outlandish monster, and dropped her head back.

Set in the ceiling directly above her was the grate of an air duct, and she knew what she should do.

Jess hopped onto the counter and grabbed the ornate, gilt iron grate to see if she could budge it. To her surprise, she was able to lift it with ease. It had not been fastened down. Forcing the universe down around her, she leapt into the duct. Happily, it had recently been cleaned. Jess would not have enjoyed crawling naked through a filthy little tube.

She replaced the grate and looked around. Ahead of her, the duct ran in the direction of the room where the man she believed was Ngo had gone, and, a short distance behind her, it turned downwards.

With only the way she wanted to go available to her, Jess began scurrying forward. She was still holding time back as much as she could, but the effort to do so and, at the same time, to creep through the dark, narrow duct soon began to tax her. Fortunately, she did not have far to go to the next vent.

When she had arrived at it, she peeked into the room below. From her vantage point she could not see everything, but she looked around as best she could.

In the center of the room was a table with a shagreen top, and a number of men were sitting around this. One was dressed in a style Jess had never seen before. Another appeared to be a nobleman from Pan Clo, and a third was the man she suspected was Ngo. She could not, however, make out the whole circumference of the table.

Jess did not know how many guards there were in the room either. She could see one standing behind the nobleman and another behind the man from Quanya, but she had no idea if there were others in places she could not get a look at.

Whether or not there were guards out of her sight, there could not have been many of them, and so Jess felt satisfied that she knew roughly what she was going to have to deal with. She returned back down the duct, jumped onto the counter, hopped to the floor, and went to the door of the toilet again.

She poked her head out, saw that the two guards were still standing there, drew her sword out from under her wig, and rushed at them.

Before the first had even realized that the figure hurtling at him like an image from a film played at too fast a speed might be a threat, Jess had grabbed him by his hair and separated his head from his neck. The second looked at her, but he too could not react in time. With a quick sweep of her sword, Jess split open his throat.

Neither had yet fallen, so Jess, having tossed the head she held onto a chair beside her first victim, grabbed him and the other man by the fronts of their coats and eased them onto the floor.

She then hurried over to the opposite door and cautiously opened it to make sure it led to the casino. It did. She poked her head out and surveyed the vast room before her. To her left she saw Uluf and the others sitting around a table.

Allowing time to return to its normal pace, she looked and nodded at them.

* * *

Uluf arrived at the casino with Ofu about a watch after Eshwurhiyo and Syo had gone inside. From the road where they had gotten out of their cab, the pair strolled down a wide walkway that ran through a forest of spires and was flanked with rows of great pedestals whereupon rested enormous statues of ferocious earthly beasts (including lions, panthers, and wolves).

The entrance to the Reef itself, at the end of this boulevard, was set in a hundred foot tall portal shaped like the head of a terrible monster vaguely like a salamander whose lower jaw was missing, having been replaced by the broad pavement. Beyond this gaping, toothy maw, and beyond its scintillating stalactite-like fangs, was a vaulted corridor hung with myriads of fluttering banners.

Uluf and Ofu, once they had entered into the dragon's mouth, passed through the first corridor and then through a series of wide halls beyond it, walking by the countless dining rooms, bars, theaters, and the like that opened upon either side of these. At the very end of such passages was an ornate arch flanked by gilded statues of lion-like creatures that stood perhaps fifty feet tall.

Beyond the arch was the heart of the Reef, its central casino. This was a circular room as big as a stadium. The walls were lined by rows of statues of sensuous women twice as tall as the lions guarding them, and the domed roof was covered in colorful erotic frescoes and supported by slim pillars shaped like trees. The floor descended into a deep pit in a sequence of concentric tiers, every one of which was filled with gambling machines, gaming tables of various kinds, bars serving food and drinks, and the odd lounging area provided with handsome young men, women, and kathoeys ready to chat with or dance for the resort's guests in return for a few kopecks. There was a gap in these tiers at the far side of the room. The highest of these were replaced by balconies supported by a metal framework, but those below were simply interrupted by an ornate portal out of which emerged an elevated walkway, a sort of catwalk, that led to the multicolored stone tower that rose, at the very centre of the room, out of its lowest circle. This structure, where Ngo's private room was located, was adorned with painted high reliefs and animatronic figures of strange monsters whose wings whirled about like the blades of a windmill and kept the air of the room circulating.

Uluf and Ofu pushed their way through the thick crowd of people that churned about this cavernous chamber. About half of the guests were from one or another of Shokai's nations, but the rest were either noblemen or bureaucrats from Nyopwa or visitors from other worlds. There were even a few homunculi and aliens.

The gangster and the toad were able to shove or wriggle their way to the edge of the uppermost tier, where an escalator led to the level below. The next escalator was located at a different point of the second tier's circumference so the two had to squeeze their way past gamblers howling in delight or (more often) disgust, naked prostitutes ready to proposition any person who passed them by, including even Uluf, and slack jawed simpletons who were overawed by the gaudy splendor around them.

Eventually, the two came to the next escalator and were able to descend to the third tier. Their way down to the center of the room continued in this way, as the escalators from tier to tier were never close to one another.

At the bottom, they quickly found the huksh table and noted that Eshwurhiyo and Syo were already seated there. Uluf and Ofu sat a few chairs away from them and began to gamble.

Once they had been there for a short time, Uluf caught a glimpse of Eshwurhiyo as she looked at him. She shook her head, indicating that Ngo had not yet arrived, and Uluf turned to Ofu and announced that he had to visit the toilet.

There the toad found Jess, and, after he had spoken to her, he returned to the table to wait until Ngo's arrival. The evening seemed to go on interminably. Uluf could think only of how ill thought out Eshwurhiyo's plan was and how likely it was that they would all be killed or captured that night. It would undoubtedly be better to be killed.

Finally, after such a wait that Uluf doubted if his nerves could bear much more, a loud drumming reverberated throughout the whole casino, followed by a blaring of conchs. The gates to the left of the huksh table were flung open and a hideously tacky procession emerged.

First came a liveried man bearing a tall staff topped with a colorfully enameled filigree medallion cast in the shape of a rose. Behind him was a uniformed soldier with a needle gun tucked into the wide red sash around his waist. He was followed by four young women dressed in long green coats and tall shakos carrying a canopy over a richly attired man, who was obviously Tsoi Ngo. The end of the procession was made up of eight more soldiers and a herd of priests mumbling mysterious sounds and sprinkling water and ashes about them.

Above this group flitted a swarm of homunculi. These strange flying creatures were like naked mole rats the size of human infants whose fore limbs had been modified into membranous chiropteran wings and whose hind legs ended in hands. In one of these each held a bag and, with the other, reached into that and tossed sparkling confetti he drew therefrom on the procession below.

When he had reached the end of the catwalk, the man carrying the staff stepped to one side of the door leading to the central chamber while the first soldier opened the door and held it as Ngo went inside, followed by the eight other soldiers. The first soldier went in after them, and the remainder of the procession turned around and went back the way it had come.

Ofu looked at Uluf and said, "I'm going to the toilet."

Uluf nodded, feeling glad and terrified that the time for action was drawing near. His whole body tingled and trembling almost uncontrollably. He decided to take a turn around the casino to relax himself.

About five minutes later, while Ofu was gone and Uluf was making his way along one of the middle tiers some distance from the huksh table, the latter noticed that five well dressed men were being led down the catwalk by another soldier, who opened the door for them and followed them into the chamber. There were now at least six gamblers inside and ten guards.

Uluf decided to make his way back to where he had been sitting, and when Ofu returned, the toad did his best to convey this information to his companion with gestures of his hands. Unfortunately, the gangster was not especially clever and Uluf did not believe Ofu understood. The toad did not, however, want to describe what he had seen out loud.

All Uluf could do now was to continue waiting. For some time, he gambled and, being terribly distracted, consistently lost, until he saw the door to his right open and Jess's head poking out at him. The time had come.

# Chapter 17
# Family Life

With two older brothers, Chac and Atu, Tsoi had never had much expected of him when he was a child, and he never did anything to make anyone suspect that much should have been expected of him. When he was very young, he simply never applied himself diligently to any enterprise because no one made him do so. Later, he avoided demonstrating undue competence at anything because he had realized that in his family younger brothers who proved themselves to be more talented than their older brothers wished them to be generally came to an unpleasant end.

Chac and Atu were both about two decades older than Tsoi, and both were the children of their father Duen's first wife, while Tsoi had been born to the man's fourth wife. The intervening two wives had not produced any male children, though Duen's numerous concubines had given his three legitimate sons more demi-brothers than any of them could keep track of. These persons, however, were, by tradition, excluded from the line of succession. (Just to make sure that none of them would think to make an exception of himself, they were also castrated as children. They did make useful officials and guards for the family.) The rulership of the Ngo would go to the eldest of Duen's legitimate children alive when he died.

Because Tsoi was so much younger than his brothers, neither of them was especially close to him, but since they saw how frivolous and childish he was, they did not come to hate him as a potential rival. When Tsoi reflected upon their indifference as an adult, he generally felt a sense of relief, knowing that he had avoided a real threat to his life. He often congratulated himself for seeing the threat his brothers posed to him when he was a child and frequently lauded himself in conversation for the foresight he had displayed in behaving like a spoiled and useless little boy. The truth was that he had been a spoiled and useless little boy who had long remained oblivious to the dangers of his family life.

By the time he had turned thirteen, according to the traders' calendar, Tsoi had become aware of these threats and so decided to stay clear of Chac and Atu. It was also around that time that he discovered how pleasurable sex with a feihi could be and devoted nearly every waking hour to those creatures. Though it was an expensive indulgence, Tsoi's bothers did not mind it. In fact, they were pleased to see Tsoi constantly intoxicated and interested only in physical delights.

Tsoi's existence was soon to change.

The Ngo, during those years, were involved in a particularly bloody feud with the O, another of the Seven Families, that had begun in the reign of Tsoi's grandfather. Over the years, this conflict had grown increasingly worse, and, by the time Tsoi had reached his teens, violent incidents were occurring regularly. One of them was to have a tremendous impact on the boy.

One night, Atu was entertaining himself in the brothels, bars, and russa dens of one of Quanya's most impoverished areas. He did not, however, think that doing so put him in much danger. That quarter was, after all, ruled by the Ngo, and he was accompanied by a troop of bodyguards. Unfortunately, he was not aware that the O knew where he was and had decided to take advantage of that knowledge. They had sent a large number of soldiers disguised as vagabonds into the area where Atu was amusing himself, and, when that man emerged from a particular whorehouse, these persons opened fire upon him with needle guns they had concealed in the bags of rubbish they were carrying. Atu and those with him were all killed.

Now that he was second in line for the succession and so more important to his family, Tsoi was no longer ignored. His father arranged for him to be trained and educated in a far more thorough way than he had been previously. Most importantly, he was to be taught how to fight.

It was in his weapons classes that Tsoi befriended his cousin, Huazheen, the son of his father's brother, Lo. Tsoi had known the boy before then, but he had never paid any attention to him, having been far more interested in his own pleasures than in interacting with others.

Since Huazheen was several years younger than was Tsoi, the former came to admire his fellow student for being slighter larger and slightly better at most everything than he was (in the way that many children do). Tsoi, for his part, enjoyed being worshipped by another and quickly took to the boy who expressed such esteem, although being respected by someone else was an odd experience for him – up till then, everyone in his family had treated him as a hopelessly stupid and entirely worthless child.

Both of the two excelled at their martial training, and both became highly skilled and dangerous fighters. To Tsoi's chagrin, however, as Huazheen matured, he diminished the difference in ability separating the pair of them so that the two were eventually evenly matched. Though Tsoi was initially irritated that the person who had previously been second best to him was now his rival, his affection for Huazheen never diminished.

Of course, he was also aware that while neither he nor Huazheen regularly bested the other with swords or daggers, Huazheen was not as clever as he was. In fact, much of Tsoi's fondness for Huazheen, from the time they had started training together, had been based on his awareness that his cousin was none too bright. Huazheen might have developed certain skills that measured up to his own, but, he was pleased to note, these never made the two equal in every way.

In those same days, after he had begun studying, Tsoi found other things besides fighting and new friends that he enjoyed. He was particularly fascinated by tales of Old Earth, even if he lacked both the patience to delve into these in detail and the memory to keep them straight. Fortunately for him, he had been captivated by a topic that was so esoteric that the shortcomings of his knowledge about it were unlikely to be noticed by anyone. Huazheen certainly never realized that when Tsoi was expostulating on the affairs of the great men who had lived in ancient times, he, more often than not, muddled one story with another and invented large parts of others. Instead, Tsoi's longwinded attempts to show off his vast learning impressed Huazheen with his friend's cleverness.

It also was at this time that Tsoi became aware of Huazheen's younger sister, Hyan. She often came to watch her brother train and quickly adopted his admiration of Tsoi. He liked her as well, since being admired by two people is twice as nice as being worshiped by one.

Not surprisingly, when she begged him and Huazheen to teach her some of the skills they had learned, the pair showed her (although they did not have high expectations of what she would be able to accomplish, for she was only seven and a half and a girl on top of that). To their astonishment, however, Hyan proved to have an innate talent for fighting. She was, consequently, at Tsoi and Huazheen's insistence, eventually included in their classes.

Tsoi would soon put the skills he himself had acquired to use. The war with the O had escalated after the death of Atu and, once he had received sufficient training, Tsoi often found himself involved in it.

There were raids on russa factories in Quanya, forays out of the city to do damage to Jaffrite preserves, and attacks on high ranking members of the O gang, all of which invariably entailed some amount of violence. At times, the Ngo were lucky and able to surprise a handful of men, slaughtering them without exposing themselves to much danger, but, at other times, they met larger forces or were themselves surprised. Then they lost their own men to the needle guns or swords of the O.

Like their opponents, the Ngo were willing to die and often did. They might flee if they had to, but when they could not escape they never surrendered.  Doing so would not, after all, have saved them.  The O would merely torture them to death if they were captured, and it was far better to be shot than to be flayed, boiled, or slowly dismembered over the course of days, weeks, or even months.

Chac did not fail to make note of his younger brother's newly discovered skills.  While he had been willing to overlook Atu's abilities because of the camaraderie he shared with his full brother, Chac was troubled when he saw what Tsoi could do.  He never acted against the boy, since he was still young, had no influence with the members of the gang, and had become well liked by his father, but he did resolve to rid himself of the new threat to his position.

At the same time, Chac was beginning to tire of waiting for his inheritance.  His and Tsoi's father, though not an especially intelligent man and never gifted with an imagination, had a talent for eluding death.  Despite his interminable conflict with the O, the man was never harmed.  He had escaped innumerable assassination attempts and was proving to be longer lived than anyone had anticipated that he would be.  This longevity was wearing down Chac's patience.

When Tsoi was fifteen, Chac decided to stop waiting and, with a group of men loyal to him, attempted to kill Duen and take control of the Ngo himself.  Once again, Duen got the better of those who would do him harm.

Duen had a thread and Chac had seen what his father was capable of with that device, and so he had ordered his best marksman to shoot him from a distance while his other followers attacked his father's closest associates. He also decided to rid himself of Tsoi.

Unfortunately for Chac, his marksman failed to hit his target, who escaped and rallied those loyal to him, and Tsoi, while just a boy, killed his own assailants.

Three of Chac's men had come upon Tsoi while he had been alone in his rooms with one of his feihi.  They had torn him away from the creature while it was still alive, before he had finished with it.  Dragging the boy from his bed and compelling him to kneel, naked and helpless, at their feet, the men, forcing down his head and baring his neck, had been about to decapitate him.  Seeing him apparently groveling before them, it had never occurred to them that he would fight back.  Tsoi's executioner was, consequently, taken by surprise when the boy lunged forward and bit his thigh with such force that a large chunk of meat was torn from his leg.

The man leapt away from the youth, as did those with him, giving Tsoi the chance to jump up and run from them.  He had only made it to the door leading to the next room when he felt a terrible pain in his back and realized that one of his would-be murderers had shot him with a needle gun.  The wound did not stop him.  Continuing his flight, he was able to close and lock the door behind him and retrieve some of the weapons he had stored in his suite.

When the assassins broke through the door, Tsoi was armed with a needle gun of his own and waiting for them, hiding behind a table.  He shot the first man in the face, killing him.  The other two fired, but their projectiles merely stuck the wall behind him.  Tsoi returned their fire and killed the second man.  The third, deciding to duck for cover, was, instead, shot in the leg.  He fell down upon the floor and Tsoi shot him again, this time putting an end to his life.

Even Chac's efforts to kill off his father's lieutenants failed.  Lo, though no brighter than his brother, was not only loyal to Duen, but was also an excellent fighter who was admired by his underlings.  He rallied them as soon as he heard that there had been trouble and handily defeated the traitors.  With the heads of those they had killed stuck on pikes or hanging from their belts, Lo's fighters hunted through the palace for more victims, and wherever they or their commander found one of the men of the latter's nephew, they took his life.

His coup having failed, Chac tried to escape from Quanya disguised as an old woman.  He was able to get into a boat leaving the city, but this was intercepted by antigravity sleds filled with Duen's soldiers.  They found Chac and returned him to his father.

Duen did not think that it would be wise for his men to see what happened to Chac after that, but he did insist upon the members of his family watching.  For the next month, Tsoi, Huazheen, Hyan, Lo, Duen, and all of his children by his concubines gathered for several hours every day to observe Chac as he was fed his dinner, the flesh of his own underlings, and was then slowly vivisected.  They watched his skin being removed, his muscles being peeled off, his fingernails being torn out, his eyes being pierced, the marrow being sucked from his bones, his feet being boiled, and various other painful things being done to him.

In the days and years that followed Chac's death, Tsoi was given ever more responsibility by his father, who was impressed both by his son's fighting skills and by his apparent erudition.  Duen was not himself sufficiently well educated to discern how superficial Tsoi's learning was.

Whatever his newfound respect for his son, Duen did not completely trust him.  He had trusted Chac and that trust had nearly been the death of him.  To provide the boy with the chance to learn some new skills and gain some valuable experience, and to get him well away from Quanya, Duen placed Tsoi in charge of a party of guerrillas he had created to raid the Jaffrite preserves controlled by the O.

Tsoi was so dispatched to the jungles of Min, where he lived under the trees, slept in caves, hollows, or primitive huts, and made trouble for his family's enemies.  He and his men fell upon the O's preserves, capturing and torturing the men working at them, slaughtering so many Jaffrites that they tired themselves from clambering over the piles of the beasts' corpses, and burning the creatures' wretched homes (as well as the storehouses where the russa collected from them was kept).  Then, leaving his enemies' mutilated bodies behind in some wrecked preserve, Tsoi would lead his followers to another to do the same deeds again.

Between these attacks, while hiding from those sent to kill them or simply resting or making their way to their next target, Tsoi and his men lived off the wretched peasants and tribesmen inhabiting the forests.  They amused themselves by ruining these people's gardens, wrecking their houses, raping their wives and daughters, and taking whatever of their possessions caught their fancy.

Tsoi did enjoy those days, though he lived without the luxuries he was accustomed to and was obliged to go days or even weeks without the embraces of a feihi. He would sometimes come across colonies of the animals living in the jungle, but they simply were not as readily available as they had been in Quanya. Perhaps because of their irregular availability, he appreciated those he did find more than he ever had the countless captive feihi that had been brought to him in the palace. He even rediscovered that the body of a human woman was able to afford him real pleasure as well.

When Duen sent his son word to return to Quanya, he was almost sad to leave his adventurous life behind, though he did look forward to returning to his palace and his old habits. He was also excited about seeing Huazheen and Hyan again.

Upon his arrival at his family's home, Tsoi learned that his father had given his thread to Huazheen and was annoyed about this for some while, since the strange device had been bequeathed to the heir of the head of the family for hundreds of years. Even his father's explanation that the thread had been passed to Huazheen as a way of thanking Lo for his loyalty and as a way of keeping Lo and his children loyal to Tsoi himself after Duen's death did not convince the youth to give up his irritation.

For several weeks, Tsoi avoided Huazheen, whom he now resented, but when his cousin, having caught him alone, freely offered to give him the thread, promising not to tell their fathers that he had done so, Tsoi was so touched by Huazheen's devotion that he insisted he keep it.

Once friendship had been restored between these two, Tsoi received Hyan as well. She had missed her cousin during his absence and, now that he had returned, was intoxicated by his wild, rough appearance. She reveled in his tales of fights underneath a roof of leafy branches that blocked out the sun and of gun battles fought in the streets of lawless towns, and she dreamt of what it would have been like to have been with him. Within a short time, Hyan was completely infatuated with Tsoi.

He had not yet returned to being exclusively interested in feihi at that time, though he was hardly aroused by the skinny girl who was constantly following him around. The armies of prostitutes and golems that were present in Quanya were far more appealing. Nonetheless, over time, Tsoi began to find himself attracted to Hyan.

When he did decide that he wanted her, he gave into such feelings completely. He was so enamored of his cousin that he could neither think of anyone else nor imagine that any other being could be as lovely, as perfect as she was. He had never before willingly surrendered himself to another person and thereby handed to that individual the power to devastate him, but when he gave himself to Hyan he lost himself in his love for her.

For weeks Tsoi rarely allowed her to leave his presence. He sought to spend every moment in her embraces and as many of those as he could within her body. Ignoring his father's annoyance about his not attending to the war being fought with the O, Tsoi's world contracted to the size and shape of his lover.

Inevitably, Duen did insist that his son continue with his lessons, that he kill his enemies and that he attend the councils where strategies were being determined. He also made sure that the boy learned how to negotiate with the Llalloi, how to conclude deals, and how to arrange shipments of russa.

Initially, Tsoi hated being so separated from Hyan, but, over time, he found that many of the activities in which his father involved him were fascinating or thrilling. He reveled in the dangers he faced when sent out to kill some member of the O gang, and he enjoyed hunting those individuals in Huazheen's company. The friendship of the pair deepened considerably in those days.

While Tsoi still spent his nights united with Hyan, his time with his father's henchmen allowed them to exercise their own influence upon him. They pressed him to drink or visit brothels with them and, eventually, Tsoi consented. He was, of course, always the focus of his companions' attentions when they went out on their forays to the taverns and whorehouses of Quanya, and Tsoi relished such a place in their society.

He continued to swear that he loved Hyan and would until his death, but he thought of her less and less and discovered that the embraces of other women could, because they were new to him, be far more satisfying than were hers. From spending every night with Hyan, Tsoi took to spending every other night with her, then but one night a week, and then even fewer than that.

Tsoi's passion finally dwindled to nothing when he was tempted by a feihi and had sex with the poor creature. The pleasure he felt when inside of it was wholly unlike anything he ever felt when he was with Hyan. Though he did not love his feihi and he was sure that he loved Hyan, he quickly thereafter lost interest in her body. She had, nonetheless, been Tsoi's first love and, over the years, he remained somewhat infatuated with her.

When Tsoi was twenty, Duen was finally killed by the O. He had taken his yacht out and was fishing with his cronies when the ornithopters guarding him suddenly exploded in the air. More ornithopters dove from the clouds above spraying the Ngo boss's craft with incendiary jelly. The whole of the boat burst into flames, and both Duen and those with him were burnt alive.

Lo wanted Tsoi to retaliate against the O as soon as his nephew had taken control of the Ngo, but the young man refused to act. Fortunately for Tsoi, though his uncle was upset with him, he remained loyal. There were, nonetheless, many members of the Ngo Family who detested their apparently useless new leader and wanted to be rid of any person who would not punish their enemies for what they had done. It was only Lo's considerable influence with his underlings that prevented the unrest of those days from growing into open rebellion.

As Lo so kept order among Tsoi's men, the young boss greatly reduced the number of attacks his family made on the O's preserves and establishments and rarely sent his men out to kill his enemies' leaders. The

O and the Ngo both began to suspect that the new leader of the latter family lacked his father's resolve and that the former would soon be able to finish their rival off.

Six months after his accession, Tsoi, accompanied by Huazheen, personally led a raid on the O's palace. He managed to kill not only the head of the gang, but all of his family and his top lieutenants as well. When he returned to his own home, Tsoi had left his enemies without any leaders.

The O quickly put together a council to run their organization, although each of its members desired to be the head of the family, which greatly reduced its effectiveness. Tsoi, having created a situation favorable to his own interests, negotiated an end to his own gang's conflict with its foes and then left them to fight amongst themselves and so weaken their position further without any effort on his part.

Lo was pleased that his nephew had killed those who had killed his father, but he was not happy with the way that revenge had been taken. He thought Tsoi had acted recklessly in personally attacking the O's palace and did not approve of his having waited so long before doing anything. The Seven Families had always made their retaliatory killings as soon as possible after their enemies had attacked them. They did not use stratagems.

Though Tsoi's uncle had little fondness for such methods, Hyan was delighted by them. She was thrilled by her cousin's cunning and was soon as infatuated with him as she had been when she had been his lover.

Tsoi was not particularly tempted to resume that relationship, however. He had sex with her a few times, but as her body simply could not give him the otherworldly bliss a feihi's could, he soon lost interest. Hyan, nonetheless, did not give up on winning her cousin over, even after she knew that she would not again be invited to his bed.

Fortunately for her, she realized that Tsoi depended upon Lo to maintain the goodwill of the lower ranking members of the Ngo Family, and she saw that her father did not approve of Tsoi. Since she also knew that her cousin was as aware of these facts as she was, she would promise him, whenever she saw him, that she would speak favorably about him to Lo.

Tsoi saw how much Hyan's influence could help him and consented to her plan. At first, she did nothing more than say the odd complimentary thing about Tsoi, but, in time, as Tsoi saw Lo's overtly expressed dislike of him easing, he resolved to make better use of Hyan. He would inform her of his plans before he would tell anyone else and then bid her speak of them to Lo so that she could convince him of their worth.

The young woman did as Tsoi wanted her to do and kept her father from ever resisting his nephew. At the same time, Tsoi started to rely upon her insight as much as he did upon her influence over her father. She so became his closest confidante and advisor.

Hyan, however, began to realize that her cousin was not as clever as she had thought he was when she had been a child. She still cared for him, but she noticed that his knowledge primarily consisted of things that he had made up and that his bravery was not so much a willingness to take risks as a foolhardy indifference to danger (In fact, she was at least as reckless as he was, but she was entirely oblivious to the inconsistency of her opinions).

At least, she thought, Tsoi was daring, unlike both his father and hers. The former had been and the latter still was so trapped in the narrow perspectives of tradition that neither had ever thought of doing anything more than preserving things in exactly the form they had found them. Of course, they necessarily failed in their efforts to keep the universe from changing.

Seeing this, Hyan would often comment upon such attitudes, noting that when something does not grow, it decays, that things never remain exactly the same. Such perspectives naturally endeared Hyan to Tsoi and cemented her position.

Tsoi even agreed to her request to be given command of a group of raiders that was being sent to punish a gang in Panjua that had attacked several of the Jaffrite preserves the Ngo ran there, although no woman had ever been granted such authority by any of the Seven Families. Actually, it was the very innovativeness of the role Hyan desired, and which she played up, that appealed to Tsoi.

He did not regret his decision. Hyan not only proved to be an excellent commander, but she also showed that the fighting skills she had demonstrated in her training were real. There was no one who went on the raid who was as deadly as she was.

Tsoi was, admittedly, somewhat concerned about her personal recklessness, her willingness to take terrible risks that apparently served only to gratify her desire for excitement,( but he could not claim that she did not consistently succeed in whatever she set out to accomplish.

Although Huazheen was, perhaps, a more skillful fighter than was his sister – he was certainly virtually unbeatable with his thread – he was not bright enough to make an effective leader. Hyan was both fierce and intelligent. Consequently, it was not long before Tsoi came to rely upon her to carry out whatever violent action he needed to be done just as he already relied upon her to provide him with advice and to sway her father.

Hyan was delighted with her new position and her increasing influence. She had become the second most powerful individual in the Ngo Family. If, she reflected, she could win Tsoi's affections back, she might even be able to control the family herself.

First, however, she needed to enhance her ability to fight. Hyan had a resonator implanted in her body and devoted herself to learning how to use it. Though she was forced to spend countless hours sitting alone in a dark cell endlessly repeating certain odd sounds, until she had so internalized them that they caused the mechanism within her to vibrate and so expand its potency that it filled her body, she was eventually able to use it to draw the external world into her mind and so subject it to her will.

---

* Tsoi was, not surprisingly, as unable to see that he was being inconsistent in condemning Hyan's love of danger as she was in feeling the same way about him.

Hyan was pleased by her newfound deadliness and by the various bloody errands she and Huazheen were sent on, and both brought her to the attention of others. Although she thereby won the respect of the members of the Ngo gang, when they saw the affection she and her brother had for one another and noted that they were almost inseparable, they began to gossip. This annoyed Huazheen, who would kill those he caught spreading tales about his relationship with Hyan, but she found them more funny than irritating. She liked the way others viewed her as some strange, terrible, but beautiful being.

What did concern her was Tsoi's concern about her ambitions.

He sympathized with his cousin and genuinely liked her. He even loved her in a way. More importantly, he needed her and he knew that. He was, however, beginning to suspect that she might eventually turn out to be as dangerous to him as she now was to his enemies.

Life as a member of the Ngo family was never uncomplicated.

# Chapter 18
# Assassination

Jess crawled back into the air duct from the sink in the toilet and made her way to the grate above the room where Ngo was. She decided to wait there just in case the others were unable to join her immediately. Luckily, less than a minute later, she heard the door to the room below open.

Before anybody said a word, one of the guards collapsed onto the floor with a needle in his throat.

Jess took hold of the grate and lifted it up. She was glad to discover it was not fastened down since she had forgotten to check it beforehand.

Slowing time and allowing space to flow gently past her, Jess wafted from the hole in the ceiling to the tabletop below her, though, to those around her, she seemed to fall with impossible speed.

Jess spun around to face Ngo so that she could cut off his head, but he was far faster than she had anticipated. He had already moved some distance from the table and was thus out of her reach.

Two guards, who had been standing against the wall behind Ngo, rushed at Jess at the same time. Swinging her blade in an arc, she lopped off the top of one man's head above his eyebrows and attempted, with the same motion, to injure his fellow. She was, however, only able to cut that person's shoulder while he jumped upon her, knocking her onto the table. As slow as Jess's opponent was while he was stuck in the syrupy time she had created, he was still heavy, and she, in the mindless excitement of the moment, was unable to push him off of her body. He tried to grab her sword arm at the wrist while he had her pinned down, but she was entirely too fast for him and avoided his hand. Quickly wearying of his fumbling efforts to seize her arm, Jess, with a swift motion, drove the point of her blade into one of the man's ears, through his brain, and out the other ear. He died instantly, and

Jess, squeezing out from under his corpse and wiping his blood from her eyes, leapt back onto her feet.

She looked around to evaluate her situation.

The room had wood paneled walls on three sides. That in front of Jess (behind Ngo) was pierced by two doors, one near each corner. Seeing these, Jess realized that there must be a corridor between this room and the vestibule where she had earlier killed the two guards. The last wall (that opposite the one with the doors) was made of a concave sheet of some completely transparent material, and in the middle of this was an ornate portal framing a pair of reinforced doors.

Eshwurhiyo, Syo, and Ofu were crouched near the door to Jess's left, each with a needle gun in one hand and a knife in the other. Two of the guards and one of the well dressed men were lying dead on the floor in front of them.

The center of the room was occupied by the large round table whereupon Jess was standing and around which the remaining gamblers were sitting. There had originally been two guards stationed at each wall behind these persons, but only half their number were still alive.

The pair who had been posted at the doorway in the transparent wall were currently rushing at Eshwurhiyo and the others, so Jess turned to deal with the other two. As she spun around, she came to face the man sitting to her right.

Jess's stomach vanished, to be replaced by a terrible, icy void. The man sitting in front of her was Tolliver.

He did not look like he was a prisoner. In fact, he was impeccably groomed, dressed in expensive clothes, and was gambling with Ngo.

Jess could not understand what she was seeing. She simply stared at the man, who was looking back at her in shock. There was no indication that he fully recognized the bone white woman in the tall beehive standing in front of him, though he did seem to be aware that he should.

Letting time return to its normal pace, Jess shouted a question at him. "Tolliver?" she asked, unwilling to believe the evidence of her eyes. "What are you doing?"

"Who are you? Jess? Oh Shit," Tolliver gasped.

Jess might not have had much of an education, but she was not stupid. It did not take her long to put the information she had together.

"You're helping Ngo," she blurted out. "You set me up."

"It's not what you think, Jess, my love."

"I can't believe you did this to me."

Jess staggered backwards. Her whole body was so weak she could not even stand, and she fell onto her buttocks in front of Tolliver. Sitting on the shagreen table, she stared at him.

"I looked all over Jezic for you. I even came here to find you. Why'd you do this to me?"

Tolliver grimaced and stood up. "Jess, you don't understand."

With tears in her eyes, Jess yelled at him. "No? I don't? What do I have to understand?"

She began to lift herself to her feet, and Tolliver, thinking she probably intended to kill him, backed away to stand behind the two guards who had previously been behind him.

He looked at the blood spattered girl squatting on the table with a vague feeling of regret, then frowned and said, "Oh shit, just kill the stupid bitch."

Jess gasped and again felt a terrible weakness sweep over her body.

When she saw the two guards raising their needle guns, however, she recovered her wits and drew the thread up from her perineum to the crown of her head, exerting her will on the world around her and commanding time to reduce its pace.

She jumped into the air, directly at Tolliver, with her sword above her head. As she did so, one of the guards was able to step into the path of her descent and she fell upon him instead of her intended victim. Jess planted one of her feet upon the crown of his head and, with the other, kicked him in the nose, smashing it into a bloody pudding. Immediately lifting herself up from that man's scalp and jumping again, Jess sought once more to attack Tolliver, but he had ducked behind the second guard and was attempting to make for the door in the transparent wall.

Unable to get to Tolliver, Jess kicked the guard intervening between her and her prey in his chest and ricocheted therefrom to stand on the floor in front of him.

Before the man could recover from the kick Jess had given him, which had knocked him back some distance, his assailant rushed at him with her sword raised above her shoulder and drove the blade into his heart.

While she was drawing it out, Jess felt a pair of thick hands wrap around her throat. The guard whose nose she had pulverized had dropped his gun when she had kicked him, but he was now trying to throttle her.

She swung her sword over her shoulder and stabbed him in his, but he did not let go. Tolliver was nearly at the door, so, in desperation, she jumped up, used the guard's own body for leverage, and kicked him in the groin. He staggered back, then forwards, and fell on top of Jess, but he did not let go of her neck.

Jess's head now felt as though it were going to burst. She had to make her opponent release her and so swung her blade around her side, stabbing him in the side of his stomach. Her energy beginning to fail her, Jess tugged on the sword with all her strength and split the man open from his hip to his armpit. He did not let go, but his grip became weak enough for Jess to be able to pry his fingers loose.

She stood up again, but staggered a little as she did so. For a moment she was both dizzy and blind and could not prevent the thread from dropping back down to the place where it ordinarily lay coiled and asleep inside her body. Time returned to its normal pace, though only until Jess had regained her composure.

Having once more slowed the universe, Jess looked around. Tolliver was already out of the door, as were most of the other wealthy gamblers. Ngo himself had just dashed through the exit, having leapt off the edge of the table, across which he had run in his effort to escape. All the guards who had originally been in the room were dead, as were several others who had entered after Jess had been distracted by Tolliver. Two of those were still fighting with Ofu and Syo and another two were coming through the door to aid their fellows. They were ignoring Eshwurhiyo, who was lying on the floor.

While Jess had been engaged in her own fight, her allies had shot the two guards who had been rushing at them, but, as soon as they had, they had been confronted by six others who had obviously been in another room adjoining the corridor outside and who had come through the same door the Tozanis had used to enter the room.

Ofu shot one of these persons as soon as he showed his face, but another three fell upon him, Syo, and Eshwurhiyo and began to struggle with them hand to hand. The remaining guards stood in the doorway with needle guns trying to get a clean shot at their enemies. Ngo, meanwhile, was standing behind the corpses of the first two men Jess had killed and watching the battle around him with a look of disinterested amusement.

Eshwurhiyo's opponent managed to knock her gun from her hand, but she then grabbed him by the throat and sent her tattoo of a centipede-like dragon crawling onto the man's face, burning it away. He fell onto the floor almost immediately, digging at his crumbling flesh with his own nails and scraping it off in large chunks.

As that man lay dying, Ngo drew a dagger and dove at Eshwurhiyo himself. She managed to evade his blow and fought back with the kuttar she was holding.

The two fought for several minutes, until Ngo, having seized Eshwurhiyo's wrist when she took a stab at him, was able to pull her forward so that she lost her balance. With a quick upward jab, he pierced her stomach, causing her nearly to double over, and kneed her in the face to send her falling onto the floor.

He then looked at Ofu and Syo. Both were still engaged in fights of their own, and so he glanced at Jess. Anger welled up inside him. It was obvious that the girl had a thread, and Tolliver had never bothered to mention that detail to him. Ngo realized that there was no way he could beat the girl and so jumped onto the table and ran for the door. He was through before Jess had noticed him.

Seeing that Eshwurhiyo, Syo, and Ofu were in trouble, Jess let Tolliver and Ngo escape and went to help her companions. She hopped onto and ran across the table, leapt from it, and, waving her sword above her brow, decapitated the guard attacking Syo. The man engaged with Ofu turned towards her in shock, and his momentary distraction allowed Ofu to run his dagger into his enemy's throat.

While Syo took Eshwurhiyo in her arms, Jess and Ofu fell upon the two remaining guards. Jess dispatched her foe quickly, cutting him in half at the waist, and then helped Ofu with his. She chopped off the man's arm and Ofu slit his jugular.

Jess looked back at Syo and Eshwurhiyo. The latter was alive and retrieving the centipede that was now dissolving its victim's cheekbones and jaw. When the tattoo was back on her arm, Eshwurhiyo, with Syo's help, stood up and looked at the others.

"We're not going to get Ngo today," Jess yelled at Eshwurhiyo. "We've got to get out of here."

Eshwurhiyo nodded and the group headed through the corridor, where they bounded over the body of a man Jess's companions had apparently previously killed there, and came to the vestibule beyond. From there, they hurried out the door leading onto the catwalk. Uluf was standing nearby, his hand in his pocket, upon his gun, guarding their exit.

Jess shouted to him, "We've got to run! Everything went wrong."

The crowd filling the casino was restive, but not yet panicky. Most of them realized that something was amiss, but they did not yet know what the problem was.

Led by Ofu, Jess and the others started running towards the nearest escalator, hoping yet to make it out the Reef's main entrance. Uluf saw the man Vijeihi had placed in the casino for them, and he nodded to the toad, indicating that he had already called the driver who was circling the streets outside to come and pick the would-be assassins up.

Before they had even reached the escalator, however, Jess and the others saw a heavy metal portcullis sliding down from the arch of the entrance to the casino, blocking their escape route.

At the same time, a soothing feminine voice announced over a loudspeaker, "Please remain calm while the resort staff escorts certain guests to a secure area. There is no need for alarm. Return to your activities and enjoy the hospitality of the Reef in the Sky."

While this voice was speaking, several doors at different points of the room's circumference were flung open and troops of silver and brass robots armed with blunderbusses hurried out of them. Every one of these machines wore a metal shako atop its spherical head, which was perched upon a thin flexible neck connected to a large, equally spherical body. Each robot's face had been made to appear vaguely human, but with its large lips, twisting copper mustachios, and projecting eyes, like the lenses of a telescope, this countenance was actually rather comical. Of course, such an automaton's reed thin arms and legs, that emerged from a body that seemed far too big for them, did not help to make it more intimidating.

A number of the casino's guests nonetheless screamed as soon as they saw the robots and attempted to flee from them. Their fear quickly spread and the whole chamber was, within seconds, filled with the confusion and panic of the seething crowd.

Jess looked at the others and shouted, "We can't get out that way! What about the ornithopters? Where are they?"

Eshwurhiyo, who was supporting herself with an arm wrapped around Syo's shoulder, replied. "Let's take the lift. Ofu, lead the way."

Ofu nodded and started running towards the doorway Ngo had originally used to enter the casino.

Before they could reach that exit, however, a pair of doors to either side of it opened up and three armed robots emerged from each.

Ofu shot at one with his needle gun, but the projectile ricocheted off the robot's head, leaving no more than a dint.

One of the robots fired his blunderbuss and sent a large dart into Eshwurhiyo's chest, knocking her away from Syo and onto the ground. As Syo knelt down in front of her, another robot fired his gun and shot her in the side of her head with a dart. It bounced off, but Syo collapsed on top of her partner, blood trickling over her ear and down her neck.

Fortunately, the mechanical men were not far away, and Jess was sure she could prevent them from targeting the others again.

She slowed time, thrust the world downwards, away from her feet, and hurled herself upon the nearest robot. Having split it in half from the top of its shako to its cauldron-like groin, she spun around and severed the head of that next to the first.

The other robots were turning to face her, but before they could she dove onto the floor, slid across the smooth stone paving, and, passing between a third machine's legs, divided the left half of its body from the right.

While the robots were distracted by Jess's attack, Ofu jumped upon the one that was nearest to him and tried to pry its head off with his dagger. The robot struck him with its gun, since it was unable to aim the weapon at him, but failed to knock the man away. Though Ofu was bruised by these blows, he, while still pushing his dagger into the space between the robot's neck and head, shoved it against its closest fellow. That robot fell on its back and lay upon the floor flailing its arms and legs in a fruitless attempt to right itself.

The last robot trained the funnel shaped barrel of its gun upon Ofu and pulled the trigger. Before the weapon discharged, however, Uluf hopped onto the mechanical man and caused it to lose its balance.

As it staggered around with the toad clinging to its head, Jess, having jumped to her feet, hurtled herself through the air and chopped off about a third of its spherical body with her sword.

She turned to help Ofu, but as he had already managed to break the head off the robot he was engaged with, she allowed time to return to its usual speed and spun around to look at Eshwurhiyo and Syo, who were both upon their feet again.

Eshwurhiyo, seeing Jess's gaze, yelled to her, "I'm fine. Just run!"

Jess nodded, sped up time once more, and rushed towards the doors in front of her. They were shut fast, but she cut through their locks with Dawn's Spine and opened them.

On the other side was a large room, and, on its far side, an elevator. Jess hurried to it and tried to open it. The elevator was there waiting for her.

She again left time to flow at the rate it chose and shouted to the others, "Come on! The elevator's here!"

They joined Jess inside and she selected the top floor. It seemed the most likely location for a hangar.

Everyone leaned against the elevator's walls and breathed heavily.

Jess asked Eshwurhiyo, "Are you okay?"

Eshwurhiyo replied, "The robot didn't hurt me. It was just a stun dart he shot at me. Somehow, it hit my necklace. It winded me but it didn't break the skin."

"How about the knife wound?"

"It's not fatal. If we can get out of here, I can patch it up."

"How about you, Syo?" Jess asked.

"I think I'm fine too. The dart hit my skull so I don't think that it was able to inject me with any poison. At least, it didn't get me with much. I'm a little light-headed, but that's it."

"I'm glad to hear it," Jess said with a reassuring smile. "Now that we've made it out of the casino, let's stay alive a little longer."

Jess looked at the dial indicating what floor they were on and saw they were approaching the top.

She said, "Everybody, move to the sides of the elevator and get your guns out. As soon as the doors begin to open, start shooting. Don't even wait to see if anyone's there."

The others nodded and readied themselves while Jess herself crouched against the wall beside the door.

"Uluf, do you have my daggers?"

"Yes."

"Give me one of them."

He took one of the daggers out of his bag and passed it to Jess, who extended the telescopic blade. She held her sword in her right hand and her dagger in her left.

When the elevator reached the top floor, the doors began to slide apart, Jess seized ahold of time, and all of her companions opened fire. There were eight guards standing immediately in front of them, three of whom fell dead, pierced with needles, before the elevator doors were even completely open.

As the others unloaded their pistols, Jess rolled out from where she was squatting to the ground between her enemies' feet and, swinging her sword in an arc around her, separated three men's legs from their ankles so that they collapsed onto the floor like felled trees.

Jess sprang to her feet behind the last two guards and chopped off their heads. These, along with their shakoes, landed upon the pile of screaming men writhing about in front of the elevator.

Before Jess could offer another sacrifice to her goddess, she felt a gust of air upon her back produced by a man rushing towards her and dropped to the floor while spinning to face him.

The guard fired a shot at her with a needle gun, but since he had aimed at where she had been standing, not where she was now crouched, his projectile missed her and struck the wall beside the elevator.

Jess separated his thighs from this calves and divided his kneecaps into even halves as Ofu and Uluf peeked out of the elevator, looking to either side. There was another group of guards standing to their right.

Both Ofu and Uluf got off a shot, although both had aimed at the same man.

This person crumbled to the ground; his companions fired at their attackers, and one of them hit Ofu in the shoulder.

Jess turned to these new opponents and saw that a couple of them were aiming at her. She jumped upon a third man and severed his jugular with her sword. As blood sprayed across her face, she drove her dagger into the man's torso, under his breastbone, and so held his corpse between herself and her attackers. When these shot at her, Jess used the body as a shield and so avoided injury.

She then threw the carcass against one of the men, who, without thinking, caught it. Jess, taking advantage of his distraction, decapitated him and the man beside him.

Four more guards rushed towards the elevator while their fellows were so dying and another two at Ofu and Uluf, both of whom were now standing in the hallway. Uluf shot his attacker in the throat, but the other man struck Ofu in the face with the wooden butt of his pistol, knocking him dazed onto the ground.

Syo met the first of the men who entered the elevator, jabbing her dagger into his heart and bathing herself in his blood. The second seized her hair, pulled her away from her victim, and threw her onto the floor. He tried to shoot her, but she rolled onto the screaming men piled in the hallway and evaded him.

The third man of this group jumped upon Eshwurhiyo, who was standing unsteadily in the middle of the elevator. She managed to slice his upper arm with her kuttar, but that injury only angered him. He knocked her pistol out of her hand and grabbed her other wrist so that she could not use her blade again.

Eshwurhiyo pressed her hand upon the man's jaw and let her centipede tattoo crawl onto his face, searing the meat from his cheeks and sending him howling onto the floor.

The last of the four men who had entered the elevator, seeing what Eshwurhiyo had done to his fellow, hit her in the nose with his fist, splattering her mouth with her own blood.

Eshwurhiyo tried to stab him in the throat, but he dodged her. She only broke the skin on the side of his neck. While rising from his dive, the man punched her in her kidneys and Eshwurhiyo stumbled backwards. Seeing that his enemy was a little disoriented, he took hold of her wrist, even though he was wary of being attacked by another acid squirting animated tattoo. When he realized that he need not worry, the man started banging her hand against the wall to try to dislodge her knife from her grip.

Eshwurhiyo attempted to dig her fingernails into the man's eyes, but he turned his head and she merely raked five red furrows into his cheek.

While he struggled with her, the guard saw the gaping wound in Eshwurhiyo's stomach and, jabbing his fingers into it, used them to grab and pull a length of her intestines out of her body. Eshwurhiyo screamed in agony, and Syo instantly turned to look at her. She could not, however, come to her lover's help as the man who had just shot at her was between her and the elevator. In desperation, she jumped at him as he fired another shot and was hit in the chest for her efforts.

As Syo fell, Jess turned away from the men she had beheaded and went to help her companions.

Ofu, Syo, and Eshwurhiyo were all helpless, but Uluf had already trained his pistol on Ofu's attacker. He fired a shot, but was struck by one of the flailing, maimed men on the ground as he was pulling the trigger. His needle still hit his target in the leg, and the man fell onto the floor. Ofu had, by that time, recovered enough of his wits to react. He bashed the man in the face and knocked his gun away from him.

Intending to save both of the other women, Jess jumped at Syo's assailant and kicked him in the side, knocking him onto the ground. She hoped that, when she landed, she would be able to ricochet from the floor into the elevator and kill the last of her enemies. Unfortunately, her feet came to rest upon the thigh of a footless guard, who jerked at her touch and sent her sprawling onto the marble paving beside him.

Before Jess could get up, the guard in the elevator closed the doors and dispatched the device back down its shaft. Syo jumped at it, but was unable to prevent it from descending.

"We've got to stop it!" Syo screamed in panic.

Jess cut through the doors with her sword and looked down the shaft. The elevator was so far down she could not even see it in the darkness.

"I'm sorry, Syo. I can't," she said.

Syo stood beside her, looking after the invisible elevator below. Jess thought she was going to jump in some deluded belief she could so help Eshwurhiyo and took her by her shoulders.

"I'm not leaving her."

"If you want to live, you're going to have to. I'm so sorry."


# Chapter 19
# Flight

Jess turned to the man Uluf had shot and shouted, "Where's the hangar? I know there's one here somewhere."

"Screw you!" he yelled back from where he lay on the floor.

"I don't have time to waste. You can tell me or you can die."

"There's no way I'm telling you anything."

Jess disemboweled the man, but she did not kill him.

As her victim wailed and tried to gather up his viscera from where they had spilled out onto the floor, Jess turned to the man she had kicked when he had tried to shoot Syo and asked him, "Will you take us to the hangar?"

The young guard was so horrified he wet himself and stammered incomprehensibly.

"Well?" Jess asked.

"I'll take you. Please don't kill me."

"We'll see about that. Get up and take us to the hangar."

The man attempted to lift himself to his feet but staggered and fell onto his knees. Ofu grabbed his arm, helped him up, and said, "Come on. Take us to the hangar."

"It's this way," the man replied.

With Ofu covering him with his gun and Jess holding her sword at his ear, the terrified guard led his captors down the corridor, away from the pile of still moaning footless men. Behind the others, Uluf, having lifted Syo's arm and put it around his shoulder, helped her keep up. She was bleeding profusely and was disconcerted with grief at having lost Eshwurhiyo.

The guard took several turns and led Jess and the others first up a flight of stairs and then through even more corridors.

Eventually, they came to a large round chamber with numerous entrances. The soiled and trembling guard took the group to the largest of these and said, "It's through here. Please let me go now."

"Not just yet," Ofu responded and pushed him through the doors he had indicated.

Beyond them was a cavernous barrel vaulted hangar that opened, at its far end, onto a wide semicircular balcony. Along the sides of the room were various sorts of barges and ornithopters.

"Where are the keys to the ornithopters?" Jess asked her prisoner.

"They keep them in an office over there," he replied while pointing towards a door to his right.

"Are there any guards in there?" the girl then asked, wiggling her sword in the man's face.

"There are usually two men posted there, an attendant and a guard. There could be mechanics too, but probably not at this hour."

"I hope you're not lying," Jess said with a smile.

She turned to Ofu and added, "Watch him. I'll be right back."

Ofu nodded and Jess, her sword ready beside her thigh and her dagger by her hip, tiptoed cautiously towards the open door of the office.

When she came close to it, she lifted her sword from beside her leg to beside her ear, but, as she did so, she accidentally tapped an empty metal canister with the blade and tipped it over. It fell onto the ground with a loud clang.

Jess hurried to stand near the wall next to the door. A moment later, she saw a man's head poke out to discover the cause of the noise. She brought her sword down upon him and cut off his face. A horrible sound came out of his throat and Jess, rushing past him, dashed into the room.

There was one other man sitting behind an image harp (a pair of lyre-like horns set on a stand) that was projecting holograms of women performing various sexual contortions. His eyes had been pulled away from these by his colleague's gurgling howls and he was looking straight at Jess. She chopped half of his head off and let his body slide from the chair where it sat onto the floor.

Jess scanned the walls. The large brass keys for the ornithopters were hanging from hooks in a cupboard to her left. She walked over to this and put down her sword and dagger, after having retracted the blade of the latter. She took off her wig and, grabbing all the keys, tossed them into it, except for one marked with a number six. This she held in her hand along with the wig.

Tossing her dagger in with the keys and picking up her sword, Jess dashed past the corpse in the office and the faceless man dying in the doorway and hurried back to her companions.

"I've got the keys to all the ornithopters," she said. Then she addressed her captive. "Where's number six?"

He pointed to one of the ornithopters. "That's it there."

"Come on. Let's get out of here," Jess announced.

The would-be escapees, shoving their stumbling, whining prisoner in front of them, rushed to the ornithopter that the man had indicated.

The squat disc-shaped body of the craft was perched on four retractable legs ending in feet like those of a cock. From one side to the other of its front extended a chrome grill, above which were six domed portholes and below which were two more. There were a further eight such portholes further back on the ornithopter, four on its top and four on its bottom. From behind the hemispherical windows on the vessel's face, both those above and those below, projected a total of four long thin antennae, each of which ended in a lamp and resembled the lure of an anglerfish. Curled above the body of the craft were two long, tapering wings that emerged from its sides and were composed of a series of overlapping, apparently clinker-built segments. The rear of the vehicle was ornamented with a twisting metal tail like that of a dog, below which was a relief of a grotesque face in whose great puckered mouth was an iris diaphragm. Beneath this was a collapsible ramp that extended to the floor.

As the fugitives came to the ramp, their prisoner, now in tears, begged them, "Please, I led you here. I helped you. Let me go now."

"Okay, you can go," Ofu replied and shot the man in the eye.

He crumbled to the floor and the others hurried up the ramp into the ornithopter.

To the right and left of the entrance were a toilet and a small kitchen and in front of the iris diaphragm was an archway leading into the craft's main room. Between the rounded, concave, wood paneled walls of this chamber, that were divided by rib-like pilasters carved into a variety of images and grotesques and set with hooks of cast metal from which lanterns dangled, were arranged a number of low tables and plush chairs and sofas.

Beyond a second, larger archway was the cockpit with its multiple hemispherical windows. Amongst these, in front of a tall, leather upholstered chair, was the semicircular control panel. This was made entirely of polished, carved mahogany and the instruments were all of shining brass.

Uluf lowered Syo, who was now little more than semi-conscious, into one of the couches, and Jess tossed her wig onto the seat of a chair.

Holding the key to the ornithopter in her upraised right hand and putting her other hand on her waist, Jess announced, "Maybe we should have asked this earlier, but does anybody know how to fly this thing?"

Uluf turned to her and replied, "I have several years' experience with ornithopters."

"Really?" Jess asked her friend. "I had no idea. I'll ask you about that later."

"It is not much of a story. The troupe of itinerant entertainers I used to belong to traveled on an ornithopter, and we all had to take turns piloting it."

"You'll have to tell me more about that some time, but, right now, would you mind getting us out of here?"

"Of course, my dear."

Uluf took the key from Jess and went over to the control console. Sitting down there, he inserted the key in a polished barrel projecting from the top of the panel and called back to the others.

"You would all be well advised to take a seat. I have no doubt that this craft will be targeted by the guns around Quanya."

As the others sat down, Uluf started flipping switches and saying, "Retracting ramp, shutting door, antigravity engine engaged, stabilizers, sensors, leg control, all engaged. Everything is ready. Let us leave."

The ornithopter walked to the balcony on its spindly legs, spread its wings, and began flapping them, lifting its weightless mass into the air.

Jess moved her foot from a pane of glass that was flush with the floor and covered the opening to one of the craft's hemispherical windows.

The brightly lit Serpent running through the middle of Quanya grew smaller and wrapped itself in the gloom of the slums that surrounded it. Soon the craft was approaching the water's edge and Jess could make out the tall towers topped with gun turrets that rose up from the waves.

Uluf called back to the others. "As soon as they realize that we do not own this craft, they will probably fire at us. Be ready for it."

A chime sounded from the control panel. Uluf flipped a switch, and a crackling, hissing voice came from a tulip shaped speaker set atop a thin stem.

It said in Uopa, the lingua franca of the Pancloan government, "Please provide your exit code."

In that same tongue, Uluf responded, "Please wait one moment. We are experiencing engine trouble."

Jess smiled at the toad's ingenuity. His deception would gain them a few extra minutes to increase their distance from the city.

The ornithopter had continued on its way for about another minute when the chime on the control panel sounded again.

Uluf flipped the same switch he had before and the same voice spoke to him, saying, "Please provide your exit code."

"I repeat," the toad answered, "we are experiencing engine troubles. Please allow a moment to make repairs."

"Please turn back. You may make repairs within Quanya's borders."

"One moment. We will adjust our course."

Turning off the communicator, Uluf addressed his companions. "Be ready. They are going to start shooting at us in a few minutes."

The ornithopter continued on its course, increasing its speed as it did so.

Again the communicator chimed, and this time the speaker said, "If you do not change your course immediately, you will be fired upon."

"We are adjusting our course. Please hold your fire. We are experiencing difficulties with our craft."

To the others, Uluf said, "That is not going to dissuade them for long."

Within half a minute, Uluf yelled out, "They have fired at us. I am going to dive."

Suddenly, he turned the nose of the ornithopter downwards and plunged the craft directly at the waves of the oceans below.

Jess grabbed ahold of her seat with one hand while placing her other arm across Syo, who, though conscious, did not seem to be aware of what was happening around her.

Just as Jess thought the ornithopter was surely going to strike the waters, Uluf leveled it off and turned it to the right so that it hurtled through the air just above the tops of the waves.

In the distance ahead of them a great white explosion flashed, illumining the night around their stolen vessel.

"Ah!" Uluf exclaimed. "They missed us."

He pulled the ornithopter up a little and continued flying in a generally southerly direction.

"They have fired a second time. Hold on."

Uluf changed direction again, forcing the craft to hurtle almost directly upwards, and then spun hard to the left while increasing his speed as much as he could.

The second explosion was far closer to the ornithopter than the first had been and shook the vessel and its occupants with some force.

"There are three more volleys heading this way," Uluf shouted.

He continued flying straight into the sky for a few moments. Then he turned again, this time back to the direction they had originally been traveling in.

"Hold tight!"

The craft dove towards the ocean, shaking wildly as a shell sailed just above it.

"That was close!" Ofu said with relief. He was repeatedly touching to his brow an apotropaic medallion he wore on a chain and had taken out from under his garments.

The other two shells passed close overhead, though not so close as the first had.

"Okay, I am going to accelerate to maximum speed."

The ornithopter's wings beat frenziedly and the vessel surged forward.

"They have fired again. There are two shells this time. If we can evade these, we should be safe. We must be reaching the limit of their range by now."

Uluf turned the ornithopter's nose towards Shokai's two moons, which were hanging close together in a gap in the clouds that covered most of the sky.

The first shell passed some distance below the escapees, but the second came too close. Their craft was seized by its wake and shaken severely.

Suddenly, as the projectile exploded in front of it, the winged contraption died.

"Hold on!" Uluf cried out.

He frantically worked the controls as the ornithopter plunged towards the ocean. The vessel started again and the toad was able to lift its nose enough to keep it from crashing.

"We must be out of their range by now," he informed the others, "but we might have taken some damage. I am going to keep the ornithopter close to its maximum speed, nonetheless, and make for land."

The ornithopter had developed a distinct shimmy from the attack, but it continued to waft its way across the ocean.

When she began to feel confident that the attack was over, Jess stood up and walked over to Uluf.

She stood behind him, placed her hands on his shoulders, and said, "That was really impressive. You're quite a pilot."

"No. I am afraid that I am not. The gunners were just especially inept. I suspect that they have never actually fired their weapons before."

"Well," Jess replied with a laugh, "whatever the case, we're alive."

Remembering Eshwurhiyo, she felt uncomfortable even before she had finished her sentence. Then she recalled Ofu's and Syo's injuries and looked around at her companions.

"I guess we need to figure out how we're all doing now. Uluf, are you okay?" Jess asked.

"Tenderized but not filleted. I have been beaten, battered, and bruised, but, nonetheless, I shall be fine. And you, Jess, how are you, my dear?"

"I'm tired. That's all. No cuts or anything. Ofu?"

Touching the medal he was wearing to his brow, he replied, "I've been shot in the shoulder, but it's not too bad."

"How about you, Syo?"

She did not respond.

Ofu answered for her. "I think she could be in trouble. She's bleeding a lot. I told her and Eshwurhiyo both they needed amulets blessed by a priest of Shyammeto."

He held up his own medallion and continued. "Eshwurhiyo was too irreligious. Now look what's happened."

Jess looked at Ofu's own wound and said, "Well, I don't know how much amulets or spells help, but, right now, we need to take care of Syo. Do you know how to fix a wound?"

"No," Ofu admitted.

"Great. I don't either."

"I believe that I could do it," Uluf chimed in.

"Do you know anything about human medicine?" Ofu asked the toad.

"I am a cook. I should be able to remove the needle from her flesh and sew up the injury."

Ofu was not pleased by this comment.

"If you can help, fine. If you can't, then don't joke around."

"I should be able to help. I am not a surgeon, but I do have some knowledge of anatomy. Besides, there ought to be medical equipment in here, and I would be amazed if there were not a device for extracting needles. The people who owned this ornithopter are gangsters, after all."

Ofu snorted in acknowledgement of the truth of what the toad had said and asked him, "In the cupboard?"

"Most likely."

Ofu walked over to one of the cupboards set in the back wall of the room and looked in it. He did not find any medical equipment and so looked in a second. There he discovered a small green canister with a painting of a man who had long horns upon his brow and was riding a creature like a lobster.

It was an image of the god of medicine worshiped in many parts of Shokai, including Tozana. In that country he was called Saagabaid, the Doctor in the Sea, both because he was believed to have died, as a man, while attending to the crew of a ship severely damaged in a storm and also because, after his apotheosis, he was supposed to inhabit a fabulous palace upon the ocean's floor.

Taking this container out of the cupboard, Ofu set it on the table in front of Syo.

"I've got the medical kit here," he said to Uluf.

The toad replied, "Good, give me just a moment while I engage the automatic pilot."

A few seconds later, Uluf got up, joined the others, and opened the canister on the table. He rummaged through its contents and found a metal tube.

With this in his hand, the toad looked at Syo's brow and stated, "She has a gash on her head. It bled quite a bit, but it appears to have stopped now. I am more worried about the needle wound."

He opened her blouse and examined her other injury, a hole in her right breast just above the nipple. There was still blood flowing out of it.

"It is ugly," he told the others, "but I do not think that it is particularly serious. The needle appears to have ricocheted off of one of her ribs. It is still in her breast and has not done any damage to her organs."

The toad placed the metal tube he held directly on top of Syo's wound and pressed a switch on its upper tip. From the other end four wire thin legs ending in little paddles emerged and spread the sides of the gash apart. Another pair of similar legs then plunged into the injury, found the needle, and, with tiny magnets, arranged it to point directly at the instrument above it. Once it was positioned in a way that it would not cause Syo further harm, another magnet in the device pulled it out of her body.

Setting his first instrument down, Uluf picked out another from the canister and used it to spray Syo's injury with a thin waxy coating.

"That," he said, "will staunch further bleeding, dull any pain Syo may feel, and prevent the onset of infection. She will heal now."

"What about the gash on her head?" Jess asked.

"I will spray some of this on there, but the wound appears to be superficial."

Uluf did as he said he would and then indicated that Ofu should come over to him.

"Take off your coat."

Ofu did so and submitted to the same procedure Syo had undergone.

When he was done, the toad turned to his friend and asked her, "How about you, Jess? Are you sure you are not injured?"

"I'm fine. I didn't get a scratch. I keep telling you, I'm too adorable to get hurt."

She smiled and Uluf put away the medical equipment.

He handed the canister to Ofu and asked Jess, "Where are we heading?"

Ofu replied, "Back to Jezic."

Jess looked at him and then at Uluf. She said, "No. Not to Jezic. They'll be waiting for us there. Don't you think Ngo alerted the authorities in Tozana? We did attack him in his casino, kill a bunch of his guards, and steal his ornithopter. If we go back to Jezic in this thing, we'll be committing suicide."

"Where to, then?" Ofu asked, feeling irritated by Jess's contradicting him but realizing that her argument was correct.

"You can do as you like, but I'm going to make sure Tolliver doesn't get away with what he's trying to do."

"What are you going to do, my dear?" Uluf inquired.

"I'm going to Tomasine Station, and I'm going to sell the information Tolliver gave me to the Llalloi."

"Did you find out what happened to him, Jess? Is he still alive?" Uluf asked her.

"Oh, he's still alive. He's just helping Ngo. I was set up, Uluf. He lied to me."

The toad looked at her with his huge moist eyes and, with a soft voice, said, "I am sorry, Jess."

She felt a knot tangle her throat and could not at first reply. She swallowed, took a deep breath, and continued. "I don't care what price the Llalloi give me, just as long as they can ruin things for Tolliver."

"How is that going to help, Jess?"

"When I was in Ngo's toilet I overheard him saying that he was planning an attack on the Llalloi. That's what he and Tolliver are going to do, so I'm going to ruin it for them."

She turned to Ofu and said, "You and Syo can go where you want. This isn't your fight."

Ofu corrected her. "It is our fight. Ngo's still after the Sing. We're coming with you."

The hairy gangster, Jess reflected, was a slave to his prejudices. He was distrustful of and hostile towards anyone who did not belong to the Sing gang and was completely disdainful of such persons' beliefs, habits, and motivations. He was also, however, utterly loyal to his fellow gang members, especially his superiors. If Gople Sing asked Ofu to slit his own jugular, the man would certainly do it.

"Anyway," Ofu continued, "what is it that you're going to do exactly?"

Jess thought about whether or not she should reveal her secrets to her ally, but then, thinking there was nothing to lose, said, "I'm going to tell them that Ngo is planning to attack them."

"How could he? Does he know where their base is?"

"Yeah. He does. Tolliver's got the information."

"That's impossible."

"No. I've got it too. Look. It's a long story, but Tolliver found out where the Llalloi's headquarters are. What really matters is that Ngo can attack them, and, if he does, the people who we all hate right now are going to win. Do we want that to happen?"

"I'm with you whether you're right or not. If you're right, this could destroy the whole Sing gang."

"Alright then," Jess said turning to Uluf, "take me to a spaceport. We're leaving the planet."

The toad nodded and Jess inquired, "Where are the spaceports on this planet?"

Uluf replied, "There are, of course, ports in Quanya and Jezic. There is also a port in Nyopwa, the viceregal capital. If we go there, however, we are bound to be caught. I would suggest that we make our way to Hwiccho. It is a long flight, but even the Ngo have little influence there. It is unlikely that we will be stopped."

"Where's Hwiccho?" Jess asked.

"It is an independent city state on the Southern Sea," Uluf explained. "Besides being the primary port for exporting and importing goods to and from every settlement across Shokai's deserts, it is also a haven for misfits and fugitives."

"Okay, let's go there."

"As you desire, my dear. To whom are you going to sell the information you have?"

"To the Llalloi boss of this region."

"Do you know him?" Ofu asked.

"I've met him once. He probably won't remember me, but that doesn't matter. I know who he is and I know where to find him."

"What's his name?"

Jess turned a thoughtful eye upon Ofu, reflected for a moment, and then answered. "I don't know if it's his real name, but he goes by Buabyue."

"What planet is he from?"

"I have no idea. Does it matter?"

"Of course. You can't trust offworlders."

"Oh, whatever."

Ofu laughed, mostly at himself. He had briefly forgotten that Jess was not from Shokai.

"I have heard," Uluf interjected, "that Buabyue is a Pancloan aristocrat. His father supposedly became involved with the Llalloi while he was the captain of a naval ship. He proved himself so useful that his masters promoted him quickly and gave him control over the region around Tomasine Station. When he died, Buabyue was given his position."

"Really?" Jess asked.

"That is what I have heard. I cannot, however, say with certainty whether it is true or not. Nonetheless, Buabyue is unusually well educated for a gangster. That, at least, would seem to hint at his origins being rather different from those of most of his colleagues."

"I had no idea about any of that," Jess confessed. "I just thought he was an old pervert."

"But you do know how to get in touch with him, right?" Ofu asked her.

"Yeah. He's got a bar on Tomasine Station. I was with Tolliver when I met him. It was really just an accident. We were meeting up with a client at the bar and our client saw Buabyue there. He knew him and so he introduced us. Tolliver and Buabyue chatted a couple of minutes and then he left. Most of that time he just spent staring at my tits and crotch. After he was gone, our client told us who it was we'd just been talking to. I hadn't known. I don't think Tolliver did either. Anyway, our client told us that Buabyue owns the bar and that he hangs around there most evenings. I figure if we go there, we can meet up with him."

"How do you think he'll react?" Ofu asked.

"I honestly don't know."

Uluf stood up and looked at each of the others in turn.

He said, "We can deal with such issues later. For now, you three should get some rest. I will attend to getting us away from Quanya."

The toad returned to the controls and resumed his position there. Ofu lay down upon one of the couches, where he quickly went to sleep, and Jess helped Syo into a position that looked reasonably comfortable. When she had done so, she walked over to Uluf and, resting her elbows on his shoulders, leaned over him.

"Are you going to be okay flying?"

"I shall be fine."

"Aren't you tired? It's been a pretty wild day."

"Someone needs to remain at the controls now, just in case we are pursued, and you and the others have engaged in far more extreme exertions than have I. Besides, I am the only one of us who knows how to fly an ornithopter, unless Syo does. Even if she does, however, she is in no condition to fly it now. I need to remain here. You need not worry about me, though. As I said, I shall be fine."

"Okay then. I'll take your word for it."

"Actually, Jess, I am more concerned about you at this moment than I am about myself. How are you holding up?"

"Well, I admit I feel like I've been gutted."

"I understand."

"Why'd he do this to me, Uluf?" Jess asked.

"I cannot honestly say. All I know for certain – from what you have told me – is that he planned to sell the information he had about the location of the Llalloi's base to Ngo and then get you to try to sell it to the Llalloi. I assume that he hoped that when the smugglers were attacked, they would think you had betrayed them. The remnants of their organization would subsequently be looking for you, not him."

Jess stood upright, placed her palms on her friend's shoulders, and said, "I can't believe he'd do that. Shit, Uluf, I loved him."

"There are people who, no matter how much you love them, are not going to return that love. Such individuals may enjoy being loved, but the person who loves them is never more than an object that gives them pleasure."

Jess exhaled loudly. She thought of how, not long ago, she had been so sure that whenever Tolliver would get excited or bored on some long journey through space he would eventually come to her, even if he did not invariably come to her first. There were, after all, other female crew members on the *Empress*, and their charms did sometimes tempt the captain. No one else, however, was able to satisfy him like Jess could, since none of the others would do the things that she would do. Knowing that, she also knew, or at least hoped, that he would always come back to her whenever he missed the pleasures she alone was capable of giving him. Apparently, she now conceded, she had been mistaken in that belief.

"Well, I guess nobody's going to love a stupid whore," she said at last.

"Please do not say such a thing, Jess. It makes me terribly sad to hear you speak like that of yourself. You are worth far more than that man is."

Jess squeezed the toad's shoulders to indicate her gratitude for his sentiments and told him, "You always know what to say, Uluf. I don't know what I'd do without you."

She stood quietly for a minute and then continued. "Are you sure you're going to be okay here tonight?"

"Do not worry about me, Jess, my dear. After all the excitement I have had today, a quiet night will do me more than a little good. Besides, tomorrow I will show you how to fly this craft."

"I don't think you want to do that. I'll probably crash it and kill us all."

"It is not as difficult as you would think it is. You will not need to land or take off. Mostly, you will just have to watch for any potential problems. The automatic pilot will take care of the rest. Even if you do fly it yourself, all that will be required of you is to maintain your altitude, and that, I assure you, is very simple."

"Okay, Uluf. I'll give it a try. Right now, though, I need to get cleaned up."

Jess gave her friend a kiss on his cheek and went to the ornithopter's toilet. There was a small shower there and she got in it. The touch of the hot water upon her skin was so good it was nearly thrilling. She washed away the layer of white powder that covered her body and kept on spraying herself well after it was gone just to relax her wearied muscles and enjoy the warm streams caressing her.

When she was done, Jess wrapped herself in a towel, gave Uluf a goodnight kiss, and, curling up on one of the ornithopter's couches, fell sound asleep.

# Interlude 8
# The Pancloan Government

The Pancloan Empire is divided into two distinct parts: the Homeworlds and the Provinces.

The Homeworlds include the capital world, Pan Clo, and the first twenty-four planets it conquered. The government of each of the latter is administered by a governor appointed by the emperor and is so directly controlled by the Pancloan state. None of these worlds has any significant autonomy.

The remaining two-hundred and thirty-eight inhabited planets of the Pancloan Empire are divided among twenty-four provinces, each of which is ruled by a governor. These governors are responsible for operations of the Pancloan Navy within their domains and supervise the viceroys below them.

Individual planets are left to govern themselves, and the empire makes no effort to determine the form of government adopted on any world within its provinces. In fact, although some planets are controlled by a single government, most are divided among several states. Each of these is free to make its own laws, to engage in diplomacy, to wage wars against other states on the same planet, and to follow whatever customs it chooses.

Legally, the emperor rules these states by right of conquest. During the expansion of the empire under Loy IV, defeated nations were made tributary to Pan Clo, the rulers of those states having been required to swear fealty to the emperor. All states that have come into existence on any given world after its conquest by Pan Clo are understood as inheriting the tributary condition and obligations of fealty of the state or states that existed when the world was subjugated. While tributary to the emperor, the states of the worlds of the provinces are discrete entities. The emperor is merely their feudal overlord.

These states are, however, subject to certain restrictions. Particular technologies are prohibited, especially those with potential military uses. No state is permitted to issue its own currency. The only legal tender allowed in the Pancloan Empire is the kopeck. No state can interfere with the work of imperial census takers, and all states must render to the Pancloan government whatever tribute it decides that state owes it. The amount of this tribute is fixed by the wealth and population of a given state as this is determined by the imperial census.

The emperor is represented on each planet in the provinces by a viceroy, who is in charge of the imperial bureaucracy on that planet and responsible for the enforcement of all the regulations imposed on the local states.

Viceroys are appointed for ten year terms and must be members of the nobility. Should a viceroy die or be accused of severe impropriety, a temporary viceroy may be appointed for a period of two years by the governor of the province in which the planet where a replacement is required is located.

From Pollidor's *Big Blue Book of Knowledge*

# Chapter 20
# In the Desert

Having stretched her arms above her head, yawned widely, and wiped the mucus from her eyes, Jess looked around from where she lay upon a plush, leather upholstered couch. It was past dawn and the sun's light filled the cabin of the ornithopter. Uluf was at the controls and Ofu and Syo were asleep on two of the other couches. Jess rolled over onto her stomach, picked up the towel she had been wearing the night before from where it had fallen, placed it under her chin, and gazed out the nearby porthole piercing the floor.

Below her was a seemingly endless expanse of green forest the surface of which, like the unmade bed of some impossible giant, rose up to form high ridges and descended to make deep chasms. The vegetation was so thick that Jess could not tell whether such unevenness was the result of the differing heights of the trees or of the shape of the land underneath them.

While so looking at this vast jungle, she did not anywhere see a town or city marring its regularity, though, here and there, a small or great river, overhung by the outstretching branches of the trees, would cut its way through the wilderness.

Even with the occasional break in its uniformity, the landscape, from the moving vehicle carrying Jess through the air, seemed to flow past the window in front of her, and its incessant undulations, like the waves of a deep green sea, mesmerized the girl. Still drowsy from sleeping, Jess's eyes grew heavy and she drifted in and out of consciousness for some time.

Eventually, her increasingly urgent need to urinate prevented her from enjoying her rest, and she was forced to stir herself. She sat up, arched her back, and, rising to her feet, hurried to the toilet. When she was done there, and was feeling much relieved, Jess walked over to the control panel and sat upon its edge.

"How are you doing this morning?" she asked Uluf. "You must be getting tired."

"I am. You should have some breakfast. Once you have eaten, I will show you how to work the controls. You can take over for me until we approach the mountains. You will have to wake me then so I can maneuver through them, but, at the least, I will be able to rest a little in the interim."

"Okay. I'll see what's in the kitchen. Do you want anything?"

"Whatever you find will be more than acceptable to me."

Jess went over to the couch where the wig she had worn the day before was lying, dumped out the keys that were in it, and looked around for Uluf's bag. Having stuffed the wig inside of this, she dug out her pink catsuit and dressed herself. Then she went into the kitchen to search for sustenance.

There was food in the kitchen and, though Jess did not know what any of it was, she gathered up enough for herself and Uluf to eat. After the toad was done with his breakfast, he quickly taught Jess how to fly the ornithopter.

"Just leave it on autopilot most of the time. You should, however, take that off every now and then and fly it yourself. That way you will develop a little confidence about handling the craft."

Jess nodded and Uluf, having left her the controls, lay down upon one of the couches and went to sleep.

About a quarter of an hour later, Syo and Ofu woke up. The latter immediately went to the toilet, followed by the former.

After Syo had been in there for about an hour, Jess began to grow concerned that the woman might have harmed herself. Eventually, Jess resolved to find out if her worries were merited, but just as she was getting up to do so, Syo finally reappeared.

Her face and eyes were red. She had obviously been crying. Nonetheless, from the look she gave the others, Jess thought it best to leave her alone. Being a gangster, Syo was supposed to be hard and tough, but, as she was not able to be so now, after having lost Eshwurhiyo, she was feeling not only devastated but also ashamed of and uncomfortable with her own behavior.

While Syo sat upon one of the chairs in the main cabin and stared out a porthole, Ofu prepared her breakfast and his own.

He was still in the kitchen when the ornithopter began to approach the tall mountains that encircled Shokai's north.

Jess got up and roused Uluf, who returned to take over the controls. His friend leaned against the panel beside him.

The slopes of the mountains facing them were covered by dense forests, and clouds of mist slid through the deep valleys between the peaks.

"Look down to your right," Uluf told Jess. "There is a Jaffrite preserve there."

Jess saw an enormous rectangle superimposed upon a muddy brown river cutting through the forest. This geometric figure was made up of a swath of ground that had been cleared of trees on either side of a tall fence. Within, the preserve was, for the most part, densely forested, but, along the river that formed its spine, there were two settlements. On the right bank of the river was a collection of domed houses and haphazardly constructed hovels like those Jess had seen in Mudtown. On the other side was a much smaller settlement mostly made up of colorful houses topped with wide roofs with upturned eaves. Behind these were a few large warehouses and an airfield.

"One of the Seven Families must have the rights to this preserve," Uluf explained.

"It's a great set up for them," Ofu added. "They keep the mudjumpers totally dependent. There are weirs up and downstream so no fish can get in, and gardens and hunting are forbidden. If the animals want food, or just want to buy some piece of corrugated tin for their nests, they have to sell their sperm. The Seven Families don't give them much for it, though. That way they make sure every mudjumper is donating as much as he produces. If he doesn't, he'll starve. It's not fair what they're making off this."

"It's not fair alright," Jess said in a whisper loud enough for Uluf but not Ofu to hear.

In a louder voice, she asked the toad, "How much money are they making?"

"I am not sure. Ofu, how much russa can one derive from a single ejaculation, and how often can a Jaffrite ejaculate?"

"They can squirt three times a day, and you can get about a hundred spoons of russa from a load."

"Well then, let us say that the Ngo control fifteen million Jaffrites. The overwhelming majority of those will be male – only about one in thirty of the species is female. That means the Ngo could collect up to forty-five million ejaculations a day. If they did, that would give them four and a half billion doses. How much do they sell the doses for?"

"The Seven Families get four groats and one cowry per spoonful of russa from the Smuggling Syndicate."

"I will have to ask the computer what that comes out to be," said Uluf as he typed the numbers into a pad in front of him.

A moment later he exclaimed, "That is over fifteen-thousand lacs a day. It would take me one and a half million years to earn that much."

"You can see why we want a part of that."

"I can also see why those who have the monopoly would be willing to do just about anything to keep you from doing harm to their business."

The ornithopter was already over the foothills of the mountains and so Uluf turned his concentration back to piloting the vehicle. He increased the vessel's altitude and wove his way through the wide and narrow valleys between the tall, mist shrouded peaks.

Over time, the thickly forested vales were superseded by high, snowy slopes. Uluf flew over these in turn and, eventually, began to descend again on the mountains' far side. There, the snows were replaced not by woodlands but by scrubby, sparse thickets and mere patches of vegetation. Even these thinned as the vessel went further south, giving way to rocky, lifeless ravines and pebble strewn sheets of barren rock.

Beyond the mountains and the hills to their south, Jess saw stretching before her a yellowish-white desert upon which not a single plant or animal could anywhere be discovered.

\* \* \*

Eshwurhiyo's hands and feet were tied with cords secured to metal loops, each of which was cast like a curling tongue and stuck out of the mouth of a sculpture of a hideous goblin adorning one of four metal poles. Armed men continuously tightened these cords, ensuring that Eshwurhiyo remained suspended (naked, spread-eagled, and facing the ceiling) several feet above the floor. While her joints were gradually separating due to such treatment, her other injuries had all been attended to in order to prevent her from dying. She was alive and suffering, although, since a gag with a bit had been forced into her mouth to keep her from crying out or biting her own tongue, she could do nothing either to end her misery or complain about it.

The room she was in was large and opulent, with bay windows overlooking the gardens of Tsoi's palace, gilt pilasters of shining red stone, numerous pieces of gaudy gilt furniture, and a sunken tiled area where Eshwurhiyo was hanging. It was obviously designed to be a place where Tsoi could watch his enemies being tortured.

After Eshwurhiyo had been there the whole of the night, and much of the following morning, Tsoi himself, accompanied by his old, decrepit major-domo and a number of servants, entered the room.

He walked over to stand beside his prisoner's head and looked at her.

He said, "Well, my pretty pet, you do seem to be in a difficult situation. I've done a little checking up on you. It seems that you're Gople Sing's sister. Isn't it a shame that it's going to end like this for you? Still, it can't be helped. We all must die some time. Even I'll die. Unfortunately for you, I won't be dying just yet and you will."

Tsoi nodded to his servants, two of whom rushed over to him, unbuckled the clasps fastening his long red frock coat, and removed it from his torso. He pointed to his crotch and they opened his trousers for him.

"It's too bad you didn't take a more honorable way out," Tsoi said while walking around Eshwurhiyo to stand between her thighs. "Now you're going to end your life in wretched humiliation. You probably don't know this, being ignorant trash, but the warriors of the ancient world always took their own lives when they knew they had been defeated. Suicide was considered to be far more honorable than being degraded by one's enemies. All the great men who were defeated, like Hitler, Napoleon, and Titus Andronicus, took their own lives. You, however, will die in agony for my amusement and that of my followers. Don't be too sad, though. I'll give you one last moment of happiness. I'll treat you to something I haven't given any human for quite some time."

Tsoi motioned to his servants and commanded them, "Bring me the juice from the feihi."

One of the men used an atomizer to spray Tsoi's genitals with fluid taken from the vaginas of several feihi and then scampered out of the pit.

Eshwurhiyo's body nearly convulsed with anger and shame when she felt Tsoi inside of her. Tears welled up in her eyes and she tried to look away from her assailant.

Within a few minutes she could feel that he had gone limp. She heard him cursing and calling to the man with the atomizer. The servant squirted more of the fluid onto Tsoi, but the gangster was unable to remain erect for more than half a minute this time.

"Damn it! It's not the same," he shouted as he repeatedly and frenziedly struck Eshwurhiyo's groin and belly with his fist.

With strides so wide they were nearly jumps, Tsoi came to stand beside her head and brought his now bright red face, that was contorted with anger, close to hers.

"You filthy, ugly animal!" he howled at the woman, splattering her with his saliva. "You're useless."

He grabbed her hair, lifted up her head, and gouged out her left eyeball with his fingers.

Eshwurhiyo screamed, though the gag kept her from making much noise. Tsoi laughed like a braying mule and wiped his bloody fingers on his victim's cheek and with her hair.

"What pleasure could I possibly find in that sewer of yours after having enjoyed the heavenly bliss of a feihi's embraces? Unfortunately for you, although my refined sensibilities have taken me beyond enjoying such a thing as you are, my men are far less discriminating. You will be entertaining as many of them as care to visit you over the next few days. Don't worry, though. I'll make certain that there's a surgeon on hand to keep you from dying before your time. You'll live through it. After all, I wouldn't have the chance to torture you if you died."

Tsoi turned to his major-domo and said, "Take this thing to the jail and inform the captain that any of my men may have their pleasure with her. She is not, however, to be killed. And make sure that there's a surgeon there to care for her."

The major-domo bowed to Tsoi, who, having been dressed by his servants, left the room followed by one of those men.

Tolliver was waiting with an armed guard outside.

Tsoi, still trembling with anger, smiled at him.

"Come here and walk with me."

Tolliver nearly dashed across the room to stand beside Tsoi, the guard remaining close behind him.

Tsoi, feeling a little better, smiled again at the quavering captain and gestured to him that they should walk together.

With a retinue of guards behind them, the pair strode out a door leading to a cloister. As they ambulated along the walkway there, past rows of liveried servant girls standing against the walls, Tsoi turned his now languid gaze upon the multicolored flowers blossoming in the quadrangle to his other side and watched the small insects flitting from blossom to blossom amongst tinted sunbeams filtering in through the stained glass roof above.

"My dear friend," Tsoi said as he enjoyed the sight of his garden, "I do wish you had mentioned that this girl of yours was going to be such a threat."

"I am so sorry, my lord. I never thought she would come here."

"Well, she did, and she could have killed me. She could have killed you as well."

"Please, my lord, forgive my lack of foresight."

"Lack of foresight? You came to me and suggested that we use this girl in our plans, did you not? Still, somehow, it never occurred to you that she might turn out to be a danger? You thought, perhaps, that her having a thread would be nothing for you and I to handle?"

"I'm sorry, my lord. I don't know what you mean when you say that she has a thread, but I didn't believe that she would come here."

"You never noticed that she can move a little faster than ordinary people? That she can jump higher and further? That she's just slightly more agile than anyone else you've ever encountered?"

"Yes, of course. She has some special ability, but she never told me what it is."

"And you never thought to ask?"

"No, my lord."

"Well, that was stupid of you."

"I swear to you, my lord. I thought she'd believe the Sing killed me. I figured she'd make some trouble for them, like you wanted, but that she'd eventually give up and just run off to sell the information I gave her to the Llalloi. I never expected her to be this persistent."

"She certainly has turned out to be very persistent. Still, she did cause even more trouble in Jezic than you said she might."

"Yes, indeed, my lord."

"Don't congratulate yourself. Haven't you wondered how she knew to come here?"

"I have no idea how," Tolliver admitted after swallowing audibly.

"Somebody made a mistake. I don't know what it was exactly. Perhaps you were seen, or someone gave you up, or maybe somebody left some bit of information behind. I can't honestly say at this moment. All that really matters though is that the Sing, and this girl of yours, found out about my involvement."

Tsoi gestured to one of his servants, and she opened a cupboard and took out a long stemmed pipe. With the help of another of the girls, she lit it and gave it to her master.

He inhaled the thick smoke and blew out a huge ring. As it wafted up to the frescoed ceiling, he said, "I appreciate the help you've given me, Tolliver, my friend. You've virtually guaranteed the success of my ambitions. Nonetheless, I will not allow you to behave in whatever manner pleases you. I have, after all, paid you very handsomely."

"Please, my lord, I didn't mean to anger you," Tolliver whimpered.

"Did you think attempting to deceive me would please me?"

"My lord, I have never said a dishonest word to you."

"An omission of a truth is just as much a lie as is any false statement if the omission is intended to lead the hearer into believing something that is not true."

"Please don't think that I intended to mislead you, my lord."

"Whatever your intentions, I am going to forgive you this time."

A wide smile spread across Tolliver's face. "Thank you, my lord. Thank you," he cried out in relief.

"However, if there is anything else that I ought to know, you would be wise to tell me about it now."

"My lord, I swear there's nothing."

"That had better be the case. I will not be so forgiving if I find that I have been lied to again."

"Yes, my lord. I understand."

Tsoi smiled at Tolliver and asked, "So then, what do you think your little friend is going to do now?"

"I don't think she'll come back here."

"Nor do I. However, I'm pretty certain she's going to want revenge. A woman's heart is filled with an all consuming fire, and, if you break her heart, you'll release that fire. You, my friend, broke this girl's heart. She's going to want you to suffer twice as much as she has. Vengeful women have brought down countless empires, after all. Look at how Mata Hari ruined Germany after being spurned by Hitler and at how Cleopatra brought Caesar's whole kingdom to its knees when he rejected her. Now, my friend, what's this girl going to do?"

Tsoi blew a cloud of smoke at his companion and smiled a cheerful if threatening smile.

"Well," Tolliver reflected, "I suppose she might go to Tomasine Station and try to get in touch with the Llalloi. She knows who their representative is there."

"There, that wasn't so bad, was it? As it turns out, I've a representative of my own there. I suspect he can arrange something for your friend when she arrives."

"My lord, perhaps you should have him take care of the Llalloi's representative before she can even tell him."

"That would be premature. I don't want them to be that forewarned. By the time your little friend arrives, there won't be much the Llalloi can do. If I kill one of them now, I might as well announce I'm planning to start a war. It's enough that we stop your girl from making more trouble."

* * *

"We seem to be losing power," Uluf told the others. "According to the instruments, the battery is not functioning properly."

Ofu asked him, "Can we make it to Hwiccho?"

"Not a chance. If the power continues to decrease at the rate it is now, the engines will stall within two hours. We need to find a new battery."

Walking over to stand behind the toad, Ofu suggested, "Check the computer for any settlements nearby. There are mining colonies scattered all over the desert. We might be able to get a battery from one of them."

Uluf spoke into a brass trumpet set atop an S-shaped copper stem rising from the control panel in front of him.

He said, "Show a map extending from our current location to points six-hundred miles to the south, east, and west. Include all settlements."

The image harp rising from the back of the panel, between the windows at the vehicle's front, immediately projected a map between its two horns.

"There," Uluf said, "about three-hundred miles to the south-west, on the edge of that range of mountains. Give me information on the settlement 'Shadow Chasm.'"

In a soft, feminine voice, the computer replied, "Shadow Chasm – mining colony – population variable. Highest recorded population: three-hundred and eleven; Lowest recorded population: nine. Owned and governed by Chac Wismang, brother of the roshpai of Min. Currently designated as an area of high danger due to recent conflicts with the local maruvazi population."

"We will land there," announced Uluf. "I am sure they must have ornithopters or barges, so they must have batteries."

"They're not going to give them to us," Ofu told him.

"Then we will have to try to buy them."

"I doubt if they'll sell. They won't want to risk being stuck out here in the desert without a way back. Besides, Ngo has probably contacted the government of Min and put a bounty on us. If they've got word of that down here, they'll kill us as soon as they see us."

Jess sauntered over from where she had been sitting to join the other two. Standing beside Uluf with her arms akimbo, she announced, "Let's steal it, then. Or maybe we can just take their ornithopter, if they have one."

Ofu laughed and said, "Yeah. We could do that. But what if we're seen? There could be three-hundred miners there. Are you going to fight them all?"

"Well, obviously, I'm not planning to just walk in and announce: 'I'm stealing your ornithopter now. Take care.'"

"Do you have an idea what you could do?"

Sticking out her tongue and rolling her eyes, Jess turned to Uluf and asked him, "Uluf, can you show me a close-up map of the colony?"

"Show a map of the area within five miles of Shadow Chasm," he told the computer.

The colony was located in a deep valley. It was surrounded on three sides by mountains and was open on the fourth.

"Uluf," Jess said while pointing to the map, "Do you see that mountain just to the north of the colony?"

"Yes."

"There's a valley on this side of it. If you bring the ornithopter in low, behind the mountains, you should be able to land there undetected. I doubt if anyone in a place like that pays much attention to who's flying around.

"By the time we get there, it'll be close to nightfall. Once it gets dark, two of us could try to sneak up to the hangar in the colony through the open end of the valley. The other two could take some guns, hike over this low part of the mountain, and hide along the top of the ridge overlooking the settlement. If the two who go in have a problem, the two on the ridge can cover them. Depending on whether there's an ornithopter or a barge there, whoever goes in can pick the others up or meet them where we land this thing. So, what do you think?"

Ofu looked at her skeptically.

"Who's going in and who's covering?"

"What do you think's best, Ofu?"

"Syo and I will cover you and the toad."

"Fine."

* * *

After Uluf had landed the ornithopter where Jess had suggested, the four fugitives dressed themselves in hotsuits they found stored in the vessel.

These were green, billow pleated garments that covered the whole of the body and were each topped by a cylindrical, tinted glass helmet set beneath a wide conical plastic hat. A network of coolant filled conduits ran through the fabric of each suit and enabled the wearer to endure the extreme temperatures of Shokai's desert.

Syo had partially regained her composure and she and Ofu armed themselves with needle rifles they discovered stored with the hotsuits. The members of the group then made sure their timepieces were synchronized. They had agreed that Jess and Uluf would try to enter the hangar as soon after the beginning of the seventh watch as was possible.

The girl and the toad set out on their walk around the mountain between the ornithopter and Shadow Chasm, and the other two departed on their own walk over the peak.

The sun was low in the sky already, so that the boulders strewn across the lifeless yellow plain stretching out to Jess's left cast long shadows. These contrasted so sharply with the blinding brilliance of the pebbles around them, which were reflecting the sun's rays, that they seemed like innumerable caves or bottomless voids, pure nothings of absolute darkness in a world of agonizing light.

Jess realized that without her tinted helmet it would be nearly impossible to see in the desert.

Of course, the place was as hot as it was brightly lit. Even with the coolant flowing through her hotsuit, Jess was soon sweating as she trudged across the uneven rocky waste. Fortunately, before long, the descending sun was hidden by one of the mountains, and this spread its shadow over Jess and Uluf's path.

They continued on their way around the spur of the mountain until they came to its southern face. In front of them was a valley bounded, to the north, south, and west, by steep rocky cliffs. Beneath the southern wall numerous rough stone buildings connected by passageways were clustered. Several of these structures were clearly living quarters, but there were also a number of larger buildings, one of which appeared to be a refinery and the others warehouses. In the very middle of the valley, surrounded by a fence, was an airfield, and, to the west of this, a hangar.

Jess and Uluf crept into a ravine they discovered near the mouth of the valley and sat there to wait until it was time for them to act.

While they did so, they kept an eye on the colony, but there did not appear to be any activity. The western cliff had already covered the little town with its shadow and there were lights visible in a number of small round windows, although not a single person could anywhere be seen.

Bored with waiting, Jess closed her eyes to get a little rest while Uluf kept watch. She was just dozing off when she felt the toad tapping her shoulder.

Jess looked at him and he indicated that she should look into the valley. Her heart sank as soon as she did. Five miners were walking down a cutback that ran up the face of the northern cliff. In front of them, their torsos bound from waist to shoulders with ropes, were Syo and Ofu.

"Oh great," Jess sighed. "This is going to make things more complicated."

She continued to watch as Ofu and Syo were taken into the colony. Then she turned to Uluf and said, "Let's just wait here until later. I guess we'll have to break into Shadow Chasm and try to get them out. Keep an eye out for any stray miners."

The two remained concealed in the ravine well past the seventh watch and the descent of night. They were hoping to see some indication that the miners were asleep, but the lights in the little round windows all remained lit.

Jess was growing tired. She rested her head upon her hands and lay upon the rocky slope of the ravine gazing at the colony.

Suddenly she felt hands grasping her arms, another wrapping around her throat, and a sharp instrument pressing into her back between her shoulder blades.

She could not act quick enough to prevent her attacker from stabbing her, so she remained still. The hands pulled her back, lifted her up, and threw her onto the ground.

Rolling over when she struck the pebbly soil, Jess was able to turn her head. Standing over her and Uluf, who had also been captured, was a mob of huge kangaroo-like creatures covered with warty, overlapping plates of leathery skin. She had never seen such beings before, but she immediately knew they must be maruvazi.

In spite of her situation, Jess could not keep herself from being impressed by her captors' stealth. She had not heard a sound when they were approaching, and they were far larger than was any human being.

They did not leave her to her thoughts for long. Almost as soon as their prisoner's backside hit the earth, the maruvazi were removing her helmet, placing a gag in her mouth, and binding her hands behind her back while pointing long metal spears at various points on her body. There was nothing she could do to resist them.

One of the maruvazi raised her shoulders off the earth and a second placed a leathern bag over her head. Jess's brief feelings of admiration began to give way to terror. The creatures clearly did not intend to kill her immediately, but she had no idea what they were going to do with her. She wondered if, perhaps, they might eat her or torture her for their amusement.

Such thoughts occupied her mind only briefly, however, for one of the maruvazi lifted her up by her feet and handed her to one of his fellows, who wrapped his arms around the girl's torso and held her upside down against his body.

Jess felt herself being carried by the huge beasts as they crept out of the ravine and across the plain beyond the mouth of the valley. Once they had gone a distance, they began to race over the desert with tremendous jarring hops that so rattled Jess she soon lost consciousness.

## Chapter 21
## Under the Sands

When Jess awoke, she found herself immersed in darkness. She blinked her eyes and tried to rub them, but her hands were tied behind her back. She remembered what had happened and realized that her head was still inside of a leathern bag.

The maruvazi were crawling instead of hopping, and she could hear them speaking to one another with breathy whistles punctuated by metallic dings.

Jess was being held upright now, but she still felt dizzy and confused from having been inverted and then shaken like a cruet. She attempted to collect her wits and to wriggle her limbs to keep them from going to sleep. Her bonds were so tight, however, that her efforts had little effect.

A few minutes later, the maruvazi holding Jess placed her upon the stone ground and removed the bag from her head.

She could see little in the dim light being given off by the foul smelling mineral burning in a pair of braziers to either side of her, but eventually discerned that she was in a room hollowed out of living stone. Uluf was sitting on the floor beside her, and there were a number of maruvazi squatting around the two of them, several of whom were pointing metal spears at their captives.

Two of those holding such weapons were standing directly in front of the girl and the toad, between them and five more maruvazi. These sat in a row near the wall of the cave, their legs sticking straight out in front of their stout bodies in an oddly comical way. Each member of this group was adorned with a plethora of bone ornaments, wore a complex apron or robe similarly made of bone, and held a long thin bone that had been sharpened at one end so that it resembled a gigantic ice pick.

One of these individuals was also holding an ancient translator tied to the top of a staff. The creature whistled into this and a crackling voice came out in a language that Jess's own translator identified and changed into her own.

The maruvazi in this way said to his prisoners, "Why were you watching the humans' buildings?"

Before Jess could reply, Uluf spoke up. "Two of our friends have been captured by those persons. It is incumbent upon us to save them."

The maruvazi replied. "We saw them watching the town as well. Why did you come here?"

"Our ornithopter is damaged and we needed a battery from the colonists."

"You came to trade with them?"

"No. We came to attack them and to take what we need."

The maruvazi switched off the active mode of the translator, and he and the other four garbed in bones spoke amongst themselves for some time.

Jess eventually grew impatient and blurted out, "Why did you attack us? What did we do to you?"

The five maruvazi looked at the girl, and the one with the translator switched the device back on and addressed her.

"You dirty our water. You hunt us while we travel across the desert. You gas our warrens."

"I haven't done any of that!" Jess shouted at her accuser.

"The humans in the valley are not our allies," Uluf added.

The maruvazi again spoke amongst themselves for a time, and, while they did so, Uluf looked at Jess in such a way as to indicate to her that she should remain quiet.

When the maruvazi with the translator spoke again, he said, "We agree that it does not seem that you belong to the same warren as the humans in the valley. If you did, you would not have been hiding and watching them from a distance, nor would they have bound your friends as they did. This could, however, be trickery."

Jess, having already forgotten Uluf's admonition, asked, "What do we have to do to convince you we're telling the truth?"

"Do you have human weapons?"

"My friend," Jess replied, "has a needle gun, and I have a sword."

"Are these all you have?"

"There are more guns in the ornithopter."

The members of the maruvazi council again spoke to one another with the translator off. When they switched it back on, the one holding it said, "We have often traded with humans at their settlements, and we will trade with you. If you will give us your weapons, we will release you to rescue your companions."

Jess answered, "We need weapons to get them out, but we'll give you what's in the ornithopter."

"That is acceptable to us, so long as you take us to the ornithopter before going to the town. That way, if you betray us, we will be able to defend ourselves."

"That's fine. It's a deal, then. Now, could you untie us? I can't really feel my hands anymore."

The maruvazi councilor addressed the guards standing over Jess and Uluf, and two of these knelt down and cut the prisoners' bonds with the blades of their spears.

"Thank you," said Uluf.

"Thanks," said Jess.

The bone clad maruvazi addressed the girl and the toad. "If we are to be allies, you will share our warren with us tonight."

"I appreciate that," Jess told him, "but we have to help our friends."

"You must wait until tomorrow."

"We can't do that."

"A dust cloud is coming. It will cover the stars tonight. Traveling is polluting now."

"You don't understand. The miners could kill them."

"Do you desire to be polluted by the spirits in the dust?"

"What do you mean?"

Uluf answered before the maruvazi could. "I believe they must have some sort of religious prohibition, a taboo, about going out when dust covers the sky."

"That's silly," Jess told him.

"Not at all, my dear. Actually, it seems a very practical belief. If one is not motivated by wisdom, one may still be motivated by fear of a bogeyman. When the stars are covered the maruvazi cannot use them to navigate, so it is not wise to go out and travel at such times. A little added dose of fear about spirits will fortify that prudence."

"We still need to go out."

"I do not think that they are going to let us do so until the dust cloud passes and they are willing to go to the ornithopter themselves."

"Okay," she replied to the toad and, turning to the maruvazi councilors, said to them, "We'll wait and do what you want."

The maruvazi looked at her and said, "Our agreement is concluded, then. Now, we must wait until the proper time. In the interim, you will remain here. I name Emerald to be your brother. He will attend to your needs while you stay with us."

One of the guards behind Jess crept over to the councilor with the translator, took it from him, and spoke into it.

He said, "I am Emerald. Follow me. I will give you food and a place to rest."

Jess and Uluf stood, though both staggered a little when they did, and walked behind Emerald towards a tunnel leading off from the room they were in.

It was narrow and completely black inside, but Emerald entered it without hesitation.

"Wait a second," Jess called after him. "I can't see anything."

"Is there something you require?"

"Light, if you don't mind."

Emerald stood in the mouth of the passageway looking at her.

"I can't see in the dark."

He still stood looking at her.

"I'm sorry. I can't find my way in the dark like you can."

"You cannot feel the earth and hear the echoes bouncing from it?"

"No. I'm sorry. I can't."

Emerald walked over to one of the braziers, picked up a sort of metal shovel lying on the floor beside it, and scooped up some of the burning mineral to use as a lamp.

As he returned to the tunnel, Jess asked him, "If you don't need light, why do you use that stuff?"

"We prefer to see if we can."

"You don't need it, though?"

"We need it for certain things."

"But not for everyday life?"

"This mineral must be mined. It is used only in the chamber of the warren council, on certain occasions, or when we perform a task requiring illumination. At other times, we do not fill our homes with light."

Jess nodded and the maruvazi led her and Uluf down the tunnel. Its rounded walls had been bored through solid rock and were worn very smooth. The warren, Jess realized, must have been very old.

She and the others continued on a gentle slope downward for several minutes, until they came to a junction with four more tunnels. Emerald went down one of these, which, eventually, opened onto a natural cavern.

With only the shovel full of dimly burning mineral to light this place, Jess could see little of it. Directly in front of her she could make out a slow moving river, and, from the sounds of the waters, she gathered it was fairly wide. The cavern extended along the bank of this stream, to Jess's right and left, though how far it went, she had no idea. Nor could she make out the roof. The light of the lamp did not penetrate that far into the gloom. She could, however, tell from the echoes of the stream resounding around her that the chamber was both very long and very tall.

Along the bank of the river, in front of a series of cage-like barriers sunk in the water, she saw a number of maruvazi squatting while holding long metal poles that ended in baskets of wire mesh. They dipped these in the stream before them and drew out white or translucent aquatic creatures vaguely similar both to fish and to insects, which they dropped into pots set on the slimy, cold stone floor.

Emerald, turning to his right, led Jess and Uluf along an even, well worn road that had been cut into the tiny hillocks and valleys that made up the ground of the riparian cavern. This path ran parallel with the river for a surprising distance. The cavern must have been over a quarter of a mile long.

Eventually, the trail veered to the left and came to an arched bridge that spanned the stream. Jess and the others crossed this and arrived, at the other side, in front of a tall portico made with columns carved into a variety of peculiar figures. Neither Jess nor Uluf was certain if these were realistic depictions of creatures the maruvazi were familiar with, beasts born of their imaginations, or abstractions.

Whatever the figures were, Emerald led his guests past them and into a wide tunnel along either side of which were numerous smaller passageways. From the noises coming from these, Jess gathered that they must be the homes of some of the residents of the warren.

Once they had traveled past at least fifty such tunnels, Emerald ducked into one on his left and continued down it for about fifty feet.

The tunnel ended in a smallish room with more tunnels leading from it. In the middle of the room, two small, immature maruvazi were squatting upon leathern pillows inflated with air and chewing upon strips of leather. Behind them was a well topped with a windlass fixed with a leathern cord tied to a leathern bladder, and along all the walls were piled a variety of tools whose functions Jess did not know.

Uluf noted a niche cut in the wall to his left that was filled with bundles of leathern strips. He walked over to this and looked at the strips. Each had been worked with some tool so that it was adorned with a series of raised designs.

The toad turned to his host and asked, "May I inquire of you, what are these?"

"Books."

"Ah," replied the toad. "I thought as much. You read with your fingers, correct?"

"Yes, of course."

"That way you can read in the dark. You have no need of light. How wonderfully clever."

Emerald turned to his guests and said, "You may rest here. I will attend to your food."

He set the lamp he was carrying on a stone shelf and left the room through one of the other doors.

Both Jess and Uluf, having stripped off their hotsuits, sat down naked in front of the two young maruvazi, who stared at them intently but did not approach them.

Several minutes later, Emerald returned with a female maruvazi. She was carrying a large bowl made of leather stretched over a framework of bone, and this was filled with a greyish paste composed of raw, pulverized meat (from the fish-like creatures Jess had earlier seen being drawn from the underground river).

She placed the bowl in the middle of the room, and all the maruvazi gathered round it. Emerald, having laid the translator across his thighs, beckoned to Uluf and Jess to join them. The maruvazi dipped their fingers into the paste and scooped up heaps of it to eat. The girl and the toad were both reluctant to follow their example, but as neither dared refuse their hosts' hospitality, they dug their own fingers into the cold, oily mush and tasted it.

To her surprise, Jess found the paste was not repulsive. In fact, after the first few bites, she actually started enjoying it.

She was curious to ask Emerald why his people would not travel while there was a dust cloud in the sky, but since neither he nor any other member of his family was speaking, she thought it wise to remain silent herself. Perhaps, she thought, it was not considered appropriate amongst the folk of this tribe to speak while eating.

When the fish paste had been entirely consumed, the female maruvazi picked up the leathern bowl and took it out of the room. While she did so, Emerald went to the well and drew some water, which he poured into a second bowl he took from a carved stone hook on the wall.

He brought this to where the others were sitting, and, once the female had rejoined them, he drank from it and passed it to the others.

After everyone's thirst had been relieved, the maruvazi returned the bowl to where it had been hanging before and then came back to sit with his family and guests.

Jess, having decided to ask her host about his people's customs, said to Emerald, "Would you mind if I ask you why you won't go out when there's a dust cloud?"

The maruvazi picked up the translator and replied, "It is forbidden to walk beneath the dust spirits."

"Dust spirits, huh? Do they attack you?"

Emerald explained. "They cover you with death. Even if they do not lead you into the wilderness to sip your breath, you will be as polluted as is an unfresh-but-undried corpse."

"Is that bad?" Jess inquired.

"Whosoever is sprinkled with death cannot return to his warren until he has been cleansed."

Jess was curious about this belief and asked another question. "Are these dust spirits the spirits of your dead?"

The maruvazi consulted with his mate and then said to his guest, "I do not understand what you mean."

Jess explained. "Some humans think there's a sprit inside our bodies and that, when we die, it comes out. It's like when an animal comes out of an egg. I thought, maybe, that's what these dust spirits are"

"You humans then believe that you have two bodies, a physical body and an immaterial body inside it, like an embryo in an egg?"

Jess nodded.

"We do not accept this idea. We are taught that every being has one body only. Maruvazi, as well as humans and other animals, have a physical body. Other creatures, like dust spirits, have an immaterial body. That is how it is."

"What do you think happens to you when you die?"

Again Emerald consulted with the female. After he had, he said, "When we die, we are dead. I do not understand your question."

Again Jess explained. "Like I said, some people think that when their body dies their spirit comes out of it."

"You think that you become the spirits that raise the dust, cool the waters, spread the rays of the sun, or push the moons across the sky?"

"Yeah, I guess some people think that. Personally, I believe that when I die, the Goddess Haya will send one of her handmaidens to lift me to her paradise. I'll rest in her garden drinking wine and listening to music forever. The only time I'll leave is when she gathers her warriors for a hunt. We'll race, drunk with excitement, across the universe taking the lives of living beings. The Goddess'll drive them to war, and we'll gather up their blood and their souls so that we can offer them up to her."

The maruvazi looked at her and said, "I do not understand what you are talking about."

"It doesn't matter," Jess assured him. "My teacher told me all that's just one way of looking at things, anyway. Actually, he said the soul isn't inside us at all. People who think it is have got it backwards. The soul isn't in the body; the body's in the soul. He said that a person's body and mind are just things made up by the Goddess and that our actions and thoughts are just like those of characters in a story she's making up. We're just roles she's playing in a game in her mind."

The maruvazi looked at Jess intently for a while, then turned his gaze upon Uluf and asked him, "You are not a human; do you see the world as this human does?"

"There are countless religions practiced among toads," Uluf replied. "I do not mean that there are many traditions amongst toads and that we belong to one or another of these. I mean that every toad takes what he desires from whatever source he desires and mixes the bits he has collected in whatever way he sees fit.

"Ah, another difference of most toad religions from most human religions is that those of the toads rarely have any supernatural elements. Toads, you see, are concerned with beauty, with the native perfection of things. We do not feel the need to think that all objects are somehow imperfect without some mystical being or another ruling over them. Instead, we realize that they are complete in themselves. We do not look at the trees and mountains as signs pointing to something else. We see them just as they are, with all their beauty and fullness.

"Certainly, toads tell stories of gods and heroes and the like, but these are no more than poetry. They are our way of praising the beauty and mystery of the world around us, and that inside our hearts and minds as well. They should not be taken literally. In fact, our tales are constantly being retold and changed. Some have been related so perfectly no toad could improve upon them, but most each toad reshapes as he sees fit. He thus takes stories that have been given emotional depth by their familiarity and transforms them in ways that will further increase their emotivity.

"We do not propitiate our gods to win their favor or to avert their anger as humans do. Our rituals are intended to bring out our awareness of the beauty of things, to focus our minds on what is immediately before us so that we can savor it. Liberation, enlightenment, for us, is nothing more than the timeless here and now experienced as it is.

"And you, Emerald, do you worship gods and spirits as men do?"

"I avoid those spirits that are polluting. I do not seek to honor them. Would I beg a falling rock to avoid me? The spirits governing the world do not listen to us, and we do not seek to sway what cannot be swayed. We are interested only in remaining pure, in avoiding what is prohibited."

After a moment's silence, Jess asked her host, "So, is this your home?"

"This is where my family lives."

"Did you dig it out yourself or did you buy it."

"There is no need to burrow in this warren. Since the humans built their town, our numbers have been declining."

"I'm sorry. I promise you we'll try to help with that. We're not all like those people there."

"The natures of two animals of the same species are often different, and the more intelligent the species is, the greater such differences usually are. I am sure humans are no exception to this rule."

"Well, some people are different, but most are pretty much the same, I suppose. Anyway, what I wanted to say earlier was that I like your home. It's really interesting."

"The nests in this warren are large, but it is an old warren. Much burrowing has been done here."

"I guess it's expensive to buy a home here, huh?"

"I do not understand."

"It costs a lot to buy your home, right?"

"To buy it?"

"You didn't buy this? How'd you get it?"

"When I took a mate, we moved into an unused nest."

"You didn't pay for it?"

"No."

"I wish it were that way with humans. So, what happens if there's not an unused nest?"

"Then the members of the tribe dig one."

"That's generous of them."

"Generous? How?"

"Well, they must do a lot of work to build a nest somebody else will own."

"A nest is not owned by anyone. I own my belongings, but the nest is a part of the warren."

"Your children won't inherit it?"

"How can they inherit a nest? They cannot take it anywhere with them. It is part of the warren."

"So, what happens to it after you're gone?"

"When someone takes a mate, he and she will come to live in it if they like it."

"I like this system. It makes things a lot simpler. I wouldn't mind not having landlords or rent or anything like that."

"I do not believe this translator is working properly. It is not giving me words for some of the things you are saying."

"Forget it," said Jess.

"Come. I will show you where you may rest for the night. If the dust spirits have passed tomorrow, you will then take us to your craft."

Emerald, having stood, picked up a tinderbox from a shelf and led Jess and Uluf down one of the corridors leading further into his home. At the end of this was a smaller chamber in the middle of which were several inflated leathern pillows.

The maruvazi told them they could sleep there and gave them the lantern and tinderbox he carried so that they would have light should they require it.

As he turned to leave, Jess called out to him, asking, "Excuse me, Emerald, where is the toilet?"

Emerald pointed to a hole in the floor at the far end of the room and left the two alone.

Jess, having emptied her bladder, lay down upon the floor and Uluf reclined beside her.

While the toad extinguished the still smoldering mineral in the little shovel, Jess arranged a pillow beneath her head.

When she was comfortable, she said to Uluf, "Do you think the maruvazi will really attack the miners if we give them the guns in the ornithopter?"

"I believe that it is very likely."

"You know, if they do, the ruler of Min will wipe out the maruvazi in this warren."

"I realize that."

"Let's help them a little. We'll destroy the colony. The roshpai of Min will blame us, and that doesn't really matter too much to me."

"How are we going to do that, my dear?"

"It's a mining colony, right? They'll have explosives. Let's set them off."

\* \* \*

When Jess awoke, she found herself wrapped in total darkness and had no idea what time it was. She looked at her watch and was surprised to discover that it was almost noon.

She felt around until she discovered Uluf lying near her.

Putting her hand upon his shoulder, she asked quietly, "Uluf, are you awake?"

As he did not respond, she shook him slightly. He began to stir and she said, "Uluf, it's almost noon. We should get up."

The toad roused himself and, using the tinderbox Emerald had given him, lit the combustible mineral in the small shovel.

The pair made their way back into the room where they had eaten the previous evening and there found Emerald and his mate engaged in different household chores.

The female maruvazi, having been whistled at by Emerald, hurried out of the room. She soon returned with another bowl of fish paste, which Jess and Uluf ate in silence.

After they were done, Jess asked Emerald, "Do your people never talk when they eat?"

"It is prohibited. The spirits devouring the flesh of dead things, that make them rot, will pollute the organs of speech."

"I see."

"Come now. You are to speak with the council again."

Emerald led his guests back the way he had taken them the night before and brought them to the council chamber.

The girl and the toad sat down in front of the bone clad maruvazi, and Emerald returned the translator to one of his betters.

This maruvazi now addressed his warren's guests. "The dust cloud has passed. When you are ready, we will take you to your craft so that you can give us the weapons in it. Then you will return here. Tonight, once the sun has set, we will take you to the miners' town."

Jess replied, "That's fine. Uluf, my friend here, and I were talking last night. We thought we might be able to help you. If we can, we'll try to destroy the colony."

The maruvazi councilors spoke amongst themselves for a time. Then the one with the translator said, "We will accept your help, but we would like to help you help us."

"Okay. Do you know the layout of the colony or how many miners are there right now?"

"There are about forty humans in the colony. You need not worry about the arrangement of the place. We will send some of our folk with you. They will tell you what is what there. They will also assist you in destroying the town's inhabitants. First, however, you must tell me what you believe can be done."

"Do you know where they keep their explosives?"

"Yes. We are always watching them."

"Great. Here's what I'm thinking we could do. I'll attack the miners to get my friends out. While they're busy with me, your people can break into the explosives store and set up charges around the colony. Uluf will be able to wire them for you. When we escape, we'll blow the whole thing up."

The maruvazi consulted with one another again, and then their spokesman said, "We will do as you suggest."

# Chapter 22
# Raid

After Jess and Uluf had dressed themselves in their hotsuits, the maruvazi covered their heads with bags and carried them upside down out of the warren. When the creatures eventually placed the two on their feet again and removed the bags, Jess was dazzled by the bright light that surrounded her. She had to sit squinting helplessly for several minutes before she could interact with her environment.

After she was able to see, Jess looked around and discovered that the maruvazi had set her down behind a rocky outcropping.

The maruvazi holding the translator crept up to her and said, "Your craft is on the other side of this formation. Two miners are standing outside of it, and there are probably more within."

"Show me," Jess told him.

Leading the girl to the edge of the outcropping, the maruvazi let her peek around. There were two men wearing baggy grey hotsuits sitting on the now extended ramp of the ornithopter. Both were armed with needle rifles.

"If you can distract them and get them to concentrate on that direction over there," Jess said pointing to a ridge of yellowish stone to the right of the ornithopter, "I can rush at them from here. I promise you I'll get them before they see me."

"Wait here," the maruvazi replied. "I will send two of my fellows. They will do as you desire."

"Okay."

A few minutes later, a heap of small rocks fell noisily from the ridge where the maruvazi had been sent. The guards heard this, stood up, and consulted with one another. They watched the ridge again. Then one of them started walking towards it while the other observed his companion with his gun ready to fire.

Jess did not waste her chance. Lifting the thread from her perineum, she let her will extend through time, bringing it within her mind and suffusing it with lethargy.

As those around her strolled about as sluggishly as sleepwalkers, Jess leapt from behind the rocky outcropping and hurled herself at the man standing behind the ornithopter.

She ran as fast as she could and then thrust the ground away from her feet so that she flew through the air, spinning head over heels.

The miner's torso was twisting round and his face was already directed towards her, but his gun was not. Before he could point it at her, Jess brought her sword down upon his neck and separated his head from his body.

Landing with a roll on the pebbly ground on the other side of the ramp, Jess sprang up using her hands, flipped herself onto her feet, and jumped at the second man. He was already facing her, but was so astonished by the blurred, impossibly quick motions of the figure coming at him that he did not fire his weapon. Jess decapitated him as she had the first man and sent his head, bouncing around inside its glass helmet, to roll across the earth.

Turning from her victim before the rest of his carcass had even collapsed, Jess ran up the ramp, opened the iris diaphragm, and entered into the ornithopter. Inside were three miners, who were rummaging through the various cupboards and below the furniture in the main cabin.

One of them, who was on his hands and knees while poking about underneath a couch, was looking at Jess, having apparently heard some noise from outside. The other two were still attending to their searches.

Jess dashed from the entrance into the main cabin, kicking the man crouching on the floor in the face, driving the bridge of his nose into his brain. She spun to her right and sliced through the body of the next miner just below his armpits, separating his shoulders from his torso and his arms.

Whipping round, she lunged at the last of the intruders, who was near the control panel. He was holding a needle rifle by its muzzle and was able to swing it at Jess as she leapt. This improvised club struck her in the side and knocked her onto the floor. The man, seeing a chance to kill his enemy, fumbled with the rifle, trying to arrange it so that he could shoot her. He was entirely too nervous, however, and, before he even had the weapon cradled in his arms, Jess was on her feet again. She smiled at the man as his mouth hung open and chopped off his head.

Jess took a deep breath and let the thread slink back down her spine to return to its slumber. Time resumed its ordinary pace, and Jess walked past the bodies to tell the maruvazi she had dealt with the miners.

Before she exited the ornithopter, Jess noticed that the door to the toilet was closed. Raising her sword to her ear, she kicked it open. In front of her, sitting on the commode with his hotsuit around his ankles, was a trembling man whose face was covered with tears. He had obviously hoped that if he remained quiet, he would not be discovered.

Jess grinned widely and said, "Finally, I get to return the favor."

The man reached out his hands as though both to implore Jess to stop and to protect himself from her blows. She chopped them off just below the elbow.

For a few moments, Jess looked at the miner while he howled in agony and then stabbed her sword into his heart.

Leaving the corpse to slide from where it sat onto the floor, Jess went to the diaphragm at the back of the ornithopter, opened it, and waved to the others behind the outcropping to join her.

When the maruvazi were inside, she showed them the weapons in the ship, and they dumped these into leathern bags.

As they were doing so, Jess told the maruvazi with the translator, "We need to clean up this mess and get rid of the bodies, just in case some more miners come here looking for this group. They'll figure something's wrong when they don't come back, but, if they don't find them, at least they won't know for sure."

"We will not waste so much meat. The carcasses will be taken back to the warren. We will clean up the blood before we depart."

"Ugh!" Jess exclaimed. "You're going to eat them? That's disgusting. "

"We will not waste so much meat."

Jess shrugged and looked at her allies with less sympathy than she had before. There was, nonetheless, work to be done, and so, having found Syo's satchel, she took out the plecostomus-like slurp cat that woman had previously used to clean blood and tossed it onto the floor. Then, forcing herself to forget her revulsion, she helped the others soak up some more of the gore she herself had splattered across the cabin. When they were done, and Uluf had picked up his, Jess's, and the two Tozanis' bags, the raiders, with their new burdens, returned to the warren.

\* \* \*

At around the eighth watch (after night had fallen), Jess and Uluf were again carried upside down with their heads in bags out of the warren. After they had been taken some distance from its entrance, the ten maruvazi with them removed the bags and allowed the girl and the toad to walk the rest of the way to the mouth of the valley wherein Shadow Chasm lay.

Jess asked the maruvazi now holding the translator, "Okay, which building is which?"

The hulking creature told her, "The long buildings to the left are living quarters. The one in the middle is where their council convenes. That is where your companions will be. Those on the far side are where they refine and keep the minerals they mine. Their barges and ornithopter are in the large building near the paved field. The small structure in the distance surrounded by a fence is where they keep their explosives."

"Okay. I want you to tell the others what I want them to do. Tell the five with the guns to stay here and cover the rest of us. They should shoot anyone who gets anywhere near us. Okay? You and the other four will go with Uluf to the explosives store. You should get as much of the stuff there as you can carry and arrange it around the buildings. Uluf will take care of wiring everything. I'll go down with the rest of you, but I'll wait until you've put out the bombs before I do anything. There might not be much time to get anything done after I go in. Now tell the others."

After the maruvazi had spoken to his fellows in a series of whistles and chirrups, Jess, Uluf, and the five maruvazi without rifles, who were armed with spears and pistols, snuck quietly towards the colony.

When they were close, Jess left the others, who made their way to the explosives store, and headed towards the building where the maruvazi had thought Syo and Ofu would be.

She peeked into one of the narrow slits that served as windows and tried to discern what was inside. All she saw was an empty office. She went to the next and found what appeared to be a mess hall.

Continuing from window to window, Jess eventually, at the very end of the building, discovered a room where two miners armed with needle guns were sitting playing dice in front of a heavy locked door.

Jess hurried around the building, to where she hoped a window into the room being guarded would be, and peered into this when she found it.

Inside was a bare cement cell and, lying naked on the floor, bound by metal collars attached to chains secured to iron rings set in the walls, were Ofu and Syo.

Both were smeared with moist and caked blood, and their faces were so battered they had been transformed into swollen yellow and black masks. Syo's thighs were especially thick with gore. She had obviously sustained some sort of severe injury, probably while being raped.

As Jess looked at them, the door opposite the window opened and five dirty miners entered. One of the jailers said something to them, though Jess could not hear what, and then closed the door.

The first of the men removed his trousers and, while one of his companions held Syo down, began to have sex with her.

At the same time, the other three forced Ofu onto his hairy, tattooed stomach and lifted his hips into the air. Two of them pinioned their victim's body and arms, and the third dropped his trousers, grabbed Ofu by the waist, and started raping him, slapping and pounding the man on the back while he did so.

Though she was trembling with the revived memory of what had happened to her on the *Cloud Cutter*, there was nothing Jess could do to help her companions at the moment, so she returned to the other side of the building, where the entrance was, and squatted behind a nearby heap of rubbish.

She watched carefully for the approach of any miner, but none of them ventured outside. At the same time, she observed the progress the maruvazi and Uluf were making with the explosives. Eventually, Uluf poked his head out from behind one of the other buildings and waved a remote control device (for igniting the charges he had set) to give Jess a signal. The time for her to act had come.

Rising up from behind the pile of refuse, Jess slunk over to the door and tried to open it. The door was locked, but Jess cut through it with her sword, opened it, and went into the narrow concrete corridor inside. This ended in a T, and Jess turned to the left, made her way to the end, and, having slowed time, threw open the door that led into the room where she had seen the two guards.

The men looked up at her from where they sat, but before they could react, she had, with a single motion, decapitated one of them and driven her sword through the forehead of the other.

Without wasting a second, Jess took the key ring from the belt of one of the guards and went over to the door leading to the cell where Syo and Ofu were. She tried one key in the lock. It did not fit. She tried a second and a third. They did not fit. She tried a fourth. It did.

As Jess opened the door, she heard one of the miners, the one holding Syo down, saying (with words that, to her, sounded like the drawn out lowing of a cow), "Forget which key to use?"

Before the man could realize that he had missed his chance to save his life, Jess was upon him, separating his head from his body. His fellow meanwhile rolled onto his backside, out from between Syo's thighs, and screamed.

There were three other men to take care of yet, so Jess turned her attention away from the shaking rapist for the time being.

The miners who had been holding Ofu were already on their feet, but Jess, spinning around, cut them both in half at the waist. The third, instead of fighting, was trying to pull up his trousers. He was so terrified, however, that he fell down onto his side. Jess jumped over Ofu, squatted beside her companion's attacker, and, while looking into his eyes, disemboweled him.

Getting up, Jess stepped over her first victim's corpse, stared at the man who had been raping Syo, and smiled. He tried to scoot away from her, but she followed him. He screamed some more. She cut off his genitals. He continued to scream, but now did so with shouts that were far louder than those that had come before.

Kneeling down beside Syo, Jess tried several of the keys on the ring she held in the lock on the collar her companion wore until she found the one that freed her. She turned to Ofu and unfastened his bonds as well.

"Come on," she said to the Tozanis. "We've got to get out of here now. Can you two stand?"

"I'll manage," grunted Ofu.

He got up slowly and unsteadily and stood beside Jess.

"Come on," she told him. "Give me a hand with Syo."

The two picked the woman up and placed her left arm over Ofu's shoulder so that he could carry her out. Her body was limp and she did not seem to have either the strength or the will to make any effort to help herself.

Ofu dragged Syo out of the room where he and she had been imprisoned, and Jess locked the door behind them, leaving the still screaming eunuch inside to wait for his imminent death.

"We've got to get out of here," Jess told Ofu and led him into the open.

Uluf was waiting behind a nearby building, having finished wiring the explosives, and rushed to join them, accompanied by the five maruvazi who had been laying out the charges. This group then hurried across the valley, over the landing field, and came to the side of the hangar.

The main doors were closed, undoubtedly to keep out the heat, and Jess did not want to try to open them. Even if she and her allies could budge them, doing so would surely make a great deal of noise. She looked around and saw a smaller door to one side. Going over to this, she cracked it open and peered within, while the others looked over her head.

Inside they saw a relatively small cargo barge and an ornithopter. The body of the latter, like the one they had taken from Ngo, was disc-shaped, perched on four legs, and held its wings curled above it. This vehicle was far less ornate than Tsoi's was, however. In fact, it was entirely unornamented. Most of it was covered with rudely bolted metal plates, and the whole of its front was composed of a single bulging, bubble window set in a metal framework.

Behind these craft, in front of a wall hung with various tools, five men in dirty tunics and loose trousers were sitting at a table playing a game that involved tossing handfuls of seeds onto a board covered with patterns.

Jess carefully closed the door and said to Ofu, Uluf, and the maruvazi with the translator, "Okay, here's what we'll do. Ofu, stay here with Syo. I'm going in and I want the maruvazi to follow me. Uluf, you wait here too. I doubt if I'll have any problem with the miners, but, if I do, set off the explosives. That'll distract them. If I don't, just hold off on the bombs. After the men in here are dead, Ofu, bring in Syo and get in the ornithopter. As soon as it's powered up and we know we can get out of here, we'll set off the explosives. Then, before we go, we can make sure there aren't any survivors. Everybody okay with that?"

Once her companions had indicated their assent to her plan, Jess opened the door to the hangar again and ran inside. Having slowed time to half its pace, the girl jumped onto a small tractor, forced the world away from her feet, and sailed through the air.

The miners stared at her in disbelief as she landed in the middle of the table where they were gambling, bouncing their seeds into their laps and faces and sending their coins to clatter upon the floor.

Jess swung her sword and decapitated the two men in front of her before they could close their gaping mouths. At the same time, two of those behind her jumped from their chairs and tried to run away while the last man scurried beneath the table.

Spinning round while she bounded onto the floor, Jess landed in a squat facing the man curled up in front of her. He started to plead with her, but, before more than the first syllable of a word had escaped his lips, Jess's sword had pierced his cranium.

She stood up and looked around. The maruvazi were hurrying after the two men who had tried to escape from her. One of the huge desert creatures, running with his spear ahead of him, pierced the first of these men through the stomach and, lifting him into the air, drove the tip of his weapon into the wall at the building's back. The miner was so pinned to the wall, his feet kicking a half yard above the floor, like an insect in some person's collection.

The last miner, confused about what he should do, stopped in his tracks and looked about stupidly. Three maruvazi leapt upon him and with their hands and hatchets tore his body apart.

Jess turned to the door, allowed time to return to its ordinary pace, and motioned for Ofu to bring Syo in. He carried her towards the ornithopter, and Jess directed her attention to the wall behind the table, trying to find the keys to that craft. She was beginning to get concerned that she was not going to be able to locate them when she heard a number of metallic clangs combined with the whistles of a maruvazi and the shouts of human beings.

Jess whirled about and saw the five maruvazi clustered around a large tractor with a flat bed. They were poking their spears underneath it with considerable energy, clearly trying to kill something there.

She hurried over to join them and, kneeling down, looked under the tractor. Three mechanics were huddled there, shouting loudly for help.

"Get them out of there," Jess shouted. "I don't want the others coming out yet."

While she was still speaking, one of the maruvazi managed to jab his spear into the belly of one of the mechanics. He pulled the squawking man towards him, enabling a second maruvazi to stick his own spear into the fellow's loins. The other three maruvazi hopped to the far side of the tractor, and the two whose spears were imbedded in one of the mechanics used that man as a sort of grisly broom to push the remaining pair out from under the tractor into the arms of their comrades.

One of the maruvazi, who was holding a hatchet, seized ahold of the first of these persons and repeatedly struck the man's arm at the elbow, until he had chopped it off. As soon as the creature had done so, he raised the severed limb to his mouth and began devouring it while the injured and screaming mechanic watched him.

Another of the maruvazi leapt upon the second mechanic, knocked him to the ground, grabbed ahold of him, and began biting large chunks of meat out of his side. The third ate the man's right leg.

As his colleagues were being consumed, the mechanic who had been speared and used to knock them out of their sanctuary was himself drawn back out. The maruvazi holding the man lifted him into the air upon their spears and held him in front of their faces in order to examine him.

Jess shouted at those two, one of whom happened to be holding the translator. "Wait! Don't kill him yet."

She then turned to the mechanic and said to him, "Tell me where the keys to the ornithopter are."

The man only grunted and tried to hold on to the spears sticking in his body to prevent himself from sliding further down onto them.

"They're going to eat you if you don't tell me."

"In the desk near the end of the wall," the man shouted.

Jess ran over there and looked inside. The keys were there.

"Thanks," she yelled out to the man as the maruvazi began to tear his flesh from his body.

Uluf, who had entered the room, looked at the maruvazi with the translator and remarked, "I thought the dead were polluting for you."

"This is still alive, though we will eat it when it has expired. Only those animals that are no longer fresh but are not yet dry are polluting. If a beast still has the smell of life, it is food. If it has dried, then it is fit to be dismembered and its skin and bones used as tools."

The maruvazi, having offered such an explanation to Uluf, returned to his meal.

"Very practical," the toad replied and started towards Jess.

She was gazing in her friend's direction and trying not to watch what her anthropophagous allies were doing. By now she was feeling thoroughly revolted by them.

When Uluf was standing next to her, Jess said, "I'm going to get into the ornithopter. As soon as you hear it start up, set off the explosives."

The toad nodded and the girl addressed the maruvazi, though without looking at them. "Once the bombs go off, open the doors to the hangar."

Jess ran to the back of the ornithopter and climbed the ladder leading to the heavy metal door above.

The inside of the ornithopter was as spare as Tsoi's had been elegantly furnished. At the front was a control panel vaguely like a pipe organ made out of battered, rusting metal, and along the walls were metal benches, where Ofu and Syo were already sitting. The center of the cabin was bare, although a toilet and a sink projected from the back wall.

Jess went to the controls and turned on the engine. Then, no more than a few seconds later, she heard and felt a powerful explosion.

While the maruvazi were still opening the hangar doors, Uluf joined Jess in the ornithopter. She gave him the pilot's seat and, under his command, the vessel walked out onto the landing field. The whole valley was now brightly lit with the flames rising from the burning ruins of Shadow Chasm.

A few miners had survived the blast and were attempting to run away, but the maruvazi were easily catching and killing them. The creatures never wasted the meat they so acquired and rarely even waited for their food to die before enjoying it.

"Uluf," Jess said, "let's get out of here. I've had enough of this place."

"As have I, my dear," the toad replied.

The ornithopter's wings spread and lifted its weightless body into the night sky while orange lights flashed into the cabin from the conflagration below and thick black smoke billowed past its windows. Within a few moments, however, the craft had left the fires behind and was flying amongst the clear milky rays of Shokai's two moons.

Jess, Ofu, and Syo soon thereafter lay down upon the floor and slept, leaving Uluf to pilot the vessel through much of the night. When he grew tired, he awakened Jess, and she remained at the controls until morning.

The girl and the toad spent the first part of the next day taking turns watching the automatic pilot as the ornithopter continued on its southward flight over the seemingly endless expanses of Shokai's deserts.

By noon, Ofu had overcome his embarrassment and returned to his normal irritable self. He began taking turns at the controls as well. Syo, however, spent the whole day lying upon the floor staring blindly ahead. Jess and the others, having failed to stir her, began to worry that she had lost her mind.

Their journey lasted the whole of the day and the following night.

Throughout that time, everyone remained largely quiet. Not only were they all exhausted and troubled by the events of the day before, but they were all ravenously hungry. Although the ship was supplied with water, there was nothing to eat onboard.

The next morning, not long after dawn, as Jess sat at the control panel listening to her stomach growling angrily at her, she saw in the distance ahead a vast brownish expanse bordered by a thin green line. They were approaching the Southern Sea.

"Come on, everybody," she announced. "Let's get ourselves ready."

After Uluf had donned a crumpled justaucorps and similarly wrinkled britches (and had helped Syo to dress herself in a grey hotsuit he took from one of the ornithopter's walls), he relieved Jess at the controls.

She went over to her bottomless bag, which was lying on one of the metal benches, rifled through it, and took out a pair of skintight pink clamdiggers, a matching halter-top, and a dark vest. Once she had dressed herself in these, Jess picked up the black wig she had worn in Quanya and undid the beehive so that, when she placed it on her head, its long tresses fell over her shoulders and down her back.

Ofu, who had attired himself in a grey hotsuit like that Syo was wearing, then said to the others, "When we land, let's meet up with a friend of mine. He's from Jezic so you can trust him. We've got to send Syo back – her mind is broken – and he can make the arrangements. He can also take care of our transportation off Shokai."

Jess nodded her approval

# Interlude 9
# Measures and Money

## Money

A single currency is used throughout human space as the Pancloan government does not permit subject states to mint their own money.

The standard unit of currency is the kopeck. This is divided into two half-kopecks, each worth six groats. Each groat is further subdivided into four cowries and each cowry into twelve pennies.

Units of one-hundred-thousand kopecks are designated lacs, although these are used only for accounting.

## Time

All space vessels use standard time, which employs a day equivalent to a day of the Earth. This is divided into twenty-four hours composed of sixty minutes each.

The Pancloan government, however, uses imperial time. This is based on the day of the capital world, which is equivalent to slightly over twenty-four standard hours. In this system, the day is separated into eight watches, each of which is split into two half-watches. Each half-watch is itself divided into sixths, and each sixth is divided into ten minutes.

Other worlds calculate days according to local rotational periods.

The divisions of a day vary from planet to planet and even from one region of a planet to another.

On most of Shokai, for example, days, which are of approximately twenty-two hours, are divided into ten watches, the first beginning roughly at dawn. These are further subdivided into four quarters of twelve minutes each.

Like days, years vary in length from world to world, generally being fixed by the time required for a given planet to revolve around its sun.

Calendars can differ from one region of a particular world to another.

Two calendars are, nonetheless, current across human space. The Pancloan year, of 397.4 local days, is divided into eighteen months of approximately twenty-two days each and is used by the imperial government. Traders' years, which correspond to Earthly years, are divided into twelve unequal months and are employed by interstellar merchants and travellers.

## Length and Weight

Although there are no universally accepted systems for measuring lengths or weights, the Pancloan government and military, as well as most interstellar traders, employ imperial standards.

In this system, a finger is the approximate width of the forefinger of an adult male. One such finger is divided into four grains, and nine fingers make a span. Three spans make a fathom. Twelve fathoms make a perch. Four perches make a furlong. Two furlongs make a stade, and four stades make a mile.

Interstellar distances are usually measured in light-years, the distance light travels in a vacuum in one traders' year.

The basic imperial unit of weight is the gum. Four gum equal one pulihyu. Nine pulihyu make a kor. Four kor equal a puha. Three puha make a gud, and four gud make a pyeha. A dozen pyeha make a mopyeha and a dozen mopyeha make a shuppuik.

Although it is not in practical use anywhere, the metric system, an archaic decimal system of weights and measures, is employed to give weights (and more rarely lengths) in the literary and religious works of many different cultures. The basic unit of weight in this system is the gram, which is roughly equivalent to a quarter of a gum. The larger units, dekagrams, hectograms, and kilograms, contain, respectively, ten, one-hundred, and one-thousand grams.

From Pollidor's *Big Blue Book of Knowledge*

# Chapter 23
# Hwiccho

Hwiccho was as drab as Jezic was colorful and as grim as Quanya was exuberant. The climate was so hot and dusty that the majority of the city was either built underground, in a warren of tunnels, or consisted of drab air-conditioned towers or prefabricated pods linked by twisting tubes.

As ugly as it was, the city was even more annoying to move through. It had grown up in such a haphazard way (under a regime that was completely unconcerned about its citizens' welfare) that finding one's way through the jumble of buildings, pipes, tunnels, and unpaved streets was a terrible hassle. Even the grey ceramic roads the usual snail-like cars raced along were more like a tangled knot than a coherent network.

After landing in the city's airport, Jess and her companions spent nearly an entire watch shoving their way through congested pedestrian passageways that dove underground, rose up to covered bridges reaching from one skyscraper to the next, wound around other buildings through twisting pipes, took ridiculous detours past factories and private buildings, and generally avoided every possible direct route.

Eventually, they arrived at a concrete building filled with a labyrinth of passageways lined with shops, bars, and brothels and lit with glaring neon signs, obscene holograms, and thin beams of light that stabbed through the smoky, dusty air from small windows set in the exterior walls.

Ofu led the others through this maze. He pushed past intoxicated locals who were staggering from one bar to the next or lying in puddles of their own waste and forced his way by gaudily made-up prostitutes who were loudly proclaiming their skills or low prices or belligerently jiggling their breasts or buttocks at the new arrivals.

Down one of the narrow, crowded tunnels, Ofu saw a place where the cement wall to the right was painted green and said, "Ah, there it is."

He promptly led the others through a warped plastic door into a grubby lounge lit only by a number of continuously roving spotlights set in the ceiling.

The place was filled with decaying couches whereupon aging, intoxicated, and dirty hookers reclined. As soon as the travelers entered, all of these women (or all of them who were aware of their surroundings) began calling out to them and tried to display what remained of their charms.

Ofu ignored the whores and crossed the room, coming to a bar that ran along nearly the whole of its width. He leaned upon this and gestured for the barkeep, an attractive if tired looking young woman with a swollen black eye, to come to him.

She asked, "What do want?"

"Is Flipper here?"

"Who are you to ask?"

"I'm a friend of his. Tell him Ofu is here. He'll want to see me."

The woman looked at him with her good eye and reflected for a moment.

"Okay," she said at last. "Hang on. I'll get him."

She went into a back room and, after a few minutes, returned.

"Follow me," she told Ofu and brought him and the others to a door set in the back wall to the left of the counter.

The walls of the room beyond were lined with divans, and that opposite the entrance was set with a series of tall thin windows that each came to a point its top. In the middle of the room was a heavy wooden coffee table that occupied most of the space between the seats. It was ornately carved but battered, stained, and slightly worm-eaten.

The woman said to Ofu, "Wait here. Flipper'll be with you in a few minutes."

Ofu nodded and sat down. Uluf helped Syo to sit beside her compatriot (since she seemed capable only of following another's lead now), and then joined her himself. Jess, having looked at the semen, food, blood, and other stains on the divans, wrinkled her nose, walked over to the windows, and looked outside.

In front of the building she was in, and extending to some distance, was a forest of tall, thin metal smokestacks that shone in the bright sunlight and were topped with multicolored flames that vomited great streams of oily black smoke into the sky. Around the bases of these was a tangled brierpatch of tubes, pipes, ducts, and the like that was so dense Jess could not make out what was below it.

Beyond this enormous refinery, and the countless other factories and factory-like buildings that made up Hwiccho, was the muddy brown Southern Sea. Continuously replenished by underground rivers, but without any outlet, the body of water was so saline that masses of pale brown froth adorned its surface and coated the rocks around its shore.

As lethal as the sea was, a number of hardy organisms had been able to survive in it. One particular plant, a thick, meaty weed composed of long vines adorned with pulpy leaves and engorged bladders, was so abundant both above and below the surface of the waters that it made the sea seem like some kind of repulsive vegetable soup.

Along the shore of the Southern Sea, to the north of the refinery (to Jess's right), was the jumbled, ugly mass of Hwiccho's center, beyond which rose the impossibly high spire of the spaceport, and, to her left, past a few more industrial structures, were carefully laid out farms green with rows of crops of a sort Jess did not recognize. Here and there, amongst these, she saw low domes rising from the ground. Since these were not high enough to be complete houses, Jess correctly inferred that they were merely the roofs of subterranean homesteads.

As she stared at the scenery before her, Jess heard the door to the room open and turned around.

A stocky, hairy man whose right arm was missing below the elbow and who was dressed in an apron like those she had seen shopkeepers in Jezic wearing had entered the room. With him was a naked young woman with very attractive features, although they were marred by a large scar that ran across the bridge of her nose and under her left eye nearly to her ear.

The man stared at Jess intently, allowing his eyes to caress every detail of her form, which was barely concealed below her skintight garments. Not appreciating his appreciation of her body, Jess sat down and crossed her arms over her chest to obscure his view.

Ofu stood up, walked over to the man, grabbed ahold of his left hand, and said, "It's good to see you, Flipper."

"And you, Ofu. It's been a long time."

"You haven't been back in Jezic for years."

"Can't be helped, friend. I don't think I'm welcome there, and I don't want to end my days being torn apart by some brass robot. It looks like you've had your own share of rough times recently."

Ofu touched his bruised face and made a sound halfway between a grunt and a chuckle.

"Yeah. Life's been a hassle recently," he said.

"Sorry to hear that. Anyway, what can I do for you?"

"Well, first of all, I could do with a good meal. I haven't had a bite in over two days."

Flipper laughed. "Of course you're hungry. What do want?"

"Bring me the best you can get."

"And your friends?"

"The same for them?"

"And the toad?"

"Him too."

Flipper snapped his fingers at the young woman who was with him, and she hurried out of the room.

Once she was gone, Ofu and Flipper both sat down upon the stained divan.

"What else can I do for you?" Flipper asked. "Besides feeding you."

Pointing to Syo, Ofu said, "I need you to arrange to send her back to Jezic. It'll need to be done pretty secretly, though, and somebody'll have to go with her. She's lost her mind. There's no way we can take her with us, and there's no way we can send her back on her own."

"How secret does this need to be?"

"Maybe take her to some city on the edge of Tozana and drive her in. Something like that."

"I assume somebody could be looking for her, somebody dangerous."

"Yeah."

"I'll have to pay her escort well."

"Don't worry about the money. I'm sending a note with her to Sing. Just tell your man to make sure Sing gets the note. He'll pay the bill when he sees it."

"Are you sure of that?"

Ofu laughed. "I'm so sure that I'll pay it if he doesn't."

Flipper smiled and replied, "Alright then, I'll do it. Now, could I get you some drinks?"

"Yeah," Ofu told him. "I could use something strong. I've had the worst luck of my life the past few days. I'm glad I had my Shyammeto medallion with me. If I didn't, I'd probably be dead now."

"You people, or whatever, want drinks too?" Flipper asked Jess and Uluf.

When both had replied they would, Flipper pulled on a tasseled cord hanging near the wall next to him, and, a moment later, the woman with the black eye entered the room.

"What would you like, sir?" she asked.

"Bring a bottle of madu and glasses for all of us."

The woman nodded and left the room to return, very quickly, with a tray with a bottle and glasses upon it. She set the glasses in front of Flipper and his guests and poured their alcohol for them.

When she had finished and returned to her post, Flipper, while eyeing Jess's figure, asked Ofu, "Now, why can't you take care of getting her back to Jezic? What's her name, by the way?"

"It's Syo, and the reason I can't is that I'm heading off planet. As soon as we eat, I've got to book a flight to the space station. Do you think there'll be one leaving today?"

"There's a flight just about every day, so I should think so. I can't imagine you'll have to wait longer than a day even if there's not."

Ofu and Flipper chatted for a few minutes while Jess and Uluf sipped the acrid and very strong madu they had been given and Syo sat quietly upon the divan contemplating her thighs.

Shortly after Ofu had finished Syo's drink, having seen that she was ignoring it, there was a knock at the door. The woman with the scar across her nose had returned with a basket stacked with plates from which a delicious aroma was escaping.

She put the basket on the table and, removing the plates from its top, took out several cylindrical tins filled with food. Having covered each plate with a layer of some pulpy greyish-green vegetable, she placed on this pieces of more appetizing vegetables and strips of a soft reddish meat. When the food had so been readied, the woman set a pair of tongs on the edge of each plate and arranged these in front of Flipper and his guests.

The girl left the room, and Jess picked up her plate and scooped some of the bottom layer of vegetables into her mouth. Her eyes bulged and her mouth twisted to the side when she did. It was horribly salty and bitter.

"What is this?" she asked.

"They call it uab," Flipper told her. "It's the main food around the Southern Sea. Hunna won't grow here, you know."

"It's terrible."

"Yeah, but if you live here long enough you'll get used to it."

"I don't want to get used to it."

"Try the vegetables or the meat. They're a lot better. I guarantee you."

Jess picked up a strip of the meat with her tongs and tasted it. It was succulent, vaguely spicy, and remarkably tasty.

"What is this?" she asked.

With his mouth full of pulverized food, Flipper told her. "It's maruvazi."

Jess prodded the meat with her tongs and looked at it for some time.

Finally, she inquired, "You eat maruvazi?"

"Not as often as I'd like to. It's very expensive."

"I've met maruvazi before. I thought they all lived in the middle of the desert."

"They do."

"How'd you get their meat, then?"

"People go on hunts, usually in barges."

"Is that how you got this meat?"

"No. This is from a restaurant down the corridor from my whorehouse."

"Oh."

"I have been on a couple maruvazi hunts, though. I even shot one once. Still, most of the meat I've had comes from professional hunters."

"Who, pray tell, are those?" Uluf asked.

"They just wander around the desert on barges with big refrigerators shooting the animals. Some of them make a pretty good amount of money at it too. It's a dangerous job, though. The maruvazi are vicious animals. They'll tear a human apart and devour him if they get a chance."

"I heard that some people trade with them," Jess said.

"Yeah. That's true. You wouldn't believe anybody would do it, but there are people who'll barter with the creatures. The maruvazi are always burrowing around, so they find valuable minerals sometimes. They'll exchange gold, jewels, or whatever else they have for different goods, especially machines or drugs."

Jess prodded the meat on her plate again. As hungry as she had been a few minutes earlier, her desire to eat had completely left her.

She looked at Flipper with disdain and asked, "How can you eat maruvazi? They have minds and cultures just like we do, you know?"

"The maruvazi don't have cultures," Flipper replied with a laugh. "They're smart for animals, but they're still animals."

Jess picked up her glass of madu and took a large drink. The potency of the liquor nearly choked her, but she managed to swallow it and glare at her host.

Ofu watched Jess with a little irritation, and, when she saw his expression, she returned his hostile stare.

Being somewhat wary of the girl, since he realized she could easily kill him, Ofu laughed and returned his attention to his food.

"Well, whatever you think, Jess, I like it."

"You're welcome to it."

Ofu looked back up at Jess, then at her food, and inquired, "If you're not going to eat yours, can I have it?"

"Go ahead," she said pushing her plate over to him.

Ofu picked it up and scraped the meat onto his own.

"You want the vegetables?" he asked.

Jess reflected a couple of seconds, then said, "Yeah, sure, why not."

Ofu pushed the plate back over to her. She picked it up and began eating the vegetables.

"There are more vegetables in the basket if you want some," Flipper told her.

"Thanks. I'll get some when I'm done with these."

After Jess had stuffed some of the vegetables into her mouth and swallowed them, she was happy she had not passed up the chance to eat. Having food in her belly felt absolutely wonderful.

Once she had enjoyed a few bites, and while she was still chewing another, she asked Ofu, "Do people in Tozana eat mudjumpers?"

Ofu laughed so hard he managed to spit a large glob of pulverized maruvazi onto the table in front of him.

"If you're stinking rich. Do you have any idea how much you'd have to pay for mudjumper meat?"

"No."

"Those animals are worth a fortune. I don't know how much a mudjumper steak would cost – I've never actually seen any being sold anywhere before – but I'll wager it's a lot. To tell you the truth, I wouldn't want to eat one even if I could. Their meat is probably nasty."

"Why is that?" Uluf asked him.

"They live in the mud. They eat carrion, slime, and the nasty little creatures living on the bottoms of rivers and the bed of the sea. Even the food they get from the land is usually the mold from under rocks or the squirming animals that live there. Mudjumpers are filthy."

"But the rich do eat their meat?" Uluf asked.

"Yeah. They eat it. I guess they have it cleaned first. I really don't know."

Jess poured herself another glass of madu, drank deeply, and said to Uluf, "You better make sure they don't eat you too."

Uluf looked at Ofu. "Do people eat toads on this planet?"

"There aren't any toads on this planet."

"Would they eat toads?"

"I suppose it would depend on what the meat tastes like."

\* \* \*

After the travelers had eaten, Ofu used Flipper's computer to book passage for himself, Jess, and Uluf on a flight leaving to the space station in two watches' time and on a vessel leaving from there to Tomasine Station.

With Syo in Flipper's care, the three left that man's brothel and went to the spaceport. The cigar shaped craft they were taking was mostly carrying trade goods to the station high above Shokai, but a section of it contained seats for passengers. Except for those reserved for the wealthy, these were all in a single large room with a low ceiling and rusting metal walls. It was nothing fancy, but it was more than comfortable enough for the brief voyage through and past the skies.

Once all its passengers were onboard (its cargo having previously been loaded), the shuttle was conveyed to the launching spire on a trolley fitted with a sort of roofed cage that kept the vessel in place on its back. The bottom of this conveyance was attached to a track at the base of the tower and, when the ship's antigravity engine had been activated, the trolley was flung, at ever increasing speeds, down the track. It hurtled up the side of the spire, whirled around its corkscrew shaped midsection, and shot along its straight pinnacle.

At the very top, the weightless ship was thrown into the sky at a tremendous speed and so required but little use of its jets to get out of the atmosphere.

The voyage to the space station was quick, and Jess's stay there only lasted as long as it took her and her companions to make their way to the mixed cargo and passenger ship that was to take them to Tomasine Station.

Jess looked at the craft, a prolate spheroid adorned with bumps, knobs, fins, and raised arabesques, through a wide, round window while she was waiting to go onboard. Although the vessel had been painted bright red fairly recently, it was obviously several hundred years old and was severely battered. It, nonetheless, was no worse than were countless other interstellar ships, and Jess gave its decrepit state little thought.

Turning to Uluf, the girl commented, "I assume they're going to stick us in a corpse tank."

"It is more than likely that we will. We did not request quarters."

"Have you ever been in one before? A corpse tank that is."

"Yes. Twice before."

"Hmm. I've never been in one. What's it like?"

"It is like being dead. You will be aware of nothing. Once you have been immersed in the tank, you will lose consciousness. When you are pulled out at the end of your journey, it will seem as though you simply closed your eyes and dozed off for a moment. Even if you were in the tank for years, even hundreds of years, it would seem like no more than a minute's nap."

"That's weird."

"Not really. The syrup, the sleeping jelly, suspends all cellular activity as long as there is a charge running through it. You will be as inert as a statue, and not a single cell of your body will age. Once you have been pulled out of the tank, you will not notice that a second has passed because, for you, no time will have passed."

"Well, this should be interesting," Jess said while smiling broadly at her friend.

Arm in arm, the pair then walked over to the hallway leading to the ether-ship on which they would be making their journey.

There, they and several other travelers were met by a steward wearing a threadbare uniform with ridiculously large golden epaulettes and a barretina that was far too small for his head. He guided the passengers along a damp, dark, mildewy passage while he and they alike carefully avoided the countless hluvess that were continuously scampering out of their way.

At the end of this corridor was a wide metal door that opened onto a large room with a low ceiling. A narrow walkway ran along the wall pierced by the door Jess and the others had used to enter the room, and, perpendicular to this (reaching to a second walkway at the far side of the room), extended a series of parallel strips of flooring each composed of a sequence of metal lids. Every third of these strips had been lifted up by mechanisms at its ends so that each was set atop the section behind it. The raised portions were actually lockers that, when lowered, fit below the level of the floor. The tops of the lockers then formed the floor itself.

Beneath the lockers was the corpse tank. The entire room, except for the walkways along its front and back walls, was placed above a reservoir filled with a viscous pink syrup. Mesh cages divided this into compartments, each of which was the size of the locker directly above it.

Jess and her companions looked at the numbers printed on their passes and, wandering along the walkway just inside the entrance, found the cages marked with the same numbers. They went down the metal path extending before them, opened up the lockers to their right, and, stripping off their clothes, placed these inside the metal boxes.

Once she was naked, Jess took from her locker a strap fixed with a metal pole topped with a ring. She fastened the strap around her chest, under her armpits, in such a way that the pole stuck up behind her head, and the others did the same.

Uluf said to Jess, "There is a sort of bit attached to the strap. Take it off and fix it to your lower teeth. When you are drawn out from the corpse tank at the end of the journey, it will send hoses into your lungs and pump out the syrup. Here, like this."

Following the toad's lead, Jess attached the bit to her teeth. She and the others then sat down upon the floor and slid into the cages.

As soon as she was submerged in the corpse tank, Jess let the pink syrup flow into her lungs. She felt a tingling all over her skin and inside her torso that soon developed into a soporific numbness. Almost immediately, her body shut down, time stopped, and she was transformed into an unaging, lifeless manikin.

While Jess was floating inertly in the pink sludge, magnets in the edge of the walkway to her side were activated and drew the pole sticking up behind her back to it. The ring at the pole's top was so lined up with those rising above the persons to the girl's right and left.

After all the passengers assigned to the third of the cages that were exposed had entered the corpse tank, the attendant watching from a window lowered the lockers that had been raised back into place and exposed another third of the cages. He did the same when this third was filled, and, when the last third had received its final cadaver, he lowered all the lockers back into place.

Heavy machines promptly entered through groaning metal doors and filled the room with crates. Every bit of the floor, except for where the rows of rings were sticking up, was so completely covered with cargo.

Lying dead in a pool of sticky pink gelatin, beneath a mountain of boxes, Jess did not notice the craft she was traveling in leaving the space station floating above Shokai nor any other event that occurred during its way to its destination.

# Chapter 24
## Tomasine Station

Had Jess been conscious when the ether-ship she was traveling in approached Tomasine Station, she might have seen the structure and thought that it resembled an enormous tree. It consisted, after all, of a sort of bulb composed of a mass of closely connected structures, a long, roughly cylindrical trunk above this, and, extending from the trunk, innumerable thin limbs, many of which divided into further limbs. The various ships that came to and moved away from the long piers might even have reminded her of birds or insects flitting about the tree's branches. Since she was floating dead in a corpse tank, however, no such thoughts occurred to her.

After Jess's ship had docked and the cargo had been removed from the floor above the corpse tank, a series of small metal devices (like robotic cicadas) that floated through the air by means of antigravity engines and were moved with tiny propellers emerged from one wall. To the back end of each of these was fixed a metal cord. The machines slowly flew across the room, and each, using sensors to determine its path, snaked its way through every third row of rings before arriving at the opposite wall and fixing itself to a connector there.

Once these devices were in place, the walkways below them were raised up. The cords were drawn taut, and the connectors moved up the walls, lifting the harnessed passengers from the corpse tank. When they were out of the liquid, the pumps in the bits they had earlier placed in their mouths spewed the pink syrup from their lungs and back into the reservoir. Then, after the tubes extending down each passenger's throat had been retracted back into the bit, the cords supporting these persons moved to the side and lowered them onto the walkway.

Although she was lying naked and wet upon the cold metal of the floor, Jess felt only a hazy sort of contentment. She was so dizzy and disconcerted that, for a few seconds, she did not have a clue where she was. She simply enjoyed the vaguely sensual feeling of floating and spinning helplessly in some undefined space.

Within a short time, Jess's eyes had begun to focus and she saw through the dim light the rusting mildewy walls of the ether-ship. The girl blinked, wiped the syrup from her eyes, and sat up. There was something scratching her shoulder. She looked down. A large hluvess was clinging to her as it returned to life. While it wriggled its myriads of prickling limbs upon her skin, Jess slapped the foul thing with the back of her hand and knocked it off of her body. The jolt roused it completely and it scurried away.

Thinking of how the hluvess must have been creeping about beneath the floor during the trip to Tomasine Station and, having lost its footing, fallen into the corpse tank, Jess glanced over at Uluf to see if he had been visited as she had. He had not and was busy simply wiping the syrup from his warted face. Once he had got it out of his eyes, he noticed Jess's glance.

"So, my dear," he asked, "what did you think of your first journey in a corpse tank?"

"How long was I dead?"

"According to the itinerary we were given, twelve days," replied Uluf while standing up and opening his locker.

"Wow. It really does feel like I jumped in the tank just a few seconds ago. That's very weird."

Ofu, turning to Uluf, said with a frown, "It's already been a couple of weeks since we got in that stuff?"

The toad took a towel out of his locker and began drying himself.

"Almost," he told his companion. "Your body was essentially dead. All molecular activity ceased during the trip."

Jess stood up, got the towel provided for her in her own locker, and began to wipe the remaining pink gelatin from her skin and hair.

"It's definitely better than sitting around in the ether-ship doing nothing for two weeks," she commented to the toad. "Don't you think?"

"Yes. It is preferable, my dear, and, what is especially nice, we have arrived at our destination no older than we were when we left."

"Yeah. I've got to preserve my youthful beauty after all," the girl laughed.

Once Uluf had donned a long blue justaucorps, an embroidered waistcoat, silk britches, and a plumed bicorne, he picked up his striped walking stick and bowed to Jess, who was wearing the same pink clamdiggers and halter-top she had been when she boarded the ship.

Ofu, having put on an apron he had bought in Hwiccho, said to Jess, "Come on. Let's go meet this Buabyue person you know."

\* \* \*

Tomasine station was even uglier than was Hwiccho. The whole place was made up of a series of dark, narrow corridors leading to terminals where crowds of pasty locals and tired travelers boarded carriages that were blown down pneumatic tubes to other terminals that led to more dark, narrow corridors.

When they had gotten off the train that conveyed them from near the bottom of the station (wherefrom the pier at which their ship was docked jutted out) to about its midpoint (where Jess said Buabyue's bar was), they finally saw a clock.

"Ah, now that is fortunate," Uluf exclaimed.

Ofu looked at the clock, but it was a twenty-four hour type, the kind interstellar travelers were accustomed to using, and he did not understand what it said.

"It's four o'clock in the afternoon. That's like fourth or fifth watch," Jess explained. "With any luck, we won't have to wait too long before Buabyue shows up. Come on now."

She led the others down a wide but dingy corridor that ended in a series of doors. Beyond these was an enormous room that gently curved away to their right and left, making a circle within the station. Both the walls of this hall, from the ground level to the uppermost of its four galleries, were filled with bars, restaurants, clubs, brothels, hotels, and countless other businesses.

Although grubby, dimly lit, and worn, the whole place was alive with multitudes of sailors, merchants, and locals, whose faces were colored blue, green, orange, red, or purple by the countless blinking neon signs above them as they searched for whatever brief pleasures they could find to relieve the boredom of life onboard their vessels or of their dreary everyday chores. As these persons, howling with drunken excitement, wandered around the floor of the ring room, along its balconies with their wrought iron rails, or across the numerous narrow bridges connecting these, hawkers standing outside one business or another tried to lure them into these establishments. Some praised the quality of the liquor available in a particular bar and the low prices for which it was sold. Others lauded the skills and cheapness of the whores displayed behind the plastic walls of some brothel. Still others droned on about how pure the drugs of a certain den were or how good the food of a restaurant was.

"Lead the way, Jess," Uluf said to his friend, and she took them through the crowd, up a glass elevator to the second gallery, and along this to a bar with a façade composed of red pilasters that framed holograms of attractive young women drinking.

"This is it," Jess told her companions as she brought them through the swinging doors.

The walls within were viewing screens that projected images of a fantastic landscape of impossibly tall, distorted mountains topped with warped trees that extended their branches below a sky of incredible pinks, oranges, purples, and other colors. Looking at these images, Jess felt as though she really was in a pavilion situated atop a great mountain, which was just the impression the images were intended to convey.

She might then have thought, had she known anything about ancient cultures, that the fantastic scenery around her resembled something Maxfield Parrish might have come up with had he adopted the styles and conventions found in Chinese landscapes. Since she knew absolutely nothing of dead civilizations or their artists, however, the thought never occurred to her.

For a few seconds even Ofu was stunned and mesmerized by the amazing dream world surrounding him, as well as by its fabulous denizens. His mouth hanging open and his eyes wide, he stared in awe both at the naked women who flitted through shining, imaginary skies upon feathery wings while being pursued by amorous men with the wings of dragonflies and at the iridescent insect-like monsters that other men and women slew with golden spears and flaming swords while they all rushed past peaks like gnarled, petrified boles.

When the travelers had gotten past their initial amazement, they went to one of the round tables set in the midst of clusters of semicircular couches with which the bar was filled.

An attractive young waitress, whose naked body was completely painted with some gold colored substance that allowed images of dragons to race and dance across her flesh, came to their table, took their orders, and, a few minutes later, returned with their drinks.

"Do you see Buabyue?" Ofu asked Jess.

"No. He's not here. Let's just enjoy our drinks. If he doesn't turn up, we'll get a room and come back tomorrow night."

Several hours later, Buabyue still had not arrived and Jess was feeling more than slightly tipsy. She had not been especially wise about the amount of alcohol she had decided to consume (though she never was), and her whole body, from her mind to her eyes to her feet, was reeling and tingling in a confusing if not unpleasant way.

Hopefully, she reflected, there would not be any problems with Buabyue. She did not know how effectively she would be able to fight when she was a little drunk.

Rubbing her eyes with her hands, Jess looked around and noticed a young man sitting nearby staring at her. When he saw her returning his gaze, he lifted up his glass as a greeting, but Jess decided to ignore him. She was not in the mood for that sort of thing.

Irritated with herself for having had too much to drink, Jess sullenly sat watching the doorway to the bar for some time. Eventually, she saw entering the establishment a short, balding middle-aged man with an unusually bulbous and pitted nose and an ample potbelly. He was dressed, in the local fashion, in a loose, fur trimmed tunic that reached to his knees and was completely covered with vibrantly colorful abstract images and geometric designs. Around his neck was a huge lace collar, and his trousers were as ornate and bright as was his upper garment.

He was accompanied by a beautiful woman about Jess's age with long black hair that reached to the small of her back. She was wearing an ankle-length formfitting black dress made out of shiny rubber that had an almond-shaped opening in the middle of the chest to reveal her ample cleavage.

Around these two were a half dozen rough looking men dressed much as was the little man they surrounded, though in far less costly garments. All of them were looking around as though they were expecting some sort of trouble and were ready and happy to deal with it.

Pointing to the unimpressive individual at the middle of this group, Jess said quietly to the others, "That's him. That's Buabyue."

"Let's go talk to him," Ofu said.

"Wait a few minutes. Let him get settled first."

Buabyue sat down at the end of a black leather sofa that wrapped around a table at the back of the bar. His companions sat beside him and the young woman upon his knee. A waitress promptly brought them drinks and, as she poured them, Buabyue undid the clasps at the back of his female companion's dress, peeled down its top, took out her breasts, and fondled them roughly. The woman stroked Buabyue's ears and cheeks with one hand and let the other caress his crotch. While he must have enjoyed her attention, and did not remove his own hands from her body, the squat little man otherwise ignored her, concentrating on talking to and laughing with his cronies.

After these persons had lost themselves in their drinks and jokes, Jess said to Ofu and Uluf, "I'm going to go over there. You two wait here."

Placing his hand upon hers, the toad began to say something.

As soon as her name had passed his lips, Jess stopped her friend and reassured him. "Don't worry. I'll be careful."

Jess swung her hips seductively as she sauntered across the room, letting several of Buabyue's men eye her as she approached. When she came close to his table, they were sufficiently aroused that they did not stop her.

Striking a sexy pose, Jess looked directly at Buabyue and said, "Hi. You might not remember me, but we briefly met once before."

"I don't, but I'm glad we're meeting now. What's your name?"

"Jess."

"I'm pleased to meet you, Jess; you are a sexy little thing. Would you like to have a seat?"

As crude as were Buabyue's intentions, his tone was surprisingly urbane and his gestures pleasantly refined.

"Thanks," Jess said as she sat next to the man. "Actually, there's something I'd like to talk to you about."

Buabyue looked at her suspiciously. "What's that?"

"Don't worry. It'll help you. Believe me."

The potbellied little man puckered his mouth and rolled his eyes.

"Go on," he told her.

"Your bosses are about to be attacked."

"Oh, really? Are you going to attack them?"

"Not me, you..." Jess trailed off, thinking she had better not say what she was about to. "I found out about a plot to attack your bosses' headquarters, and I came here to warn you about it."

Buabyue laughed. "That seems very unlikely to me."

Jess pulled out a slip of paper she had stuck in her halter-top and put it down in front of Buabyue.

"Are those the coordinates for your headquarters? If they aren't, I'll leave now, but, if they are, you should listen to me."

Buabyue looked at the paper and his plump face went limp, his piscine lips dropping open as though he were a carp getting ready to devour a worm.

He turned his gaze back to Jess and, pushing the young woman from his knee, began to stand up. Jess stood up along with him.

"Come with me," he told Jess and gestured to three of his men to follow behind.

Buabyue led the others to a door at the back of the bar that was set in an image of a pavilion perched atop of a thin outcropping of rock hanging over a deep gorge at the bottom of which ran a tumultuous stream.

Beyond was a long corridor with sickly green walls of padded leather. There were several doors along either side of this and one at the far end. Buabyue took the others to the most distant door.

The walls of the room past this were made out of sheets of plastic set in fake wooden frames, and each of these sheets was painted with images of hideous grinning or threatening demons with dagger-like fangs, curling tusks or horns, wildly rolling eyes, and green, red, or blue skin.

On the right hand side of the room was a writing desk and in the middle a low table surrounded by plush chairs.

Buabyue sat in one of these, indicated to Jess that she should do the same, and motioned to his men to stand behind the girl.

When everyone was settled, Buabyue asked his guest, "Where'd you get this?"

"I used to work on a smuggling ship. My captain, Tolliver, came across it in a message."

"And I suppose you want me to pay you for it?"

"You do what you like. I'll take your money, but that's not why I'm here."

"Care to elaborate?"

"Tolliver, my captain, sold the coordinates to Tsoi Ngo, and he's planning to attack you."

Buabyue again puckered his flabby mouth between his round cheeks. "Why are you telling me?"

"Tolliver was my…I…He tried to set me up. He wanted me to blackmail you, but he'd already made a deal with Ngo. When you got attacked, you'd think I was the one who sold the coordinates to Ngo and you'd come after me. You wouldn't even have a clue about Tolliver."

Buabyue smiled. He believed the girl. A desire for revenge was a motive he could understand.

"If you're telling me the truth," he said to her, "I'll make sure you're rewarded, but if you're lying to me, you'll die."

"Fine."

Buabyue looked at Jess intently while examining the situation in his mind. After a few minutes, he asked her, "When's this attack supposed to take place?"

"I have no idea, except that it's probably going to be soon. I don't have any details."

"Okay then. I'm going to go to our headquarters to warn my superiors. You can come with me."

"That's fine with me. I'm not quitting this now."

"Good. I'll arrange for fifty million kopecks to be deposited into your account in the Imperial Bank after we leave. I assume you have an account there. Will that be a sufficient reward for your efforts?"

Jess nodded calmly, although, after something like an electric shock had surged from the crown of her head to the tips of her toes, her body went so numb that she actually wet herself a little.

"If we're attacked, or we find out that an attack was planned, or even that Ngo has the information you say he does, you'll be rich. If you're lying to me, you'll never enjoy the money."

"Yeah. You already said that. Look. All I want is to keep Tolliver from getting his way. If you want me to go with you, that's fine. Like I said, I'm not walking away from this just yet. When you're attacked, I'll even fight alongside your own soldiers. I'll do whatever I can to make sure Tolliver doesn't win in this."

Buabyue smiled at her and then said to one of his men, "I want my ship readied as soon as possible."

"Yes, my lord," the man replied and left the room.

"You have your own ether-ship?" Jess asked. Buabyue must be very rich, she thought.

"Yes."

"We're taking it to the Llalloi's base?"

"Yes."

"I hope there's enough room on it for my friends?"

"What do you mean?"

"I have two people with me who will be wanting to come."

"Who?"

"One of them is the cook from the ship I used to work on. Tolliver betrayed him too. Anyway, he's not going to let me go on my own. He's my friend, after all. The other one works for a gangster on Shokai named Gople Sing."

Buabyue's chubby face contorted into a grin. "Sing? You came here with a man working for Sing?"

"Yeah."

"Who is it?"

"His name's Ofu."

"Don't know him. Well, Jess, why didn't you tell me you were working with Sing? It would have prevented a lot of suspicion."

Jess realized at once that Buabyue must have some arrangement with the Sing, although she did not know what it was. Hoping not to give her ignorance away, she merely said, "I'm not here representing Sing. I'm here on my own. Your business with Sing and his gang is between the two of you. I'm not involved. If you want to talk to Ofu about it, go ahead. Just don't think that I'm part of any deal there. I'm here for myself."

Buabyue suspected from the girl's defensive speech that she did not know about his arrangements with Sing, but he kept that realization to himself.

"Come," he said while standing up. "While my ship's being made ready, let's have a drink together. We'll invite your friends over and we'll all have a nice talk."

"If it's okay with you, I'd like to get cleaned up. I've been in a corpse tank and my whole body's sticky from the jelly."

"I'll take you back to my own home. You and your friends can shower there. When you're done, one of my men will show you to my ship. It won't be but an hour or two before it's ready and maybe another hour before we can get clearance to leave. First, though, I need to transfer the money I promised you to your account. Do you have a credit wand with you?"

Jess took her wand out of her halter-top and handed it to Buabyue. He walked over to the writing desk and inserted the wand into the mouth of a brass frog sitting there on a pedestal from the back of which rose a thin metal stalk topped with an open lotus blossom. It was Buabyue's computer.

He said to it, "Transfer, in twenty-four hours time, fifty million kopecks from the primary business account to this account. This transfer can be stopped by me, but by no one else."

The metal frog's lips moved around the wand, as though the creature was holding a cigar in its mouth, and, in an inappropriately feminine voice, it said, "This transfer will be performed as commanded. You may remove the wand."

Buabyue addressed the frog again. "I also need three guest passes to the upper residential sector, valid for today."

Three orangish tickets emerged from the side of the computer's base and Buabyue, taking these in his hand, gave them to Jess along with her credit wand.

He gestured to one of his men, a nervous individual with a pointed, rat-like face, and said, "Luhit, take this girl and her friends to my house. Give them access to my bathroom and let them get cleaned up. When they're done, bring them to my ether-ship."

"Yes, my lord," the man replied.

He then led Jess back into the bar, and she went over to Uluf and Ofu.

"Come on," she said. "We need to get cleaned up. We're leaving in a couple of hours."

Turning to the man in whose care Buabyue had left her, Jess asked, "So, why do we need passes to go to your boss's house?"

"Buabyue lives at the top of the station."

"Could you elaborate a little?" Uluf asked him.

"Yeah," Luhit replied as he waved his arms about and led his charges out of the bar onto the crowded balcony beyond. "Only rich people and their servants are allowed at the top."

"Really?" asked Jess. "I've been here a couple of times and nobody ever kept me from going anywhere."

"Where'd you go?"

"Here and to the warehouses and piers."

"Yeah. Travelers are allowed to visit the lower parts of the station," Luhit replied, relishing his chance to show off his knowledge and emphasizing his words by flapping his hands about his face. "The lower parts are where you'll find the warehouses where ships unload their goods so they can be transferred to other vessels, the repair facilities to keep the ships running, and whatever else space travelers need. Yeah. That's right."

"Oh. Okay."

"How is the remainder of the station laid out?" Uluf inquired. "I assume we would not have been allowed to visit all its parts."

"No, you wouldn't have. Above the lower section is this one, where you'll find the shops, brothels, bars, hotels, and so on. Of course, you could have come here. The next level is where the free residents live. Yeah. Then there are the levels for the station's slaves. The bottom ones are for the low ranked slaves and the top ones for the high ranked slaves. At the top of the main cylinder is the upper residential sector. It's the priciest part of the station and access to it is strictly regulated. Yeah. That's where Buabyue lives. Last of all, sticking out of the cylinder are the government buildings and the palace of the Ivé family."

Turning to Jess and nearly jabbing her eyes with his long, sharp nose, Luhit informed her, "They definitely wouldn't have let you in there. Yeah. You definitely wouldn't have been allowed in there."

"Who are they? The Ivé I mean." Uluf inquired as the group continued along the gallery.

"They own Tomasine Station."

Jess leaned close to Uluf and whispered, "Hey. There's a guy who was in the bar earlier following us."

"Do you think he is up to some sort of mischief?"

"I'm not sure. He looked like he just wanted to have sex with me earlier, but maybe he wants more. He's the one with the long braids. Keep an eye on him."

"I will," the toad promised.

Luhit turned into a train station, followed by the others, and they all boarded the next train that came to stop in the transparent tube in front of them, as did the man from the bar.

While Jess and the others were sitting inside the carriage and heading down the side of the station, Uluf asked Buabyue's henchman, "Are there many slaves here?"

He laughed and threw his arms up into the air. "Everyone who works at the station is a slave."

"Are you a slave?" Jess inquired.

"No. I work for Buabyue, not the Ivé. Only the people who run the station are slaves. Yeah. Most of the shops are rented out to free residents. Some of the top officials working for the Ivé are free too, and most of their security teams. Everyone else, from longshoremen to mechanics to clerks to government officers, is owned by that family."

"That must keep costs down," Ofu noted.

"Yeah. I'm sure it does. They don't buy any slaves, either, so they don't spend money even for that."

"Where do they get their slaves, then?" Uluf asked.

"Most of them are born to other slaves. The rest they get from residents who default on their taxes, especially the air tax. It's pretty steep."

"The air tax?" Jess asked.

"Yeah. Yeah. If you stay here longer than a month, you'll have to pay it. It costs money to run the oxygen plants, you know. If you don't pay it, you become the property of the Ivé."

"How's that?" Jess exclaimed.

"It's on the documents you signed when you came onboard the station. Yeah. You should have read them. I don't suppose it matters, though. You'll be leaving in a few hours anyway."

Just then, the train arrived at the travelers' destination and they and their guide got off, though without being followed by the man who was shadowing them earlier. Once they had shown their passes to a guard standing at the exit to the station, they stepped into a vast open room.

The walls were lined with rows of ornate stone buildings and, above these, a balcony upon which was situated another row of similar buildings. A third tier of structures rose from a balcony placed upon the second tier, and a fourth and a fifth had been constructed yet further up.

There were also, in this cavernous chamber, wide, tree lined walkways in front of all the rich buildings, and those built above the lowest level were attached, with graceful bridges, to islands of similar structures that rose up in the middle of the room.

Jess stared in wonder at this place, and at its equally impressive roof. This was formed of a multitude of viewing screens (set in a metal framework) on which were projected images of a blue sky filled with gently drifting white clouds.

"Who lives here?" she asked.

"Drug barons, smugglers, exiled dictators, rich traders, war criminals," her guide explained with exaggerated gesticulations. "Yeah. If you've got money and need to be at the center of interstellar trade, or just need to get away to a place that doesn't care what you do, so long as you can pay your bills, this is where you need to go."

As Luhit said this, he led the others to a moving pavement, which conveyed them beneath rows of blossom laden trees, past fountains and gardens, and beside elegant eateries and cafes to a spiraling escalator that took them to the very top tier of buildings.

"This is Buabyue's place," the travelers' guide stated while the group approached one of the most impressive of the houses, a substantial edifice of polished pinkish stone.

Luhit knocked upon the green copper door, and, when a young woman in skimpy livery opened it for him, he gave her Buabyue's instructions. The serving girl let her boss's guests into the man's ostentatiously sumptuous home and led them to a marble bathroom that, by itself, was many times larger than were most of the residences Jess had ever been in.

There the servant and Luhit left the three, allowing these persons to shower and clean themselves.

# Interlude 10
# Space Travel

If the universe were imagined as constituting the surface of a sphere, faster than light interstellar travel could be imagined as being accomplished by piercing the sphere at one point, departing from its surface, moving through its interior, and emerging again upon the surface at another point.

The interior region of this imaginary sphere, that through which interstellar travel occurs, is actually a separate universe. This was designated the Emmenthal by early scientists who noted its resemblance to the honeycombed cheese. At about the same time this region was so named, the network of passages running through it came to be known as the Warren and the individual passages as ducts. All of these terms, or variations of them, have remained in use up to the present day.

Most interstellar travel takes place along repeatedly traversed routes since movement through a duct results in the widening of that duct and since the wider a duct is the less resistance it will give to the passage of an ether-ship. Because of these effects, a vessel can move faster through a wide duct than a narrow and will require less energy to do so.

Fortunately, ducts do not contract after they have been widened. Humanity has consequently been able to make use of a network of passageways connecting countless solar systems that was created by ancient space faring species. The majority of the ducts currently traveled by humans were, in fact, merely rediscovered by men.

While ships can form new ducts by burrowing directly through the body of the Emmenthal, this involves the expenditure of a substantial amount of energy and is much slower than moving through a pre-existing duct. It is, as a result, rarely done.

Movement through the Warren is not, however, the only energy intensive activity required to travel through space. Piercing or tumbling into the Emmenthal also consumes energy in considerable quantities. Smaller ships, therefore, are rarely equipped with the devices, called divers, required to do so.

Such vessels, to enter into the Warren, make use of gates called rabbit holes that are set up in nearly every colonized system. Larger ships will often, in order to conserve their fuel, make use of rabbit holes as well.

These gates are always located on the outskirts of solar systems as the gravity well created by a sun causes distortions that make the pathway from this universe to the Emmenthal unstable. Passage through a rabbit hole located within a gravity well is thus exceedingly dangerous and is best avoided.

Once within the Emmenthal, a vessel ceases to exist in ordinary space and cannot even be detected from our universe. Nonetheless, movement within the Warren can be detected by other vessels present in it.

In the first days of rapid interstellar travel, it was discovered that ships journeying through the Emmenthal caused the walls of the Warren to resonate – much like sea going vessels produce a wake in the water they are moving through. Unlike the wake of a watercraft, however, an ether-ship's ripples extend both before and behind it. Such a vessel can, consequently, be detected not only by those following after it, but also by those it is approaching. To date, only two known species, the shiyu and iliyo, have developed engines capable of moving a ship through the Emmenthal without creating a resonance.

Although such effects have been noted and studied, relatively little has been learned about the physical laws of the universe wherein they occur. The Emmenthal remains largely mysterious to this day.

Nothing, for example, is certainly known about the existence of life within the Emmenthal outside of the Warren.

Within the Warren, however, a number of non-intelligent species can be found.

Several of these are parasitic and harmful to space craft. Like barnacles, such beings often take up residence on the hulls of vessels, and their colonies can form significant encrustations. When made up of members of species that produce corrosive chemicals, these colonies can cause mild or severe damage to a ship.

The different species of such parasites are collectively referred to as mites since the Emmenthal is infested with them just as cheese is sometimes infested with ordinary mites.

From Pollidor's *Big Blue Book of Knowledge*

# Chapter 25
# Down the Rabbit Hole

When she had bathed, and washed away the stickiness of the syrup from the corpse tank, Jess dressed herself in her black tube top, red skirt, and dark vest and walked out onto a balcony adjoining the bathroom. Ofu was already sitting in a chair there, and she sat in another near him to wait for Uluf to finish getting ready. She knew from experience that the toad was fond of preening himself and would surely take some time to do so in such an exquisite toilet.

The town before her, with its various levels, connecting bridges, quaint houses, and tree lined streets, was genuinely lovely. Jess watched as uniformed servants rushed about laden with packages, as wealthy, elegantly dressed men and women wandered through gardens, and as young men reclined upon green lawns with the women they were trying to seduce.

She also noticed, leaning against a tree across the street from Buabyue's house, a nicely but not richly dressed man smoking a long glass pipe and occasionally glancing in her direction. Shortly after he saw Jess on the balcony, the man walked away and disappeared, leaving Jess feeling distinctly uneasy.

Perhaps, the girl reflected, she was being unduly suspicious, but she still thought it wise to remain a little more conscious of her environment than she usually was.

Whatever precautions she was going to take were not, however, going to interfere with her present appreciation of her surroundings. As she gazed across the vast room below her, the screens set in the ceiling changed from blue to golden, washing the buildings with a dazzling yellowish radiance.

Stunned by this artificial dusk, Jess muttered to herself, "Just so, just so."

Several minutes later, after having cleaned and beautified himself (and after having put on a woman's summer kimono), Uluf joined his companions. They then found Luhit, who led them from his master's house back to the station. There they boarded another pneumatic train, and this conveyed them to the level where the lowest of the slaves lived.

Getting up from his seat when the carriage had stopped, Luhit urged the others to rise as well. "Come on, now. Come on. Yeah. I have something I need to buy in case the boss wants me to go with you."

The travelers followed their guide down a rusting metal tube that was lit by flickering yellow lights and opened on either side onto a series of small rooms. Each of these was equipped with a sliding metal screen that could be used to close the room off from the walkway, but it was so warm and stuffy inside that most of the screens had been left open.

Within these grubby, dimly lit apartments, men and women sat or stood about watching picture vats or image harps, talking on telopticons, chatting with one another, playing games, drinking, shouting at their children, or otherwise living their impoverished lives.

Luhit led the others down a series of corridors, past many such habitations, until he came to an apartment where a skinny (or rather skeletal) woman was squatting on a plastic stool suckling a greasy baby at her withered, pythonine breast.

"Is Ingric here?" Jess's guide asked the woman.

She stood up, walked to a doorway in the back of the room, pulled aside a cloth hanging across it, and shouted for Ingric. A few moments later, a man wearing a tunic and trousers printed with geometric designs obscured with oil and food stains came out.

"What can I do for you?" he asked.

Luhit rubbed his twitching hands. "I might be going away for a while. Yeah. That's right. I need about ten ounces of chu."

"I don't have that much."

"How much do you have?"

"About eight ounces, I think."

"I'll take it. Yeah. I'll take it."

"I'll give you six, but I need the rest for myself and my other customers."

"Seven."

"Six and a half."

"Fine. You got the money?"

With broad, overly dramatic motions, Luhit took a handful of coins from a pouch hanging at his waist, sorted out several of them, and handed these to Ingric.

"Hang on," that man said as he went back into the room where he had come from.

A few minutes later, Ingric returned with a vial filled with a black paste and gave this to his customer.

"Have a nice trip," he said.

Luhit smiled, baring his prominent yellow teeth, patted his supplier on the shoulder, and led Jess and the others back down the way they had come.

As they were walking, Jess asked the man, "Why are you buying that stuff from a slave? You work for the Llalloi."

"I don't know what you're talking about."

"You don't have to play dumb with me."

"Even if I did work for the Smuggling Syndicate, they don't deal with chu. It's not worth the trouble for them. It's a poor man's drug. Yeah. There's not enough profit in it for them."

Jess thought about that and realized the man was certainly correct. Chu was a mild hallucinogen and produced a pleasant sense of euphoria. It did not provide the wild experiences russa did. It was not as addictive or as rare as russa was either.

"So," she asked, "I guess chu's not legal here, huh?"

"Yeah, it is, but the taxes on it are too high. Good thing is there's always someone trying to unload a little contraband. Why pay premium price when you can get it for cheap from some slave? They're happy to sell whatever they've got to anyone who'll give them a few groats."

While they were talking, the travelers lined up one behind another and walked close to the wall to allow an approaching group of surprisingly well dressed men to pass.

These persons were squeezing by Jess and her companions when she caught a glimpse of a glint of metal from one of the men's right hand.

Without thinking, she pulled the thread up through her spine, slowed time, reached her own hand inside of her vest, and placed it upon her sword.

Sensing motion behind her and spinning around, Jess saw one of the men who had already passed her turning back to stab her with a kriss.

She dropped into a squat, pulled out her sword, and allowed the segmented blade to slide from the hilt.

Before the man in front of her could react, Jess jumped at him and sliced his legs off immediately below the groin.

Her victim's torso had just fallen onto the floor beside his still vertical legs when the man who had first caught Jess's attention jumped at her and tried to stab her with a knife. She dove to the side and decapitated him as he moved past her.

Five of the remaining men lunged at her at once, two from one side and three from the other. Jess, twisting the universe around her and drawing one of her daggers, ran up the rounded wall across from her companions, over the ceiling, and jumped down behind the two men who were further down the corridor in the direction she had just come from.

Her enemies' backs were towards her when Jess chopped off one man's head with Dawn's Spine and drove her dagger into the brain of the other through the spot where his cranium met his spine.

Before that second person had collapsed onto the floor, Jess threw her dagger at the closest of the three men in front of her, hitting him in his throat. He made a nasty gurgling sound as he sprayed the corridor with blood.

Ofu, while this individual died, jumped upon one of the two men standing next to him, who, Jess noted, was the person she had seen ogling her in the bar earlier, and snapped his neck. Luhit tried to do the same to the last of these three, but his enemy knocked him down instead. Buabyue's henchman would then have been killed had his attacker's body not suddenly been shredded by a volley of needles.

There were four more men standing a little further down the hall, between Jess and the station she had been heading towards, and one of them was holding an automatic needle rifle. His first attempt to use it had led to the death of one of his companions, but he was raising it again to make a second attempt.

Ofu, Uluf, Jess, and Luhit all jumped out of the corridor into whatever apartment was nearest as the man with the rifle began firing at them.

Jess, her heart thundering with alarm, was able to find cover behind a table, where she discovered a girl of about sixteen already cowering.

From the increasingly loud noise of the nonstop impact of the needles in the table, Jess realized the man with the rifle was coming towards her.

She looked at the terrified, whimpering girl beside her. The teenager, she thought, was a pretty thing, even with her face contorted with fear and covered with tears.

"I'm really sorry about this," Jess told her as she grabbed the back of the collar of the girl's dress.

Using the thread to project her will onto the world outside, as though it were merely an extension of her self, Jess pushed the young woman into the air and held her in font of her own body. Then, mentally offering up the girl's blood and life to the goddess Haya, Jess rushed across the apartment.

The rain of needles tore through the poor, weeping creature's flesh, causing her to flail about so wildly that Jess had some trouble keeping the girl's torso between herself and her assailant. She was, nonetheless, able to hang on to the collar of the now shredded dress the dying teenager was wearing and, still using her as a shield, lunged at the gunman standing near the entrance to the apartment.

When she was almost upon him, Jess threw the nearly dead body of the girl at her attacker, knocking him backwards. Before he could aim his weapon again, Jess had lopped off both his hands at the elbow.

The last three men only had knives, and, when they saw Jess rushing towards them, they turned to flee.

Trapped in slow motion, they did not make it far. Jess decapitated two of them with a single swing of her sword and would have dispatched the last had Luhit not leapt from the apartment where he had sought cover and jabbed a dagger into the man's eye.

Jess let time return to its ordinary pace and shouted to her companions, "We'd better get out of here fast."

Luhit, though frantically whirling his hands about in a wide arc before his chest, replied to her with a calm voice, "You needn't worry about that."

"A lot of people just saw what happened," Jess said while recovering her dagger. "Aren't the authorities going to come after us?"

"I shouldn't think so. These people know who I work for, and they don't want to get him angry with them. Besides, low level slaves are pretty desperate. Yeah. They could sell the bodies for their organs. If rumors about what they do are true, they might even eat them. I don't know. But I do know that they're not going to cause us any trouble. Yeah. That's right."

Jess shrugged her shoulders and put away her weapons. "Okay then. So, who were these people?"

"I have no idea. I was hoping you'd know."

"They're dressed like people from here."

"They were probably working for Ngo," Uluf noted. "Remember, my dear, he has Tolliver with him, and the captain might have guessed that you would be coming here."

"Yeah," Jess admitted. "That's true. Well, I'm definitely not going to forget this."

The travelers made their way back to the station, and, from there, continued their journey on the pneumatic train, quickly arriving at one of the station's docks.

"Here," Luhit said to the others as he gestured wildly for them to come to the window he was standing beside.

In front of him was a long pier that extended from the central cylinder of the station. This branched off into smaller piers, and, at these, various ether-ships were docked.

He pointed. "That's Buabyue's ship there."

The vessel he had indicated appeared to consist almost entirely of a series of petal shaped sails that radiated out from a central point in such a way that the whole vessel looked like an open rose. From the midst of these huge sheets, and dwarfed by them, three narrow cylinders, a larger one flanked by two smaller ones containing the vessel's engines, projected like great metallic stamens.

A young woman with lime green hair and wearing a skimpy blue rubber dress approached the travelers. Her figure was so perfect and her complexion so flawless, Jess knew at once that she had to be a golem. She was.

The machine looked at the pink haired girl and inquired, "Are you Jess Ichikawa?"

"Yeah. That's me alright."

"Buabyue is waiting for you on the *Salamander*. Please follow me."

She led Jess, Uluf, Ofu, and Luhit into the ship, took them down its oak paneled corridors with their parquet floors and gilt metal pilasters cast in the shapes of various animals, men, and grotesques, and brought them to a beautifully carved teak door.

The woman knocked upon this and, a moment later, a man opened it for her.

In front of her, Jess saw Buabyue reclining on a green leather sofa. In one hand, he held a drink and, in the other, the breast of a golem shaped like a young woman with bright red hair wearing a tiny, skintight, yellow dress made of shiny rubber. Behind the smuggler, a pair of thugs was leaning against a bar and another two were sitting in chairs at the opposite side of the chamber.

Buabyue motioned to Luhit to join his fellows and to his guests to sit down in some of the chairs situated around the room. As Jess did so, she bent her neck backwards and looked in wonder at the view above her.

The ceiling of the room consisted of a number of screens set in an ornately cast gilt frame, and on the screens were projected images of the stars shining outside the ship. These were so clear that the ceiling seemed like the roof of a glass dome rising from the top of the vessel. In fact, when she first entered, that was exactly what Jess had thought it was. It was only when she expressed this belief that Buabyue corrected her and told her how the room was actually constructed.[*]

"Your ether-ship," Uluf said to Buabyue, "is lovely."

"Yeah," Jess added. "It's incredible. It's a lot nicer than the *Empress*."

"Thank you," the man replied with a flabby grin.

"You must be really rich," Jess noted.

"I do well for myself."

"Do you have your own diver?"

"Yes, but we'll be going through the station's rabbit hole."

Uluf inquired, "Are those solar sails on your ship?"

"Yes."

Ofu, not being accustomed to space travel, was surprised by this. "There's no sun out here. How are we going to move?"

Buabyue laughed. "The *Salamander* is able to project beams of light onto the sails when it's outside of a solar system."

The man was interrupted by a slight jolt, but then went on. "We seem to be casting off. Can I offer you any drinks while we make our way to the rabbit hole?"

---

* Though Jess had traveled on the *Empress* for over a year, she was still quite innocent about such things. Her education, as she would have admitted, had not been especially impressive.

As the vessel slowly pulled away from the pier, Jess was able to see Tomasine Station. From her perspective, it looked like a tree the size of a mountain with its base above and its branches below.

She did not, however, pay it much heed, as she had seen it before and had been handed her drink by the green haired woman who had showed her into the room. Although Jess had no idea what this stuff was, it had a pleasant spicy sweetness that was neither too spicy nor too sweet.

While sipping the slightly frothy liquor, she noticed that Buabyue's eyes were caressing her body from her face to her feet, though they did seem to linger on certain parts longer than on others. Jess was accustomed to such behavior, but, after a few moments, she nonetheless began to grow uncomfortable with his stares.

Seeing his friend's annoyance, Uluf decided to distract his host. "Sir, if you do not mind my asking, what do you intend to do upon arriving at our destination?"

Looking away from Jess's thighs, Buabyue said, "Ah, well, I'll tell the Llalloi Council what your friend told me. It will be up to them to decide what to do. Hopefully, if she's right, Ngo hasn't attacked yet."

"What if he has?" Ofu asked.

"You needn't worry, my friend. Your boss isn't ruined yet, and we're not abandoning you."

"If Ngo's crushed your lot, what can you do?"

"Ngo isn't going to break the Llalloi with one strike."

"How can you be sure of that?"

Buabyue was beginning to get irritated. "Even if Ngo cut off the head of the Llalloi, we wouldn't die."

Jess had a pretty good idea how the Llalloi were organized from Tolliver's dealings with them. They had some sort of mysterious cabal at the top, but nobody knew anything about it, or even, until Tolliver's discovery, where it was located. This inner echelon handled some of its business directly, but, more often than not, its members left the running of their empire to representatives in charge of different regions. Buabyue was one of these. He coordinated the shipping of russa in his area, but even he did not do so directly. He sent the information for setting up shipments, making payments, taking deliveries, and so on to a vast number of dummy corporations that were no more than computer programs, and these conveyed the information to other similar companies. Such instructions were eventually sent to companies operated by independent contractors who, in turn, hired various ships to make deliveries. The captains of these ships, and the bosses of the companies that hired them, knew what they were doing, but they did not have any way to implicate the Llalloi if they were caught. The most they could do would be to give their interrogators the name of the company from which they had received a contract. But, since the Llalloi would have heard about the problems that company had encountered, they would already have closed the dummy corporation down.

As long as a few of their higher officers survived, or even their regional representatives, the Llalloi would not be wiped out by any single attack on them. Of course, without their hierarchy in place, those that survived could wind up turning on one another and finishing off their enemy's work. If they did help one another out, however, with all their contacts and their loose but effective organization, the Llalloi might not only survive, but could potentially still defeat their attackers.

After so reflecting, Jess noted, "Yeah, but you still need someone to supply you with russa. I thought you only had a deal with Ngo."

Buabyue looked at Ofu, who looked back at him vacantly. The smuggler realized that Sing's henchman had no more idea what was going on than did the girl. He had no intention of sharing what he knew with them, either.

The Llalloi had built up enough of a stockpile of russa to last for years, but all they really needed was enough to tide them over until they had set up a new government in Tozana and handed the mudjumpers in that country over to the Sing. They would then have a new supplier, while Ngo would still have to make deals with innumerable local gangs and set up a distribution system from nothing.

Actually, Buabyue thought, this whole situation could provide the smugglers with the means of getting rid of the Ngo. If it did, with the Sing under their control, the Llalloi's profits could soar. More importantly, his own profits could.

"You needn't worry," he told Jess. "We're going to take care of things. Ah, the rabbit hole is just ahead."

Jess and the others immediately looked at the viewing screens that formed the ceiling and saw this structure before them.

The rabbit hole was an enormous, complicated ring floating some distance from Tomasine Station.

As the *Salamander* came near it, the middle of the ring filled with a flickering light that soon resolved itself into a silvery, shimmering sheet of something that did not seem to belong to the ordinary universe. It was more like an animated painting of a turbulent sea than it was like anything that might be encountered in reality.

Within a few minutes, the ether-ship was piercing through the rabbit hole and entering into the complex of ducts that made up the Warren.

As the *Salamander* so tumbled, Jess briefly lost any sense of up or down, inside or outside. Everything became a colorful maelstrom in which she could not discern what was her body and what the objects outside of it, nor what the relationships were between any of these.

This sensation passed quickly, as it invariably did when she left reality and entered into the Emmenthal, and Jess looked back up at the image screens above her head.

Though she had traveled through the Warren on many occasions, Jess still found the way it looked a little unnerving. The ducts were gigantic tunnels that appeared to be part of some living organism. Their walls seemed soft and frequently undulated with slow or spasmodic contractions. Being in the Warren, Jess thought, was like passing through the intestines of some giant monster.

If this impression were not sufficiently disconcerting, the very oddness of the Emmenthal could make it even worse. The walls of the ducts were made of a substance that did not look like anything in ordinary space. Traveling through the Warren was, consequently, an almost hallucinatory experience, like finding oneself wandering inside of a painting or an animated film. There was something thrilling about the weirdness of this neighboring universe, but it took some presence of mind not to be horrified by it.

Jess, fortunately, was accustomed enough to the Emmenthal not to be frightened by it, but was not so accustomed to it that the sight of its wonders failed to thrill her.

Her heart racing with excitement, she craned her neck to hunt for new spectacles or for the chance to see sights so strange they consistently enthralled her no matter how many times she had seen them before.

Upon the quivering wall of the duct, Jess spied a flock of peduka feeling about with the two sets of antennae projecting, like sprays of colorful feathers, from their mile long bodies, which were sheathed in chitinous, spiked, segmented shells that shone with shifting, variegated lights.

As she watched these unearthly creatures hunting down countless thousands of creeping beasts and sweeping them into their great mouths, Jess caught sight of a swarm of suapu floating upon the invisible currents surging through the Warren.

"Look at that, Uluf," she cried out excitedly and pointed at one of the screens.

The toad followed her finger, as did several of the others in the room, and gazed upon the slow but graceful movements of the suapu as they moved alongside the *Salamander*.

Each of these creatures was vaguely like a slug, though its white, translucent body, filled with red and yellow organs, was thick and round at its front end and tapered to a point that branched into a number of root-like tentacles at the other end. They were utterly alien and quite beautiful.

Jess grabbed Uluf's arm and exclaimed, "That's the most I've ever seen at one time. They're really amazing."

"They do have an otherworldly loveliness," the toad replied.

"Yeah. It's unbelievable that they can live out there."

"The creatures of the Emmenthal are certainly like nothing that exists in our own universe."

The girl and her friend sat watching the suapu for several minutes, until the *Salamander* had accelerated to such a speed that it left them behind.

"Now," Buabyue announced, "I think I will retire to my bed and get a night's sleep. Then it's to my corpse tank for the remainder of the voyage. There are others available if any of you would prefer to remain preserved through the journey ahead."

"Why are you going to go sleep first?" Jess asked.

"I've been awake a whole day, and lying in a corpse tank isn't like sleeping. My body needs to be rested for when we arrive."

"Oh. That makes sense. I guess I'll do the same. I am pretty tired."

Gesturing to the buxom women with brightly colored hair standing around him, he added, while looking at Ofu, "If you'd prefer to stay awake, my golems will attend to your needs, whatever they may be."

Jess did not miss her host's point and asked, "Do you have any male golems?"

"No, my girl, I am afraid I do not."

"Fine. I'll just get some sleep and get into a corpse tank, then."

"As will I," added Uluf.

Ofu decided to entertain himself with Buabyue's golems for a while before he entered one of the tanks.

# Chapter 26
# Torment and Travel

Eshwurhiyo's naked body, or what was left of it, as both her right hand and her left leg below the knee were missing, was supported by a dozen thin metal rods that pierced her flesh and kept her hanging a few feet above the floor. These rods, bent like the legs of a spider grasping its prey, came together in a mechanical box behind the woman's back. Above the box was a sort of halo of metal tubes (arranged like a starburst set upon a series of concentric circles) that ran from the box to a collection of globular glass containers suspended over Eshwurhiyo's head. These were filled with blood and various chemicals that were regularly pumped into her body to prevent her from dying.

The eyelid of her remaining eye had been cut off and a tick-like robot that had burrowed into her skin above that eye had to continuously spray it with water to keep it moist. Other robots, like nasty metal spiders, crawled all over Eshwurhiyo's body, squirting each new wound they discovered with chemicals to staunch any bleeding and so prevent the injuries the woman suffered from killing her.

As wretched as Eshwurhiyo was, she could not offer any resistance, since her arms and legs were each grasped by the long fingers extending from the arms of the mechanism holding her. She could not even curse her tormentors, for all her teeth as well as her tongue had been torn out of her mouth, which was itself held in place by a vice that had been driven into her facial and jaw bones.

Although the woman's condition was horrifying to see, the room she was in was not some grim abattoir, but was luxuriously if gaudily decorated. At intervals along the walls were gilt pilasters shaped like trees adorned with jade leaves, hung with glass fruits, and inhabited by clockwork birds and squirrels, and the spaces between these were painted with scenes of a green woodland filled with multicolored beds of blossoming flowers past which diverse animals wandered.

At one end of this sumptuous, tacky room, beneath a pergola smothered in pink roses, was a recess surrounded by concentric circles of colorfully tiled steps, and it was in the middle of this that the machine restraining Eshwurhiyo was situated.

Standing beside her was her torturer, a pleasant looking man with a smiling round face, expressive eyes, and red cheeks. He was dressed in a white apron that was saturated with Eshwurhiyo's blood and had fastened around his waist a belt from which hung a variety of knives, tongs, picks, and other cruel instruments.

He appeared to be taking pleasure in his activities (which he was) and merrily whistled a song. From time to time he glanced over his shoulder, grinning at those positioned behind him, hoping to see that they approved of his efforts. While only one of them seemed to be enjoying himself, there were three spectators present and he was performing for all of them.

At the opposite end of the room, an attractive young woman was playing a pungi, the strident notes of which filled the air. The poor thing, who was naked except for a plumed toque, was chained in a niche in the wall facing the torturer and his dying prisoner, and, although she was trying hard not to look at either of them, she was, nonetheless, visibly trembling (both from cold and from fear). She clearly did not appreciate the performance being given.

Before this girl, however, was the one enthusiastic member of the audience, Tsoi Ngo. The gangster was dreamily watching Eshwurhiyo while reclining in a plush chair smoking his long stemmed pipe and nibbling on pieces of candy that, using his long enameled artificial nails, he picked up from the trays and compotes arranged on the table in front of him.

The last person in the room, the torturer noted, was possibly the least happy to be there. He was an offworlder named Tolliver and was squirming about in a seat near Tsoi and looking simultaneously disgusted and terrified. Seeing such behavior, the ruddy, cheery man with the knives thought that it was very likely that, in the near future, he would be working more intimately with this uncomfortable individual.

A door opened and Tsoi's ancient, withered major-domo hobbled into the room and bowed before his master.

Tsoi asked him, "Have you sent the message to my dear cousin telling her to expect our guest's friends?"

"Yes, my lord. The message has been sent."

"Wonderful. Hopefully, of course, my representative on Tomasine Station will have attended to the girl by now."

As Tsoi spoke, the torturer gently held Eshwurhiyo's hand and caressed her palm. Then, one at a time, he bent each joint of each of her fingers backwards until it snapped. When he was finished doing so, he chopped off each segment of each finger and tossed these to a pair of strange monsters secured with gilt chains to a metal post that rose up in a cushion-lined depression that was surrounded by a low fence of gold filigree and situated between Tsoi and Eshwurhiyo.

The body of each of these creatures was shaped more or less like that of a dog, but its naked, warty hide was thick and leathery. Each had a long prehensile tail resembling that of a rat, comically short legs, little round ears, a drooping beard hanging from its chin, and a great gaping maw from the top and bottom of which emerged saber-like tusks.

While the two animals yipped and burped and gurgled, they greedily snapped up the tidbits they were given, licked their snouts, and begged for more.

Mechanical spiders sprayed Eshwurhiyo's mutilated hand with coagulants while the torturer patted her cheek and softly told her not to worry. He pulled a knife from his belt and cut a slice of meat from her thigh. Holding one end of this in his hand and supporting the other end with his blade, he showed the steak to Eshwurhiyo before handing it to the animals to eat as the woman watched.

Tolliver attempted to arrange himself in his chair so that he would not be able to see any of this. The sight of what Ngo was having done to Eshwurhiyo was making him nauseous, and he was afraid that he was going to be sick. He had no desire for that to happen, not only because he did not want to throw up, but also because he was afraid of what Tsoi's reaction might be if he did.

Tsoi noticed that his guest was trying not to look at Eshwurhiyo. "Now, now, my friend. You've been brought here to learn a lesson and you're not paying any attention."

"I'm sorry, my lord," Tolliver replied weakly.

"I hope this is proving to be instructive for you."

"Yes, my lord. It is."

"Well, isn't that nice," Tsoi said and inhaled the smoke from his pipe. Blowing out a thick ring, he continued. "Have you met my cousin, friend?"

"Huazheen? Yes."

"No. His sister, Hyan."

"No. I have not, my lord."

"Well, that's a shame," Tsoi stated as the torturer peeled the skin off of Eshwurhiyo's rib cage. "She is quite a lovely creature and very clever. She's also as deadly as your little friend. Oh, maybe she can't fight like that girl can, but she can come close, and I'll wager that she's far brighter than that girl of yours is. Both she and her brother really are wonderful. They do help me out in so many ways. Huazheen, I suppose you noticed, isn't so intelligent, but he's the best fighter I've ever seen. If anyone can take on your girl in a one on one duel, it's him."

"I'm relieved to hear that, my lord."

"Yes. If my man at Tomasine can't dispose of this nuisance you've burdened me with, those two certainly can."

Looking up at Eshwurhiyo, who was staring at the torturer as he fed the two animals her skin, Tsoi gave the woman a bright smile. "I suppose you must be getting hungry yourself."

"Feed my guest," he instructed the torturer.

The man let the animals have the rest of the skin and walked back over to Eshwurhiyo. He made an incision around her ankle and flayed the skin from her foot. He put it in a glass bowl fixed to the top of a brazen machine and then removed the flesh from her metatarsals, tossing this into the container as well.

When he was done, while the mechanical spiders sprayed the chains of bone and tendon dangling from Eshwurhiyo's leg with coagulants, the man pressed a button on the machine holding the meat. This activated a motor that propelled a blade that pulverized the flesh.

The torturer grinned at Eshwurhiyo, turned the screw of the vice in her mouth, and opened her jaws. Drawing a nozzle from the mechanism he was holding, he shoved its tip, which was bristling with sharp metal legs, into her throat.

Eshwurhiyo felt the spiky tips of these tiny limbs piercing her esophagus and crawling downwards, dragging the tube to which they were attached into her stomach. At the same time, a pair of spiders connected to the ends of other tubes descended from the halo behind her head and settled beside her nostrils.

The torturer flipped a switch on the device he was holding and the flesh from Eshwurhiyo's own foot spewed into her belly. Her body heaved with convulsions, but, with the tube in her throat, she could not vomit.

Once her fit had given way to a pathetic trembling, the man withdrew the tube from his victim's mouth. When its tip passed her lips, it sprayed these with a film that sealed them shut.

"I hope you enjoyed your meal, my pretty pet," Tsoi called out to her.

Eshwurhiyo began to vomit, but, since her mouth was closed up, she merely squirted some of the stuff out of her nose and choked on it. The two spiders perched beside her nose crept up her nostrils, down her throat, and brought their tubes into her lungs to prevent her from suffocating.

The woman's body continued to heave for some time, until even Tsoi began to be repulsed.

Letting clouds of smoke he had inhaled from his pipe drift out of his nostrils, Tsoi grimaced and said to Eshwurhiyo, "Ah, you are disgusting, my pet. It really does make me sick to watch such a foul creature. I suppose you were never taught any manners as a child. Filthy little beast."

As he spoke, he noticed that Tolliver was staring at the ground, not at Eshwurhiyo.

"My friend," Tsoi said, "you are not an attentive pupil."

He turned to his major-domo and gestured at Tolliver. "Show him out of the room and bring in the castellan."

"Yes, my lord."

The major-domo led Tolliver away and returned in the company of a man in his early forties dressed in expensive garments cut in the style favored in Quanya.

Tsoi, his eyes fixed on the hairy tip of the man's nose, motioned for him to occupy the seat Tolliver had vacated.

He blew a cloud of smoke at the castellan and then inquired, "What news do you have of my dear Soniyo?"

"My lord, it appears that she is intending to act soon."

"Explain."

"Our representatives in her household inform us that she has moved several thousand of her own soldiers into Jezic and provided them with a significant cache of weapons."

"What do you think her chances of success are?"

While the torturer scraped the flesh from the bones of Eshwurhiyo's right forearm and let her watch as he fed each strip of meat to the animals chained in front of her, the castellan said, "There can be little doubt that a large proportion of the first estate in Tozana will support her, as will certain factions in the military and bureaucracy. Moreover, civil unrest in Jezic is becoming severe, so it is likely that a coup will be met with approval by most of the common people as well."

"Do you think she'll succeed, then?"

"If she acts without hesitation, she should be able to take power. My concern is about her ability to hold onto it."

"Go on."

"Does she have the wits and the foresight to break the Llalloi's allies?" the castellan asked.

"I have repeatedly stressed the importance of doing so in my conversations with her, so I hope so."

"As long as she does what you have told her to, my lord, she could keep the throne. She just needs to move quickly and eliminate any threats to her position."

The torturer severed the tendons connecting Eshwurhiyo's ulna to her elbow and, holding the bloody bone in his hand, playfully tapped the woman's forehead with it before tossing it to the animals to gnaw.

Tsoi, having bent his head backwards, began shooting smoke rings from his mouth towards the ceiling. "And if she drives out the Kuma and then devotes herself to throwing lavish balls and planning her coronation?"

"The Llalloi have bought many friends in both the military and the bureaucracy. They've also used the Sing to smuggle in a substantial arsenal. Should Soniyo fail to act quickly to discover who her enemies are, and to remove them, they could well have the support and the means to dispose of her."

"We will remind her to take the appropriate measures, then."

"Yes, my lord."

"Incidentally, do we know who the Llalloi are employing?"

"None of the persons we are certain about are that important. We do have suspicions about some more significant individuals, but nothing definite. The problem is that if Soniyo treats them too roughly, or if we turn out to be wrong about some of these persons, others who weren't willing to help the Llalloi, who might otherwise have supported Soniyo, could turn against her, and us. It's going to be tricky to handle the situation effectively."

"I have complete confidence that you'll ensure Soniyo does not create any problems," said Tsoi while Eshwurhiyo's torturer plunged an enormous syringe into one of her thighs and used it to suck the marrow out of her bone.

The woman's body convulsed so fiercely that the smiling man bent over in front of her was having some difficultly keeping his tool in place.

"Please calm yourself, pet," Tsoi said to her. "You needn't worry yourself unduly. We aren't going to let you die. I do so want for your brother to see you again, after all."

As tears rolled from Eshwurhiyo's eye and gurgling noises came from her throat, the torturer squirted her marrow into a bowl to give to the animals in front of him.

Tsoi, meanwhile, took a deep draught from his pipe and stood up, followed by the castellan.

"Give her a little break," Tsoi told the torturer. "Just use the pain machine on her. We'll chop her up some more later."

The gangster and his servant walked to the door opposite the one through which the latter had entered while the torturer jabbed a wand into the back of Eshwurhiyo's neck.

This device directly stimulated her brain and filled the whole of her body, inside and out, with a sensation far more agonizing than that of being on fire.

A servant opened the door in front of Tsoi, and he and the castellan stepped onto a balcony overlooking the sea that was set high in a wall of the Ngos' incredible palace.

Leaning over the banister, Tsoi said, "I hope that you will not disappoint me."

"My lord, I invariably endeavor to do my best to satisfy you."

"Pay close attention to the situation in Tozana."

"I will, my lord."

"I cannot depend upon Soniyo. The woman is an idiot. I am afraid that the moment she's overthrown the Kuma roshpai she'll settle into the palace, start picking robes for her coronation, and forget about everything that could help ensure she retains such things."

"You can rely on me, my lord," the castellan said, and Tsoi allowed a cloud of smoke to drift out of his mouth and be carried away by the wind.

"I do hope so. Now, have you received any news of my uncle and cousins?"

"Yes, my lord. Your allies have joined them and the lot are on their way to Suturik."

"The major-domo has just informed me that he's let them know about Tolliver's little friend, that she might be arriving there to meet them."

"I doubt if she will be much of a problem, my lord."

"That girl has been nothing but a problem. Oh, we'll still chop the Llalloi's head off, whether she's there or not – I've no doubt about that – but I don't want to underestimate the trouble that child could cause us."

"Huazheen and Hyan are both excellent fighters, and your allies are among the best in the known universe."

"Yes, but it would be foolish not to take whatever precautions are required for us to win."

\* \* \*

Beside one of the wood paneled walls of the dimly lit cabin, near a little round porthole, was a polished metal platform with a round lid fixed to its top. A pair of nearly naked female golems with blue-green hair opened this and lifted Jess from the cylindrical corpse tank below, in which she had lain dead throughout the journey.

After she had recovered her wits, Jess asked one of the plastic automatons, "Are we out of the Emmenthal yet?"

"Yes. The *Salamander* emerged from the Warren seven hours ago."

"How long was I dead?"

"Six days."

"That's really weird," Jess exclaimed as the two golems began toweling off her body. "I feel like I was in Hwiccho on Shokai yesterday morning, but I know it's been more like two weeks. More than that, actually. This is definitely a better way to travel than sitting in your cabin and staring at your feet."

One of the golems smiled at her and asked, "Would you like something to eat?"

"Yeah. That sounds great. Come to think of it, I really haven't eaten anything since I was in Hwiccho."

"What would you like?"

"Is anybody else going to be eating with me?"

"You will be dining with Buabyue and your companions, should the latter care to join you."

"Okay. Well, I'll have whatever everybody else is."

"I will convey the message to the cook," the golem informed her and left the room.

The other machine finished wiping the pink syrup from Jess's body and brought over a red dress made of a paper thin rubber-like substance.

"You may wear either this or the garments you brought with you."

Jess took the dress in her hands and examined it. "I'll wear this."

The golem helped her put on the skintight garment, the long skirts of which reached to her ankles and were slashed nearly up to the hip on either side.

Jess looked at herself in a full length mirror set in one wall and smiled widely. "Ooh, I'm pretty sexy in this, huh?"

"Yes, you are, madam."

Jess turned to look at the golem. Her eyes were slightly larger than were those of an ordinary human and her features more regular, but she could easily have passed for a woman.

"You look really real," Jess noted. "May I touch you?"

"Certainly, madam."

Jess ran her fingers along the golem's arm and then felt her cheeks. The automaton felt just like a person. Biting her lower lip, smiling wickedly, and raising her eyebrows, Jess squeezed one of the golem's breasts. It felt like an ordinary breast. Being a little embarrassed, she pinched the golem's nose and laughed, hoping thereby to relieve her own tension.

The golem echoed her laughter in a way that reminded Jess the young woman in front of her was a machine and her reactions the results of a behavioral program.

"Are you like a person in every way?"

"Externally, I am similar but not identical to a human being."

"How are you different?"

"My eyes are larger than are those of most humans. My legs are longer. My hips are wider. My bust is larger. My waist is narrower. My skin is not affected by the presence of fatty tissue or scars. I do not have body hair."

"No body hair? Really? Why not?"

"Golems are cast in a mold. All hair is added after the body has been produced. The hair on the head, the eyebrows, and the eyelashes can be attached with one appliance for each of these. Body hair would have to be implanted one hair at a time. That would be prohibitively expensive."

"May I see?"

The golem held out her arm and Jess inspected it closely. There was not a hair on it.

"You're solid inside, right?" Jess inquired.

"That is correct."

"How far does your throat go, then?"

"It extends through the neck to the top of the torso."

"What about those?" Jess asked pointing to the golem's crotch.

"The vagina extends to a mock cervix and the rectum is approximately nine inches in length."

"May I see?"

"Certainly," said the golem as she sat upon the bed against the cabin's back wall and lifted up the skirts of her dress.

"It's very realistic," Jess noted. "Thanks."

"Is there anything else you would like to see, madam?"

"No. That'll be fine. Anyway, I guess I should go get something to eat now."

"As you desire, madam. Please follow me."

The golem led Jess out of the room and through a series of luxurious corridors to an elegantly decorated dining hall. There she saw Buabyue already sitting at the end of a long oak table.

Looking up from his food, he gestured for Jess to join him.

"You're the first to arrive," he said. "Your friends have been awakened, though. I'm sure they'll be here shortly."

The golem with Jess pulled out a chair for her and she sat down, thanking the machine for her efforts.

"Would you like some coffee?" Buabyue asked.

"Yes, please."

Addressing another of his scantily clad golems, this time one with purple hair, Buabyue said, "Fetch some coffee."

The golem bowed and replied, "Yes, my lord."

A few minutes later, she returned with a tray, placed a cup in front of Jess, and filled it with steaming coffee.

As Jess sipped this, Buabyue asked her, "How is it?"

"It's really good."

After a moment's pause, she said to her host, "I guess you're worried about your home."

"My lieutenants will attend to things there for me."

"Sorry, I wasn't talking about Tomasine Station."

"Do you mean Suturik?"

"Is that where we're going?"

"You didn't know?"

"Actually, no. I had the coordinates, but I never got around to looking up the planet, never mind the exact location on the planet."

"Well, there's no harm in telling you. We're going to Ekeya. It's a city on Suturik. However, that's not my home."

"I thought you were part of the Llalloi. Isn't that where they're from?"

"Yes. It is. However, few of their regional representatives are from Ekeya. If we're especially successful, we might wind up there, but we come from other places and start with other positions in their organization."

"Really?"

"Yes. Don't you think if we were all from Ekeya that somebody might notice and realize that's where the Llalloi are based?"

"Yeah. I guess that's true. So, the Llalloi don't really run their own organization?"

"The Llalloi aren't a family like the Ngo. They're more like the other gangs in Quanya. You're a Llalloi if you're a member of the organization. The top levels of the Llalloi are based in Ekeya, but the rest of the organization is spread out."

"But the people in Ekeya run the whole thing, right?"

"That's correct. They control the money and make all the decisions. Ah, your friends have arrived."

Uluf and Ofu entered in the company of a pair of female golems. The automatons led the man and the toad to the table and seated them there.

Buabyue instructed one of his golems to bring food, and, a few minutes later, she wheeled out a cart laden with plates, which she set out in front of each of the persons at the table.

Jess found the meal, that consisted of slices of fish and vegetables wrapped in a kind of slightly sweet bread, to be quite tasty and greedily gobbled it up.

While his guest was consuming her food, Buabyue, who was letting his eyes rove over every visible curve of her body, whether convex or concave, said, "Jess, I've got a proposition for you."

The girl looked back at him suspiciously. "What?"

Buabyue laughed. "As much as I'd like to, that's not it, my darling child. Luhit told me what you did in the slaves' quarter."

"Okay. Go on."

"I won't be allowed to bring any of my own men into Ekeya and there could be trouble there. In fact, there's almost certainly going to be trouble."

"And?"

"I want to employ you to provide me with protection."

"You mean as your bodyguard?"

"As you will."

"I'm assuming that Ngo's planning to do something big on Suturik, and that's got to mean that he's going to be doing something pretty bloody. I want to get back at Tolliver, but I don't want to die."

Actually, Jess had every intention of making as much trouble for her former captain as she could. She, nonetheless, thought she might as well make as much money as was possible while she was doing so.

Jess popped another piece of wrapped fish in her mouth, and Buabyue said, "I'm not asking you to die for nothing. I'll add ten million kopecks to your account. All I'm asking in return is for you to provide protection for me if I find myself in trouble. Who knows, maybe nothing will happen. You'll still get the money."

Jess, pretending to consider Buabyue's proposition, twisted her face into what she (falsely) believed was a thoughtful expression, turned sideways in her chair, and gazed out one of the windows beside her. For a few moments she examined the vast petal shaped sails of the *Salamander* as these caught the rays of Suturik's sun, which so pushed the vessel towards that planet through the empty ocean of space.

Having spent enough time at her game to appear clever, Jess answered. "Okay. I'll do it."

She then gobbled up another piece of wrapped fish and exclaimed, "Why not, after all? Maybe it'll be exciting. At the least, I'll be making things just a little bit harder for Tolliver."

"Wonderful. I'll transfer the money into your account when we arrive at the spaceport. But you'll only have access to it if I'm still alive when we leave. Got it?"

Jess, who was now leaning back in her chair (not in order to appear introspective but because she had eaten so much that she was feeling more than a little unwell), nodded her head.

"Fine," she informed Buabyue while she squeezed her stomach.

As the girl slowly sank down into her chair, wishing she had shown a little more restraint, Buabyue, glancing out of one of the portholes behind her, said, "We should be arriving at Suturik shortly."

Jess turned around and saw, floating in the blackness outside the ethership, an almost entirely blue planet with pale pinkish icecaps and wrapped in pink clouds.

"Is that Suturik?" she asked.

"Yes."

Uluf, who had stood up and walked over to one of the portholes, noted, "It is an exceptionally pretty world."

"I like the pink clouds," added Jess, though she was not then able to appreciate them fully.

"They match your hair, my dear," the toad said to her as she lurched up to join him.

Looking at Buabyue, he went on, "I have not encountered such clouds on a planet with a breathable atmosphere. What is that of Suturik like?"

"Oh," answered the smuggler, "you can't breathe it. The cities are all in domes. If you venture outside, you'll have to wear a mask."

"I see," replied the toad.

Buabyue stood up. "If you will excuse me, I must leave you now to make preparations for my meeting with the councilors of Ekeya. You may return to your cabins if you'd like, or, if you'd prefer, my golems can take you to the ship's lounge. You'll be able to watch our approach there."

"Thanks," Jess said, still holding her stomach. "I'll do that."

"As will I," added Uluf while looking at his young friend.

Ofu, however, asked his host, "Could I borrow one of your golems again?"

"By all means. Take two or three if you like. They're very easy to clean."

# Interlude 11
# Suturik

**Human Settlement**

The colonization of Suturik began in 198 S.A. and was carried out by all of the major terrestrial nations of the Commonwealth. Since the atmosphere of the planet is poisonous to humans, these colonies were built within protective domes. Settlement on the planet has, as a result of the restrictions of the environment, tended to be concentrated in relatively large urban centers.

After Suturik was given independence in 322, the world quickly fragmented into a number of city states, each controlling substantial, sparsely populated stretches of territory. Such political entities have survived until the present day.

**Fauna**

Most of the species inhabiting the planet resemble terrestrial insects or crustaceans insofar as they possess an articulated exoskeleton, multiple compound eyes, and six or more legs. Body types are, however, variable. Some species have undifferentiated, segmented bodies like those of millipedes, centipedes, or woodlice. Others have bulbous bodies like those of ticks or mites. Others still have bodies divided into two, three, or more distinct segments, like those of spiders, ants, or shrimp.

Certain species also possess bladders that can be filled with buoyant gasses. These bladders, which can often be inflated and emptied at will, enable the creatures possessing them to become airborne. The majority of such species maneuver by means of two or three pairs of membranous wings.

One of Suturik's most unusual species is the brimu. These creatures resemble hollow, purple maggots approximately nine-hundred feet in length and spend their entire lives floating through the skies. Each brimu allows air to pass freely through its gaping maw and filters out and devours the various creatures, whether large, small, or microscopic, that enter into it.

**Domesticated Animals**
Several species indigenous to Suturik have been domesticated as livestock while others are used as mounts or draught animals.

Gheau, a species larger than elephants but vaguely similar to triops in appearance, are raised across Suturik for their meat, as are the slightly smaller sufine, that resemble dust mites, the similarly sized sea urchin-like eshoque, the thousand-foot-long caterpillar-like hiika, and the marginally larger sea cucumber-like cuheiya.

The locustian bureine are used as flying mounts, as are the thrip-like huvinku, the dragonfly-like kurushyi, and the vicious, barely controllable hryttha, which look remarkably like winged silverfish.

Certain non-flying species are also used as steeds, including the quick, agile, earwig-like osu, the heavily armored taaka, that are much like gigantic seed shrimp, the ferocious, lumbering moyu, which resemble oversized Cooloola monsters, and the hopping psicca, that are similar to wingless cicadas with the legs of fleas.

From Pollidor's *Big Blue Book of Knowledge*

# Chapter 27
## Ekeya

Hyan was sitting in her huge bathtub, that was perched atop its four gilt feet in the middle of a large room designed to look like a gazebo. Instead of glass walls, however, the chamber was furnished with viewing screens projecting images of a carefully manicured garden under a bright blue sky across which flocks of colorful birds flew and mountainous white and grey clouds drifted.

Although she would have preferred to have spent the entire journey in her corpse tank, and did spend a large part of it there, Hyan had so many arrangements to make that she frequently had to remain alive. Even if she had to be conscious, she was not, however, going to endure living in the wretched quarters she had found in the *Star Hopper*, the ether-ship Tsoi had purchased. In fact, as soon as she had seen the drab vessel, she had insisted upon making a few quick alterations to her suite. The fanciful gazebo with its beautiful if unreachable gardens at least gave her a place to relax when she was not dealing with the ship's crew or her allies, whose own craft the *Star Hopper* had recently joined.

A young woman was standing behind Hyan massaging her shoulders when another entered through the door opposite, kowtowed, and said, "My lady, your brother."

Huazheen entered the room, crossed over to the tub, rested his arms upon its rim, crossed his hands upon his arms, lowered his chin onto his hands, and looked at his sister.

"So, what's going on with those people who tried to kill Tsoi?" he asked.

"His agents on Tomasine got themselves killed. I've been told that our friends are on their way to Suturik."

"What're you going to do about them?"

"I'm going down to the planet before we attack."

Huazheen laughed and raised his chin from his arm. "Father's not going to like that."

"It's not up to him."

"Are you going to try to kill them all?"

Brushing her plaited hair from her eyes, Hyan replied, "I'll try to thin them out a little."

"The girl has a thread, though."

Hyan frowned and splashed her brother. "I'm not stupid. You don't think that I'm going to try to take her on, do you? I'll leave her for you."

"You'll let me get killed instead, huh?" he replied while splashing his sister back.

"Better you than me," she told him with a laugh.

Huazheen now frowned, stood up, and leaned his back against the tub, turning away from his sister.

"You're adorable when you're petulant," she informed him.

Huazheen, she realized, was none too bright and probably thought she was being serious.

Hyan decided that she ought to explain herself before he became unduly cross. "I'm just joking with you, Huazheen. I'm not serious. Don't fight the girl if you don't want to."

That comment did not improve his mood. "You think I'm a coward, then?"

"Now, now, Huazheen. You needn't get testy with me. I'm only having a little fun with you. It's entirely up to you whether you fight the pink haired girl or not. If you do, I'm sure you'll chop her into pieces. Why, after all, you're almost as good a fighter as I am."

"I'm better."

"That's only because you have a thread and I don't. You know, it's really not very fair uncle gave it to you. I only got passed up because I'm a sweet and delicate girl."

"I'm better whether I have the thread or not."

Hyan pushed herself across the tub, lifted herself out of the water, wrapped her arms around her brother's waist, and implored him with a pouty expression, "Come now, Huazheen, let's not fight. I so hate it when we fight."

He scowled down at her from over his shoulder.

"Huazheen, please. I have to leave the ship on the shuttle tomorrow to make it to Ekeya in time to meet our friends, and I don't want to spend our last day together squabbling."

Huazheen turned around and rested his hands and forearms on his sister's head. "What do you mean by 'our last day together'? Do you think something's going to happen to you?"

"To be honest, I don't know."

"What exactly are you planning to do?"

"I've decided to go after the man from Jezic. I don't know how important he is, but since Tsoi wants him dead I'm going to kill him. If I can, I'll go for some of the top Llalloi too."

"What're you going to accomplish by doing that?"

"I'll do a little of what Tsoi wants me to do and I'll have some fun at the same time. Isn't that enough?"

"Still, isn't this kind of risky?"

"It's ridiculously risky."

"You could get caught."

"That's true. I could also arouse the Llalloi's suspicion and give us away."

"Doesn't that make this kind of stupid?"

"Well, I suppose it does. If you mean that going down there on my own and trying to kill a couple of my enemies isn't very prudent, I guess you're right. Still, it's going to be tremendously entertaining, I'm sure."

"Don't let them find out who you are."

"I won't. I like a little danger, but I'm not foolhardy. It's one thing to take risks. It's another thing to commit suicide."

"So you say, but this whole plan of yours is pretty dicey."

"That's the fun of it."

"I hate it when you do things like this."

"I'm a hunter, brother. That's just who I am. What's life without a little excitement, after all?"

"You don't have to put yourself in danger like this, though."

"I most certainly do need to! What's the fun of sitting in some sky barge picking off stupid, helpless animals below you? When I hunt, it's one on one. I'm like a lioness killing an elephant. I give my prey the chance to fight back. It's not really exciting otherwise."

"You are stubborn, Hyan."

"Stubborn, beautiful, and deadly."

"And alive. So stay that way."

"I'm going to take precautions, brother."

"Then you're going to wear your mask, right?"

Hyan laughed again and again splashed her brother. "Like I said already, I'm not stupid, Huazheen. Even if there's nobody there who would recognize me – and it's always possible someone would – I'm sure the Llalloi know what people from Panjua look like. I'm definitely going to wear my mask. Happy?"

"Yeah. I don't want you dead, you know."

"I know that. I just want to have a little fun. That's not so bad, is it? Let your little sister hunt some humans. Please."

Taking Hyan's chin in his hand, Huazheen asked, "What're you going to do to them?"

"I'm going to gobble them up with my killer cunt."

Huazheen laughed and splashed his sister. "You're insatiable, Hyan, and incorrigible."

"Well, of course. That's what people say about any girl who wants to enjoy her life."

Huazheen hopped onto the rim of the tub and sat there looking at Hyan. "How are you going to get into some place where you can meet these people you're planning to kill, then?"

"That's already arranged. I'm going down with a changeling. We're going to impersonate a wealthy merchant from another city and his daughter. I'll be the daughter. That'll take care of the language problem too."

"You're joking with me," Huazheen said with disgust.

A changeling was a hybrid creature produced by inserting a demi-ape (a type of homunculus made up of little more than a brain and a few rudimentary organs) into a reanimated human corpse. The demi-ape was able to link its own nervous and circulatory systems into those of its host so that it could control the corpse and receive sustenance from it.

"What's wrong with a changeling?" Hyan asked.

"They're just revolting. You know it's a dead body, right?"

"I know, Huazheen. What am I supposed to do, though? I've been told that women don't have very high status in Ekeya, so I'm not going to be able to get into the places where I want to be on my own."

"Why a changeling though, Hyan?"

"The body's from Suturik, so it'll be completely authentic."

"Where'd you get it?"

"I brought it with me. I was thinking about going down to Ekeya even before Tsoi informed us of his latest whim."

"What about your mask? Have you worked out how it's going to look yet?"

"Yes, I have. Would you like to see it?"

"Sure."

Hyan stood up, clambered over the rim of the bathtub, and then down the steps set against its side. After her serving girl had dried off her body, Hyan sat down on a chair near one of the room's walls.

"Bring me my mask" she told her servant.

The women handed Hyan a disk shaped container something like a huge compact. Hyan opened it and looked at the odd creature sleeping inside.

It was a flat, oval thing vaguely like a ray pierced with three holes that made it resemble a face. Hyan lifted it up and briefly glanced at the countless tiny tendrils wriggling on its underside. These would soon be worming their way through the skin of her face and attaching themselves to her nervous system, thereby enabling her to manipulate the mask just as she would her own body.

Though it was a separate organism, the mask had been grown from Hyan's own cells and was, as a result, nearly impossible to detect.

She pressed it against her cheeks, forehead, and brow. For a few seconds, her weirdly distorted visage resembled a Noh mask, but, as her nervous system was joined to that of the mask, she was able to force it to spread out in some places and to thicken in others. While the odd creature could not make the face smaller where it was supported by bones, it could press against cheeks to make them thinner or fatten itself to make them rounder. It could, by building itself up, lengthen a person's chin or make cheek bones appear higher or a forehead wider or more prominent. It could even increase or decrease concentrations of melanin to lighten or darken its complexion.

When she was done contorting the mask into the shape she wanted, Hyan picked up a looking glass and examined herself. Her face was now unrecognizable and her skin much lighter than it had been before.

"I rather like this face," she said. "Maybe I'll keep it for a while. I will need to powder the rest of my skin, though. What do you think of it?"

Huazheen, who was still perched atop the rim of the bathtub, replied, "It's nice. You won't have a hard time seducing your victim."

He jumped off the tub, stretched his arms above his head, and announced, "I'm going to get some rest. Don't leave without telling me, okay?"

"Don't worry. I won't."

Huazheen left the room, and Hyan began to take off the mask. She decided not to, however, and instead admired her new face in her mirror.

"This is going to be fun," she told her reflection.

Although she had not been convinced about the wisdom of Tsoi's plan, she did appreciate both the chance it would give her for a little excitement and the potential it had to make the Ngo the richest of the Seven Families. It was even possible that Tsoi might be able to run the others out of business and win a monopoly on russa production. Of course, she thought, as daring as the enterprise was, having Tsoi pulling the strings did entail a few risks.

Hyan had long ago decided that Tsoi was an idiot who just happened to be convinced he was a genius. He was, nonetheless, the first member of the Ngo family in hundreds of years who had any imagination. Whatever his inadequacies, at least he had ambition.

In fact, Hyan would have loved to be married to him. She could not, being a woman, head the family herself, but she could run it through Tsoi if she could wed him. Eventually, she knew, he would have to think about taking a wife. If he did not, he would not be able to produce an heir. Hyan just had to make sure that she was the one he chose. After that, she could find some way to gain control of the man.

It was a shame that he was so addicted to feihi. Things would have been so much easier if he were interested in human women.

Still, even if she was unable to wed Tsoi, as long as he never married anyone else, and so never produced a successor, things were likely to go her way. Lo was next in line to head the house and, after him, Huazheen.

Although Hyan had no desire to see her father in control of the Ngo – in the matter of the succession, he was, for her, merely the means by which Huazheen could be advanced – she did need him. In fact, her life would probably have been difficult without him. Most of the members of the gang had little affection for Hyan or her brother, and some actually thought the two of them were more affectionate with one another than they ought to have been. Nonetheless, almost everyone was loyal to Lo, and that kept him and his children safe from Tsoi, who, whatever his affection for Hyan and Huazheen, could be entirely ruthless.

What was more, her influence over Lo made her useful to Tsoi. He needed Hyan to keep himself safe from her father. The man's popularity was always a threat to his nephew.

Actually, Hyan thought to herself, she would miss her father if he died. He exasperated her, but she did love him.

Be that as it may, he would make a terrible boss. He would be just another uninspired moron satisfied with the way things had been for generations. It would, she admitted, be better for the family if Lo were gone before Tsoi. She would just have to make certain that her own position was secure by that time.

Of course, Hyan reflected, even if Lo did die before Tsoi, if she had not married her cousin by then, she would have to wait until that man was dead before she could run things through Huazheen. She could very well be an old woman by that time, and that would undoubtedly spoil her ability to enjoy such a position. What fun could she possibly have as a decrepit old hag?

Hyan was not yet sure what she should do to guarantee her future status, but she did decide that she needed to come up with a plan soon. Either she would find a way to convince Tsoi to marry her or she would figure out how to remove him and Lo from her life.

For now, however, there were a number of preparations for her little vacation that still needed to be made.

* * *

The sky of Suturik was a deep, rich green across which bright pink clouds swirled and through which vermiform brimu wafted like gigantic carp shaped kites. The rugged landscape spreading out beneath this emerald dome was covered by a dense jungle of multicolored vegetation. The ground was coated by a soft, mossy blue carpet, and from this rose twisting blue trees, groves of blue fungus, and thickets of blue mold, all of which were adorned with innumerable orange, yellow, green, pink, lavender, or red blossoms, spikes, filaments, gills, or fans. Many of these strange plants were, however, shrouded by the lavender mists that curled their ways through the glens, crevices, and other low places of the wilds.

Through this incredible landscape, herds of lumpish sufine and bristling eshoque gamboled while men riding leaping psicca or stealthy osu prodded some lone hiika or cuheiya with bolts of crackling electricity they threw out from rods tipped each with a metal ball, so driving the hill sized caterpillars and sea cucumbers before them.

As he gazed in awe at such incredible beasts lumbering through this strange countryside, Uluf murmured, "Just so, just so."

Jess, hearing him, thought the same and, placing her hand upon her friend's forearm, said, "Just so, alright."

These two, Ofu, and Buabyue were sitting upon cushioned sofas arranged inside an elongated glass bowl that was hanging beneath a metal engine from the top of which sprouted six long, arched, multi-jointed, stilt thin legs. Except for a pathway that circled around the vehicle's furnishings, the cabin was entirely transparent and gave the travelers the opportunity to look in whatever direction they wanted at whatever object caught their fancy.

About a quarter of an hour after this transport had left the spaceport behind, it passed over a range of translucent, crystalline hills, like half melted honeycombs interspersed with inverted icicles, and entered a wide valley. There before her Jess saw Ekeya.

The city was built underneath a transparent shield that was so tall it more closely resembled a pointed bell jar than it did a dome.

The buildings on the outskirts of this metropolis were relatively tall, but they were dwarfed by the incredibly high, impossibly thin skyscrapers at its center, the innermost of which reached to the very pinnacle of the clear canopy and actually pierced it.

Near the base of the shield was a ring of circular gateways connected to metal tubes that reached to the ground. Though Jess did not know it yet, it was through these that the city's airborne cavalry was able to issue forth and engage with its enemies.

As Jess stared at these marvels, the multi-legged vehicle she and her companions were riding in conveyed them along a road that appeared to be made of silver cobblestones and that was alive with innumerable other vehicles, each moving along on its own unknown errand. There were transports similar to the one Jess was in, as well as long, low mechanical wagons like gigantic centipedes and carriages pulled by moyu, gheau, and sufine.

After a time, the city before her having grown large as she approached it, Jess noticed an elegant gateway composed of two pillars topped by a pair of crossbars that was set in the front of a sort of fifty foot tall bell jar projecting from the side of the main dome.

When the visitors arrived at this, they found a queue of vehicles and were not able to enter the city until an officer whose body had been made weightless by a small antigravity engine and from whose back sprouted a pair of iridescent mechanical wings, like those of a dragonfly, flew up to the glass bubble atop the vehicle. The driver was seated there, and he showed to the guard the paperwork that gave permission to his passengers to pass.

Once the vehicle had entered into the glass vestibule, along with various others, those that were drawn by the giant insects were led down ramps that descended under the city. When the last of these creatures had disappeared into the tunnels, metal gates closed over their entrances and the venomous air that filled the glass room was sucked out and replaced with breathable air. A glass door then slid open in front of the travelers and they were able to enter the city.

Jess was genuinely impressed by Ekeya. Many legged vehicles walked down its wide streets under tall, thin skyscrapers, not one of which was dully utilitarian or garishly ornate. Each building was different, but nearly all were composed of distinct vertical sections, each of which either had white or pastel walls set in a dark framework or was adorned with colonnades of bright green pillars. Like those of pagodas, every one of the levels of these towers was shaded by beautifully adorned and gracefully upturned eaves.

Had Jess known anything about ancient Earthly cultures, she might have thought that the sensitively restrained elegance of the buildings of Ekeya was reminiscent of that of the structures of China or Japan and that they were entirely devoid of either the showy gaudiness of European architecture or the monotonous drabness of American. She had no familiarity with such things, however, and the thought never occurred to her.

She did, nonetheless, notice that the loveliness of these structures was enhanced by their setting. As close as the city's towers were to one another, the gardens, groves, and ponds amongst which they were situated gave Ekeya an aura of contented repose. Each building, like some fairy castle, rose up from a charmingly distorted landscape of steep little hills, precariously overhanging cliffs, deep valleys, and narrow ravines.

The travelers continued along the broad thoroughfare cutting through the very middle of the city for some time, until, at last, their vehicle came to Ekeya's central and tallest building, whose parti-colored walls were entirely covered by porcelain tiles painted with images of sinuous plants and charmingly realized beasts.

"This is it," Buabyue said. "This is the City Palace."

"Is that where the Llalloi live?" Jess inquired while squirming around and trying to adjust her skintight red dress.

"It's the seat of the government."

Jess looked at him waiting for further clarification.

"The elite of the city are the Llalloi and the government here is the organization that runs their smuggling operation."

"Don't the people know what's going on, then?"

"No. The common people have no part in the government. Besides, they're absurdly loyal to their tribal chiefs."

"Huh?"

"The people of Ekeya are divided into sixteen tribes. Each tribe is ruled by a king, and the kings are the ones sitting on the council."

"So, they're the only ones who know that the city is the headquarters of the Llalloi?" Jess asked with a laugh.

"No. The royal families do. I suppose some of the retainers might as well."

Jess stared at him without understanding.

"The families of the kings have grown large over the years and not all of the chiefs get their position by inheriting it. Some are elected by their whole family. Even in those tribes where kings do inherit their throne, their families are powerful. They're not going to be excluded from the Llalloi. You can believe me on that. I also know of a few powerful retainers that have been let in on the secret, but I don't think it's that common. I'll tell you more later. It looks like we've arrived."

The vehicle stopped in front of the palace's colonnaded entrance and lowered its glass carriage onto the pavement before a row of enormous brass robots. Each of these was shaped like a ten foot tall flea with the legs and pincers of a crab, and all of them began to twitch and click their claws as Jess and her fellows emerged from their transport.

A porter standing at the base of the stairs approached them and inquired about their business. Buabyue presented him with a card, seeing which the man led the travelers into the building and delivered them to a guard who, in turn, took them up a lift, down a series of corridors, through a sliding door, and into a pillared room with a vaulted ceiling.

Sitting in the middle of this chamber upon a large round cushion was a man in his fifties wearing a long, heavily brocaded jacket. He was occupied painting a picture upon a large sheet of paper spread out on a low desk.

He bid his guests sit upon a number of pillows in front of him, and, when they had done so, he spoke.

"What brings you to the city, Buabyue?"

"I urgently need to speak to the Council."

"What about?" the man asked as he continued to paint.

"I am sorry, Ongkri. I can't tell you. I have to address the Council first. This is extremely important."

"The Council is meeting in a few hours. I will inform them that you are here and need to tell them something."

Buabyue touched his head to the floor, and Ongkri, putting down his brush, went on. "You may wait in a guest suite until the Council calls you. If there is anything you require, please tell the serving girls. You may leave."

"Thank you."

Buabyue again touched his brow to the floor, urging Jess and the others to do the same, which they did.

Ongkri rang a bell and a young woman wearing a brocaded sarong and a cloth band beneath her breasts appeared to stand to the man's right.

"Take them to a guest suite."

"As you desire, sir," she replied with a bow.

Then, addressing the others, she said, "Please follow me."

The woman took Jess and her companions to an elegantly simple suite of rooms that opened onto a balcony planted with a lush but unostentatious garden. There they were provided with drinks and food and allowed to relax until they were called to address the Council.

# Chapter 28
## The Hospitality of the Llalloi

The guard led Jess and her companions through the corridors of the City Palace to a large hall, at one end of which was a pair of wide, ornately carved wooden doors.

He gestured towards the rows of cushions set against two of the walls and bid the members of the company seat themselves.

Buabyue turned to Jess and informed her, "When we're inside, I must ask you to remain quiet. Women aren't allowed to speak to the councilors when they're in the audience hall. If you have to say something, whisper it to me and I'll tell them."

Jess contorted her face and replied, "Fine."

The travelers had not been waiting long when the wooden doors opened and a man emerged. He was carrying a staff topped with a lantern and wearing a jacket that had long skirts and was embroidered with images of stylized insects.

He nodded to the persons in front of him and said, "The Council will see you in the Hall of Private Audiences."

The travelers stood up; the man asked them their names and then instructed them to follow him.

The Hall of Private Audiences was a large but by no means overwhelming room that was made to seem far smaller than it really was by the forest of pillars crowded within it.

Jess and the others walked through these and seated themselves on cushions set on the floor in the middle of the room. Before them, on a platform at the end of the hall (the steps of which were adorned with sculpted faces), were two tall, brightly painted pillars carved with various images. Between these was a beautifully painted screen pierced near its base, at the middle, by an oval portal. It was through this that the councilors soon made their entrance.

Each of these persons, all of whom were men, wore a huge, colorful hat shaped like the head of a stylized terrestrial animal. One was a frog; a second was a pelican; a third was a lion, and still others resembled other animals, including an otter, a cuttlefish, a rabbit, a desman, and a walrus. Though Jess had never been to the Earth, she recognized some of these creatures from the faces of different species of homunculi. There were, however, a few she could not figure out. Most of the animals' visages were, after all, wildly distorted. For a brief moment, she wondered if this was because the people who had made the hats had never actually seen the animals they were depicting or because they were attempting to create fanciful representations. Either way, the hats were very odd looking.

The councilors' other garments were rich, but were not nearly as dramatic as was their headgear. Each man wore a close fitting waistcoat that was buttoned up the front, had skirts reaching to just below the knees, and was bound at the waist with a wide sash. Over this, each wore a houppelande with a long train that was being held by a young woman wearing a sarong and a strip of cloth around her torso, just below her breasts, as a sort of support for her bosom.

The councilors sat in a semicircle upon round cushions arranged on the platform, and the young women sat, with their heads bowed, behind them.

The man positioned at the end of this group, to Jess's right, whose brow was decorated with the head of a carp with a huge gaping mouth, addressed the man who had brought the travelers into the room.

"What business have we here?"

The man with the lantern replied. "This is Buabyue, the representative on Tomasine Station. These others are Ofu Not, a member of the Sing gang in Jezic on Shokai, Jess Ichikawa, a smuggler, and her companion, Uluf. They have come, my lords, because Buabyue says that he has urgent news."

The councilor looked at Buabyue. "You may tell us your news."

Buabyue, having first touched his forehead to the ground, said, "My lords, I am sorry I must do this, but I have to inform you that I have learned that you are in danger."

"How so?" asked the councilor who had spoken before.

"This girl, Jess Ichikawa, has informed me that she was employed by the captain of a smuggling vessel who discovered your location. He gave her this information so that she could blackmail you, but he did so only in order to prevent your noticing him. While deceiving and using this woman, he himself sold the information to Tsoi Ngo."

"Go on."

"Jess Ichikawa didn't follow through with her captain's plan and overhead Ngo himself saying that he was planning to attack you."

"And how could she have heard him say so?"

"She broke into his casino in an attempt to kill him."

The councilor laughed. "Ah, now that's a brave girl."

"Indeed she is, my lord."

"Why did she do it?"

"Revenge. She was jilted, after all."

The councilors laughed and shook their heads in understanding.

"My lords," Buabyue interjected, "I implore you to take action. I have seen the coordinates this woman's captain has. They are those for Ekeya."

"You needn't worry. Ngo's attack has already begun."

"My lord?"

"One of our neighbors, Padangkpei, declared war upon Ekeya only yesterday."

"My lord, I do not think…"

The councilor interrupted him. "We have had a trifling disagreement with Padangkpei for several years about grazing in a particular valley in the hills between our cities. It has never been a matter of great importance, but, yesterday, they sent soldiers into the valley, killed our herdsmen there, and took their animals. Now they are marching against us. We did not, at first, understand why they would so attack us, especially since they have neither the army nor the skills needed to defeat us, but this news of yours would explain their motives."

"My lord?"

"They must be receiving help from Ngo. That would make sense of the current situation. I can only assume that our enemies will be well armed and, perhaps, aided by mercenaries. We will have to be very well prepared. I thank you for your information, Buabyue. We might not have dealt with this attack in an adequate manner had we continued to believe Padangkpei was acting alone."

"You are welcome, my lord."

"Nonetheless, I would like for you to accompany our army to provide them with advice about any offworld mercenaries that may be with the Padangkpeians. It is, after all, possible that you will have some familiarity with any mercenaries that have been hired."

"As you desire, my lord."

"Now, have you rewarded the girl?"

"Yes, my lord. I gave her fifty million kopecks."

"Good."

Addressing Jess, the councilor then said, "Although your motives were not unselfish, you have done us a considerable favor, and we are grateful for it."

He looked at all the persons sitting before him and continued. "Nonetheless, I must ask you to remain in the city for the duration of this war."

Hearing this, Buabyue spoke to the man, saying, "My lord, if you wouldn't mind, I would like for Jess to accompany me when I leave with your army."

"Why is that?"

"She has experience fighting Ngo's men. She did try to kill Tsoi after all."

The head of the council frowned. "I am not certain that would be wise."

Forgetting Buabyue's warning, and much to his chagrin, Jess decided to speak up.

"If it's all the same to you," she said, "I'd like to go with your army to see the battle. Maybe I can help. Besides, I do have an interest in how all this turns out, you know."

The councilors collectively smiled at this. Their leader said, "You should not speak in here."

"Yeah, I know, but I don't want to get stuck waiting around doing nothing."

"You may so desire, but your wish is not possible. Our soldiers will not have time to care for you."

"I don't need anyone to take care of me. I can fight."

"Can she?" the councilor asked Buabyue.

"I have not seen her, but I have heard she can," he replied while looking at Ofu.

The Tozani told the council, "She can fight like nothing I've ever seen. In one day, she's killed more men than I have in my whole life."

The councilor smiled and with a laugh told Jess, "You may go with our army, but don't expect to be pampered. We cannot allow our soldiers to die just to protect you."

"Fine," Jess replied. "That's all I want."

"Good. For now, however, you all should rest."

Indicating one of his fellow councilors, the man said, "You will be placed in the care of Jiru's sister, the Queen of the Podgohani."

Jiru pressed the palms of his hands together before his face and addressed Jess and her companions. "My attendant will lead you to my sister's palace."

The woman behind Jiru (who was quite lovely but rather formal) moved to his side and kowtowed to him. He touched her head, and she crept away from him on all fours. When she reached the edge of the platform, she lowered her feet onto the floor and stood up, without ever turning her back to Jiru.

The woman bowed again, turned around, and, having nodded to Jess and those with her, stood before them. "My name is Ghoryi. I am pleased to be able to offer my services to you."

The leader of the council then addressed this group. "You may depart with the thanks of the council. As long as you remain in this city, you will be our guests and will want for nothing. After your departure, should your words have proved to be true, you may live your lives with the knowledge that you have our gratitude – and all that is entailed by that. You may go to your quarters and rest."

Ghoryi bowed to the head of the council and gestured for the travelers to rise and follow her out of the audience hall.

As the woman led Jess and her companions through various hallways in the City Palace, Jess asked her, "So, this Jiru's sister is the queen of her tribe, right?"

"Yes. That is correct."

"Why is it she's allowed to be a queen but can't be on the council?"

"She is the queen, but her brother is the ruler."

"I'm confused."

Buabyue (who seemed very eager to ingratiate himself with Jess) explained while examining her breasts. "Property passes from mother to daughter here, but the women don't control the property. If a woman's mother's brother is alive, he runs things. If he's dead, then her brother does. When he dies, her son takes over."

Ofu was surprised by this arrangement. "How did that happen?"

Buabyue replied, "Marriage disappeared from Ekeya long ago. They don't have wives here. I suppose it was easier to pass property from mother to daughter and to let sons and brothers manage it than for fathers to try to figure out who their sons are."

"There are similar customs in human cultures on many different worlds," Uluf interjected. "In truth, it has been my experience that such arrangements are, perhaps, the most common currently to be found."

Ofu paid the toad no attention and asked Jiru's attendant, "Is that how it happened?"

"I don't know. That's how things have always been."

The group came to a doorway leading onto a long bridge lined with lampposts that reached from the City Palace to another tower near to it.

Jess hurried out to lean over the railing and gaze at the lush gardens and curving roads far below her.

"This place really is pretty amazing," she exclaimed.

Uluf came to stand behind Jess (though he remained a good distance from the edge of the bridge), reached out his arms, and placed his hands upon her shoulders, partially to express his affection and partially to reassure himself that she was not going to plummet to her death by misadventure.

"The city is lovely from here," Ghoryi noted.

"Yeah," Jess replied without having heard a word the woman had said to her.

The Ekeyan walked over to Jess, stood beside her, and surveyed the city.

Pointing in the direction towards which the bridge was heading, she said, "Do you see that stream there? The area north of it is where the Podgohani live.

Uluf inquired, "The entire tribe lives there?"

"Yes. That is our district."

"You don't live with people from other tribes?" Jess asked.

"No. Each tribe has its own district."

Jess frowned, though she did not turn her face towards the others. "Where do people who don't belong to a tribe live?"

"There is a foreign quarter, but you can't see it from here. It's on the other side of the City Palace."

Uluf was growing increasingly uncomfortable with standing on the bridge (it was extremely high above the ground) and said to Jess, "Perhaps we ought to be continuing on our way now."

Jess turned around and smiled at him. "Sure. I guess you're right. Come on."

As the group continued its way along the bridge, Jess asked Jiru's attendant, "I hope you don't take offense, but I've been wondering, what's with the animal hats the councilors were wearing. Do you know?"

"They are the emblems of the tribes. Each tribe is guarded by the spirit of a particular beast from the ancient world."

Uluf was curious about this. "They have religious significance, then?"

"Yes."

"That is interesting. I am surprised to see earthly animals so venerated here. If you do not mind my asking, how did that come about, my dear?"

"It is all the result of what happened when Ekeya was founded."

"How's that?" Jess inquired.

"I can tell you the story if you'd like."

Jess grinned. "Please do. I love stories."

"When men first came to Suturik, the world had a single queen. The first queen had two daughters and each of her daughters had a son and a daughter.

The title passed through the senior branch. The daughter of that line became queen and her brother became the governor. His most trusted advisor was his cousin, who had become a bishop, a kind of wizard in the old religion. He was, however, an evil man who desired that the senior line should be destroyed so that his equally wicked sister could be queen and he could be governor.

"The true queen did not have any daughters, only a son, and it seemed the bishop would eventually have his desire. But after everyone had given up hope that the queen would give birth to an heir, she did bring forth a daughter, who was named Dyanu. Unfortunately, the queen died giving birth to her baby.

"Dyanu's uncle at once decided that he must be rid of this child and, when he gave the girl her first bath, as was his right as a bishop, according to the ancient custom, he consulted his book of spells. With a terrified expression, he proclaimed to the governor that his book prophesied that the child's progeny would form an army and that they would slaughter all the rest of their family.

"The governor was frightened and asked his cousin what could be done. The bishop told him he must kill Dyanu, but the governor could not bring himself to do so. Thinking quickly, the bishop then suggested that the girl be locked in a tower and placed in the care of his sister. Dyanu would thus see no other person but this woman and so would never have a chance to bear children. Thinking this advice wise, the governor shut Dyanu up in a tall tower to which only the bishop's sister had a key.

"The bishop still desired that Dyanu should be killed, however, and ever thought of some way that this might be accomplished.

"Years later, when Dyanu first menstruated, she believed that she suffered from some terrible ailment since she had no experience of the world beyond the walls of her chambers. She told her keeper of her trouble and this vile woman, seeing an opportunity to be rid of Dyanu, told the girl to put cottage cheese between her legs, claiming that doing so would cure her of her sickness."

The travelers came to the end of the bridge, where their path led through a wide cylindrical tunnel that pierced the tower in front of them and continued, at its far side, over yet another bridge.

"Once Dyanu had done as she was instructed," Ghoryi went on explaining, "the evil woman told her brother of her plan and then went to the governor. She informed him that she had seen a man enter Dyanu's chambers secretly and have intercourse with the girl. He should, she said, ask the girl what she had done and, if she would not confess to him, should feel her genitals to see if they were moist.

"The governor, fearing for his life, hurried to see Dyanu and, when she was before him, asked her if she had been with a man. She replied to this individual, who was a stranger to her, that she had never seen any person but her keeper. The governor, believing that she was lying, put his hand upon her genitals and felt the wetness of the cheese there.

"Overcome with anger, since he believed Dyanu had but recently had sex, he drew his sword and decapitated his child. She did not, however, fall down before him. Instead, her body picked up her head from where it lay upon the floor and held it before her chest.

"She accused her father of imprisoning and murdering her when she had done nothing wrong and then, her head in her hands, made her way out of the palace and the city unopposed.

"Emerging into the atmosphere outside, she was not burned, but continued on her way until she reached a spot where a spring flowed from beneath a great boulder.

"She lay down in the water and the blood flowing from her neck filled the stream. Up to this very day, it runs red. If you go there, you will see this for yourselves.

"Several drops of Dyanu's blood were, in those moments after her death, devoured by a fish. In this creature's belly, the drops were transformed into sixteen sons and sixteen daughters.

"They grew inside the fish until they were old enough to walk. Then the beast threw itself out of the river at the very spot where Ekeya is now built. The fish promptly died, but the children continued to live in its belly, where the air remained sweet."

The woman stopped briefly to emphasize the importance of what she was about to say. "Now I will tell you about the animals that are the emblems of our tribes. As the children could not venture outside of the fish into the venomous air of Suturik, Dyanu, who was, in truth, the Great Goddess, Daheiren, sent to them sixteen pairs of spirits ruling sixteen kinds of beasts from the old world. These spirits cut off Dyanu's children's heads and replaced them with their own since, being spirits, they could survive in the poisonous atmosphere. Each pair that had the same sort of head afterwards counted themselves as full siblings and the others merely as their half siblings. These couples began the sixteen tribes."

Jess and her companions, having emerged from the tunnel, walked onto the next bridge, which was thinner but, with its graceful arch, far more charming than was the first. It ended in a many roofed, porcelain tower that was so narrow it seemed as though it should have been impossible for it to stand.

Ghoryi gestured to the others that they should proceed towards this structure and then, as Jess gazed around in amazement, went on with her story.

"Ever since that time, each tribe has been protected by its tutelary spirit, and that is why the people of a tribe venerate the animals whose visages the councilors wear."

The woman smiled at Jess when she had finished her tale, but the latter put her hands upon her head and exclaimed, "You can't leave it like that. What happened next?"

"After the sprits descended to our world, the people of Ekeya were born," Ghoryi continued, looking like a young schoolmarm who, though formal, was fascinated with her topic and loved speaking about it to others.

"Because the thirty-two siblings were still little more than infants, their mother appeared before them and bid each pair of them create a garden in the ground before the fish's mouth and sow it with their blood. When they had done so, she said that they were to go and find a nest of lyupua, a sort of predator that lives in these parts, kill the parents, take the ninety-six young, and feed them with their own blood.

"In time, the three male and three female lyupua raised by each couple were transformed into human beings. The men were fierce and loyal and devoted themselves to protecting the pair of Dyanu's children who had raised them. They were the first of the retainers.

"Meanwhile, the plants that grew in the garden bore fruit shaped like human children. These matured into the first tribesmen. From that time, they have loyally served Dyanu's children, working for them and providing for their needs.

"Eventually, when the sixteen sons of Dyanu had reached maturity, they returned to their mother's home and killed their father, their uncle, and their aunt. There has not been a single ruler over Suturik since then.

"The society of Ekeya, however, has survived unchanged from the day the city was founded. The royal families, each descended from one of the pairs of Dyanu's offspring, are on top. They own all the land, control the government, and receive the veneration of the people. Their retainers are in charge of actually running the administration, although their main duty is still to fight during wars."

Buabyue interjected at this point, "You can believe me, there are a lot of wars here. They're very belligerent and obsessed with honor in this area of Suturik. The retainers are frequently put to use."

After the potbellied smuggler had said this, Jiru's attendant continued. "Under the retainers are the ordinary tribesmen. They work as everything from physicians to teachers to guards to laborers."

Again Buabyue spoke. "They don't have any say in how things are run, but they're insanely loyal to their royal houses."

Jess clasped her hands behind her head as she walked backwards, facing Ghoryi. "That was a great story. There's nothing like that where I come from. In Hosak, people would say that you're gossiping about the gods. They wouldn't like it."

"That, my girl, is very silly," Ghoryi informed her.

"You don't need to tell me that. Religion in Hosak is all about rules, rules, and rules. It's crap. The only thing religious people there are interested in is telling you to eat some certain food, to wear some specific sort of clothes, to be a good little girl, or whatever. It gets old fast. To be honest, I can't say I was ever thrilled with any of their rules. My own mother didn't really give a fuck about religion, but, take my word for it, I still got to hear plenty about how evil I was. That's always encouraging."

Ghoryi laughed and ran her fingers through Jess's hair, removing the girl's bangs from her face. "I'm afraid you've come from a terribly savage place. But then, if people there don't know how things came about, how could they know their place in the world?"

"I guess that's kind of how I feel now," Jess replied. "Mostly, I agree with Uluf. He's very spiritual."

Turning to her friend, she asked, "What is it that I believe?"

The toad took Jess's hand and looked at Ghoryi. "Among my own folk, narratives are understood to be the most poetic, and hence the best, way of expressing one's awareness of the numinous, of the mysterious profundity of things as they are in themselves."

"You don't think they're true, then?" Ofu asked him while scowling disapprovingly.

"I believe that myths are truer than mere historical accounts. Because they do not refer to events beyond themselves, their truth is not dependent upon their accurately reflecting such events. They are true in themselves, in the same way poetry is true. A poem simply consists of particular words that arouse a certain awareness, and a myth is the same. Neither requires anything extrinsic. What is more, the truth of an historical account is not just dependent on things beyond itself, it is dependent upon things, events, that, having passed away, no longer exist. History is, in a way, essentially false, while poetry and myth are eternally true."

Ofu snorted, and Ghoryi said, "I cannot say that I agree with you – I do believe in the historical truth of my people's myths – but your perspective has a certain appeal."

Jess nodded in general sympathy with her guide and turned around to walk facing forwards. Although she did not understand everything Uluf had said, his arguments sounded good to her. She also knew that, whenever she lifted her thread from its resting place, she could feel the goddess Haya flooding through her body, drowning her and possessing her entirely. She so knew about the immediate experience of the numinous, even if she could not express it poetically.

Arriving at the end of the bridge, the group stood in front of a post and lintel gateway made out of bright green wood, within which a pair of heavy doors about twenty feet tall were set. Before these were guards in colorful uniforms carrying halberds and needle guns.

When they saw Ghoryi, the soldiers opened a smaller door set in one of the larger ones and let her and those she was leading enter.

"This," she said, "is the royal palace of the Podgohani. Please follow me. I will take you to the queen."

She led her charges down a series of hallways to a long simple room, where she bid them wait as she continued through a sliding door at the far end.

A few minutes later, she returned and beckoned the others to follow her through that same door.

Beyond was a wide semicircular balcony planted with a garden, in the middle of which was a pavilion. The woman took them to this structure and bid them enter into it.

A lovely woman slightly younger than was Jess was sitting behind a low table whereupon she was arranging flowers, and, behind her, along the walls of the room, several female attendants were sitting quietly and four armed guards were standing solemnly.

The woman at the table looked up from her flowers and said, "I am Hyuka, the Queen of the Podgohani."

Buabyue immediately rested himself upon his knees and kowtowed to the woman, indicating to his companions that they should do the same.

"You may rise," the woman said.

When her guests had lifted their brows from the floor, she continued. "I understand that my brother has placed you in my care."

"Yes, your majesty," Buabyue replied.

"I also understand that you will need to remain in the city for some time, except you two." She indicated Jess and Buabyue with a nod in the direction of each.

The queen went on while looking at Jess. "I give you over to Ghoryi, Jiru's attendant. She will take care of you until you leave with the army."

Turning to Ofu, she said, "You will be looked after by Ghaheitthu from the First Guard Squad."

"You," she went on while looking at Buabyue, "will be watched over by Daheijjyi, from the same squad."

Now turning her gaze to Uluf with an expression of uncertainty, she asked, "You, are you male or female?"

"Male, your majesty."

"Then you will be looked after by Jarsu from the First Guard Squad."

Looking at the entire group in front of her, the queen continued, "You are all free to do as you wish while you are here. Wander about the city; enjoy a play; do whatever you like. Just don't try to leave your caretakers. Do you understand?"

The visitors nodded that they did.

"Wonderful. Ghoryi will show you to your rooms. You may leave now."

Following Buabyue's lead, the travelers bowed to Hyuka and then followed Ghoryi from the pavilion, being careful not to turn their backs upon their royal hostess.

Once they were in the garden again, Ghoryi told a guard to fetch the three men the queen had assigned to her guests and bring them to the guest suites on the blue floor. She then led Jess and the others to a lift, which conveyed them to a hallway whose walls were made of powder blue panels set in ivory hued wooden frames.

She showed the men and Uluf to one of these rooms and, when their attendants had arrived, took Jess to hers.

Inside, beyond a simple chamber with walls made of cream panels set in frames of dark wood, was another equally austere yet elegant room. The only furnishings in this were a large brass lamp, a cabinet filled with books, and a pile of thick pillows and blankets.

Jess, exhausted from her travels, immediately dove onto these and took a nap.

# Chapter 29
# The Temple of Eheiku

When Jess awoke from her nap, she had Ghoryi take her to the suite where the men were staying since Uluf had her bottomless bag, and so her clothing as well, with him. There, in the toad's room, she changed into her black halter-top, black shorts, and tall boots.

Once she was dressed, Jess went out into the sitting room the bedrooms surrounded and hopped onto one of the pillows strewn around a low table piled with food. The others were already there nibbling the refreshments and drinking a dark, brownish, frothy alcoholic liquid.

Turning to Uluf, Jess said, "So, what do you want to do tonight?"

"My dear, whatever you would prefer will be fine with me. I am mostly interested simply in seeing the city."

"Ghoryi, what's there to do here?" Jess asked while pouring herself a glass of the brown liquor.

"Tomorrow the weapons of the army will be blessed. That's always an impressive ceremony."

"How about now?"

"What would you like to do?" she inquired in a formal but friendly way as Jess grimaced at the bitter taste of her drink.

"Ah, what is this stuff?" Jess asked, looking at the liquid.

"It's bruy. Drink more. You'll like it."

"I'm not sure about that."

Jess took another sip, puckered her mouth, closed her eyes tightly, and continued. "Anyway, what are my choices for things to do?"

"Would you like to have a drink, watch a theatrical performance, take a boat trip, have sex, see a wrestling match, or perhaps something else?"

"What about the sex?"

"I could take you to the Temple of Eheiku."

"What's that?"

"It's the temple of the goddess of the Podgohani."

"And they'll let me have sex there?"

Ghoryi laughed. "Of course."

"Sorry, but you're going to have to fill me in."

"When a woman wants to have sex, but doesn't have a lover or, at least, wants someone different from any of the lovers she does have, she goes to the temple of her tribe's goddess."

"Nobody minds if she does that?" Jess asked before taking another sip of her drink.

"Of course not. Who would mind? The goddess enters into the woman's body and participates in her pleasure, and the woman, quite possibly, adds to the goddess's lineage."

Jess looked at her with an expression of complete incomprehension.

Buabyue (who, though a gangster, was a well educated one) interjected, "Jess, people don't marry here. A woman may take as many lovers as she wants to – although these are almost always from the same class that the woman is from. She doesn't have any obligations to any of the men, either."

"Really?"

"Yes. It's true. In Ekeya a man and a woman can be sexual partners without their having feelings for one another. Even if they do, it would be extremely unusual for their relationship to be exclusive. Besides, if a woman wants something different, she can always go to one of the temples Ghoryi just mentioned and have sex with any man she meets there."

"Who takes care of the children?" Jess asked, wiping the froth from the last sip of her drink from her lips.

"The mother's brother or uncle, whoever is the senior man in her family," Buabyue told her.

"And he won't mind if his sister or niece or whatever just has sex with anybody?"

"What concern is that of his?" Ghoryi said.

"That's definitely different from where I grew up. A respectable woman didn't go out of her house without her father or her brother. No sex before marriage for women there, and probably none after. I think that's why there were so many whores, like me."

"It's not like that here."

Jess picked up an ocher dumpling from the table in front of her and took a tentative bite from it. She had no idea what she was eating, but it was wonderfully spicy and smelled vaguely like cinnamon and cumin.

Popping the whole thing into her mouth, she asked while chewing it, "Don't men mind if their sisters keep getting pregnant and they have to pay for the children?"

Ghoryi replied, "Those are their heirs. Why would they mind?"

"Besides," Buabyue added, "if a man knows he's the father of a child, he'll usually give the mother a gift. He'll also generally give gifts to the child as well, although I don't think many men have close relationships with their offspring."

"What's more," Ghoryi said, "it is better for a woman to have many lovers. It brings honor upon her family and demonstrates her worth."

Ofu snorted. "No woman of mine is going to have sex with another man."

Ignoring him, Buabyue asked, "Even if it didn't, don't women usually get a lot of gifts from their lovers?"

"Yes," Ghoryi answered. "They do. If a man wants a woman to take him as a lover and wants to retain her affections after she has done so, he has to give her gifts."

Jess laughed. "I could live with that, being showered with presents and free to do what I like."

After emptying her cup of bruy in a single draught, which kept her from speaking for a few moments as she recovered from its overwhelming bitterness, Jess inquired, "So, who's coming with me? How about you, Uluf?"

"My dear, of course I will accompany you. I would not want to leave your side, although I am sure that there will not be a lady toad at this temple to interest me."

"I'm sure there won't be," Ghoryi admitted.

"What about you two?" Jess asked Ofu and Buabyue.

"I'm afraid I have business to attend to," the latter replied.

"Like what?"

"I'm far too old to win over a pretty girl at the temple, so I'll go somewhere where the women are young, lovely, and amendable to gifts."

Ofu laughed. "I'll go with you."

"As you desire."

Jess stood up and announced, "Okay then, let's get going."

Uluf, Ghoryi, and Jarsu stood as well.

Ghoryi said, "Follow me," and took the others out of the tower and into the city.

The group wandered through crowded streets under tall spires and beside sedate gardens, until, at the end of a wide avenue, Ghoryi stopped.

"That is the Temple of Eheiku," she said pointing ahead.

The structure she indicated consisted of a wall about sixty feet high surmounted by a tiled roof with upturned eaves that enclosed a large circular space. From the wall rose, at even intervals, six towers so thin they were almost poles. These extended to an impressive height and supported a conical roof that covered the whole of the structure far below it. In the very center of this place, rising over the wall but not coming close to the gigantic baldachin above, was a many roofed octagonal tower whose corners were adorned with brightly painted sculptures.

Ghoryi led Jess and the others under a bright purple torana that was built into the outer wall, through a passageway, and into a broad circular plaza. The insides of the walls were completely covered by five levels of colonnades, and behind each of these arcades were innumerable doors.

In the wide, open garden within the walls and around the tower in its middle, which was the temple itself, countless men were wandering around an equal number of women resting on the large stones and small boulders strewn around the place as seats.

"Do you see those women?" Ghoryi asked Jess.

"Yes."

"We will join them. If you see a man you like, you may go to him and ask him if he would like to join you, just as he may ask you if he sees you first. Should you both agree, the man will rent a room from the temple and the two of you may use it."

"How do they do that?"

Pointing to stone booths topped with little onion domes located near each of the spiral stairways leading up to the balconies stretching along the walls, Ghoryi said, "Go to one of those kiosks. There's an attendant there with the keys to the rooms. The man will give him some money and he'll give the man a key."

"Okay," said Jess. "Let's have some fun."

The group walked across the wide courtyard – that was alive with countless flowers, bushes, and trees – and came to a little artificial hill topped with an oddly shaped boulder with a hole through its center. Jess immediately clambered to the top of the rock and sat there cross-legged looking down at the others.

"Come up here, Uluf," she called to the toad and reached out her hand for him.

He took it but lifted himself only onto a shelf in front of the hole in the rock, where he sat with his striped cane across his knees and Jess's shins and feet wrapped around his neck.

"I am quite fine here," he assured his friend.

"Coward," she retorted.

The remainder of the party leaned against the boulder or reclined upon the slope of the hillock.

"So, what now?" Jess asked Ghoryi.

"If you see a man who takes your fancy, beckon him to come to you, or, if a man asks you to join him, and you are willing to do so, follow after him."

Jess craned her neck around and peered at the various men wandering about the courtyard. She did not immediately see someone who appealed to her. She, however, apparently appealed to virtually every man who saw her and was repeatedly propositioned. Since none of these persons struck her as someone she would like to be with, she turned them all down.

"You are certainly arousing considerable interest among the male visitors to the temple," Uluf noted.

"Of course," Jess replied while arching her back, tilting her head, and placing one hand behind her neck. "I am gorgeous, you know."

Ghoryi smiled at her. "It's not often that a woman who's not a Podgohani comes here, let alone someone from another world. You're very much the novelty."

"Well, that too."

At that moment, an old woman wearing a colorful shawl over a robe tied with a sash approached the group. To her waist was secured a line fastened to a large metal balloon painted with images of men and women with exaggerated genitals engaging in different sexual acts, and this was floating just above the level of her head. On her other side hung a basket filled with crude clay cups.

"Cup of veingu?" the old woman croaked.

"What's that?" Jess asked Ghoryi.

"It's a drink."

Turning to the hawker, Jess inquired, "How much?"

"One groat a cup."

"I'll take one."

The woman took a cup from her basket and filled it using a small hose with a nozzle at its end that was fitted to the metal balloon. This, Jess then realized, was actually a jug of veingu supported by a small antigravity engine.

The vendor handed the cup to Uluf, who passed it to Jess while she, having taken a groat coin from the small pouch hanging at her hip, passed this down to the woman.

As the others purchased cups of their own, Jess gazed at the liquid she had bought. It was a pleasant golden color, if somewhat suspiciously thick. She cautiously sipped it and discovered that, although both very sweet and potent, it was rather pleasant.

"This is pretty good," Jess told Ghoryi.

"Yes. I like it myself."

Jess was still drinking her veingu when she saw, a short distance away, a young man whose face she liked.

"Oh, that's the one I want," she exclaimed and waived her free hand frantically to get his attention.

The man noticed her and, with a second youth, came over to the rock where Jess was sitting. He nodded to her, motioned for her to come with him, and she, returning his nod, finished her drink, jumped down, and entwined her arm with his.

Turning back to Uluf, she said, "I'll be back in a little while. Hopefully not too little of a while, though."

The second man asked Ghoryi to join him. She assented and said to Uluf's attendant, "Jarsu, keep an eye on the girl while I'm away. Make sure she doesn't wander off somewhere."

"As you wish."

Jess, Ghoryi, and their temporary companions made their way to one of the stone booths, where each of the men gave the attendant two kopecks for a key. Each of the couples then proceeded on to a low door made out of some orange colored substance (that Jess assumed was taken from a local plant), unlocked this, and went inside.

The rooms were small and plain. Except for a futon against one wall, a washing basin against the other, and an image of a goddess Jess took to be Eheiku set in a niche in one of the stone walls, they were entirely empty.

"You're the first woman I've been with who's not from Ekeya," the man told her.

"You're the first man I've been with who is," Jess replied with a laugh. "Don't worry, though. All the important parts will still be compatible."

She stripped off her boots, shorts, and halter-top, tossed them onto the ground in one of the room's corners, and walked over to the man.

Standing on the tips of her toes, she kissed him and began undoing the clasps first on his jacket and then on his trousers.

She pulled the latter down around his ankles so that he could step out of them and, laying his penis across her palm, examined it carefully.

"I'm going to drain you of every drop of juice you've got," she told him, but as her translator was buried under her clothing and could not pick up her words, he did not understand what she said.

"You have no idea what I'm telling you, do you?" she commented as she saw that the man, having heard words that were no more than gibberish to him, was staring at her dumbly.

With a another laugh, Jess pushed him onto the futon, leapt upon his body like a tigress upon her prey, and went on to have the most fun she had experienced for some time.

* * *

After Jess had returned from her tryst, she found Uluf, Ghoryi, and Jarsu waiting around the rock she had been sitting upon earlier.

Feeling unusually happy, Jess was excited to see the city, so Ghoryi took the others around, showing them the sights of Ekeya until the sun had set and the green sky turned black.

As the group was wandering beneath rows of dim streetlights, they came upon a wide square, part of which was enclosed by a barrier made of sheets of cloth hung between tall poles.

"What's that?" Jess inquired.

"They're putting on a play," Ghoryi told her. "It's part of our celebration of the war."

"Can we watch it?"

"It'll probably cost you a half-kopeck."

"That's fine. Let's go see it."

Jess and her companions, having paid the price Ghoryi had said they would, entered into the enclosure. It was filled with a crowd of men and women who were resting on mats spread out on the ground and drinking cups of veingu or bruy being sold by vendors wandering amongst them.

At the far end of the enclosure, behind a group of musicians sitting on the pavement, was an elevated stage whereupon colorful marionettes were being moved by puppeteers concealed by a roof decorated with gargoyle-like figures. To either side of the stage was a kind of dock. In one of these stood a man and in the other a woman. These two were singing in nasal tones the dialogue of all the puppets.

Ghoryi led the others to a free mat, where they reclined, bought veingu, and watched the performance.

"What's going on?" Jess inquired.

"It's an ancient story. You see, long ago, when Ekeya was still young, the king of the Aheika clan had a niece, Mihu, who, it is said, was the most beautiful woman who has ever lived. She was, of course, desired by every man who saw or even heard of her. Eventually, word of her loveliness spread to the distant city of Mangkcheun, which was then ruled by a cruel tyrant named Onyiniru. This fiend came to Ekeya to look at Mihu and was immediately overcome with lust for her. She, however, wanted nothing to do with him. Being the child of a demon, he was not only grossly fat, with six long breasts that swung about his ankles, but he also had three heads, six eyes upon each head, and noses like sausages. He'll be on stage shortly, and you'll see how vile he is."

"What happened then?" Jess asked.

"Mihu rejected his advances, but Onyiniru was maddened by his desire for the girl. Since she would not give herself to him, he decided to take her by force and carried her back to Mangkcheun.

"As soon as Mihu's eldest brother learned that his sister had vanished, he set off to find her and, eventually, discovered her in Mangkcheun. When he snuck into Onyiniru's palace to recover her, however, the demon killed him and devoured his body. Mihu's second brother then set out to find the missing girl, but he too was murdered and eaten. Sadly, the third and youngest brother, though wise and benevolent, was crippled and could not himself help his sister. He feared that there was nothing he could do, but, happily, a young man named Ghasuhu from my own tribe, the Podgohani, was in love with Mihu and offered his help to her brother."

"Did he save her?" Jess asked with the excitement of a child.

"He did find her in Mangkcheun and was able to free her from her abductor and take her home. Unfortunately, this only enraged the fiend, who followed after Ghasuhu and Mihu with an army. Ekeya fought a terrible war with him, in which three out of every four men died, but we won in the end and killed the demon."

"To what part of this tale has the play come?" Uluf inquired.

"The eldest brother is just now searching Onyiniru's palace. In a moment, he will find his sister and speak with her. Then the demon will arrive and kill him. Watch."

Even as she spoke, a bejeweled, impossibly thin marionette with a stylized face came upon a lovely, delicate female puppet.

"That's Mihu!" Jess exclaimed.

"Yes, you are correct," Ghoryi told her.

Each of the two characters, or rather the man and the woman standing at the edges of the stage, performed complex, interlocking songs for some time, but these were eventually interrupted by a grossly fat three headed marionette.

"That must be the demon," Jess said.

Ghoryi nodded.

The fiend lifted up a sword and, after battling Mihu's brother for some time, struck the man's head off. The woman standing beside the stage gave a mellifluous, oddly graceful scream for the female puppet, which then collapsed before her monstrous abductor.

"The music is quite lovely," Uluf noted.

"Yes. It's very old fashioned, but it is pretty," Ghoryi replied.

The remainder of the play, which Jess and the others watched while drinking copious amounts of veingu, followed the narrative that Ghoryi had related and ended with the slaying of Onyiniru by Ghasuhu, whose body was dismembered and buried in separate graves around Ekeya.

When the play was over, Ghoryi said to the others, "Perhaps we ought to return now. Tomorrow, I will take you to see the Blessing of the Arms. My sister has a flat overlooking Tribo Plaza, where the ceremony will take place. I will bring you there if you like."

Jess smiled and nodded. She did not say more, however, since she was feeling more than a little tipsy from all the veingu she had consumed. Her stomach was none too settled, either. The liquor was very strong and very sweet.

Uluf replied, "That would be delightful, thank you. I am always intrigued by the customs and religions of human beings."

"You will be impressed with the rite, then," Ghoryi informed him.

On her way back to the tower where she was staying, Jess remained quiet and made it a point to hold onto Uluf's arms so that she did not fall over.

*　*　*

Tsoi blew a cloud of smoke out his pursed lips for it to be carried away by the wind as he leaned against the wrought iron railing of the balcony projecting from the side of his pleasure barge. So smoking his long stemmed pipe, he watched a nondescript antigravity sled approaching his vessel (as both hung in the skies high above the open ocean) and felt distinctly uncomfortable about meeting with the craft's passenger.

Although the vehicle before him was simple and unimpressive, the individual within was the viceroy of Shokai himself.

What made Tsoi especially anxious was his awareness that that man undoubtedly had something important on his mind if he wanted a face-to-face meeting, as he did now, for the viceroy had no desire for his dealings with Tsoi to be known. In fact, he always took great pains to make sure they were kept secret.

The sled passed around the side of the barge to land out of Tsoi's sight, and the gangster returned inside. Closing the door to the balcony behind him, adjusting his long, enameled, artificial nails, straightening his colorfully embroidered frock coat, and examining his Pharaonic eye make-up, Tsoi took a deep breath and sat upon the back of a crouching young woman.

A moment later, there was a knock at the door and a servant entered the dimly lit, wood paneled room leading a middle-aged man wearing the white cassock of an official from Tozana.

"Please have a seat," Tsoi told this person while the servant left and closed the door behind him.

The official lowered himself onto the back of a second young woman and touched his belt. His body, garments, and face suddenly dissolved. They had only been a hologram projected as a disguise.

In their place was a wheaten complexioned individual wearing an elaborate wig composed of rows of curls upon which rested a bejeweled kamilaukion. A lace jabot hung from his neck, and a web of cords and sashes supporting numerous ribbons and medallions was draped over a printed waistcoat that was largely covered by a long embroidered justaucorps. Below these garments, the man wore baggy trousers cinched at the ankle with ribbons, and his feet were shod in ridiculously long poulaines.

Adjusting the sword and the dagger hanging from his waist and resting his extended right hand on the top of an intricately carved cane, the viceroy eyed Tsoi with disapproval.

"I hope you are well today, your immanence." Tsoi said to his guest.

The gangster gestured to a table to his right laden with ewers and inquired, "Would your immanence care for something to drink?"

The viceroy nodded without speaking. He detested Tsoi, but the man was, almost certainly, richer than was any human being other than some member of the emperor's own family.

As demeaning as it was to deal with such a creature, the viceroy did have terrible debts and his arrangement with Ngo would not only clear those but would make him wonderfully wealthy as well. Of course, he reflected, he would have to stay alive to enjoy such benefits.

Tsoi gestured at a pair of naked young women standing next to the table, on either side of a brass post, to which they were bound with golden chains fastened to collars around their necks. Each of the women hurriedly filled a cup with wine. One of them then handed her cup to the viceroy, who laid his cane across his lap, and the second handed hers to Tsoi.

"Why, may I ask, did you desire this meeting today, your immanence?"

The viceroy, taking a sip of his drink, replied, "I have two concerns I would like to discuss."

"Please go on."

"I have heard rumors that you have acquired an armed ether-ship."

Tsoi flinched. The viceroy must have well placed spies in his palace. When he returned, he would have to ferret them out and bring their lives to an unpleasant end.

"You needn't worry about that," Tsoi assured his guest while blowing a ring of smoke towards the ceiling. "Every precaution is being taken."

"I needn't remind you what the consequences will be for you if it is discovered. You will be tortured and your entire family exterminated. I would not be able to protect you if you were caught by my superiors."

"I realize that, your immanence, just as I realize what the consequences would be for you."

The viceroy's fingers touched the hilt of his dagger. If the temptation of the wealth he could acquire by helping Ngo had not been so considerable, he would surely have jumped from his chair and driven his blade into his arrogant host's heart. His whole body itched and burned with anger at having been so threatened by the vile hoodlum.

Tsoi watched his guest carefully, uncertain what he should do if the viceroy attacked. The man had surely been trained in the use of arms, but Tsoi was confident enough in his own abilities to believe that he could best his assailant. Even if he did, however, he would only be preparing himself for a far nastier death at the hands of the Pancloan government. The punishment for killing a viceroy was sure to be grisly.

Tsoi smiled widely, emptied his cup of wine, and announced, "Please do not be unduly concerned about the ship, your immanence. I have placed it under the command of my uncle, Lo, and he is a very cautious man. He won't let it be discovered."

"I certainly hope not."

"Besides," Tsoi said, casually tossing his empty wine cup at one of his servants, "it's quite possible that I won't even have to make use of it. I only needed it in case my allies didn't show up, but I've been informed that they've honored their obligations and have joined with my own people. The ship will, I hope, never be seen. It will merely remain in reserve in case it is needed. You must admit, your immanence, that would be the wisest strategy. It is, after all, well known to all good generals that having some sort of reserve force can be the key to winning a battle. Just look at the great general Shih Huang Ti, the conqueror of the ancient land of China. While he was subduing his enemies with one army, he kept a second army, an army of golems, buried underground, ready to be called up whenever it was required."

The viceroy marveled at his ally's silliness, exhaled loudly, and leaned back. "Whatever the wisdom of having this vessel – and I do not think that it is wise at all – I trust you will keep its existence secret. Do not ruin this operation. I am providing you with protection, but there is only so much I can do."

Annoyed as he was at having to behave obsequiously towards a man he was, after all, paying, Tsoi still managed to reply graciously, "I understand, your immanence."

He then took a deep draught of smoke from his pipe and inquired, "What else, may I ask, has brought you here?"

The viceroy, resting his left hand on the head of the girl he was sitting upon and sipping at the cup of wine he held in the other, looked at a large painting on the wall behind Tsoi. It very realistically portrayed a pair of lovers reclining in a copse below a craggy mountain.

Twisting the edge of his mouth in contempt and disgust, the viceroy reflected on what such a piece of art said about his ally. Like virtually all men without taste, Tsoi obviously thought that a painter was talented if he was able to slavishly mimic the forms of the external world. He could not grasp the subtle truth that it was the painter's capacity to draw out the emotive essence of objects that determined his worth. Tsoi really was a crude individual. Still, the man was rich and he was generous with his bribes.

With a sigh, the viceroy said, "My agents in Tozana have informed me that the situation there has become extremely volatile."

"That was our intention," Tsoi responded while shooting a series of small smoke rings at one of the naked serving girls in order to make her cough and to cause her eyes to water.

"I have little doubt that your pet, Soniyo Dogrue, will be able to act soon, and will probably succeed. However, I still have concerns about the state of affairs in Tozana."

"Would you mind elaborating, your immanence?"

"As I am sure you are aware, the Llalloi have been funneling arms and money into Jezic. They've got someone of their own they're planning to put on the throne, although I don't, as yet, know who that is."

"Ah, yes, your immanence. That is almost certainly the case."

"Do you think your Dogrue woman can get rid of such persons? For that matter, do you think she'll be able to calm the ordinary people after she takes over? She could easily end up being toppled by riots herself."

Tsoi took a draught from his pipe and let the smoke ooze out of his nostrils. "Your immanence, I must confess that I am less than confident in Soniyo's abilities. I am afraid that I may have to call on your help if she isn't able to manage the situation."

The viceroy emptied his cup and held it out to be refilled by one of Tsoi's serving girls, whose completely depilated body glistened with oil. "Are you still hoping to handle that eventuality as we'd previously planned?"

"Yes, your immanence. I am no expert on interstellar affairs, but I assume that the Iridescent Blossom Society is still fighting its little revolution."

"Indeed, it is. Actually, Tsoi, the rebels have made significant advances since we last spoke. They're threatening the fleet in several provinces. Oh, and they do seem to be financing their revolt, at least in part, with money from drug smuggling operations."

"That's convenient."

"Yes. It doesn't make much sense to me that they're becoming smugglers and drug dealers for their cause – considering that they're supposedly fighting to bring in some perfect age ruled by their goddess that's going to be nothing but peace and equality for all mankind. Nevertheless, it is convenient for us."

"I'll make it look like the Sing are supplying the Society with russa, then. No one will blame you if you send your army into Jezic under such circumstances. If anything, they'd blame you if you didn't."

"That's true enough," the viceroy conceded.

Drinking his wine, he added, "Still, you'll need to fabricate a sufficient amount of evidence to justify my actions, and you'll have to make it believable."

"That shouldn't be a problem. My people have produced some beautiful forgeries."

"We can settle the details of how you'll inform me when you need me to act later."

"As you desire, your immanence."

"I do wish you had selected a different conspirator in Tozana. I'm sure that Soniyo Dogrue is going to be a problem. Even with the best evidence money can buy, I'd still prefer not to act overtly."

"It couldn't be helped, your immanence."

"Yes. I suppose that's true. You'll have my army when you need it. Just keep that ether-ship of yours well hidden."

Tsoi smiled broadly and wished he did not need the viceroy. Dealing with the man was always demeaning. Be that as it may, his help virtually guaranteed that Tsoi would win in his fight with the Llalloi.

The viceroy consumed the last of his wine, set his cup on the head of the girl he was sitting upon, stood up, and walked towards the door. He said, "I hope that you will keep our discussion entirely private."

Tsoi stood himself, took a draught from his pipe, and replied, "It goes without saying, your immanence."

"What about this lot?" the viceroy asked pointing to the serving girls and the women being used as furniture.

"Their discretion is assured."

"Good. I will send you the particulars for letting me know when to send my army into Jezic."

The viceroy reactivated the hologram that disguised him as a Tozani official and left the room.

Tsoi, having taken a draught from his pipe, pointed to one of his serving girls and commanded her, "Get on your knees."

She knelt and her master looked at the second woman. "Strangle her with her chain."

The standing girl, though whimpering and crying, wrapped the chain binding her colleague around that woman's neck and throttled her until she was dead.

"That's a good girl," Tsoi informed the woman as he walked over to stand behind her. He caressed her shoulders, squeezed her breasts, kissed her ears, horripilated her skin with the touch of his artificial nails, and slit her throat with his dagger.

The two women fastened to the chairs had both begun crying and both struggled fruitlessly to get out of their bonds.

Tsoi sat on the back of one of them, stroked the girl's hair, and opened her jugular.

While blood was still gushing onto the floor from her wound, Tsoi went to the last woman still alive, who was now screaming and weeping uncontrollably. He killed her just as he had the others.

Then, having used the girl's hair to wipe her blood from his hands, Tsoi walked over to a telopticon set in one of the walls, switched it on, and said, "The ship's steward."

A moment later a man's face was looking at him from the image harp.

Tsoi said to it, "Send me a maid, several actually, and a knacker. The serving girls here have died."

"As you desire, my lord. Would you like them sent immediately?"

"Yes. I'm afraid the girls have made quite a mess. Also, tell the knacker he can grind up the bodies I've left him and feed them to the servants. It's been a while since they've had any meat, well, except for that feihi. I think they deserve a treat."

# Interlude 12
# The Smuggling Syndicate

After the discovery of the intoxicating effects of Jaffrite semen, the use of that substance as a drug quickly spread from Shokai to numerous other worlds. As the demand for russa increased, more and larger organizations arose to produce, ship, and sell the drug, in spite of its possession having been made illegal in almost all the places where it was consumed.

The majority of the gangs controlling the production of russa did not become involved in the shipping of their product to other planets. Instead, they made arrangements with persons who had experience smuggling illegal goods.

Initially, a wide variety of organizations and individuals purchased russa from its producers and shipped the drug to different worlds. In time, however, roughly twenty large smuggling gangs gained more or less complete control over its transport.

This number was reduced to a dozen by the Russa War, as many of the smugglers were unable to endure the difficult circumstances of that period.

After the Treaty of Hudaipwa, the surviving groups prevented others from encroaching on their trade, but they did not cooperate with one another. In fact, the wars they fought among themselves eventually led to the destruction of all but five of the smuggling gangs.

During this same time, each of the smugglers' organizations formed a stable relationship with one or two of the Seven Families. As such pairings inevitably made allies of particular gangs, conflicts among the smugglers often involved the Seven Families as well. Simultaneously, competition among smugglers undermined the value of the product they were transporting and so led them to quarrel with the Seven Families about the purchase price of russa. Not only did these situations create tensions between russa smugglers and producers, they also increased tensions among the producers, who were forced to compete with one another.

In 1579, under pressure from the Seven Families, the heads of which desired an end to this state of affairs, the five smuggling gangs came to an agreement with one another and formed the Smuggling Syndicate.

Each would subsequently purchase russa only from certain families (three smuggling gangs bought from one family each, and two bought from two families each), and each would sell russa only in a specified area of human space. The worlds of men were divided between them, allowing room for future expansion, and each of the smuggling gangs consented not to impinge upon the territory of any of the others. Additionally, they agreed to ask a single standardized price for the russa they purchased from the Seven Families.

Once this compact had been made, the five remaining trafficking gangs came to be referred to collectively as the Smuggling Syndicate, although they never developed any central organization. Their alliance has been strained by a number of conflicts, some of them armed, but the profits they have made when not competing have inclined them to maintain amicable relationships with one another. They have even been known to cooperate in destroying any group that has attempted to involve itself in russa smuggling.

All of the smuggling gangs are extremely secretive and few specifics about their organizations can be given. Most, however, appear to rely on complex networks of false companies, independently contracted smuggling vessels, exclusive contracts with the Seven Families, extensive connections with russa dealers, and the control of enormous amounts of money.

In most cases, neither the locations of the bases of operation of the smuggling gangs nor the identities of the persons or groups controlling these are known with certainty.

From Pollidor's *Big Blue Book of Knowledge*

# Chapter 30
# The Blessing of the Arms

When Jess arrived in the suite that had been given to her, she collapsed onto the pillows strewn upon her bedroom floor and nearly fell asleep. As her still slightly drunk and weary mind slowly sank into darkness, however, a sudden wave of sadness flooded over her body. She had been thinking in a confused, half-dreaming way of what she had done in the Temple of Eheiku when, apparently from nowhere, she saw the man who had attacked her in the *Cloud Cutter*.

Tired as Jess had been seconds before, that image immediately awakened her. She lay in bed feeling agitated and disgusted. No matter how she tried to force her mind towards other objects, it kept returning to that man until she realized she would not be going to sleep any time soon.

Conceding defeat, Jess stood up and stepped onto the balcony outside both her room and that of her male companions. It was planted with trees, shrubs, and flowers set amongst little mounds, oddly shaped rocks, tiny streams, and shallow pools. As she walked naked into the pleasantly cool, moist air, she heard gentle musical notes drifting towards her through the semi-darkness.

She looked around and saw Uluf sitting cross-legged upon a large stone playing his portable sarangi and singing with tones and timbres impossible for any human being. The girl walked over to him, leaned against a nearby tree, and listened to the toad's song.

> *My childhood's past;*
> *My youth is gone,*
> *But more than death*
> *Is yet to come.*
>
> *The summers' days*
> *Of sizzling heat*
> *And cooling streams*

*Await me still.*

*The winters too,*
*With freezing winds,*
*With dripping ice*
*And glowing snows,*

*Delight my soul*
*And seize my thoughts,*
*Possessing me*
*With all their charms.*

*I'll not forget*
*The loveliness*
*Of all the world*
*Surrounding me.*

*Regrets indeed*
*May haunt my mind,*
*And I may wish*
*For days gone by,*

*But I'll not ignore*
*The shining stars,*
*The flowers near,*
*The river's smell,*

*The laughing girl,*
*The taste of food,*
*Nor other joys*
*The world can give.*

*I'm drunk with life;*
*I'm filled with love*
*Though I may die*
*With any breath.*

Uluf's words suffused Jess with a pleasant melancholy, and as she let them slide and wriggle through her being, she tilted her head backwards so that she could look at the sky.

The dome above her was almost completely transparent, though it reflected the lights of the city, which shone like stars hanging midway between the ground and the black vault of the heavens. Above these, high in Suturik's venomous atmosphere, Jess could see the greenish glow of the bioluminescent brimu as they were gently carried by the winds like living, carnivorous clouds.

When her neck began to grow tired, Jess turned her gaze upon the city itself and examined the half-visible shapes of its buildings as these were revealed by the greenish, golden, or pinkish glow of streetlamps, open windows, or glowing archways. Although not brightly lit, Ekeya was not dark and forbidding like the slums of Quanya were, and, although speckled with different colors, it was not gaudy as that city's center was. Even when shaded by night, it had a mysterious elegance that hinted at the presence of gorgeous shapes and that filled the person fortunate enough to see such details with a desire to discover more.

"This place is really pretty," Jess said to Uluf.

While continuing to play his sarangi, the toad replied. "Indeed, it is. It is more like Faerie than a town of human beings."

"For some reason, it's so beautiful that it makes me sad to look at it."

"How so, my dear?"

"It's kind of a jumble of different things. I wouldn't even be here if Tolliver hadn't decided to set me up as a decoy so that he could get rich. The whole reason I'm here is kind of sad, I guess. Even so, I kind of wish Tolliver was here with me. I'm not going to let him get away with what he did to me, but, at the same time, I miss him. Actually, I suppose I still love him in a certain way. I know things like that don't make sense, but I still can't get them out of my mind."

"We have certainly been witnesses to or participants in a variety of terrible things recently."

Jess could not help but laugh. "Now that's the truth."

After a pause, she went on. "Sometimes, I wish I could just jump out of my body and leap back in time so I could start life all over again."

Jess wiped her eyes, which, she noticed, were getting moist. "I suppose it'd all be the same, though. I'd need a whole new family if things were really going to be different. Still, as long as I'm dreaming, I might as well wish for a real childhood and all that stuff."

She looked down at her feet for a few moments and then turned her face back to Uluf. "I know I'm being stupid, but I do want a new life. I don't like this one so much."

She grew suddenly quiet as she thought about what had happened to her on the trip to Quanya and to Syo and Ofu in the mining camp.

"I wonder what happened to Eshwurhiyo," she said.

"I am afraid that I do not know for certain, my dear."

"You don't suppose she could still be alive, do you?"

"I would not think that it is likely, I am afraid. However, anything is possible. So far as I am aware, she is alive and well with her brother back in Jezic."

Jess smiled to lighten the tragedy. "I don't think that's very likely."

"No, I am afraid that it is not."

Jess made a silly face and then laughed again. "You see what I mean? That's why I feel a little sad."

"You should have listened to the song I was singing, my dear."

"Why's that?"

"As it said, do not burden your appreciation of beauty with irrelevant worries. Simply immerse yourself in your enjoyment of what is before you."

"Okay, but even if you can forget all that stuff, you still know that no matter how happy you are, it's going to end."

"That is true, my dear," said the toad while still playing upon his sarangi. "However, the evanescence of beauty merely makes it more precious. Lose yourself in the eternity, the timelessness of each brief moment. Experience each thing merely as it is in itself, with all its native beauty, and do not bind it with connections to other things beyond it, whether from the past, the present, or the future."

Jess arched her back and stretched her arms above her head. Then she squatted in front of Uluf, leaning her shoulders against a tree.

"I wish it were as easy as that. It's hard to let go of things; for me it is, at least. I'm haunted by the ghosts of my past. They're always there, even if I don't see them, ready to jump out and show me how ugly they are. I know I'm whining, but there's a lot I'd like to forget about my life. Actually, I'd like to forget most of what's happened in the last two weeks, or four weeks, I mean. Maybe you can let go of things like that, but it's hard for me. Whenever I'm happy, it seems like, out of nowhere, I see that man on the *Cloud Cutter* shoving his prick into me, or one of the thousands of dirty, stinking old men who did the same to me before I met Takenac. Believe me, it doesn't stop there. I don't even want to talk about the things I remember from when I was a little girl. There's always a ghost lurking inside my mind waiting to jump out and spoil my happiness. To tell you the truth, I don't think I even deserve to be happy."

"Everyone deserves to be happy, Jess."

"Well, even if that's true, it's hard to accept that whatever happiness I get is going to last. Like I said, it's going to end sooner or later."

Prompted by her own comment, Jess's mind wandered back to the thrilling, magical times when she had been with Tolliver and to all their poignantly experienced sensations and emotions. She remembered how he had tasted when he was inside her mouth and how he had felt when he was inside her body. She remembered how happy she had been when she saw him trembling with pleasure and how excited she had been upon convincing herself that he would never leave someone who could make him feel that way.

Then, as quickly as such images came to Jess, a heavy emptiness filled her breast. She had hoped so hard that she would be able to keep the captain's love, but she had failed so miserably. Not only had their relationship and its joys come to an end, but Jess's memories of them had also been spoiled. Now, she wondered if Tolliver had ever loved her at all.

"And as I told you, my dear," the toad said, interrupting her thoughts but guessing what they were, "you should not allow the pain of one moment to seep into and spoil the joy of another. Though you will, of course, suffer if you lose someone you loved, you do nothing but pointlessly add to that pain if you forget all the happiness you experienced before that loss. People often remember only their miseries and so allow them to drown their recollections of their joys. They claim that all ends in sorrow because years of pleasure are sometimes followed by weeks of pain. As a result, their future joys are spoiled and they are left only with suffering."

"I suppose you're right. It's better to enjoy things and keep them separate from your problems."

"Yes. Now you see. Why mingle your pleasures with your troubles? Immerse yourself in the wonder of the world around you."

"Is that what you're doing now?"

The toad smiled at her. "You are correct. Ekeya is a beautiful place. I came out here to enjoy its charms. After I had sat here for a while, I was so carried away I could not restrain myself. I simply felt compelled to express my joy with music."

\* \* \*

The wide road Jess had traveled along when she had first entered Ekeya had been closed to traffic, and now, from both the city's outskirts and its center, companies of soldiers goose stepped down it towards a circular plaza about midway between these extremes.

Standing upon a balcony projecting from a tower near this place, Tribo Plaza, with Uluf, Ghoryi, and Jarsu, Jess was able to see those men clearly and was surprised by their odd attire.

Over their shaggy green tunics the soldiers wore colorful breastplates. On their legs were equally colorful grieves, and upon their brows they wore as helmets the husks of gigantic legumes. These were wildly multihued and bizarrely shaped, but, Jess would later learn, were also harder than any metal.

Amongst such troops marched men sounding loud, wailing notes upon buisines and bagpipes or beating rhythmically upon great kettle drums. The sounds of these instruments, having been amplified by microphones, made every solid object in the city, as well as its very air, reverberate.

When the first of the companies reached the edge of the circular plaza, those on the right marched to the left side of the road while those on the left marched to its right side. The companies behind these did the same and the whole army formed itself into two rows facing one another along the thoroughfare.

While Jess was watching the events below her, from one of a row of semicircular balconies projecting from the wall of a nearby skyscraper adorned with countless eaves, a beautiful young woman who had long black hair that hung loosely around her shoulders and who was wearing a sarong and a band of cloth below her breasts stood leaning over a balustrade looking at the same things. She held a bowl filled with the bitter brown bruy that was popular in Ekeya and sipped at it from time to time through a straw.

Behind her, reclining in a chair, was a man dressed in a style that was similar to that of Ekeya but was clearly not that of the city.

The pair had the features of persons from a region of Suturik across the sea to the east of Ekeya, but they were both frauds. The woman's face was created from a living mask and she, Hyan, was from Shokai. The man was a changeling. His body was that of a person from Suturik, but it was just a puppet being operated by an homunculus.

Hyan was enjoying the spectacle below her. Actually, she liked just about everything she had discovered in Ekeya. It was a shame, she thought, that these people were her enemies. The city was a far more pleasant place than was Quanya.

She looked back at her companion. "Why don't you come and join me, Chongmuri?"

"No thank you, my lady. I would prefer to remain here."

"Don't call me that, you silly monkey. My name's Chun."

"I am sorry, Chun."

"That's better. Well, you do as you please. I'm going to watch the parade," she said, turning back around.

"I might as well enjoy this place before it's gone."

From the tall gate of the temple built next to the City Palace, a group of naked young women whose bodies were painted bright red and who wore wigs made of golden thread had emerged and, passing before a multitude of long tables that had been set in the plaza in front of the palace and the temple, had started making their way down the main thoroughfare. A few of these persons were carrying banners, but most of them held halberds festooned with flowers, from each of which weapons a bowl was hung by a string.

Adjusting her pink halter-top and tugging at her pink shorts, Jess leaned over the railing to get a better view.

"This is very impressive," she informed Ghoryi.

"Do you have similar rites where you come from?"

"No. People in Hosak wouldn't like this. They'd think it was corrupt or something."

"What do they do there to participate in their religion?"

"Mostly, they go to temples on certain days and listen to a priest telling them how evil they are and lecturing them on what they should do to be less evil."

"It sounds very dry."

"It is."

"The way Jess describes it," Uluf added, "religion in Hosak is more or less like attending a series of speeches given by an embittered schoolteacher. I have never been able to discover anything religious in it."

"Me either," Jess concurred.

As she spoke with her companions, Jess saw, in the midst of the red dyed women, a pair of moyu with glass spheres over the heads (that allowed them to breathe their own atmosphere). These were pulling a cart whereupon a large number of young men rode. One of these individuals was crowned with a wreath of flowers, dressed in rich robes, and bore a staff topped with a lantern. The rest, though similarly crowned, were otherwise naked and chained to posts.

There were no rituals like this in Quanya, Hyan reflected. Everything there was tacky and garish. No one had any sense of the sublime.

A parade of hideous images rushed through her mind. She saw, to her disgust, hundred foot tall animatronic icons wiggling about in giant, gaudily decorated temples, thugs drilling holes in their tongues to expiate their failures, and aging molls wailing ridiculously upon finding patches of mildew, puddles of vomit, or clusters of warts that had miraculously taken the shape of their favorite deity.

"Oh, Chongmuri," she said while trying to bring her attention back to the procession moving down the street below her, "there are some things about Quanya that I don't miss at all. Still, I'd rather be the queen of a land of dimwits than an ordinary person anywhere else."

After the red women came an enormous wagon covered with an opulent baldachin supported on Churrigueresque columns being pulled by genetically modified warthogs that were at least twelve feet tall at the shoulder.

Upon this cart stood a man in a jacket of the kind fashionable in Ekeya that was sewn from silver thread and, over this, a houppelande of golden thread. His face was painted blood red and upon his brow was a conical hat onto the back of which was attached a thin metal platter that seemed to encircle his head like a halo. In front of him was a huge mace, and he rested his hands upon this as he stared fixedly ahead.

"Who's that?" Jess asked as this vehicle came close enough for her to see it clearly.

"That is Hrahei, the general of our armies," Ghoryi replied with a prideful tone.

"Why's his face red?"

"He has come from the temple of Daheiren, the Great Goddess. He has seen her visage and been possessed by her. Now he is burning with her divinity. That is why his face is as red as the sun, why a halo shines behind his head, and why he is garbed in silver and gold."

When the red women arrived at the plaza, they arranged themselves in a circle facing its center, where a huge cauldron filled with some sort of frothy soup had been set upon a pile of burning logs arranged not far from a wooden catafalque adorned with silver medallions and colorful streamers. One of their number meanwhile went to the wide gates of a temple built on one side of this open space and knocked upon it with the end of her halberd.

The doors opened, and a man wearing colorful robes and a bright sombrero emerged accompanied by a host of bare-footed old women in heavy black gowns and a number of naked men, several of whom were bearing curved swords. This group went to the middle of the plaza where the cauldron was while the cart bearing the young men stopped on the opposite side of this.

Hyan was mesmerized by the occurrences happening before her. She felt herself drawn from her body by the ritual's beauty. The actions of the persons on the thoroughfare were so perfectly choreographed, like those of dancers, that these individuals seemed to live in some rarefied, liminal reality that stood outside of time. For a moment, as she would when watching a beautifully animated movie, Hyan forgot herself and trembled with the excitement that the performance in the street below stirred up within her.

Once the wagon where the general was standing had arrived at the plaza, it stopped between the cauldron and the road leading to the City Palace, with the other wagon to its right and the priest and priestesses to its left.

"What's in the big pot?" Jess asked.

"Biru. It's fermented milk."

The young man wearing the wreath stepped down from his wagon and stood before the cauldron. The old women went to him, poured oil upon his head, daubed his lips and brow with an orange paste, and handed him a dagger.

Leaning over the rim of the cauldron, while being supported by the priestesses, the young man brought the blade to his neck and slit his throat so that his blood sprayed into the biru to the rhythmic chanting of the priest standing before him.

"Why'd he do that?" Jess demanded in horror.

"He's a brave hero."

"Why'd they let him kill himself, then?"

"That was his desire."

"He chose to die?" Uluf inquired.

"Of course."

"Why?" Jess insisted.

"The other men on the cart are prisoners we have taken. They will be sacrificed to the goddess. Our hero, the man who has just offered up his life, will guide them to her as a gift from our city."

Although she could not clearly see everything that was happening in the plaza, Hyan was fascinated by what she could see. The body of the man who had just slit his own throat was now being carried to the other side of the cauldron, where it was placed upon the catafalque before the priest.

"I wish I knew what they were doing," Hyan told the changeling, eager to involve herself even more deeply in the spectacle she was watching.

"You can't see?" the corpse asked.

"That's not what I meant."

"I don't understand."

"Oh, shut up, you stupid monkey."

The priestesses, having clambered onto the catafalque and arranged themselves, like great vultures, on perches along its sides, squatted around the corpse of the man who had sacrificed himself, split open its belly with a knife, peeled back its skin, and examined its innards. After a few minutes of doing so, they pounced from their roosts and began ululating wildly while dancing about the cadaver as though possessed.

"What are they so happy about?" Jess asked.

"They have inspected the victim's entrails."

"Okay. Go on."

"They have seen victory in them. We will surely win this war."

Two of the guards who had come out of the temple with the priest and priestesses went over to the cart where the prisoners were chained, released one of the captives, and brought him over to the cauldron.

The men held their prisoner fast and one of the aged priestesses anointed him with oil while another spread the same orange paste upon his forehead and mouth that had been placed on the first man. After this was done, the guards held the man's head over the cauldron and a third priestess cut his throat with a knife so that his blood gushed into the biru.

Once this victim had been exsanguinated, his body was given to the men with swords, who chopped off his head and stuck it atop the halberd carried by one of the red women encircling the plaza. The body itself was thrown to a place between the cauldron and the road leading out of the city.

The same procedure was followed with each of the men chained on the wagon, until there was a great heap of corpses on the opposite side of the cauldron from the general (who was overlooking this whole ritual) and the milky biru had become deep red.

The various priestesses then came close to the boiling, bubbling liquid and stared at it for some time.

"What are they doing now?" Jess asked with a slightly tremulous voice. She was beginning to feel a little queasy. She was even beginning to wonder if the religion of Ekeya was as appealing as she had first thought it was.

"They are watching the biru to detect the patterns of its writhing. That way they can confirm if their earlier prophesies were correct."

Once the old women were satisfied that all was well, they raised their arms and howled like wild beasts.

"Ah," said Ghoryi. "Everything is fine."

One of the priestesses took a ladle from a brass clasp fixed to her robe, dipped it into the cauldron, and poured the biru and blood into a vessel held by a second priestess. This woman carried the liquid to the general and gave it to one of his attendants, who handed it to the man himself. The general lifted the bowl before his face in acknowledgment and then drank its contents.

"Oh my!" Jess exclaimed. "That's disgusting. What's he doing?"

"He is gaining all the strength and bravery of the men whose blood was poured into the cauldron."

"Are you sure it works like that?"

"Certainly."

Jess leaned over and whispered in Uluf's ear. "You know, I think people are crazy everywhere."

"My dear, I am inclined to agree with that."

Having cast the bowl upon the ground, the general bid his driver take his carriage to a place between the temple and the priest, facing the cauldron. When he had arrived at his destination, he bowed to the priest and priestesses, and they bowed to him in return.

One by one, each of the red women fixed her halberd into a hole in the paving (these were imperceptible from where either Hyan or Jess was watching), took the bowl hanging from the weapon, walked over to the cauldron, and allowed the priestess with the ladle to fill it with biru.

As the musicians played upon their instruments and raised a great clamor, the red women went to stand between the cauldron and the roads extending from the plaza to the city's center and its edge.

The hosts of soldiers lining the thoroughfare then marched in companies to join the women, who, holding their bowls before the lips of every man who approached them, allowed him to sip the bloody milk. When he had done so, each cupbearer dipped her own fingers into the frothy red liquid and anointed the man's weapons with it.

Hyan, while pinning up her hair with a pair of lacquered chopsticks, looked back at her companion.

"I wish you could access your host's memory so you could tell me what's going on."

"I'm sorry, Chun. I don't have that ability."

"Never mind. It doesn't matter. In a couple of days this city won't exist anymore. It's really quite a shame. I do like this place. Still, what has to be done has to be done."

Her bowl emptied, each of the women returned to the cauldron for more and continued doing so until every man in Ekeya's army had drunk some of the biru and his weapons had been marked with it.

The great wagon the general was standing upon was then daubed with blood by the priest using a sort of mop that he had dipped into the cauldron of biru. After that, the priest chanted something before the general and each man bowed to the other.

The general commanded his driver to take the wagon around the cauldron and down the thoroughfare leading to the city's edge. Preceded by the priest, priestesses, and red dyed women, and followed by the hosts of soldiers who had been lining the road leading to the city center, he made his way towards the great glass dome.

As the last of the men marching behind him passed their fellows standing along the street, these persons fell in behind the others and joined in the great parade.

When the army had reached Ekeya's gates, it turned onto a road leading to the right, and this brought it to the front of a large and ornate temple, where the soldiers were blessed by a group of priests. From there, the host followed the same road in a great circle back to the gates, whence it made its way back up the main thoroughfare until it came to the plaza in front of the City Palace.

There, the general stepped down from his vehicle and walked to one of the tables that was set at the top of the steps leading into Ekeya's central building, where the councilors were already seated beneath the ranks of their brazen flea-like guards. After he had joined them, he beckoned to all who could see him to come to him.

"Come," Hyan said to her changeling. "Let's go down to the plaza. It's time to hunt."

"As you desire, Chun."

At the same time, Ghoryi, Jess, and Uluf left the balcony where they were standing and headed for the same place.

# Chapter 31
# Festivities

An enormous communal bowl carved in the shape of a worm with a human face at either end of its body had been set upon each of the tables in the plaza in front of the City Palace. Inside, every one of these was heaped with a variety of different foods, and from them the multitudes of congregated men and women took whatsoever they wished to eat.

To ensure that all were mirthful as they so feasted, there were also, around the sides of the plaza, countless casks of bruy as large as small buildings, and each person helped himself to as much of this drink as he desired so that, after a short time, most of the revelers were at least a little tipsy and many were completely drunk. Everywhere, they were eating and laughing and dancing to the loud sounds of horns and drums.

Although Jess did not care much for the bitter liquor of Ekeya, she did get a bowl of the stuff and was soon feeling pleasantly lightheaded. She did not, consequently, notice the attractive young woman and the grim faced merchant wearing foreign clothing who were never very far from her.

Instead, while musicians played loudly upon their instruments and innumerable people formed themselves into great circles and danced ecstatically, Jess, overcome with enthusiasm and alcohol, rushed off to join them, dragging Uluf by the hand.

As the dancers whirled around the edges of the plaza and down the middle of the street leading to it, Jess gyrated wildly, threw back her head, and laughed with excitement. She leapt and spun about, waved her limbs, shook her body, and turned her face towards her companion again and again, beaming at him while sweat saturated her hair and poured in rivulets down her cheeks. The dangers that lay ahead of her vanished in her joy. Intoxicated by the bruy, the music, the fever of the crowd, and her own energy, she lost herself completely in the frenzied dance.

Eventually, however, Uluf drew close to her and told her he needed to rest. The two left the circle and went to lean against a wrought iron fence enclosing one of the temples facing the plaza.

Jess, having got herself some more bruy, continued to wiggle to the sounds of the music that filled the air while Ghoryi and Uluf watched her.

After a time, though she was still enjoying herself, Jess became increasingly tired and increasingly drunk. She clung tightly to Uluf's arm to make sure she did not fall down and, as she drank even more, chatted with her friend and with Ghoryi.

"You people actually make war seem like it's fun," she informed her supervisor.

"It would be wrong not to celebrate the heroism of our soldiers," Ghoryi replied. "Many of them will be dying over the next few days. They ought to enjoy their last moments. Besides, it will give them a taste of the paradise they will enter if they die and so will inspire them to fight more bravely."

"Well," Jess replied, "if that's what motivates them, then let's motivate them some more. I'm having a great time here."

"So I see."

Uluf looked first at the woman and then at Jess. He did not like Ghoryi's tone. For a second he wondered what had prompted it. Perhaps, he thought, she disapproved of Jess's drinking. He quickly rejected that possibility, however. Though Ghoryi was not nearly as drunk as Jess was, she was hardly sober.

He turned his gaze upon those around him and watched as they enjoyed themselves with as much abandon as Jess did. Her behavior was nothing unusual, at least as far as the toad could tell.

Uluf then noted that the garments and mannerisms of the members of the crowd filling the plaza were different from Ghoryi's or Jarsu's. The people around him, he realized, were commoners, not retainers. All the revelers of that class were congregated near the steps of the palace.

He examined the man and woman assigned to watch over Jess and himself. Both, but the latter in particular, were clearly uncomfortable and seemed not to know what to do with themselves.

Suddenly, he understood. Ghoryi (and Jarsu) did not approve of making merry with her (and his) social inferiors. Visiting the temple of the tribe's goddess was acceptable, but dancing in the street with ordinary folk was not.

The toad smiled within as he watched Ghoryi cringe to be surrounded by those she saw as being beneath her. It was not that he had any animosity towards her, but he himself had been despised by so many human beings over the years in just the way Ghoryi despised those around her now that, in spite of his awareness of the pettiness of his feelings, he was still pleased to look at her squirm.

His musing was interrupted when Jess asked him, "So, Uluf, are you coming with me tomorrow?"

"Do you need to ask, my dear?"

"I don't completely take you for granted, you know."

"I realize that. I only meant that you ought to know that I have no intention ever to abandon you."

"I know that, Uluf."

She smiled at the toad, patted his cheek, and went on. "Anyway, I'm glad you're coming with me. How about you, Ghoryi?"

"No. I will remain here. You will be given a new handler for your journey."

She turned to the toad. "I will inform his majesty that you will be traveling with the girl and that her supervisor will need to watch you as well."

"Thank you, my lady."

The toad bowed graciously over the ornate top of his cane and Ghoryi smiled at him.

Jess continued talking with the others for some time, although she never stopped drinking as she did so. Her vision had, as a result, become more than a little blurry, her speech somewhat slurred, and her legs entirely unsteady when she heard someone greeting her.

Even after scanning the faces of those around her, she did not, for a moment, recognize any of them. Having eventually focused both her eyes and her thoughts, however, she was able to recognize Ofu. Once she had seen him, she saw Buabyue as well, who was the one who had addressed her.[*]

Both of the men were dressed in the style of Ekeya, and both were accompanied by arrogantly strutting but beautiful young women. These two were garishly dressed. Their hair was piled upon their heads in outlandish fashions, and little golden bells dangled from their pierced nipples and from bands on their upper arms.

Ofu looked at Jess and commented, "You've had a few."

"And I'm feeling great."

"I see that."

"So, how are you two doing?" Jess asked while looking at them from under heavy eyelids.

Ofu smiled broadly and, roughly squeezing his companion's breasts, exclaimed, "Not badly. The women here are real whores. Toss one a half-kopeck and she'll be on her knees."

Jess frowned at Ofu, but he went on. "I like these girls a lot better than the aristocratic women we saw at Hyuka's palace."

"So, you just got some prostitutes?" Jess asked.

Buabyue replied, "They're not prostitutes. Women here accept gifts from their suitors. These women just happen to be poor, so they're a little more inclined than women from the retainer class to be persuaded by presents. Fortunately, they don't insist upon very large gifts, either."

"Well, I hope you're having fun," Jess informed him.

"I always enjoy my visits to Ekeya," Buabyue said.

"I guess you'd rather be staying here tomorrow."

"Yes. Nevertheless, if the Ekeyan council wants me to advise Hrahei, their general, then that's what I'll be doing."

"And you, Ofu?" Uluf asked.

"I'm staying here. This isn't my fight."

"Suit yourself," Jess told him.

She still had not noticed Hyan, who was sipping a cup of bruy and leaning against one of the green lampposts that encircled the plaza.

Reaching her arms above her head, grabbing the metal post behind her, and arching her back, Hyan spoke to her homunculus. "Have you seen Ghasuhu?"

"Yes, Chun."

"Go over to him and introduce yourself."

---

[*] Their handlers were following behind them.

"As you wish."

Hyan hoped that the homunculus would do a decent job of impersonating a wealthy merchant. If it could, it might be able to talk Ghasuhu, the king of the Sakahei (one of Ekeya's tribes), into joining it for further discussions about a possible business deal. If the creature could do that, it might get the chance to kill the man. Since Ghasuhu was in charge of Ekeya's defenses, not only would his death further Hyan's plans, but the homunculus would be able to get from him the codes that would give Hyan access to the city's security system.

"Are you going to do something about the girl while she's drunk?" the creature asked.

"I was thinking about that, but I'm not sure."

"Why not?"

"I can't decide if she's an idiot or if she's up to something."

"What do you mean?"

Looking at Jess, Hyan explained. "She'd have to be a moron to get as drunk as she seems to be. If she's as lethal as Tsoi thinks she is, she couldn't be that stupid. Maybe she knows something is going on."

"Or," Hyan continued while turning to face the homunculus, "she might just have no sense. After all, she must be a little mad to have tried what she did in Quanya."

While Hyan was saying this, Jess decided that, as drunk as she was, she wanted to dance some more. She grabbed Uluf's hand and pulled him along after her to one of the circles of revelers.

"That decides it," Hyan said. "I'm going after the man from Jezic. You take care of Ghasuhu."

The woman and the homunculus separated, each heading towards his quarry.

Hyan went over to Ofu, nodded to him, and looked at him with a sidelong glance. He looked back at her and was immediately excited. He had already realized how readily available the women of Ekeya were and, seeing that this one appeared to be interested in him, hoped he would be between her thighs shortly. Hyan, letting her eyes stray across her prey's crotch, saw how aroused he obviously was and approached him.

Sipping her drink, she placed her hand upon his arm and inquired, "Where are you from?"

"I'm from Jezic."

"Where's that?" she asked, coyly twirling her hair.

"It's in Tozana, on Shokai."

"Oh, really? You're the first one I've met from Shokai."

"Hey," snarled the woman with Ofu. "Can't you see this one already has a girl?"

Hyan brushed her hair away from her face, tilted her head, and gazed up at Ofu.

"You already been inside this one?" she asked him while pointing at the other woman.

"Yeah. What of it?"

"You want to crawl back into the same hole or do you want to try something new?"

Ofu smiled broadly. "When you put it like that, the choice is pretty obvious."

He looked at the woman he was already with and, appreciating her charms, suggested, "Why don't we all have some fun together?"

Hyan pressed herself against him and took his genitals in her hand. "I don't want to share. I want this thing for myself."

Ofu pushed the other woman away and informed her, "Sorry, beautiful. You're on your own tonight."

"Screw you, you clot," the woman snarled, making a gesture with her hands. She then spat upon the ground and, tossing her head back, strutted away.

After watching her rival leave, Hyan said to Ofu, "Okay then. Let's have some fun. My name's Chun, by the way."

"Yeah, whatever."

Ofu gestured to his keeper and, when that man had come up to him, said, "We're going back to my room."

"Where's that?" Hyan asked.

Her quarry pointed to the palace of the Podgohani. "In that tower over there."

"Let's just get a room nearby."

"Fine."

* * *

Ofu was lying on the pillows strewn about the hotel room Hyan had suggested he rent, his head propped up on his elbow so that he could watch the young woman in front of him untie her sarong and let it fall onto the floor. He stared at her as she walked over to him, stood over his hips, and slowly lowered herself down onto him.

Hyan leaned forward, pressing her breasts against Ofu's chest and kissing him for several minutes.

When she raised herself up again, she noticed the medallion resting between the man's hairy, tattooed collar bones.

"What's that?" she asked him.

"It's an amulet of Shyammeto."

"Is it magic?"

"It protects me."

Hyan laughed. "And you think it's going to protect you from me? I don't think so. I'm voracious."

The woman fiercely bit Ofu's neck and his nipples before lifting herself up on her knees and staring at him lustily, her long hair drifting about her face like a black storm cloud swirling around the moon. He returned her gaze and watched her intently as she took his penis in her hand and slid it inside of her body.

Ofu had never been with someone so skilled. Hyan was able to grip him with her vagina – she was wonderfully strong – and knew exactly when to do so. After a while, the pleasure he felt was so intense it actually began to hurt. The pain, however, merely added to his delight. His mind reeled from the bliss that suffused him and nearly drove him mad. His ecstatic agony grew more and more overwhelming, until, suddenly, it became so extreme that it lost its pleasurableness and simply became pain.

Ofu arched his back and began to lift himself up on his elbows when his whole body convulsed in agony. He felt as though his penis were being simultaneously stabbed with several knives and torn apart by a grater.

He fell backwards and started to roll onto his side, but, before he could do so, a cutting sensation at the root of his genitals startled him into his senses. He reached out to grab the woman sitting on top of him. She leaned back and then stood up, out of his reach.

Ofu looked at his crotch but could not see his penis.

The woman stepped forward to stand over his head, squatted down over his face, and allowed his severed member to fall out of her vagina onto his forehead.

Ofu gasped in horror and would have grabbed the woman had he not seen her genitals. Her labia were drawn apart like an open mouth and within them were myriads of little legs (like those of an insect) adorned with saw-toothed spines. The orifice of her vagina itself was even worse. It was filled with tiny, triangular fangs and was repeatedly opening and closing with a nasty slurping noise.

Just as Ofu opened his mouth to scream, Hyan sat down upon his face and let the crotch spider she had placed within her begin eating him.

It was a genetically modified animal that had been directly linked with her own nervous system so that it obeyed her will. It did not attack and feed when she did not desire it to, usually being sustained not by dining upon its victims through its syringe-like legs and teeth but by its connection to Hyan's own circulatory system.

While Ofu lashed about to the sound of his own muffled cries, Hyan pulled the chopsticks from her hair and drove them into the man's ears. He briefly convulsed and then died.

The chopsticks were, in fact, control spikes, and Hyan, turning Ofu's head, stabbed one into the base of his skull.

Stroking the corpse's cheek, Hyan whispered to it, "I guess your magic trinket wasn't much help after all."

She stood up, wrapped her sarong around her waist, and said, "Get up and get dressed."

Ofu's corpse did as she commanded it, and, when it was back in its clothing, she gave it another order.

"Tell the guard to come in here."

While the zombie walked over to the door and beckoned to Ofu's keeper to enter, Hyan uttered that particular sound that caused the yoke she wore to resonate beneath the artificial skin that was currently concealing it. She repeated the sound, over and over again, until she felt the universe succumbing to her will. The vibrations of the yoke pulsed through space and time transforming these into extensions of her body. Time slowed as she desired it to, and Hyan leaned against a pillar with her remaining chopstick in her hand.

"What do you need?" Ghaheitthu asked Ofu as he walked into the room.

Before he even suspected that anything was wrong, Hyan leapt from where she stood, faster than a bolt of lightening, and drove the spike into the man's heart. He staggered backwards and grasped at his chest, but his attacker had drawn out her weapon and was already plunging it back in above his hand. Again he grasped at it, but again he was too slow. Hyan stabbed him in the heart a third time, and Ghaheitthu, falling onto the ground, died while making a foul gurgling noise.

She rammed the control stick into the back of the cadaver's head and said to it, "There's a furnace in this building. We're going to be visiting it. Now get up."

The corpse stood and Hyan went over to a wardrobe, where she found a clean dressing gown for it to put on. Once Ghaheitthu's body was wearing this and Ofu's had wrapped a scarf over its mutilated face, their killer commanded them to follow her to the furnace.

The woman and her zombies went down into the basement of the tower, without anyone who passed them noticing anything unusual.

Once they were standing in front of the furnace, Hyan ordered Ofu to open a door set in its side and to stand in front of this. She pulled the control stick out of his brain and instructed the other zombie to push him into the flames. After Ghaheitthu had done so, she removed his control stick and pushed his body in after the first.

Closing the door behind them, she commented to herself, "That was disappointingly easy."

Hyan left the tower and returned to the rooms where she was staying, where she found her homunculus waiting for her.

"How'd it go with you?" she asked.

"Ghasuhu was interested in the offer I made to him. I asked if he would like to discuss it in greater detail. He said that he would. We went to a restaurant and talked. After the sun had set, we left. As we were walking in the street, I slit his throat."

"Did anyone see you?"

"No."

"Are you certain?"

"As certain as I can be."

"Did he provide you with the security codes?"

The homunculus removed a metallic device from his pocket and handed it to Hyan.

"He was very fresh when I put the control stick in his brain. When I told him what I wanted, he didn't have any trouble accessing the information. The security blueprints are in the wand and so are the pass codes we'll need."

"Good. What did you do with the body after you were done with it?"

"I walked it to a pond I had seen nearby and pushed it into the water."

"Wonderful. We'll be having worlds of fun now."

# Chapter 32
## On the March

"Before you leave with the army," Ghoryi told Jess as she handed the girl a green box, "you'll need to put these on."

Jess took the box, set it on the low table in the middle of the lounge outside of her bedroom, and asked, "What is this?"

"It's a protective suit. The atmosphere of Suturik is venomous and corrosive. You'll need it if you're going to be outside the city."

"Should I put it on now?" Jess inquired.

"Yes. Your next supervisor will be arriving shortly to escort you to the carriage you'll be traveling in."

"Okay," Jess replied and began stripping off her clothing so that she could put on the garments provided for her.

Once she had dressed herself in the dark blue, skintight jumpsuit made of some paper thin, glossy, rubber-like material, Jess placed over her head a glass orb like a fish bowl, from the top of which projected two short, thin golden antennae and from the back of which emerged, just above the neck, a brass, trumpet-like funnel that collected oxygen from the atmosphere.

Ghoryi smiled and tried futilely to keep herself from laughing. "You don't need to put on the helmet yet."

"I just wanted to see what wearing it would feel like," lied the pink haired girl.

As Jess, blushing brightly, was removing the globe from her head, there was a tap upon the outer door. Ghoryi opened it and Uluf, Buabyue, and a man Jess had not previously seen entered the room.

The toad and the gangster were wearing garments similar to that Jess had on, and the other man was attired in a colorful formfitting jacket that had long skirts and appeared to be made from rubber. His right hand was resting upon the hilt of a dagger hanging at his hip, and, under his left arm, he held a tall conical sallet with a projecting visor.

"This is Jess Ichikawa," Ghoryi informed the man in her graceful, formal way.

He nodded to her, and Ghoryi told Jess, "This is Misheya. He will look after you while you are with the army."

Jess nodded her head to the man in return.

Looking at the other two, she said, "I guess Ofu's not coming, huh?"

Uluf answered, "He does not appear to have changed his mind since yesterday."

To this, Buabyue added, "He didn't return to our suite last night. He must still be with that woman he met."

"If you will follow me," Misheya told the others.

Then, while Jess was tying round her waist the cords of the bottomless pouch containing Dawn's Spine and her daggers, he added, "We should be joining the army now."

"Thanks for the tour, Ghoryi," Jess said as she left the room.

Ghoryi nodded to acknowledge the sentiment.

Misheya led his charges out of the tower to a large and ornate carriage, the body of which was similar to that of an ancient stagecoach. It was paneled with a bright yellow substance not unlike wood and adorned with elaborately carved pilasters of another, nearly black wood-like material. These rose above the flat roof and were topped with lanterns themselves capped with iron finials. From the front of the cabin emerged a thin stalk upon which rested a smaller compartment made of panes of glass set in a metal framework similarly topped by lanterns.

As elaborate as this vehicle was, the parts of it that caught Jess's attention were the six long, black, arched, and segmented legs (like those of a spider) that it was perched upon. These, she realized, would raise the vehicle high into the air when it was traveling. At the moment, however, it was resting on the ground to allow the passengers to enter into it.

Misheya gestured for the others to step into the carriage while an attendant held the door in front of them open.

Inside, there were two plush couches facing one another and a table in the middle. Above the latter, set in the wall directly opposite the door, was a telopticon designed to look like a flower. At the tip of its stem were lacquered pink petals from amongst which rose a pistil (that was actually a microphone) and a pair of white stamens that formed the image harp.

When everyone was inside and seated, Misheya switched on the telopticon and said, "We're ready to leave."

"As you command," replied a voice, that of the driver, coming from amongst the flower's petals.

The vehicle lifted itself up from the ground and lumbered down Ekeya's main thoroughfare toward the wall of glass.

Once it was outside the dome, it joined with various others that were assembled just beyond the city's gates.

Misheya informed his fellow travelers, "We will remain here as the army is mustered."

Jess looked around and noticed that large numbers of people had gathered along the perimeter of the city and were watching what was going on outside. Most seemed to be facing Ekeya's gates, so Jess watched these as well.

The inner gates of the vestibule leading into Ekeya were then closed and the outer gates opened and left so.

For a few moments, there was quiet. Jess felt a thrill of anticipation, which was quickly heightened by the sound of blaring buisines and rumbling drums.

From out the trapdoors set in the floor of the vestibule emerged an eight-legged carriage similar to the one Jess was in but with glass walls. Within this Hrahei sat upon a throne holding a staff topped with a spray of what looked like feathers, though these were actually the multicolored gills of one of Suturik's great insects.

This vehicle turned to the left and began to circumambulate Ekeya.

After it, out of the trapdoors, swarmed a stream of gheau, sufine, and osu drawing chariots that were either supported on wheels or wafted through the air by means of antigravity engines. These, following the general, made their way out of the city and began to circle round it.

Behind them came prawns as large as busses to whose backs gun turrets had been strapped, and, behind these, Ekeya's infantry.

A few of the common soldiers flew upon wings like those used by the guards Jess had encountered when she had first entered the city, but most were on foot.

Both the ground and the air infantry wore the shaggy garments and odd helmets made from giant legumes they had donned the day before, though all now additionally wore a mask with a long curved snout shaped like the beak of a raven, above which was a pair of huge goggles with black, opaque lenses.

As this host moved around the city, Jess heard a groaning noise coming from behind her. She turned around and spied, for the first time, a shining silver gate set between two rocky outcroppings.

When this had slid open, there spilled forth a procession of mountainous hiika, and each of these pulled an entire metal castle that, with its antigravity engine, floated above the earth.

These creatures fell in behind the infantry and followed them as they moved around the city.

Jess was genuinely awed by the spectacle before her. Not only were the beasts of the army impressive on their own, but every one of these various monstrosities was festooned with brightly printed ribbons, draped with ornately woven tapestries, dripping with strings of gems and pearls, and adorned with plumes and fluttering banners. The sight was simply astonishing.

Even Uluf, who was never impressed with martial displays, could not keep himself from muttering, "Just so, just so."

After Hrahei had completed his circuit of the city, he brought his carriage to a place facing Ekeya's gates and remained there while his host formed itself into two columns, one on his right and one on his left.

After a few moments' wait, the shutters closing the tubes that ran between Ekeya's dome and the ground just within it opened up. From these flew swarms of huvinku, kurushyi, hryttha, and bureine, all of which were ridden by fancifully attired soldiers.

"Those are the royals and retainers from amongst Ekeya's tribes," Buabyue told Jess.

She nodded in response, gazed fixedly up into the sky, and gawked, with her mouth hanging open, at the multitude of enormous insects swirling above her head. The smuggler, meanwhile, admired her breasts, carefully examining how their every contour was revealed through the girl's thin, tight suit.

The cavalrymen flew their mounts around the city as the others had circumambulated it, and then formed themselves into a cloud above the main body of the army.

Sixteen members of the city's air cavalry, all of whom were mounted upon kurushyi, separated from the others and landed upon the ground in front of Hrahei's carriage.

"What's happening now?" Jess asked.

"They're the generals in charge of each tribe's army," Misheya explained. "They're paying homage to their commander, swearing that they will obey him in every way during the campaign."

Once the huge dragonflies had settled themselves upon the ground, their sixteen riders dismounted and kowtowed before the general, who indicated with his staff that they should rise.

The men remounted their steeds, returned to the air cavalry, and led it away, through the sky, toward Padangkpei.

Once they were some distance ahead, the army began to march. The column to the general's right set out first, followed by Hrahei himself, and then by the other column.

"Now we and the baggage will set out," Misheya told the others.

Along with the vehicles around them, they fell in behind the army.

Jess looked back and noted that more carts drawn by huge insects were emerging from the trapdoors in the vestibule and that several ornithopters were walking out of the same gates whence the hiika had come.

While these craft lifted themselves from the ground and flew above the army, Misheya addressed his charges.

"We should be engaging the army from Padangkpei tomorrow."

Jess nodded to him and pressed the side of her face against the window next to her to see the strange world around her.

Almost immediately, she felt the glass reverberating with something other than the machinery moving the vehicle and wondered what this was. She listened carefully and so made out the sounds of some sort of song.

"It seems like they're singing something out there," she said to the others.

"Probably a marching song," Misheya informed her. "Wait just a moment. I'll turn on the outside microphones. You should be able to hear it."

Misheya switched on the telopticon, adjusted it, and sat back.

"There," he said with a gesture of his hand.

The cabin was immediately filled with the tones and rhythms of the soldiers' singing, though their voices were made tinny and peculiar by being filtered through the microphones of their protective suits.

With the help of her translator, Jess listened to their words.

> *Off to the war I march, my love,*
> *And lift my banner high.*
> *But in my dreams I'll see your face,*
> *And wake at night and sigh.*

*Oh! Oh! Oh!*
*I miss my sweetheart so!*

*I'm sure to meet some foreign girls*
*And wrap them in my arms.*
*I'll hold their hands and taste their lips*
*And savor all their charms.*

*Oh! Oh! Oh!*
*I miss my sweetheart so!*

*Yet all the girls from distant lands*
*Are quite unlike my love.*
*When you would scream you'd pull me close,*
*But they'll just push and shove.*

*Oh! Oh! Oh!*
*I miss my sweetheart so!*

*Finding myself between their thighs,*
*My thoughts will be of you.*
*Whatever pleasures they can give,*
*I promise I'll be true*

*Oh! Oh! Oh!*
*I miss my sweetheart so!*

*I'll leave their brothers with my sons*
*To wash and feed and see.*
*They'll need to wipe their sisters' tears*
*For they will dream of me.*

*Oh! Oh! Oh!*
*I miss my sweetheart so!*

*I'll be a hero when I'm back,*
*Unlike those ancient men*
*You used to sate your youthful lust,*
*And we'll make love again.*

*Oh! Oh! Oh!*
*I miss my sweetheart so!*

As Jess enjoyed such martial music (without really understanding what the song was about), her carriage continued on its way behind the army through the weird landscape of Suturik.

She moved past dark blue orbs that were as big as elephants and were adorned with myriads of tufts of scintillating pink whiskers, below pastel blue tree-like columns topped with clumps of lavender sausages, around thickets of midnight blue canes crowned with translucent fans that fluttered in the wind, and near various other odd wonders besides these.

Though such plants intrigued Jess, the planet's animals were even more bewitching. High above her, the girl saw locustian bureine, silverfish-like hryttha, and thrip-like huvinku flying. Creeping upon and below the blue vegetation that surrounded her, she spied countless other insect or crustacean-like creatures of innumerable different species, and even discovered, floating weightlessly through the air (but not far from the ground), many that were neither quite like insects nor quite like fish, but were rather a mixture of the features of both these sorts of animals.

As she sat staring at such marvels through the window beside her, Jess realized that she had not seen a single settlement since leaving Ekeya. She had caught glimpses of a number of herdsmen tending flocks of different sorts of gigantic insects, but had yet to encounter these persons' habitations.

When this thought occurred to her, she asked Misheya, "Where do the people I keep seeing live? It doesn't seem like there are any towns."

"There are villages here and there. Do you see the ridge just ahead?"

"Yeah."

"Wait till we get past it. There's a settlement there."

Once the army had passed through a valley cutting into the high ground Misheya had pointed out, Jess alternated between craning her head around to see what she could through the windows on the opposite side of the carriage and pressing her face against the window beside her.

With a laugh, Misheya pointed through the window next to Jess and said, "It's over there. Do you see it?"

"Oh, okay. I see it now."

At the center of this town was a glass dome, like that of Ekeya but much smaller and filled with far more modest buildings, while, around this, were a number of low tumuli. These, Jess could tell, were actually the roofs of underground houses and must, she surmised, be connected to the others with tunnels.

Beyond such habitations were a great many pens, wherein herds of insects were confined, and a large number of long, low greenhouses. Each of the latter was encircled by a palisade of metal spikes and topped with metal ornaments shaped like the leaves atop of a pineapple.

Seeing her looking at these structures, Buabyue (hoping to win the girl's favor and so eventually gain entrance into her body) explained. "The spikes keep the huge insects indigenous to this world from landing on and ruining the greenhouses."

Jess nodded, looked at him out of the corners of her eyes (since she was well aware of the man's desires), and said, "That makes sense. Why do they need the greenhouses, anyway? Can't people eat the plants here?"

Buabyue turned to Misheya, who said, "A few are edible, but most are not."

"What of the animals?" Uluf inquired. "Are they raised for food?"

"As a rule, yes. Their flesh is generally poisonous, but some of the beasts can be eaten. The poison can be removed from the meat of a number of the insects. The flesh of others is not entirely venomous. As long as the good parts are separated from the bad, such creatures are edible."

Thinking that eating one of these insects would be like eating a hluvess, Jess grimaced. With her brow furrowed, she asked, "What do they taste like?"

"Each is unique. I'm sure you've had some sort of meat since you arrived here."

"Do you remember the ocher dumplings?" Buabyue asked her.

"Yeah."

"Those were made from sufine."

"What are those?" Jess inquired with trepidation (not being sure she wanted to know the answer).

Buabyue looked out the window over Jess's shoulder and pointed to a pen filled with bulbous, lumbering beasts like giant dust mites.

"See the animals there?"

"Yeah."

"Those are sufine."

"I ate one of those?"

"Yes," Buabyue replied while trying not to laugh at Jess's nauseated expression. "It was pretty tasty wasn't it?"

"It was before I knew what I was eating."

Jess leaned back in her seat and returned to looking out the window, hoping to forget this revelation about her recent diet.

Except for a brief stop in the middle of the day, the army continued on its journey until the evening, when it made camp on top of a hill surrounded by a forest of pulpy blue plants sprouting brilliantly red tendrils that branched out like blood vessels and arteries suspended in the air.

The vehicle Jess was riding in set itself upon the earth, and Misheya said to her and Uluf, "Come, I'll show you how to ride a walker. It's possible we could get caught up in the fighting and, if we do, you'll want some kind of mount."

Jess and the toad both nodded to him.

"Thanks," the girl replied. "What's a walker? Is it a kind of insect?"

"No," Misheya said while putting on his helmet and indicating to Jess, Uluf, and Buabyue that they should do the same. "Riding any kind of insect requires skill. You haven't the time to learn. A walker is a machine. I'll show you in a minute."

Misheya turned on the telopticon and spoke a number into it. A moment later a man's face appeared between the artificial stamens.

"This is the chief machine driver."

"This is Misheya-Ku of the Cheuni. I need a walker at my carriage."

"I'll send it over immediately, your grace."

"Thank you."

Turning off the telopticon, Misheya opened a cabinet set in the wall beside the door and took out four pistols. He handed three of them to the others and kept one for himself.

These were similar to the needle guns used on Shokai (in that they consisted of a metal barrel set in a wooden stock). However, unlike the guns of that other planet, which were more or less banana shaped, these were so slightly curved that they were almost cylinders.

After everyone had a gun, Misheya gestured to Uluf that he should open the door to the carriage. The toad did so and discovered that outside of it there was an iridescent bubble large enough for all of the passengers to stand within.

Misheya then walked through the bubble, which reformed behind him unbroken. The others followed after him.

Jess looked around. The army was setting up a lavish encampment. Nearly the whole of the hill was covered with brightly colored tents of various outlandish shapes, almost all of which were topped with fluttering banners or poles supporting the image of some goddess or god.

Closer to the travelers than the soldiers' bivouac, the wagons of the baggage train had stopped, but even this part of the camp was made impressive by its bustling activity. From some of the nearby vehicles cooks rushed into hastily erected tents and began preparing the soldiers' food. From others, animal handlers scurried out to deal with the cavalry's mounts, and from still others dashed the various servants required by the officers to attend to their persons.

Most importantly, the great tower-like, colonnaded wagons housing the army's brothels arranged themselves before open spaces so that the soldiers could come and gaze at the naked whores wiggling behind innumerable bubble windows before entering these establishments and paying for whatever girls pleased them best.

"Is this a needle gun?" Jess asked Misheya when she was able to draw her attention away from the sights around her.

"Basically, yes. It uses a magnetic pulse to fire a projectile, but that, unlike an ordinary needle, is equipped with a small incendiary. The flying insects here are able to become airborne by producing hydrogen and storing it in sacks inside their bodies."

Jess's eyes widened on hearing this, and she interrupted him with a question. "How do they land?"

"They fly downwards. They do have wings. When they reach the ground, they simply cling to it with their claws. Anyway, what's important about this is that if you are able to shoot an insect and create a spark inside one of those pouches, you can blow it up. Don't aim at the head. Aim at the body. That's where the hydrogen sacks are."

Jess could not help but laugh.

"This is going to be interesting!" she exclaimed.

"Remember what I told you," Misheya continued. "Ah, the walker is here."

Jess turned in the direction towards which Misheya was looking and saw the vehicle approaching her.

The walker was supported on six long, thin, arched legs, like those of a giant harvestman. Its shimmering cloisonné body was shaped roughly like a teardrop, the tapering forward end of which came to an upturned point like the horn of a rhinoceros beetle, and atop of it was a sort of saddle.

The machine, having stopped in front of Jess and the others, rested on the ground, and the driver hopped off of it. He bowed to Misheya, who dismissed him.

"Would either of you care to try it?" Misheya asked Jess and Uluf.

"Sure," the girl answered with a wide grin. "But – I will warn you – I don't have any idea how to drive this thing."

"It's simple. Sit in the saddle."

Jess climbed on top of the walker.

"Put your feet in the stirrups."

Jess slid her feet into these, which were like a pair of nacre covered boots hanging from the sides of the vehicle.

"It's controlled by mechanisms in the stirrups," Misheya said. "If you want to go forward, press your right foot forward. If you want to stop, press your right foot backwards. If you want to turn right, press your right foot towards the right. If you want to move left, press your right foot towards the left. If you want the vehicle to move up, press your left foot towards the left. If you want it to move down, press your left foot towards the right. The harder you press in whatever direction, the faster the walker will move in that direction. Got it?"

"It sounds simple. I don't know how easy it will actually be to do it, though."

"Give it a try."

Jess cautiously pushed her left foot towards the left, and the walker rose from the ground. She then pressed her right foot forward and the vehicle began to move. She was impressed by how easy it was to control and was soon wandering amongst the vehicles of the baggage train as though she had been driving a walker for years. Nevertheless, Jess did not take it into the main part of the camp or outside the palisade the soldiers had erected around its perimeter. She assumed that going to either of those places would not have been appreciated.

The girl still had a tremendous amount of fun riding the walker. Although it did sway about quite a bit as it moved, in a way no other vehicle Jess had ever been on did, she actually found this rocking to be rather pleasant. What was more, looking down from her high seat upon the various persons scurrying about their chores and gazing out across the vibrantly colored forests of Suturik imbued her entire body with a tingling excitement.

After about an hour of entertaining herself so, Jess returned to the carriage she had been traveling in and found that a tent with a conical roof topped with a green banner had been erected beside it.

Lowering the vehicle to the ground, Jess dismounted and walked over to the tent. There was a small vestibule at its front covered with a membrane like the one that had earlier sprung from the side of the carriage. She walked through this and noted that it reformed behind her. At the back of the little room she was standing in was a second membrane, and she passed through this into the tent proper.

There, reclining on pillows around a low lacquered table covered with trays of food were her three companions. Jess sat down beside Uluf, picked up a morsel of food, and examined it carefully to make sure that it was not made of meat. Once she was satisfied that it was not, she popped it into her mouth and relaxed with the others.

# Interlude 13
# Languages

Although an exact figure is impossible to give, the number of languages currently in use could be in excess of two million. A few of these are used on several planets, but the overwhelming majority are confined not just to one particular planet or another, but to one region of that planet. Only three languages are important throughout human space: Twituboch, Uopa, and Naval Tongue.

Twituboch is the lingua franca of interstellar traders. Its grammar and core vocabulary are derived from Vietnamese, an ancient language that was spoken on the Earth, but it incorporates words from a variety of other tongues, especially Hindi and English.

The language currently referred to as Twituboch has changed significantly over the centuries, to the degree that its earlier forms are not comprehensible to speakers of its later forms, but its role as the language of space merchants has never been threatened.

In the second half of the Sixth Century, as interstellar travel became routine again, one company, Green Star Shipping, which was based in a region of the Earth then known as Vietnam, came to play an increasingly important role in the reemerging trade between worlds. At that time, such commerce was limited, largely consisting of the export from the Earth of technological and luxury items in exchange for exotica produced on the colonies. Because there was not a sufficient amount of trade to support a large number of competitors, once Green Star had gained its dominant position, it was able to maintain a virtual monopoly on interstellar commerce.

To facilitate its trading operations, Green Star, during the period of its ascendancy, built and staffed space stations throughout that part of the galaxy then occupied by humanity.

Since the crews of these and of the company's ships were primarily recruited from Vietnam, the language of that country was used by nearly all persons engaged in commerce between worlds.

Green Star, perhaps because of its dominance, eventually became unwieldy and internally fragmented. By the early Eighth Century, it had splintered into several companies. As the volume of interstellar trade increased, other entities even came to compete with these.

The employees of Green Star's successors were, however, still being recruited from Vietnam. Many, in fact, were former Green Star workers. Their language, consequently, continued to be used almost exclusively among interstellar merchants.

Over time, especially after traders from different parts of the Earth or from other worlds increased in number, the Vietnamese spoken by space travelers changed. Having been simplified grammatically, having lost its system of tones, and having incorporated words from other tongues, it became Twituboch.

The usefulness of having a single language spoken by all interstellar traders, as well as the development of this occupation virtually into a segregated caste, has guaranteed the survival of their language.

The second language spoken across human space, Uopa, had originally been the vernacular of an empire that had covered about a third of Pan Clo during the time of the Confederacy. After the fall of this empire, Uopa remained the language of learning across the regions it had ruled.

When Pan Clo was unified, Uopa was used as the language of government, even though it had by then ceased to exist as a vernacular. With the later establishment of the Pancloan Empire, Uopa came to be employed throughout human space. Since it was the language of administration and justice, it also came to be known as Cuapa or the Language of the Court.

The final widespread language, Naval Tongue, is artificial, though it is based on several related vernaculars spoken around the capital region of Pan Clo. It was created by linguists in the early days of Pancloan expansion to provide military personnel with a common language.

In order that it might best fulfill such a function, Naval Tongue was made grammatically simple, precise, and suited to giving commands. It has, nonetheless, been enriched over the years by numerous slang terms and irregular constructions introduced into it by its speakers.

From Pollidor's *Big Blue Book of Knowledge*

# Chapter 33
# On to War

While Jess and her companions were eating, a soldier poked his head into their tent.

"Excuse the intrusion," he said. "Is Buabyue here?"

"I am he."

"General Hrahei would be pleased if you would come to his tent."

Buabyue stood up, and Jess asked him, "Can I come with you?"

"Certainly. If the general doesn't want you there, he can always send you away."

Jess jumped to her feet, took Uluf's hand, and lifted him up after her. Putting on their spherical glass helmets and following Buabyue, who was himself following the soldier who had summoned him, the girl and the toad left the tent and made their way through the lanes between the round, conical, and onion shaped tents of the encampment.

As they were walking, Jess saw floating through the air near her a school of creatures like multicolored fish adorned with countless waving tendrils and glowing whiskers.

Captivated by their beauty, the girl reached out to touch one of them. Seeing her do so, Buabyue shouted out, "Don't do that!" Unfortunately, Jess's fingers were already upon the side of one of the fish when she heard his voice.

No sooner had Jess made contact with the creature than an electric shock surged through her body, leaving her feeling empty and weak. She jumped backwards and nearly ran into another of the fish in the process.

"Watch out for those," Buabyue told her. "They defend themselves with electricity. They won't kill you, but getting shocked is never pleasant."

"No, it's not," Jess agreed.

The soldier who was leading the travelers took them around a corner, to a large pink tent topped with six conical peaks surrounding a seventh, and brought them into this structure.

Inside, a number of men wearing rich garments of the style favored in Ekeya and crowned with tall plumed hats adorned with colorful enameled medallions cast in the shapes of the totemic animals of the sixteen tribes of that city sat upon cushions around a low table whereupon a map was spread.

The soldier, removing his mask and helmet, dropped to his knees and kowtowed to one of these men, who was, perhaps, in his middle thirties and was wearing a lavender jacket and a hat with an image of a rabbit upon it.

When the soldier raised his head again, he said to this individual, "My lord, I have brought you Buabyue. The other two are his companions."

Buabyue, having taken off his own helmet, kowtowed as well, followed by Jess and Uluf, who assumed it would be wise to follow his example. When the smuggler rose, he told the general, "I am Buabyue, my lord. This girl is Jess Ichikawa and the toad is named Uluf. It is Jess who brought me the information I gave to the council. I ask you to forgive my bringing them here."

The general dismissed Buabyue's concerns with a wave of his hand and then informed him, "I am aware who these two are, Buabyue, and you needn't worry about having brought them here. They could, after all, be of use to me. At any rate, they have already been of considerable use to the council. Now, seat yourselves comfortably."

Hrahei turned to one of the men resting near him and instructed him, "Inform our friends of the current situation."

"As you wish, my lord," the man replied.

Turning to Buabyue, he pointed at a line of mountains on the map between two cities. Jess correctly assumed that the city to the east of this range was Ekeya since there was an ocean just to the east of it. She had noticed, while she had been making planetfall upon the vessel that had taken her from the orbital station where Buabyue's ether-ship had landed, that Ekeya's spaceport was built not far from an ocean.

The officer continued. "Our scouts have located the Padangkpeian army here. They're making their way along the mountain range, heading east."

With his finger he traced upon the map the army's movements, emphasizing that the southern part of the range curved to the east and came very close to Ekeya itself.

"It would appear," he said, "that they don't want to stray far from the safety of the mountains. They're going to try to follow them until they can get close to Ekeya itself."

"Are they supported by any mercenaries?" Buabyue asked.

Hrahei responded, "Our scouts have not seen any, but that doesn't mean there aren't any hiding somewhere in the mountains."

"So what are you going to do?" Jess blurted out.

The general smiled and told her, "I'm going to split our army. One part will hurry to the south of the force from Padangkpei. They'll cut them off so they can't flee from us. The second part, which I'll be leading, will then approach them from the north."

He pointed to a pass in the mountains. "We're going to try to engage them at the end of Takinu Pass. Our own army is substantially larger than is that of Padangkpei, so, if they are not supported by mercenaries, it will be advantageous for us to engage them on open ground. They'll have little chance against our superior air cavalry and larger infantry. However, if they do have allies, we could be outnumbered or outclassed. If that's the case, and we're near the entrance to the pass, we can retreat into it. The valley is narrow and would allow a small force to fight a large one on equal terms. Of course, we must make sure that, if we are superior, they are not able to enter the pass. Now, Buabyue, you are an offworlder, what sort of mercenaries might the Ngo have hired?"

"I beg your forgiveness, my lord, but there is no way I can say. I will have to see them first. But I can say that they probably won't have much of an air cavalry. If they have any, it'll be light. They could have men with personal fliers or wings and antigravity engines, but that should be it. I'll be able to give you more specific information when I see them."

The general leaned back. "Is there anything else you can tell me?"

Buabyue reflected for a moment and then said, "I think you should count on there being mercenaries in the battle. Tsoi Ngo isn't going to leave something like this to some minor city. He's going to do whatever he can to make sure the job's done properly."

"I assumed as much," the general replied.

"It's also likely – In fact, it's almost certain – that he'll have sent somebody close to him to take charge of the situation."

"Who?"

"Probably either his uncle, Lo, his cousin, Hyan, or his castellan."

"Go on."

"Lo is brutal, brave, and well liked by the Ngo gang, but he's not especially bright and he's set in his ways. Tsoi often relies on him, but he doesn't have much confidence in the man. I think he's the least likely of the three to be here. If he is here, expect plodding, straightforward strategy, but a readiness to fight."

"And the others?"

"The castellan's cunning, but he's not a soldier. He'll probably rely on the mercenaries' leader for strategy. Hyan's the one Tsoi's probably sent, though."

"And what's he like?"

"Hyan is a woman, my lord. She's Tsoi's cousin, Lo's daughter. She's very smart. In fact, she's probably the smartest person in the Ngo family. She's also reckless and takes terrible risks. Those are probably the traits that endear her to Tsoi the most. After all, he's like that too. If she is the one he's sent, expect your enemies to be daring and to try dangerous strategies."

Buabyue, Hrahei, and the latter's officers continued to discuss their options for the coming battle in great detail, until Jess was bored witless. After a while, her brain was so numbed that she started having trouble keeping her eyes open, and it was only Uluf's frequent pinches and nudges that prevented her from dozing off and tumbling over.

Eventually, Hrahei noted how bored his young guest was and, smiling, told Uluf to take her back to her tent.

The toad placed Jess's helmet upon her head and his own upon his. He lifted up his half conscious friend, wrapped one of her arms over his shoulder, and walked with her back to the tent where they had been before. There, he set her down upon a pile of pillows, took off her helmet, and let her sleep. He then went to get a little practice riding the walker, just in case he would need to use it later.

\* \* \*

The Ekeyan army resumed its march towards the mountains the following morning and, having reached their foothills, continued onwards under the tall quartz spires that projected from amongst the soft, spongy blue vegetation that surrounded them.

As the host proceeded along its way, Jess spied a number of villages, every one of which had been destroyed. The central dome of each was smashed; the pens were filled with slaughtered gheau or sufine, and smoke billowed out of the ruined subterranean houses.

When the vehicle in which she was riding passed the first of these, Jess asked Misheya, "Did the Padangkpeians do that?"

The man was clearly trying to restrain his anger and merely nodded in acknowledgement. Jess thought it wise not to press him and fell quiet again.

The army continued moving southwards throughout the day, stopping only briefly at around noon to rest. It was able to reach Takinu pass by early evening, but, when it arrived, the force from Padangkpei was nowhere in sight.

Hrahei ordered his forces to make camp, and Misheya left the others so that he could inquire about what was happening. When he returned, he informed Jess, Uluf, and Buabyue that the army of Padangkpei had attempted to avoid the smaller body of soldiers the general had sent to block its march. That other force was now, however, driving Ekeya's enemies back towards the mountains. The battle would be fought the following morning.

Almost as soon as she had awakened the next day, Jess was told by Buabyue to get into the carriage, to which the walker, its automatic driver having been activated, was now secured with a tether.

Once the army of Ekeya had broken camp, it was positioned directly in front of the entrance to Takinu Pass. To its south, and heading towards it, was a much smaller force, and behind this, pursuing the second army, were the soldiers Hrahei had previously divided off from his main force.

A body of foot soldiers and cavalrymen was placed near the pass to guard against any possible attack from that side. The baggage train, along with the carriage Jess was riding in, was placed at the back of the army, to its north, with a body of infantrymen just in front of these noncombatants. Before this host, ranks of lumbering moyu and taaka were arrayed, and the great metal castles bristling with cannons that were drawn by enormous hiika were scattered throughout the army.

While the air cavalry and air infantry rose up into the sky above the main body of the army and the forces of Padangkpei began to draw near, Jess felt a wave of excitement rush through her flesh. She grabbed Uluf's hand and pressed her nose against the window as if she thought that by doing so she would be able to see the terrible events about to occur before her eyes more clearly.

When their enemies were not too far away, the rows of Ekeyan moyu and taaka sprang forward and raced towards the Padangkpeians. Their counterparts in the other force did the same, and these armored behemoths collided with one another midway between the two armies. The shells of many of the monsters split open when they crashed into others of their kind, and their pinkish organs and greenish blood spilled out upon the ground. Others slipped in this slimy mess of viscera and rolled upon the earth, where they were trampled by both their fellows and their enemies.

The riders of the huge beasts, at the same time, fired their rifles at their foes, aiming either for their human enemies or for the heads of their steeds. Some of the men so shot fell dead upon the earth. Others, still alive, were smashed underfoot by insects racing around them. Those whose mounts were killed or wounded fared no better. Their bodies were crushed and torn limb from limb when the giants collapsed onto the ground. Even those few who were thrown clear were reduced to a gelatinous pudding within seconds of being unseated.

The heavy cavalry forces were still fighting when, from each army, countless men riding osu and psicca charged at them. These beasts, smaller and faster than the moyu or the taaka, swirled around those brutes, biting at them with their fierce mandibles as their riders shot at their counterparts with long, brightly painted needle rifles.

Eventually, the Ekeyan cavalrymen were able to cut a path through their enemies and a great many moyu and taaka rushed at the body of Padangkpeian infantry in front of them.

They pulverized those men beneath their feet, squashing their torsos into jelly, cracking their skulls like eggs, and grinding them into the earth. Behind the giants swarmed slithering osu and leaping psicca, that themselves eviscerated their foes while their riders, like mounted hunters, shot at the Padangkpeians with their guns.

Even as this struggle continued, the air cavalries met in the sky. Jess watched with fascination as the giant insects whirled and dove beneath quickly moving pink clouds and gently undulating brimu.

Some of the flying mounts, hit with incendiary projectiles, exploded in bursts of flame. Others tore the soldiers of the air infantry (the men with artificial wings and antigravity engines) limb from limb, devouring their vivisected carcasses, and still others grappled viciously with one another in the air. At the same time, the beasts' riders shot at their foes with rifles or pistols, tried to stab them with long, tasseled halberds, or sought to crack open the thick chitin of their adversaries' mounts with becs de corbin or pollaxes.

As fierce as was the battle in the sky, a part of the air cavalry of each army was able to disengage from its counterpart and fall upon the ground forces below. Although many of the flying beasts were shot by the foot soldiers, so that they exploded in the air and rained burnt gore down upon their killers, others escaped their assailants and allowed their riders to cast grenades amongst the men beneath them, blowing their bodies apart and leaving substantial holes in their ranks.

One such group of Ekeya's flying warriors came to the aid of the ground cavalry driving deep into the army of Padangkpei and enabled the latter to split off a large portion of the enemy army from the rest. These persons, seeing their isolation, panicked and began to flee to the north and east.

Misheya smiled as he watched them. "If they have reinforcements hiding, they'd better use them soon. It looks like they're heading for a devastating defeat."

"Are you certain?" Buabyue asked him.

"What?"

"Look again."

Misheya peered out the window. The force that had been fleeing moments before had managed to circle round to the side of Ekeya's army and was now charging at it.

"They've tricked us," Buabyue said. "They're attacking our flank and we're completely unprepared for them there."

Misheya grimaced as the Padangkpeian force, which was composed of both ground infantry and ground cavalry, drove into the Ekeyan army not far from where his carriage was.

"We could be in danger where we are," Buabyue noted. "They're heading right for us."

Misheya swallowed audibly. "We've got to do something. The army's too far behind us. The Padangkpeians will be all over the carriage before anyone can get here to help."

Jess put on her helmet. "I'm going out."

"Jess, please do not," Uluf implored her.

"They're heading right for us, Uluf."

"Besides," she added while glancing at Buabyue, "I've got to earn my groats."

Buabyue smiled at Jess, but Misheya looked at her with scorn.

"What do you think you can do?" the latter asked.

"Oh, you'll see," she replied.

"Good luck, then. Here's the key to the walker." Misheya handed her a brass key he took from a pouch hanging from his belt. "The keyhole is in a box on the front right foot. Turn the key and the walker will lower itself for you."

He switched on the telopticon and instructed the driver to lower the carriage to the ground.

"Thanks," Jess replied as she opened the door. The toad was staring at her with a worried expression.

"Don't worry, Uluf," she added. "I'll be fine. You keep forgetting what I'm always telling you: I'm too cute to die."

"Be careful all the same, my dear," the toad responded.

As the girl stepped outside, Uluf stood and, with his gun in one hand, took her arm with the other. "Wait, my dear. I am going out with you. I will do my best to provide you with cover."

"Stay in here. You're always telling me you're a terrible shot."

"Well, I will concede that when I was with my old troupe of entertainers, I was never comfortable shooting at the girl on the spinning wheel, even though she often chose me as her partner when her usual partner was unavailable. Still, however skilled or unskilled I may be, I am not such a coward that I will not, at the very least, endeavor to protect my own life."

Buabyue rose from his seat. "Your toad's right. I'm going out as well. I have no desire to cower in this vehicle and wait for the Padangkpeians to come and kill me. How about you, Misheya?"

The man nodded and he, Uluf, and Buabyue placed their helmets upon their heads.

Passing through the iridescent film that had formed around the door and into Suturik's poisonous atmosphere, Jess's companions took shelter behind the arched legs of the carriage and began firing their weapons at the approaching army.

Jess herself left them and rushed over to the walker, that was fastened with a cord to the back of the carriage. She found the box with the keyhole, opened it, and, having inserted the key, turned it. The walker at once lowered itself onto the ground and allowed Jess to mount its back.

Taking a deep breath to calm her shaking body, the girl slipped her feet into the stirrups and commanded the vehicle to lift itself up. Jess turned to face her foes, who were now very close, and took the pistol Misheya had given her out of the infinitely spacious pouch hanging from her waiste and held it in her right hand. She then drew Dawn's Spine from that same pouch and, holding it in her left hand, extended the blade from the hilt.

Wriggling about in the saddle to make sure she was secure, which she was thanks to the walker's stirrups (they gripped her feet very snuggly), Jess surveyed the situation around her. A body of Ekeyan foot soldiers was approaching from behind her, supported by a castle drawn by a hiika, but these would not reach her before the Padangkpeians would. Fortunately, the drivers, bearers, handlers, and others working in the baggage train had armed themselves and were crouching behind their wagons or the huge gheau, sufine, or other beasts pulling these and firing on their approaching enemies. They were not especially skilled, but they were at least slowing those persons down.

That, however, was about all they were accomplishing for, although most of the Padangkpeians were infantrymen, at their front were nine warriors riding Cooloola monster-like moyu, and these beasts were smashing through all the wagons, men, and draught animals in their path.

Her heart thundering in her breast (with both excitement and fear), Jess pressed her foot forward as hard as she could, sending the walker sprinting at an incredible pace towards the enormous creatures heading in her direction.

As the machine raced at the stampeding insects, Jess raised the thread inside her body from her perineum, where it had been resting, to her brow, turning the universe inside out as she did so. She immediately felt as though she were swallowing the whole world, drawing everything that had, seconds before, seemed to be separate from her into her mind, into which all such things melted. Time ceased its hurried rush forward and her hurtling vehicle began to move with graceful slowness amongst a host of soldiers who were fluttering about like pieces of down upon the wind.

The girl looked at the men she was approaching. They were wearing robes made of shaggy plant fibers and brightly painted, wood fronted masks carved into the faces of fierce birds with hooked beaks, leering, tusked fiends, and snouted, porcine goblins. In their hands were colorfully painted rifles or pikes decorated with banners or plumes, and with these weapons they shot or pierced their unskilled enemies.

Jess aimed her pistol at the first of the riders in front of her and pulled the trigger. The man fell backwards in his saddle, but, as his leg caught in his stirrups, he did not drop onto the ground. The moyu he was riding continued on its path, not noticing that its master was dead.

Without hesitating, Jess fired again and killed a second rider, who, like the first, was not unseated and kept on his way into the host of his foes.

A flame burst from the chest of third, and he tumbled onto the ground, where his corpse was squashed and torn apart by the beasts following him.

Jess spun her head around quickly and saw her three companions peeking from behind the legs of their carriage and shooting at their attackers. Uluf was clearly covering his friend, and she knew at once that the toad had killed the man who had just fallen before her.

Smiling at the thought of having someone looking out for her well-being, and thinking that Uluf was not as bad a shot as he claimed to be, Jess looked forward again and made ready to resume her fight.

As much as she had slowed time, the Padangkpeians were coming at her so fast that she did not have time to shoot the next cavalryman from a distance. His moyu was turning to charge her walker and the man himself was raising his rifle to fire at her. Jess, however, carefully aimed her own weapon at him as he moved so lethargically it seemed that he was weighed down by some invisible burden. She squeezed the trigger and the needle pierced the lens covering his right eye, which exploded into a little stream of flame when the incendiary in the projectile ignited.

The man's corpse flopped backwards before convulsively lurching forward to lie across the pommel of his saddle.

Just as that soldier's life came to its end, Jess's entire body was shaken. Everything in front of her was suddenly transformed into a conflagration. A vast wall of seething flame rose up before her, engulfing three of the remaining moyu.

After a moment's shock, she realized that the castle that was approaching from behind had fired a shell and that such an explosive had landed amongst the moyu.

At the very instant she knew what was happening, she heard the drawn out sound of several more cannons firing. Seconds later, she watched as explosions tore great holes in the mass of infantry that was following behind the cavalry.

Both of the remaining riders were to her left and were already past her, so Jess spun around to face them. She saw that one of these two was dead, shot, she assumed, by one of the persons hiding behind a baggage wagon. The second, having crashed through one of these wheelless carts, was heading in the general direction of the carriage where Uluf was.

The toad, the gangster, and the soldier were firing at the cavalryman coming towards them, but none of them was able to hit him. Misheya did wound the moyu itself upon its shoulder, but this wound merely enraged the beast. It did not slow it down.

Jess, concerned about her friend (her only friend), rushed after the rider coming at him, her arm raised in front of her, and fired her pistol. The needle struck the man in the back and he jumped in pain. He did not, however, die. Jess fired again, and this time her needle passed through and flambéed her enemy's heart. He collapsed onto his saddle and his mount smashed into a wagon, crushing both the driver huddling behind it and the gheau anxiously fidgeting in front of it.

Before she could turn around to face the body of infantry that had been behind the moyu, Jess felt an intense pain in her right shoulder that knocked her out of the walker's saddle.

# Chapter 34
# Battle

Jess grabbed ahold of the pommel in front of her in time to prevent herself from falling off the walker and then looked up. A hryttha like a winged silverfish was passing beside her. Its rider, she noted, was holding a halberd. Realizing that she must have been struck with this, Jess examined her arm. It hurt, but it was not cut. Her attacker must only have hit her with the weapon's shaft, not with its blade.

Exhaling in relief, Jess lifted her gun and fired at the insect her assailant was riding as it slithered in a circle through the sky in order to attack her again. She aimed for its body, and, when her projectile hit it, the great flying creature burst into flame, splattering the girl with hot gore. Fortunately, thanks to the protective suit she was wearing, she was not burned.

Wiping the green blood and pink entrails from her helmet so that she could see, Jess turned around and looked up at the sky. It was filled with a swarm of various sorts of insects.

"Oh, lovely," she exclaimed.

Two more hryttha were flying straight at her. She fired at the first of them, hitting it and causing the hydrogen in its body to explode violently.

The cascade of viscera that pummeled her nearly knocked Jess from the walker, but it also threw her other attacker off its trajectory, causing it to strike another insect flying nearby. This creature was cast onto the ground, where it and its rider were shot dead by the workers in the baggage train.

The man who had intended to attack Jess regained control of his mount and swung it round in order to approach her a second time.

Since it was heading directly towards her, Jess could not aim at the creature's body. She instead pointed her gun at the rider's throat and pulled the trigger. A plume of fire erupted from his larynx along with bits of meat and various tissues. The hryttha continued towards Jess, despite its rider's demise, and the girl was forced to duck to avoid its bite. While it passed beside her, she swung her sword and split it in half midway along its length.

No sooner had she dispatched the insect than Jess felt a disturbance in the air beside her. Someone had shot at her with a needle gun and had missed her helmet by inches.

She looked to the east. The Padangkpeian infantry was fast approaching her, and it was now supported by more cavalry. About a dozen osu were slinking over and between the wagons to her left.

Another needle ricocheted off the walker next to her leg and a third grazed her helmet, leaving a deep scratch upon its glass.

Though time was still moving at the reduced rate Jess had determined, leaving her to act with extreme rapidity, the girl's vehicle was trapped in the same temporal treacle as were the Padangkpeians. As a consequence, she was as easy a target as were any of the other combatants.

Sweat poured down Jess's brow and into her eyes. She blinked and automatically raised her hand to wipe it away. Striking her helmet instead, she remembered the head band that had been provided with her suit.

Unfortunately, she had forgotten to put it on earlier. She shook her head vigorously in an attempt to dislodge the sweat running into her eye sockets, but merely slapped her cheeks with her saturated hair.

While the castle behind her fired its canons again, obliterating the front ranks of the infantry coming close to her, three of the enemy's osu emerged from amongst the wagons and squirmed about the walker's feet. Their riders raised their guns to shoot at Jess, but, before they could do so, she pulled her feet from the stirrups and leapt out of the saddle.

Jess drew the ground towards her slowly, aiming her pistol at one of the riders below her. As she gently fell, she fired, hitting him in the head and killing him instantly.

She then grabbed one of the walker's legs, used it to spin around in midair (so that she was facing the second of her opponents), and shot the man in the heart.

Jess pushed herself away from the vehicle's leg, somersaulted through the air, and landed upon the back of the third osu, in front of its rider. With a single stroke of her sword, she separated her adversary's head from his torso and watched as his body collapsed twitching at her feet.

Four more osu rushed out from amongst the wagons and came at Jess, their riders firing their weapons at her as they approached.

Taking Dawn's Spine in her right hand and the pistol in her left, the girl jumped from the back of the insect she was standing on and crept along its side, allowing her enemies' needles to pierce the beast's carapace and kill it rather than her.

Once she had come to its flailing, pitchfork tail, Jess forced the universe down around her and lunged at the nearest of the riders ahead of her. She waved her sword in circles around her head, planted her feet upon the osu's back, and chopped its rider in half at the waist.

The second rider died almost immediately thereafter, shot in the stomach with an incendiary projectile. Although she was not sure who had killed him, Jess felt a certain happiness at the thought that Uluf might have helped her again.

The third cavalryman, meanwhile, fired at her, and though she was fast enough to prevent the needle from killing her, she was unable to avoid it entirely. It glanced off her helmet with enough force that it knocked her off her feet and sent her crashing onto the ground beside the riderless osu's many feet.

For just a second, Jess was disoriented and, forgetting herself, allowed time to return to its normal pace. As soon as she heard the ordinary sounds of the world, undistorted by their passing through the atmosphere at half their usual speed, as they did when time was slowed, she gasped in shock and fear and raised the thread back up her spine, re-submerging the world in the syrup of her imagination.

Jess rolled under the lethargically churning legs of the osu beside her, jumped to her feet on its other side, and then leapt from the ground onto the creature in front of her. The rider who had just shot at her looked up at her face and flinched with surprise. Jess, giving his blood to her goddess, separated the upper half of his skull from the lower half and hopped off of the osu to stand beside the last of these whose rider yet lived.

The creature began to turn toward her, but, while it was still doing so, Jess sliced its body in two midway along its length. The rider fell into the heap of entrails that had squirted out of his mount's corpse and tried to grab ahold of the insect's body to pull himself out of this mess. As he so struggled, Jess chopped off his arms at the elbows. The man crumbled onto the ground howling in agony.

Thinking the Padangkpeian infantrymen must almost be upon her, Jess spun around to face them, but the open area in front of her was empty, except for the corpses of those who had already been killed. Her closest enemies had taken shelter behind several of the nearby wagons and others, as they approached, joined their fellows.

Jess looked back at the Ekeyan army and saw that a large body of infantry supported by a regiment of psicca riders was rapidly approaching and firing upon their foes. They had already surrounded the carriage where Uluf and the others were and so stood between those persons and their attackers. At the same time, the hiika drawn castle had moved closer and was repeatedly hurling shells upon the Padangkpeians, annihilating great numbers of them.

Realizing that she was exposed where she stood and likely to be killed by the shots fired by one or the other of the armies, Jess dashed into a narrow space between a pair of wagons. She dropped onto the ground and looked around as best she could. A short distance away there were several men, though Jess, being able only to see their legs, could not tell if they were Ekeyan baggage handlers or Padangkpeian soldiers.

She crawled underneath the wagon in front of her, between its huge spoked wheels, and made her way across an open area to another transport that floated in the air with the help of an antigravity engine. Next to this was a squat, hulking gheau making frantic clicking noises, and Jess hid herself behind the forest of its many legs.

She breathed deeply for several seconds, trying to regain her strength and composure. Her stomach moved rapidly in and out with each exhalation and inhalation, and her heart drummed so violently in her chest she felt as though it would shatter her ribs and tear itself loose from her body.

Once she was feeling a little better, she shook her head about inside her helmet, in the hope of getting a little of the sweat off of her face and out of her eyes, and looked around, ready to resume her fight.

The half dozen persons ahead of her were, Jess now saw, Padangkpeian infantrymen. Three of them had climbed onto the running board of a baggage wagon heaped with sacks of grain and were firing their long red rifles (decorated with images of various abstract animals) at the Ekeyans, while three more were standing on the ground. One of the latter was slitting the throat of a driver he had caught and the other two were rifling through the garments of a man they had already killed.

Jess rolled out from under the wagon, swinging Dawn's Spine in an arc. The torsos of the two men squatting beside the corpse were sliced in half below the sternum and the cadaver's head was lopped off in the process.

Jumping onto her feet, but remaining close to the ground, Jess amputated the legs of both the third soldier and his victim.

The three men hanging onto the wagon had heard her, but, caught in temporal treacle, they were only beginning to turn around to face their enemy.

Before they could attack, Jess lunged at the first of them, disemboweling him. Then, leaping to the side to avoid his entrails, which were spewing out of his body, she cut the second man in half from one shoulder to the opposite hip with a downward motion of her blade,

The last man, though unable to aim at Jess, did manage to hit her with the barrel of his rifle, knocking her off her feet and onto the ground. He himself, however, lost his grip on the side of the wagon and fell onto his backside next to her.

Jess quickly sprang to her feet and leapt on her attacker. He was fumbling with his rifle and so gave her the chance to remove his head from his body.

The girl was still rising up when she was jolted by the impact of a needle upon the trumpet-like funnel emerging from the back of her helmet. The blow knocked her forward, causing her to bite her tongue, and that sent a bolt of anger surging through her body. Looking up from under her contracted brows, Jess saw huddled amongst the bags on top of the wagon her victims had been clinging onto two more soldiers. One was facing her and the other was turning in her direction so that he too could shoot at her.

As the first man fired at her a second time, Jess leapt backwards, flipping head over heals, ricocheted off another wagon behind her, and propelled herself onto the top of the wagon where her assailants were.

Without giving the first of these men a chance to realize what was happening, Jess separated his head from his neck. The second, meanwhile, jabbed the pink haired young woman in the chest with the muzzle of his rifle, knocking her onto her buttocks.

Her breath expelled from her lungs, Jess was unable to focus herself and let the thread sink down her spine and time return to its normal pace.

The man in front of her dove at her while she was incapacitated and hit her in the stomach with his rifle. Jess gasped in agony, but did roll to one side to avoid a third blow. Her attacker swung his weapon like a club and bashed Jess in the shoulder. She yelped like an injured dog and rolled backwards over the bags of grain, nearly falling off the wagon.

Jess's enemy, thinking he was about to kill her, jumped carelessly at the girl. She, however, having recovered her wits, raised up her thread, slowed time, dove to one side, and cut the man in half.

Even as the upper and lower parts of his body fell onto the bags and slid thence onto the ground, Jess heard a loud noise above her. She turned her head upwards and saw a vast multitude of insects flying through the sky.

"Oh, this is just great," she said to herself before sighing and offering up the lives of all those she was about to kill to the goddess Haya.

Many of the insects circled over the advancing Ekeyan troops, their riders dropping grenades on those forces and doing them great harm, though many were shot and blown up as they so attacked. Others, however, passed over the soldiers and rushed at the metal castle behind them. Within moments, this huge structure, bristling with so many cannons that it looked like a giant robotic hedgehog, was almost completely covered with swarms of hryttha, bureine, huvinku, and kurushyi.

Jess did not have the luxury of watching the battle behind her since five bureine were coming at her from the sky. Her heart racing with excitement and her mind wholly focused on her actions, the young woman slowed time as much as she could without exhausting herself. She took her pistol in her right hand and fired at the first of her most recent assailants. The insect's body exploded, knocking away the others to either side.

Jess fired again and blew up a second bureine. While pieces of its burning meat drifted through the air of the slowed world around her, Jess realized that she could not kill all three of the others before they reached her.

Focusing her will, she seized ahold of the atmosphere surrounding her body and pushed it away from her. The shock wave smashed into the giant locusts hurtling towards her, sending two of them spinning into the ground and one of them onto the top of a wagon.

Jess shot at the pair on ground, blowing both of them up before they could right themselves. The last, meanwhile, had been able to lift itself off the wagon and into the air, but, before it had raised itself up more than a couple of feet, Jess swung round and fired an incendiary into its body. It exploded as the others had before it.

Crouching down to avoid, as much as was possible, the chunks of meat and bits of exoskeleton raining down upon her, Jess also avoided a volley of needles that was fired at that same moment by the Padangkpeian infantry.

She heard a loud noise and, turning around, saw a dozen friendly psicca hopping amongst the wagons in her direction. Remaining low to avoid the continuous fire Ekeya's enemies were directing at these leaping cicada-like beasts, Jess also avoided being struck by the insects, which were soon jumping over her.

Lifting up her head, Jess watched the creatures falling upon their foes and tearing them apart with their mandibles while their riders shot other men with their rifles. Jess herself took aim with her pistol and killed at least two men, maybe three, before the Ekeyan infantry swarmed through the alleys winding between the wagons around her and, engaging with the Padangkpeians, created such a maelstrom of bodies that she was no longer able to get a clear shot.

Jess took the opportunity to recover her strength and lay, breathing heavily, upon the sacks of grain heaped on the wagon, though these were sticky with blood and entrails.

Suddenly, she heard a loud explosion behind her, jumped up, and whipped around. The castle that had been lobbing shells into the Padangkpeian army had burst into flame and the incendiaries within it had begun blowing up. Many of the insects that had been clinging to its side, to allow their riders to fire their weapons through the slots out of which the fortress's cannons projected or to cast their grenades through these, were caught up in the series of explosions that tore large portions of the metal walls away. Others, however, were able to distance themselves and either circled about the structure or began attacking the infantry surrounding it.

Their success was short lived. Before the castle had even been completely disabled, two more approached it from behind. Both of these, once they had come close enough, started firing their cannons, with devastating effect, into the Padangkpeian forces attacking the flank of the Ekeyan army.

Jess turned her eyes towards the carriage where Uluf was and was relieved to see that, though it had been stuck by a few stray pieces of the wrecked castle, these had not come anywhere near her friend. He and the others were still crouching behind the vehicle's legs and firing at their enemies.

The infantrymen of the invading city, their numbers now sorely depleted, then began fleeing, pursued by the foot soldiers and psicca riders of Ekeya.

Though the swarms of flying insects that had just taken off from the destroyed castle had, up to that moment, been heading towards its replacements, when their commanders saw the predicament their ground forces were in, they turned their mounts around and went to help those men extricate themselves from their current danger.

The air cavalry flew low over the wagons, the riders shooting at whatever Ekeyans they saw, whether these were soldiers, baggage handlers, or huddling, terrified prostitutes.

Jess watched this cloud of buzzing insects and tried to crawl down behind the heap of sacks below her to shield herself from their riders' fire. Several did shoot at her, but none of their needles came close.

About half the swam had passed over Jess when one of the cavalrymen, upon seeing her, and realizing that he did not have a clear shot at his enemy, spun the huvinku he was riding around and forced it to alight upon the wagon.

The multi-legged creature, like a thrip the size of a rhinoceros, crept onto the side of the pile of sacks and its rider took aim at Jess with his long red rifle. The girl, though briefly horrified by the face of the monstrous insect gazing at her and gnashing its mandibles (that were bigger than her torso), did not let such fear paralyze her. Still holding back time, she dove beneath the huvinku's body and, swinging her sword in a circle, chopped off its legs before rolling out from under it.

She slammed down upon a full sack, from which she propelled herself with a leap, and landed on the back of the creature, in front of its rider. He turned his masked face towards the young woman looking at him, but, before he could react, she, offering up his life to the goddess Haya, split the right side of his body from the left.

Jess turned to jump from the back of the now flailing huvinku onto the ground, but, as she did so, four more insects came upon her so quickly that even she could not avoid them.

The foreleg of a dragonfly-like kurushyi struck her waist, causing her to double over onto its back, her own legs dangling in the air as the creature rushed over the wagons just beneath it.

The kurushyi's rider recoiled in astonishment as he gazed down at the young woman looking up at him. That surprise delayed his reaction enough to give Jess the chance to regain her breath and recover her wits. While the man started to point his rifle at the girl, she, dropping her own pistol, seized ahold of the pommel of his saddle, drew herself upwards, and swung at him with her sword.

The blade cut off the end of the rifle's muzzle and the hand with which the rider was holding the weapon. He screeched in pain, threw the rifle butt at her, and thoughtlessly pulled upon the reins he held.

As the kurushyi soared straight upwards into the sky, Jess nearly fell from its back. She was only saved by landing on the chest of the man who was now between her and the ground. He started striking her with the stump of his forearm, and she wrenched the reins from his hand. Pulling them in the opposite direction she had seen him draw them, so that the huge insect returned to a nearly level course, Jess lay her sword along her enemy's throat.

"If you don't want me to kill you, take us to the ground," she yelled at him.

The man had lost any ability he had to reason, however, and, drawing a dagger from his hip, attempted to stab Jess with it.

She bent to the side to avoid his blade, swung her own, and cut her enemy in half at the waist. His body then fell upon Jess, knocking her backwards, onto a pair of the kurushyi's iridescent wings.

The rider's torso was still on top of the girl and causing her to slip downwards, so, almost in a panic, Jess swung at it with Dawn's Spine. She divided it into two parts, which fell away to either side, but, as she did so, she also sliced off one of the insect's wings.

The great creature immediately began flying crazily towards the earth, Jess barely clinging to its rough, chitinous back.

"Oh, this is just lovely," she commented to herself as she saw the wagons rapidly approaching her.

Jess readied herself to leap from the insect's back just before it struck, hoping she would be able to manipulate the world enough to survive. But, instead of hitting the earth, the kurushyi slammed into a pair of hryttha. Both of these beasts were severally mauled by the impact, but they stopped the kurushyi's dive.

Gritting her teeth in anticipation of her delayed plummet to resume, Jess was surprised to discover she was actually rising upwards. The kurushyi appeared to be dead or unconscious, but, since it was no longer propelling itself at the ground, the hydrogen in its body was lifting it into the sky.

It did not take Jess long to realize that such an ascent would, ultimately, be even more dangerous than her earlier rush towards the earth. She looked downwards. One of the hryttha the kurushyi had run into was still fluttering around beneath it, though its rider was clearly dead and the insect itself appeared to be severely wounded.

Whatever its condition, it was, nonetheless, Jess's only chance. She jumped from the kurushyi onto the hryttha below and grabbed the reins still held by the dead man, whose crushed body was slipping from the saddle. Pushing this to the ground, she tried to direct the creature downwards.

The insect obeyed, although its flight was erratic, and was soon a short distance above the earth. Unfortunately, another soldier of Padangkpei's air cavalry saw Jess riding the wounded beast and directed his own bureine at her.

He fired a shot at the girl with his rifle, but missed, giving Jess the chance to stand upon her mount and leap from it onto that of her attacker. The man was shocked to see Jess do this and offered her no resistance when she decapitated him.

Shoving his body from the saddle and taking its place, Jess tried to fly the bureine towards the ground. She was nearly there when two more bureine riders flew at her, firing their rifles as they did so.

"Oh, come on!" she yelled. "Give me a chance to get back on the sweet ground. Can't you see I'm tired of flying around like this?"

Jess, now more irritated than furious, spun her mount round, amazing herself that she was able to do so successfully, and attempted to fly over the attacker to her right. Instead of just passing over the other beast, her own snapped at its rider and tore off a large part of his head.

While feeling glad that she had not allowed herself to get within the reach of any flying insect's mandibles, Jess pressed herself down against her mount's back to avoid the shots the other man was taking at her and continued her descent.

Not being a skilled rider, Jess slammed the bureine into the ground, smashing its body so that its pink entrails and green blood gushed out upon both the soil and its rider's body. The impact also threw Jess from her seat, though she was able to curl herself into a ball and roll along the ground, so preventing herself from being injured.

She managed to regain her feet just as the other bureine dove at her. While jumping to the side, she swung her sword, slicing the insect's side open along the length of its body. The beast crashed into the ground a short distance away.

Its rider started to pull himself from his saddle, but, mired in the slowed time Jess was forcing upon the world, he was not able to free himself before the girl, who moved like a character in a sped-up film, had rushed upon him. He looked up in time to see her sword split his chest open and bisect his heart.

Jess immediately raised her sword beside her head, ready for the next attack, but, instead of discovering a new enemy, she found herself isolated amongst the wagons. She spun her head around, but did not see anyone nearby. The remnants of the Padangkpeian force that had attacked from the east were fleeing, and the Ekeyan forces that had been sent to drive them away were close on their heels. Even the two castles that had arrived to help the first were moving away from the smoldering remains of that structure to join the main body of the troops of their army.

Looking in that direction, Jess saw that the battle was still undecided, even if the little struggle she had been caught up in was over.

Exhausted but relieved, Jess shook her head in another attempt to get the sweat off of her face and walked back towards the carriage where Uluf, Buabyue, and Misheya were.

Her three companions were no longer crouching behind the vehicle's legs, but were standing in front of these surveying the grisly scene around them. Uluf, Jess noted, was looking directly at her. Although she knew how her friend felt, Jess could not help but feel surprised and touched whenever she was presented with evidence that any living being actually cared about her. As far as she could recall, the toad was the only person who had ever shown any concern for her without being primarily interested in getting her to spread her thighs.

Upon coming to her friend, Jess put her arm around his spherical body, happy that they were both alive. She then opened the door to the carriage and, with the others, went inside.

While Jess was taking the glass globe off of her head, Misheya, smiling broadly, exclaimed, "That was amazing. I've never seen anybody fight like that."

Jess grinned at him, slid down her seat, and rested her head against its back.

"At least I've got a couple of talents," she replied as she wiped away the puddles of sweat that had accumulated on her face.

"How are you, Jess?" Uluf asked her. "Are you injured?"

"A little battered and bruised, but I'm fine."

The toad took her hand in his own and squeezed it.

"I am glad to hear that."

Brushing her drenched bangs from her eyes and running her fingers through the rest of her equally saturated hair, Jess asked, "So, how's the battle going?"

Misheya looked out the window, appraising the scene around him, and said, "We've certainly had some trouble, but now that that's been taken care of, it looks as though we're winning. Look over there. We're crushing the Padangkpeians."

"No sign of any reinforcements?"

"No. I don't see any. If they don't show up soon, it won't matter if they do."

Jess pressed her face against the window beside her and watched as the Ekeyan army pushed its opponents backwards, though the latter continued to resist and to inflict substantial damage upon their assailants.

For some time, Jess observed the conflict raging on the plain below the mountains. The fight never again approached the carriage where she was sitting, and she soon found herself so relaxed that she felt more like a spectator at some incredible show than a participant in an actual battle.

About an hour after she had returned to the carriage, Jess heard the telopticon chime.

Misheya answered it and the face of a young soldier appeared between its artificial stamens.

The man asked, "Is Buabyue there?"

"I'm here."

"I have an urgent message from General Hrahei."

"Continue."

"We have received a communication from Ekeya. The city is under attack by an offworlder ether-ship. You have been ordered to return to the city immediately to provide advice to the defenders."

"Who's attacking?"

"I don't have that information."

"How's he to get back?" Misheya interjected.

"A high-speed ornithopters is being dispatched to you now. Prepare yourself to be picked up immediately."

"I'll be ready when the craft arrives," Buabyue told the man, who then ended his communication.

Turning to Jess, he told her, "You'll come with me. I could require your help."

Jess placed her hands behind her head, smiled widely, and replied, "Sure. Why not?"

# Chapter 35
## The Fortunes of War

After Jess, Uluf, Buabyue, and Misheya had been picked up by the high-speed ornithopter (which looked somewhat like a great, metal manta ray), it conveyed them through the skies towards Ekeya. Within a very short time, the passengers could see the bell jar that enclosed the city rising in the distance.

As they got closer, they noticed a strange craft hanging onto the side of this glass structure with a long metal stem, as though it were a flower emerging from a transparent rock.

It was odd to see such a large ship suspended in the air, but the vessel itself was as peculiar as was its position. It consisted of two long hulls (on different levels) joined, like those of a catamaran, by a series of bridges. Rising from both of these were several tall masts from which were hung numerous shimmering metallic sails in an arrangement as complex as that of any clipper ship.

"I've never seen a vessel like that," Jess commented. "It's very pretty, though. Have you seen one, Uluf?"

"No, I have not, my dear. At least, I have not seen one physically before my eyes. I have seen images."

"Oh, what is it?"

"It is an iliyo raider."

Jess had never encountered an iliyo or one of their ether-ships before, but she was aware of the aliens' reputation.

"I've never heard of the iliyo raiding this far from the frontier," Misheya said.

"And I've never heard of them working for humans before, but here they are," Buabyue told him.

"What do you mean?" Misheya asked.

"Don't be thick, man. They're working for Ngo. These are the mercenaries we were expecting."

"Why didn't they help the Padangkpeian army, then?"

Buabyue looked at the soldier with astonishment. "You can't be serious. The Padangkpeians were a distraction. They drew out your army so the iliyo could attack Ekeya. Even if Padangkpei is defeated, it's still going to win this war."

"Don't exaggerate. I'm sure we can defeat the iliyo. You've had experience with people and creatures from different worlds. What can we do?"

"Refuse to fight."

"Don't be absurd."

"I'm not. The iliyo find war very entertaining, and the more difficult their opponent is to defeat, the more thrilling it is for them. If someone isn't a threat, they won't be interested in him."

Turning to the pilot, Buabyue instructed him, "Inform the city that unless it's absolutely necessary, no one should engage with the iliyo. Retreat and hide. Anyone who wants to survive is going to have to be weak and helpless. Anyone who fights back is going to die. Send the message."

The pilot communicated this information to the city, though Buabyue suspected that his advice would not be followed.

The potbellied smuggler then turned back to Misheya. "Can we get into the City Palace quickly?"

"There's a pneumatic train that runs between the hangar where we'll be landing and the City Palace."

"I'm sure," Buabyue explained, "that Ngo's going to want the councilors targeted. The iliyo will be hunting them. There's no way we're going to defeat the creatures, so, if the councilors are going to survive, we're going to have to get them out of the city."

"I'll get you to their chambers," Misheya promised.

"Jess," Buabyue said to her breasts, "I want you to cover our retreat if we can get the councilors together to get them out of Ekeya. Do you understand?"

She nodded.

The ornithopter flew just outside of the dome covering the city, and Jess and the others peered at the place carefully. There did not seem to be much damage, although they could see evidence of fighting in several places.

"It doesn't look that bad," Jess noted.

The craft dove into a ravine between two craggy hillocks and through a passageway so narrow the tips of its beating wings nearly touched both of the walls. Having arrived at a large underground chamber, the ornithopter landed upon its four outstretched feet.

Jess and the others hurried out of the vessel to a train sitting in a pneumatic tube at the back of the cavern. This conveyed them through a tunnel to another stop, where, at Misheya's bidding, they emerged to be greeted by a troop of soldiers wearing the shaggy garments and legume helmets favored in Ekeya.

One of the men stepped forward and addressed Buabyue.

"The Council requires your presence," he said.

"Are they preparing to escape?" Buabyue asked.

"You will have to ask them what their plans are."

Buabyue nodded and the soldiers led Jess and her companions to an elevator. This took them to a room filled with nervous guards ready for a fight they apparently expected to lose. From there, they made their way down a corridor that led to a second elevator, and this conveyed them to another corridor. Having hurried down this passageway, the group came to a second chamber alive with restless soldiers, at the back of which was a heavy, reinforced door.

The captain of the men leading Jess and the others spoke into a communicator shaped like a small flower set in the wall beside the door, and this, after a few seconds' delay, opened up to let them pass.

Within, the members of Ekeya's ruling council were sitting around a picture vat, upon which various scenes of fighting from around the city were being shown.

The head of the council, who had spoken to Jess and her companions when they had first arrived in the city, was next to this device. Upon seeing the offworlders enter, he raised his head and, with a shaky voice barely loud enough to be heard over the rumble of an explosion coming from somewhere else in the city, addressed his guests.

"Buabyue," he said, "come and sit."

The smuggler sat near the older man, and Jess and Uluf seated themselves close by, though Misheya thought it proper to remain standing in the presence of his superiors.

The councilor addressed Buabyue. "Our soldiers are being defeated everywhere they meet the iliyo. Do you know what we can do?"

"Escape. I have no doubt that the aliens are here for you and the other councilors. If you run, they might give up. It's really your only chance. You're not going to defeat them."

"It's not so easy, Buabyue."

"My lord, we had no difficulty landing and the way from here to the hangar has not yet been blocked."

"You have only just arrived. You haven't seen what's been going on."

"Please tell me, my lord."

"The iliyo are letting any vehicle land, but they've got small craft of their own circling the city. These are shooting down any vessels that attempt to flee."

"Oh, that makes sense," interjected Jess.

Buabyue looked at her and explained. "Actually, my girl, it does make sense for the iliyo. They won't mind if anyone comes into the city. That'll just give them more people to fight. Normally, they wouldn't care if cowards fled – they're no fun, after all – but Ngo must want to make sure the Council doesn't get out. That's surely why they're shooting down any escaping vessels."

"I guess that makes sense," Jess conceded.

"Is there another way out of the city?" Buabyue asked the councilor.

"Yes. There are several. Unfortunately, the iliyo have blocked the paths to every one of them."

"Do you think they did so deliberately?"

"Yes, but I don't think they know exactly where the passages are."

"What do you mean, my lord?"

"When they first attacked the City Palace, they took the lower levels, destroyed most of the elevator shafts, and cut off all the escape passages. We're just fortunate that they hadn't smashed the shaft you used. I'm sure that they realize we have escape routes, and I'm just as sure that they're trying to prevent us from reaching them."

"But you don't think they know exactly where those passages are?"

"No. They've been too indiscriminate in their attacks. If they knew where the routes are, they would have targeted them more specifically."

"Good. If we can fight our way through, we might be able to escape."

"And how do you think we're going to be able to do that?"

Buabyue looked at Jess. "Her. With the help of the soldiers you've got outside, she can do it."

The councilor looked at him incredulously.

"We don't need to defeat the iliyo. We only need to run through a few corridors to an escape route. If you don't do this, you're going to die. I assure you."

Grimacing, the councilor called up a blueprint of the City Palace on the picture vat in front of him

"Here," he said pointing at it. "There's a tunnel with a small pneumatic train that runs from here to the spaceport. The route there is fairly simple. The elevator that would have taken us directly to the train has been destroyed, but, if we take the elevator you used earlier, we can get off on the fifth floor and go along this corridor to these stairs. They'll take us to another corridor, here, in the third basement. It runs along this way, past this intersection with another corridor, to a mechanical room. If we follow it nearly to the end, it'll take us to another set of stairs. These will take us to the train. The problem is that the iliyo have taken everything below the third floor."

"Could they have got to the train itself?"

"No. The door leading to it is concealed."

"My lord, are you certain they couldn't have found it?"

"Yes. The door is alarmed. Had it been opened, it would be indicated on the map we're looking at now."

"Good. That's the way we'll go, then."

"Do you have a plan in mind?"

"Yes. I plan to do this quickly."

"That's it?"

"That's what's going to matter. We've got to get past whatever iliyo we meet before more know we're there."

"Go on."

"Jess and some of your soldiers will lead the way."

"Hold on a second here," Jess exclaimed. "I don't think I agreed to defend everybody. I'm here to accomplish my own goals, not to be some kind of heroine."

"If you're a good girl and help me out, I'll fuck you till your toes curl."

"That's tempting, but I still didn't sign on to protect every person in this city."

"Nonetheless, you're the only one who's going to have a chance against the iliyo."

"Still," Jess replied.

She glared at Buabyue and the councilor for a moment, crossed her arms over her chest, and blew her hair from her eyes. "Well, at least don't make any plans for me. I want in on making some of the decisions."

"As you desire," the councilor told her.

Buabyue then addressed Jess. "Don't worry. We'll send a team of scouts ahead of you so you won't run into any surprises, but you'll still have to fight. The Ekeyan soldiers aren't going to be much help, either."

"That's reassuring."

"It's the best idea I have, Jess."

"Go on," she told him, unable to think of anything better herself.

"Once you've cleared a given corridor," Buabyue said, "the rest of the soldiers will follow, with the councilors in their middle."

He turned to the city's ruler. "What do you think, my lord?"

"We'll do as you suggest."

The man called to his fellow councilors and explained Buabyue's plan to them. They consented and sent one of the soldiers with them outside to inform the troops standing guard what they were going to do.

Once everything was settled, Jess stood up and started to leave the others and join the soldiers who would be acting as scouts.

Uluf grabbed her shoulder. She turned around, and the toad said to her, "Be careful, Jess. This is not really your fight."

"I know, Uluf. I don't plan to get killed yet. This isn't finished, after all, and it won't be until Tolliver's paid for what he did to me."

She squeezed the toad's hand and left him.

Jess and a dozen soldiers went to the elevator and descended to the fifth floor.

Surrounded by men who were fidgeting nervously in anticipation of their deaths, Jess strove to calm her own fears. She was aware of what the iliyo were supposed to be able to do and knew that she could be facing the most formidable enemies she had yet encountered.

Taking a deep breath and wiping away the anxious sweat dripping from her brow, nose, and chin, Jess struggled to draw the thread up from her perineum. She was, however, so fearful that she felt as if little insects were creeping through every cell of her body and gnawing at her every nerve. Though she seized the thread over and over again, it was as slippery as an eel and repeatedly escaped from her.

Eventually, Jess got a grasp on the ancient device and pulled on it fiercely.

The thread, piercing the length of her body and flooding her being with a terrible radiance, suddenly expanded the potency of her will, enabling her to slow the pace of the entire universe.

Jess was ready to fight.

When she and the soldiers had arrived at the fifth floor (which was silent save for the grumbling of distant explosions), five of those men looked around to make sure there were no enemies nearby while the others, and Jess herself, who had drawn Dawn's Spine and one of her daggers, remained just outside the elevator waiting for the next group of persons to join them.

After the elevator had made three trips from the councilors' chamber, the city's dignitaries and their guards were all on the fifth floor.

The scouts went on ahead to the doorway leading to the stairs the group was going to take and checked for any surprises that could be waiting for them on its other side. They indicated everything was clear and the others followed them to the fifth floor landing.

From there, the scouts hurried down the stairs and again checked for enemies. Once they were sure they were alone, they sent for those following behind, who ran down to the door leading to the third basement.

As soon as she had arrived at the bottom of the stairs, Jess opened the door there a crack and peeked into the corridor on the other side. It was a narrow passageway made of plastered stone with pipes running along its vaulted ceiling. Though the place was poorly lit and curved off to the right, the girl decided there was nobody in the vicinity.

Shutting the door, Jess allowed time to return to its normal pace and addressed the six scouts in a whisper.

"You three," she said (indicating who she meant with a nod of her head), "go on straight when we come to the intersection. The rest of you turn to the right and check things out. Make sure there aren't any iliyo around who could attack us from behind. Don't engage with them if you see them. Just come back and let me know they're there. I'm going to go down the corridor to the left and check it out. Got it?"

The scouts showed that that understood, and Jess gently opened the door. She looked back at Uluf with a smile and, as she slowed time again, entered the hallway.

Jess and the six soldiers quietly closed the door behind them and made their way down the curving corridor.

When this group arrived at the intersection with the other hallway, it split up as Jess had decided, and she herself headed down the corridor to the left.

The girl could not see far ahead as the passage bent to the right. Nor could she hear properly since she had reduced time to a creeping pace. Ready to be confronted with an enemy at any moment, she held her sword beside her ear while listening to her heart thundering in her chest and her breath howling like a gale in her nostrils.

Trembling with anxiety, in a way she had not done since her first fights in Hwakash after leaving Takenac's house, she tried to focus herself, to remind herself of her own skills, but she could not banish the sense of dread that suffused her whole body.

Jess saw a light coming from further down the corridor and, pressing herself against the wall to her right, slowly crept forward, knowing that there was something ahead of her.

She peeked around the bend and saw a room filled with large, grey metal pipes that emerged, like the tentacles of an octopus, from a gigantic potbellied boiler. In front of this, a short distance from where the corridor opened onto the room, lay a man wearing a rough blue tunic and loose trousers. Both of his legs had been cleanly amputated, and he had lost much blood as a result, though he was still alive.

Not seeing anyone else around, Jess crossed over to the dying engineer. Weak as he was, he turned his head to gaze up at her through dim eyes and appeared to try to say something.

Pitying the poor creature, whose body was shivering with shock and pain, Jess quickly decapitated him so that he would not suffer any more.

She knew that there must be an iliyo nearby. The man she had found had been mutilated only a few minutes before. She did not, however, see her enemy anywhere in the room.

Since she was able to move more quietly when she had not slowed time, she allowed it to return to its normal pace and slowly walked over to a tangle of pipes that extended from the right side of the boiler and ran across the room to pass through its wall.

Jess peeked between two of these when she reached them and saw a strange being standing, with its back to her, looking through a doorway in the opposite wall. She had never seen an iliyo before, but she was absolutely certain she was looking at one now.

It was not what she had expected. The creature was very small, shorter even than Jess herself was, and looked remarkably fragile, like some graceful ornament rather than a fearsome killer.

At first, all Jess could make out of the iliyo was the back of its thin, tubular, but tapered body, which was covered by a glossy black carapace that appeared to have been lacquered and that was painted with sinuous floral and abstract images. After a few moments, however, the creature turned from the door and began to walk to the right, along the wall, with bobbing, distinctly comical steps like those of a bird.

Its front, Jess now saw, was divided into two rows of roughly square segments of soft white flesh (that made its belly look vaguely like an embroidered quilt). The skin covering the lowest three pairs of these segments was translucent and glowed with some bioluminescent material.

Above these greenish patches was a pair of stick thin legs covered with a black exoskeleton that had two sets of joints, each of which was protected with a mass of yellowish spikes. Its feet were long, soft, pointed, without separated digits, and looked like poulaines, though each had a sharp spur at the heel.

From the top four segments of its body emerged four arms. These were much like the legs, but ended in clawed hands that consisted of a pair of opposed palms without thumbs.

In the midst of these upper limbs, attached to a stem that jutted out from the creature's chest, was a complex, colorful organ composed of a mass of orbs, tendrils, and claws that vaguely resembled a bunch of grapes. This, though Jess did not know it, was the iliyo's reproductive organ.

Its torso was topped with a chasuble-like shell, and out of the center of this projected a thin neck that blossomed into six fleshy and bright red flower petals.

The iliyo's head, which was set amongst these, was like that of a prawn, though it was adorned with a pair of feathery antennae resembling those of a moth. Below and extending past the tip of its long rostrum was a broom-like mass of silvery whiskers, and from out of these dangled a curled up siphon similar to the proboscis of a butterfly.

Though the iliyo was unclothed, tasseled cords were draped around its body, as were ornate pieces of jewelry and numerous bright ribbons.

As strange as the being in front of her was, Jess could not help but think that it was still beautiful.

Such admiration did not, however, prevent her from noticing the sword it held in one of its hands. She looked carefully at this thin grey rapier and realized that it had a monomolecular blade and would be as deadly as was Dawn's Spine.

Slowing time and taking a deep breath to steel herself, Jess dove between the pipes in front of her, pushed herself through the air, and lunged at the iliyo, hoping to slice it in half before it was even aware that it was being attacked.

While Jess's body was still hurtling through the air and she was yet bringing the blade of her sword down upon her victim, the iliyo turned towards her and, with impossible rapidity, moved to one side.

Jess was astonished. She had never seen any living being move so fast without the assistance of a thread.

Ricocheting off the wall and spinning round, she again tried to strike her enemy, but as her sword approached its throat, the alien ducked and avoided it.

No sooner was she standing on the floor in front of the iliyo than it endeavored to strike her with its own sword. Jess was, fortunately, able to parry its attack. She jumped backward and pushed the creature with her blade, trying to knock it off its balance.

Her attempt did push the iliyo away from her, but accomplished nothing else. The alien lunged at the girl, making sounds that, though distorted by the lethargic time in which she had submerged the world, must have sounded like a flute and a shawm playing at once.

Jess, barely avoiding her enemy's sword, leapt to one side, thrust the universe down around her feet, and rose up into the air. Propelling herself with as much force as was possible, she sought to kick the strange organ emerging from the middle of the iliyo's chest.

Although she did not know it, a blow to the iliyo's genitals would have debilitated the creature. Unfortunately for Jess, the iliyo stooped down and her foot only made contact with the top of its torso.

The blow did cause the iliyo to stumble, and Jess, having landed, spun around, seeking to kick it again. This time, her blow struck the center of the alien's body, sending it reeling backwards.

Jess spun again, like a top, trying to kick the iliyo a third time, but instead found herself stopped midway through her intended motion. The iliyo had grabbed ahold of her ankle.

It would have amputated her foot had Jess not parried its blow. That threat countered, she sent herself soaring upwards and, while the iliyo was still holding her, kicked its bewhiskered face.

The alien released her, and she kicked it just below its skinny neck to propel herself backwards.

Landing in a squat, Jess immediately bounced back up and tried to strike her enemy with her sword. The iliyo not only eluded her weapon, but also, when it lunged to one side, reached out with one of its arms and grazed her shoulder with a set of claw-like barbs emerging from its knuckles.

Jess looked down at her bleeding wound and swung at the iliyo as it sought to move behind her. The creature again ducked beneath her blade, although, as it did so, she was able to grab ahold of one of its arms.

The girl pulled her foe towards her while parrying its attempts to decapitate her, but it jumped upwards, spun backwards, and sought to gore her with its spurs.

Drawing her waist back, and so keeping the iliyo from making contact with her body, Jess sliced through two of its arms, which spayed her with thin, pinkish blood. The alien did not, however, jump away, as she had expected it to. It lunged at her again.

Once more, Jess parried the iliyo's blow, but she was so astonished by its tenacity that she did not pay close enough attention to her footing and fell backwards. As she plunged towards the ground, Jess realized that she was about to die and felt an intense sadness sweep over her body.

The iliyo, seeing her momentary helplessness, did not attack. Jess heard it making various musical noises as it moved away from her.

While she did not know what to think of the creature's actions, she resolved not to waste her opportunity to live.

Jess jumped back onto her feet and rushed at the iliyo.

The creature yet again blocked her attacks, but Jess's energy did drive it backward. Her sword pressed against her foe's, the girl jabbed her dagger into its genitals. The alien shook convulsively and staggered away from its attacker.

Jess promptly seized the iliyo's sword arm and, while holding this, chopped off the hand gripping its blade.

In agony, and expecting death, the iliyo swung at Jess with its remaining fist, cutting her left arm below the elbow, but otherwise not harming her.

The girl did not allow this wound to distract her. Instead, she swung her sword in an ostentatiously wide arc and separated the iliyo's head from its neck.

For a few seconds she looked down upon its corpse in admiration. Jess had never before faced an enemy so skilled.

She offered up the iliyo's blood to Haya (while hoping that the goddess would accept the life of such a beast) and bowed to her adversary.

Then, turning away from the alien's body, she hurried back to see what the other scouts had discovered.

# Interlude 14
# The Iliyo

The iliyo control a significant area of space to the northeast of the region inhabited by humanity. In spite of the extent of their domain and their extreme aggressiveness, because the species does not possess a single government and individual political entities are rarely able to cooperate with one another, they do not pose a significant threat to mankind. Their frequent raids are, however, a considerable nuisance.

While most human interactions with the iliyo are hostile, men have visited their worlds and traded with them. A fair amount of information has so been gathered both about their biology and their cultures.

Physically, iliyo lack human beings' muscular strength, but they are generally acknowledged to be the better fighters. Not only are they far more agile than are humans, but their senses are also considerably more acute.

The iliyo, strictly speaking, have only one sex, as they produce but a single type of reproductive cell, two of which are required to produce an offspring. Nonetheless, they have six different types of reproductive organs, and these are not all mutually compatible physically.

After a successful mating, one or both of the iliyo involved will produce thousands of eggs. These eventually hatch as non-sentient larvae, which, rather than being cared for, are left to fend for themselves in the wilderness. In fact, adult iliyo frequently hunt their larvae for sport or food.

After a period of time, the larvae become chrysalides and metamorphose into adults. During this period, they are retrieved and carefully tended by adults of their species, although these are not necessarily related individuals.

The environmental conditions under which a chrysalis matures will determine its nature as an adult. The moister it is kept, the more emotional, and the more aggressive, the adult will be. The warmer it is kept, the more intelligent. Certain special individuals, often called either poets or berserkers, can be produced by submerging a chrysalis in heated water. The resulting adults are emotionally unstable and uncontrollably aggressive, but they are also highly intelligent, sensitive, and creative.

Different combinations of heat and moisture produce the "castes" of iliyo society. These, it should be noted, are divisions of individuals according to intellectual ability and emotional sensitivity; they are not hierarchical.

Members of a given caste can be identified by the color of the "petals" around an individual's neck, which color is determined by the heat and moisture a chrysalis was exposed to. Moderate temperatures produce no color; higher temperatures produce blues and lower temperatures yellows. Greater amounts of moisture tend to produce reds and lesser amounts whites. Iliyo castes and petal colors are as follows:

**Poets**: Magenta.

**Intellectuals** (from more to less emotional): Purple, lavender, and blue.

**Craftsmen** (from more to less emotional): crimson, pink, and white.

**Laborers** (from more to less emotional): orange and yellow (there is no highly aggressive type of laborer).

There is also a leader caste produced by coating a warm, moist chrysalis with a particular gum. Adults of this caste, who have green petals, produce pheromones that incline others to follow their commands.

All iliyo, irrespective of caste, have little ability to restrain their emotions. Interpersonal conflicts, as a result, almost invariably lead to violent confrontations.

To minimize such bouts and allow for social interactions, the iliyo place an enormous emphasis on etiquette. The behaviors of individuals are thus largely guided by intricate rules of conduct, although these are specific to each of their numerous different cultures.

The creatures' proclivity towards violence is also curtailed by their symbiotic relationships with certain types of trees.

After emerging from its cocoon, an adult will, for some time, feed exclusively on the sap of a tree. Although, initially, an iliyo can consume the sap of any type of tree, it will eventually restrict itself to a single tree. Once it has fed on that tree long enough, it will no longer be able to digest the sap of any other kind of tree.

At the same time, the iliyo will become physically and psychologically dependent upon the smell of and environment provided by such a tree. Later, it will make its home among the roots of the same species of tree and will not be able to survive for long without its sap and aroma.

Because of their need for such habitations, iliyo cities are composed of forests of trees used as dwellings set among gardens and surrounded by enough wilderness to provide the colony with animals to hunt.

Population densities are thus kept low and opportunities for interpersonal conflict are reduced.

In fact, members of the species are extremely individualistic and prefer not to interact with one another.

A given iliyo, of whatever caste, will usually perform its functions apart from others, cultivate its own food, and live alone. They do not take long term mates. Sexual relations are completely casual.

In spite of such unsociableness, once a chrysalis has matured, the young adult is placed in the care of an adult of its own caste and raised as a member of a colony. In a number of iliyo cultures, an adult is permitted to leave the colony that adopted it, but, in others, it is expected to remain a member of that colony throughout its life.

Such colonies, sometimes called clans, are the basic unit of iliyo society and are composed of anywhere from a handful of individuals to as many as twenty or thirty thousand. The governments of different colonies are extremely varied, but all are centered around a structure called a lodge, which is also generally the focus of iliyo religious life.

There are two primary types of larger political institutions.

From time to time, members of a colony will break away and form a new colony. In some iliyo cultures, this new group will retain a relationship with the original colony, whether as equals or as feudal vassal and superior, respectively. In the latter case, as colonies fragment, complex hierarchies of colonies can develop.

The other primary type of large organization is the alliance, which is usually an association of independent colonies that have agreed to engage in certain cooperative activities.

In either of these cases, the highest authority remains a lodge. In feudal cultures, subsidiary colonies are generally understood as possessing branch lodges. The new colony's real lodge is that of the original colony. Among alliances, high-lodges are established in which representatives of member colonies can meet. Such a high-lodge may or may not have religious functions.

These large institutions rarely govern their members and, for the most part, exist only to provide them with the ability to mount raids on other such groups or on other species.

Although the iliyo are not acquisitive (in fact, even the leaders of colonies live among the roots of trees without wealth, servants, or many possessions), they are such slaves to their emotions that they can think of nothing but their own pleasure. Unfortunately for other species, while they devote much of their existence to artistic pursuits, they are also enamored of the thrill of battle and regularly send raiders far from their own worlds to attack those of their neighbors.

They do so acquire technological items and novelties for their amusement, but their primary reason for engaging in piracy is simply that they find fighting pleasurable.

From Pollidor's *Big Blue Book of Knowledge*

# Chapter 36
# Running the Gauntlet

Jess met the Ekeyan scouts at the intersection and asked them what they had found. Neither of their parties had discovered any enemies, so the girl ran with impossible speed back to the stairwell where she had left the councilors, their soldiers, Buabyue, and Uluf.

Allowing time to return to its ordinary pace, she beckoned to these persons to follow her, and they hurried through the corridor, past the intersection, and down the hallway beyond it.

The group stopped near a door at the end of the corridor that led into a dark room from which came the low, rhythmic rumbling of machinery, and the soldiers' commander moved to the smoothly plastered wall to his right and tapped out a complex code.

The wall slid open and revealed a landing from which descended a spiraling flight of stairs.

Jess turned to the head of the council and said, "Go ahead. I'll stay up here with the scouts. We'll make sure no one comes up behind you."

The councilor nodded and, having sent several of his soldiers ahead of him, started down the stairs himself. The others followed after him, except for Uluf, who moved to the side to stand beside Jess.

"You have been injured, my dear," the toad observed.

"Yeah. Sorry about that, Uluf. I guess I'm not completely indestructible after all. I am alive, though."

While more of the councilors and soldiers went past them, Uluf asked, "Was it an iliyo that did this?"

"Yeah. It was incredible. I've never fought anyone like that. It could move on its own nearly as fast as I can when I use the thread."

Before the toad could reply, he and Jess heard cries coming from the stairway leading to the train. Moving her friend to one side, Jess jumped onto the landing and looked down.

A group of iliyo with magenta petals round their necks and human soldiers wearing colorful armor and plumed helmets had jumped out of the carriage resting in the pneumatic tube that ran through the chamber beneath her. The former were cutting down the men at the bottom of the stairs, leaping upon their corpses, and attacking those behind them, while the latter were firing needle guns at those persons higher up the flight.

Jess leapt back into the hall, barely avoiding a needle shot at her, and exclaimed, "I guess they did know about this route. We're not going this way."

Several Ekeyan soldiers rushed past Jess, but she grabbed ahold of the first of the councilors to come through the door and pulled him to her.

"Is there another escape route? One that's not in this building?"

"Yes," replied the young man as he pushed his ornate headgear, adorned with the image of a pig, off of his face.

"Where?"

"It's in my family's palace," he said as two more councilors and about a score of soldiers ran past him.

"Can we get there from here?"

While Buabyue and a few more soldiers, including the captain, escaped their attackers, the man responded. "If we go back up the way we came, we can cross a bridge to it."

Pushing the terrified councilor away from her, to encourage him to run, Jess yelled, "Lead on!"

She peeked around the edge of the door, but the soldiers' captain, who was standing on its other side with one of his men, gestured for her to move back.

He said to his subordinate, "The councilors are dead. Kill their murderers."

The man took from his belt a wand attached to a hose that led to a small tank hanging at his hip. He aimed this at the iliyo running up the stairs and pushed a button on the device. From a nozzle at its tip spewed a burning jelly that covered the iliyo and the mercenaries behind them. Their bodies were instantly wrapped in flames, as was the entire room they were in.

The men below, finding their armor to be insufficient protection, howled in agony. The iliyo, however, remained silent as their flesh was consumed and their carapaces audibly cracked. Realizing that they were going to die, they lifted up their swords and decapitated themselves.

The captain tapped the wall in a particular place and the door shut.

"Come on," Jess said to him. "We've got to get out of here."

Taking Uluf by the hand, she ran down the corridor to the flight of stairs, following the surviving councilors and their guards and followed by the captain and his subordinate with the flame thrower.

The survivors hurried back up the way they had come and took the same elevator upwards that they had earlier used to descend, though this time there were few enough of them to require but a single trip.

The young councilor who had told Jess he knew of another escape route said to her as the elevator came to a stop, "We need to get off here. There's a bridge on this level that'll take us to my palace."

"Lead us there," she replied.

\* \* \*

Hyan was reclining upon a pile of cushions heaped up in a stone pavilion in the middle of a garden enclosed by a glass dome set in a bronze frame. This place, which was perched upon a balcony projecting from a tower about midway between Ekeya's center and its edge, afforded her a view of much of the battle being fought in the streets below.

Her allies had taken the lower parts of the City Palace, but a number of the giant, flea shaped brass robots guarding the structure's main entrance were still functioning and tearing apart a group of mercenaries who had allowed the machines to get close to them. Other soldiers were, however, on their way, and these, firing explosive projectiles at the robots, blew them up, sending smoking, twisted, and melted bits of casing and mechanical parts scattering across the plaza.

Elsewhere, Ekeyan air infantrymen darted about upon iridescent wings, plunging from towers to attack bands of Hyan's soldiers. Some of the winged men, the young woman noticed, were skilled fighters, but there simply were not enough of them to defeat their enemies.

Whatever advantages the locals might have won in one fight were invariably undone by their defeats elsewhere. Hyan had little doubt that she would shortly have control over the city.

She took a draught from the long stemmed pipe she held, smiled, and looked over at the iliyo( standing nearby beneath a blossom laden tree just outside of the pavilion.

While playing upon a complex musical instrument (something like a bagpipe combined with a harmonium), the small, delicate creature was enjoying the fragrance and intoxicating effects of the curling wisps of smoke that rose from a sort of censer it was holding in one of its hands and that drifted up amongst its silvery whiskers and over the sky blue petals ringing its head.

"Why is it," Hyan asked the alien while blowing out a cloud of smoke, "that your kind have such difficulty following orders?"

The iliyo looked at her, though without putting down its censer or ceasing its playing upon the instrument it held.

The translator hanging from one of the cords looped around its body transformed the musical notes of its own speech into Panjuan. "It is easier for humans to obey than it is for us since your species does not possess emotions."

Hyan raised her eyebrows. "We certainly do have emotions."

"That is incorrect. It is a scientifically established fact that humans lack emotions."

"And how is that?"

"We have studied your species extensively and found no evidence that you have emotions. You do have words for what seem to be emotions, but these, in fact, merely describe certain physiological reactions, not emotions properly speaking. For us, emotions have both physical and mental effects. For you, they are not like that."

"I beg to differ."

Hyan blew a great cloud of smoke at her ally and savored the surge of excitement it had sent coursing through her body.

"I believe you are simply confused. If you really had emotions, you would act upon them, and yet, even though you say that you feel joy or fear, you do not show evidence of feeling such things."

Hyan smirked. "We can control ourselves."

"That is absurd."

"No. I hardly think so."

---

* Hyan's liaison with the aliens' leaders.

"I suppose you believe that you can also stop your heart or even activity within your cells."

"That's a little bit different," the young woman noted before sending several smoke rings towards the ceiling of the pavilion.

"No. It is not."

"Well then, what about your species? I admit that the group that I sent to get the councilors couldn't control themselves, but you obviously can. That pretty much shows some of you aren't slaves to your feelings, even though some of you are."

"Those were poets you sent. Their emotions are particularly intense. They feel things far more poignantly than I do. I cannot control my emotions better than they can. I simply do not have the emotional depth they do."

Mulling over the iliyo's comment, Hyan realized she had made a mistake when she had chosen who she was going to dispatch to capture the councilors. When she had asked the iliyo's leader who his best warriors were and he had told her his poets, she had told him to send them. Although she had known that her allies could be unstable, it had never occurred to her that some of them were insane.

"I wish one of you had mentioned that your best fighters wouldn't have any self-control. Now the whole operation could wind up as a disaster."

"I fail to see the connection, but I agree that it would have been better if we had been able to fight with the city's army."

"What are you talking about? I mean your lot didn't get the councilors for us. We needed them to get information about the Llalloi organization."

"I understand. I thought you meant that you had not enjoyed yourself."

It would perhaps, Hyan thought, be best not to mention every one of her decisions to Tsoi. The perspectives of the iliyo were more alien and their goals less compatible with her own than she had anticipated. While her failure to foresee such differences was entirely understandable, Tsoi might not see that.

Brushing her hair from her face, Hyan, with a slightly chagrined tone, said, "I certainly get the whole idea of enjoying life – believe me, I do – but is there anything more for you than propriety and pleasure?"

"Yes, but those principles guide us, just as grasping guides human beings."

"What? We're much more rounded than you are."

"No. You are the ones who are limited."

"Oh? How so?"

"You are completely dominated by your need to grasp things. It is the most important trait of your species and is central to your being."

"I think we're a little more complicated than that."

"I have watched humans myself. You are obsessed with seizing things and holding onto them. Everything else, even pleasure, is subordinated to that. Your whole culture is based on grasping, from your governments to your economies to your interpersonal relationships. Look at your object here. Is it not to seize something and then to hold onto it?"

Before Hyan could answer, the door leading from the garden into the tower opened and Huazheen, dressed in a long blue frock coat cut in the style preferred in Quanya and printed with images of white clouds, flying birds, and, along its hem, gnarled trees and fanciful hills, stepped out together with a pair of iliyo, one with green petals and the other with pink.

He instructed the aliens to wait beside the entrance, his translator converting his words into the sounds of flutes, shawms, and bagpipes that were used as speech by that species, and left them behind.

Huazheen made his way down a trail of stepping stones, moving past Chongmuri, who was squatting on a boulder, sat upon the railing of the pavilion, and looked at his sister. Though she had removed her mask and wore her own face again, she was still dressed in the sarong and breast band favored in Ekeya.

The young woman, turning away from the liaison, took a deep draught from her pipe and felt the smoke pervade her body, infusing it with a ferocious but dizzying energy. Smiling at this sensation, Hyan cast her eyes upon her brother and said, "The pink haired girl is here."

"She's finally turned up?"

"Yes. A team of the mercenaries are fighting with her and the councilors on a bridge leading out of the City Palace."

Hyan stood up, leaned across the railing of the pavilion, and gazed at the palace.

"That one there," she said pointing.

Huazheen looked where his sister was indicating and saw a wide, semicircular balcony from which extended a long, narrow bridge.

"I see them."

"Are you going to fight her?"

"Yes. She's going to die today."

Hyan smiled, patted her brother's cheek, and said to him, "Do be careful, Huazheen. She's deadly, after all."

"I will."

"Oh, and one more thing."

"Yes?"

"There are three councilors with her. Make sure they're captured, not killed."

"I will."

"Please do."

She looked back at her liaison, who was playing upon his instrument, and scowled. "I just received word that there's been a fight in one of their little escape tunnels. It sounds like most of the councilors were killed by those stupid iliyo."

"Didn't you tell them not to kill the councilors?"

"Of course I did, but apparently they forgot."

"I thought they were supposed to be obsessive about keeping their word."

"They are, so far as I can tell. Unfortunately, they also seem to go a little mad when they're fighting. I don't think they have any self-control, especially when they're unduly excited."

"I understand. I'll use the mercenaries against the Ekeyans. At least they can follow orders."

"That sounds fine. I'm sure you'll capture as many of the councilors as are still alive. Return to the iliyo's ether-ship with them when you've got them. I'm going there now."

Hyan embraced her brother and went to lean against one of the carved pillars at the pavilion's entrance.

"Remember, Huazheen, I'm depending on you. If we don't bring back at least one of the councilors, Tsoi is going to be very irate with us."

"I'll do my best, Hyan."

"I know you will. Now take care."

Huazheen walked over to his sister, bent over, and kissed her black stained lips. Then, turning with a smile, he rejoined his two iliyo guards and with them left the garden. The three made their way to a hangar where they boarded an antigravity sled that took them to the bridge leading to the balcony where his enemy was.

* * *

Jess and those with her, all of whom were hiding behind the pillars of an arcade that opened onto a balcony projecting from the side of the City Palace, saw Huazheen's craft land on the bridge.

When they observed that the top of the sled was covered by a protective bubble and that the man and two iliyo within it were not getting out to join in the fight, they turned their attention from these individuals back to the troop of mercenaries huddled behind a large fountain in the middle of the balcony.

Jess kept her eye upon the small red flags (decorated each with an image of some kind of animal vaguely like a winged fish with a human head) that were attached to poles rising from the mercenaries' shoulders and that fluttered above the rim of the fountain's basin.

When she noticed a pair of these rise, the girl focused upon them and then watched as one of her enemies exposed himself in order to aim his needle rifle. Like his fellows, the man was wearing a plumed bascinet, red armor covered with elaborate decorations, and long, pointed sabatons.

Jess, ignoring his finery, fired the rifle she was holding, striking her enemy in the throat and killing him immediately.

While the mercenary collapsed onto the ground, the girl noted that the man sitting in the sled was speaking into a communicator. She could not hear what he was saying, but she was sure he was creating more trouble for her.

The man and the two iliyo got out of the sled. Each of the aliens was holding a sword in one of its four hands and a metallic globe in another. Around each of these orbs was an oval hoop that seemed to hang in the air and was nearly as tall as was the iliyo and slightly wider. At first, Jess did not know what the objects were, but, when several of the Ekeyan soldiers fired upon the iliyo, she saw that the creatures moved the globes and that the needles stopped when they reached the plane extending between each of these and the hoop around it. The devices, she realized, must generate some sort of force field.

The man in the blue frock coat, who was standing safely behind the two aliens, was holding a translator attached to the end of a wand. When he spoke into this, it amplified his voice so that he could be clearly heard even by those at the far end of the balcony.

He said, "Jess Ichikawa, I wish to speak with you."

Although she was surprised to be so addressed, the girl yelled in reply, "What do you want?"

"I want to kill you, Jess Ichikawa."

"Well, come over here and see if you can."

"Don't be silly. Let's fight out here in the open so everyone can watch."

"No thanks. You can come and get me if you'd like."

"Oh, come now. Don't skulk about back there. You ought to come out and fight me properly."

"No, I don't think so."

"Why not? It'll be so much fun."

"I don't plan to get shot by your men."

Huazheen laughed. "My love, I swear they're not going to shoot you."

"Sorry if I don't have complete confidence in you. I think I'll just wait over here. If you really want to, you can come and fight me."

"Okay, I've got a bargain for you."

"What's that?"

"Let's come to an agreement. If you can defeat me in a fight, you and your companions may leave the city. If you lose, I'll just kill you all."

"You think I'm going to agree to that?"

"Why not? You're going to die anyway. You can't kill all of us. I've just sent for more soldiers. They'll be coming up behind you in a few moments. Can you kill a hundred men?"

"Maybe. I wouldn't say it's impossible."

"My, you do take some convincing, don't you? Well, in that case, I'll just have to try to persuade you to do what I want."

"Go ahead."

"I'll make the choice simple for you. How about that? You can come out and fight me or you can watch me butcher everyone with you. Then, when I'm done, I'll kill you too."

"Oh, now that sounds likely."

Huazheen struck a balletic pose, with one hand on his hip and the other before his face, his fingers extended and his palm upwards as though he were holding some invisible object.

Gazing in Jess's general direction, the young man transformed the pillars behind which the Ekeyan soldiers were hiding into extensions of himself. Their externality so burned away, they became mere phantasms he had conjured up and were made wholly subject to his will.

Suddenly, when Huazheen commanded their molecules to tear themselves apart, several of the pillars shattered with a tremendous crack, scattering fragments of stone across the balcony and injuring a number of the Ekeyans and a few of the mercenaries as well.

Jess looked at the young man in shock. He had to have a thread. There was no other way he could have done something like that.

Two of the soldiers, made brave by their desperate fear, leapt up from the ground and pointed their weapons at Huazheen. He, however, standing with his arms akimbo, tore off their heads with his mind. The pair fell to the ground dead.

Behind them, two more men tried to scurry for cover, but Huazheen saw them. He twisted one man's neck so that his head faced backwards, and the second he tripped by shattering his thighs. The wounded soldier looked up in horror and tried to drag himself towards the stump of a column with his hands, but the youth at the other side of the balcony pulled off his arms.

Another man, having snuck a short distance behind a fallen column, emerged to run at Huazheen while shooting at him with his needle gun.

The youth smiled and with a thought caused his attacker's eyes to explode.

As this person crumbled, howling madly and clawing at the blood and jelly oozing down his cheeks, Jess felt the organs inside her torso melt away into a nauseating void. She stared at the young man with her mouth hanging open. Her body was heavy and limp. She even wet herself a little.

In all the time since Takenac had given her the thread, she had never fought another person with such a device. She had never had the chance to do so. Now she was going to have to fight someone who not only had a thread but was far more accomplished at using it than she was. There was no way she could do even a fraction of the things the young man before her was capable of.

Huazheen was amused by Jess's surprise and smiled widely at her.

"Will you reconsider my offer? It still stands. I really do want to fight with you."

"Okay," Jess said, thinking she was about to die. "Tell your soldiers to put down their weapons and to honor our agreement when I kill you."

Huazheen did so and Jess stood up and walked towards him.

As she moved past the fountain, she set her needle gun on its rim and took Dawn's Spine in her hand, extending its telescopic blade.

The man in front of her pushed past the two iliyo and stood where the bridge met the balcony.

The sun, made lime green by Suturik's strange atmosphere, was hanging low in the sky, to Huazheen's left, and its rays gave his face an emerald glow.

From his belt hung a covered handle, and from this extended a band of flexible steel held in curled loops by a tasseled cord. He removed the string, lashed the weapon about, and let the band, which was actually a whip-like blade with razor sharp edges, extend to a length of about five feet.

Jess gazed at the man's young, handsome face as he smiled benignantly upon her. She saw no trace of animosity in his expression. He did not appear to look at her as an enemy at all. He actually seemed to be enjoying himself immensely.

As nervous as Jess already was, there was something about her enemy's manner that unnerved her even more. She felt her heart beating within her breast with such ferocity that it seemed to make her whole body reverberate. Her hands were actually trembling a little as she approached her foe.

For the briefest of moments, Jess almost panicked when this anxiety prevented her from stirring the thread from where it rested at her perineum. Happily, she was able to gather her wits and lift it up her spine to her brow. Drawing the world around her into her mind, once the thread had exploded through her body, Jess slowed time as much as she could and readied herself for what, she expected, was going to be a genuinely dangerous fight.

When she was close to her enemy, Jess shouted wildly and thrust the world towards her back, hurtling herself through the remaining space between them as fast as a needle could fly. Her sword beside her ear, she prepared herself to slice the man in front of her in half, but, just before she came to him, he ducked to one side and avoided her.

Flipping head over heals in order to land on her feet on the bridge behind Huazheen, Jess spun around and looked at the man with an expression of nervous anger.

Huazheen sighed, thinking his opponent was not going to be as entertaining as he had hoped she would be.

Then, raising his eyebrows and brushing his hair from his face, he swung his sword around his head and body as one would a whip and dove at Jess.

The long blade flew towards the girl, and she was only able to avoid it by diving to one side and rolling across the bridge.

She jumped up beside the railing, spun around, and found herself looking at the serpentine sword racing at her through the air a second time.

Once more, Jess dropped to the ground, though now, when she rolled, she did so in Huazheen's direction. He was smiling widely again.

As she came near his feet, she swung Dawn's Spine and attempted to chop through his ankles, but he leapt straight up and escaped her attack.

While hopping onto her feet, Jess grabbed ahold of the atmosphere around her and shoved it at her attacker, knocking him backwards while he was still hanging above the surface of the bridge.

He was cast against the railing and would have gone over had he not lashed out his sword and wrapped its blade around that of Dawn's Spine. Using Jess herself as leverage, he pulled himself forward.

Jess, unbalanced by the man's weight, staggered towards Huazheen, but, once she had regained her footing, she used him as he had used her. Drawing herself towards him, she jumped from the pavement and kicked Huazheen in the chest with both her feet, sending him crashing onto his rump.

The young man, leaping back up almost at once, pushed the world away from him and flew backwards along the bridge to land on the balcony. There, shaking his head to recover his wits, he yelled at Jess in words so fast that only she could understand them. "You are good, my love. You're probably the best I've ever met. Even the iliyo aren't that fast."

"Why don't you just give up, then?" Jess shouted back.

"Don't be stupid. This is great fun. Besides, you may be good, but I'm better."

Huazheen rose up into the air and, extending his arm, let his blade fly out at Jess. It barely missed her as she jumped forward and over it. Spinning her feet upwards over her head from behind and whirling them round, Jess slammed her heels into her enemy's throat. At the same time, she brought her sword down upon him, though he, injured as he was, was still able to dodge the blade.

Jess bounced off of her opponent's chest, pounding upon his breastbone with the soles of her feet, and landed in front of him as he staggered backwards gasping for breath.

Anger shot up through Huazheen's body and he lashed at Jess with his sword, looping the blade around her body. She, however, dove into the air, arching her back over the circle the sword had formed, and landed on her left hand, which she used to push herself back up so that she came to rest crouched upon the pavement.

Huazheen drew his sword back to him, whirled it around his head and prepared to strike at Jess again. Before he could do so, the girl reached into her pouch, pulled out a dagger, extruded its telescoping blade, and threw it at him.

The man leaned to one side and escaped being struck, but, in the time it took him to do so, Jess was able to get close to him.

She swung her sword at his belly. He bent his body and remained alive. She swung at his chest. He leaned backwards and was not hurt. She swung a third time, at his crotch. He jumped nearly twenty feet behind where he had stood.

Jess ran at him, twisting her body to prevent his sinuous blade from touching her, but when she was near him and preparing to strike him with her own sword, Huazheen spun round and kicked her hand. Dawn's Spine nearly flew from Jess's grip.

Fumbling to keep a hold on her weapon, Jess leaned too far to one side and almost fell over. Huazheen kicked her in the stomach with one foot and, immediately after that, in the crotch with the other.

Jess collapsed onto her hip and had to roll back and forth across the pavement to avoid the lashings of Huazheen's sword.

As she listened to the man laugh while he so teased her, Jess raised Dawn's Spine and used it to catch her enemy's blade. Huazheen's weapon wrapped around the girl's sword the next time he tried to strike her. She pulled the blade downwards, causing her enemy to lose his balance, and then regained her own footing.

Smiling broadly at Jess, Huazheen said, "This really is the most fun I've had in some time. You are a delight."

"And you're a nuisance. Just die already."

Jess was not really enjoying their contest. She was actually more than a little worried that it was going to be her last.

Huazheen hopped onto the railing of the bridge and casually walked along it while whipping his blade about in intricate patterns.

"Come now," he said. "That's not how it's going to happen. We both know that I'm going to kill you. Perhaps I shouldn't say that, though. I don't want to discourage you."

Jess glared at him while he smiled at her, but she waited for him to make the next move. He did not. Instead, Huazheen staggered to the side and nearly lost his footing on the railing.

At first, neither he nor Jess was sure what had happened. It was only when Huazheen looked down at his body and wiped blood from the side of his belly that either of them realized that one of the Ekeyan soldiers had shot him with a needle.

No one else yet knew what had happened, and Huazheen was so surprised he merely stood looking at his own injury. Jess decided to take advantage of the opportunity given her. She dove at him, swung her sword, and chopped off both the man's legs at the knee.

Her blade was so sharp that for a moment Huazheen remained standing where he was. Then blood squirted out of his wounds and his thighs slipped from his calves. He desperately swung his blade hoping to kill the enemy who had killed him, but he attacked so clumsily Jess easily eluded his blows.

Huazheen fell backwards, off of his legs, and towards the earth far below, his feet soon following after him.

Jess turned around to look at the balcony where the others were and saw the two iliyo, their rapiers in their hands, capering over to her while making what must have been a lovely music with their complex vocal organs.

Jess, having allowed time to return to its normal pace, said to the iliyo, "There's no reason for this. I had an agreement with your boss."

When both of the creatures were standing in front of the girl, the one with green petals around its neck performed a number of intricate gestures with its four arms while producing a sequence of musical notes. The translator hanging from a cord at what would have been its shoulder (had it had shoulders), converted these into a human tongue, which Jess's own translator converted into Twituboch.

The iliyo informed her, "You are deliciously skilled. I ask you to fight with me."

"What?"

"Will you fight with me? There are few opportunities in life to face an opponent as dangerous as you are."

"I had an agreement with your boss. He told you to let me go without a fight."

"If you do not believe I would be a worthy opponent, I will not detain you. My lodge consented to follow Huazheen, and he has instructed us to let you go. I have no desire to behave improperly. If you wish to leave, I will curl up in sorrow, but I will not humiliate myself with dishonesty."

"Then let me and everybody with me pass," Jess replied.

"I am saddened that I will not be able to fight you. Your sort are usually so clumsy and easy to kill, but you are a marvel. When I return to our vessel, I will sing of you."

The tiny, fragile creatures hopped away to stand beside the red suited mercenaries. From there they watched as the councilors, soldiers, Uluf, and Buabyue cautiously emerged from behind the pillars where they were hiding and hurried over to join Jess.

Looking at the young councilor she had spoken to before, Jess said, "Lead the way. We need to get out of here before someone else decides to stop us."

# Chapter 37
## From the Sky, through the Fire, and into the Earth

Hyan was sitting upon what looked to be a twisting root that emerged from the living wood out of which the whole of her cabin was formed. With its uneven surfaces, dark recesses, and strong but pleasant aromas, the room was like the hollow of a tree.

Huazheen had earlier mentioned to her that he found the narrow passages, the unnecessary bulges and nooks, and the countless shadows of the iliyo ship to be both oppressive and strange, but Hyan liked the vessel. There was something magical about the little chamber the aliens had given her that made her feel like she had left her everyday life behind and entered into some liminal reality human beings ordinarily only visit in their dreams or their imagination. In fact, the whole craft was a joy.

In the way that men shaped bonsai trees, the iliyo had sculpted a genetically modified tree (which generally lay no more than an inch thick upon the metal of the hull) into an endless variety of captivating shapes. They so created a warren of small, winding spaces where they could rest upon gnarled, deformed, yet graceful and sinuous roots and be sheltered by an uneven ceiling composed of thick and thin branches woven together or allowed to wind their way whithersoever they would.

"It's very odd," Hyan said to Chongmuri, who was standing near the doorway, "and very beautiful."

"The iliyo vessels are certainly different from those of men, Chun," the changeling replied, speaking loud enough to make himself heard over the sounds of the hurdy-gurdy-like instrument Hyan's iliyo liaison was playing as it squatted upon a curving root across the room from the woman.

"You needn't call me that anymore, you stupid animal," she snapped at the demi-ape.

"As you wish, my lady," the corpse replied as its mistress turned from it to gaze for a while longer at the room she was in.

"So," she said to the iliyo, "why do you go to all this trouble with your ether-ships?"

Without ceasing his musical performance, the alien asked her, "What do you mean?"

"Why all the wood?"

"We require its scent and sap. We cannot travel without our trees."

"I suppose the design is purely for the sake of beauty."

"Yes. We would not be able to enjoy our raids if we could not travel in decent accommodations."

"You know, I do sometimes think your people are all insane, but there are things about the way you look at life that are appealing. Maybe you could be a little more practical, but you do at least enjoy your existence. I've certainly met few humans who are as devoted to relishing life's experiences."

"As I previously informed you, my species has emotions, which yours does not. We cannot simply function as automatons like you can. We need music, poetry, fine food, beautiful quarters, and the like to survive."

"You can be quite exasperating. I previously informed you that we do have emotions, and I am getting a little annoyed about being told that I don't."

"That very statement proves that you do not."

"Oh?"

"If you were truly angered, you would not sit there speaking to me. You would attack. Since you do not, I must infer that what you describe as anger is merely a physiological reaction, not something present in your consciousness."

"Okay then, what are you feeling right now?"

"Sadness that I was not able to participate in the fighting."

"And how is it that you can feel that without acting upon it?"

"I am acting upon my feelings. I am playing a musical piece to give life to my sorrows."

Hyan laughed. "Well, you certainly do know how to appreciate every feeling."

"What other reason is there for living? We are not like you. We cannot endure merely by eating and reproducing. Life is not all practicality for us. Animals are concerned with practicalities. We are concerned with the useless, with the relishing of existence. You would understand if you had emotions."

"Never mind," Hyan said to the creature and turned her attention back to her environment.

After so admiring her surroundings for some time, the young woman, inhaling the intoxicating smoke produced by the herb burning in the bowl of her pipe, leaned against the rough bark of the wall and gazed out the little window next to her head, letting her thoughts pass from the room she was in to the city outside.

She wanted to enjoy the last few moments of Ekeya's existence. As soon as Huazheen returned with the city's councilors, she would be leaving and destroying the place.

Still, there was nothing she could do about that. The Llalloi had to be broken.

As she so reflected, Hyan heard a knock on the door to her cabin, or rather on the wood forming the room's small round entranceway.

Turning round, she saw one of the mercenaries, his bascinet under his arm.

"Is Huazheen back?"

The man swallowed audibly. "My lady, I am sorry to inform you of this, but your brother has been killed."

Hyan looked at him without expression for some time, until the man, growing uncomfortable, continued.

"He was defeated by the pink haired girl he went to fight."

Looking away from the man, Hyan felt a sickness rising up within her. She tried to reply, but her mouth only fell open and hung limply. Whatever words she attempted to form merely came out as jumbles of incomprehensible sounds.

The man was still staring at her, but Hyan was unable to control herself. Tears began pouring from her eyes, vomit surged up into her mouth, and her body convulsed with sobs.

At first, the soldier started to move forward to console her, but then, thinking it would probably be wiser if he did not, turned away and tried not to look at the young woman as she cried.

Hyan looked up, her face red and twisted with grief. With more tears seeping from her eyes, she addressed the mercenary, though she frequently choked and her breath was often cut off by the heaving of her chest. "Send a troop of iliyo after her. I want them to kill that little whore. She's not going to live, not after what she did to Huazheen."

The man turned back to face her and protested, "My lady, the iliyo are not reliable. They could kill the Llalloi as well. Your cousin will be upset if one of them is not brought to him."

Hyan screamed in a voice so tremulous it was difficult to understand. "I don't care! Bring me that girl's head or I'll have yours! It's one or the other. You choose."

"Yes, my lady," the man replied and turned to leave the room in a hurry.

Looking at Chongmuri, Hyan screamed, "Go with him and make sure he does as I wish!"

"Yes, my lady."

Perhaps, the iliyo observing all this reflected, some humans did have emotions.

* * *

The young councilor who had been directing Jess said to her as he, she, and the others with them entered a large chamber, "There's a corridor at the far end of this room. That'll take us to the room where my family's private elevator is. We can use that to get to our escape tunnel."

"Okay," Jess replied as she waved to the others to follow her into the great hall.

When they had crossed about half of its length, a door at the far end opened and a group of ten iliyo hopped into the chamber to stand between them and the way out.

The Ekeyan soldiers raised their needle rifles and began firing, but their projectiles, like fingers pushed into a rubber balloon, were slowed and stopped by the iliyo's shields.

While the aliens spread out and began running at them, the captain instructed the two of his men with flame throwers to use their weapons.

The soldiers let loose a torrent of gelatinous fire upon the iliyo, incinerating half their number and transforming most of the room into an inferno.

Fiery tongues raced across the floor and up the walls, meeting upon the ceiling, where currents of flame swirled and undulated wildly. Jess and the others instinctively crouched low and covered their faces, but the iliyo did not pause.

As Jess took her fishbowl helmet from Uluf, who had been holding it for her, and fastened it over her head so that she could breathe amidst the conflagration, the first of the five remaining aliens jumped upon one of the soldiers holding a flame thrower, grasping the man's hair with one hand, his shoulder with another, and planting its feet upon the man's chest.

The soldier looked at the iliyo with his mouth hanging open as the creature swung its sword and separated his head from his body.

Hopping back onto the floor and tossing the head it held into the flames, the lavender petalled iliyo whirled about like a dancer in a ballet (or like a beetle on a hotplate), severing limbs from shoulders, heads from necks, and legs from hips.

Jess would have gone to fight the gracefully savage being had its fellows not then fallen upon her and her companions.

Reducing time's passing enough to make the sheets of flame darting around her seem like slowly twisting, wispy clouds, the girl leapt to the side and then to the back of a pair of iliyo. She rose into the air brandishing her sword and, with a single stroke, cut each of them in half midway up its torso.

A third (green petalled) iliyo saw what she had done and raced towards her almost as fast as she could move with her thread raised.

The creature swung at her, but she parried its sword with her own. Drawing back and jumping to one side, the iliyo again struck, but Jess again parried. It hopped up, kicked her sword hand to one side and, with one of its free hands, grabbed her wrist.

Jess gasped as the alien brought its blade down towards her shoulder, but she was able to drop into a crouch, reach up her left arm, and seize its wrist.

The iliyo rested its feet upon Jess's chest and, with the edge of its shield, struck her shoulder where it met her neck, just below her helmet,

Biting her lip to distract herself from the pain of being so hit and feeling fear welling up in her stomach, Jess tried to stab her opponent with Dawn's Spine, but the iliyo's shield was in her way. She swung frantically to one side, seeking to dislodge her attacker. It, however, seized her shoulder and held on tight.

"Let go of me, you stupid bug," Jess shouted at the iliyo.

It did not release her, so she jabbed her sword beneath its shield and chopped off the glowing end of its body.

The iliyo made a loud noise that, in the slowed time Jess inhabited, was strangely serene and lovely, but, even as its organs began dripping out of its wound, it did not let go.

"Let go!" the girl shouted again as she shoved her helmeted head past the iliyo's shield and rammed it into the complicated genitalia hanging from its chest. That knocked the creature off of her.

In spite of its injuries, the iliyo was on its feet again almost immediately and was able to parry Jess's blows with surprising ease.

She was growing exasperated with her enemy's resilience and thrust her body at it with all her strength, slamming into the iliyo with such force that both of them tumbled onto the ground. As they rolled past patches of burning gelatin, grappling with one another, Jess drove her blade into the creature's body and split it open along nearly the whole of its length. At last, the iliyo died.

Jess stood up, looked around, and felt her stomach melt into a painful void. Not only were there two pink petalled iliyo still alive and busy killing her companions, but a group of mercenaries wearing red armor followed by a single man richly dressed in a style favored on another part of Suturik had also entered the room through the same door the aliens had used earlier. Although they were not firing upon the Ekeyans, the soldiers had positioned themselves along the wall with the door leading to the escape route.

Taking a deep breath and exhaling it forcefully, Jess shook her head to try to scatter some of the rivers of sweat pouring down her face into her eyes and mouth. Her efforts had little effect, so she blinked a few times, picked up the dead iliyo's shield, and ran towards one of its surviving companions.

With its acute hearing, the iliyo was aware of Jess's approach, but it took the alien a good five seconds to dispatch the three soldiers it was already fighting so that it could deal with its new enemy. That time was sufficient for Jess to split the iliyo into upper and lower halves.

She turned towards the only one of the creatures left alive. It had just amputated the arms of a soldier who had been guarding one of the councilors and was now jumping at the dignitary.

While the iliyo knocked the kriss the councilor had drawn from his hand and thrust its sword into the man's forehead, Jess dashed at the alien with her own sword held beside her ear.

The iliyo gracefully twirled around, parried Jess's blow, and struck at her in return. She dove backwards, avoiding its blade, fell to the side, and jabbed at the creature near where its right leg was connected to its body.

Dawn's Spine pierced the iliyo's soft flesh, though not deeply, and the tiny being silently hopped backwards. It did not, however, retreat. Instead, the iliyo immediately leapt at Jess, trying to drive its sword into her stomach. She moved to one side and swung her own blade, cutting off both her enemy's feathery antennae.

That injury sent the iliyo into a fit. It shook its head wildly, wriggled its body, and hopped up and down in a comical way.

Jess did not allow it time to recover its wits. She lunged forward, grabbed one of the iliyo's arms, and, holding it steady, cut off its head.

No sooner was the last of the iliyo dead than the mercenaries began firing upon Jess and her companions, hitting several of them.

"Get down," she shouted while letting time flow as it usually does.

The others dropped to the ground and Jess, again slowing the universe, held the iliyo's shield in front of her and hurtled herself through the conflagration separating her comrades from the mercenaries.

She fell upon her foes before they had even accepted that the young woman's impossibly fast movements were real.

With a single, spinning motion, Jess kicked the man to her left in the throat, sending him sprawling, and decapitated the man to her right, though she inadvertently let go of the iliyo shield when she did so.

She jumped over her victim's corpse, chopped the next two men in half, and cut open the cranium of the man behind this pair.

The others in front of Jess had now had time to train their rifles upon her, but, as they fired, she dove to the side, rolled along the ground, and let their needles pierce the bodies of the man she had kicked and those near him.

Before they could aim again, Jess was swinging her sword from where she was crouching and so cut four of her enemies' legs off halfway along their shins.

There were still more soldiers ahead of her and a few yet alive behind her, so Jess jumped up onto the wall in back of these men, ran along it, and returned to the floor between the last of her foes and the door they had used to enter the room.

The man directly in front of her lost his head as she landed beside him, as did the two next to him as they started turning to face their killer.

The mercenary who had been standing behind this pair had had time to whip around while Jess butchered his fellows, and he lunged at her before she could do the same to him. He struck Jess's body with his shoulder and knocked her to the ground.

Trapped beneath an enemy as slow and as heavy as a Galapagos tortoise, Jess did not try to dislodge him, but instead grabbed the plume atop his helmet, pulled up his head, and slit his exposed throat.

Blood sprayed across her own helmet from his jugular while Jess focused her will upon his body, thought of it as no more than an extension of her own, and tossed it aside as she would wiggle a finger.

On her feet again, Jess looked at her remaining enemies. Several of the mercenaries, she noticed, had been shot by the Ekeyan soldiers, but a number of them were still alive.

One of them, who was clearly their captain, spun around when he saw Jess stand up and faced her with a determined resignation. Though he assumed he would die if he attacked this deadly young woman, he knew Hyan would not forgive him if he let her go. What was more, the Ngo woman might not just kill him. She might, he reflected, decide to spend her journey home torturing him.

The captain, with such thoughts racing through his mind, drew a kuttar from his belt and rushed at Jess, but, trapped as he was in a universe made of treacle, his approach was so lethargic that she had no trouble chopping off his head.

There were only three men still fighting after the captain's corpse fell to the ground. The Ekeyans shot down two of these in the time it took Jess to disembowel the third.

The girl spun around again and gave her attention to the man from Suturik. She was glad she did so. He was training a needle gun on her. Jess bounded to the side, leapt into the air, and kicked him in the face.

The blow knocked the man back but did not appear to have done him any harm. Jess lunged at him again, and he struck her breast with his gun. The pain Jess felt briefly disoriented her (and caused her to loosen her grip on time, which returned to flowing at its ordinary rate), but she recovered her composure fast enough to prevent her enemy from ramming the muzzle of his weapon into her ribs and shooting her.

She grabbed his wrist, moved his hand to the side, and swung her blade, splitting him in half at the waist.

The two parts of the body collapsed onto the floor, and Jess started to turn away from it. Then she realized that the cadaver's torso, head, and arms were still alive and that the thing was actually aiming the gun it still held in its hand at her.

The girl chopped off the arm pointing in her direction and split the torso open from its base to its throat.

Among the various organs she revealed, Jess saw something squirming. She poked around inside the body with Dawn's Spine, prompting something like a mess of slimy organs dangling loosely from a spine and what vaguely resembled the eyeless, earless face of an ape to creep out and try to wriggle pathetically across the floor.

For a moment, Jess was so repulsed by this creature that she did not act, but that very disgust quickly impelled her to stomp upon it without thought. The fluids and blood filling the imp squirted out and Jess, feeling distinctly sick, wiped her foot on the trousers the man from Suturik had been wearing.

Jess stuck out her tongue, shook her head, and looked back through the burning room at her companions. She could barely see them through the flames. These had so spread and grown in intensity that she could only catch brief glimpses of unidentifiable figures standing somewhere near the middle of the great hall.

Focusing all her will on the scene before her, Jess seized time and grasped the flames with her mind, as though the latter were merely fanciful creations, and drew them to either side. She walked between the roiling billows of fire that decorated her face and body with flickering light and stood before the others, all the while maintaining the chasm running through the inferno.

Letting her eyes rove over her companions, she found Uluf and felt a nearly orgasmic happiness rise up through her body when she saw that he was not hurt.

Most of the others, however, were dead. Only Buabyue, two soldiers, and an elderly councilor had not been injured, although one more soldier and the young councilor in whose palace they were standing were yet living, if with severe injuries. The first had been shot in the face and a large part of his jaw was missing. The second had lost his right arm below the shoulder.

Releasing time from her grasp, but keeping the thread raised so that she could hold onto the flames behind her, Jess said to the surviving soldiers, "Help up the councilor."

Uluf pointed to the wounded soldier and asked Jess, "What about this one?"

"He's not going to live," she replied as she walked over to the man.

"I'm sorry," Jess told him. "There's nothing I can do."

Offering up his life to Haya, she cut off the soldier's head.

"Come on, everybody. Let's get out of here," Jess shouted while grabbing a cord that was draped around one of the dead iliyo.

Still holding back the conflagration, Jess ran with the others through a tunnel of fire to the other side of the room and passed through the door the councilor had earlier pointed out.

Once they were on the other side and had shut the door behind them, Jess let go of the thread inside her so that it sunk back to her perineum, and the world that had been inside of her slipped outside again. She breathed a sigh of relief, bid the others stop their flight, took off her helmet, handed it to Uluf, and went over to the young councilor.

She looked at his arm. It was bleeding profusely and would soon kill him.

"Hold him still," Jess told the soldiers and tied the cord she had taken from the iliyo around the man's stump.

"That'll have to do for now," she said and then addressed the youth himself. "Can you hear me?"

He nodded.

"Which is the door to the suite you mentioned?"

"The one at the very end of the corridor."

"And the entrance to your escape route?"

"It's in the bedroom, in the back wall."

"How do we open it?"

"There's a button," he said weakly and then let his head drop.

"Where?"

The man did not respond.

Jess shook his chin and repeated her question.

Opening his eyes and looking at her, the councilor said, "On the pillar, in the eye of the kurushyi."

"Okay," Jess said to the others, "let's run."

They did and quickly passed from the corridor into the elegant suite beyond it. Though the councilor had lost consciousness again, they found the bedroom.

Jess spied a sculpture of a kurushyi carved into the top a pillar and, as it was out of her reach, told Buabyue to press its eye. When he did, a panel slid open in the back wall and the group entered into an elevator concealed there.

This took them to a small pneumatic train that ran through a tunnel deep below the ground. The group boarded the carriage, and it was propelled by a burst of air through the tube in which it was set.

When the vehicle eventually stopped, at the end of the tube, the group got out, carrying the injured man with them.

They had arrived at a small cavern little bigger than the glass tube sticking out of one of its walls.

There were two doors opposite the tube and Jess went to one of these, opened it (revealing a narrow tunnel cut through the living rock), and looked back.

The soldiers were laying the councilor on the ground, so she addressed Buabyue. "Go and see what's on the other side of that door. I'm going to check this one."

Though not pleased that Jess was giving him orders, Buabyue nodded to her and went to the door.

While Jess walked down the tunnel in front of her, which was lit by a number of small, gem-like fixtures set in the ceiling, she was startled by the sensation of something touching her shoulder.

She spun around, ready to fight, but was confronted by Uluf.

Putting both her hands on the toad's shoulders, leaning forward, and resting her forehead on his, she said, "Don't do that, Uluf. You scared me to death. I'm a little edgy at the moment, you know."

"I do apologize, my dear," the toad replied. "Come. Let us see what is ahead."

The girl took her friend by the hand and the pair walked along the corridor to another door, this one made out of thick metal.

Jess turned the screw set in the middle of the door, swung it open, and stepped into a small cave.

Light was coming through several small slits that pierced the wall opposite her, so Jess walked over to one of these and peered through it.

The window provided a view of Ekeya, though the city was some distance away. Jess looked around as best she could with the limited range of vision the slit permitted her and realized that the chamber she was in had to be inside one of the hills between Ekeya and the spaceport.

She gazed carefully at the domed city to try to discern what was happening there and quickly noticed that the iliyo ship had lifted itself up from where it had been resting and was floating in the sky.

"What's going on?" she asked Uluf, who was now standing beside her looking through another slit.

"I am afraid that I do not know for certain. It appears that the battle is over, but I cannot say why the iliyo are not departing."

"I think they're going now," Jess said.

The alien vessel was slowly rising through the atmosphere directly above Ekeya.

"That appears to be the case," the toad agreed.

No sooner had Uluf said this than he and Jess saw a flash of curving light, like an electric arc, blaze forth between the ship and Ekeya's dome. For several seconds this blinding ray danced about, until, suddenly, a part of the dome shattered, leaving a great hole in it, through which the breathable atmosphere inside poured out and the lethal atmosphere outside poured in.

"They're killing everybody!" Jess shouted. "Why are they doing that? Is that what they came here to do?"

"I do not know, my dear."

"I suppose Ghoryi's over there somewhere. That's too bad. I liked her. She was nice."

"Yes. It does seem unlikely that she would have left the city. Nonetheless, her doing so would not have been impossible."

"And Ofu too. I guess he came all this way for nothing. He should've gone back to Jezic."

"He was probably in Ekeya as well."

"Poor guy. I admit I didn't like him all that much, but I still feel sorry for him."

The graceful ether-ship, topped with countless shimmering sails, continued to float up into the sky, past undulating brimu and cotton candy clouds, until, when it was little more than a silvery spot scintillating in the green vault, something metallic glimmered beneath it.

"They've dropped something," Jess noted.

For a moment Uluf was silent. Then, grabbing Jess and pulling her away from the window, he said, "Do not look."

A burst of brilliant light sent beams like knives through the windows, piercing the darkness of the chamber and causing Jess to jump into the toad's arms.

When the light had faded, she leapt back over to the window and saw a fiery mushroom rising where Ekeya had stood.

Though it was obvious, she still informed her companion, "They've blown up the city."

Uluf took Jess's hand. "Come, my dear. Let us leave."

The pair returned down the tunnel, where they saw that the young councilor who had guided them out of the city had died.

Jess knelt beside him and stroked his cheek. "I'm sorry I wasn't much help. Best of luck wherever you are."

Buabyue returned a few minutes later and, seeing Jess, asked her, "What did you find?"

She stood up, turned around, and faced the smuggler. "They destroyed Ekeya. They dropped a bomb on it."

Buabyue looked at her, not knowing what to say.

Finally, he asked, "Are you sure?"

"Yes. Of course, I'm sure. The city is completely gone."

"Ah, now that is a disaster," Buabyue said while wiping his brow. "Still, everything's not lost yet. The tunnel I went down leads to an apartment this fellow has at the spaceport."

Buabyue looked at the man to whom he was referring and saw that he was dead. "It leads to an apartment that he used to have at the spaceport."

"We can get out of here, then?" Jess asked.

"Yes. Let's go."

The last remaining councilor of Ekeya looked at him and, with tears in his eyes, asked, "Why? We're ruined. There's nothing left."

"We're not dead yet," Buabyue replied in what was nearly a shout. "You, my lord, are now in control of the Llalloi. You're the last of the bosses, but your organization is still intact. And don't forget what we're doing on Shokai. We can still break Ngo. We just have to get to that planet to take charge of things."

The old man looked up.

"Yes. You're right."

"Come on, then. The *Salamander*, my ether-ship, is at the orbital station. We can get a shuttle there and be heading out within a couple of hours."

Jess smiled at Buabyue.

"That's the spirit!" she exclaimed. "Let's go make Tsoi miserable. Besides, I'm not done with Tolliver yet."

"What about the iliyo?" the old councilor asked. "Are you planning on using your ship to chase them?"

"No. It can't be done," Buabyue replied. "Iliyo ether-ships don't make the walls of the Warren resonate. That's one of the reasons they're such good raiders. It's impossible to detect them coming, and it's impossible to track them. We're better off just heading to Shokai."

"Then let us leave," the old man conceded.

"One last thing," added Buabyue.

"What?"

"The body of your fellow councilor."

"What of it?"

"If Ngo has any more men on Suturik and they find it while it's still fresh, they'll be able to put it in a juicer and extract information from it. I'm sure he knew secrets you wouldn't want Ngo to hear."

"I suppose we must ruin the brain."

"Yes. Would you like me to do it?"

"No. One of my soldiers will. You, take care of it."

The soldier the old man had indicated found a large rock and used it to smash the head of the corpse lying at his feet, reducing its brain to a chunky jelly.

# Chapter 38
# Back to Shokai

Once he had ejaculated, Buabyue lay on top of Jess's naked body until he had recovered his breath and could lift himself off of her. He sat on the edge of the bed and wiped away some of the sticky pink syrup that had stuck to his flabby chest and rounded stomach.

With a smile, he stood up and beckoned for a pair of golems shaped like curvaceous young women to dress him in the fur trimmed tunic and trousers (decorated with brightly colored abstract designs) that were fashionable on Tomasine Station.

There would be numerous dangers he would have to face in the coming days, but Buabyue was not frightened. If anything, he was excited by the possibilities being presented to him.

He walked back over to the bed where Jess was lying and looked at her dead face. Her mouth and nostrils were covered with a mask that kept the sleeping jelly in her lungs and prevented her from waking up. Running his hand across her body, he could feel that life had returned to her skin, but her mind was still motionless. She was still as good as dead.

Shaking her body so that her breasts wiggled, Buabyue said to the unconscious woman, "You've got lovely tits, Jess. I've had a marvelous time playing with them. Too bad you weren't able to enjoy this as much as I did."

He stood up again and told his golems, "Clean out her genitals and put her back in the corpse tank."

The golems bowed to him and, while they removed any evidence of what Buabyue had done to Jess, he walked over to a telopticon like an oval frame that was set in one wall and said, "The steward's office."

A moment later, a man's face appeared in the frame as though it were actually there looking at Buabyue from a hole in the wall.

"My lord," the face said.

"Is Frunso in his corpse tank yet?"

"No, my lord."

"Ask him to join me in my lounge. Tell him there's something important I need to discuss."

"Yes, my lord."

"And send Luhit there with a sharp knife and a juicer. Tell him to put the latter somewhere Frunso won't see it."

"As you desire, my lord."

Buabyue switched off the telopticon and turned around to watch his golems lower Jess back into her corpse tank.

"I assume you cleaned her thoroughly?" he asked.

One of the golems, who had emerald green hair, replied, "Yes, my lord."

"Fine. Clean the room; change the sheets on the bed, and switch off the lights when you're done. You can wake her up in fifteen days. Just make sure to get her out of the corpse tank about twelve hours before we arrive at the station so that she can get some proper sleep."

"Yes, my lord," the two golems replied in unison.

Buabyue checked to make certain that he had a needle gun in the pocket of his tunic and left the room.

When he entered his lounge, he found Frunso, the elderly Ekeyan councilor, sitting there sipping upon a drink and Luhit leaning against a wall behind that man while rubbing his sweaty hands together anxiously.

Taking a drink of his own from an impossibly busty orange haired golem standing behind the bar, Buabyue sat down facing the last living boss of the Llalloi.

He gulped down half of his drink and looked up at the domed roof above him. Its viewing screens were showing images of the void outside the ethership. Suturik was no longer visible, though its sun could still be seen as a small shining light. The radiance pouring forth from it appeared to be no more than a trickle, but it was still sufficient to fill the *Salamander*'s vast sails and push the ship through the emptiness.

The smuggler turned his eyes towards these sails, that rose up from the edge of the dome, and admired their graceful efficiency. They were higher than was any earthly mountain but were as thin as a membrane and capable of propelling a vessel at nearly the speed of light.

Still staring above his guest's head, Buabyue said to that man, "We'll soon be far enough away from the sun to open up a rabbit hole and tumble into the Emmenthal."

Frunso scratched his stomach and asked, "Are you sure this is safe?"

"The *Salamander*? It's a wonderful ship."

"No. Going to Shokai."

"Don't worry, my lord. We won't be going to Tozana. I own a refinery and several buildings in Hwiccho. We'll be staying there with my employees. I assure you that we'll be safe."

"Good. Thing's could get violent in Tozana."

"I'm certain they will, my lord."

The old man sipped his drink and Buabyue said to him, "My lord, I'm sorry to bother you with practical matters so soon after the loss of your home, but I'm afraid that they simply can't wait."

"Go ahead, Buabyue. I understand the need completely."

"Thank you, my lord. There are going to be many expenses in Tozana while we're funding our little revolution. Plus, you're going to have to control the entire Llalloi organization on your own. Before we continue with our plans, I have to ask you if you have access to all the Llalloi accounts and corporate information. I hope you will forgive me for such intrusiveness. I would never have asked were our situation not so desperate."

Frunso waved his hand in front of his face to dismiss Buabyue's anxiety. "You needn't worry. Though I do have access to everything we have, your concerns are legitimate. We are in severe trouble at the moment."

Buabyue, looking relieved, smiled and said, "Some of us in more than others."

He then pulled the needle gun from his pocket and, while the old man looked at him without understanding, shot him in the heart.

Shifting his gaze towards Luhit, Buabyue said, "Cut off his head and hook it up to the juicer."

Luhit, grinning widely and franticly shaking his head up and down, drew a hilt from his pocket, touched a switch on it, and, when its telescopic blade had rushed out, used its monomolecular edge to decapitate the old man sitting in front of him.

As he did so, the golem standing behind the bar bent down, picked up an odd looking device, and set it on the counter.

Holding Frunso's head upside down to minimize the mess the blood dripping from it would make, Luhit went over to the bar and placed his burden, the right way up, upon a metal plate covered with syringes and tubes.

This, and the whole of the contraption, the juicer, was supported on a low tripod, while between its legs, under the plate the head was resting on, there was suspended a glass sphere filled with a pinkish substance that looked like sleeping jelly. This was actually a preservative that would keep the head from rotting. It would not, however, stop all molecular activity in the way sleeping jelly did.

Rising from either side of the plate, and extending around the head, was a metal hoop, and, from the outer edge of this, a series of small vials filled with various liquids projected like the rays of a starburst. When Frunso's head was secured onto the plate and filled with the pink preservative liquid, needles automatically extended from the vials, from the inside of the metal halo, and stabbed into the man's flesh.'

Within seconds, the head's eyes opened and stared blankly ahead.

Buabyue looked at his golem and said, "Begin recording."

"Yes, my lord," the plastic machine replied and set a microphone in front of Frunso's mouth.

Turning his gaze to the head, Buabyue commanded it, saying, "State all known details about all Llalloi accounts, one account at a time."

The corpse began rattling off information about various accounts. After listening to it for long enough to know that it was providing the details he wanted to know, Buabyue turned away and gestured for Luhit to sit in one of the empty chairs.

"When we arrive on Shokai," Buabyue informed the younger man, "I'm sending Jess back to Tozana to be my emissary to Gople Sing. She's proved to be wonderfully useful and she's known there. However, I want you to accompany her, to make sure she's reliable."

"As you wish, my lord."

Buabyue continued while watching his underling first use the back of his hand to wipe his snout-like proboscis and then his tunic to remove the mucus so gathered from his knuckles. "Before she leaves, I'm going to be giving her this message wand."

He pulled a small metal stick out of his pocket and held it up between his thumb and forefinger.

"It has the instructions I'm giving Sing on how to proceed. Make sure the girl gives it to him."

"Yeah. Of course, my lord."

Buabyue then revealed a second tube he was holding in his palm and tossed this to Luhit.

"This is a duplicate. I'm giving this one to you, Luhit. If the first gets destroyed or Jess doesn't hand it over to Sing, you're to give this one to him. But, more importantly, I want you to look at it and make sure he does what I've told him to do. Understand?"

"Yes, my lord."

"I'm also giving you access to several of my private accounts. If you require money to carry things through, get it from those. Don't be shy to use them, either. Remember, if we succeed in this, I will be the Llalloi."

Buabyue leaned forward and looked at Luhit. "Since you're one of my top men, you're going to be richer than you ever dreamt you could be. Of course, if you fail, Ngo's going to kill both of us."

"I won't disappoint you, my lord. Yeah. That's right."

Luhit's mouth curled into a wide smile below his long, sharp, and twitching nose.

"I hope not. Now go look at the information I've given you and rest in your corpse tank."

"Yes, my lord." Luhit rose from his seat and started to leave the room.

When the man had reached the door, Buabyue called out to him. "Oh, Luhit, send in a couple of golems to clean up this mess."

"As you desire, my lord – yeah – yeah," the man replied as he waved his hands about in front of his face.

When Luhit had gone, Buabyue leaned back in his seat and gazed at the images projected upon the viewing screens above him.

He watched as the *Salamander*'s vast sails were drawn in, like the closing petals of a flower, and as a spherical device attached to the end of a metal tentacle emerged from the vessel's back end and slowly extended towards its front.

When it had moved past the prow of the ship, the sphere expanded, changing into an ever widening hoop that, eventually, was wider than was the craft itself.

Suddenly, the hoop filled with a flickering, otherworldly light and the *Salamander* tumbled through this into the Warren beyond.

As the lounge passed through the rabbit hole, Buabyue lost himself in a confused whirl of strange colors and weird sensations. He barely noticed the end of the ship moving through the great ring and then pulling the hoop through itself with the long metal tentacle that was holding the device.

After he had regained his composure, Buabyue allowed his eyes to rove across the walls of the duct his craft had entered and thought about what he would do once he had defeated the Ngo. Such reflections soon so captivated Buabyue that he barely heard the droning of Frunso's head behind him or the efforts of the golems in front of him to remove that man's corpse.

* * *

Wearing her black tube top, her pink shorts, and her loose vest, Jess stood with her arms akimbo looking at Buabyue.

The blazing light of the noonday sun flooded through the skylight above her and filled the large, gaudily decorated sitting room with an almost unbearable brightness.

Buabyue was reclining upon a divan sipping a cup of some hot drink and looking back at her.

Uluf and Luhit were nearby, drinking from cups of their own and watching the potbellied, aristocratic gangster and the skinny girl who just happened to be an accomplished killer.

"Why aren't you going to Jezic yourself?" Jess asked Buabyue.

"There's been a coup. A woman of the first estate, Soniyo Dogrue, has overthrown the former ruler and proclaimed herself roshpatni."

"So?"

"We have no doubt that she's being financed by Tsoi Ngo. She's already struck against the Sing gang. Gople himself is alive and in hiding, as are our more respectable allies, but it is simply too dangerous for me to visit the city at the moment. If I were to be caught, we'd all be lost."

"What about me? You paid me to protect you, and even though you're not going, you want me to go to a city where I could wind up getting captured and killed?"

"You're the best fighter I've ever seen. You can take care of yourself."

"I still didn't agree to be your errand runner."

"As you say. I will pay you an additional ten million kopecks for your service."

Jess raised her eyebrows, lifted her arms, placed her hands behind her head, and clasped her fingers together. Exhaling loudly, as though to clear her mind, she wandered over to the wide window stretching across the wall to her right.

She leaned against the sill and surveyed the tangled pipes and tall smokestacks of Hwiccho's factories, its grim housing blocks, and the endless, shimmering desert that stretched out beyond these all the way to the horizon.

"Before I agree," she said without looking at her employer, "tell me what you want me to do."

"Gople Sing is still alive, like I said, and we're still in contact with him. You will meet with one of our agents, and he will take you to see Sing."

"Go on."

"I'll give you a message to deliver to Sing. Once you've done so, you'll remain with him and make certain that he adheres to the plans I have outlined in that message."

"Could you give me the gist of it?"

"Certainly. We are going to remove Soniyo Dogrue from the throne and replace her with Somnat Malotrue. He's a general in Tozana's army and is well respected by his fellow officers. They'll follow him if he rebels against the new roshpatni. He's also an aristocrat, like she is, so he can count on his high born friends to help out."

"What're we going to do to help?"

"I've provided Gople Sing with enough money to buy arms, hire mercenaries, and pay bribes. We've already got significant caches of weapons in Jezic and a fair number of soldiers. With that wand, Sing will be able to pay off a good many of the troops who might not have risen against Soniyo. That'll keep them out of the fighting, even if they don't actually join us. I've also told him how he can get into the palace. He's going to send in a squad of raiders and try to grab or kill Soniyo. While they're in there, Malotrue will get word of the attack. Actually, he already knows about it, but he'll pretend to get word of it. Claiming he's come to protect his ruler from her enemies, he'll bring some troops to the palace. It's being guarded by Soniyo's personal soldiers, so he'll need to arrest or fight them. Either way, he's going to take control of the palace. If our raiders haven't caught or killed Soniyo, Malotrue should get her. Bribes and our mercenaries ought to be able to take care of the remainder of the soldiers in the city."

"So, what am I supposed to do?"

"Like I said, you should make sure that Sing doesn't deviate from my plans."

"What's it matter? You have the army helping you."

"No. I don't. I have some generals in the army helping. Most of the troops have been removed from Jezic and replaced with Soniyo's own retinue. Malotrue will only have a few soldiers at his disposal. He's going to have to rely on men provided to him by Sing. If Sing doesn't cooperate, the result could be a disaster."

"Okay. I'll keep an eye on him. Is there anything else?"

"Yes. I'd like for you to take part in the raid on the palace."

"I thought you were going to say that."

"Jess, your skills are ideally suited to such a task."

Turning round and leaning against the window, Jess crossed her arms beneath her breasts and said, "Okay, I'll do this for you. If nothing else, maybe I can tick Tsoi off enough so that he'll blame Tolliver for all the trouble I've caused and kill that wretched vermin."

Buabyue grinned like a wolf ready to devour a rabbit and exclaimed, "Wonderful! Now, here's the message wand I want you to give to Sing."

The man took the metal tube out of his pocket and stretched out his hand, offering it to Jess.

She stared at him from where she stood at the window for long enough to allow the man's arm to begin to get tired and then walked over to him and took it.

Once she had examined the tube, she slid it into the pouch hanging at her hip and asked, "So, there's been a coup? I assume that means there's going to be a lot of soldiers around Jezic. How am I supposed to get into the city? They could be looking for me, you know."

"You needn't worry about that. I have already arranged for you to be smuggled into the city."

"Okay. Go on."

"You'll take an antigravity barge from here to Beelwaro. It's a town on the Hwikeihi River. I have someone there who'll meet you and take you into Jezic."

"They aren't going to be on alert in this Beelwaro?"

"No. It's deep in the jungle, far from the capital."

"How am I getting from there to Jezic, then?"

"You'll take a boat. The Hwikeihi flows through Jezic."

"They're not going to be looking at traffic on the river? I mean the soldiers working for the new ruler."

"We will be taking every precaution, Jess. I don't want you to fail in this, after all."

"Not half as much as I don't want to be killed."

Buabyue laughed.

"I promise you, you needn't worry unduly. My man in Beelwaro is expecting you."

"Okay. I'll go along with you on this."

"Wonderful."

"So, when's my barge leaving?"

"This evening, at half past the sixth watch."

"Where's the airport?"

"Don't worry about that. I'll take you down there myself."

"I assume you're booking my passage too."

"Yes. I've already reserved rooms for you and Luhit."

"Luhit?"

"Yes. He'll be accompanying you."

Jess looked at the man, feeling vaguely uncomfortable about him without knowing why.

"Fine," she said at last.

"Jess," interjected Uluf.

The girl looked at her friend and waved her hand.

"I'm sorry, Uluf, but I'd rather you stayed behind this time."

"Why, my dear?"

"If something happens to me, I don't want all this money to go to waste. You've got access to my accounts. At least you can enjoy being rich if I don't make it back."

"My dear, I…"

"Don't argue with me. I'm not changing my mind."

The toad saw that this was the case and merely said, "Do at least be careful for me. No amount of money would be sufficient compensation for losing you."

\* \* \*

That evening, Jess, Uluf, Luhit, and Buabyue went to Hwiccho's airport, a rambling complex of grubby buildings squatting beside a dusty plain that had been cleared of large boulders, but which was nearly concealed by the wriggling waves of heat produced by the glaring sun hanging in the sky.

From the terminal, they were conveyed across the airfield in an air-conditioned carriage drawn by a team of chained maruvazi whose eyes were covered with blinders.

"That's the *Jewel of the Sands*, the barge you'll be taking," Buabyue said while pointing out the window.

The others looked and saw a large vessel with six levels, all of which were encircled with glass enclosed, pillared balconies. From the top of the ship emerged a pair of black smokestacks, and at its back and on a pair of poles projecting to either side were propellers.

It was an impressive craft, Jess thought, though its white painted hull was everywhere peeling and it did seem to have endured a great many rough trips.

When Jess and the others arrived at the *Jewel of the Sands*, its balconies were already packed with dirty miners and factory workers dressed in hot suits, pyjamas, or long, loose robes and chatting loudly while smoking clay pipes and drinking liquor from large jugs.

Pushing through these persons on her way to her room, Jess attracted a great many lewd comments and propositions, while Uluf, who was still with her, and wearing a brightly colored brocade sticharion and a plumed kamelaukion, captivated every one of the rough, ignorant men who saw him.

Fortunately, Buabyue had booked an individual cabin for Jess, and she was able to close the door and shut out a little of the noise and most of the attention of her fellow passengers.

Jess collapsed on the bed and leaned against the brittle, flaking paint on the metal wall behind her, dislodging several large and numerous small pieces of this, which fluttered down onto her legs and the sheets below her.

"By the emperor's backside, it is hot in here!" she exclaimed.

"The controls for the air-conditioning are over here," Uluf said to her as he manipulated them.

Cold air blasted out of a duct directly above Jess, who tried to fan herself by rhythmically tugging on her tank top.

"Ooh, that's better."

There was a knock on the door.

"Who is it?" Jess called out.

"Buabyue."

Uluf walked over to the door and let the man in.

He wiped his brow with a handkerchief, sat upon a rickety chair next to a worm-eaten writing desk, and looked at Jess.

"Where's Luhit?" she asked.

"He's in his cabin. It's next to this one."

Buabyue leaned back in the chair and noticed several men peeking through the room's windows in order to ogle Jess. He got up, closed the shutters, and reseated himself.

Though he could still see a number of men trying to peep through the slats, Buabyue ignored them and said, "Jess, you'll be arriving in Beelwaro in six days. This is for the trip."

He took a small purse from a bag he had slung over his shoulder, bounced it in his hands so that the rattling of the coins inside of it could be heard, and tossed it to Jess.

"There should be more than enough money in there to last you while you're on the barge."

"Thanks."

Uluf filled three cups with water from a spigot set in the wall above a wash basin and handed one of these to Jess and another to Buabyue, keeping the last for himself.

"So," Jess asked, "how am I going to recognize this man of yours in Beelwaro?"

"Luhit knows him."

"But how am I going to know him?"

"He's very tall and very skinny, and all his teeth are rotten. He's also going to address you as Nino and Luhit as Hanju."

"Okay. That'll work."

"Also, I've brought these for you."

Buabyue reached into his bag, pulled out a small round tin and a black wig, and tossed these into Jess's lap.

"What's this?" Jess asked while examining the tin.

"It's dye for your skin. You're too light complexioned to be from Tozana. Rub it all over your body before you arrive there. With that and the wig, nobody's going to notice you."

"Fine."

"Good. I'd better be off soon. I won't be in contact with you for a while, so take care of yourself."

"Okay then," Jess replied as she hopped off of the bed and went over to Uluf.

She embraced the toad, who ran his knobby, webbed fingers though her pink hair and, resting his chin upon her shoulder, said to her, "Do be careful, my dear."

"I will, Uluf."

She pushed him away a little, though the two were still holding one another's waists, and, imitating a serious voice, informed him, "I keep telling you I'm too cute to die. Why don't you listen? Get it into that head of yours, okay?"

# Chapter 39
# From Hwiccho to Jezic

Tsoi caressed the face of the dead feihi lying next to him in his bed, feeling sad that such a beautiful thing had been lost. Still, he reflected, the poor creature's very transience, that required it to be appreciated immediately or never, that gave it a fragile preciousness, made it even more beautiful than it would have been had it been more durable.

Even so, he wished he could have enjoyed the feihi a little longer. He had been unusually rough with it and had quickly wrecked its delicate internal organs. Of course, Tsoi had been very upset earlier when he had received word about Huazheen from Hyan, and sex with the feihi had made him feel much better. It really had been helpful.

His mind was yet reeling with the drug produced by the creature's genitals when, with a sigh, he resolved to tear himself away from his only source of consolation and attend to the pressing concerns of the world.

Tsoi rolled over, activated the telopticon fasted to a circlet on the brow of a naked young woman kneeling, shackled to the floor, beside his bed, and looked at the face of the man that appeared between its harp-like horns.

"My lord," the face said.

"Send me the castellan."

"Yes, my lord."

Tsoi leaned forward, wiped the feihi's genitals with his fingers and examined the mixture of sexual juices and blood that was dripping onto his sheets. He licked it, and though it tasted rather foul it did send a surge of pleasure through his body, like an electric shock transformed into an orgasm.

He lay back upon his pillows and relished the sensation for a few moments as he gazed at the nacre eyes of a voluptuous female figure in the bas-relief that completely covered the golden walls of the room, until he heard a knock upon the door.

Once Tsoi had gestured to another of his nude female attendants and she had dashed over to and opened the entrance to her master's bedroom, his castellan walked in and bowed to him.

"My lord," the man said.

"Come here and help me up."

The castellan walked over to the side of the bed and lifted Tsoi to his feet.

"Dress me," Tsoi added.

"Yes, my lord."

The castellan went to the wardrobe on the other side of the room, took out a thin white shirt, a shining, iridescent, pink frock coat with a tall embroidered collar, and a pair of loose silk trousers sewn with complex, interweaving floral designs.

Returning with these to where Tsoi was standing and laying the shirt and coat over the back of a crouching unclothed woman who was held in that position with gold restraints, the man knelt before his master and began putting his pants on him.

While the castellan did so, Tsoi said to him, "I received a message from Hyan earlier."

"I hope all has gone well, my lord."

"It has not."

"I am sorry, my lord."

"Shall I tell you what she said?"

"If it would please you, my lord."

"Well, it wasn't all bad. The Llalloi have been nearly wiped out."

"That's good news, my lord."

"It's not that good. Hyan wasn't able to capture any of them, and she even said that a few of the Llalloi might have escaped. She wasn't certain, but she said it was a possibility."

"At the very least, their organization must be severely compromised."

"Now that's true," Tsoi conceded as the castellan stood up and began draping his master's shirt over his shoulders. "However, they're not broken yet. Let's not forget what happened to Kublai Khan when he tried to conquer Japan."

"I'm not familiar with that story, my lord."

"It's history from Old Earth. It's very ancient. Somebody like you wouldn't know it, but I'll enlighten you. There was a great king, you see, named Kublai Khan, and he had conquered almost the whole of the Earth, but his enemies, desperate to survive, gathered together on a little island called Japan and dropped an atomic bomb on him when he tried to rid himself of them. They would never ordinarily have done such a thing, but they thought it was their only way to survive. Desperate, terrified men will do desperate and terrifying things. It's a lesson you shouldn't forget. I won't. We need to be very wary of our enemies right now. There's nothing they won't be capable of."

"As you say, my lord," replied the castellan as he began dressing Tsoi in his coat.

"That's not the worst of it, I'm afraid," Tsoi said with an ostentatious sigh.

"My lord?"

"You see, my dear cousin Huazheen has been murdered by that same girl who tried to kill me."

"I'm sorry, my lord. You have my sincerest condolences."

"Thank you, my friend."

While fastening the buckles running up the front of the coat, the castellan asked, "Is there anything I can do for you, my lord?"

"Yes, there is, and that's why I've called you here."

"My lord?"

"It's likely that the Llalloi, and possibly that horrible pink haired girl, are going to act against Soniyo Dogrue in Tozana."

"That does seem probable."

"I'm afraid that I don't entirely trust that woman's judgment, or her abilities. I've made arrangements to take care of things if she loses control of the situation, but I'm hoping that it won't come to that. I want you to go to Jezic and keep an eye on the situation there."

"As you desire, my lord," the castellan said and straightened Tsoi's garment.

"Don't bother with it," Tsoi told him. "Get rid of that thing."

Tsoi pointed to the body of the feihi.

The castellan, having picked up the corpse, carried it over to the chute leading to the incinerator, and Tsoi continued.

"You shouldn't announce your presence. I wouldn't want Soniyo to know you're there."

The castellan dumped the feihi's body into the chute and replied. "As you desire, my lord."

Tsoi picked up his long pipe from a table, packed it with ando, his favorite intoxicating herb, reclined before an oriel window set in the wall beside his bed, and lit the pipe. After he had inhaled the smoke and briefly savored the dizzying sense of gladness it sent washing through his body, he said, "Be unobtrusive but observant. Keep an eye on whatever that woman does. I want to know everything that happens in Jezic before anyone else does. Do you understand?"

"I do, my lord. You can depend on me."

"Let us hope so."

* * *

Seven days after the *Jewel of the Sands* left Hwiccho, rather than the six Buabyue had told Jess it would take, the barge approached Beelwaro.

Wearing a long black wig and having dyed her skin so that she would not attract attention, Jess looked at her naked, bejeweled body in a mirror hanging on the wall. She was impressed at how authentic she appeared. Even her facial features were not remarkably different from those of most of the people of Tozana, though she did more closely resemble the Ngo she had seen in Quanya. Nonetheless, she doubted if anyone who saw her would think that she was not a native.

Satisfied with her disguise, Jess stepped out of her cabin and leaned over the railing running along the balcony outside (the windows having been opened after the vehicle left the desert behind).

She looked back for a moment at the tall mountains that circled Shokai's northern regions, out of a pass through which the barge had just emerged. Then she let her eyes wander over the endless expanse of forest that covered the plains below these. There was hardly a column of smoke rising from amongst the trees or the scar of a highway marring the jungle's beauty.

The girl was at once mesmerized and delighted by the undulating canopy beneath the skyliner. As she gazed at this incredible wilderness, gusts of wind surged across the deck, causing the strands of her wig to whip about and the gaudy ornaments wrapped around her torso and limbs to jangle wildly. These flurries threatened to blow everything upon her body away, but, at the same time, they also seemed to dislodge all her anger, regret, self-doubt, and self-hatred, so promising to leave her pure and naked within and without. Only the dregs of her unpleasant emotions were left to stir – virtually unnoticed – underneath the shining, peaceful surface of her awareness. Whatever dangers were yet ahead of her, she was, at least for a moment, suffused with a sense of dreamy, pleasant calmness.

Exhaling in satisfaction, Jess spied, directly below her, a river that meandered through the wilds, and, following this, she saw, not far ahead, a sprawling city rising up from amongst the trees. This, she at once realized, must be Beelwaro since it was the only urbanized area for many miles around.

The city was mostly located on an island in the middle of the wide, muddy, and sluggish Hwikeihi River, but had spilled over onto both of its banks. A large part of Beelwaro was even built directly over the reddish-brown water. Innumerable structures had been erected on stilts in the river and could be reached only by boat, though some were connected to one another or to the dry land with narrow wooden gangways. Some of these structures were actually rather elegant and pretty, with the upturned eaves Jess had seen on houses in the towns to the north, but most were wretched hovels cobbled together with whatever materials their inhabitants could find. The buildings raised on the ground were little better. Even the few tall minaret-like towers similar to those of Jezic were grubby and weathered.

After the *Jewel of the Sands* had landed at the city's airport and Jess and Luhit had disembarked, they were met by a tall, scrawny man with a handful of grey, yellow, and black teeth hanging precariously from his blackened gums.

"Welcome to Beelwaro, Nino," he said to Jess with a bow. "I'm Hojun. I've been asked to take care of you while you're here."

Jess bowed in return and the man continued. "I'll take you to your hotel."

"Thanks," Jess replied.

Hojun led the pair out of the airport to the shade beneath one of the few raised highways that cut through the city. Walking past the snail-shaped taxis parked there, he approached a rickshaw, paid the puller a groat, and bid the others seat themselves in it. The three then set out towards their lodgings through the sweltering, humid air that seemed to be pervaded with both smoke and the smells of humanity.

Almost all of the locals, Jess noted, were members of Tozana's lowest estate, but the tattoos with which virtually every person decorated his or her naked body were different in style from those she had seen in Jezic. A few were representational, though these were always crudely done, but most were of complex, interwoven abstract designs that were actually rather attractive.

Here and there, usually emerging from the front of some tiny shop or another, she also saw persons of the fourth estate. She even noted the odd member of the third estate riding in a rickshaw or sitting behind cast iron railings on the balcony of some building. There were not, however, nearly as many individuals of these classes as there were in Jezic. She did not see a single person of either of the top two estates.

As impoverished as Beelwaro was, it was also alive with activity. Barges and riverboats jostled with one another, and with incredible flotillas of tiny gondolas, upon the surface of the Hwikeihi. The streets were choked with pedestrians, rickshaws, and heavily laden wagons pulled by gigantic squamous creatures vaguely like the mwags Jess had seen fighting in Jezic and Quanya, though these used their trumpet-like snouts to scavenge the ground in front of them for refuse and had long, fatty antennae that stuck straight up from their brows and wiggled spasmodically in the air.

"There's a lot going on here for a place in the middle of the forest," Jess commented.

"All the ores and minerals from the mines in the mountains and all the products of the jungle come through Beelwaro on their way to Jezic and the rest of the North," Hojun explained. "Not only that, though. There are a lot of wild mudjumpers that live by the tributaries of the Hwikeihi or by other rivers around here, so there are also a lot of smugglers."

"I thought the penalties for that were pretty severe in your country. Yeah. I did," Luhit said, running his constantly moving fingers through his oily hair.

"They are. It's a risky business, but it pays a lot too. You'll even find some men who go out and trap feihi. Now that's risky. Of course, if you can trap just a few of them in a year and sell them off without getting caught, you can live it up in a place like this."

Wiping his face, since the heat and humidity seemed to have trapped every particle of dust, refuse, smoke, and oil that came into contact with him in his pores, Luhit looked around at the garbage filled streets, the sweating laborers, and the crumbling buildings and rolled his eyes in doubt.

As they continued on their way through the congested streets of Beelwaro, Jess noticed a Jaffrite's carcass hanging at the front of a butcher's shop. Then, before she had even decided that she was sure about what she had seen, she saw another in a second shop.

She grabbed Hojun's arm, shook it, and asked him, "Do people eat mudjumpers here?"

"There are people who hunt or trap the wild ones living in the forest."

"Really?"

"Yes. They're one of the best game animals."

"Isn't that kind of gruesome?"

"What do you mean?"

"Well, they are intelligent after all. They have some kind of worth."

"That's a very strange thing to say. Maybe you're thinking that the mudjumpers here are as valuable as the ones in the preserves. They're not. They're just wild animals here."

"That's not what I meant. Forget about it."

Once they had arrived at their destination, a formerly elegant but now squalid hotel, the balconied front of which provided the numerous prostitutes living there with a place to display their charms (or, at the least, their availability) to all passersby, Jess and Luhit were shown to their rooms. Though these were hardly elegant and, not being air-conditioned, were more than a little hot, they were not unpleasant.

Jess did not, however, feel like resting and so went down to the hotel's restaurant, where Hojun had said he would be. Joining that man, who was drinking a bottle of liquor, she asked him to show her around the city.

"You should stay here," he replied. "We're a long way from Quanya or Panjua, but that doesn't mean the Ngo don't have men here."

Jess leaned back in her chair, crossed her arms, and glared at the man.

Finally, taking a spare cup from the center of the table, pouring some of Hojun's liquor in it, and raising this to her lips, she said, "Fine. I suppose you're right."

"Drink up," Hojun said and swallowed the contents of his cup.

Jess did the same, though the liquor nearly made her gag. It was very strong and tasted terrible.

Tapping on her throat, she asked, "So, what's your plan to get us to Jezic?"

"I'm putting you on a riverboat leaving for Jezic tomorrow, but you won't go the whole way on it."

"Why not?"

"I'm afraid the army might be checking passengers when they arrive in the capital."

"So, how are we getting there?"

"You'll take the boat as far as Sika; it's a town just south of Jezic. My cousin lives there. He's arranged the last part of your trip."

"Go on."

"He's going to pay a local fisherman to take you into the city. Nobody's going to notice some poor fisherman when he shows up in Jezic. You'll be completely safe. I've already sent word to Sing that he needs to have someone meet you when you arrive in order to smuggle you across the city. That's going to be the dangerous part, but there's not much we can do about that. They say the army's all over the city now."

Luhit, who had just arrived at the table, nervously asked, "What have you heard?"

"Soniyo's arrested every member of the Sing gang she could find and has been executing them as soon they've been caught. The Kuma family, the old royal family, mostly got out of the capital and back to their estates, but a few of them are in the roshpatni's jails. So are a lot of the generals and top government officials. I don't think she's been killing any aristocrats, but she's got them locked up if she's afraid of them."

Jess felt a little concerned when she heard about the situation she was heading into, but, taking another drink of Hojun's liquor, she exclaimed, "Well, if we could be dying soon, let's at least enjoy ourselves tonight."

She ordered another bottle of liquor and sat in the hotel restaurant drinking with her two companions until she grew so bored with them that she was more interested in getting some sleep than in consuming more alcohol. Hojun and Luhit were both disappointed to see her leave, as each had hoped the girl would get drunk enough that she would be willing to have sex with him.

The following morning, Hojun hired a rickshaw and took Jess and Luhit down to the river, where they boarded a large passenger boat.

Leaving Beelwaro behind, the pair traveled downstream for three days before arriving at Sika. It was a smallish, unimpressive town and did not tempt Jess the way Beelwaro had.

The two travelers were met there by Hojun's cousin, who gave them beds in his own home to sleep in that night. The next morning, he brought them back to the river, to a small wooden fishing boat mounted with a single lateen sail, and introduced them to its naked, grey-haired, gap-toothed owner.

That man, in turn, took the pair down the Hwikeihi along with a cargo of salted fish.

Shortly after nightfall, as the lights of Jezic were being lit not far ahead, the aged fisherman bid his nude, sunbaked passengers hide themselves in a small compartment at the boat's stern. There, in that hot, close space, the two remained for several hours, bathing themselves in their own sweat and absorbing the aromas seeping from the mountain of preserved fish that was heaped up around their ankles.

Eventually, Jess felt the little boat banging against a pier and almost cried at the thought that she would shortly be getting out of the compartment where she was hiding.

A few minutes later, the door to this opened and a dark figure reached out its hand and helped Jess onto her feet. In the light of Shokai's moons she could vaguely discern the features of the fisherman and was relieved she was looking at him and not at some soldier come to arrest her.

Another man, who was standing on the pier, gestured to her as the fisherman helped Luhit up, and Jess walked over to him, watching her step carefully so that she would not slip on the piles of fish that filled the boat.

When she was near this person, Jess could see that he was dressed in the apron worn by members of the fourth estate.

"You Nino?" he asked.

"Yeah. That's me alright," Jess replied.

"Come with me. I'm here to take you to Gople Sing."

When Luhit had joined this pair, the man in the apron led the travelers to a warehouse perched above the river.

"This building's owned by a friend of ours. We can sleep here tonight."

"We're not joining Sing right now?" Jess asked him.

"No. There's a curfew. If we're caught out after dark, we'll be shot on the spot. We'll be safe in here."

Inside the warehouse, the man brought them to an office where several mattresses had been placed on the floor.

"I got some mattresses from the workers' dormitory earlier. We can sleep on these tonight."

"Is there anything to eat or drink, especially to drink?" Jess asked him. "I feel like I'm about to die."

"Yeah. I'll get you something from the refectory."

After the man had fed her and Luhit, Jess, exhausted from her journey, lay down upon one of the mattresses on the floor and immediately went to sleep.

When she awoke the next morning, she cleaned her face and body as best she could in the sink in the toilet adjoining the office, retouched her skin with the dye Buabyue had given her, and arranged the wig upon her brow.

Seeing his guest was done readying herself for the day ahead, the man who had met her and Luhit fed them breakfast and took them to a car parked outside the factory.

Opening the door, he leaned inside the vehicle and lifted up the cushion of the back seat, revealing a hidden compartment.

"Oh, not another hidden compartment," Jess moaned.

"This is how we've got to do it," the man told her.

With a sigh, Jess said, "At least the car's air-conditioned and there aren't any fish."

The ride was cramped, unpleasant, and seemed to go on forever, but, fortunately, the vehicle was never stopped.

When the cushion above her and Luhit was removed, Jess found herself outside what looked like an abandoned apartment building.

The man who was smuggling Jess informed her, "This is an abandoned apartment building."

"Oh really?" the girl asked, feeling a little bit tired and irritable.

"Yes. There's an entrance to the sewers here."

"Excuse me?" Jess said.

"We're going through the sewers."

"Why?"

"They empty into Mudtown."

"Okay. Lead the way."

The man took Jess and Luhit into the crumbling building, down a flight of rickety stairs, and to the basement. There, he found a manhole, removed its metal cover, and told the others to climb down the ladder within. This took them to a wide tunnel with a vaulted roof through the middle of which, between two narrow walkways, ran a sluggish, foul smelling stream.

The man from Jezic came down the ladder behind the others, produced a torch from a pouch hanging at his waist, and said, "This way."

Jess followed him, but, naked as she was, she did her best not to touch the slimy wall to her side or any of the often unidentifiable but invariably filthy objects that were scattered along the path before her.

The group walked through the sewer for some time, until Jess had grown quite tired. She was, consequently, relieved when she saw a circle of sunlight ahead of her.

The end of the sewer was a large tube that simply stuck out of the side of the hill atop which most of Jezic was built and emptied the waste it carried from above onto one of the streets of Mudtown.

Beside the stinking river that flowed between the shanties and domes where the Jaffrites lived, Jess saw a pair of the creatures standing next to a cart.

Her guide motioned for her to go to it. "Here, get in the back of the wagon, under the tarp."

Jess and Luhit did as that man had instructed them and he joined them as soon as they were concealed. The Jaffrites then grabbed ahold of the long poles projecting from the front of the cart and pulled it through the street.

They shortly turned from that road and thereafter made their way through countless narrow, filthy pathways and alleys until they arrived at a dilapidated dome in front of which stood a half rotted carved pole propped up with several pieces of broken timber and a sheet of discarded metal.

One of the Jaffrites tapped on the side of the wagon, and Jess's guide told her, "We're here. Get out and get inside the door as quickly as you can."

Jess hopped out and dashed inside the domed house, followed by the two men. The Jaffrites remained outside.

# Chapter 40
## Concealment

Within the Jaffrite dome, past the vestibule, three of those creatures were squatting on the dirt floor between the rough pillars used to support the roof.

When they saw the new arrivals, one of them gestured to Jess's guide. He went over to the rubbery beast, which led him, Jess, and Luhit through a low passage at the back of the chamber and into a second dome beyond. Walking past four more Jaffrites which were squatting there, they crept through another passage and entered a third dome.

There Jess saw Gople Sing sitting, together with several of his followers, upon a low platform that ran around the edge of the chamber.

Jess immediately thought of Syo and scanned the room to see if she was there. She was not, which saddened Jess a little, as she would have liked to see that Syo was well. Then she remembered Eshwurhiyo and immediately felt waves of anxiety spilling out of her mind to pervade the whole of her body. She was not eager to explain to Gople what had happened to his sister in Quanya, and she was afraid that the gangster might blame her for the disaster there.

Standing up, Gople walked over to his guest and said in his deep, booming voice, "Jess Ichikawa. How are you, love? Well, I hope."

"I'm fine. This is Luhit. He works for Buabyue."

"I'm Gople Sing," that man informed Luhit.

"Yeah. Yeah. I'm pleased to meet you, sir."

"I hope you two have brought me good news. Things have not been going well here."

"So I see," Luhit noted, his hands flopping about before his face.

"Yes. I assure you I don't usually live in such accommodations."

"I have a message for you from Buabyue," Jess interjected.

She took the message wand Buabyue had given her from the bottomless pouch hanging from a gold chain enwrapping her waist and handed it to Gople.

He held it up and said, "If he says what I think he will, we should be able to act within a few days. I'll look at it right now. Why don't you two have a seat? I'll have some food brought for you. I'm sure you must be hungry."

"Yeah, I am," replied Jess, who was feeling both relieved and concerned that Gople had not yet mentioned his sister.

"Please rest yourselves." Gople motioned to the platform running along the wall.

Jess and Luhit both sat down and Gople left the room. A few minutes later, another gangster entered carrying a tray of food and set this between the two newcomers.

Luhit looked at the piles of pea-green noodles and chunks of things he did not recognize. Then, moving the dish rapidly up and down, he asked, "What is this?"

The gangster looked at him. "Haroko gnwi."

Jess's translator did not translate this phrase, taking it as a proper name, but Luhit's obviously did.

"Green noodles?" he asked. "Yeah. I see that. But what are they made of?"

"Hunna."

"Yeah. And what's that?"

"Don't worry about it," said Jess as she picked up a bowl and began sucking up the noodles in it. "It's just a plant they grow here. Eat your food. It won't kill you."

Luhit grudgingly did so and the two consumed their meal in silence.

Shortly after they had finished, Gople returned and sat in a chair that one of his underlings had carried in for him.

"I've looked at Buabyue's message," he said. "I'm very pleased, and Malotrue will be as well."

"I'm glad to hear it," Jess said with a smile.

"We should be able to act by the day after tomorrow, by Tuesday."

Luhit scratched his brow with one hand and let the other flail about in front of his face. "That soon?"

"Yes. Most everything is already prepared. With Buabyue's money, we can pay off enough people to reduce the odds against us considerably, and with his information we can get into the palace. We just need to distribute the bribes and make contact with his accomplices. That should be done by tomorrow."

"At least we don't have to wait long," Jess added.

"Now," Gople said, "allow me to treat you to a cup of madiro. It's very nice."

"Thanks," Jess replied.

A tattooed gangster entered the room holding a tray whereupon rested several cups and a clay jar with a round belly. He set the tray on the platform beside Luhit and poured a slightly pinkish liquid from the jar into each of the cups, handing these to Jess, Luhit, and Gople.

"What is it?" Jess asked.

"Madiro."

"I mean, what's madiro?"

Gople laughed. "It's fermented hunna, love."

Jess sipped hers and commented, "It's very sweet. I like it."

"I'm surprised you haven't had any since you arrived on Shokai."

"I had a bottle of something that was a lot stronger than this when I first came here. It wasn't this tasty, though."

"It was probably shobat. That's also made of hunna, but it's much stronger than madiro is."

"Maybe that was it, then. I like this better."

Jess took a deep breath and said, "About Quanya..."

Gople interrupted her. "You don't have to explain. I don't blame you. Eshwurhiyo knew she might not be coming back when she left Jezic."

"What about Syo? How is she?"

"She's alive, and she's doing a lot better than she was when you sent her back from Hwiccho."

"I'm glad to hear it. I felt really bad for her."

"She's here with me now if you'd like to see her."

"I'd like that actually, but only if she doesn't mind seeing me."

"I'm sure she feels the same as I do."

Gople turned to one his henchman and instructed him, "Send Syo in."

The man nodded, left the room, and, a few minutes later, retuned with Syo.

Naked and wrapped in jewelry, Syo walked over to the others with an air of sensual (if somewhat melancholic) dignity and sat down next to Jess. She looked much better than she had the last time Jess had seen her, although she lacked the vivacity she had had when she had been with Eshwurhiyo.

"How are you, Jess?" she asked.

"I'm fine. How are you?"

The woman was smiling, but Jess thought (or maybe just imagined) that there was something venomous in her tone or in the shapes her eyes assumed when she looked at her former companion.

"Everything's good," Syo informed her. "Gople's really helped me get over what happened. He's even taken me as his woman. I guess that means that if everything goes well over the next few days I'm going to wind up very rich. Yeah, things have worked out for me."

Jess was sure Syo was holding something back. Her speech was painfully insincere. Was she unhappy being Gople's lover? Undoubtedly. Could she think Jess was responsible for Eshwurhiyo's death? Probably. Did she want revenge? Possibly. It would be wise, Jess thought, to watch Syo carefully. Not only was she a good fighter, but she also knew many people in Jezic and was sleeping with Gople Sing.

For now, Jess smiled pleasantly at her. "I'm glad to hear that, Syo."

Gople poured the woman a cup of madiro.

"I assume Ofu didn't come back with you," she said to Jess.

There was ire in that!

"I think he died when the iliyo destroyed Ekeya."

"The iliyo?"

"Yeah. Ngo hired one of their clans as mercenaries."

"Did you know that, Gople?" Syo asked.

"Yes. Buabyue sent me a message. Now, I must excuse myself. I have preparations to make."

The gangster stood up and looked at Jess and Luhit. "Until we're able to act, you'll need to stay in hiding."

"Where?" Jess asked.

"Here in Mudtown. You're going to be staying in a mudjumper den."

His hands and rodent-like face all twitching, Luhit asked, "Can you trust those creatures?"

"They know that Soniyo's going to clear out Mudtown. They're either going to be killed off or sent to a preserve run by Ngo."

Luhit was still unconvinced. "Yeah. Yeah. But are they smart enough to realize that's not going to be good for them?"

"Even animals can figure out that they aren't going to want that. Besides, I've made some deals with the mudjumpers' leaders. They're going to provide us with shelter right now. When Buabyue's friends are in power and we're taking over Ngo's place, they're going to get a cut of the profits. Don't get me wrong, though, it won't be too much. Come on. I'll send you to your new home."

Gople motioned for a handsome but severe looking young woman to come over to him. "Karino, love, take Jess and Luhit to the quarters I arranged for them."

"Alright," the woman replied with a bow.

Jess turned to Syo as she left and grasped that woman's hands. "It was good to see you again, Syo. I'm glad you're okay."

"I feel the same," the other replied.

The woman into whose custody Gople had delivered Jess and Luhit led that pair back the way they had come, then bid them wait by the front entrance while she stepped outside. A moment later, she returned and motioned for them to exit the building.

In front of the door was a cart like the one that had conveyed them from the sewer. Knowing what was expected of them, Jess and Luhit crawled under the tarp covering its back, together with their most recent guide, and set off on another journey through the stinking alleys of Mudtown.

* * *

The complex of interconnected domes where Gople had sent Jess and Luhit was much like the one the gangster himself was hiding in.

Taking her charges inside, Karino addressed a Jaffrite sitting beside the entrance. "Gople Sing's sent you these two. You're supposed to hide them until we're ready."

The Jaffrite replied to her with a sequence of whistles and clicks that Jess's translator did not understand. The creature then gestured to one of its fellows, who was squatting in the middle of the dome, the dusty, smoky recesses of which were only half lit by the beam of light shining through a narrow opening in the roof.

The second Jaffrite approached Jess and the others and bid them follow it, leading them through the dome, a passage on its other side, a second dome, and a second passage. This last ended in a door made of corrugated metal that was fastened shut with an enormous padlock.

The Jaffrite lifted a key hanging as a sort of decoration from one of the chains it was wearing as jewelry, opened the lock, and bid its guests enter.

In the room before her, Jess saw a pair of Jaffrites hunched over a wide, low bowl set upon a tripod. In this vessel was a clutch of dozens of grey, leathery eggs, and the aliens were continuously whistling and clicking over these in an odd but musical way while scattering upon them flower petals and what appeared to be spices.

Jess looked at the creatures and realized that they were different from any of the others she had previously seen. Each was roughly the same size as any other adult Jaffrite, if noticeably fatter, but its tail was black and featureless instead of being colorful and complicated.

At first Jess thought the pair had been mutilated, but Karino, seeing her confusion, said to her while sitting down upon the low platform running along the dome's wall, "They're sows. We're going to be staying in the seraglio."

She laughed and shook her breasts vigorously. "We're going to be a mudjumper's whores."

Jess smiled and sat down next to Karino while Luhit stood over the females examining them and rubbing his greasy head with both his hands.

"You should be pretty safe here," Karino continued. "Except for Songbird, the head of the house, the one who let us in, no one is allowed in here, not even the other members of the house."

"Really?" Jess asked. "Why not?"

"Something like ninety-seven percent of mudjumpers are male, so these sows are precious. They've got to be sequestered and guarded. Besides, just look at them, aren't they gorgeous?"

Ignoring the last remark, Jess replied, "Yeah. Uluf, a friend of mine, did mention that most of them were male."

A few minutes later, the door was unlocked and opened again. The same Jaffrite that had shown them to the room, the one Karino had called Songbird, entered carrying a bottle and a stack of cups.

He set these in front of Jess and the others and lifted a translator set on a wand hanging from one of his gaudy chains. "I have brought you something to drink, my lord and my ladies."

Jess poured herself a cup. It was madiro, but this bottle was not nearly as good as was that Gople had provided. Still, she did not complain.

Jess put down her cup, took a handkerchief from the pouch she wore at her hip, and wiped her face. It was sticky with oil and dirt and sweat, as was the whole of her body.

Turning to Karino, she asked, "I don't suppose there's any way I could have a bath in here, is there?"

"Songbird, bring us a tub of water."

"As you desire, my lady," the Jaffrite replied and lurched out of the seraglio, closing and locking the door behind him.

A few minutes later he returned, whistled at the females, and watched them as they lit fires in several bowls of scented wood, placed these in front of a screen made of woven reeds that concealed about a quarter of the room, and crept behind that partition to cover themselves.

When they were hidden, Songbird whistled again and a pair of male Jaffrites carried in a large round tub made out of the stiffened hide of some animal.

They set this near Jess and left the room. While the girl was still inspecting the cauldron they had brought, the pair returned with leathern bags filled with water, which they poured into the tub. The two left and returned with water several more times, until they had completely filled the tub.

Jess tested the water with her hand. It was not warm, but as hot and stifling as the room was, she hardly minded. She was not even concerned that the water did not look particularly clean. It was water and that was all that mattered.

She did not waste any time adding more sweat to her sticky skin. She threw her wig onto the ground and crawled into the tub.

Dunking her head under the water and lifting it up again, Jess exclaimed, "Now that feels good."

"I guess I'm doing a fine job of watching over Sing, huh?" she added with a grin.

The two Jaffrite females and Songbird were watching Jess as she enjoyed her bath, and, seeing them staring at her, the girl suddenly felt uncomfortable.

She did not mind that Karino and Luhit were scrutinizing her, but she was bothered by the Jaffrites' doing so.

Their gaze reminded her of a time when she had been working in the brothel in Hosak and one of her clients had brought his dog in with him. The animal had sat on the floor and, with its head cocked to one side, had intently observed Jess and its master the entire time they were having sex. Although she was never sure why the dog's curious voyeurism had bothered her, it had.

"Do they ever leave?" Jess asked Songbird while gesturing at the females of his species.

"No, my lady."

"Oh."

Jess looked at Karino. "Is that true?"

"Have you ever been in Mudtown before?"

"Yeah. The last time I was in Jezic."

"Did you see any females here?"

"No. Actually, I didn't."

"There you go."

"Songbird," Jess said looking at the Jaffrite, "why do you keep your females locked up in here?"

"They belong to me. I am not going to let anyone else mate with them."

"Don't they have a say?"

Karino interjected. "The sows aren't just the patriarch's property, they're his treasure. The mudjumpers consider their females to be extremely valuable. For our slimy friends here, wealth comes down to how many females you have. They don't waste them, believe me. When an old mudjumper dies and hands over a house to his son, he hands over the kid's mother too. The new head doesn't just let her sit around after that, either. He starts mating with her. It seems disgusting, but I guess, since they're animals, it's okay.

"I wouldn't want to be a female mudjumper," Jess commented.

"Don't feel too bad for them, Jess. The boars don't have it so great, either. The sows may belong to the head of the house, but then, in a way, so do all the males living with him."

"Are they slaves?" Luhit inquired.

"No. Every mudjumper belongs to a house. They don't have proper families. It's like they're part of a herd, I suppose."

"Really?" Jess asked.

"Yes. The females produce a mess of eggs, but they'll almost all hatch out as males. They don't go off and marry or something like that when they get older. They stay and serve the head of the house they were hatched into. When the head dies, he picks one of his sons to succeed him. The way they look at it, the old boar gives his slimy little boy everything that 'pertains to the females.' That includes the sows themselves, the complex they live in, and everything in it. They see this whole place as nothing but a seraglio and a bunch of guardrooms. Anyway, the new head has total authority over his brothers, uncles, cousins, and whatever other males are in the house. Later on, when he has sons of his own, he'll have authority over them too."

"So all of the mudjumpers living in these connected domes are part of the same house?" Jess asked.

"Yes, and they all obey their head like his word is a command from heaven. They're totally loyal. How do you think their king has managed to stay around? He doesn't have any real power, but they still let him rule them. I suppose some insects are like that. Actually, it makes things simpler for us. We only have to deal with the head of a house. He speaks for all his followers."

"Could you hand me my drink?" Jess asked Karino.

"Hey," that woman called out to Songbird as she threw a clump of earth she had dug out of the platform at him. "Give Jess her drink."

"Yes, my lady."

The Jaffrite picked up Jess's cup, refilled it, and handed it to her.

Jess smiled at the creature and said, "Thanks."

"Songbird," Karino asked, "you'd obey your king, right?"

"Yes, my lady."

"If you had an argument with some other mudjumper and you two couldn't settle it between yourselves, you'd take it to the king, right?"

"I would send my underlings to fight anyone who attacked our house."

"Yeah, but you're a gangster. What would an ordinary house do?"

"The head of a house would go to the king. He will settle the disputes of his subjects if they cannot."

"What if one of them doesn't like the king's decision?" Karino asked. "Will he still do what the king says?"

"Yes."

"Even though the king can't really do much to him?"

"He would obey."

"See," Karino said to Jess. "There you go. They're like insects. Obeying is an instinct for them."

Jess turned to Songbird. "Why would you obey the king? What would happen if you didn't? Does he have police?"

"If I disobeyed the king, I would sever myself from his sanctity and be polluted. No other Jaffrite would deal with me. My house would be cut off from society until I submitted and cleansed myself."

"See," Jess said to Karino. "They have reasons. It's their religion."

"Don't be silly, Jess," Karino replied.

Jess sipped her madiro and scowled at her supervisor.

"Would you like some?" she asked Songbird.

"No, my lady."

"They don't drink that," Karino explained. "Songbird, why don't you go get some of your own marsh juice?"

"If my lady would like me to."

"Go get it."

The Jaffrite left the room and Karino told Jess, "You've got to see what they drink. It's disgusting."

"Have you tried it?"

"Certainly not."

"So, anyway, why do you call him Songbird?" Jess asked.

"Isn't it obvious? He loves to chatter."

"He's hardly said anything," Luhit noted.

"The name's ironic," Karino explained while rolling her eyes. "Just try to get him to say more than you few words. It can't be done. I suppose that's why Gople sent us to him. That and he has a huge family and sells a lot of russa to us."

While Karino was speaking, Songbird reentered the room carrying a large bowl. He set this down between the tub Jess was bathing in and the platform where Karino and Luhit were sitting.

The two offworlders leaned over to look at the marsh juice. It was a greenish, frothy sludge.

"It look's like mucus," Jess commented.

"What is it? Yeah. What is it?" Luhit asked.

"There's a kind of slug that swarms across the bottom of the ocean. The mudjumpers dive down and collect them. Then they crush the slugs' bodies into a pulp and ferment the slime. Isn't it repulsive?"

Jess had to admit that it did look unpleasant.

"How can you drink that stuff, Songbird?" Karino asked, but, before the Jaffrite could answer, the woman grabbed the container and tossed it onto the ground.

"Why'd you do that?" Jess snapped, angered at the woman's treatment of her host.

"You shouldn't get upset, Jess," Karino retorted while jangling some of the jewelry Songbird was wearing. "They're just animals, even if they like to pretend that they're humans. Stupid animals."

"I heard from my boss – yeah – he told me that they had civilizations before we did," Luhit said. "Yeah. That's what my boss told me before."

"Don't be ridiculous," Karino answered. "What kind of civilization are mudjumpers going to have? They don't use metal. They don't have machines. They barely even build fires."

"Whether they're animals or not isn't that important right now," Jess interjected. "Actually, I mostly want to know if it's going to be safe to stay with them here tonight."

"It'll be safe. They know how bad the situation is right now."

"I understand that. It's not what I was worried about, though."

"What then?"

"They're not going to try to eat us or anything like that, are they?"

"That's a strange concern."

"Well, what do they eat, then?"

"I don't know. Dirty things from the bottoms of rivers or the sea, I guess."

"In that case, could you get me some more madiro? I'm going to sit in my bath and get completely drunk."

# Chapter 41
## Coup

The day following Jess's arrival in Mudtown, a naked man covered with tattoos depicting various beasts fighting with one another and draped with gaudy jewelry was shown by Songbird into the seraglio.

Addressing the three humans he found there, the man asked, "Jess Ichikawa?"

Jess, naked except for a string around her waist, stood up from where she was lying on the platform by the dome's wall, scratched her head, arched her back, and yawned.

"Yeah. That's me."

"Sing wants you to go and get ready for the attack."

"Is the coup today?"

"We're going to be attacking tomorrow, just before dawn."

"Well, lead on," Jess said before picking up her black wig and arranging it on her head.

The man brought Jess out of the Jaffrites' complex to the street beyond, where she saw a wagon drawn by a pair of the rubbery creatures.

The gangster started to say something, but Jess interrupted him.

"Yes, I know. Get into the back of the cart and hide under the tarp."

"Good girl," he replied as she got into the back of the cart and hid under the tarp.

Once the man had joined her, the Jaffrites pulled the wagon through the streets of Mudtown for some time.

Tormented by the sun glaring down at Shokai and the ubiquitous cloud of dirt and smoke hovering across the Jaffrites' city, Jess thought she was going to expire before she had faced a single enemy. Sweat ran from every pore of her body, saturating her hair and making her feel grossly filthy. The trip was entirely unpleasant.

Eventually, as Jess was thinking that had her pores not been completely clogged with oil and dirt she would surely have sweated out every drop of water in her body, the wagon stopped. One of the Jaffrites lifted up the tarp at its back and motioned for Jess and the gangster to get out.

They had arrived at a tunnel leading to one of Jezic's sewers, though it was not the same one Jess had previously used to come to Mudtown.

Trying to avoid the stinking water that was flowing out of the wide passageway and down the street of the Jaffrites' town, Jess followed her latest guide into the sewer.

He led her down the narrow path that ran along its edge, holding a torch in one hand to light their way.

"Where are we going?" Jess inquired after they had traveled far enough for their voices to be inaudible to those outside.

"To Somnat Malotrue's mansion. He's the one we're helping to put on the throne."

"Yeah. I heard about him."

After wandering through the sewers for what seemed a lifetime to Jess, the man ahead of her turned off into a narrow side passage.

There was no ledge in this tunnel, and Jess was forced to wade (in her sandals) through a half inch of dirty water, occasionally stepping on squirming things that she was glad she was not able to see in the nearly complete darkness.

The two had gone down this way for a time when they arrived at a hole that had been dug through the stone wall to their left.

"Through here," Jess's companion instructed her.

She entered into the tunnel after him and saw, in the dim light of his lantern, a rope ladder hanging from a vertical shaft in the ceiling.

"We have to go up there," the gangster said. "You go first."

"Fine," Jess replied and began scaling the ladder, while her companion illumined both the girl's way and her naked body, the posterior end of which he carefully examined as it swung back and forth in front of his face.

At the ladder's top was a solid piece of wood. Jess tried to move it but it would not budge.

"Knock on it four times, pause, then knock twice more."

Jess did so and, a moment later, heard the sound of something heavy being slid across the top of the wood. Then the wood itself was moved and a hand reached down from above to help her up.

Once her eyes had adjusted to the brilliant sunlight around her, Jess realized that she was standing under an awning that extended from the wall of a courtyard.

A group of naked men whose bodies were decorated with elaborate patterns of gold paint were standing around her.

One of the men helped Jess's companion out of the sewer, bowed to him, and asked, "This is the girl?"

"Yes."

Another of the gold adorned men bowed to Jess and told her, "Come with me. I'll take you to the people you'll be helping."

Having looked up to see that the courtyard wherein she was standing was attached to the base of a pale green mushroom-like tower, Jess followed the person who had addressed her through a wooden door set in the wall to her right.

This opened onto a corridor that, in turn, led to a large refectory where a group of men wearing budenovkas and elaborate, colorful garments decorated with ribbons, medallions, and lace trim were sitting at a long table eating noisily and talking loudly with one another.

They looked up when Jess entered the room, and one of them, their captain, inquired of the man with her, "Is this the girl who's coming with us?"

"She's the one."

The mercenary, who was obviously not from Shokai, motioned for Jess to come to him. She did so while the gold painted servant remained standing at the entrance to the room.

As she sat, Jess noticed blond hair coming out from under the man's cap.

"You have yellow hair," she said to him. "That's unusual."

"Not where we come from."

"Is it real?"

"Yes."

Jess reached out her hand and pulled a lock of the man's hair out from his budenovka so that she could inspect it.

"Is your hair this color everywhere?"

The man placed one of his feet on the bench he and Jess were sitting on, pulled up the leg of his trousers, and showed her the blond hair covering his calf and shin.

Jess smiled and said, "That isn't the place I was wondering about, but I guess it answers my question."

The man grinned back at her. "I'll show the other bit later. Right now, I ought to tell you what our plans are."

"Go ahead."

"It's pretty simple, really. Every morning, just before dawn, a truck delivers fish to the palace kitchens. We're going to be in the next shipment that arrives."

"Great. More fish."

"Sorry. What's that?"

"Forget it. Just go on."

"Anyway, our friends here have paid off the guards who'll be watching the gates we'll be going through, so we shouldn't have any trouble there. They've also paid the kitchen worker who accepts the delivery. He'll let us into the palace."

"Will he be the only one there?"

"No. We'll have to try to avoid the other workers."

"Why didn't they pay some more of them off?"

"The more people who know something beforehand, the more chances there are for us to be betrayed. One accomplice in the kitchen is enough to get us in. If his friends see us, we'll deal with them then."

"That makes sense."

The captain took a piece of paper out of a pocket at his hip. When he had unfolded this, Jess saw that it was a map of the palace.

The man continued. "We'll go through this passage here. That'll take us out of the kitchens. Then we have to make it up these stairs and down this corridor, and this one. Our target, Soniyo Dogrue, the new ruler of this country, should be in here. This is her suite, and this is her bedroom. We're going to capture her if we can, but, if we can't get her out of the palace, we're just going to kill her."

"It sounds simple enough."

"It's a long way from the kitchens to Soniyo's bedroom. We're going to have to be careful we don't meet a guard. There are troops wandering through the palace. Once we've got our target, it's going to get even harder. She's likely to make a fuss and could easily alert her soldiers."

"How are we actually getting out?"

"While we're in there, some soldiers working for our patron are going to show up at the palace to help with the trouble there. They're supposed to create enough of a distraction for us to get behind them."

"Okay."

"Just follow my lead while we're in the palace."

"I will."

"Good. Now, why don't you have something to eat? There's a window in the back wall. I'm going to sleep when I'm done with my food. I suggest you do the same. Your friend back there will come and get you in the middle of the night when it's time for us to get ready."

\* \* \*

When Jess rejoined the mercenaries later that night, she found them all dressed in black armor made of interlocking pieces of some dull plastic-like material. To the front of his budenovka each had fastened a veil, and each had daubed the area around his eyes with black paint.

The mercenaries did not have armor that would fit Jess, but one of Malotrue's gold decorated servants provided her with a black catsuit sewn from threads capable of giving her some protection against needles and edged weapons.

Jess took off her black wig, handed it to a naked servant, and asked for a budenovka. One of the mercenaries took a spare from a pouch he carried and handed it to her.

Covering her face with a black veil, Jess informed the others, "Okay, let's go."

The mercenaries went into another courtyard, where they waited in the moist, relatively cool night air. After about a quarter of an hour, a gate opened and a truck shaped something like a snail with a long, spiraling shell extending far behind its head slid into the courtyard.

"This is it," the captain said to the others as the driver got out of the vehicle and opened a door in its side.

Jess followed the mercenaries through this, making her way over heaps of refrigerated fish, and entered into a small compartment at the very back of the vehicle. There the group huddled as the truck left Malotrue's mansion and rushed through the streets of Jezic to the roshpai's palace.

As nervous as she was, Jess felt as though the journey happened so fast that it was over almost as soon as it had started. She had not realized that they had been motioned through the palace gates by the guards posted there and had arrived at the kitchens until the driver had opened the compartment behind his cargo of fish and the mercenaries surrounding her began pouring out.

They were in a garage in front of a loading dock opening onto a cavernous kitchen.

A young man wearing an apron gestured to the mercenaries to follow him.

He led them into the kitchens, which were then only occupied by three other cooks, all of whom, Jess thought, must have been bribed, in spite of what the captain had told her. The worker guiding Jess and her companions then took them to the other side of the vast room and pointed to a door.

"Through here. Hurry," he hissed, urging the assassins forward.

They, two abreast, with Jess and the captain forming their second rank, rushed down the unadorned corridor beyond the kitchens and came unopposed to a flight of stairs.

There was no one about. The passage was obviously intended for the use of servants, and none of them had as yet begun his daily routine.

The mercenaries made their way up the flight of stairs at the end of the corridor as quickly and quietly as they could.

When they had come to the landing at the top of the stairs, the captain moved in front of his men and, cracking open the door there, peeked through.

He motioned for the others to follow him as he went on, and the group, resuming its earlier formation, stealthily made its way down the hallway, over shining marble floors and past stone walls decorated with bas-reliefs set between pillars carved into the shapes of lovely young women.

They came to another corridor leading off to the left under an arch of alabaster filigree, and the captain looked around the corner.

He jerked back and held up two fingers, indicating that there were two guards. Having touched his own chest and pointed to one of his men, he held up his palm to the others.

The captain and the man he had chosen, each bearing a kriss in one hand and a needle gun in the other, crept around the corner and tiptoed down the darkened corridor towards the two men leaning against the walls at its far end, on either side of the pair of wide doors that led to Soniyo's suite.

The captain and his soldier intended to attack the guards at close quarters and slit their throats before they could cry out, believing that those men, being at most half awake, would be easy to kill. Unfortunately, just as the mercenaries were nearly upon them, one of their intended victims stirred and caught a glimpse of his enemies.

He was not able to cry out before the captain jumped upon him, covered his mouth, and drew his dagger across his prey's jugular.

The noise the mercenary made, though slight, was enough to rouse the second guard. Without need of thought, he flipped a switch on a mechanism on his belt and then died as his blood sprayed out of his throat, the captain's companion having slit it.

Iron bars fell from the lintel of the door before the assassins, blocking their path.

The pair immediately drew lasers from their belts and began to cut through the bars.

Jess, along with the other mercenaries, ran to the two and, seeing what they were doing, said, "Get back. I'll open it."

She extended the blade of her sword from its hilt and swung it across the top, the bottom, and both the sides of the grille, cutting the iron bars as though they were made of paper.

Two of the soldiers grabbed the barrier and tossed it onto the floor while the captain opened the doors.

The group entered into a large but unoccupied sitting room, and the captain led the others through it into a second sitting room. At the far end of this was another door blocked by iron bars.

"Soniyo should be through here," the captain shouted.

Jess hurried to the door in front of her and cut through the bars blocking their passage as she had done before.

One of the mercenaries swung the door open, but immediately collapsed onto the ground dead.

The others dove to take cover.

Jess dropped behind a nearby chair, barely avoiding several projectiles fired in her direction.

Taking a deep breath, she peeked out from behind the chair and saw in the next room a number of teal uniformed men armed with needle rifles surrounding a naked and attractive young woman holding a dog by one of his hind legs.

While several guards were hurriedly leading the frightened woman away, the mercenaries began firing at the half dozen who remained behind, shooting down two of them.

As the guards shot back and killed one of the would-be assassins, Jess lifted the thread up her spine, using it, when it was alive and quivering inside her body, to lasso time and hold it captive as though it were on a leash.

Imposing her will on what she ordinarily perceived as the external world, but which she knew was entirely within her mind when the thread was roused, Jess forced away the air in front of her. Though it took a great amount of energy to do so, she in this way scattered the needles that were shot at her as she jumped from where she had been crouching.

She flew with impossible speed towards her enemies and fell upon them unharmed.

The torsos and arms of three of the guards were all cleft in two with a single swing of her sword. The last man, while yet moving to train his gun upon his attacker, died when his cranium, and both of his eyes, were bisected by Dawn's Spine.

Her foes dead, Jess looked around and saw the door through which had fled the naked woman (who must, she knew, have been Soniyo).

Jess raced to this and threw it open. On the other side was another sitting room, but, as this was empty, she hurried across it, at a speed twice that another human being could move, to the door facing her.

She opened this in turn.

Jess did not notice if Soniyo was in the corridor beyond. She was far too distracted by the great mass of soldiers running towards her.

She closed the door immediately, while her foes were still raising their needle rifles to fire at her, and turned to rush back into the bedroom.

Several of the mercenaries were a short distance behind her, including the captain, and Jess, having let time return to its usual speed, shouted to them, "There are more soldiers coming. We've got to get out of here fast."

Shoving two of the men to get them moving, Jess ran past them and retraced her steps through Soniyo's suite, repeating her words as she passed more of her companions.

The captain was just behind her and, as Jess entered the corridor outside the roshpatni's room, she heard him say, "Go back the way we came! It's the quickest way out."

The intruders raced down the hallway, but, when they arrived at the stairs, they were met by ten soldiers carrying needle guns.

Jess, again reducing the advance of time to a crawl, dove at her adversaries before they could aim their weapons and decapitated four of them. The captain jumped after her and buried his kriss in one man's throat. Two more of the guards fell under the fire of the remaining mercenaries.

While turning round to take a second life, the captain let a knife penetrate his breast and staggered back. A second blow, this one to his neck, brought his days to an end.

The man who killed him did not, however, outlive him by long. Jess split him into separate right and left halves and then did the same to one of his fellows.

The last of her foes, seeing what the girl had done, collapsed onto the ground at her feet and began to wail and grovel. Jess did feel sorry for him when she saw his fear, but she still divided his torso from his hips.

Leaving the captain's corpse behind, Jess (who released time in order to let her comrades keep up with her) hurried with the others back down to the kitchens (now filled with cooks lighting ovens and laying out the ingredients of the dishes they thought they would shortly be making) and came to the garage.

At the far end of this was a large wooden gate. Jess ran to it, cut a way through it with her sword, and dashed out of the palace. There was a wall in front of her, but this was pierced with another gate set between a pair of sentry boxes.

Not waiting for her companions, Jess slowed time again and hurtled towards the sentry posts so fast her feet seemed to rest upon the air itself rather than the cobblestones beneath her.

She came to the structure to her right and stabbed the man standing in it through his neck. The other soldier tried to aim at the girl in the catsuit as she nearly flew at him, but he fumbled with his weapon in his fear and allowed her to sweep her sword from his right shoulder to his left hip and chop his body into two separate parts.

Jess looked out in front of her at a wide square surrounded by beehive-like temples and bullet shaped houses.

For just a moment she thought she was going to be able to flee without having to fight again. Then, as soon as she had let time return to its ordinary pace, she saw a large body of men streaming into the square from a street opening onto it on her right.

Each of these persons was wearing a conical hat tipped with a red plumed spike, shoes with curling toes, baggy red trousers decorated with a ridiculously large, armored codpiece, and a dark blue tunic with swallow tails, loose sleeves, and a big, red collar.

Jess had seen such persons when she had first arrived in Jezic, both at the spaceport and at the March of the Dead, and knew they were policemen.

They organized themselves directly in front of Jess, blocking her path, though they did not seem to take any notice of her, and pointed their plumed halberds in the direction whence they had come.

After them, another body of uniformed men, who were obviously soldiers, marched into the square and positioned themselves directly in front of the policemen. All of these individuals were wearing tall, pointed hats (like medieval hennins) and close fitting orange jackets with flared skirts (like great bells) that reached to their ankles,

A man capped with a golden miter adorned with white plumes and riding an antigravity sled then came up from behind the soldiers and positioned himself in front of them. He held a microphone before his mouth and addressed the crowd of policemen.

"Do not block our path. We have received word that an attempt has been made on Roshpatni Soniyo's life and have come to protect her from her enemies. Any effort to detain us will be understood as an act of treason."

When the man had spoken, one of the policemen made his way to the front of his fellows and, without a microphone, yelled out in response, "And we have been commanded by her majesty's castellan not to let anyone into the palace. No exceptions are to be made."

"I then declare you to be rebels against the queen," the man in the sled called out and motioned for his men to advance upon the others.

As the policemen drew their needle guns, held their halberds pointed towards their foes, and readied themselves for a fight, Jess heard shouts coming from behind her. She looked around and saw a group of palace guards rushing at her.

Unable to flee from these persons, since the policemen blocked their way, the mercenaries began firing at their assailants while Jess held Dawn's Spine by her ear and readied herself to kill them once they had come closer.

She did not get the chance to do so. The policemen behind were being slaughtered by the trained soldiers attacking them and were breaking rank in increasing numbers. Many of them were fleeing wherever they could see what looked like a promising escape route, but many others were simply falling back. As they shuffled across the square, they approached Jess and the mercenaries, until they were virtually on top of them.

Jess, seeing policemen coming at her, slowed time and fell upon the nearest of them. She severed one head after another, racing up and down the ranks engulfing her, but as many of the constables as she slew, still more replaced them. They were far more terrified of the soldiers attacking them from the other direction than they were of a single girl with a sword and so kept retreating in her direction. Jess, whatever her skill, could not kill as many people as could an entire army.

Seeing how the policemen were being handily dispatched, the palace guards who were attacking the mercenaries turned around and fled the way they had come.

The failed assassins took the opportunity to flee themselves and escaped from the square into a road opening onto it.

Having been separated from her companions, Jess was unable to join them in their retreat. However, as the force of policeman had now completely dissolved and the surviving men were either doing their best to get away from their attackers or surrendering to them, she was in little danger.

The soldiers of Tozana's army rushed past Jess as she stood in the square watching the end of the brief battle that had been fought there. She saw the orange clad warriors fighting with those few guards who offered them resistance; she saw them binding those who surrendered, and she saw them pushing their way into the palace.

It would not take them long to overrun it. Although Soniyo might have escaped with her life, she was not going to escape with her position.

# Chapter 42
## Between Storms

T soi was gazing out across the expanse of the ocean and admiring how the waters shone in the night with the lights of Quanya and the rays of Shokai's moons. He felt surprisingly relaxed (considering all his current worries) while looking at such a vision and leaning against the railing that ran along the edge of the long semicircular balcony that projected from one of the skyscrapers of his palace.

This particular building, that rose up behind its dreaming owner, was carved into a series of figures like a thousand foot tall totem pole. One of these sculptures was of a young woman who held in her hand a vessel from which a fierce beast was drinking. The vessel formed the base of the balcony, and the mouth of the beast formed a great arch at one of its ends.

Tsoi turned around, rested his backside against the railing, and exhaled loudly in an effort to clear his mind of a brief annoyance that had intruded upon his thoughts. He had suddenly recalled how his executioner had allowed Eshwurhiyo to die (even though he had wanted her to live long enough for Gople to see her being tortured) and how her body had been fed to his servants without his having authorized it. Still, those who had been responsible for the latter error were now themselves being consumed by their fellows and the torturer had been suitably punished. Tsoi smiled and let his mind turn back to what was now before his eyes.

A short distance away, Hyan was reclining on a couch idly toying with one of her braids while chewing upon the tip of another. Her father, Lo, was walking across the balcony, over the pornographic mosaics with which it was paved, towards one of the statues that held the lanterns that lit the place. These sculptures were arranged in a row along the top of the railing and were shaped like pairs of male, female, and transgendered lovers in different combinations, though every couple was intertwined in sexual embrace.

In one of his hands Lo held a pile of nuts and was eating these as he took to looking out over the ocean, discarding the shells into the waters with jerky motions that revealed his current irritation.

"You needn't be so angry, Uncle," Tsoi informed him after watching the man for a few moments.

"Things are getting worse and worse. We're heading for a catastrophe, and we've only just avoided one."

"What? Do you mean my fighting ship? You didn't even have to use it."

"But we still have it, and, if we're caught with it, we're all dead."

"It's safely put away now. You shouldn't worry so much, Uncle."

Lo turned at him with an infuriated expression.

Visibly calming himself, he said, "You're ruining us, Tsoi. Whatever you think you've accomplished on Suturik has been undone in Tozana. Besides, that whole expedition to Suturik was foolhardy. Show some sense."

Hyan, still chewing on one of her braids, looked up at the pair. She did not say a word.

Tsoi smiled at her and turned back towards the ocean.

"You will have to wait, Uncle," he said. "I assure you, we're not beaten yet."

"My lord," announced Tsoi's prune-faced old major-domo as he emerged from the entryway.

"What?" the man's master replied.

"Soniyo Dogrue has arrived."

"Bring her to me."

"Yes, my lord."

The major-domo left the balcony and returned a few moments later with Soniyo, who was elegantly dressed in a tight white choli and an equally tight pink skirt that emphasized the curves of her body.

As attractive as he found her figure, Tsoi still could not prevent himself from being distracted by her oddly pointed head and the plate-like whorl of hair sitting upon its peak.

The woman sauntered across the balcony, trying to appear simultaneously seductive and angry, but, when she noticed the obscene images formed by the tiles below her feet, she nearly stumbled and dropped the hadishyen she was carrying under one arm.

Distracted, she stood looking at the figures for a moment. Then, remembering her purpose, she continued over to stand in front of Tsoi.

"Hello, Tsoi," she said with a venomous smile.

"Hello, Soniyo."

"Roshpatni Soniyo."

"Whatever."

"No, not whatever. Roshpatni Soniyo."

"I think not."

Soniyo's face was turning red. She screamed, "If I'm not, it's your fault!"

"And how is that?"

"What about the help you promised me?"

"Your majesty, I'm afraid that you've proved to be less competent than even I expected you would be. It's certainly not my fault that you took hardly any precautions after you seized the throne. I was originally going to help you out, but I thought better of it."

"Oh, you're not going to sit by and leave me to crawl away somewhere and hide. I know what you've been up to."

Lo, who had been concerned with staring at Soniyo's breasts, suddenly looked at her face.

Tsoi grimaced, in spite of his efforts to remain unaffected, and seeing this, Soniyo grinned at him maliciously.

"Don't you remember our last meeting? You told me you'd found out something about the Llalloi, where they were, and you said you were going to take care of them. Maybe you thought I wasn't listening? I'm not stupid, Tsoi. I have ears in your palace just like you have ears in mine. I heard what you were up to."

"You are beautiful, your majesty," the hadishyen interjected.

Soniyo slapped its cranium and went on. "Oh, I know about your little ether-ship, the one the Pancloans will kill you for if they find out you have it."

Tsoi swallowed audibly.

"So, don't you think you should help me out?" Soniyo asked. "Let's help each other. How about that?"

"The beauty of the stars pales before that of your shining eyes, your majesty," the hadishyen informed its mistress.

"Shut up, you repulsive little animal," Tsoi snapped at it.

"Don't you talk to my dear little friend like that," Soniyo barked back.

Tsoi, giving in to his frustration and anger, snatched the hadishyen out of Soniyo's arms and tossed it off the balcony to fall a thousand feet into the sea or onto the rocks along its shore.

Soniyo stood with her mouth hanging open staring at Tsoi for so long he actually began to feel uncomfortable.

He was turning away to leave her when she unclasped a silver rod attached to the top of her skirt just below her navel. It was not some sort of buckle, as it appeared to be, but the handle of a dagger.

Soniyo extended its telescoping blade and lunged at Tsoi before he realized what was happening, burying her weapon in his stomach up to its hilt.

Tsoi hit her nose with his fist and knocked her onto the floor.

"You clot! You whore!" he shouted while looking at the knife handle projecting from his torso.

He removed his artificial nails, grabbed Soniyo's hair just below the whorl at the top of her head, and yanked her onto her feet. She looked at him in panicky terror, but did nothing to resist.

Tsoi shoved her against a statue of a man and a kathoey and began pummeling her face with his fist, until little could be seen of her smashed features beneath the blood gushing forth from her injuries.

Eventually, Tsoi regained his composure and, though still holding onto Soniyo, stopped hitting her. He stood looking at the woman with contempt and annoyance.

She, crazed with humiliation, pain, and fury, took the opportunity Tsoi so gave her and lunged at him, raking bloody furrows into his left cheek with her fingernails.

Reacting to his own pain without thought, Tsoi seized ahold of Soniyo's head and started pounding it against the statue behind her.

"You whore!" he screamed at her as he repeatedly slammed her cranium onto the stone.

The woman flailed about impotently and attempted to scratch at her attacker, without success, until, with an unpleasantly wet popping sound, the back of her skull cracked open.

She made a gurgling, gulping noise and looked up at Tsoi with wide eyes that shone white in her dark red face.

Her assailant was not moved to pity by her gaze. He continued bashing her head on the statue, feeling and listening to her skull crumbling as he did so.

Pieces of Soniyo's brain and slivers of her cranium splattered around her, and her blood seemed to spray everywhere, soaking both her clothes and Tsoi's. He did not, however, stop, but, instead, continued his attack until nothing remained of her head that could be recognized as such.

Exhausted by the emotional intensity of Soniyo's killing, rather than by his physical exertions, Tsoi let the woman's body slide onto the floor and staggered backwards, to rest against the statue behind him.

Hyan and Lo were both staring at the head of their house. The former was still lying upon her couch chewing on one of her braids, but her father stood with his mouth hanging open and his brows pinched with anger.

"Don't you think her people are going to say something about your ethership now that you've killed her? You really have ruined us now, Tsoi."

"Uncle…" Tsoi started to reply, but, before he could finish his sentence, Lo had pulled a kuttar from his belt and was running at his nephew.

Tsoi drew a dagger of his own and jumped to the side, an action that sent rays of pain slicing through his body from the knife burning in his stomach.

Lo spun round and lunged at Tsoi again, but the younger man hit his uncle in his left eye with his fist and managed to cut the man's left shoulder with his blade.

"There's no need for this, Uncle," Tsoi wheezed while holding the handle of the dagger sticking into his body.

"I'm not letting your nonsense go any further!" Lo shouted back. "My son is already dead, and the rest of us will be soon if I let you keep this up."

Tsoi again avoided Lo's attack when that man again rushed at him, and again wounded his assailant, this time across his breast. The injury was superficial, however, and only increased Lo's wrath.

The older man bent over and ran at Tsoi as though he intended to ram him in the stomach, but, as Tsoi stabbed downwards, Lo revealed his move to be a feint. He seized his opponent's wrist, swung him against one of the statues rising from the railing, and tried to stab him in the breast.

Tsoi was able to grab his uncle's wrist, and the pair stood face to face with Tsoi pressed against the statue and each of the combatants' blade inches from the other's body.

Tsoi felt his heart racing as he stared at his uncle and saw the irrational fury in the man's face. He knew he would not be able to overpower his enemy. His body was already weak from his injury and from the blood he had lost.

The panic that was beginning to well up inside of him suddenly gave way to confusion when Lo staggered backwards and released his wrist. Tsoi looked down and saw the tip of a blade pointing at him from where it emerged from Lo's heart.

Once the blade was withdrawn, Tsoi, letting go of his dying uncle's wrist, watched as Lo slowly turned round to see Hyan standing before him with her long, grey scimitar in her hand.

"I'm sorry, Daddy," she said.

Tears were pouring from her eyes as she again drove her sword under her victim's ribs and pierced his heart a second time.

Once Hyan had pulled out her blade, Lo fell onto the ground. His daughter knelt beside him and placed his head in her lap.

"I'm so sorry, Daddy. I just couldn't let you kill Tsoi. No matter what you think, we don't have a future without him. What could I do?"

Lo did not answer her, though he was still alive. He merely looked into his daughter's eyes and opened and shut his mouth dumbly.

Tsoi lowered himself onto the floor beside Hyan and smiled at her.

"I should marry you for this," he informed his cousin. "And maybe I will someday."

With the back of her hand, she tried to wipe her father's blood from where it had splattered across her face in a diagonal line extending from the left end of her mouth to her right temple, but only managed to smear the gore.

"I hope you do someday, my lord."

"Yes, I will, my dear, but, for right now, I'd like for you to fetch my surgeon."

\* \* \*

Jess was so excited when Uluf arrived at the airport that she was jumping up and down like an overeager puppy. As soon as the toad had stepped off of the ornithopter that had brought him from Hwiccho, Jess, wearing her black halter-top and pink clamdiggers, ran over to her friend, twined her arms around him, and gave the warty amphibian a kiss on his mouth.

"I told you I was too cute to die, didn't I?" she asked him playfully.

"Indeed, you did, my dear," the toad replied. "Nonetheless, it is a relief to see that you are still alive and well. I cannot entirely refrain from worrying about you, Jess."

Wrapping both her arms around her friend again, Jess walked him away from the ornithopter and to the multilegged wagon that would take them back to the terminal.

"Come on," she said. "Let's celebrate your arrival."

"Certainly, my dear," Uluf responded as he carefully lifted up the hem of his sky blue cheongsam to step into the centipede-like vehicle in front of him.

The two took their seats, though Jess, pressing against Uluf and holding his hands in her own, could not keep herself from squirming.

"What are things like in Jezic now?" Uluf asked.

The wagon began walking back to the airport terminal.

"It's been pretty calm, actually. There hasn't been any fighting since the coup. Still, you should've waited a while longer before you came here."

The toad had left Hwiccho three days earlier, immediately after hearing that Soniyo had fled Tozana.

"The situation, from what I have heard during my flight, has remained calm. Is that not true?"

"It's true, but you still should've given it more time."

"No, Jess. We will face whatever dangers are ahead of us together."

"Okay, but today let's have some fun. We never really got to see the city together. Why don't we do that?"

"I am sure we will have a marvelous time. We will simply have to postpone our troubles, trails, and tears until another day."

The girl kissed the toad again and continued chatting with him on the way to the terminal.

From the airport the two took a taxi into the city and got out in a large public square surrounded by multicolored pastel skyscrapers, the pediments of which were filled with a variety of shops.

Uluf noticed that, in many of these, pamphlets bearing titles like "The Sins of Soniyo" were being sold.

The toad picked one of these up and looked at the picture on its cover. This depicted Soniyo seated at a lavishly set table feasting on a human infant she had taken out of a pile of babies arranged on a charger in front of her.

"What is this?" he asked.

"Oh," answered Jess with a chuckle. "That's how they got rid of Soniyo."

"Please go on, my dear."

"Okay. The way Buabyue arranged the coup was supposed to make it seem like Malotrue was just rescuing her from me. Later on, after he got into the palace, he claimed that he found evidence of all kinds of crimes she had committed. He came on the picture vats and made a big announcement about them."

Adopting a deep voice meant to imitate that of a man, Jess went on. "I have learned that the woman I risked my life and the lives of my men to save is really a monster. She has taken control of our fair country so that she can indulge her grotesque vices. We have found conclusive proof that she has been eating the flesh of babies, bathing in the blood of virgins, and having sex with men, women, and animals. I declare her reign to be over."

In her normal voice, Jess then said, "After that, the army asked him to be the roshpai and he humbly accepted."

"Those are some pretty wild lies. Do the people really believe them?"

"Yeah, I guess so."

Looking at the pamphlet Uluf was holding, but being unable to read the writing in it, Jess asked, "So, what's it say in that, anyway?"

"Pretty much what you just said."

"Oh, they're releasing a movie about her reign today. You want to go see it?"

"It could be fun. Why not? I assume it is going to be about all these crimes of hers."

"I'm sure."

"They certainly did not wait long to put out some propaganda. The movie must have been animated before the coup."

"I guess. There's a theater over here, on the other side of the square."

Uluf put the pamphlet he was holding back on the counter of the stand in front of him, and he and the girl began walking to the cinema.

"What are you going to do now, my dear?" the toad asked.

"I'm not sure. I know you're going to think I'm being stupid, but I'm not done with Tolliver yet. I'm going to kill him."

"Jess, he could already be dead. You have ruined his plans and caused Ngo a great deal of trouble. I do not think that such a person is going to forgive someone for causing him as many problems as Tolliver has."

"Still, that's just guessing. I'm sorry, Uluf, but, when things calm down a little bit, I'm going back to Quanya."

\* \* \*

The face of the viceroy of Shokai was staring at Tsoi from between the horns of the brass telopticon mounted on the brow of a naked woman squatting on the floor in front of the gangster.

Adjusting the kamilaukion resting on top of his mane-like wig, the viceroy said, "What is this news you have for me?"

The words he spoke to Tsoi Ngo were entirely scripted. The two men's plans had been finalized shortly after their last meeting and their current conversation was nothing more than a game, a mere bit of playacting. They were really talking only so that Tsoi could inform the viceroy that he needed the help that man had been bribed to give him while, at the same time, providing both of them with the appearance of honesty and innocence.

Tsoi was lounging upon a broad throne situated in the middle of a wide stone platform that itself was in the center of a lush garden spread out under a vast glass dome. Hyan was sitting on the floor, leaning against the side of the throne, smoking a pipe, and watching the telopticon.

"Your immanence," Tsoi said, "I have received word from my contacts in Tozana that the recent revolution there was engineered by the Iridescent Blossom Society. The rebels are planning to take control of the production of russa in that country and use the money generated from the sale of the drug to finance their insurrection against the emperor."

"Can you provide me with evidence of this?"

"I am forwarding the information to you now, your immanence."

"I will review the proof you have sent. If it is legitimate, I will immediately dispatch five-hundred soldiers, five-thousand scorpions, and three castles to Jezic."

"Your immanence, I have a significant amount of property in that city. Would you allow me to send a team of representatives with your army to safeguard my interests?"

"Ordinarily, I would deny such a request. However, given that you have provided me with the information that will enable me to prevent Tozana from becoming a source of money to the Iridescent Blossom, I will allow it. I will have my adjutant contact you shortly with a rendezvous point, should an army be sent."

"Thank you for this indulgence, your immanence."

"And I thank you for the service you have provided."

The viceroy ended his transmission and Tsoi called his major-domo.

The man's face took shape in the middle of the brass lyre and said, "My lord."

Hyan picked up a pipe from a tray lying beside her, packed and lit it, and handed it to her cousin.

"Send in Tolliver," Tsoi commanded.

"Yes, my lord," the major-domo responded.

Tsoi turned off his telopticon, took a draught from the pipe Hyan had given him, and thanked her while running his hand along the cornrows on her scalp.

"I want to go to Jezic with them," she said.

"No. It's too dangerous."

"My lord, please. That girl is there, and I want to kill her. She murdered Huazheen."

"I don't want to lose you, Hyan. Enough of our family is dead already."

"My lord, please. I promise I won't fight her myself. I know I can't beat her, anyway. Just let me watch her die. Please."

Hyan looked up to Tsoi with tears in her eyes and his resolve collapsed.

Stroking her cheek, he said, "Okay, Hyan. You can go, but don't fight, especially with that girl. Do you promise me?"

"Yes, Tsoi. I do.

As Hyan kissed her cousin's hand in gratitude, Tolliver entered the garden flanked by a pair of guards and followed by a bull-headed homunculus who held a chain fastened to a collar around the former captain's neck.

Tsoi motioned for the girl crowned with the telopticon to move to the side, and Tolliver, having been brought before him, was thrown onto the ground at his feet.

"Tolliver," Tsoi said with a smile, "you have been useful to me. I will not deny that. However, your plan has proven to be riddled with problems. You failed to mention how deadly your girlfriend is, and she has given me a great deal of trouble."

"My lord…" Tolliver started to say, but the homunculus kicked the back of his head and, placing his hoof on the man's neck, forced his face into the floor.

"Do shut up, Tolliver," Tsoi continued while letting smoke drift out of his nostrils. "You should know that I've received word from my castellan. He's in Jezic right now. I suppose you've heard what happened there. My precious little Soniyo has been overthrown. Now the poor creature's dead. It's your fault, Tolliver. You know why? Hmm? Well, guess who was sent to kill her. Who do you think? Was it my mommy? Was it, maybe, a magical ghost? Hmm? Who do you think?"

Tolliver did not answer so the guards standing over him kicked him in the kidneys.

He started to lift his head to reply, but, when the homunculus forced it back down with his hoof, Tolliver spoke with his lips pressed against the stone paving.

"Was it Jess, my lord?"

"Good guess, my friend. It was her. That horrid pink haired girl has caused me even more trouble. It's too bad you had no insight into her character whatsoever."

"I'm sorry, my lord."

Tsoi jumped up, kicked Tolliver in the face, and began pacing back and forth in front of him while smoking his pipe and clicking his long, enameled artificial nails.

"I'm giving you one last chance, Tolliver, and that's it."

"Thank you, my lord. What can I do?"

Tsoi kicked him in the face again.

"Shut your mouth. I want you to kill Jess Ichikawa. I want you to kill her, and I want you to bring me her head. If you don't, I'm going to shred your body, and I'm going to take years doing so. Do you understand, my friend?"

"Yes, my lord."

"That's great. Now, I know you're no warrior like that girl is, so I am going to give you some help. I'm sending fifty of my best men with you, as well as my beloved Hyan."

She smiled at him and took a draught from her pipe.

Tsoi sat back down upon his throne, reached down his arm to rest his hand on his cousin's shoulder, and continued addressing Tolliver.

"They'll help you with your quarry, but they'll also be keeping an eye on you to make sure you don't try anything silly. We wouldn't want you to run off, after all."

Hyan stared at Tolliver while making her eyes as big as she could.

"Don't be naughty now," she informed the man. "I'll gobble you up."

"And she will too," Tsoi added.

# Chapter 43
## Counterrevolution

"Jess, get up!" Uluf cried out while shaking his friend.

Rubbing the mucus from her eyes, the girl asked, "What is it, Uluf?"

"You have to get dressed now. Please, my dear, hurry."

"Okay, Uluf. What's going on?"

"Get up and look for yourself."

Jess stumbled out of the bed and, still naked, walked over to the large window to her left to gaze out at the city, which was illumined with the orangish rays of the dawn.

She had been out drinking with Uluf the previous evening and had only returned to Gople Sing's apartment, where she was staying, after half the night was gone. With so few hours' sleep, her head remained clouded and her body was still exhausted. She did not want to wake up.

What she saw outside the window ended that feeling instantly.

Three metal castles with towers and turrets extending both upwards and downwards and bristling with cannons hung over the city and, between and to either side of them, were five troop carriers flying white banners each emblazoned with a stylized flower.

"Oh shit," she muttered.

"Gople says that the flower is the device of the viceroy!" the toad shouted in near panic. "We have to get out of here, Jess."

"Yeah. I guess so."

She dashed back over to the bed and picked up her black shorts, pink halter-top, and vest from the floor beside it, where she had left them before going to sleep.

Once she had dressed and tied her bottomless pouch to her waist, the girl took out Dawn's Spine and one of her daggers.

Jess started to run for the door, but then stopped and looked at Uluf.

"Where are we going?" she asked.

"Through the basement and into the sewers. We can make it through those to the sea. Sing has a submersible there that can take us away from Tozana. Please, Jess, you have to hurry. Sing is not going to wait for us."

The girl was no longer looking at her friend, but was staring out the window. One of the troop carriers had floated past.

She hurried to the window and looked down. The vessel had landed at the tower's base and a swarm of scorpions each as big as a horse was streaming out of it.

"If we're going down," she said, "we're going to be fighting our way to the sewers. Hmm. This whole situation seems very familiar."

"This way," the toad said as he led her out of her bedroom, down a hallway, and into another room, where Gople, Syo, Luhit, a dozen of Gople's men, and as many of his women were equipping themselves with weapons.

* * *

Hyan took a deep draught from her pipe as she reclined upon a couch set within a mirrored pavilion that was itself situated beneath a silver onion dome on the top of a tall tower rising from the side of one of the castles floating above Jezic.

Having exhaled the smoke and tasted the excitement it aroused in her, she adjusted the ankle length, flared skirt of her skintight, pink, military style jacket, smoothed out a couple of spots where the shiny rubber material had bunched up, and admired the lines of her thigh high black boots.

Once Hyan was satisfied with her appearance, she tugged roughly upon the thin chain she was holding, that was fastened to a collar secured around

Tolliver's neck. The man, so jarred, looked up at the woman from where he was squatting on the reflecting floor.

"What's wrong, little Tolliver?" Hyan asked.

He merely stared at her with a grim expression.

"I suppose you think you're about to die. Is that it?"

The man still did not answer.

"Or do you think that I'm not treating you well? Is my little pet feeling humiliated?"

Tolliver looked away from Hyan, and she kicked him. He did not return his gaze to her so she kicked him again.

When the man still did not raise his head, Hyan handed the leash to one of the mercenaries standing behind her dressed, like his fellows, in pink and blue armor. She then stood up to lean precariously far over the railing.

The new roshpai had sent out all of his military ornithopters, and great numbers of them were zipping across the sky above the city. Unfortunately for Malotrue, they were rapidly being shot down by the far superior weapons of the viceroy's castles. Some, their wings flapping uselessly and their antigravity engines wrecked, plunged to the earth to explode amongst Jezic's buildings. Others, too damaged to fly but with their antigravity devices intact, continued moving in whatever direction they had already been going. Of these, a few crashed, a few spun away into the distance, and a few soared into the sky, where, eventually, their pilots would suffocate.

Leaning even further over the railing, Hyan examined the castle itself. Its base was composed of towers and battlements just as its top was so that, when looking at its lower half, she felt as though she were looking at the reflection of a castle in a clear pool of water. The metropolis below it then seemed to her like some strange fairy city built far below the surface, in some magical submarine kingdom.

It was no land of idyllic peace, however, but was alive with conflict.

A fierce battle was being fought around the roshpai's palace. Tozana's troops were doing their best to protect their new ruler, but they did not stand a chance against the viceroy's army.

Numerous scorpions swarmed over the palace walls and crept over its roof, crashing through windows and entering into the structure. Others attacked the roshpai's soldiers, slaughtering them with needle guns, impaling them with poisonous stingers, or tearing them apart with huge pincers.

Hyan, though fascinated by this struggle and accustomed to violence, was a little repulsed, in spite of herself, when she noticed that many of the scorpions were devouring their fallen enemies, even though these persons were often still alive.

Tearing herself away from this spectacle, Hyan called out, "Castellan."

"Yes, my lady," he replied.

"Where are we going?"

As the man walked over to join his mistress at the railing, the mercenary holding Tolliver's leash pushed him onto the floor with his foot to get him out of the way. Ignoring the defeated individual crouching at his heels, the castellan pointed towards the east.

"Over there. One of the troop carriers is already on its way. Watch it and you'll see exactly."

"This is going to be fun, I think," Hyan told the man with a grin.

"My lady, please don't take any unnecessary risks. I have been informed that you swore to your cousin that you wouldn't…"

Hyan interrupted him. "I know. Don't worry about it. Now, why don't you get your soldiers together? We ought to be going down soon. Inform me when you're ready."

"Yes, my lady," the castellan replied and began turning away.

"Wait a second," she told him.

"My lady?"

Hyan knelt beside Tolliver, cupped his chin in her palm, and, while looking at him, said to the castellan, "Take this one with you. Give him over to the captain of the mercenaries. Inform him that he is to tell his men to follow Tolliver's orders when it comes to fighting. But make sure they know not to let him go. If he tries to get away, they can kill him. Oh, and I want his head if they do. Do you understand?"

"Yes, my lady."

The soldier holding Tolliver's leash yanked the man up onto his feet and pulled him along as he followed the castellan down the stairs leading away from the pavilion. Hyan leaned against the railing, watched them go, and then, turning around, returned to looking at the battle.

\* \* \*

"Good. You're here," Gople said when he saw Jess and the toad. "We're about to leave."

"You can't go into the basement," Jess informed Gople, who was pushing past her into the hallway she had just left behind. "The bottom of the building is filled with scorpions."

"I know. Come on," he yelled back without stopping.

Jess followed him as he explained. "There are hangars for antigravity sleds halfway up Sunshine Towers. We're heading for those. We might make it there before the scorpions do, or, at least, before many of them do."

Rushing to catch up with Gople, Jess told him, "They'll shoot you down if you fly out."

"Not if we're quick. We'll leave from the side of the building opposite the castle and we won't go far."

"Even so, where are we going?"

"To my offices. There's another way into the tunnels there."

"Are they far?"

"No. They're on the other side of the big square south of Sunshine Towers. It's not that far. We can make it there."

They reached the end of the hall, and one of Gople's men opened the door. It led onto a stairwell.

"Come on. Down this way," Gople said to Jess. She realized that the viceroy's soldiers would surely have seized the elevators and that the stairs were their only way down.

"Watch out for anyone coming up the stairs," Jess advised him as she went through the door

"The stairs only reach to the hangars," Gople replied and hurried down the steps, Jess and the others at his heels. "As long as we don't waste time, we'll make it to the hangars before the scorpions."

Jess looked over the railing and saw that Gople was correct.

Unfortunately, she did not notice that a scorpion had climbed up the outside of the building and was pressed against the tall window that spanned the height of three floors and provided light for the stairwell.

She heard a loud crash and turning her head saw the scorpion break through the window and scurry onto a landing between her and the door to the hangars.

Several of the gangsters leaned over the railing and began shooting at the monster with needle guns, but their projectiles ricocheted off its carapace without doing any harm. They did, however, get the scorpion's attention, and it aimed its own automatic needle rifle and began firing, killing four of the men in seconds.

"Through here!" Gople shouted. He opened the door leading to the floor above the hangars and sprinted through it, followed by his underlings and the rest, while another scorpion that had scaled the face of the tower crawled through the shattered window and joined the first of its kind.

Jess ran to catch up with Gople and said to him, "Tell me where we're going. I'm faster than anyone else here. I can scout ahead. I've actually had a little experience at it, you know. This situation isn't exactly new to me now."

He did not argue with her. "Go through the door at the end of this hallway. There's a central lobby there. Go through that, through the door at the far end. That'll take you to another corridor like this one. There's another stairwell at its end. But watch out, that one leads to the bottom of the building."

"Okay," Jess responded and raised the thread from her perineum to her brow.

Then, slowing time as much as she could, she set off running down the corridor like a character from a children's cartoon.

She opened the door to the lobby, glanced through, saw that it was empty, signaled to the others to follow, and went through herself.

Cracking the door at its far side open, Jess peeked into the corridor beyond.

In the hallway before her she saw a pair of yellowish scorpions with their great stings raised above their backs and their pinchers, which were of unequal size, twitching before them. In the smaller of these, each of the creatures held an automatic needle rifle, while the other, much larger claw spasmodically opened and closed. The latter, Jess thought, looked powerful enough to chop a man's body in two with ease. Each beast's hairy, bulging chelicerae (which were far larger, in proportion to the rest of its body, than were those of an ordinary scorpion) were, however, even worse. They were surely more than sufficient on their own to rend their victims into small pieces.

Between these monsters stood a soldier who was speaking into a communicator.

He wore a close fitting, emerald green coat with long, loose skirts that reached to his ankles and a sallet with a visor that covered his forehead and extended a good two feet in front of his face. The helm was further adorned at the temples with colorful lamellae from which projected plumes of whisker-like beaded cords.

The man's communicator was fastened to the front of his uniform, below his chin. It was a brass device shaped like a cornu, the funnel of which opened towards his mouth. He was speaking into the end of the horn.

Jess allowed time to return to its normal pace and listened as the man said, "I'm on the fifteenth floor. I'm sending the scorpions ahead."

He then flipped a switch below the communicator and addressed the scorpions. "Search this level and kill everything you find."

Jess quickly and quietly closed the door, slowed the universe, ran back through the lobby, and, letting time return to its normal pace, grabbed Gople, who was about to enter that room. "There are two scorpions coming. We're trapped."

"No, we're not," he replied and kicked open a door beside him that led into an apartment.

"This way," Gople shouted and hurried out of the hallway.

Jess followed him, pushing Uluf in front of her, just as the scorpions that had blocked their original route smashed through the door leading to the corridor.

The last of the gangsters tried to lock the door to the apartment, but the latch had been broken.

"Forget about it," Jess yelled at him. "I'll keep them back. Go on ahead."

The man nodded and dashed after the others.

No sooner had he done so than a side door opened and an elderly man walked into the room.

"Who are you?" he asked Jess. "What's going on today? It sounds like there's a war being fought outside."

"Run!" Jess screamed frantically at the man, but he just stood where he was looking at her and asking her questions.

Not having the time to answer him, and being genuinely terrified of her newest enemies, Jess lifted up her thread and slowed time once more.

At that very moment, the first of the scorpions burst through the door in front of her.

She did not wait for the beast to look around and aim at her. Instead, Jess lunged at it and, tracing out a huge eight with her sword, chopped off both its pinchers.

The scorpion thrust its stinger at her, but Jess jumped to one side and amputated it before the horror could withdraw the gigantic poisoned dagger. The scorpion raised itself up upon its legs, and Jess drove her sword into its face.

It still did not die, but it did begin jumping around the room in pain, forcing Jess to dive under a table to avoid its flailing.

The old man stood watching the creature in shock, and he still was when another scorpion entered the room. The first thing it saw was this person and so jumped upon him, stinging him in the chest and clipping off one of his arms with its larger pincher.

Jess slid out from under the table in order to attack the second scorpion as she had the first, but, before she could do so, the first scorpion, which was still throwing itself around the room, slammed into the newcomer.

This beast immediately turned upon its fellow and the pair began wrestling and fighting with one another, though the newer arrival, having claws and a stinger, fared better in their fight.

Jess did not wait to see the outcome, but instead rushed through the door the others had gone though, closing and locking it behind her.

She found herself in a hallway with many doors, but as that at the end was open Jess knew that Gople and the others must have gone that way.

She ran into the room at the corridor's end. Its walls were lined with shelves laden with books, and it was filled with expensive looking furniture. Directly across from the entrance there was an archway, in which was set a glass door leading to a small room with a door at its back. Syo was standing in front of this.

"Over here, Jess!" she cried out.

Jess, having already released the thread within her, rushed over to Syo and said, "Come on. We've got to hurry up."

Syo smiled and took a deep breath.

"Jess, good luck with the scorpions," she said.

"What?"

Syo hit the side of Jess's head with a bookend she had picked up.

Everything suddenly went black for Jess and she staggered backwards and fell onto the floor.

Jess would have died there had she not chanced to see, through the dark blobs racing about in front of eyes, that Syo was aiming a needle gun at her.

Slowing down time and rolling to the side, Jess avoided the projectile the other woman fired. When she tried to stand, however, the dizziness produced by her injury sent her back onto the wooden floor.

This time she was fortunate enough to fall behind a couch, and this shielded her from Syo.

As Jess listened to Syo walking across the creaking wood, she crawled around the couch to keep it between her and her attacker.

"Why are you doing this, Syo?" she called out.

"Fuck you, Jess," the woman responded while firing several needles into the couch separating her and her quarry.

"Thanks. That explains a lot."

"Don't even bother denying anything, you stupid, crazy whore."

"Okay," Jess said, shaking her head in an attempt to recover her vision and her balance.

"The scorpions'll be here in a minute. If you don't want them to eat you, you should come out from behind the couch. At least, I'll just shoot you."

"Thanks for the mercy, but I'll stay here."

Syo continued to circle the couch, and Jess continued to crawl around it.

"Maybe I should just leave you for the scorpions."

"You do that."

Her voice trembling as she started to cry convulsively, Syo screamed out, "It would serve you right! I know Tsoi didn't just kill Eshwurhiyo. He would've tortured her first. I loved her and she died in agony."

"I'm sorry, Syo. I really am."

"Fuck you, Jess Ichikawa. Fuck you."

Syo fired numerous shots into the couch before continuing. "Don't even pretend with me. You left her there. You left her to die. Then you left me to be raped by I don't even know how many men. Come out from behind there, damn you!"

Having recovered her wits enough to focus her thoughts, Jess raised the thread up from her perineum to her brow and kept it there.

"Come on, Syo. I didn't want any of that to happen. I did my best, I swear."

Syo's body was heaving with sobs when she howled, while repeatedly firing her gun, "Fuck you! Fuck you! Fuck you! You let the only person I'll ever love die and you think 'I did my best,' is going to make any difference. No. I don't think so."

"You may not remember this, Syo, but that wasn't exactly a fun filled vacation for me either."

"Fuck you, you stupid, crazy whore."

Syo started firing at the couch again, and Jess realized that she was not going to persuade the woman to put down her weapon.

Seizing ahold of time, Jess leapt from where she was crouching, hurtling from the side of the couch at Syo.

The woman had time to fire at her, but her shot was high and did not hit Jess.

The pink haired girl swung her sword and chopped off both of Syo's feet, sending her tumbling to the floor.

When Syo hit the wood, the impact knocked the air from her lungs and sent her weapon flying from her hand.

Jess rushed to grab the gun, but, as her hand closed upon it, she saw, out of the corner of her eye, a scorpion entering the room.

She looked at Syo and wished she could dispatch her before the monster got to her, but she did not have time.

To escape the scorpion, Jess bolted for the glass door and closed it behind her. The huge creature slammed into the transparent barrier, but, fortunately, the glass was reinforced and did not break.

For a moment the scorpion banged itself against the doorway, and Jess noticed that it was beginning to crack. Then it heard Syo, who had begun to scream uncontrollably, and turned around.

The scorpion pierced the woman with its stinger as Jess looked on. She could see Syo's face and could make out that her eyes were still moving and her mouth still twitching. The woman was almost completely paralyzed, but she was still conscious as the scorpion tore into her body with its huge chelicerae and began to devour her.

Jess vomited on her feet and had to brace herself against a wall to keep herself from falling down.

She did not look back again, but she knew that the scorpion would soon be following her. Gathering all her resolve, Jess righted herself, opened the door opposite that leading to the library, and ran down the stairs on its other side.

# Chapter 44
## Into the Maelstrom

At the bottom of the stairs leading away from the library Jess found a doorway. She went through it and saw before her a cross shaped hangar opening onto all four sides of the building and filled with antigravity sleds.

"Where's Syo?" Gople asked as soon as he had spotted Jess. "She stayed behind to let you know which way we'd gone."

"Syo's dead, and we will be too if we don't get a move on."

"Yeah. This way," Gople replied and led Jess towards one of the sleds.

Uluf and five of Gople's henchmen were already sitting in it, and the rest of the people Jess was escaping with were piling into a larger vehicle parked beside the first.

While they were still getting into the sleds, a pair of doors opened at the side of the hangar opposite them and a scorpion rushed into the room.

"Hurry!" Gople shouted, but the monster had already begun firing its needle rifle.

The pilot of the larger sled and three young women sitting on the red leather bench beside him were instantly killed and slumped down covered with blood.

"Don't leave without me," Jess instructed Gople. She then raised the thread within her, slowed time, and, swinging Dawn's Spine, jumped at the scorpion.

It did not have a chance to react and prevent its attacker from slicing off its sting, grabbing ahold of its tail, and landing on its back.

The creature reached up with its larger pincher to snatch Jess from where she was crouched, but she chopped off first that set of claws and then the other.

Wanting to dispatch her enemy, the girl repeatedly stabbed it where she thought its brain might be, but was wrong every time. The scorpion was merely enraged by her actions and threw itself about so wildly that it eventually dislodged its attacker and sent her rolling across the hangar's floor.

Standing up quickly, so she could avoid the wounded scorpion if it cast itself in her direction, Jess saw another, the one that had eaten Syo, emerging from the door through which she and the others had entered the hangar.

The gangsters were shooting at it with their needle guns, without effect, and it was shooting at them in return, killing four more of the women and one of the men from Gople's entourage.

Jess ran at it from the side, hoping to avoid the rain of needles, and ducked behind its back. With a swing of her sword, she lopped off the creature's tail at its base and tried to scurry onto its back. Its writhing body tossed her onto the floor instead.

The scorpion began turning towards her to rend her with its claws and chelicerae and to devour her, but Jess slid underneath its body. There, as the beast's feathery pectines flapped about her face, she jabbed it with her sword. Reacting instinctively to the pain, the scorpion raised its body up, and this gave Jess the chance to swing her sword in an arc and split its front part from the rear.

Thrusting upon the ground with her feet while pushing it away from her with her mind, Jess popped out from under the scorpion before its entrails spilled across her body. She flipped end over end, landed on her feet, and ran back to the sled.

The seat next to Gople, who was piloting, was empty and Jess plopped down into it and told the man, "Go before any more of those things show up."

Gople had already started the sled and it was floating about a foot above the floor. At Jess's word he engaged the propeller and flew the craft out of the hangar followed by the other with the remainder of his dependents.

Keeping the sled behind Sunshine Towers, the gangster sought to avoid being seen by and so drawing the fire of either the floating castles or the troop carrier that had landed on the building's other side. While the other craft trailed the one that Gople was piloting, the two rushed towards the ground, stopping their descent only when they were about twenty feet from the pavement.

"We'll stay low," Gople explained to his passengers, "and fly along that row of trees. Those and the towers should give us enough cover to reach the far side of the square. Once we're there, we can move down some of the side streets. They'll give us cover until we reach our goal."

Concealed by the pastel towers or by rows of trees, the two sleds had made it halfway across the distance to the further end of the square when an explosion rocked the first of the vessels and sent it hurtling into the sky.

For an instant, Jess thought they were being attacked, but the explosion had been produced by a shell fired at a group of orange uniformed soldiers who were marching down a street the sleds were crossing.

Jess, having seen these men rushing towards Sunshine Towers, looked back at the building itself and saw a cannon operated by a team of the viceroy's troops, who were dressed in uniforms like the one the man she had seen with the scorpions wearing.

As the sled spun through the air, its passengers clung to their seats and Gople frantically manipulated the controls, hoping to regain command of his vehicle. Once he had, Jess, though dizzy, was able to look around more carefully.

It appeared as though the war was being fought in several different parts of Jezic. One of the floating castles was hovering above the roshpai's palace and the other two over the city center. All three were firing rockets and lobbing shells at their enemies below them and shooting down any vehicle that dared raise itself into the air.

Much of the city was, as a result of the castles' bombardment, veiled with thick clouds of smoke and debris. Although Jess could not make out what was happening within these, from the popping sounds of explosions coming from them, she was sure that a fierce battle was being fought.

She wondered why the viceroy would have sent his soldiers to help Ngo as she looked at the damage these persons were causing. At the same time, she realized that, even though they were facing soldiers of the Pancloan army, Malotrue and his followers would not quickly surrender their newly won positions.

Such ponderings were interrupted when the sled passed between two more buildings on its way back to the earth and exposed itself to another cannon that had been unloaded from the troop carrier.

This fired at them as soon as they came out from behind the skyscraper with such accuracy that, Jess later thought, the weapon's crew must have seen them earlier and been waiting for them to appear again.

The shell glanced off the side of the sled and sent it careening through the air, away from Sotru Square, between a pink and a green tower, and towards the metallic highway running down the center of a wide boulevard.

Jess closed her eyes, thinking that she was going to die, but, somehow, Gople regained control of the damaged sled and set it down upon the ground. The landing was rough, but no one was more than jarred by it.

A moment later, the other vehicle, having circled round, began descending to pick Gople and the others up.

The sled did not reach them. When it was not far away, an energy ray fired between two towers from one of the castles struck it. The craft exploded, sending Jess and her companions jumping behind or underneath whatever cover was immediately available to them.

After the last pieces of debris and charred human remains had fallen to the earth, Jess climbed out from a vagrant's shanty to look at Uluf.

"You okay?" she asked him.

"I am fine. How are you, my dear?"

"Still alive and as cute as ever."

"How about you, boss?" one of Gople's last living henchmen asked him.

"Great," the gangster replied while looking around.

The situation in which he and the others found themselves was not any safer than that they had faced in the air.

The streets were filled with panicking men, women, and children, who were fleeing madly from their homes or shops, away from Sotru Square, in a jostling, violent mob. They were shoving and bumping against their fellows, and, whenever some person happened to fall, the others paid no attention to him. Instead, they simply ran over him, trampling him beneath their feet.

Through this roiling mass of people, Jess saw an orderly formation cutting its way and approaching from the south.

Behind a row of multi-legged tanks like gigantic rhinoceros beetles each of whose horns had been transformed into a cannon and a flamethrower, a body of orange uniformed soldiers was marching down the street to attack the scorpions that were swarming around and up the sides of Sunshine Towers.

Another group of soldiers was, at the same time, coming near to the sled.

Their captain yelled out to the people who had crashed in front of him. "Get out of here now! You want to get yourselves killed?"

Without waiting for a reply, he turned and led his men down the next road running to Sotru Square.

Gople tried to restart the sled, into which he and the others had climbed, but it was no longer working.

"Come on," he shouted to the others. "We're going to have to go on foot."

The gangster and his passengers hopped out of their vehicle and ran down the boulevard, towards the soldiers led by the tanks and past the street onto which the other company had marched.

"This way," Gople informed his companions as he guided them into the next road and started taking them back towards Sotru Square.

Though they tried to keep low and remain inconspicuous while they were running, they could not help but look up and see, in the next street, a furious confrontation.

A dozen scorpions had fallen upon some soldiers there and had begun tearing their bodies apart with frightening speed and savagery.

The beetle-like tanks groaned forward, and each, having reached the end of the side street, sprayed a combustible jelly out of its flamethrower. This stuck on both the human soldiers and the scorpions attacking them, burning them until they collapsed in death on the ground, where their corpses were wholly consumed by the flames.

"Hey!" someone shouted from behind Jess, and she turned around to see thirty soldiers dashing towards Gople.

One of them called out again.

"Are you Gople Sing?"

"Yes."

"I've been sent to inform you that these soldiers are here to provide you with protection."

"Good. We could use it."

"Now, you will come with me."

"No. I've got to get to Sotru Square."

"I'm afraid not. That's where the fighting is."

"Nevertheless, our only way out of here is through there. If we don't go that way, we're going to die."

"I'm sorry, sir, but I've been instructed to…"

Gople interrupted the man by suddenly raising his needle gun and pointing it at the soldier's face.

"You and your men go on ahead of us to the lavender building on the southern end of the square."

* * *

"The building there is Sunshine Towers," the castellan said to Hyan while pointing through one of the round windows set in the front of the jet propelled troop carrier they were traveling in.

"That," he continued, "is where Gople Sing resides."

"What about the girl?"

"My informants tell me that she is staying there with him."

"Good."

Adjusting a thick, rubber coated wire that ran from his right ear to a brass globe fixed to the panel in front of him, which was next to the pilot's controls, the castellan added, "The Pancloan troops have secured the bottom of the building. Gople and his lot can't get down now."

Hyan twisted her face into a pouting frown. "That's a disappointment. I was hoping to see the girl fight, and I was hoping to see her die."

The troop carrier was hovering close to Sunshine Towers, allowing Hyan to watch numerous scorpions crawling up its walls and smashing through its windows to get at the people within. Nobody inside that building was going to be alive for much longer.

"My lady," the castellan said.

"Yes?"

"I've been told that two antigravity sleds escaped from the tower's hangar a few minutes ago."

"Is it the pink haired girl?"

"I don't know. Both of the vessels were hit. One was destroyed and the other forced to land. The persons who were riding in the second craft are moving back towards Sotru Square, the plaza where Sunshine Towers is."

"Why?"

"Gople's office is in a building there."

"Which one is it?"

The castellan pointed and said, "They must be heading there, if that's them. One moment. They've killed four scorpions! That's impressive."

Hyan smiled. "That's the girl. Take us to the tower with Gople's office. We're going to wait for them there."

* * *

439

Jess and her companions were rushing down the street leading back to Sotru Square when four scorpions and a dozen green uniformed Pancloan soldiers leapt upon them from an alley running between two structures to the right.

The Tozani soldiers opened fire on the creatures with their needle rifles, without effect.

"Shoot the men in green," Jess shouted to her most recent allies. "I'll take care of the scorpions."

Raising the thread to her brow and opening up her awareness to the briefest moment, Jess ran at the scorpions, which were not yet firing their own weapons, and chopped off the pincers of the first one of them she came to. It reeled backwards when so struck and, in a panic, landed upon another of its kind, stinging that beast frantically.

Jess spun around, as the Tozani soldiers and gangsters began exchanging fire with the men from the Pancloan army, and slid under one of the remaining scorpions.

She rolled from one side of its body to the other, slicing it in half as she did so, and then, having regained her feet, fell upon the last of the creatures.

It was attacking the orange clad soldiers and had already stung one of them and torn the body of another in half with its pincers.

Approaching the monster from behind, Jess sliced off its tail, kept to its side while it tried to spin around and face her, and lopped off four of its legs. The scorpion fell onto the ground, unable to move itself, and Jess crouched behind it to avoid being shot by the viceroy's troops.

There were still three of them alive when they decided to retreat, though one more of them was shot as he ran away.

"How many have we lost?" the commander of the platoon asked one of his men.

"Five, sir. Three shot and two killed by scorpions."

"One of the Pancloans has a flamethrower. Go get it."

"Yes, sir," the man replied and ran over to the corpse to take its weapon.

"Come on," Jess shouted, having allowed the thread to sleep again. "We've got to hurry."

She hopped over to Uluf and took his hand. Together the pair ran with the others down the street, until they came to the edge of the building at its end, which stood between them and Sunshine Towers.

The group ran off the road and huddled at the structure's corner, peeking around to see what was happening.

A large part of the plaza was occupied by a long, cylindrical troop carrier that, with the two huge round windows at its front, looked like a giant fish that had been cast onto the earth, an impression that was furthered by the fact that its hull had been decorated with the features of a fish, including fins, scales, and a gaping mouth that held the front grill.

Between this vessel and Sunshine Towers there were a number of soldiers and a few scorpions, but most of the square was empty, except for the still smoldering corpses of those persons who had attempted to flee across it from the buildings along its sides.

Gople, putting his left hand on the platoon commander's shoulder, pointed with his needle gun at a lavender tower the podium of which was enclosed by a colonnaded veranda topped with three pillared balconies.

"We've got to get in there," Gople said.

"We'll have to move through the square."

"Let's hide behind that." The gangster pointed to a long, narrow platform planted with trees that ran nearly from the east side of the plaza to the west.

"Okay. I'll send one squad there first. Then, the second squad will accompany you and your companions. I'll follow with the last squad. You'll have cover from both sides."

"Sounds great to me."

The commander looked at three of his men and said, while turning his gaze from one to the next, "You go first. You, go with Sing. You, stay with me."

Ten soldiers, their weapons ready, dashed out from behind the building, across one corner of the square, leaping over the corpses and pieces of corpses that littered the ground, and ducked behind the platform.

"Go," the commander said to Gople.

He, his remaining henchmen, Jess, and Uluf followed the soldiers as quickly as they could while surrounded by more Tozani troops.

Although the ground was uneven because of the bodies strewn upon it, and the flagstones were slick with blood, making it difficult to move either rapidly or inconspicuously, they were, nonetheless, nearly able to reach the platform. Unfortunately, just as they came upon it, one of the Tozani soldiers slipped in a puddle of entrails and fell backwards. He involuntarily yelped when he hit the ground, and several of the scorpions standing near the troop carrier heard him.

Without waiting for commands, four of the gigantic monsters raced towards Jess and the others.

She turned around and shouted, "Does someone here have the flamethrower?"

"Yes. I've got it," came a voice.

"Use it on the scorpions. Come on, hurry."

The man stood, aimed the weapon at the beasts, and sprayed a stream of burning jelly onto their bodies.

The creatures writhed about, spinning round and round upon the ground, but they could not extinguish the flames.

"Ooh, good work," Jess told the man.

"Thanks."

Their problems were not, however, over. More scorpions emerged from both the troop carrier and Sunshine Towers.

A dozen of these, being directed by the Pancloan soldiers behind them, turned to attack the commander of the platoon and the squad that had remained with him. Tearing limbs from bodies with their pincers, paralyzing with their stings, and ripping open bellies with their chelicerae, the scorpions did not take long to slaughter and consume their victims.

The remainder of the creatures were racing at Jess and those with her.

One of the soldiers yelled to Gople, "You and your friends run to the building. My squad will cover you."

Then he turned to one of his fellows and said, "You and your squad stay with him."

Jess, Uluf, Gople, his five henchmen, and nine soldiers ran towards the tower while the remaining soldiers fired at the approaching scorpions. The man with the flame thrower killed many of them, but others followed faster than he could set them on fire.

While Jess passed through the heavy wooden doors at the tower's front, she turned around and saw the soldiers who had remained behind being eaten alive.

She shook her head to cast that image from her mind and hurried into the tower.

Within was a large corridor ending in another pair of impressive doors. A short distance before these, on the wall to the right, was a smaller but still richly carved door, and Gople was running towards this.

"Through here," he shouted and went into the room on the door's other side, followed by four of his henchmen.

Just as Uluf had passed through the doorway, Jess and the others still outside were knocked off their feet by an explosion.

Although thick dust filled the room, concealing much of what had happened, Jess was able to discern that there was a substantial hole in the ceiling near the door Gople and Uluf had gone through.

Standing up, the girl started to follow them, but, as she leaped over the corpses of several soldiers, first one then another scorpion fell out of the hole in the ceiling.

Uluf poked his head out the door and Jess saw him.

"Close the door!" she screamed. "I'll follow you in a minute."

The toad did as the girl wished, barely avoiding a scorpion that had been hurling itself at him from one side.

At that very moment, mercenaries in blue and pink armor began leaping from the hole above after the scorpions.

Jess, raising the thread and slowing time, jumped upon the first two of her human foes to enter the hazy room and decapitated them both. Another pair joined their dead fellows almost immediately, but she chopped off their heads as well.

More soldiers quickly descended, and though several of them were shot by the Tozanis, many of them were not.

Speeding through the clouds of dust, Jess lopped off arms, severed heads, amputated legs, split open bellies, and divided torsos in half.

She separated the front end of one scorpion from its tail, stamped upon its head, and leapt into the air, slicing off the heads of two mercenaries before her feet were upon the ground again.

Spinning round she cut off a pincer grabbing at her, as well as the chelicerae gnashing behind it, then dove to one side and hacked off an armored soldier's feet.

Suddenly, another explosion sent her flying against a wall. Shaking her head, Jess stood up and saw that one of the Tozani soldiers had set off a grenade, killing the rest of the mercenaries in the room along with at least three scorpions.

The battle was not, however, finished, as more of the crawling monsters were pouring out of the hole in the ceiling.

One of these fiends jumped upon a surviving soldier and clipped off his head with its larger pincer. Another fired at several others as they tried to regain their feet. A third sucked the liquefied innards of Gople's follower from his stomach.

More jumped from the ceiling to join these and participate in what killing was left to them, until there were so many of the monsters between Jess and the door she needed to go through that she realized she could not fight them all.

She struck off the stinger of one of the creatures as it tried to jab her and then cleft off its pincers. The scorpion threw itself at the girl, intending to bite her with its sharp fangs, but Jess lunged to the side and split open its body from the front end to the rear.

Even with that enemy dying, others were ready to replace it and were already rushing at her. Jess ran to the back of the hall, opened one of the ornate doors there, and slipped inside. She closed the door behind her, without looking for what new danger she might be facing, and, finding a latch, locked the scorpions out and herself in.

# Chapter 45
## Satisfaction

In the foyer outside of Gople's office, the gangster looked from his four remaining underlings to the toad and said to the homunculus, "Come on. We've got to go on. She'll find us if she lives."

Before Uluf could object or Gople could continue on his way, a door at the other end of the room (at the top of a platform reached by a flight of steps running from one wall to the other) opened and a young woman in a tight pink uniform entered with a group of armored mercenaries.

Hyan drew her sword and began moving towards Gople.

One of her soldiers stood in front of her and protested, "My lady, you swore to your cousin that you wouldn't fight."

"I thought I promised I wouldn't fight the pink haired girl. I don't remember saying I wouldn't fight Sing. Now get out of the way, because I'm going to kill you if you don't."

Hyan began reciting the sounds that activated her resonator and felt the vibrations it sent through her body. Quivering with excitement as she devoured the world around her and forced time to move at the pace she chose, the young woman smiled down at her victims.

Gople's four remaining henchmen placed themselves between their master and Hyan, aiming their pistols at her.

She took the iliyo shield she had hanging at her waist, activated it, and ran at them. Their needles struck the shield and fell from it onto the ground without harming her.

When she was close to her enemies, Hyan began swinging her scimitar about her head. She decapitated the first of the men she fell upon and dispatched the second in the same way. The third man tried to stab her with a dagger, but she cut off his hand and slit his throat.

As his warm blood sprayed across her face, Hyan thrust him away with her shield and stabbed the last man in the belly, splitting him open so that his viscera spilled out onto the floor.

Hyan turned to Gople and, having let the vibrations of her resonator slowly fade away, permitted time to resume its ordinary pace.

She addressed her enemy. "You must be Gople Sing. I'm Hyan Ngo."

"I'm aware of who you are. I've heard about you and your brother."

She almost laughed to hear that such gossip had made it as far away as Jezic.

"Today's the end of your life, Gople," she informed him.

Brandishing his dagger in front of his chest, he shouted back, "We'll see."

"You're not going to fight me with that, are you? Well, this is hardly going to be fair if you do."

Hyan tossed her scimitar (and her shield) onto the ground and drew a hilt from her belt. She pressed a button on the device, and the blade of a kriss wiggled out of it.

The mercenaries' captain called out to Hyan from behind her, "My lady, don't be foolish."

"Hush! As long as I'm here, I might as well have a little fun."

Smiling at Gople, she said, "Now, my friend, let's see which one of us is going to kill the other. I think I'm the one who's going to be doing the killing. How about you? What do you think?"

Gople lunged at her, but Hyan, even without her resonator activated, was fast enough to avoid him.

She spun around and kicked the man in the small of the back as he moved past her and then coyly brushed her plaits from her eyes.

"You're going to have to do better than that, Gople, if you don't want me to kill you too quickly."

The gangster dove at her again, swinging his knife back and forth in front of her face and screaming. Hyan fell backwards without striking a blow at her enemy, until, tired of his efforts, she kicked him in the groin.

Gople doubled over and nearly dropped his weapon, but Hyan did not attack him. She merely stood back and watched him as he cupped his injured testicles in his hand and glared at her hatefully.

"I hope you've already had children, Gople," she laughed. "Did I crack them? If I didn't, I'll be sure to cut them off when I'm done with you.

Maybe I'll let you live. I'll just take your toys instead of your life. How about that?"

The gangster lunged at the young woman again and again she avoided him. This time, as he fell past her, she grabbed one of his necklaces, jerked him back, and sliced off the tip of his nose.

Gople howled in pain and rage. He tried to stab Hyan in the chest and almost succeeded. She was only barely able to catch his wrist and divert his blade.

Looking at Gople with surprise, and a slight admiration, she complimented him. "That was actually close. Better luck next time."

Then she poked out one of his eyes with the tip of her own dagger.

Gople grasped his face and swung madly at Hyan. She fell back, ducked to one side, jabbed her kriss under his ribs, and twisted it to let him feel the pain of being injured.

"How's that, Gople? Hurts, huh?"

He tried to stab her face, but she slipped behind him, thrust her left hand between his legs, and grabbed his penis. Before Gople was able to react, Hyan reached her right hand around his waist and severed his organ at the root.

The man stumbled forward and fell onto the ground screaming wildly.

Hyan walked over to him, kicked his weapon out of his hand, kicked him in his chest, knocking him onto his back, and stood above him.

"Sorry, Gople, but it's time to die," she said while tossing his penis at his face.

"My lady!" Hyan's captain shouted.

"What?"

"Jess Ichikawa is here."

Hyan looked around and saw the pink haired girl running straight at her. She would have liked to fight Jess, but since she had promised Tsoi she would not, she picked up her sword and sped back to her soldiers, half of whom were advancing to meet her.

Seizing the captain's hand, Hyan commanded him, "Kill her or die. I don't really care which. Just give me a good show."

* * *

At the far end of a huge oval room filled with gaming tables, Tolliver and five mercenaries in pink and blue armor were standing on a stage framed with sculptures of trees with intertwining branches and trunks that were shaped like voluptuous, naked nymphs.

Jess quickly looked around to see if there were any more persons in the room she was going to have to fight, even glancing above her at the domed roof composed of a gilt framework supporting image screens that were projecting moving pictures of a blue sky filled with white clouds.

She did not see any additional attackers, though she knew there might be some concealed somewhere in the jumble of tables and gambling devices that surrounded her.

Unfortunately, the sight of Tolliver had so upset her that she was unable to concentrate on anything but her feelings. Her body, drained of vigor and youth, trembled with rage, regret, love, sadness, hatred, and self-loathing.

Stepping into the casino, Jess screamed in a broken falsetto, "Why don't you just come down here, Tolliver? Come on."

"No, Jess. I don't think so."

The girl, upon hearing his voice, felt her anger flood through her veins, drowning or sweeping away every other emotion, and was rapidly overcome with a blinding madness. Forgetting everything but Tolliver and her desire to put an end to his existence, she ran towards him, without even raising the thread within her.

When she had covered about half the distance to the stage, Jess saw several shimmering images rise up like mirages from behind and beneath the tables around her.

She immediately realized that these were mercenaries wearing camouflage armor able to project, on any given side, images of whatever the person viewing it would have seen had the man wearing the armor not been there. Though such a device would not render its user invisible, it would transform him into something like a human shaped mass of heated air.

As furious as she was, Jess regained her composure when she saw these enemies, lifted the thread to her brow, slowed time, and forced the world down around her feet.

She soared above her attackers and kicked the face of one of them and the chest of another, sending this pair staggering backwards.

Sliding back down to the earth behind a third man, she wrapped her arms around his body, embracing him closely so that she could thrust her dagger under his helmet and into his neck.

Dark red blood spewed from the mirage, splattering three of the others in front of it, as the man the shimmering air really was fell convulsing to the floor.

Another mercenary behind Jess fired a needle gun at her, but since he missed, he only managed to gain her interest.

The girl spun around, swinging her sword in a wide arc and chopping the man in two at the waist. Now entrails spilled from the distorted air as the other such mass had earlier produced blood.

Two more nearly invisible mercenaries lunged at Jess, from opposite sides, and she, with a single motion, stabbed at the one in front of her with her sword and kicked at the other approaching her back with her left leg.

The man ahead fell dead when Jess withdrew her blade from his cranium, and the second stumbled back, dropping his own almost wire-thin dagger.

Before she could fall upon this man and put an end to his life, two of his mirage-like fellows lunged at her. She chopped off one man's right arm and kicked the other in the chest, knocking him onto his backside.

Impatient to be done with these persons, who were nothing but obstacles on her path towards the only thing she desired, Tolliver's corpse, Jess started to move towards the mercenary she had last kicked in order to finish him off.

Before she came to him, however, the man from whom he had distracted her grabbed her from behind.

He wrapped his arms around her torso, pinned her arms against her sides, and screamed to his fellow, "Kill her! Kill her!"

That man jumped from the floor and with one of his cobelligerents dashed at Jess. She, pushing up and backwards, and using the man holding her as leverage, kicked at first one and then the other of her attackers. Both stumbled back, and the one with his arms around the girl lost his balance and fell down.

The impact caused him to loosen his grip on his diminutive adversary, who hopped up, spun around, and cut off his head.

Jess would have turned upon the last of the camouflaged mercenaries had she not heard Tolliver screaming, in low, drawn out tones distorted by the lethargic time in which he was trapped, "Shoot her! Shoot the whore!"

Reacting at once, Jess dove under one of the tables and heard the grunts of the mercenaries she had not killed as their fellows' needles pierced their bodies.

Jess scurried towards the stage under the cover of the tables of the casino, moving like a cartoon squirrel scampering from tree to tree. Though her attackers continued to shoot at her, they did so without success.

The girl jumped upon the stage in front of them and killed three of the men at once. The other two, unable to react quick enough to save themselves, Jess dispatched next, so clearing her path to Tolliver. He, however, was retreating towards a door behind him.

Jess, having let the thread slide down her spine to rest in a coil upon her perineum, threw her dagger at Tolliver. It hit him in his left thigh, and he stumbled forwards and nearly fell down.

"You worthless whore!" Tolliver shouted at her as he grabbed the hilt sticking out of his leg. "Can't you just die?"

Hearing this, Jess was so enraged that she did not go to the man and simply decapitate him. Instead, she picked up a stone (carved into the shape of some erinaceous animal) that was being used to hold down the cloth draped over a table placed in the middle of the stage and threw it at him.

It hit Tolliver's arm when he tried to block it and bounced onto the parquet floor.

Nearly deranged with grief and anger, Jess ran towards her former love, leapt into the air once she was halfway to him, and kicked the man in the throat.

He fell backwards choking as Jess landed with a roll behind him, jumped onto her feet, returned to him, and sat down upon his neck, her legs to either side of his head.

She held the tip of Dawn's Spine a fraction of an inch from Tolliver's right eye and said with a shaky, gasping voice, "You know, I thought I'd like doing this, but I don't. It actually makes me sad. Damn you, Tolliver. I loved you. I guess I still do in some stupid way. I've been with thousands of men – and that's thousands more than I wanted to be with – but I thought you were going to be the last. I thought I was going to grow old with you.

Sometimes I even thought I might have a baby with you. How crazy is that?"

"Jess, we could still be together," the man whimpered.

"Oh, please. That's just pathetic. You betrayed me. You used me. You even tried to kill me. I don't think I can get over all of that."

Jess started to cry, but managed to go on. "I would've given my life for you if you'd asked. Why did you have to do this? I loved you so much."

"If you can't forgive me – and you should, my love – then just come on and kill me. Get this over with."

Jess was trembling so much that the tip of her blade wiggled and sliced a gash across Tolliver's forehead.

"Damn you, you stupid whore!" he shouted. "Just end this. Why do you have to be so neurotic about everything? Stop babbling and just kill me."

Jess looked at him.

Tolliver screamed in terrified frustration.

"Let me make this simple for you. I enjoyed fucking you, and I admired the way you could fight. That's all you are or ever were to me, you dumb cunt, a good fuck and a great killer."

Jess felt her chest begin to heave and stood up above Tolliver's hips.

He gazed up at her, lifted himself onto his elbows, and said, "Oh, and I figured you were stupid enough to fall for my little scheme. I guess I hadn't counted on how crazy you are. Come on, finish it."

Jess, her now red face curled into a frown, swallowed deeply, raised Dawn's Spine above her brow, and brought it down across Tolliver's head, slicing his skull into upper and lower parts.

Suddenly, the girl lost all self-control. She began screaming and chopping at the man's body wildly, hacking at it over and over again until she had reduced it to such small pieces that it was barely recognizable as having ever been human.

When she finally regained her sanity, Jess stumbled backwards, used her vest to wipe away some of the blood that had splattered across her face, and exhaled loudly.

A sense of relief mingled with a terrible sadness swept over her, but, as swiftly as it had arisen, it disappeared, dispelled by worry. She remembered how she had left Uluf and thought of how he could have been killed.

Not wanting to lose her only friend, Jess jumped off the stage, ran through the casino, threw open the doors (carelessly forgetting that there could yet be scorpions outside, though there were not), dashed across the hallway, and passed through the door leading to Gople's office.

* * *

Jess spied the gangsters' corpses as soon as she had entered the room and a sudden panic rose up within her. She turned her head to either side, saw Uluf pressed against a wall, and exhaled in relief.

Then she noticed the young woman standing over Gople's body and the two dozen mercenaries with her.

Raising Dawn's Spine above her shoulder, the sword's blade pointed forward, Jess ran at the woman whose long black hair was plaited into cornrows. She, however, jumped backwards and retreated behind her soldiers. While half of them remained clustered around her, the other half of their number rushed towards Jess, each with a sword in one hand and a needle gun in the other.

Jess, reacting without thought to their assault, chopped off the heads of the first two men she came to, spun around, and decapitated both of the men standing to either side of them.

Ducking to avoid the blows of their fellows, she severed one man's feet, pivoted on her heels, and, as she rose up again, split a sixth man from his groin to the crown of his head.

Then, while Jess amputated the hand of a soldier who had tried to stab her and twirled about to skewer another coming at her from behind, Hyan began walking forward.

The mercenaries noticed her approach and one, being briefly distracted by it when he was attempting to shoot Jess with his needle gun, missed her and accidentally shot one of his fellows.

Jess turned around and cut off his hand while another of his comrades fell dead beside him, shot by Uluf, who had himself picked up a needle gun.

The last man stared at Jess for a moment before turning to run back to his comrades on the platform. She was not going to let him go, however, and, racing after him, sliced into his back deep enough to open up his spinal column.

Hyan, who had now circled round Jess, stepped over the body of one of her dead soldiers and crossed over to squat beside a loudly bawling man whose hand Jess had amputated. She unlatched his helmet, took it off, and gently stroked his hair.

"My lady," one of the uninjured mercenaries called out. "You are not supposed to fight that girl."

"Shut up! Are you going to stop me? I'll warn you now, if you get in my way, I'll kill you."

No one else raised his voice.

Resting her scimitar on her shoulder, Hyan stood up and glared at Jess, who had let time return to its usual pace. "You murdered my brother."

"I'm sorry about that, but I don't even know who your brother is."

"And that makes it better? I loved him more than I love myself, and you killed him."

"I've killed a lot of people's brothers."

Rage welling up within her, Hyan began uttering a sequence of strange sounds, and these activated the resonator wrapped around her shoulders. She stared at Jess with complete hatred and readied herself to draw the universe into her mind.

"You can't live after what you did to him," she snarled in a tremulous voice.

While her remaining soldiers stood dead still, transfixed by the scene before them, Hyan grabbed the one handed man at her feet by the hair and decapitated him. Before Jess knew what her enemy was doing, Hyan threw the head at her.

It struck Jess in the chest, knocking her backwards and winding her.

No sooner had she recovered her wits than Hyan leapt threw the air, raised her sword beside her ear, and swung it in a wide arc.

Jess seized ahold of time, ducked, and avoided her adversary's attack.

Seeing this person's movements, Jess realized that the woman must have some device like a thread. Although it was clearly not as good as was a thread, it was still sure to make her opponent formidable.

Inhaling deeply and readying herself for a dangerous confrontation, Jess, without delay, tried to stab Hyan in the belly, but the woman bent to one side and swung her sword again.

Jess parried, struck (only to have her own blow parried), blocked another blow, and then struck again.

Hyan slipped to the left and kicked Jess's feet out from under her. The girl fell onto the floor, rolled, and hopped back up behind her foe. She, however, whirled around and brandished her sword in a circle, attempting to bisect Jess into upper and lower halves.

Jess threw herself into the air, spun head over heals, and came down upon Hyan, kicking her in the cheek once and upon the chest several times.

Hyan did not leap back, as Jess had anticipated she would, but clutched the girl's leg and twisted it around, hurling Jess, face down, onto the ground.

Her breath knocked out of her and fear surging uncontrollably through her body, Jess barely escaped being skewered by her enemy's scimitar. Then, as soon as Jess had regained her feet, Hyan soared into the air and kicked her chest several times, causing her to stagger backwards.

Even if she had not had some sort of thread-like device, this woman, Jess thought, would still have been good. She was not nearly as skilled as the man Jess had fought on the bridge in Ekeya (who was probably the brother she had mentioned), but she was not approaching her fight as a game like he had. That, by itself, could easily make her as deadly as he had been. She was clearly determined to kill her brother's killer.

Jess, however, being equally determined not to die after all the ordeals she had recently endured, kicked Hyan between her legs and brought her sword down upon the woman.

Hyan parried the blow and hit her enemy in the cheek with her fist.

Jess, a hot blast of anger exploding in her breast, grabbed Hyan's hand and pulled it downwards. The women's blades slid across one another, and their torsos slammed together.

Jess hit Hyan in the kidneys, and Hyan hit Jess repeatedly in the chest.

Both women forgot their thoughts and lost themselves in the deadliness and pain of their struggle. Jess was aware only her desire to live, her fear she would not, and of the actions that she took, while Hyan knew nothing beyond her overwhelming hatred and anger, that were impelling her to attack the woman before her.

The two threw themselves apart, Jess diving for the ceiling and Hyan for the floor. Then, from their perches, they launched themselves at one

Melting Worlds

another, repeatedly striking and parrying with their swords while they grappled and twisted through the air.

As they crashed into a wall, Hyan seized Jess's hair, drew her face close, and bit her ear. Jess screamed and, since Dawn's Spine was pressed against her enemy's blade and both weapons were trapped between the combatants' bodies, punched the side of the woman's torso.

Hyan gasped, fell back, spun around, and, howling madly, tried to decapitate Jess.

The latter, fortunately, fell to one side and swung Dawn's Spine upwards, cutting off Hyan's sword arm just below the elbow.

Looking at her hand twirling weightlessly in the air, disconnected from her body, Hyan yelped like a wounded puppy and, without a thought, jumped backwards to land and collapse at the feet of her remaining mercenaries.

Jess let go of time and sought to catch her breath.

Hyan sat upon the floor screaming uncontrollably and shaking her head from side to side so that her long plaits flew wildly about her face and shoulders.

After watching her for a moment, Jess picked up Hyan's severed hand, shook it to make it drop its weapon, and threw it at the woman.

"Don't forget this," she shouted.

When the hand hit Hyan's shoulder, she stopped screaming, picked it up, and then shrieked at her remaining soldiers, "Kill her! Kill her! Kill her!"

The mercenaries in unison aimed their rifles at Jess and fired at her. She, however, leapt straight up into the air and landed, like a spider, upon the ceiling, where she snatched up time and wrapped it in her will.

Jess ran, upside down, towards her enemies, threw herself at the ground, and decapitated two of them.

Hyan, seeing what she did and now overcome with terror, motioned for a pair of her guards to help her up. The two hurried to her, placed her arms upon their shoulders, and carried her, crying but still holding her amputated hand, out of the room.

Jess would have liked to follow Hyan, but there were still eight men trying to kill her.

Three of these jumped at her at once, but Jess leapt from the floor onto the shoulders of a man who was not wearing his helmet. She kicked him in the face, driving the bridge of his nose into his brain, and, with a single motion of her sword, cut off the tops of the heads of the other two.

While Uluf fired his needle gun from where he was standing and killed one more man, Jess spun backwards – head over heals – from the shoulders of her dead mount to land on her feet behind another of her opponents.

She split him open from his crotch to hip, let his entrails spill out upon the floor, dove over these, and pierced yet another man through the heart.

The last remaining mercenaries, both of whom had soiled themselves, collapsed onto their knees and dropped their weapons, hoping to receive mercy from an enemy they knew they could not defeat. She instead offered up their blood to Haya and decapitated them both.

Jess, her mind dizzy from excitement and her chest heaving from her exertions, let the thread slide back down to the base of her torso and walked over to Uluf.

Though she was spattered with blood, she could not restrain herself and hugged him tightly.

"Come on," the girl said to the toad. "Let's get out of here."

"Yes, my dear. I do believe that would be the wise thing to do."

"How's he?"

"I am not sure," Uluf replied as he walked over to Gople.

The toad checked the man and said, "He is alive."

Jess and Uluf helped Gople up and put the gangster's arms over their shoulders so that they could carry him the rest of the way out of the city.

As they began to make their way to the submersible, Uluf held out his hand and showed Jess Gople's penis.

"I found this. What should I do with it?" he asked.

"Where'd you pick that up?"

"Back there. It was lying on the floor."

"Just throw it away. What're you going to do with it, after all?"

"I thought that it could, perhaps, be reattached."

"It'll be rotten before we get him to a surgeon. Besides, I'm pretty sure they can just grow him a new one."

Uluf tossed the penis onto the floor and the group hurried on its way.

As injured as he was, Gople was able to direct the others to his offices and to the passage leading into the sewers.

Once they were underground, he told Jess she should walk straight ahead and look for a ladder the bottom rung of which had been painted red. That would lead them to a cavern connected to the sea. There, in a lagoon, they would find his submersible.

As soon as he had given Jess such instructions, Gople lost consciousness.

The girl and the toad carried the man as they trudged through the dark underground passage, though their burden quickly grew heavy and, eventually, had them staggering.

By making several stops to rest, the two were able to continue on. They were always wary of pursuit and listened carefully for the sounds of scorpions scampering upon the stone or of booted soldiers running through the stinking waters flowing beside them, but they never heard a sound besides that of the stream itself and those of the various sorts of vermin living in it.

Several hours later, Uluf spotted the ladder with the red rung. He and Jess roused Gople, and he, with their help, was able to climb down the ladder into the cave.

Inside, moored to a stalagmite, was a small craft, no bigger than a car, shaped like something halfway between a fish and a grasshopper.

Gople tried to use the key hanging from a chain around his neck to open the vessel, but was too weak from loss of blood to control his own fingers. Uluf did it for him and the three entered the submersible.

It was easy to operate and took them, unseen beneath the waves of Shokai's single ocean, away from Jezic.

While still conscious, Gople told the others, "Take us to Min."

"Why?" Jess asked. "What's there?"

"Safety."

"Okay. How do we get there?"

"There are coordinates available on the computer," the gangster told her.

Later that day, Gople died, and Jess and Uluf continued on their way to Min.

While she sat beside one of the submarine's little round portholes, gazing at the strange creatures dwelling in the waters, Jess smiled and whispered to herself, "Just so."

Uluf went over to his friend and sat down in the seat beside her.

"Well," said the toad to the girl, "that was a complete disaster."

Jess looked at him quizzically and replied, "What do you mean?"

"It appears that Ngo has won everything and we barely got out of Jezic alive."

"Uluf, we have seventy million kopecks. The two of us are rich and Tolliver's dead. How could things have turned out better?"

The toad patted the girl's thigh and nodded his head.

"So," she asked, "where do you want to go?"

www.ingramcontent.com/pod-product-compliance
Lightning Source LLC
Chambersburg PA
CBHW020924020726
47495CB00002B/330